Best Wishes -

Ted Leverin

The Other Side
of the Bridge

TED LEVERING

Illustrated by Ann L. Winterbotham

Published by
Willowmead Publishing Company
4030 Skates Circle
Fort Myers, Florida 33905

Library of Congress Catalog
Card Number: 91-91144

Designed by Dave Gorrell

Printed in the United States of America

First Printing November 1991
Second Printing January 1992
Third Printing January 1994
Fourth Printing October 1996

ISBN 0-9640957-7-7

DEDICATION

For everyone who ever loved islands ...
past, present, future.

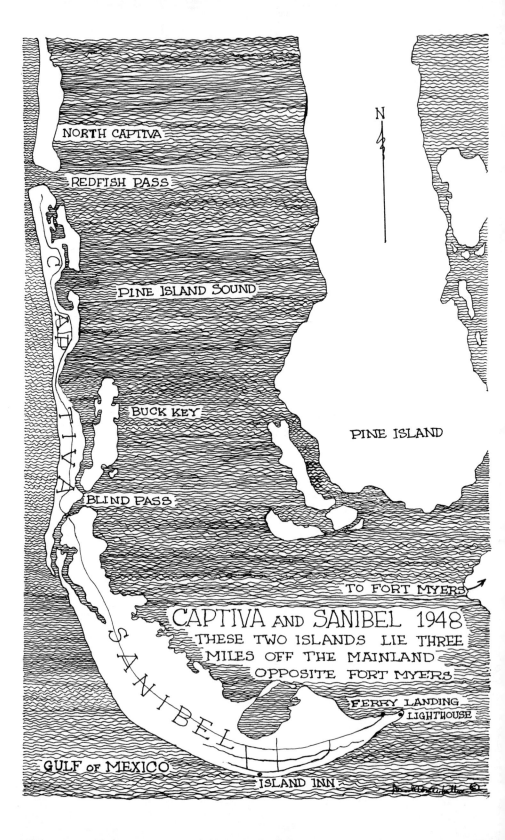

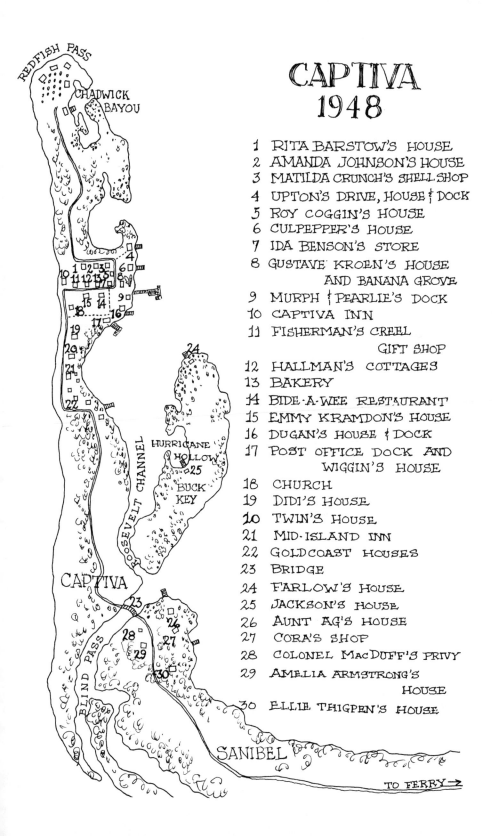

CAPTIVA
1948

1 RITA BARSTOW'S HOUSE
2 AMANDA JOHNSON'S HOUSE
3 MATILDA CRUNCH'S SHELL SHOP
4 UPTON'S DRIVE, HOUSE & DOCK
5 ROY COGGIN'S HOUSE
6 CULPEPPER'S HOUSE
7 IDA BENSON'S STORE
8 GUSTAVE KROEN'S HOUSE
            AND BANANA GROVE
9 MURPH & PEARLIE'S DOCK
10 CAPTIVA INN
11 FISHERMAN'S CREEL
                GIFT SHOP
12 HALLMAN'S COTTAGES
13 BAKERY
14 BIDE-A-WEE RESTAURANT
15 EMMY KRAMDON'S HOUSE
16 DUGAN'S HOUSE & DOCK
17 POST OFFICE DOCK AND
            WIGGIN'S HOUSE
18 CHURCH
19 DIDI'S HOUSE
20 TWIN'S HOUSE
21 MID-ISLAND INN
22 GOLDCOAST HOUSES
23 BRIDGE
24 FARLOW'S HOUSE
25 JACKSON'S HOUSE
26 AUNT AG'S HOUSE
27 CORA'S SHOP
28 COLONEL MacDUFF'S PRIVY
29 AMELIA ARMSTRONG'S
                    HOUSE
30 ELLIE THIGPEN'S HOUSE

AUTHOR'S NOTES

GENERAL:

It's a long trip back to 1948. Without notes, my memory has undoubtedly played tricks. Certain liberties have been taken regarding events and timing, always to further the story line.

From the onset, I was advised by legal counsel to change the names of participants as a protection against invasion of privacy. I have reluctantly done so.

The characters, in large part, are real, as are the majority of the episodes. Readers familiar with the period and the people may enjoy trying to figure out who is who.

APPRECIATIONS:

It would have been impossible to ready this manuscript without the help of friends, acquaintances, local business people, and those in distant places who responded so willingly to my requests for help. Some spent hours sketching, editing, and correcting. Others supplied enthusiasm and jogged my memory when I became discouraged or dried up.

Ann L. Winterbotham's charming illustrations visually lift the script immeasurably. Jean Culpepper supplied early enthusiasm and support, and endless hours editing the maturing manuscript. George Campbell's technical advice has been invaluable. Paul Everett searched out dangling participles and hidden grammar infractions. My brother, Jack, guided me with pertinent episodic realignment and character honing. Dave Gorrell acted throughout the 3 1/2 years of this project as a supportive sounding-board.

Additional support and enthusiasm have been given me by Bob Chaudoin, Roman and Esther Parulski, Robert and Madonna Gorrell, and Father W. H. T. Williams.

I am indebted to all of you, and thank you.

Ted Levering
East Fort Myers, Florida
December, 1991

Prologue

June, 1991

Cars moved swiftly through Southwest Florida along Route 41 and approached Fort Myers. They sped past ornate restaurants, fast-food drive-ins, used car lots, gas stations, branch banks, shopping centers and motels. As they neared the four-lane bridge spanning the wide river the bumper-to-bumper flow slowed briefly, then rushed purposefully across the water and raced on southward.

Once over the bridge, the sleek sedan turned out of the right lane and took the down-ramp to McGregor Boulevard. At a traffic light, the driver leaned on the steering wheel and drew in his breath.

"Look at this cross-traffic! Must be an accident ahead."

His passenger seemed unperturbed by traffic noise and fumes. With eyes closed and a dreamy smile, she lounged back with one hand outside the open window.

"I'd forgotten," she said, wiggling her fingers up and down.

"Forgotten what?" he asked, inching the car slowly forward.

"This air. How soft it is." She reached out as if to grab a handful. "Not like Minnesota. The air back there is sharp, bracing. This is sensuous. I just love it. I feel like a cat. Want to stretch and purr."

"You'll have plenty of time to stretch and purr if this traffic doesn't open up."

"Now, Jerry, don't be grumpy." She snuggled up against him. "We waited so long to come back, don't spoil it by being impatient. Look — there's Edison's Home, just as it was. And these royal palms along the road look the same, even if thirty years have slipped by."

They experienced a small sense of reassurance as they proceeded south. They could recognize some of the old homes with their well-manicured lawns and bright bougainvillea. And the high water tower at the Country Club ... and the gentle rise and bend of the road as it crossed Whiskey Creek. The first shock was the imposing overpass leading to Cape Coral. Driving under the heavy concrete arch, Jerry grimaced.

"Progress," he muttered.

From there on, southward to Punta Rassa, they recognized little except an occasional ranchland still stubbornly playing host to scrawny Florida cattle. Most old landmarks had disappeared, replaced by tarmac and parking lots and apartment complexes, all seemingly stamped from a single mold. Not one gladiolus spike thrust skyward through the fertile sandy loam of the former P&X Bulb Company. Instead, a golf course spread into the distance, with small groups of people riding golfcarts from point to point.

The old country store at Barrett's Corner had disappeared. The sign now read "Miner's Corner", and a four-lane highway split left to Fort Myers Beach and right to Sanibel Island. They drove right. They no longer talked but sat silently looking out the windows. Everywhere were huge shopping malls, apartment buildings, parking lots. And people! People were everywhere!

Further south, at the final bend before Punta Rassa, bill-boards lined the road so close together it was difficult to see beyond them to the open Gulf.

She kept her eyes focused on the road ahead.

"This is depressing, isn't it?" Her voice was very low, barely a whisper.

Around a bend they found themselves lined up behind dozens of other cars at the tollbooth for the Sanibel Causeway. She gave a tiny moan and raised a hand to her eyes as if to fend off a blow.

He glanced quickly over at her.

"What's wrong?" he asked.

"I've been dreading this." she replied. "Of course I knew things would be changed. After all this time they'd have to be. But I don't have to like it." A little smile etched the corners of her mouth, softening the distress in her eyes. "Remember the little ferryboat ... and Captain Bumpter and his pipe? Even the ferry slip is gone. They've pulled up all the pilings. Look at that monstrous building they put up where the slip used to be." She jabbed a finger out of the window as if to poke a hole through the tall complex wall. "And this hideous mess in front of us!"

"It isn't hideous if you've nothing to compare it to," he remarked. "The sweep of the Causeway and its bridges is beautiful in its way."

The traffic moved slowly and they moved slowly with it. Finally, over the bridge and on the Causeway, Jerry cut his speed even further. The driver behind blasted his horn, and Jerry pulled over onto the sandy shoulder and stopped.

"Now this is hideous!" he said. "Look at that jam of people. Like a miniature Jones Beach!"

Blue-green water lapped gently at the Gulf-edge of the three-mile Causeway linking the mainland to the southern tip of Sanibel Island. The sandy shoreline was blanketed with people, a frenetic carpet of teeming activity. Sunbathers stretched out on bright blankets. Radios blared. Children darted in and out, screaming and tossing sand at each other. A group of old men, scantily clad and unpleasantly hairy, lumbered back and forth after a volley ball. People swam, snorkeled, scuba-dived, wind-surfed or shot in and out among the bathers on swift and noisy jet-skis.

Didi glanced at her husband's set face, and leaned her head onto his shoulder.

"Everybody has to live. Time doesn't stand still, you know."

He nodded. "I know. I know."

"Come on, Jerry, let's go on," she breathed. "Let's just drive on down the road to Captiva as fast as possible."

They inched at a snail's pace along the Causeway and down the single road bisecting the island, boxed front and back by other motorists. The five-mile stretch from the Causeway turnoff to Tarpon Bay Road was lined on each side by a solid mass of stores, gift shops, restaurants and gas stations. Both Jerry and Didi stared in disbelief as they drove slowly along.

Twelve miles further they reached a spreading rental conglomerate, where a large sign announced 'The Rendezvous'.

"Amelia Armstrong's home!" Jerry pointed. "And somewhere back there, opposite, must be Ellie Thigpen's. My! How she could fish. Remember?" A huge smile creased his face.

"And up ahead, just a bit to the right, at the foot of the bridge, is Aunt Ag's ... our ... home." Didi was trembling with excitement. "Let's go. I can't wait!"

They drove into the yard and sat silently, looking around. She drew a deep breath and expelled slowly.

"Jerry, how marvelous!" Her eyes glowed with emotion. "It's just the same. The old house! Cora's shop! The path lined with conch shells. Even that huge hibiscus!"

He took her head between his hands and kissed her.

"Welcome back, Didi," he breathed into her neck, hugging her tightly. "Welcome back."

Since Aunt Ag's death in '56 and their own departure to St. Paul and Minnesota Mining in '58, they had kept the island place intact, refusing even to rent. They wanted it ready, at a moment's notice, in case they decided to visit.

Once inside, they explored the old house.

"I asked the people at the Island Realty office to have it spruced up for us. Looks nice and clean, doesn't it?" Jerry stopped speaking and watched her as she wandered about the old room, adjusting things, smoothing pillows. She paused by the west window and gently pushed the old rocker. It creaked a little as it moved back and forth.

"Maude! Aunt Maude! Do you ever think about her, Jerry?"

"All the time. Just about every day. Aunt Maude was a great influence in my life. I loved her very much."

"Yes," Didi agreed, mentally drifting back the years. "She was great. I loved her, too." With a sigh, she turned to the door. "Well, let's unpack."

3

"No. Let's take a walk first." He motioned her to the door and held it open. "Let's cross the bridge and walk the beach."

The old wooden bridge was gone. A wide two-lane cement span had replaced it. Colonel MacDuff's little outdoor privy was gone, replaced at the moment by a sun-tanned fat lady on a green beach towel. There was a small county-maintained beach on the west side of the bridge, at the south end of Captiva, into which, it seemed, at least 500 bathers were squeezed.

"Good heavens!" Didi said, holding fast to Jerry's hand as they stood at the road-edge. "Why do you suppose they don't drive on north along the beach where it's not so crowded?"

A sunbather overheard her.

"We would, lady, but this is the only place to park. All the rest is private property."

"Good heavens!" she repeated.

The sand spit that had stretched from the end of Captiva south along Sanibel was gone too, and with it the terns and Maude's old pine. Sick at heart, they turned around and retraced their steps back across the bridge.

Later, resting from hauling in suitcases, Jerry stood staring out of the back window.

"Maybe we shouldn't have come," he said meditatively. "Maybe it's not wise to reach back. I wanted to recapture the old days, to romp with you again in the Gulf ... to wander the beach and maybe find another golden olive. But it can't be, now. It's gone forever. We can't drag it back."

Didi, perched on a bar-stool, stopped sipping iced-tea and looked at him.

"That's not necessarily true, Jerry. We can drag it back. We have two whole months down here in this comfortable, familiar old house, with the sun and the air and all our memories. Let's tell people how it was. Let's tell the story of those old days ... how your Aunt Agnes came to this remote little island and how she opened that tiny gift shop with her two friends, Maude and Cora. You came down in 1948 to help them ... didn't you? What were you ... sixteen?"

He held up a cautionary hand, and shook his head.

"Come on, now, Cutie. Be sensible. I couldn't remember all that. Its been forty-three years. Where would I start?"

Her enthusiasm continued to bubble over.

"I can help you remember. Start at the beginning, when you arrived at Aunt Ag's dock in Sonny Steven's air taxi, and go on from there."

He shook his head a second time.

"No. I couldn't. So long ago. I'd never be able to handle it."

"I'll help, Jerry." Didi's face was aglow. "Come on. It'd be fun!"

He looked steadily at her for a long moment.

"Are you serious?" he asked.

"Yes."

"You really want to?"

"Yes."

4

He gave her a second long look, then his face broke into a gentle, loving smile.

"Did you pack my tape-recorder?"

1

September, 1948

I t was low tide as the little plane slipped and slid along the air currents, just inches above the mangroves, plopped like a fat duck into the shallow water and taxied toward the shore. As they bumped along Jerry could see Aunt Ag standing on her little bay-side dock, one hand shading her eyes against the setting sun and the other holding fast to a shiny red bicycle.

An unfamiliar shyness dropped over Jerry as he climbed out of the plane. He wanted to rush over to Aunt Ag and squeeze her but he seemed all hands and feet, and he hung back.

Aunt Ag took no notice. All in one quick motion she planted a kiss on Jerry's head, thrust the bicycle at him, waved goodbye to Sonny as the plane pulled back into deep water.

"Goodbye, Sonny. Thanks. Don't forget to get Jerry's luggage over to Captain Bob, and I'll pick it up tomorrow at the mail-dock. It's really quite safe, I suppose," she added, more or less as an aside, gazing after the little plane, now only a speck in the twilight. "Still, somehow ... I don't think I would want to ..."

"Aunt Ag, what's that fuzzy stick you keep banging me with?"

"Mosquitoes, Jerry. Mosquitoes. This is a horse's tail. Cora makes 'em. She has one for you. If you don't swish yourself constantly about the ears and legs, especially the legs, you'll be a sight in no time. Come on, now, let's get inside. Bring your bike with you."

"Oh, Aunt Ag. It's mine? Gee, thanks! A new one, too! Thanks." His entire face smiled.

"It's not new. I had Evan paint an old one, that's all. Come on, now, in we go."

The screened door on the porch opened a bit and someone inside started horse-tailing the opening.

"Come on, now. In we come."

Aunt Ag smiled as she herded the boy and the bike onto the porch. "That's Cora. She likes to repeat."

The introductions were over pretty quickly. Jerry had been worried about this situation. He hated meeting people, or rather, he hated for people to meet him.

A pastel little lady, thin and dainty, held open the door.

"This is Cora Chisholm, Jerry ... my nephew, Gerald."

"I'm Cora Chisholm, Gerald, and I'm pleased to meet you."

"How do you do."

"You can call me Aunt Cora."

"Thank you."

A vast bulk appeared from back along the porch and a deep voice boomed.

"And I'm Maude ... Maude Appleton, Gerald. If everyone else is doing it, I suppose you'd better call me Aunt Maude ... and I imagine you prefer to be called Jerry, don't you?"

"Yes'm."

And that was that. It was all over.

The house sat on a finger of sand, jutting into the back bay off the northern end of Sanibel. Surrounded on three sides by water, the only entrance was toward the south, out a hibiscus-lined path to a small parking area where the car was kept. The sand road that ran from the Sanibel ferry slip, seventeen miles to the south, aimed exactly at Aunt Ag's house, touched her lot line, then veered at a 90-degree angle to the west, crossed the little hump-backed bridge over Blind Pass and on to Captiva.

The house itself was simply built of board and batten, comfortable, roomy, airy. A wide screened porch completely encircled the inner living area of large kitchen, slightly formal parlor, bedroom and bath, with a guest room on the second floor ... one of those square enclosed widow's walks seen all over the Florida back-country.

"Jerry, you can have this whole big room to yourself," Aunt Ag explained as she led the boy up the staircase. "You can see all about, three sides, and you'll have plenty of sea air. I've put shirt and shorts of Uncle Will's out for you to change to. If they don't fit, don't worry, we'll pin. Your own things will get here tomorrow and we'll go together to pick them up. Now, freshen up a bit and come down to supper. Will you be comfortable here?"

"Yes'm."

"And, Jerry," Aunt Ag paused, one hand on the door-knob. "I'm so pleased you're here with me."

Later, downstairs again in his makeshift clothes and facing the three ladies and a table laden with food, Jerry's shyness disappeared. The meal was huge. First there was a mango salad, then fried fish and mounds of mashed potatoes, fresh peas, milk, and a fat sweet potato pie.

A lot had happened that day, and the lad was tired from all the excitement. Soon after supper he excused himself and went to his room.

Not much conversation passed between the three ladies during the cleanup chores. When Maude had returned to her rocker by the window and Cora was stirring the soaking tub filled with palm fronds softening for tomorrow's mosquito swishers, Agnes leaned against the doorjamb and looked for a minute at her two friends.

"Well, girls, what do you think?" she asked, drying her hands on a dish-towel.

"Pretty puny's what I think."

"Now, Maude." Cora pushed back a loose strand of hair, a sign that she was preparing to rationalize. "He's been very sick, remember. He seems quiet and polite. He certainly ate a good supper."

"Wolfed it down you mean."

"There you go again. Why are you always so negative. Why can't you ..."

Agnes cut in. "Now, Cora, please."

"I only meant ... "

"I know, Cora." A sympathetic smile removed any edge to Agnes' remark and she slowly nodded her head.

Cora caught the smile, and dipped her head in response.

"Do you two think I made a mistake," Agnes questioned, moving along with her thoughts, "bringing the boy down here, in all this September heat, and the bugs, and the frenzy of readying the shop for December ... all those endless trinkets you make, Cora ... and your long hours of shell-gathering, Maude?"

Maude had stopped rocking and was watching Agnes closely. "Don't forget those hot walks to the lime grove and my tomatoes. I'm not getting any younger, you know."

In an effort to erase the tension, Cora said brightly "Now, Maudie, you've years left ... years!"

Maude spun on Cora, her mouth snapping open for a stinging retort. With visible effort, she turned away, shrugging her shoulder. Grabbing an over-sized fly-swatter, to lessen her irritation she began banging the screen wire where she could reach it.

"I'll never get used to all this buzzing," she said. "The filthy things, clinging so thick to the wire, poking their nasty sharp little noses right through, ... no air can get in. Listen to 'em buzz. The northerners say the noise keeps 'em awake at night, like someone snoring. Oh, I forgot to tell you, in all the comings and goings ... the Nickerson funeral has been postponed a week, something about family gathering and some mix-up over the casket."

"How do you know?" Cora had stopped stirring the fronds and was all attention.

"Emmy Kramdon stopped in for a moment on her way back from Ft. Myers and told me. Emmy is always on top of things like that, you know."

Cora had the bone and began gnawing. "What will they do with the corpse? I mean ... won't it ... won't it ...?"

"Rot? Do you mean rot, Cora. Why don't you say it outright, if that's what you mean? No, it won't. They've finally added a refrigerator room to the City morgue, thank heaven. They can keep 'em frozen down for weeks ... even years, I suppose."

Cora gave a little moan.

"All of which reminds me," Maude went on, settling in for a vigorous chat, "of the rather disastrous burial of old Captain Jones in the Captiva graveyard. Several years back it was, in '40, before you two came here."

Cora's attention had strayed a bit and she was sprinkling lye onto her fronds. "Why bury him there?" she asked, offhandedly.

"Because he was dead," Maude snapped at her, overlooking Cora's rather vacant gaze and wrinkled brow. "It was really a bad time," Maude rushed on. "That flash hurricane was on us without the least warning, tides surged around, the Sanibel ferry escaped up-river, the mail-boat couldn't run ... we were cut off completely. At the peak of the fury, a great limb from that huge Australian pine just opposite Hurricane Hollow ... you know the one, Agnes, it still stands over there ... well, old Captain Jones had been trying to work his mullet boat into shallow water and apparently leaned up against this tree for protection. The gales tore loose this big limb and it crashed down onto Captain Jones, squashing him like a june-bug!"

Cora moaned again and sagged back into her chair, eyes fluttering.

Agnes leaned toward Maude and rapped her on the knee.

"Now, Maude, we don't want to hear any more, if this is going to be another of your horrible stories. We've other more important things to talk about tonight."

Maude, however, plunged on.

"How could this be horrible, Agnes? It happened, didn't it?" The lack of logic in that remark missed her entirely, as she rocked back and forth like a large Fate savoring her memories.

After a minute or so, Cora, somewhat recovered, breathed softly ... "then what happened?"

The effect on Maude was immediate.

"What happened? I'll tell you what happened. In those days there was no ice-box big enough for a body to be put in, not in Ft. Myers and certainly not on the island. Old Jones had to be buried right away or he would have started to decompose, there under that broiling sun. Murph Suggs had a few boards and Evan had some sticks and those two nailed together a coffin of sorts. Roy Coggins dug the hole ..."

"Grave," Cora whispered.

" ... dug the hole," Maude didn't pause for a second, "and the rest of us, six others, gathered that afternoon at the Chapel-by-the-Sea for the funeral. Sam Wooten agreed to read something or other from his Bible ... <u>BUT</u> ..."

Maude came out with this word like a cannon shot and both Cora and Agnes came bolt upright in their chairs.

" ... when they went to place the lid on the coffin," Maude went on, "it rocked. Everyone had forgotten all about old Captain Jones' huge nose, famous all about these parts. The lid tilted and they couldn't nail it down.

The men conferred a bit and then asked all us ladies to sit awhile in the Chapel."

"While they gathered more wood." Cora was now body and soul into the narrative.

"No. There was no more wood. Anyway, about a half-hour later they called us out, the lid was on and the burial proceeded. See, I told you this wasn't horrible, Agnes. Now, was it?"

Agnes looked steadily at her friend and asked the inevitable question.

"Maude, how were they able to nail down the coffin lid?"

Maude nodded affably, as if all the pieces were falling into proper position.

"I heard later, from Sam," Maude continued, "that they found they couldn't twist the old gentleman's neck as rigor mortis had set in ... so they just took the hammer and smashed off his nose."

Cora started to whimper, and Agnes stared fixedly at Maude.

"You ought to be shot, Maude, right as you sit there ... making up that bizarre story just to frighten Cora."

"No, Agnes. No. It's a true story. Every word Gospel!" She began to bristle at being doubted.

"All right, Maude. I believe you. But no more stories — at least not tonight."

"Wait a minute." Cora had come to life and was puzzling over something with a distant look. "If they smashed his nose off with a hammer, did anyone ever find it?"

"Find what?"

"The nose."

A silence settled in.

Later on, the three were sipping cocoa in the kitchen. Maude was worried about her friend. "Ag, relax, honey. It'll all work out just fine. You didn't make a mistake. Jerry will be a great help to each of us. We'll fatten him up, get him tanned, and he'll fit in just splendidly. I can't wait to get enough muscle on him so he can haul those water buckets for me."

Agnes nodded her head. "I know, but I worry he'll be lonely."

Maude gathered up the cocoa cups and put them in the sink. Then she turned and smiled. "He'll be so busy from now to December he won't be able to think, believe me. After that, the tourists will be back 'til Easter and we'll have to maybe pair him off. Don't fret. And don't mother him Agnes. Let the boy grow up. He's in the best possible place for it. Everything is still raw here and he'll bump into reality, into simplicity, and the good weather, and the bad weather ... and himself. Don't hang over him. Give him space. Don't mother. Come on, Cora, let's go home."

Cora was headed for the door, horse-tail flicking, when she stopped and turned. "I have the oddest feeling I've forgotten something."

Maude was abrupt. "You have. You didn't give Jerry the swisher you made for him. You can give it to him tomorrow, if you don't forget."

Left alone, Agnes sat at the table and pondered. Suppose he does get lonely ... suppose he gets sick again ... all that cool sea air ... better run up and check if he's all right.

At the top of the stairs, with her hand outstretched to open the bedroom door, she stopped. Then she turned and quietly went back down.

2

The next morning, as the first light appeared in the east, Jerry was up and struggling into Uncle Will's shorts. He sank to his knees in front of the largest window and waited eagerly for the dark to dispel so that he could see out. The night air lingered, chilly and carrying a tantalizing tang of salt. Did he smell it ... or taste it? Was it wet against his cheek or was he imagining it? Were those leaves out there a bit more distinct?

As the darkness became grey, and the sky lightened somewhat, he found he could see across the inlet from Aunt Ag's yard to the mangroves growing on the other side, lush and moist, with trunks in the shallow salt water and aerial roots hanging in profusion, tangled and twisted together. Interspaced stationary roots were festooned with heavy clusters of what he supposed were blooms, lumpy and whitish.

A large black and white bird swooped by on silent, effortless wings, dragging its long red bill in the water as it skimmed along. It turned and retraced its path and was gone in a twinkling, leaving a little rippling on the water's surface. Farther north, to his right, the boy could just make out a tall dead pine tree, spiking the sky.

All at once, the morning sky burst suddenly into color. Startled, he pulled back and watched in awe his first day-break on the Gulf.

Behind him in the east, an edging of the rising sun peeped over the horizon, deep red and already hot. Searching rays touched the bottom of the fat gray cloud cover, causing it to blush a faint pink. As the sun rapidly changed from red to burnt-orange, the entire sky was suffused in deep pink, a color so vivid even the green mangroves across the inlet appeared pink.

The sun seemingly leaped up over the edge of the world, as if God's Hand pulled it along on invisible wires. The cloud cover began to disperse, change from pink to scarlet, with streaks of orange and yellow. The Gulf water, stretching as far as Jerry could see, reflected the red-orange and yellow of the sky, with highlighting of silver atop each gentle wave.

Just when he felt he could stand no more ... it was gone. The sun was up, yellow-gold and beaming. The Gulf was blue. The mangroves were again green. The world was normal. The day had begun.

The boy sighed deeply and settled back on his heels. It was several moments before he realized that bustling noises from the kitchen below were seeping up the staircase, along with the smell of fresh coffee. He was ravenous, and rushed down the stairs.

"Well, young man, you look pretty good." Aunt Ag was putting breakfast on the table and stopped to smile. "Did you sleep well?"

"Yes'm. Very well." Jerry drew out his chair and sat down. "I guess I was real tired, all the excitement yesterday, and all. I slept great."

Aunt Ag stood in front of the boy, her hands on her hips, all solicitation. "Jerry, I don't want you doing too much right off. No leaping into things. You've been pretty sick, you know."

"Yep. I mean, yes'm. I was. But I'm not now. I can't remember ever being this hungry. No matter what you've got, I can eat it all."

Aunt Ag returned to the stove, laughing.

"Well, we'll fill you up, you'll see."

"Gee, Aunt Ag, do you have sunrises like this every day?"

"Oh, no," Aunt Ag replied, moving things about and dishing up. "No. This morning was rather special. I saw it, too. Beautiful. Somedays, it's just a sunrise. Then others, like today, it's as if the heavens open and angels sing." She placed a heaped-up plate in front of him and patted his shoulder. "Has something to do with how wet the night was, I think."

Jerry was only half-way through the eggs and pancakes when Maude came bolting through the screen door and plopped a large box onto the table.

"There," she exclaimed, straightening up and tugging at a wide leather belt around her waist from which hung a hatchet and a knife. She was wearing pants with the legs stuffed deep into thick stockings. Her heavy boots clunked on the floor as she moved about. Jammed on the back of her head was a wide-brimmed hat, from which dangled wisps of green netting.

Jerry's expression of disbelief threw Maude into a series of deep guffaws. Rocking with laughter, she flipped the netting forward and it completely engulfed her head and face, draping onto her shoulders. Her voice was slightly muffled as she wandered the room, chuckling.

"Don't smile, now," she said. "Your outfit is in the box there. It's a gift from all three of us. We pitched in and bought it for you. We got it from way up north ... L. L. Bean ... and it's actually a blackfly outfit for northern deer-hunters but it works fine for mosquitoes, too."

"Isn't it hot?"

"Yep. But I'd rather be hot than bloodless."

Jerry reached out and flipped the hatchet handle.

"What's this for, and the knife?"

Maude drew out the knife and hefted it.

"I have to have a knife. Always had one, since I was a kid. A machete. But here on the island, things aren't all that primitive, now, and I kept sticking myself in the leg when I stooped over to pick up shells. So I traded my machete for this knife. The locals call it a pig-sticker. The hatchet comes in handy for chopping driftwood. And, of course, snakes."

Jerry was all eyes.

"Aren't you afraid to get close enough to a snake to chop it? That isn't a very long handle."

"I don't chop. I throw." Maude was well aware of the effect of all this on the boy and she played it out to the end. "As a young girl, I spent a lot of time with the Seminole Indians, deep in the Everglades, and they taught me how to use it. Its come in handy many times, though rattlers are sluggish. If you stomp hard on the ground when you run across one, it'll coil and look around in a slow fashion and there'd be plenty of time to chop. But somehow I never could bring myself to do it. Closeup killing is not for me. I'd rather throw. More impersonal."

Leaving the boy's head spinning with impressions ... Indians ... tomahawks ... snakes ... she finished her coffee and headed for the door.

"Jerry, I'm off up the road to tend my limes. Cora'll kill me if I don't water 'em this morning, as I missed for several days. If you want, you can meet me here when I get back in a couple of hours, and we can wander over to the beach. Would you like that?"

Jerry agreed eagerly, and Maude was out the door and on her way.

Agnes called after her. "Maude, take the car. It'll be easier for you and I won't need it until mail time."

A faint "Okay" drifted back.

The box contained heavy twill pants, a twill shirt, woolen sox, gauntlet gloves, a wide-brimmed hat, and army boots with "collars" on them that laced around the ankle. In one corner, in a protective envelope, was a green netting.

In the midst of the trying-on activity, Cora arrived, with armloads of palm fronds.

"Oh, good. I see Maude gave you the box, Jerry." Cora began busily sorting fronds. "I hope everything fits. You'll think we're crazy but you'll need it all when you're fishing from the bridge, especially at night. The beach can be unbelievably buggy too, on a dark day and if the wind is from the land. There won't be many mosquitoes this morning, though. The day is brilliant and they're not happy in hot sunlight."

Agnes was gathering up the box wrappings and she smiled as the boy climbed in and out of garments.

"He's going to meet Maude in a bit, Cora, and they'll be going to the beach. I guess all he'll need will be his swisher, don't you agree? They won't be gone long."

Jerry looked up.

"Aunt Ag, where's this beach Aunt Maude spoke of? I'm all turned around. How do we get there?"

"Well, now, Jerry, let's see. Come over here to the window for a second. Cora, see if these directions are clear. Jerry, you go along that path, past our little parking area, to the road. Turn right and cross the bridge."

Cora butted in ... " It's wooden, humpbacked, and narrow. Cars can only travel one at a time whatever direction. It's call Blind Pass Bridge because it crosses Blind Pass." She nodded her head at the aptness of the name.

Without acknowledging the interruption, Agnes went on. "This house sits on the northern end of Sanibel. When you've crossed the bridge you're on the southern end of Captiva. There's a narrow extension of Captiva stretching south from where the bridge touches down and it runs parallel to Sanibel for two miles or more. The islands are separated by a deep channel that narrows to about a hundred feet wide. It's called Blind Pass because the Gulf entrance is so difficult to locate from open water. All the back bay waters filling this section of Pine Island Sound funnel under the bridge and out this channel to the Gulf. Do you understand?"

The boy nodded.

"So," Agnes went on, "that's the geography lesson. Part-way along that finger of Captiva, left of the bridge, is a tremendous blown-down pine, lying on its side and half covered with sand. Maude likes to sit there and gaze out over the Gulf and meditate. You and she will most likely end your beach exploration trip right there. Look." She motioned the boy to her side. "You can see the beach and open water from this window, off there to the left."

Jerry peered out and shook his head. "I've never seen so much water. It just goes on and on, doesn't it?

"Yes, it does," Cora said, walking over to join them. "The Gulf of Mexico is pretty big, you know. Straight off there, much farther than we can see, is Mexico. Imagine!"

"Imagine!" the boy echoed.

"Haven't you ever seen an ocean? Didn't you ever travel to the Atlantic coast with your folks?"

"No, we never did. I never even imagined." Jerry had become quiet. "Must be lots of critters messing about in all that water. I can swim and all that, but I couldn't swim fast enough to get away from anything big. Scary, isn't it?" he mused.

Aunt Ag patted his arm and went over to the table where the fronds were spread out. "Now, don't worry your head about that, Jerry. I've never heard of anyone being hurt while swimming around here."

" 'Course, there's always a first time," Cora offered, with a little giggle.

Aunt Ag looked up and a quick little frown flecked her forehead.

"Let's not stir up trouble, Cora. The boy has enough adjusting to do, getting used to the island ways, without worrying about imaginary beasts lurking in the water. Jerry, please give me a hand over here with these fronds until Maude comes back. I agree with her ... splitting these things is a bore. Come on, now."

By the middle of the morning the boy had sat long enough, and he decided to explore the backyard.

"Not barefooted, Jerry." Cora stopped him at the door. "The yard is full of sand spurs. They stick in your feet and you'll fester. Nasty things. Maude's been too busy these past few days to scuffle 'em. Wear shoes. And don't climb on the oyster beds at the water's edge. Their shells can cut, if you're not careful. And take your swisher."

After Jerry had gone out, Cora turned to Agnes with a rueful little smile. "Seems all we're doing is warning him about the uglies, when we should be pointing out the pretties."

"Oh, I don't know, Cora." Agnes was deep in thought. "He'll bump into everything, both good and bad, before too long, on his own, I suppose." Her voice trailed off as her mind was on something else. "Cora, the three of us are fairly intelligent. I mean, we've got good minds. We are imaginative. Are you listening?" Cora nodded swiftly, though she wasn't. "We should put our heads together and come up with some simple gadget to split these fronds quicker, and more easily. This sticking in a pin and slicing one little strip at a time is really stupid. Think of the hours we waste. Maybe Jerry could dream up something. When he comes in, I'll ask him."

Later, when Jerry came back from his yard tour, Agnes turned to him, holding aloft a sliced leaf, but before she could go into the problem Maude banged through the door.

Jerry looked eagerly at Maude. "I've already got swim trunks on under my pants. I'm ready, Aunt Maude."

Maude sighed and settled into a chair by the table. "Just a minute. Just a minute. I've been weeding and hauling water for the better part of two hours. Let me recover a bit. Is there any tea?"

The boy was eager to share his discoveries.

"The dock is great, Aunt Ag. It reaches out into really deep water. I tossed in an old oyster shell and it sank way, way down, sort of fluttering as it went. There's an old pelican that didn't like me being there. He perched on one of the end pilings and watched me move toward him. When I got closer than he wanted, he jumped off, spread his wings and scooted along just above the water. Golly, I like him. Real great. When I backed up, he'd circle and land on his piling again."

Cora said, "That's Hiram. We feed him. We always clean our fish there, on that flat board nailed to the end of the dock." She put down her pins and leaves and went to fix tea. "He eats fish. Did you see that big pouchy beak on him? That's how he catches fish. Pelicans are very interesting birds."

Maude nodded. "Interesting, but dirty. Course, most birds are. Jerry, when we get to the beach in a bit, you'll see 'em feeding."

"Aunt Ag, do those green bushes across the channel bloom on top, too, or just at the water level?" Jerry asked.

Aunt Ag was still sticking pins into palm leaves and slitting them from top to bottom. "Jerry, those are mangroves. They're not really bushes, not like you're used to back in Evanston. They're actually trees, of sorts. Instead of one central trunk, they expand from a runner root system, and every so often they drop other roots down into the water. When floating leaves and branches get caught in those roots, that helps build new islands. Out in the bay, away from people, the mangrove islands serve as nesting sites for many water birds. I'm sure Maude will tell you all about that, which she loves to do." Agnes glanced fondly over at Maude, who was accepting a cup of tea from Cora.

"And Maude is very smart," Cora tossed in. "She's practically an authority on that stuff."

Maude looked embarrassed. "Pooh!" she muttered.

Agnes sat up straight and stretched her back. "I'm sorry, Jerry. I didn't answer all your question. Those 'blooms' you asked about — those aren't blooms at all. They're oysters. Coon oysters. Small, tasty and sweet. Already salted by the water slapping up over them as the tides change. We always carry a couple of oyster knives and old gloves in our skiff when we troll for snook and redfish. Then, when the wind is right and we're hungry, we tie up among those roots and eat our fill. Delicious." Anticipating the boy's next question, Agnes added, "Called coon oysters because the raccoons love them. At dusk, if you're quiet and watchful, you can sometimes catch sight of one or two, slipping along the bigger roots to the water's edge, and eating the small oysters. They don't shuck them as we do, of course — they bite a hole in one end and suck out the meat and juice."

Maude abruptly stood up. "I'm ready. Give me my swisher and get yours. We're wasting time. Let's go."

"Speaking of time," Agnes called after them, as they hurriedly crossed the porch, "Please be back by noon at the latest. I've got to drive to the post office to get Jerry's luggage, and I'd like him to go with me. Maude, have you got your watch?"

"Yes, I have. We'll be back on time," Maude called over her shoulder as the two of them reached the road and turned onto the bridge.

"Wait a second, now." Maude grabbed Jerry's arm to slow him down a little. "Want you to notice this spot. We're dead center of the span, at its highest point, and at high tide the water is about twelve feet down. Sailboats with masts or fancy-rigged small yachts can't go under. They have to turn around and go back past the post office and then Murph's dock and on up to Redfish Pass to get out to the open Gulf. The fish, of course, can go through and at high tide they do. Then, some six hours later, back they come on the in-coming tide. Both of those times are the best times to fish from here." Maude pointed back toward Sanibel. "Elmira Thigpen fishes here most every day or night, high and low tides, all winter long. She rents one of Amelia Armstrong's cottages in that cluster over there — you can just see 'em. They're about a quarter-mile up the Sanibel road from your Aunt's house. I'll introduce you to Ellie Thigpen when she gets down and you can fish with her. In about six-eight weeks, around the middle of November, she gets in."

17

Jerry peered down at the water rushing by. The surface ripples flashed silvery highlights across the miniature waves, acting as a light barrier to his casual glance. Then his eyes focused beyond the surface into the deeper water below. He reached for the woman.

"Gosh, Aunt Maude, look! Look down there! Hundreds of fish, all heading in the same direction. What are they? Can I catch 'em? Must be hundreds! Maybe more!"

Smiling at the boy's enthusiasm, Maude leaned on the bridge railing and watched the fish.

"Those are mullet. They travel in schools like this. You're right. Hundreds. You can't catch 'em on hook and line — they only eat vegetation. The fishermen net them. They're a food staple for the whole southern coast, especially the natives. Fried mullet is heavenly, but you have to know what you're doing when you cook it."

"Why?"

"It can be greasy if it's handled wrong."

"Can we maybe catch some?"

Maude nodded and prepared to move. "Don't know why not. There's a cast net somewheres around the cottage. I saw it just the other day. Have to see if it needs mending. Old man Jackson will fix it for us, if it does."

"Who's he?" Jerry was still staring down at the dense school of fish.

"A mullet fisherman. Lives in a palmetto and tin shack on Buck Key, over there. You'll see, later on. He mends nets. We often give him one of Cora's key lime pies."

They meandered on across the bridge to the open Gulf and turned left to walk parallel to the water. The breezes cooperated and blew just enough to discourage mosquitoes.

Jerry stopped stock still, stunned by the picture in front of him.

"Oh, Aunt Maude, look!" His eyes shown with delight. "It's the most beautiful place I've ever seen."

Maude's arm gave a little twitch, as if she would reach out to the lad. The impulse was gone in a flash. With visible effort, she kept her hands by her side.

"As you get to know this island, Jerry," her voice was gruff with emotion, "a lot more places will be the most beautiful you've ever seen." She fell back a step or two, watching him.

Stretching straight ahead, the beach appeared endless. There were no dunes as the sand barrier was not high enough. Palms fringed the upper beachline, their fronds rustling in the sea air. Clutches of green unripe coconuts hung in the tops. Brown ripe ones, with their casings slightly split, lay about on the dazzling white sand, which was much finer than the sand at the water's edge. Having previously been blown inland by gale winds, this exceptionally fine sand had been trapped by the roots and stalks of sea oats, which grew in clusters between the palms. An occasional stunted pine struggled for mature growth in an unsuccessful battle with the salt spray and the blistering sun.

Seashells were everywhere. Inland from the water, just before the palm line, mounds of sun-bleached shells lay in wild profusion, intermixed with old seaweed, sticks, bits of dried sponge, strands of old netting, and other items cast up by high waves during storm action.

At the water's edge was a glistening array of newer shells, most having been left on the beach by yesterday's tides. Big shells, small shells, brightly colored shells, dull shells, a few still alive, strewn about in wild abandon, all gleaming and shining in the morning sunlight from their bath by the last incoming wave. As lace-edged wavelets coasted gently up the beach, paused, deposited a sparkling foam-line that disappeared into the sand, and then returned again to the waiting sea, the wetted sand seemed to bubble a bit as tiny holes appeared, announcing the presence of creatures living below the crust. Sandpipers and plovers scurried about, probing the sand excitedly, bobbing up and down and chattering loudly to each other. Snow-white terns hovered above the waterline or plunged into the shallow water just beyond, to soar again on throbbing wings, tiny alewives held in their beaks. Further out, in deeper water, brown pelicans fed, sailing along on effortless wings and diving headfirst into the waves, their bills slightly open. Still further out, in open water, every so often a huge fish rolled, gleaming an iridescent blue in the sunlight.

Wordlessly, the boy slipped off his shoes and moved slowly forward, across the sand avenue between the two rows of shells, the old and the new. He dug his toes experimentally into the warm sand a few times and then tossed back his head and yelled aloud in glee, pirouetting round and round.

An energetic wave swept in and foamed around his legs.

Again, Jerry was stunned.

"Aunt Maude, look! It's warm. It's not cold at all. It's warm, like the sand."

"Yes," Maude said, finding herself mesmerized. In a low voice, "Yes, it's warm." She had forgotten how beautiful it all was — the blue water, the white-gold sand, the green trees, all spangled by the multicolored shells, the birds, the peace. She hadn't seen it for a long time now. She passed this way nearly every day, but she hadn't seen. Looking at it all now as the lad must be viewing it, she was overcome by the tranquility of the lovely place.

With the boy laughing and darting about, and the older woman moving more slowly, the two made their way along the beach to Maude's favorite spot, the tumbled-down old pine. Here she settled among the branches and watched the youth cavort on the beach. She leaned forward, elbows on her knees and hands hanging between her legs. Reaching down for a handful of sand, she hour-glassed it from palm to palm, musing about the boy. Puny. Waist not much bigger than she could span with a grasp. Have to get some flesh on him. And white, dead white! An hour or so in the sun more than enough this time. Lovely lines on him, though. Straight legs, wide shoulders, splendid set to his head. The crisp, golden-brown hair and russet eyes bespoke tomorrow's tan. In no time at all, he'd be gleaming red-brown from top to toe. Heads would turn, bound to. Hope he'd never know. What was there about him that so quickly got under the skin? Was it the openness, the enthusiasm, or maybe that strange blend of innocence and complexity? She'd had a moment back there when emotions long suppressed had gushed to the surface and she had instinctively moved to touch the lad. Mustn't. Must not, ever. But what prompted? Odd! Why had memories of the scrub, the north Florida lumber camp, surfaced at the same instant, the physical hardships she had endured when she was just his age, working with an adored father too gruff to show affection, to ever hug her, though she waited day after day, and hoped. Was her urge to touch this carefree lad in any way allied ...

Jerry's shouts of glee broke Maude's reverie. He was splashing in and out of the warm Gulf edge, chasing the plovers which fluttered along the beach just beyond his rushes.

"Aunt Maude, come on down here. Didn't you wear a suit? It's great. Come on."

In a sort of trance, Maude reached down and slipped off her shoes and socks. She hadn't done this for years. How wonderful the warm sand felt around her toes. She moved slowly down the sloping beach to the water's edge and sank to her haunches. Jerry flopped on his stomach in the water in front of her, moving to and fro with the gentle rise and fall of the waves.

"Look at all the action right here," he said, tracing the edge of a wavelet with one finger. "As the water goes back out, all these little shells get tumbled around and every so often something alive gets uncovered. Look. Look there! There's something running down after the water and then it disappears. Where does it go? Huh?"

Maude hunched forward, left arm clasped around her knees. With her free right hand she scooped deep into the sand, withdrew a handful and mounded it in front of the boy.

"Look at all _that_ action, Jerry. See those tiny shells? Watch as they thrust out their tongues. Actually, it's not tongues at all but their bodies. That's the way they move about. They're called coquinas. Shore birds love 'em."

Jerry was fascinated. "They're so beautiful. All those different colors and stripes. Why are they all so different?"

Maude probed with her finger along with Jerry. "I don't know. I've always wondered, too. Maybe the coloring has something to do with what they eat."

"There must be thousands of 'em, Aunt Maude. Thousands. Maybe even millions."

"Oh, I agree. Millions. When you consider you can uncover hundreds by just grabbing at the wet sand here, and all this beach, and all the beaches all over the world. Unbelievable, isn't it?" She smiled as she spoke.

20

Jerry was intent on scooping. Suddenly, in front of him, a white bug about the size of a large grape scurried toward the receding water and buried itself in the wet sand.

"What was <u>that?</u>" he wanted to know, drawing back in alarm.

Maude chuckled aloud. "It's okay, Jerry. That was a sand flea. Won't hurt you. Dig around and catch one and hold it in your hand. Its little feet tickle. There's one. Grab it, but be gentle, Its little body is very frail and you'll crush it if you're not careful. The sandpipers and the plovers, even seagulls if the weather is rough, they all love sandfleas. There, doesn't it feel strange?"

Jerry nodded as the little creature dug frantically at his palm with its tiny feet. "I don't mind 'em, but I don't really like 'em," he said, gently releasing it back into the water. He moved out deeper. "Gee, this is sure different from Lake Michigan. I can float so easily. And it's so warm. I could stay in all day."

"Yep," Maude agreed. "But not today. Your Aunt Agnes wants us back by noon and we mustn't be late. Off we go." She straightened up with some difficulty.

Jerry was silent on the way back down the beach and across the bridge. He'd been here not even a full day and so much had happened, and it was all so new. When they reached the house he was glad to sink into a chair beside Cora, who was fiddling with fronds.

"And just why are your pants wet, Maude?" Cora smirked over her discovery. "I do believe you've been in the water. I'm right, now. You have been in the water, haven't you?"

Maude had been heading for the kitchen but she spun around and went out the porch door. Her answer was testy. "Yes, Cora, you're right again. I've been in the water."

Cora watched her disappear down the little path.

"There must be something wrong with me," she speculated. "Lately, most everything I say sets her off. Maude never used to be like that. I'll have to be careful."

"Aunt Maude was great over on the beach." Jerry kept the conversation alive, though he felt a short nap would be great. "Where's she heading, anyway?"

"Oh, she's going to our house, I suppose. Your Aunt Agnes has two other little huts on this property besides this house, both sheds originally." Cora was delighted for the company and the chance to ramble. "Agnes had the larger of those two rebuilt a bit, and Maude and I live there. It's small, only a kitchen, bath, one bedroom. I use the bedroom and Maude sleeps on the porch. The other former shed is our gift shop."

"It's all screened, I hope." Jerry looked at Cora quizzically.

"Oh, yes, of course. We may be primitive here on the island, but we're way past smudge pots and smoke. No one uses that any more to keep mosquitoes out. Maybe Sally-Anne and Doobie still do, but if so, they're the only ones."

"Who are they?"

Cora had the tabletop covered with frond bunches by this time and was beginning the intricate business of binding the handles. She leaned back in her chair for a minute and looked vacantly at Jerry.

"Who are who?"

"You were talking about some Sally-Anne and Doobie people. Who are they?"

"Oh, yes." Cora dragged herself back to the subject. "Sally-Anne cleans house and does laundry. Doobie's her husband. He does yards. They're negroes, the only black family on the islands ... Sally-Anne and Doobie Denkins. They're very nice. I think they smudge their windows, not so much because they can't afford screening but windows always were smudged and they like to cling to the old ways. Itty, bitty people. You could put both of 'em together in your hip pocket and never know you were carrying anything."

Jerry chuckled as he thought this over.

"Aunt Cora, that's silly."

"Well then, just you wait. Both Sally-Anne and Doobie do for Agnes here and will appear in a day or so, at dawn. You'll see!"

Jerry switched the subject.

"Aunt Cora, Aunt Agnes is taking me with her to the post office. Where's that?"

"The post office is in Bertha Wiggins' living room, in the old Island Hotel. When Bertha got the job as postmistress several years back, Evan, her husband, partitioned off the front half of the living room and made a post office. It's real nice. The other half of the living room is still large enough for the Wiggins' family to use, though where they all sit, all those kids, I'll never know. Whoever built it there sure made a wise choice — the old hotel, not the post office. It's almost dead center of the island, and the bay is only a step east. You can toss a shell into the bay from the post office stoop. That's where the mailboat docks. The Gulf is west, down a winding path about 800 yards long. All cathedralled over now — the path, not the post office. Run down, though." Cora nodded and then added, "the post office, not the path."

Jerry was frowning as he tried to keep all this straight.

Cora never paused. Agnes would be back any minute, and then she would lose her audience.

"That mailboat thing sure has me puzzled. I never have understood exactly what they mean. Everyone tells me you have to order two days before you want something ... but I'm never sure if it is actually before or after. I mean, I know what you have to do. If you want things delivered say on Wednesday, you have to order on Monday. That's clear. But the before or after business, that's tricky. It all depends, in my mind, on which end is which, doesn't it? You order two days before, but the stuff arrives two days after. See what I mean? And poor Mrs. Olney, the Captain's wife, she gets the order a day before but she shops and puts the stuff on the mailboat a day after. As far as I'm concerned ... "

Jerry never knew the answer to this latest concern of Cora's as Aunt Agnes appeared at the screen door and beckoned him out.

They climbed into the car and crossed the bridge, heading for the post office.

3

S tanding well back from the bay shoreline in a surrounding grove of coconut palms and Australian pines, the old Island Hotel sagged gently on one side and, like an aging dowager permanently down on her luck, seemed content to bask in the sun and dream of yesterday's triumphs. A close observer, however, looking beyond the rotting banyan draped in cereus and strangler fig aerial roots, could still discern evidence of former finery, of an expansive columned piazza, of a generous double-door entryway handsomely carved, of wide windows gazing out across the bay. It took little imagination to conjure up the gaiety and excitement, the swaying lanterns and bustling servants, the smoke-filled dining room where the millionaire guests replete from a banquet of endless variety, sagged back in their chairs with their rum and Havanas and told again of the huge fish that got away.

The Island Hotel was built in the early 1900's, soon after Captiva Island was chanced upon by the likes of Teddy Roosevelt, Rex Bell and Jack London. It soon became a favorite fishing locale for the very select and the very rich. A wide, sturdy dock was thrust into the bay some 200 yards from the hotel's front door. Gleaming white yachts anchored to this snug harbor, tugging gently at their hawsers and rocking back and forth with the tide, while their owners gambled and gossiped in the hotel lounge.

By 1947 the old hotel was in need of serious repair and a coat of paint. It had, for years, been the home of the Wiggins family. Evan was the island handyman and his wife Bertha was the Captiva postmistress. The daily mailboat, the Santiva, tied up at the Wiggins dock each day but Sunday, just past noon. The arrival of the mailboat touched off the peak of daily excitement, and everyone who could manage to get there assembled for the thrill.

The Santiva was rounding the end of Buck Key and heading toward the dock as Aunt Ag inched her car into the post office parking area and braked beside two others.

"Were you driving slow to keep from throwing dust?" Jerry asked, gazing all about.

Aunt Ag smiled fleetingly and then looked serious. "No, dear, not exactly. It's that I am always fearful of running into one of the Wiggins children. There are so many and they all seem so small. There's the youngest, over there under the banyan, all over mud. She's so dirty she blends into the sand. She could just as well be squatting right in the middle of the roadway. I might, somehow ... " Aunt Ag's voice trailed off and she gave a little shudder, shaking off the unpleasant thought.

"Look," she said brightly, "everyone is here. See that crowd out on the dock?"

Jerry looked. "Aunt Ag, I see only eight people."

"Right. Let's see, now ... Evan is off working for Amelia Armstrong, Roy is on Sanibel wiring the Community Hall, Murph and Pearlie are tending shop at their own dock, Amanda never joins in, and Jasper Dugan is home with Peggy, who is ill. That's seven ... and these eight make fifteen, which is right. Fifteen in all."

"What about you? You and Aunt Cora and Aunt Maude?"

"Oh, we don't count." Aunt Ag looked meditative. "The fifteen I named are Captiva people. We don't count. We live on the other side of the bridge."

"Aren't there any kids on Captiva?"

"Of course. A few. But they're at school. You'll meet them later."

Aunt Ag slid from under the steering wheel and waved a hand toward the dock. Jerry hung back.

"You go on, Aunt Ag. I'll wait here."

"Now, Jerry." She was all sympathy. "I know how you feel but sooner or later you'll have to meet the islanders. Here they are, nearly all. You can get it over with all at one time, in about five minutes. Come on, let's go."

As they approached the end of the dock, Aunt Ag put her arm around the boy's shoulder. "Good morning, everybody. This is my nephew, Jerry Marshall. He'll be with me this winter."

Aunt Ag was right. It didn't take long at all. Six women were grouped more or less together, several sitting on piling, all talking at once and busily swishing their horses' tails around their ankles and upper torsos. Every so often, catching sight of a mosquito feeding on someone else's neck, one would lunge forward and swish a neighbor's face. This never seemed to bother the swished or interrupt the conversation, which flowed on without pause at a furious pace.

Two men squatted at the end of the dock, making imaginary tracings on the weathered boarding with their fingers. As he drew near, Jerry saw one gentlemen shake his head violently, exclaiming in a strong, positive tone "No, no, Gustave. A mast forward of center in a stiff breeze can cause trouble ..." Aunt Ag's hand on his arm steered him away from this interesting conversation and over to the women.

"Jerry, this is Mrs. Crunch." In an undertone, "She has the only shell shop on the island."

Jerry shook hands with a tiny woman, crouched so far over he first thought she was sitting. When he looked closely he could see she was, in fact, standing. A tremendous coal-black hairdo rose in a pyramid above her face, the highest beehive Jerry had ever seen. Several tightly curled ringlets slid coyly across her shoulders and down her front.

The other introductions were routinely acknowledged. "Mrs. Benson, my nephew" ... "How do." — "Mrs. Upton, Mrs. Bartowe, my nephew." ... "How do." — "Mrs. Kramdon, Mrs. Wiggins, my nephew, Jerry." ... "How do."

Jerry scarcely heard any of it. His eyes were focused on Mrs. Crunch's hair. How did she get it to stand up like that? So high! Did she wear something under it, a kind of cone arrangement, and pull the hair up around it? Once she had it up, did she leave it like that all day? All week, maybe? Longer?

Aunt Ag tugged at his arm.

"Jerry, stop staring at Mattie. Look, the boat is docking. Maybe you can help."

There was a little bump as the boat brushed the dock. Ropes were tossed fore and aft, deft hands flashed over piling, and the Santiva was lashed in. Then, everything was motion. Those on the dock all rushed at the boat and clambered aboard, patting the Captain on his shoulder as they passed him, and grabbing packages and bundles that were stacked on the floor. The Captain was laughing at everybody as he bobbed up and down, white teeth gleaming in a deeply tanned face, blue eyes twinkling in easy good humor.

"If you don't find everything, ask me, ask me," the Captain called, as he handed out a large package to Mrs. Crunch.

"Oh, Jerry," Aunt Ag beckoned, "Can you take that from Mrs. Crunch, please, and put it in our car. We'll give Mattie a lift home. That's much too heavy for her to carry all that way."

"Yes'm," Jerry said, as he gathered it up and headed inshore. "Oh, boy," he thought to himself, "if I sit in the back I'll get a really close look at that top-knot."

While everyone was sorting out their orders, Captain Olney tossed out a large canvas bag, which Bertha Wiggins seized and carried to the post office.

The Captain then perched on a piling and accepted orders from anyone wishing anything from the mainland ... delivered in two days, not tomorrow ... and the islanders grouped around him. Aunt Ag stood quietly to one side, waiting for all this to finish.

"Captain, did Sonny deliver any luggage to you? My nephew's suitcases? Two, I think. Wasn't it two?" Turning to Jerry and discovering that he was already aboard the Santiva, Aunt Ag made airy introductions, moving her hands back and forth ... "Captain Olney, my nephew Jerry."

The Captain shook Jerry's hand heartily. "Yes'm. It was two. I've got 'em hatched in, to keep the spray off. Lad, lift that back seat cover. There. In there."

Back at the car, squeezed in the back between his luggage and Mrs. Crunch's package, Jerry felt a bit dazed.

"Aunt Ag, is it like that every day?"

Mrs. Crunch turned around in the front seat, twisting her whole body apparently because of a stiff neck.

"Good Heavens, boy, today was easy. Wait til Christmas and the snowbirds are all here. Gets positively frantic then." She laughed with a thin, high-pitched raspy sound, like winter wind tossing dried reeds.

The Captiva Shell Shop was located a half-mile farther along the sand road from the post office. Jerry carried the package through the shop and into the kitchen behind. As he went, he glimpsed cases of seashells, boxes of assorted souvenirs, bottles with lizards and snakes floating in liquid, shellacked turtle shells, old fishing netting, and he made a mental note to return to this haven at the first possible chance.

Back at Aunt Ag's, after luggage and packages had been hauled in and disposed of, Jerry joined Cora and Maude on the porch.

"We can't wait!" Cora bubbled.

"How'd it go?" Maude rumbled.

The ladies were hunched over a long worktable, sorting pine cones into neat little piles.

"What are you doing?" Jerry asked.

Maude swooped a large pile into her apron and rose to carry it off.

"Careful, Jerry, or she'll tell you," she said.

"I certainly will." Cora's face was alive with the chance to explain. "You see, Roy Coggins dropped off this croker sack full of pine cones while you and Ag were gone. He collects 'em for us up on Sanibel. For some reason, the real piney pines don't grow down here. All we have here are Australian pines which give these itty bitty round cones," and she held out a seed cone about the size of a ripe blackberry. "But they're perfect for faces and heads. These big ones make fine bodies, so we have to sort 'em into proper sizes, big and small. You see?" Her busy hands never stopped or hesitated as she rushed along, sorting, piling, discarding.

Jerry looked a bit startled.

"What do you do with 'em?"

"Oh, didn't I tell you?" A vague expression crossed Cora's face. "We make souvenirs with them. We take heart shells from the beach ... you can gather those for us, later on, as Maude complains about all that stooping over ... and we glue a big cone to the edge of the shell, glue a little cone to the top of the big cone as its head, fix an auger shell on as its nose, paint eyes, add 'Captiva Island' to the base and we get 50 cents for 'em. The winter folk snap 'em up, though I don't know why. I wouldn't give one shelf space in my cellar."

27

Maude agreed, inelegantly, "Me, neither."

"We call 'em monsters" Cora added, with a chuckle.

Jerry wanted to help, and dragged up a chair, but Maude held up a remonstrative hand. "We've just about finished here, Jerry. You can help Cora later with her tails. They have to be shredded, and that's a bore. Right now, we want to know what went on at the post office. Something always does."

Aunt Ag had joined the group. "Not much, really. Everyone was there. I introduced Jerry around. He hated it. Dennis Upton and Gustave Kroen are still squabbling on where to put the sail on their bayou skiff." Turning to Jerry, "they were the two men kneeling at the end of the dock. Dennis is Tabby's husband. You met her. Mrs Upton. They're from Massachusetts and of the Boston Sailing Gang. Kroen is our token Russian Refugee. Fishes mainly for shark, which he chops up and buries around his banana plants. Must work. I've never tasted such bananas. Lady fingers and lots of 'em."

Maude nodded in agreement. "Lots of flies, too."

"Oh, Maude, now ... even Eden had its snake," Cora said.

"For mercy sakes, Cora. Don't drift off into one of your philosophic moods, now. There's lots to be done. You've all these swishers to work over before the fronds rot ... and I'm way behind with my rocking." She had the grace to smile gently.

Jerry glanced over at Aunt Ag. "I didn't meet Mrs. Upton, did I? Which one was she?"

"The tall one. Very thin. With the straight gray hair cut across her forehead in bangs."

"Oh, now I remember." Jerry looked faintly puzzled. "The one with something wrong with her chest. She kept digging at it."

Cora laughed aloud. "Oh, I always thought so, too. Then one day, Tabby and I were strolling along the beach, shelling, and we were pretty confidential and I asked her what was wrong with her chest. Nothing! Nothing at all. She isn't digging at it. She's twirling a button. She's ashamed because her bust is so flat and feels a hand up there hides it all. Every dress she buys has to have a button just below the neck. If it hasn't she sews one on."

Maude was rocking now. "Takes all kinds! With that voice, she needs all the help she can get!"

"Maude. Be kind. Tabby can't help that whiny tone. She says she jumped off a hay-stack when she was a girl and jammed a stalk down her throat, which did something permanent to her vocal chords. She's very sweet and does a lot of good and you know it. You just let up, now." Cora toyed with the idea of pursuing the situation and maybe become more outraged. Then she decided to let it slide ... there was so much to do. Besides, with Maude, there'd soon be another bristly moment. Always was.

"Did you run over any of the Wiggins kids?" Maude wanted to know.

Aunt Ag handed a package and several letters to Cora, and then glanced over at Maude.

28

"No, but it seems only a matter of time. I was saying to Jerry that Bertha ought to take a little more care. Too-loo ... "

In a simultaneous aside, Cora explained to Jerry ... "Bertha says that she has so many kids, and it's such a bother to hunt around for names, that she long ago decided to name 'em after flowers. This one, the youngest, is really named Tulip. She calls herself Too-loo, so we all do."

" ... Little Too-loo," Aunt Ag went on, "was playing in the dirt alongside the parking area, and if it hadn't been for that faded red ribbon on her hair I'd most likely never have seen her at all."

Maude had stopped rocking and taking up a pair of binoculars she focused on a tunnel cut into the mangroves through which she could see the Sanibel end of Blind Pass Bridge.

"Cut that tunnel herself," Cora whispered to Jerry. "Always knows who comes and goes." She chuckled under her breath.

Jerry chuckled with her.

"What's in your package, Aunt Cora?" he asked.

"Name stickers," she answered. "I had 'em printed in Tampa. Last year we didn't have any and I keep feeling we've lost a lot of business in the shop because people don't know a name. I keep getting letters addressed to 'that little gift shop by the bridge'!"

Jerry took one of the stickers and read 'The Grab-Bag, Captiva, Florida' and under that, in smaller print and in quotes was "where the two islands join ... by the bridge."

Jerry looked thoughtful.

"Aunt Cora, maybe you should have added your phone number."

Cora laughed and patted the boy on his shoulder. "My goodness, didn't you explain to him, Ag? There aren't any phones on the island. If you must phone out, you go to the ferry, seventeen miles up the road, cross to the mainland and there's a phone there. Mostly, we learn to do without." Cora smiled over at Jerry. "There's a heap of things you'll have to get used to, Jerry. No phone is just one of 'em. Maybe, if Aunt Ag hasn't anything for you to do just now, you would help me for a bit with these palm fronds?"

Aunt Ag nodded and Cora crossed to the end of the porch and sank down beside two large tubs. Pushing her sleeves back, she plunged her hands into the floating green-brown mixture, explaining to the boy as she worked her hands up and down, back and forth.

"I heard awhile back that some folks used palmetto fronds but I've always found those too brittle. The little streamers break off after a very short time and I don't want that. I use coconut fronds. Palmettos are easier to come by, actually, but a whole dollar is a lot to pay and I feel people should get the best return possible for their money. Coconut fronds are best. You have to be careful cutting. The tree might die if you cut off the central yellow-green fronds, as they are actually the bud. No need to risk killing a tree when it's not necessary. Maude never cuts the low fronds, either — they're too dried and brittle to plait successfully. Then, back here, we slice the leaves from the

29

back rib and soak them overnight. A couple of spoons of lye seem to speed up the bleaching process, and that's what I'm doing now, mixing it all about. I never should have left these so long, or put the lye in so soon. I usually leave the lye-water on the leaves less time, but with you coming and all the excitement and such, I'm mixed up on my schedule. We'll have to rinse several times, and hope." Cora was intent on her chore and didn't notice the puzzled expression on Jerry's face.

"What happens to the stuff then?"

Cora looked at her fingers, which were beginning to pucker. "Too much lye. What do we do now? Well, as I said, we rinse. Then we drape the leaves over that drying rack outside there, and we let 'em dry. Not fully, you understand ... maybe halfway. Then the whole batch gets dunked in salt water, which gives the leaves body. Then we dry 'em again. Once all that is done, we slit each leaf into six or seven thin strands with a pin or something, tie the strands into bunches, bind several bunches at one end ... and you've got another horse's tail. We sell 'em to the winter visitors for a dollar each."

Jerry's hands were in the mix by this time and he agitated the water vigorously. "How did you learn all this, Aunt Cora? How long have you been here on the island?"

"Not all that long," Cora answered. "I've been in southwest Florida for many years, over in Ft. Myers and around, since the time the City was a sleepy little village at the intersection of two dirt roads. I learned this and other little things from an old lady who lived deep in the scrub. Mr. Chisholm, my second husband, and I would bunk at her place when the men hunted wild pigs. I went along but I didn't hunt. I had lots of free time and so did Anna Barnes. When her chores were finished, we'd sit and rock on her porch and she'd teach me. Loved it, we both did. Bill Chisholm died several years back. I met your Aunt last year and we became friends at once. And here I am. I've been on Captiva a bit better than a year, I suppose. Maybe a year and a half, or so."

She dragged one tub over to the edge of the porch and up-ended it, letting the water run off through the screening. "If you'll turn on that faucet, Jerry, and grab the hose over there, you can wash off the floor ... and haul me the second tub, please."

So they worked and talked, and the afternoon wore on.

"What about Aunt Maude," Jerry wanted to know. "Was she a friend of yours?"

Cora straightened up, stretching her back and brushing at a stray lock of hair.

"No, not a friend like you mean. I knew her, of course. She's been hereabouts for years, was born somewhere near, I think. No, I didn't bring Maude here. One day she simply appeared. Just right out of the bushes, seemed like. There she wasn't, there she was. Big. Hands on hips. Agnes and I were repairing the dock and Maude appeared at the end. I nodded and Agnes said "Hi" and Maude just stood there and looked. Then she took the hammer from my hand, murmured something about doing it faster and started nailing. I guess Ag and I more or less pulled back and Maude finished the docking by herself. She never left. She stayed. Still staying. She's a great help, a very great help, and a good friend. We love her."

Jerry nodded thoughtfully.

"Of course," he said, "I guess there's lots of work, without men."

By this time they had hauled all the wet palm leaves out to the drying rack and returned to the porch, slapping at the pesky mosquitoes buzzing all about.

"I guess you never get used to these things," Jerry muttered, swatting at several mosquitoes that had gotten inside.

Aunt Cora handed him his swisher.

"Here," she said, "use this. You can tell yours because I wove red and blue cord into the handle to make it different."

The inner door opened and Agnes stuck her head out.

"Cora, I'm going to run down and visit Peggy Dugan and take her some of that fish chowder we had for lunch. I'm sure she's sicker than Jasper reported. I think Jerry should come, too. He can meet both the Dugans and while I'm visiting Peggy, he can run over to Murph's dock and see that. And that'll be the end of it, Jerry. You'll have met most of them ... and tomorrow you'll be on your own."

Jerry squirmed as Aunt Ag reached out and hugged him tightly.

"You'll love Murph and Pearlie and the dock." Cora's face was bright with interest as she explained. "It's the only place on the island to have fun. They sell cold drinks, and beer, and they have a juke box and folks dance Saturday nights and everything. Bare-footed!"

As Agnes and Jerry drove into the Dugans' yard with its modest cottage and two small rental units nearby, Jasper Dugan was tending his coconuts, which were buried in rotting seaweed at the high tide line.

"Look at all them coconuts, spread out there in the sun, every last one's sproutin'. They like the salty water to dunk 'em twice a day, and the rest of the time they lay dry. Most folks don't know that, and I don't tell 'em. That's my secret. That's why I have such good luck with my coconuts ... that, and always marking north on 'em when I transplant. North to north, every time. Else they waste more than a whole year trying to twist themselves back in line like they was when they first sprouted. Funny, eh? You'd never think of a plant figuring that out. Plants is smart. Another thing most folks don't know, and I don't tell 'em." He shot a fierce stream of black tobacco juice into the bay and it made a little splash. He brushed at his chin where a dribble of juice glistened.

Jerry was threading his way along the water's edge toward Murph's dock when Jasper called after him.

"You, boy. You ever need any coconuts, you let me know. Mighty fine lady, your Aunt. She's been thoughty to Peggy, and I owe her. You let me know now, you hear?" And he waved a gnarled hand after the boy.

Murph's dock stretched out from the shoreline into the bay about 150 feet. At the far end was a weather-beaten, lop-sided shed with a rusted tin roof. It took concentration for Jerry to walk those 150 feet, as the dock was more or less thrown together. The support piling were thrust into the muddy bay bottom at haphazard angles, the cross supports weren't level, the planking was of varying thicknesses, and many boards were warped and turned up at the end. Every so often there was a gaping hole, where some merry reveler had plunged through.

Murph was out after mullet, and his wife Pearlie was queening it up all by herself when Jerry peeped around the corner and into the dock-house. Pearlie spied him right away. Setting her beer can down on the counter and wiping her mouth with the back of her hand, she motioned him in.

"Hi. Who're you?"

"My name's Jerry," he said shyly, as he walked in. Gosh, he thought to himself, this is a big, big woman.

Pearlie heaved herself out of her chair and reached for a fan. It was hot as blazes, with the afternoon all but over and the early evening breezes not yet up.

"That's fine," she exclaimed, tugging at her bikini top and fanning down inside it. "And where's your home?"

"I live in Evanston, Illinois."

"Where're you staying here on the island?"

"On the other side of the bridge. Mrs. Agnes Trumbull is my aunt. I'm staying with her this winter."

"Oh. I see." Pearlie's voice tended to trail off. She wasn't all that excited by the conversation. What she really wanted was another beer. "That's nice. You're pretty runty. The sun will bake that white skin black if you don't watch out."

"I've been sick."

Pearlie nodded. "Bet ya have, at that. Most people are." Her head sagged for a moment, then jerked up. "Thirsty? Like a soda? Back there in that tub of ice, behind the bar. Help yourself — and bring me a beer, that's a love."

Gulping his soda, Jerry looked all around and every glance proved better than the one before. Windows were everywhere, on all four sides, screened against the bugs and with the usual wood awnings propped outward by stakes. Old fishing nets were draped about. A huge juke box stood in the corner opposite the bar. Tables with rickety chairs were scattered here and there. The bay threatened to flood in along one side, the floor was built so close to the water. Outside, benches were placed under the wide eaves in such a manner that people could sit there and fish with one hand and still reach into the bar with the other for a fresh beer without getting up.

Jerry loved it all and hated the thought of leaving, but he didn't want to keep his Aunt waiting.

"I have to go now, but I sure like it here. Thanks for the soda. Can I come back?"

Pearlie's face creased into a warm smile. "Lord love ya, of course you can. Any time. Whenever you're over this way, you look in, you hear? If you're going now, how's about fetching me another beer on your way out, that's a love."

4

Roy Coggins was the island electrician. He'd been a medic in World War II. When that conflict ended Roy returned to Captiva, built himself a palmetto shack between the Gulf and the bay, took a correspondence course in electricity under the G. I. Bill of Rights, practiced local wiring and repairing as the course progressed, and he prospered. Now, two years after his monopoly was established, any island problem remotely connected with electricity was turned over to Roy.

He worked from six a.m. til two p.m. from an ancient flatbed Ford truck, eating his oatmeal and mullet lunch on the job and by three p.m. each day he was swimming in the Gulf opposite Captiva Inn.

It didn't take Jerry long, as he bicycled about the island, to discover Roy's routine. From then on, when Roy appeared for his afternoon swim, Jerry was usually leaning up against a swayback palm tree on the Gulf edge, waiting for him. They became friends quickly and Roy was responsible for Jerry's first steps along the road to future financial success.

One afternoon, as they lazily floated together over the sandbar 200 feet out from the shoreline, in water four feet deep, watching the porpoises jumping and rolling farther out, Roy announced that Jed Staines, up on Sanibel had an old army ambulance he'd offered Roy in exchange for wiring a shop Jed was building.

"He's set on this shop up there. Plans to sell bait. Who to, I don't know. Us year-rounders don't need to buy bait. We net all we want. The winter folks dribble in for only three-four months each winter and they mostly sit in the sun and snooze. Only a few seem to be lively enough to go fishing. Anyway, he's building the thing and I'll wire it for him. And if I can take it out in trade, you can have my old flat-bed."

"Whaddaya mean, whaddaya mean?" Jerry's eyes bugged with excitement, and he ran all his words together in disbelief. He failed to see a foaming wave, which slapped his head, pushing him under. As he sputtered back up,

Roy was spitting a long stream of water high in the air as he floated serenely about.

"Just like a porpoise" he grinned over at Jerry.

"Whaddaya mean, huh?'

"Well," Roy said, "I've been thinking. With all the rain this time of year, I've got to either stop work and meet the mailboat every day to pick up my supplies, or let 'em sit there on the dock and get soaked, so if you had the flat-bed you could pick my stuff up for me and deliver it to my shack. If you hustle you could most likely pick up and deliver other stuff, too. Captain Bob charges five cents for each package and he makes out okay. If you charged five cents per package, you could cover your time and gas for the truck and have some jingly in your pocket. You can drive, can't you?"

"Sure." Jerry nodded his head for emphasis.

"It wouldn't take all that much time," Roy went on, "You meet the mailboat most days anyway, don't you? To load the stuff on the truck and tote it about wouldn't take much more than an hour or so most days, and you could still meet me here afternoons, like you do now. What about it?"

"Yea," Jerry agreed, "it might be great. I'll have to talk to Aunt Ag first though, before I decide. I'll let you know tomorrow, okay?"

"Sure," Roy answered. "That'll be okay. I'm not going anywhere. Hey, look out there, at those porpoises. They're playing around with a school of mullet. Watch 'em. Sometimes I've seen 'em play football that way. One porpoise will take a mullet and toss it high in the air and before it hits the water another porpoise will grab it and toss it back up. They move on along the coast that way with the tide, tossing and catching, until they disappear from sight, that poor old mullet never once getting wet again. Ye Gods, they're moving this way. Stand still, now, they may come close."

They did come close. All at once, mullet were everywhere, swirling about, bumping each other, flipping in and out of the water, in a frantic dash to escape the porpoises. They hit Jerry's stomach and entangled his legs, splashing water all about. The Gulf seemed to boil with fish. Suddenly, a huge dark form streaked in, slamming into Jerry's side, throwing him flat. The air was knocked from his lungs, his side ached, and the rough Gulf bottom cut his knee. He sputtered back to the surface, with Roy helping him.

"What was that?" he wanted to know. Then he noticed a large grayish form several yards off, lying motionless just below the surface, facing him. "There it is. What is it? Let's get out of here!"

He'd have headed for shore in alarm but for Roy's quiet voice and restraining arms. "Don't thrash about so, now. We'll go slow-like." Roy spoke gently to reassure the boy. "That's the porpoise that accidently swam into you. It wants to make sure you're okay before it swims away again. Porpoises are very intelligent and very gentle. There was a case not too long ago over at Ft. Myers Beach of a porpoise that saved a young girl from drowning by pushing her ashore. It swam under her and kept lifting her up. This one wants to be

35

sure you're okay. If your leg wasn't bleeding there'd be no need to go ashore, but no sense taking chances. Let's go."

They swam slowly toward the beach, with the watchful porpoise following.

"What do you mean, taking chances? What chances, if that porpoise is safe?" Jerry was moving slowly.

"Sharks. They smell blood. Never heard of one in here, but we don't want the first, do we?"

Jerry's speed suddenly increased, and he sighed in relief as he reached the beach.

"Whew, that was something" he said, resting at the water's edge. The porpoise was watchful for a second longer, then seemed to swim a bit backwards, turned with a tremendous burst of speed and a fountain of spray and streaked off after his fellows, by this time way down the coast.

"Aunt Ag is never going to believe this" Jerry muttered to himself as he climbed on his bike and headed for the bridge.

Later that evening, his leg secure under a layer of gauze dipped in iodine, administered by a solicitous Cora, Jerry discussed Roy's offer. There was instant approval all around, and the delivery business was born. On the side of the flat-bed Jerry painted "Island Delivery". Evan Wiggins erected a frame of sorts to support an old tarp to keep out most of the rain. Maude and Cora wrote enough small notices for Bertha to drop one in each island postal box and two days later Jerry started systematically canvassing the island for individual reactions.

His first call was to Mr. and Mrs. Upton, and here he bumped into a stumbling block. In her high-pitched voice and fumbling at her chest, Mrs. Upton wanted to know whether, since she and Mr. Upton both drove, the proposal was to charge five cents for each of their packages even if they picked them up themselves. This was an angle Jerry hadn't run into so he told Mrs. Upton that he would plan further and let her know.

After several late evening discussions between Jerry and his ladies, the business format emerged. The Island Delivery proposal was that Jerry would meet each incoming mailboat. Those packages still uncalled for by the time the boat left would be hauled to proper destinations for a fee of five cents per package, regardless of size. Building supplies and furniture were not included. These commodities would be hauled under Special Arrangements. Jerry was to keep individual records, in duplicate, one copy to remain in his record book and one copy to accompany the delivery. Monthly billing would be submitted, itemized by day, the last day of each month. The bill was to be paid by the fifth.

Before too many days passed, everyone on the island had signed up for this delivery service, except old Mr. Jackson the mullet fisherman and Amanda Johnson. Mr. Jackson felt all this delivery business was unnecessary, just one more indication of commercialism creeping in. Besides, he lived on an island and Jerry couldn't deliver there, anyway.

36

Amanda Johnson was a different matter. She wrote Jerry a note, refusing his services as she felt she couldn't afford them.

●

Ellie Thigpen returned to the islands several weeks earlier than usual. Maude was delighted, on driving past Armstrong's cottages with Jerry on the way to the lime grove, to spot Ellie stringing fishing line back and forth between two poles, scanning each inch with a practiced eye.

"Hi, there," Maude yelled from the truck cab. "Didn't expect you 'til next month."

"Couldn't stand it one day longer," Ellie yelled back. "Got to thinking about all those lunkers swimming around out there, teasing 'come and get me, Ellie' so I just packed up and headed south. Got in late last night."

"Come to supper tonight, and we'll catch up."

"Love to." Ellie waved a hand at the disappearing truck and reached for another rod.

They bounced along over the sandy road, Jerry and Maude, and turned in to the abandoned key lime grove where Maude tended two dozen or so trees ... enough to provide all the lime juice Cora needed for those pies everyone loved. Just beyond the trees Maude had a small tomato patch.

The lime trees were not finicky, as fruit trees go. They didn't require the fertilizer that orange trees needed, being more big bushes than actual trees. They did very well in a sand-loam soil, providing weeds and carpenter ants were kept from their root systems, which was close to the surface. However both trees and tomatoes required a great deal of water. Because of the high shell content of the soil, water tended to leach on through rather quickly. Maude did a little hoeing and soil bust-up, as she termed it, while Jerry hauled buckets and buckets of water from an old artesian wellhead, hung with a yellowish beard of sulphur. The air smelled of rotten eggs from the water except when the trees were in bloom, at which time the air was thick with a sweetness reminiscent of orange blossoms mixed with the cloying perfume of gardenia.

"Ellie Thigpen has forgotten more about pole fishing than all the experts ever knew. She's the best. She'll show you what to do on the bridge. It's a buggy business, night fishing, but mighty exciting, with the quiet and the moon and the night birds swooshing by and the water lapping and the fish feeding with popping sounds like pulling a cork from a bottle. As with most everything else, the only sour note is man." Maude chopped and talked, pausing every now and then to lean one arm on the hoe handle and shake her head.

Jerry was only partially listening. He was wondering how much merchandise might arrive on the mailboat. Today's delivery was special. Captain Bob had promised to loan him a bug duster. Roy had one and was able to keep the mosquitoes away from his shack pretty successfully. Jerry wanted to surprise Aunt Ag, as she was bothered far more than most by the critters.

That evening was hot and humid. A summer storm formed across the bay and lightning streaked the sky. The supper was light but ample, highlighted by one of Cora's lime pies, a twelve-incher mounded high with meringue, white and fluffy. For the occasion, Cora had added a fine dusting of grated chocolate. At the first bite Jerry understood all the comments. It was so light he thought it would float off his plate. He ate slowly to stretch the eating out as long as possible.

Ellie Thigpen voiced everyone's sentiments.

"Oh, my. I could sit in a bath-tub full of Cora's lime pies, and pull 'em up around my chin!" She patted her stomach and stretched her feet. "It sure is good to be back. I always say you can exist anywhere, but you come back to the island to live."

Night chores took over. The conversation moved along slowly, as when good friends are comfortable with each other, well fed and drowsy. Cora and Jerry worked at the center table, pasting and labeling items for the shop. Maude helped Agnes with the meal clean-up, and Ellie sat in Maude's chair and rocked. In the bayou behind the house a loud sucking, popping noise broke the silence, and Ellie came alive.

"Maude, how's the snooking off the bridge?" she asked.

"I don't really know, Ellie. I haven't been fishing lately."

Ellie was aghast. "Mercy, whyever not?"

"Well, I just haven't had time lately. Jerry got in just at the front of the month and we had to get him organized. There's been a blow or two and the two of us have spent time shelling for Cora. The limes and the tomatoes, you know. It takes a lot of effort to round up all those palm fronds Cora needs for swishers, and a lot of fiddling with the stuff once you get it. I don't know, Ellie. Seems there's nothing much to do here but I never have any time."

There was no rancor in these remarks, no petulance, just a quiet statement of fact.

"Besides," Agnes cut in, "We knew you'd be back sooner or later and catch 'em all. We need some, too. The freezer's empty."

"I'll soon take care of that for you." Ellie pulled her legs in and straightened up. "What time is it."

"About six o'clock" Cora threw in.

"Let's see. The tide will be flooding in an hour, and an hour past flood is when I like, but I'm all sixes and sevens in my shack just now. Jerry, let's fish tomorrow night, how about that? Proper time tonight is about eight o'clock, so tomorrow night about nine will be fine."

Maude leaned over and breathed in Jerry's ear "Tides are an hour later each day, give or take a bit."

"Have you got any equipment?" Ellie went on. "Must have the proper stuff, and in first-class condition. I can't abide equipment that busts or nets that are frayed or rotting. I've a pole I can lend you but you'll have to fix up one for yourself pretty quick. Guess we'll have only one lamp and one net tomorrow night, unless Maude comes along. You coming, Maude?"

"Sure."

"Then you can drag along your lamp and net and that'll be plenty. Jerry, remember, a fisherman needs his own gear. Remind me tomorrow and I'll see if I can rustle up a cane pole for you. I've got a number of 'em in storage somewhere. All you'll need is some rope and wire. Hooks, of course. You can get all that stuff from Murph down at the dock. Bob Olney can get you a Coleman Lantern from Main Street Hardware in town. Remember, order a two-mantle one."

Ellie was a great organizer. She liked to do it and did it well.

"There's this business," she went on, "of the blasted bugs. You'all must have gotten Jerry an outfit soon as you knew he'd be with you." Both Agnes and Maude nodded. "So, we'll be wearing that stuff. Hot! But you'll get used to it. If the fish are biting, it'll be worth it, believe me." Ellie jumped up and began pacing about. "I'm all charged up. I'm ready to go right now."

Agnes soft-pedaled a bit. "Not tonight, Ellie. Tomorrow night will be fine. Jerry can save up on his strength a bit and get used to the idea. This is all new to him, you know."

"Aunt Ag, I'm fine. I really am. I don't feel at all shaky, any more. But you can trust me. If things get too much, I'll rest." Jerry turned toward Ellie, who had crossed to the window and was looking off across the bay. "What do you do, Mrs. Thigpen, with the fish you catch? How big are they?"

"These can be some size, Jerry. Where'd you say you are from? ... Illinois? I suppose you caught sunnys up there. Maybe a trout or two. That would be bait for these fish. Average one weighs in at six-eight pounds, and on up to twelve. Sometimes, if there's been a heavy rain and the tide is extra strong, you might tie into one on up to fifteen pounds, but that's a whopper. No mistaking when you get one on ... they fight like crazy. Long, solid fish, something like a northern pike, if you know what that is. Snook have a solid black stripe down each side. Undershot jaw. Beautiful fish."

Jerry nodded. He was hanging on to every word Ellie Thigpen said.

"I use a heavy cane pole," she went on, "with a lot of whip to the end. Twelve feet of clothes line is tied to the end about a foot in, and some six feet of heavy wire is tied to the rope. No reel. This isn't sport fishing, this is eating fish fishing. We want 'em and we want 'em quick. Once they strike I strike back and immediately haul 'em up onto the bridge. No messing around. No ceremony. Just snatch 'em up. Lay 'em in the center of the bridge, lengthwise, so any cars happening along can straddle 'em. It's all got to be fast, 'cause when they start feeding it's mostly over in a half-hour or so." Ellie held up a remonstrative hand. "And no talking! You can't seriously fish and chatter. You have to concentrate, to attune yourself to the fish. You have to sense when one is eyeing your bait and slowly circling it to strike. You can't see him, but you must 'feel' him. Then, when he strikes, you strike back. If you're lucky, you got him. All very fast."

"By the way, Ellie." Maude had almost forgotten to tell her. "Jerry has an old truck. He's started a delivery business on the island, so he can haul your fish to Murph's ice-house and you won't have to."

"Well, that's a relief, sure enough. That'll be just great. I'm off home now. Thanks for everything. I'll clear things away tonight and be ready for tomorrow. It's almost here, you know." And Ellie left in a rush.

With Mrs. Thigpen and her intensity gone, the others worked along quietly. Jerry mentally went over all the fishing information he'd been told and came up with several questions.

"Aunt Maude, Mrs. Thigpen mentioned a net and a lamp. What are they used for? I don't understand."

"I agree, Jerry. Ellie didn't go into all that very clearly. This is the way it works. It's night and you want to go fishing on the bridge. First, you gather together all the things you'll need, and you light your lantern inside before you go out. It'll be a pump-up gasoline pressure lamp with two special mantles or 'bulbs' that light from a match and glow brightly. They're called Coleman Lamps and campers use 'em, usually in the north. Then, dragging all your gear and the lamp, out you go to the bridge. The lamp is tied to a support strut and lowered to just clear of the water. This is tricky, as you want it as close to the water as possible but high enough so it won't get splashed if wind comes up and riles the bay. All kinds of little fish immediately circle around the light, curiously enough always swimming counter-clockwise, isn't that odd? Where was I?" Maude was getting sleepy. "Oh, yes. You let down the lantern, tied to the bridge. A long thin fish about the size of a flat pencil, seven or eight inches long, called 'hound minnow', they circle into the light, too. You take the net and swoop 'em up. That's your bait. You hook 'em in one eye and out the other and they live quite a long time. You drop 'em back into the water and move 'em about just clear of the light circle. If the moon is bright, you can dangle 'em back and forth in the water the entire length of the bridge. Ellie Thigpen moves hers in a large figure 8. Says it excites the fish feeding nearby. I don't know. But I do know that the fish, immediately he's hooked, tries to dart back under the bridge. I suppose he feels safer there in the shadows. Your line is apt to get fouled in the barnacles on the piling, and if you didn't have that six feet of wire on the end of your rope, your line would be cut through and the fish would escape. End of lesson. Next lesson tomorrow night, on the bridge." Maude's eyes closed and her head sagged.

But Jerry wasn't finished. "How many can we catch?" he wanted to know.

Aunt Ag glanced over at Maude, nodding in her chair, and took up the narrative.

"Well, now, Jerry, that depends. Sometimes only one or two. If everything is right, quite a few. One night, Ellie pulled in fifteen, all by herself."

"What happens to them, then?" This was Jerry's first encounter with wild life slaughter, and he was instinctively repelled. "One person and fifteen fish! She didn't need all those."

"That's Ellie's livelihood, Jerry. She catches fish and sells them. People eat them. There never are enough fish caught to supply the market. We take these and gut them. Then we drive to the dock and sell them. To Murph, at so much per pound. Murph in turn stores the fish on ice in a small shed connected to his main dock-house. Twice a week the Punta Gorda Fish Company sends a boat to collect whatever's stored, buying 'em from Murph, and dropping off ice. The fish end up in markets all up and down the east coast. It's necessary. People need the fish."

Maude wasn't asleep. She studied Jerry through half-closed eyes, sensing his revulsion. "There are millions and millions of fish in the oceans, Jerry. All down through history, they've been a main source of food. The Bible is full of fishermen and fish. I'd be against it, too, if it was all waste. But it isn't. These fish go to market, and some child in Brooklyn, say, has a meal. So it goes."

Jerry nodded, as he moved toward the staircase. "I know all that. But I've never ... well ... done any killing. I mean, I've never been responsible for ... I mean ... " His voice trailed off as he moved up the stairs to his room.

A strained silence hung in the air.

Maude rested her head on the back of the rocker and stared upward. The boy would be all right, once he'd had time to digest this brush with reality. Especially after he'd had his first snook hooked and fighting. Visions crowded her mind of a young girl, years before, crouching in the brush as lumbermen returned to camp lugging three fresh-shot deer. Blood dripped from slashed throats, heads lolled from side to side, glazed eyes, already festooned with flies, stared at her. The air suddenly smelled wild and untamed and hot. "Come here, girl, and give us a hand," her father called, but she shrank back deep into the brush, shuddering. The loud laughter of the men drowned the sound of her retching. Maude shook her head and expelled deeply through her mouth. Don't dwell on that stuff, she told herself ... all over and done with, thank God. Forget it ... Today! Concentrate on today.

5

From the time she was very young, just able to talk, Sally was out of step. The youngest of nine children, she was born in 1891 on the banks of the Ashepoo River, sixty miles south of Charleston, South Carolina. Though other members of her family and outside acquaintances projected an easy air of shuffling, smiling, yassah-nosah, this child held her head high, her back stiff. She seldom smiled. Her air of self-sufficiency kept others at arms length. People did not understand this strange behavior and marked her down as pushy, and uppity, and headed for a fall. They went their own way, and Sally went hers.

The tobacco and cotton fields around Ashepoo were fertile, the crops plentiful. With the wharves of Charleston easily accessible, the export prices remained substantial, not yet reflecting the depressed values of the inland areas. The children of plantation owners lived well and ate well, playing through their carefree days.

Not so this small black child! Not yet in her teens, Sally's tiny hands were formed to a hoe handle. Into the fields at dawn, she hoed alongside the others until the sun dropped low. A simple meal, usually grits and fatback, was her daily reward, after which she flopped onto one side of the bunk she shared with her two sisters, her thin body twitching in exhaustion throughout the night's sleep.

As the years went by, Sally watched silently as her brothers slipped off, one by one, heading for the excitement of Charleston and the good life. They did not return. Sally did not miss them. Each departure was evaluated not as a loss but as one less mouth to share the meager daily food. Occasionally, after another disappearance, Sally would lean on her hoe, staring down the row of tobacco plants she was weeding, and wonder.

The winter of 1905 was exceptionally mild and Sally decided it was her time to leave. Her brothers had all headed north, to the towns and the bright lights. She would head south, keeping to the fields she knew and felt comforted by. One night, with a bright moon sailing high, she slipped from her bunk and gathered her few possessions into a bandanna bundle. Then, with the bundle tied to her hoe, and the handle across her shoulder, she trudged down the lane and disappeared into the moonlight. She was fourteen years old.

The trip southward was slow and covered six years. Sally worked the spring and summer of 1906 in the melon patches of Coosawhatchie, then moved on south, crossing into Georgia in the vicinity of Springfield. She spent a year alongside the Ogeechee River, working in a large, dusty peach orchard. Then a passing wagoneer gave her a ride into Fargo where she caught a barge plying the Suwanee southward to the Gulf.

One sunny March afternoon in 1908, Mrs. Anne Newton glanced up from pruning her roses and caught sight of a small dark figure leaning on her gate.

"Mercy, child, you gave me a start! Do you want something? Don't be breaking down my gate, now."

"No'm, I won't." Sally said slowly, gazing straight at Mrs. Newton. "Could ya spare me a drink o' watah, Missus? I'se thirsty."

Sally stayed with Mrs. Newton for three years, working as all-round house servant. Those were happy years. Mrs. Newton taught the girl to cook, to clean and to read. The strong affection each felt for the other was never shown but the girl's eyes grew warm and deep.

However, the wanderlust persisted and by 1911, at the age of twenty Sally was restless once again. Reluctantly, Mrs. Newton wrote a letter to her brother in Fort Myers, a partner in the P & X Bulb Company, and gave Sally a farewell present of a steamer ticket from nearby Suwanee down the open Gulf and up the Caloosahatchee River to Fort Myers. As they shook hands and said goodbye, Mrs. Newton never knew from the girl's solemn face that deep inside she was torn apart. In memory of her friend, Sally added Anne to her name.

Hoeing the flat sandy-loam fields of gladiola under the broiling sun of southwest Florida didn't bother Sally-Anne at all. She loved the warmth, she loved the beautiful flowers which seemed to spring out of the earth, straining and reaching upward with their spiky flower-heads, all brilliant colors. She was happy again, and peaceful.

Here she met Doobie. One afternoon, when it was time to quit the fields, Doobie reached out and took her hoe, walking beside her to the collection station and the shanty-bound wagons.

"What they call you, girl?"

"Sally-Anne."

"Where you from?"

She had to wait a moment to settle her heart. Her breath seemed to be gone.

"I'se a Carolina gullah, way back."

Doobie snorted. "I'se a Georgia geechee, myself."

She sneaked a sidewise glance. This would be a fine man for her. Not much bigger than she was. She liked small men, dark men, and he was small and dark. Ugly, too, which was good. He'd stay home nights. She might as well grab him.

Never one to pull back from a decision, Sally-Anne married Doobie Denkins several week-ends later. Holding hands, they exchanged simple promises and with hesitant smiles, crept deeper into the palmettos along-side the river.

A year or so later, when the Rigby Brothers expanded their vast trucking farm on Sanibel, Sally-Anne and Doobie applied for work. They crossed the sound on the Punta Rassa ferryboat, and even before touching down on the island, while still out on the gentle, clear, blue-green water, with porpoises rolling and playing off to one side, and white birds swooping and diving, a sense of deep contentment suffused her entire body.

Sally-Anne had finally reached the end of her journey.

●

The morning following the encounter with Ellie Thigpen and all the bridge-fishing talk, Jerry was up at dawn, ready for the day ahead. He yanked on his shorts and raced down the stairs and fell over Sally-Anne. She was flat on the floor, half under the sink, repairing the plunger of the cistern pump-handle, her legs thrust toward the stairs. Foggy with sleep and his mind elsewhere, Jerry didn't notice and tripped over her feet.

There was instant pandemonium. Sally-Anne jack-knifed her legs and tried to sit upright, crashing her head into the bottom of the sink.

"Lawd a-mercy," she cried. "What's goin' on out there? Ain't nothin' sacred these days?"

Jerry, covered with confusion and trying to apologize, patted at her legs and kept repeating louder and louder to top Sally-Anne's voice.

"I'm sorry. I'm sorry ... "

Aunt Agnes rushed out of her room because of the commotion, took one look at the two sprawled on the floor and laughed out loud.

"Whatever are you two doing, down there?" she wanted to know, and she stretched out a hand to help Sally-Anne up.

"Don' tech. Don' tech me. I ken do it." Sally-Anne was on her feet like a safety-pin suddenly snapping open. "My," she said, brushing ineffectively at her gingham skirt, "looks like it's gonna be a upset day, sho' 'nuff." She flexed her legs up and down. "Nothin's broke. Is you broke?" and she turned to the boy.

"Sally-Anne, this is Jerry, my nephew." Aunt Agnes explained, on her way to the stove to start breakfast. "He arrived awhile back."

"Yes'm." Sally-Anne nodded. "I 'spected so."

"Is something wrong with the sink?"

"Yes'm. I was gettin' cistern water, fixin' to make coffee and only a little drizzled through. That ole plunger's stuck agin."

Agnes was busy now at the stove, readying bacon and eggs.

"Well, after we eat, maybe you can fix it. Can you fix it?" Sally-Anne nodded and Agnes went on. "Maybe Jerry can help. Show him what you do and then he can fix it if it goes bad when you're not here. Can you do that?"

"Yes'm." Sally-Anne went outside to check on Doobie, scuffling sand spurs somewhere in the yard.

Jerry wolfed his food, and Aunt Ag watched with disapproval.

"Jerry, what's all this rush? You're eating as if you've never seen food before. Things are supposed to be peaceful and quiet and slow, here on the island. Why are you gulping?"

"Aunt Ag, there's so much to do. I don't want to miss anything. I've got to pick up Aunt Maude and drive her to the limes ... Aunt Cora asked me to go with her for more palm fronds ... I have to meet the mailboat, especially today, as I'm getting the ... as I'm expecting lots of packages to deliver ... Roy is expecting me for a swim and Mrs. Thigpen has promised to take me fishing on the bridge tonight. And now you've asked me, first off, to help Sally-Anne fix the sink. I gotta get moving or I'll never get it all done on time."

Agnes smiled at the boy's vitality. He seemed over his bout with pneumonia, thank goodness. He certainly didn't look sick any longer. Another week of sun and sea air and he'd be fine. Wonder what he is expecting Captain Bob to bring him on the mailboat. He stumbled a little, just now, and looked a bit guilty. Must be up to something ...

Sally-Anne and Jerry were at the sink.

"Fust, you pulls out this here pin." Sally-Anne showed him how. "That turns loose the inside stick from the handle. Grab holt of it tight-like or it'll slide on down the pipe and git away from ya. Then yank her outen the top, like this. Here's the trouble. This ole piece o' leather dries out and curls. Won't suck water ifen it don' fit the insides o' the pipe, sos I beat on it with my iron. I wet it fust an' beat on it, and beat on it and flatten her out. Onst she's flat agin an' wet agin I puts her back inside the pipe, put the pin back in the handle an' pump her. Oh, I fergit. Onst she's back together I pours water down the pump. Called primin'. Don't use the water from the spigot there. That's salty water and will sperl the drinkin' water below. Use water from that ole gallon jug under here. Onst she's workin', don' fergit to fill up that bottle agin, fer the nex' go roun'."

Maude had come in by this time. She crossed to the sink, grabbed the pump handle and worked it violently up and down. Water gushed into the sink.

"What's the trouble? Works fine," she said.

"Coursen it do." Sally-Anne moved her head with a slight air of grandeur. "I fixed it." Muttering to herself, she went up the stairs to clean Jerry's room.

Agnes rolled her eyes at Maude and motioned toward the coffee pot.

45

"Thanks," Maude said, getting herself a cup. "Jerry, I loaded my gear into your truck but I'm not putting it on just now — there's a stiff breeze blowing and the bugs may hold off. We'll see. Can always put it on later. Better bring your own stuff, though. By the way, I told Cora I'd go with her for those darn fronds, so you can forget that. We'll be a little longer than usual at the grove this morning. I want to hoe 'em out real good and really souse 'em with water. Then we won't have to go back for awhile." Maude was standing by the kitchen window, gazing out into the back yard. "I suppose we should trim back that gumbo out there. It's too huge now and the way it leans over the house is dangerous. Every time I come in the back door I keep thinking we'd better cut her back." Maude mused aloud. "Old Sammy Two-Boars would kill me if he knew I was even thinking of it." She slowly shook her head as she remembered. Turning back into the room and getting a fresh cup of coffee, Maude gestured at Agnes. "You know, Ag, you're just too lenient. Doobie is sound asleep in the gazebo. I saw him as I came in. Why do you let him get away with it? The yard's a disgrace. Sand spurs and weeds everywhere. Could be neat as a pin if he'd scuffle it. Want me to rouse him?"

"No, Maude, thank you just the same. Let him snooze. I know what he's doing and so does Sally-Anne. If he's not up and about in a little while, she'll tend to it. Besides, the slower he works, the faster she goes, so it all levels out. It's not exactly a fortune I'm paying them, you know."

Maude nodded and added with a touch of sarcasm ... " and Doobie's so 'wore out' or he's 'feelin' porely.' Doobie's always 'wore out'."

"Of course he is." Agnes was stacking dishes in the sink. "He's spent his whole life dodging work, and that wears out a man. Anyway, before they leave, most of the yard will be tended. If not, Sally-Anne'll grab a scuffle-hoe and catch it up. You'll see. Same thing, every week."

"But why do you put up with it, Ag?"

"Because that's the way it is down here." Agnes was talking now more to Jerry than to Maude. "It's a question of my adjusting and their dignity. It's all a part of the larger picture. We need them. They need us. Doobie has to feel he's getting away with something, or his self-image is disturbed. Sally-Anne has to feel she's protecting him. I have to put aside my heavy Nordic shoes and adjust to the gentle flow of life on the island. If one maintains a proper attitude, it's all of no great importance. Should I have a serious problem, I can go to them and they'll help me. They can always call on me for help. It's not a thing that's talked about, but we all understand."

"But, Ag, you've made it so easy for them." Maude swung around to Jerry, still at the table, silently absorbing this exchange. "Do you know what your Aunt did? She had Evan repair and screen in that old potting lean-to of your Uncle's. Just behind that gumbo-limbo out there, it is. Put in a table and two chairs, just so Doobie could sit there, out of the bugs, and sleep!"

"No, Maude. So Sally-Anne and Doobie could eat their lunch there ... with dignity. Always remember dignity."

Maude didn't acknowledge Agnes' interruption. She went hurriedly on.

46

"Then, when she found she could stand here and see them, she had Doobie plant those two big hibiscus to block off her vision."

"To give them privacy, Maude."

"Why couldn't they eat inside here?" Jerry wanted to know.

"Ah, you see." Agnes smiled at the boy. "Now, it becomes a question of my dignity. I wouldn't mind, but Sally-Anne won't have it. She says it's because Doobie is too hot and dirty from sweating in the yard, but the real reason is that Sally-Anne feels it wouldn't be 'fittin'. The way we've worked it out, everybody wins. When they head for home, Doobie can swagger a bit, because he's put one over on me. Sally-Anne can give me her slight little bow, which says 'no, he didn't. I fixed it even' ... and I can look forward to their coming next week, even before they're out of the drive."

On the way to the grove, Jerry asked Maude about the drinking water.

"I don't understand all that about drinking water and salt water and the things Sally-Anne was telling me. Why is there salt water coming out of the faucet and city water from the pump?"

"Oh, no. It doesn't work like that. City water?" Maude laughed as she spoke. "No city water within miles of here. Ft. Myers, yes, but not on these out-islands. Everybody out here has a cistern. Mostly a cypress tank on stilts alongside the house. Your Aunt's cistern is under the house, made of cement blocks with the walls white-washed and parafined so it won't leak. Rainwater is collected there, and used for drinking and cooking. The water runs off the roof into gutters along the eaves and then down a pipe into the cistern. All of it has to be cleaned once a year. I've done it and it's no fun, believe me. That rain water is too valuable to use for toilets and the shower and dishes and so on, so a screened pipe called a sand point is driven down into the yard, deep enough to reach below the water level, and water from that is piped in for the plumbing and the sink. That's salt water."

"Is that why the soap won't lather in the shower?"

Maude nodded. "Yep. And that's why the dishes are on the sticky side. Clean but sticky. One more get-used-to down here. It's also why the plumbing wears out so soon."

Jerry worried along with the idea. "Suppose there's dirt on the roof ... bird droppings and lizards and so on?"

Maude glanced at the boy. "Very smart," she acknowledged. "There always is. That problem is taken care of by a by-pass valve about half-way along the down-spout. When it's closed which it always should be, the water is blocked from entering the cistern and flows instead out of the valve opening, letting the first flush of rain rinse the roof of all the varminty stuff. Then if the cistern is low, someone inside the house braves the storm, and dashes out and throws the valve ... usually first standing under the valve spigot and washing his or her hair. Hair can get mighty gluey from swimming and salt showers."

"When I came down this morning, I was the first up but Sally-Anne was already working in the kitchen." Jerry said, as he turned off the dirt road and

47

into the grove, and drew up under an Australian pine in the shade. "How'd she get in? Has Aunt Ag given her a house-key?"

"Don't need one." Maude shook her head. "Nobody on the island locks anything. Houses are open, cars have keys left in 'em. It's different out here from in town or in Evanston," she went on. "People depend on each other. Suppose, for instance, you needed help or had to get in someone's house, or use their car ... can't fiddle around with keys or run the risk of being locked out, you know. If folks need a tool or a car, they leave notes that they took such and such, and bring it back when they're done. It'll be time for me to get off the island when folks have to lock up."

The older woman and the young boy worked smoothly together. Maude was proven correct about the bugs. There were none at all. With the hoeing finished and the trees all soaked with water, they sat under the pine to rest a bit.

Jerry had another question. "Aunt Maude," he asked, "who is Sammy Two-Boars?"

Maude chuckled. "You heard that, did you? Well, now let's see!" She broke off a twig and began scratching in the sand between her feet. For some time she was silent. Jerry didn't make a sound.

"Before I tell you this story," Maude finally said, "I must explain that it came to me as an ancient Indian folk tale. It might not even be authentic, I don't know. Way, way back, maybe some true event sparked the fable, maybe an Indian child felt sick and faint, and in a weakened condition had a vision, as happens in other religions, and the story was passed down. I don't know. If you believe it, it's true. Old Sammy certainly did. He was very old, and very wise and very honorable."

There was another long pause and more scratching in the sand. Then, in a quiet tone, still hunched low, Maude began:

"It was years ago, and I'd gone deep into the Everglades with Bill Thompson, the Indian Agent from Tallahassee. I'd known Bill since I was a tiny girl and we'd often gone into the 'glades together. This time there had been rumors of harbored aliens and Bill was sent in to investigate. Not a thing, however, came of our search and the final afternoon, as we were preparing to pull out, Bill decided to spend the night with Sammy Two-Boars, one of the Indian elders, whose headquarters was nearby. So we pushed our way through the hyacinths and nosed in to the hammock's little beach. I remember it was shady and cool as we stepped ashore and several little children ran down to greet us. In the center of the clearing grew a huge gumbo-limbo tree, the largest I've ever seen. Really mammoth, with thick lower branches spreading far out, and a leafy center soaring to the heavens."

"We had a regular feast that night, under the gumbo — spitted alligator tail, maize and sweet potatoes. We were brought mangoes covered with wild honey afterwards. Later, leaning against the tree trunk and resting, I was fighting off sleep when the old man leaned toward me and tapped me on the knee."

"Tonight ... full moon ... he come, maybe!"

"I didn't understand a word of the Seminole language, so Bill had to translate, which added an additional haunting quality to the evening ... the old man's low, guttural voice rising and falling in the cadence of age-old storytelling, underlined by Bill's whispered translation:"

'Long, long ago, back when the earth was young and there were few people, the heavens were controlled by the Four Winds. The cold, blustery North Wind was the eldest and the decision-maker. It was he who controlled the winter and the snows. The West Wind and the South Wind controlled the rains and the storms, the flooding of the rivers and the heaving and pounding of the seas. The East Wind, younger than the others, and tranquil where they were fearful, blew gently across the land, rousing the flowers in the Spring, causing the grasses to nod and bow together as they talked in whispers, and teasing the nesting birds by swaying their nests and raising their feathers.

One afternoon, as he moved across the Everglades, East Wind glanced down and saw a maiden in a dugout, poling a waterway at the edge of a lake. She was beautiful, tall and graceful, and her raven-black hair glistened to her hips. As she emerged from the cattails, she saw on the lake shore a golden youth, dressed all in white, bathed in a shimmering light. He beckoned, and she went.

They frolicked all summer in the hammocks and the waterways. They could not leave each other. East Wind neglected his duties. The Seasons were grumbling. North Wind called together his two brothers. East Wind must give up this maiden. She was a mortal and would grow old. He was a Wind and would stay forever young.

The three dominant Winds were in agreement. The maiden was imprisoned inside a gumbo-limbo tree where she would remain forever — tall, beautiful, young. East Wind could visit her whenever he happened that way, blowing affectionately around her, as she tried to capture him by entangling her branches. And so it is to this day.'

"Hours later, a rustling awoke me. I was in my sleep-bag in the bright moonlight and could see the whole clearing. Old Sammy was on his knees, placing a dish heaped high with food under the gumbo-limbo. I did not move. He did not know I saw.

"The following morning, we said our goodbyes and thank-yous and went on our way. As I passed the tree, heading for our boat, I noticed that the dish was empty!"

For some time Jerry didn't look up. He was watching a small brown-green lizard perched on a root of the pine bob it's head up and down and blow out it's chin-pouch. When the lizard darted away, Jerry looked at Maude. His eyes were smiling gently.

"That was a lovely story, Aunt Maude. Did you make it up?"

"Not all of it, no." Maude shook her head from side to side. "Of course not."

"Who ate Sammy's food? The Maiden?"

"That doesn't really matter, Jerry, does it? Some one or some thing was hungry. The important thing is that if we have too much, we should put a little out. We have to help, as we go along our way. Maybe, after all, it was the maiden!"

●

That noon, Captain Bob handed the duster across the boat railing to Jerry and brushed aside any thanks.

"If you can repair it, you're welcome to it." He winked at Jerry. "Hate things taking up space that don't work. It's most likely the impeller, 'cause it doesn't put out dust regular. If you can't fix it, maybe Roy can. Or Evan. Anyway, it don't do me any good. You're welcome to it."

That afternoon, instead of swimming, Roy and Jerry operated on the duster, taking the long metal dusting tube off the canister and then dismantling the housing. Sure enough, the flat ribbed disk that served to force the insecticide power from the canister out the tube was missing several ribs. While Roy rummaged around in his electrical supplies, hunting nuts and screws, Jerry whittled replacement ribs from two old shingles. Before the afternoon was over, the duster was nearly as good as new. Jerry hung the canister belt around his neck, adjusting it so that the duster rode on his left hip, and filled the canister with insecticide dust which Roy gave him. Then he ran about, grinding the canister handle, and a gratifying cloud of powder blossomed from the nozzle.

Promising to meet Roy the next afternoon for a swim, Jerry headed back toward Aunt Ag's. He was anxious to surprise her.

"You do what, with what?" Aunt Ag indeed was surprised. "What is that stuff you're squirting all about? What's it supposed to do? Don't get it in the house, Jerry. I hope it's fit to breathe." Agnes was quite skeptical as she watched the boy darting about the yard, in and out among the bushes, leaving a fog of dust behind him.

"It's okay, Aunt Ag. It's been approved by the U. S. Department of Agriculture, and farmers are beginning to dust crops with it, and grove owners use it on fruit. It won't hurt humans or wildlife or fish or anything. It's called DDT." Jerry stopped to recover his breath. "I should be dusting before the sun is up and while everything is still dewy. Roy says it will keep mosquitoes away 'till the afternoon, unless it rains and washes all the dust off. It's expensive, so I thought I'd mostly fog the doorways and the path to the parking area, and squirt some around your car and my truck."

"Are you sure it's safe, Jerry?"

"Yes'm, it's safe. Everybody is using it. If it works, it'll certainly take the place of that sticky 6-12 that came out during the war. 'Course, we'll still have to smear that on for fishing on the bridge at night and times like that — dust wouldn't be effective there in all that breeze. I'll try early tomorrow morning, and we'll see if it works."

Maude had been watching this exchange, leaning against a porch upright, and Agnes looked quizzically at her as she came back inside.

"This world and the next" Agnes exclaimed, rolling her eyes up.

"It's quite alright, Ag. I've been reading about this DDT. The government releases are touting it to the skies. It will revolutionize the whole business of insecticides, it seems. Bad bugs will disappear in no time at all, now."

Agnes, the quintessential conservationist, was unconvinced. "I've never known any such panacea! What will happen to all the good bugs and the birds and little animals, and the fish, all of which eat up those so-called bad bugs? What about that dust settling on the roof and washing down into the cistern? Has any government official tested this DDT to see what happens if you drink it?"

"Come on, Ag. The government says this stuff is fine ... harmless. We have to go by some authority and that's the authority we go by. The label is Progress. You know."

"I'm not so sure I do!"

As Jerry ran in the house, Maude grabbed him by the arm. "Early supper, Jerry. Ellie Thigpen mentioned fishing at nine o'clock, but if I know her she'll be out there by 7:30 if the tide's right or not, fishing up a storm. This'll be your first trip and it'll take a bit of getting used to, all those clothes and the fishing gear and all. Let's eat soon's we can and I'll help you get yourself together. It's gonna be a hassle, at best."

It was a hassle, but amicable. Everybody got involved, laughing together and making friendly jokes as each new item was brought out. Jerry and Maude cut the fool, jousting at invisible enemies and leaping about in various threatening postures. Jerry didn't know which was worse, the netting around his face that not only cut off the air but his vision as well, or the thick gauntlet-gloves that turned all his fingers into thumbs.

"Aw, come on, now, Aunt Maude. Nobody can fish in all this stuff. I can hardly move at all and I can't see. Can't I go out in just my regular clothes?"

"Sure you can. But you'll only do it once. Then you'll rush pell-mell back inside and be laid up for days. Those bugs are mean. Thick and mean. But wear what you want. Don't go by me." Maude was on her knees, fussing with her gas lamp. "I haven't lit this thing for months. Hope it's still working." She pumped the pressure handle until it stiffened, then locked it down and opened the jet. A hissing sound escaped.

Cora reached over with a flaming home-made taper and the mantle ignited and burned with a bright white glare.

51

"I love to light 'em but that's all. Won't carry 'em around. Afraid they'll explode" she said, timidly.

As the fading daylight turned first to dusk, then abruptly into inky darkness, Maude and Jerry stomped down the path and out onto the bridge, lugging lamp, net and poles.

Agnes and Cora, arm in arm at the window, watched them disappear around the bend. Agnes chuckled as she squeezed Cora gently.

"I've often wondered what the winter visitors think they're seeing when they first spot one of our night fishermen. Gives 'em a start, I'll bet."

Ellie Thigpen was already on the bridge, a dark blob at the far end, leaning across the railing and reaching downward. She'd lowered her lantern to just above the water and a round patch of light some eight feet in diameter reflected from the surface.

"Got anything?" Maude asked.

"Nothing yet," Ellie answered. Her voice was muffled and Jerry could barely hear her. "Too early. Go away, Maude. I'll keep Jerry here with me."

Maude took no offense at the abrupt dismissal but returned to another section of the bridge before lowering her own lamp. She appreciated the unspoken rule of never crowding into another's 'territory' and could well remember Ellie's long-lasting fury when some northerner once rushed up to where she was fishing, plopped his bait nearly on top of hers, and breathed beerily at her 'What ya catchin' here, huh?' Ellie had pulled back her head and stared at the intruder in total disbelief. Then, without a word, she'd pulled in her bait, yanked up her lantern and relocated herself to the other end of the bridge. Days later, still sputtering, she had said to Maude "Can you believe the gall of that ass?"

Ellie drew Jerry to her side. "Nothing to tell you about the lamp. Any fool can lower it. Just be sure you allow for splash. Wouldn't do to get it wet. Now, watch down there. See all that stuff, bustling about? That little thing that sort of flicks in and out of the light, that's a shrimp. Too small for bait unless a giant happens along. We're not after any of this teeny stuff. There! Look there! See that swoosh of light streaking along below the surface, stirring up the phosphorus? See it suddenly boil in and swirl away? That's the boy we want, a snook feeding deep."

"Let's catch him" Jerry exclaimed, excitedly.

Ellie snorted. "Not a chance" She said. "He was too deep and by now he's halfway to Mexico. No hurry. Should be a good night. No wind and the moon'll be up soon. The pass'll be full and they'll be top-feeding. You can tell by the sound they make, sucking in the bait ... like corks popping out of a bottle. Gimme that net, now. Mr. Minnie's coming soon, I can tell in my bones."

Ellie grabbed the net from Jerry and then quickly swooped low with it.

"There. See that? Told you he'd be along and he did and I got him." Ellie swung the net over the railing and onto the bridge, where it flopped up and down a bit. Then she handed the net handle to Jerry.

"Might as well start right here" she said. "Slip off your glove and reach in there and grab that boy. I'll get my pole." She darted away down the bridge to where she'd left her gear.

Jerry could see a thin form flopping in the net. Feeling like he was thrusting his arm down a dark tunnel where some monster could lunge out and bite it off, he reached gingerly under the edge of the net and gabbed the little fish.

"I've got it! I've got it, Mrs. Thigpen. See?"

Ellie was back with her pole. " You sure have" she said "but its hind part before. I need the head. Turn it around."

Jerry opened his hand to do so, and the fish was gone. With a surprisingly hefty wiggle for so small a thing, it flipped out of his grasp, landed on the bridge decking and slid through a crack. All in a second, it was gone.

"Gosh! Gee! I'm sorry!" Jerry was horrified. Mrs. Thigpen smoothed it over. Taking up the net, she led the boy back to the lantern.

"No harm. Too bad he escaped, 'cause he had 'ten-pound snook' written all over him. No, I'm just ragging you, Jerry. Here, take the net and scoop up another one. Listen now, watch for a long, thin, greenish fish, about the size of a pencil, with goggle eyes and a long hair-like snout. They'll dart into the light and hesitate for a second. That's when you swoop. So you have to hold the net half in, half out of the water and absolutely still. There's one, now. Swoop!! Swoop! ... see, you missed. Come from their rear, always net fish from the rear, if possible. I feel that gives you a second's edge, as they're peering forward ... or should be."

"What are the ones we're after called?"

"Hound minnows. But never mind that. Just get me one."

The next swoop was successful and Jerry lifted up the net. Mrs. Thigpen took it and dropping the handle end to the bridge, leaned the rest against the railing so that the net hung over the water.

"Maybe this will be easier, Jerry. Now, reach in there and grab it. Remember, have the head sticking forward. If you grab it wrong end to, keep your hand in the net to switch it around. Then, if it flips out of your hand, which it may do several times, it'll still be in the net. Understand? Now, bring it out. Don't give it to me. You keep holding it. I want the head. Stick the head toward me and hold it still."

Ellie reached out with her left hand and grabbed Jerry's holding the minnow. Then, in a quick motion, she took her hook and stuck the end in one eye, through the head and out the other eye. Holding her line with the fish impaled on the hook and swaying back and forth like a tiny pendulum, Ellie laughed and exclaimed "There, ain't she a beaut?"

Maude had joined them by this time and now she motioned to Ellie and said "Why don't you go on and fish, Ellie? I'll continue Jerry's education. After all, with us it's more or less just fun, but for you it's serious. Go on. Catch a whopper." Ellie moved on down the bridge, holding her bait just on top of the water and moving it in a large figure 8.

"Aunt Maude, did you see what she did to that poor little fish? Right in one eye and out the other. Ugh!"

Sensing the boy's repugnance, Maude experienced another flash-back to her childhood in the piney scrub ... a small child yelling with rage when she happened upon a black snake swallowing a toad. Grabbing a pine bough, she had lunged at the snake, but her father was quicker. He seized the snake's tail and cracked it through the air like snapping a bull-whip, sending the head flying in one direction and the mutilated toad in another. She had reached down to gently gather up the poor broken little thing, but her father's huge foot came down on it, twisting and squashing it to a bloody pulp. Horror-stricken, she'd screamed and fallen to her knees, rocking back and forth as she moaned in agony. Her father stomped on ahead, calling over his shoulder 'lay off that bawling, girl. One hoppy-toad one way tuther don't make no never-mind' ...

Maude decided not to sympathize with the boy. He'd get used to life's little horrors sooner or later. Better be on the casual side.

"Come on, now, Jerry. Remember what the cigarette ads are claiming — 'Nature in the raw is seldom mild'. 'Course, that's nature against nature and this is man against nature. So it seems different, but it's not, really. Man has always survived by taking what he wants. Always has, always will. If that hound minnow hadn't been netted, but had gone on rushing to the sea on the strong tides, some predator fish would have gobbled him up in no time. This way, Ellie will most likely land a snook and we'll eat it. It's not the end result that's so distressing, but the procedure."

"Aunt Maude, if I stay here I'll be agreeing to all this and I think I'm against it. I don't think I can stay. I gotta go back."

Just at that moment a tremendous disturbance occurred at Mrs. Thigpen's end of the bridge. A furious splashing and thrashing boiled the water, and Maude and Jerry raced that way. Mrs. Thigpen wasn't making a sound, but was holding on to her cane pole for dear life. The rope and the wire leader were taut and moving violently first this way, then that, as the hooked fish tried desperately to break free. A full moon was peeping over the pines edging the pass and night birds were swooping by on silent wings. A feeling, wild and exciting and primitive, beautiful and scary all at the same time, filled the air and communicated with the boy. He grasped the bridge railing and watched raptly as the fight raged ... the silent, determined, hooded figure and the frantic, frenzied fish. The bent pole exerted a constant pressure upward against the fish's downward pull, and the fish soon tired. Sensing this weakening, Ellie Thigpen heaved upward with all her strength and the snook broke water and sailed high over the railing and landed flapping on the bridge.

"Oh, boy! Oh, my gosh! How exciting, "Jerry yelled, rushing for the fish. Falling to his knees, he held the snook with both hands to keep it from thrashing loose. "Aunt Maude, look. It's so huge. I want to catch one. Can I? Can I?"

Maude smiled in her hood. "I thought you were disgusted and going home" she said. Jerry didn't answer, and she didn't press the point.

Staring at the flopping fish, Jerry reached out a tentative finger and traced the black streak down its side from just behind the gills to where the tail joined the body. Running his finger back toward the head, he was surprised when Maude jerked his hand away.

"Have to be careful of the gills," she explained. "The leading edge is sharp as a razor. Another reason for that long wire leader on the pole. His gills and his mouth. Watch out for both. See him snapping there? If he comes down on your hand, he can give you a very bad time. He's no toy, remember."

"He's just beautiful. Just beautiful. And so big. All I've ever caught is sunnies and a gudgeon or two. Never anything like this. What's he weigh, anyhow?" Jerry turned to Maude, forgetting he couldn't see her.

"Well, let's see." Maude held out her hand, full length and with the fingers held tightly together. "One hand, four pounds. He's about seven-eight pounds. Perfect for eating. I can feel my taste buds squirting already."

All this time Ellie Thigpen had been busy, back at her lamp and her net. "Come on, you two." she called. "Time's awasting and we came to fish. They're beginning to pop all over. Let's get in there and get some."

When Jerry netted himself another hound minnow, he asked Maude to hook it for him, and turned his head to one side as she did. Then, figuring he might get in Mrs. Thigpen's way, he dropped his bait on the opposite side of the bridge and started slowly walking up and down, trying to maneuver his minnow in the pattern Mrs. Thigpen used. Back and forth, back and forth. Nothing happened. The moon was up full by now and bathed the scene in silver light. He could hear fish feeding all about, sometimes close in, sometimes far out in the pass. Nothing happened.

Mrs. Thigpen landed two more snook and Maude landed one and lost one. Jerry stopped walking about and rested against the railing. It had been a long, busy day and he was tired. He moved his bait about in a desultory manner, half asleep, and was annoyed when it stopped. He gave a little tug but it didn't move. Darn. Must be hung up on a branch or a piling or something. He gave a sharp, strong tug and the world came alive. The cane pole nearly slipped from his slack grasp before he had time to tighten his grip. No question he had somebody down there. Back and forth, up and down, sideways, the fish thrashed, then seemed to quiet down and just hung on his hook. Felt like a hundred pounds, just hanging there. Then, on the move again and around a piling. Jerry held on and tugged. The fish reversed itself from under the bridge and headed down the open pass.

Maude and Ellie had come up to watch the struggle.

"Hold his head up. Keep a tight line. Don't let him jerk. Keep a constant pull. Hold on. Pull. Hold on." Jerry didn't know who was talking or much of what was said. He wanted that fish. Gosh, how he wanted that fish. He'd never wanted anything so much.

Suddenly the tired fish gave up and floated on his side up to the surface. Huge. Jerry took one look and backed hurriedly away across the bridge, pulling the fish up out of the water as the line tightened.

"Oh, my God, no." Maude screamed. "You'll lose him. His mouth will tear."

But Ellie Thigpen had gone into action. She leaned far down over the railing, wrapped the rope around a finger and lifted upward. Slowly, slowly, without jerking, smoothly she lifted the fish up and over the railing. It flopped onto the bridge.

"What did I do wrong? What did I do?" Jerry was jumping up and down, half hysterical.

Maude quieted him. "You didn't do anything wrong. There he is. You got him."

Ellie patted the fish. "Lovely. Lovely, Jerry. You've got yourself a beautiful redfish. Must be ten pounds if it's an ounce. Only thing better than a snook is redfish. See that circular black mark on his tail? It's on both sides. That's the redfish mark. As soon as he dries out he'll lose the red tinge he now has, but he'll keep the tail mark. He's a beauty. Just beautiful. I'll clean him up for you and ice him down and you can come over tomorrow and get him. Let's all go home, now. We've got gear to collect and fish to lug and I'm tired. For the first bridge outing of the season, it's been great. But enough's enough. Let's go."

6

October

One mid-October afternoon the incoming packages and supplies were heavier than usual and Jerry was so busy loading everything onto the flatbed he didn't notice the slight figure drawn back into the shrubbery. As he climbed into the truck to drive off, a tentative hand reached out and timidly touched his shoulder.

"Could you please give me a ride home? I've got money and I can pay. I'm Amanda. Amanda Johnson."

"Yes'm I know." Jerry had seen Amanda once before, but only from a distance. She'd been hurrying along the lane from the post office northward, her head bent low, her swisher flicking mosquitoes and one hand clutching the handle of a large woven basket. He wasn't at all prepared for the shy creature with the beautiful flashing teeth and the large soft brown eyes.

"I live down the lane, just behind Mrs. Crunch's shell shop."

"Yes'm, I know. Climb in. I'll be happy to drive you home. Have you any packages?"

Amanda gestured toward the bushes, and a half-smile chased across her face, flaring her nostrils and slightly lifting one corner of her mouth. "Just those few things. I could carry them but you see, it's my foot."

Jerry glanced down and saw that her foot was bandaged up over her ankle. It seemed quite a large bandage.

"My lithograph machine collapsed on one side and caught my foot. Tabitha Upton drove me to the hospital. The doctor says that I broke a small bone in my arch. He gave me a crutch but I left it on the dock in town when I caught the mailboat this morning. A body can't walk in sand with a crutch." Again the fleeting smile, and a small sound of embarrassment, sort of a humming, came from her throat. "He put a cast on it."

Jerry helped her into the truck and retrieved her packages. Not a word was spoken as they drove along the sandy lane, across Palm Avenue, on past the shell shop, around the corner and into Amanda's yard. Jerry helped her inside and then stacked her packages on her porch.

She was rooting about in an old suitcase. "I've some money in here, somewhere. I know I have."

"That's okay," Jerry exclaimed, waving goodbye and turning to climb back into his truck.

Again the sudden smile and the deep humming sound, and the cottage door softly started closing, blotting out more and more of Amanda's face, until the door latched shut, and she was gone.

Later that afternoon, swimming with Ray and discussing the episode, as they splashed about on the sand-bar, Jerry turned pensive.

"It would'a been kinda spooky, if she wasn't so shy and gentle."

"And beautiful," Roy added. "Don't you think she's beautiful?"

Jerry jumped a small wave, wishing it was bigger. "Yeah. I suppose she is. But not exactly like a woman, somehow. More like an animal. A deer. A fawn — that's it. She's going to be my fawn lady." He plunged under the water and upended Roy. They both came up gasping. "My very own fawn lady. I'm going to protect her forever."

"From what?" Roy wanted to know. "Everybody always wants to protect Amanda. Make no mistake about it, though. She can be tough as nails under all that shyness. You betcha."

"Roy" Jerry stopped charging about and looked seriously at his friend. "She said her foot was broken because some sort of machine fell on it. What was she talking about, anyway? Do you know?"

"Sure I know. Her lithograph arrangement sagged to one side, I guess from all the thumping and pressure that goes on, and tore loose part of the framing, which smashed down on her foot. I know 'cause Mrs. Upton had Evan and me go in last night and fix the press."

"What does she do with it, the machine thing?"

"She etches with it. Pictures. She draws pictures. It's very technical and I'm not sure I can explain it right. She has these two huge flat stones, one above the other, the bottom one in a stationary frame and the other suspended above it in some sort of wind-down arrangement. First she rubs the stationary stone smooth with a pumice block, like cooks do a grill. Then she spreads a thick coat of grease, Vaseline I think, all over it and with a thin wire she draws a picture, whatever she wants, in the grease. Fine lines are left where the wire removes the grease an' she pours muriatic acid into them. The acid eats out the stone along those little lines but doesn't spread because of the grease. Next, she cleans the stone, pours ink in the lines, wipes the stone clean again, and finally lays a sheet of special porous paper on top. When all that's done, she lowers the top stone and presses it in place with the wind-down handle, like a reversed car jack. The stone is very heavy to begin with, and the handle exerts a lot of pressure. Then she opens up the press and carefully peels back the paper, and on it in ink is the drawing. Mrs. Upton says Amanda is very talented as an artist and would make a lot of money if there was any way to show her stuff."

"I knew she was special when I first saw her." Jerry was alive with interest. "Does she store the stones? Her cottage floor must be pretty solid to carry all that weight."

Roy shook his head. "Oh, no. She says she gets only eight-ten pictures — she calls 'em 'impressions' — from one stone. Then it's worn out or something, and she has to do it all over again. She only has two stones, the bottom stationary one and the suspended one. Just the same, when Bob lugged 'em across from the city on the mailboat, it took four of us to get 'em from the boat to her house and set up. We had to revet the floor with cement blocks."

"Gee. Do you suppose she'd show me some of her pictures?"

"Sure." Roy was amused by the boy's eagerness.

"Imagine!" Jerry went on. "Way out here, on this tiny island, a real artist. Gee!"

They both were suddenly aware of hammering down the beach.

"Who's building something? I can hear hammering."

Roy chuckled. "That'll be Buster. My brother. Turns up every so often. Came in last night in his flat-bottom. Says he's here for the winter. I told him one night was one night too many for me, to get himself some place to stay if he was staying, so he's throwing up a wickie. Says he's gonna sleep on the beach. Wait'll you meet Buster. You won't think <u>he's</u> beautiful, believe you me!" And Roy gave a loud guffaw.

"Whaddaya mean 'came in a flat-bottom' ... what's a flat-bottom?"

"A kind of boat. There're many kinds of boats y'know ... in-boards, out-boards, sails with keels ... you know. Well, a flat-bottom is just that — a wide, wooden boat with a flat bottom instead of the usual V-hull. Has an in-board motor and can move about in shallow water. Buster uses his for taking tourists after bonefish in the Keys, where there're lots of mud flats and oyster bars, and the water is often very shallow."

"Golly," Jerry exclaimed. The two of them were resting on their elbows at the water-edge, running sand through their hands. "It must have taken some time for him to come up from way down there. How fast is that boat, anyway?"

Roy waved at Buster who'd started down the beach toward them. "He drove up to Fort Myers Beach. Had his boat in a repair yard there. Then he crossed over the sound to Sanibel and came on down the bay side. Still, took a smart bit of time at that, I guess."

Buster proved to be no beauty. He sauntered up and joined them, with a nod toward Jerry. He was thin and angular, tall and somewhat stooped. Both shoulders had flowery tattoos on them. His face sported several days beard growth, and he was chewing tobacco. Yet there was an air about Buster, a devil-may-care, rakish quality, that added zest and excitement.

"Claims the ladies go wild for him, down in the Key West area," muttered Roy under his breath, as Buster languidly stretched out on the sand near them. "He's an on-again, off-again fishing guide. Works out of Islamorada, mostly."

Jerry was fascinated.

Buster, meanwhile, was gazing off across the Gulf and spoke to Roy without turning his head. "You'll have to put up with me for one more night, Bro. That wickie won't be done 'til tomorrow night. I'll pay you off in mackerel."

"Humpf," Roy grunted. "Just where're you gonna get all those mackerel? It'll take a heap."

"Out there. Look at 'em, shining and flashing and cutting the water. They're moving north in big schools. Look at the birds. You can always tell by the birds. I'll fix up and push out about dawn, and fish until noon. Wanna come along?"

Roy nodded. "Sure, I want to, but I can't. I gotta work. Jerry, here, might be able to get free and go with you, if that's all right?"

Buster never took his eyes off the fish. "Sure. Okay. Where do you live, Jerry?"

"Illinois."

"No," said Buster. "I mean here. Where here on the island?"

"Oh, I'm sorry," Jerry answered. "I'm visiting my aunt, first house on the other side of the bridge."

"Can you be ready by seven a.m.? Meet me at Murph's dock. Sharp, now. I hate to dawdle."

Jerry's eyes were open so wide they threatened to fall out and his lips quivered with excitement.

"Sure. Yeah. What'll I bring? I've got a bamboo pole."

Buster smiled at Roy and turned to Jerry. "I've got stuff — you can use mine. By the way, offshore, out in the open Gulf, we use rods. Rods and reels. Poles are for bridge fishing and such. I'll show ya. See ya tomorrow at seven at the dock. I'm going back and fight that shelter." And he was off up the beach. As an afterthought, he called back "Bring some food."

Aunt Ag looked skeptical. She knew Roy, of course, but she didn't know Buster. She was about to refuse permission for Jerry to go when Maude came in and smoothed things over. She did know Buster and her endorsement eased Agnes' mind.

Cora promised to pack a lunch.

"A lot, Aunt Cora. And for two, okay?"

"Yes, dear. I'll tend to it. Why don't you work on some shop gadgets 'til supper time?"

The next morning at six-thirty Jerry was at Murph's dock, hunched under an eave, his cap pulled way down over his eyes, beating at mosquitoes with his swisher. Both Cora and Maude had cautioned him about being too early, but in his eagerness he couldn't wait. As Buster nudged into the dock Jerry sighed with relief and climbed aboard, dragging the lunch basket.

"Hey. The bugs are sure fierce. Will we have 'em all the way?"

"Nope," Buster answered. "Soon's we get up a bit of speed, we'll leave 'em behind." He shoved off, circled away from the dock in a wide turn, and headed toward Redfish Pass, several miles to the north. "What's in your box?"

"Food."

Buster grinned. "Great," he said. "I'm already starved. Don't know why I'm never hungry when I wake up but as soon as I get out on the water I could eat a horse." He grabbed up a sandwich and munched into it.

The bay was flat in the clear early hour. An occasional disturbance showed here and there as a mullet broke the water or a pelican splashed headfirst after a shiner. The bow of the boat, now slightly out of the water, cut the surface smoothly and left a gentle wake behind them, which leveled out and was absorbed by the quiet expanse of the sound.

As they moved along, the island slipped by on their left. Lush, emerald-green mangroves overhung the water, dotted with white where egrets roosted or adjusted their perches, not yet active for the day. No noise disturbed the peaceful, serene atmosphere except the putt-putt of the boat motor.

Jerry sat quietly, slightly hunched, trying to absorb it all, holding his breath for fear that any sudden movement might shatter the moment. Buster stared straight ahead, eating a second sandwich.

When they were broadside to the pass, Buster swung right into the open bay, surprising Jerry.

"I thought we were heading out into the Gulf."

"We will be, after a bit." Buster was fiddling with two small ropes, lashing the tiller to one side, steering the boat in a wide circle.

"There," he exclaimed, when everything was to his liking, "that'll keep us going 'round while I show you every dang thing there is to know about a rod and reel. Think you can learn?"

"I can try."

"Okay, then. Here we go! This here is a rod. This big arrangement here is a reel, and it's screwed down onto the rod by these little twisters here." He reached down and picked up a duplicate set and handed it to Jerry. "You'll be using this set-up, so you'd best hold it now, and you can follow me as I explain. First off, this is an all-purpose rod, light enough to catch small stuff and medium to fairly heavy stuff but not great big fish. You hold it with the reel up, like this, and the handle on your left side, and your left hand slightly forward of the reel, holding the rod here. You're right-handed, aren't you?"

Jerry nodded, and Buster fussed with the rod until Jerry had it correctly. The boat circled slowly.

"Okay. Next. Your right hand holds onto this little handle on the side of the reel, which turns the center spool and winds in your line. This little latch up here on the reel releases the line and let's it out. Ya with me?"

Jerry nodded.

"Okay. Next, the line," Buster went on. "For this kind of small fishing I use twenty-pound test. That means if you tied one end to something stationary and pull against it twenty pounds worth, it'd break. Anything less, it'll hold. Got it?"

Jerry was concentrating. "I understand. If I catch a fish weighing less than twenty lbs., the line won't break, right?"

"Wrong. Has nothing to do with how much the fish weighs, but how much it pulls. Some huge fish swimming in the same direction you're going might not exert much pressure at all, while some small fish can pull many times its own weight. A yellow-tail jack, for instance. Soon's he gets hooked, he turns sideways and swims against you and feels like a whale. Anyway, you don't have to remember all that while you're fishing, it's just background. So, lemme see, now. That's all you need to start you off. Oh, I almost forgot the most important thing of all ... the drag. Look at this little gadget. Here. On the right side of the reel, this five-armed little sprocket. That's called a drag and it's just that. It's a 'brake', like in your truck. It tightens up and squeezes down on the center spool, and stops the free release of the line. Here, lemme show ya."

Buster quickly relashed the boat tiller so they were running straight into the bay. Then, taking Jerry's rod he snapped forward the release latch on the reel and fed line out into the water. Next, he opened the drag until there was no pressure on the spool. Handing the rod back to Jerry, he motioned toward the line, feeding freely from the end of the boat.

"See, if you caught a fish now, you'd have no control. Your line is free and the fish could go just about anywhere he wanted. So we tighten up this little sprocket and more and more it slows down your line's free flow. We tighten it to just under the breaking point of the line, and if the fish pulls less than 20 lbs. you can wind him in. If he pulls more than 20 lbs, the line will feed out against the reel. Here," and Buster reached over and grabbed Jerry's line. "Now, I'm a fish. Wind me in!"

Jerry snorted with laughter and wound his reel, pulling Buster's hand closer and closer. Suddenly, Buster pulled back extra hard and the line started stripping out.

"Wind me in. Wind me in!" he yelled.

Jerry clasped the rod tighter and wound like fury, and though the reel handle turned to wind line in, the line kept feeding out.

"See," Buster exclaimed, "That's how the reel works. Adds weight to the fish and tires him out."

Jerry was jumping about.

"Yeah. Yeah. Yeah." he cried. "Now I understand. I really do. I understand. What else?" In his excitement he nearly went overboard.

Poking about in the lunch basket, Buster grabbed another sandwich.

"Boy, all this teaching makes me starved." He grinned over at Jerry.

"What about bait?" Jerry asked, glancing around the boat.

Buster went on. "Well, that's easy. We'll be out in the open Gulf, out there." He pointed eastward. "For mackerel you troll. The boat keeps moving slowly, so we don't use live bait, we use lures. These little things." He held out a small silver, slightly bent piece of metal, with a hook screwed to it. "Called Huntington drones. They come in graduated sizes from one through eight. We'll use number twos. They drag along about fifty feet behind the boat and twist and flash. Feels like a little throb through your rod."

Buster had previously put together several drones with short wire leaders and swivels and he now attached one to Jerry's line and tossed it overboard.

"There," he said. "Now you're all set. Let your line on out and feel the throb. If it stops bumping you've picked up a weed, so you have to wind it in and clear it."

"How much do I let out?" Jerry wanted to know. He was nervous now, and his voice quavered.

Buster was back with the motor and tiller, and he glanced out and waved his hand. "That's far enough. Flip your reel latch up and just hold on. Here we go." He swung the boat around and headed out the pass.

All of a sudden, there was a sharp, strong tug on Jerry's line, and a tubular, greenish fish jumped out of the water and violently shook itself side to side.

"I got something. I got something," Jerry screamed and sat frozen while the fish leaped about.

Buster cut the throttle and let the boat drift.

"Wind it in, man. Turn that handle. Feel it pull. Ain't it great? You've got yourself a good-sized ladyfish."

"How can you tell from this distance?"

"Tell what?"

"That it's a lady fish."

"Aw, come on." Buster looked at Jerry in disbelief. "Come on. I'm not talking about its sex. The name of the damn thing is ladyfish. L-a-d-y-f-i-s-h. That's what it's called."

By this time Jerry had brought the fish tight to the boat, and Buster reached over and grabbed it in one hand, twisted the drone from its mouth with the other and flipped the fish back into the water.

"No good to eat. Away it goes." He straightened up and threw back his head. "You've now been broken in, so let's get out of here and get some good stuff." He slapped the motor throttle and the little boat swung around and headed out to sea.

The tide was running in strong through the narrow pass, causing a roiling of the water where the rushing flow met the calm bay water. The flat-bottom bumped and tossed as it chugged through this turbulence, and Jerry felt apprehensive when he glanced over the side and saw the bubbling surface only inches from the gunwale. He moved gingerly from the side to sit on the motor cove beside Buster, whose complete disregard for danger was reassuring. Breaking through the choppy water, Buster steered slightly to the right, to miss the sandbar lying across the Gulf-side entrance to the pass, and swung round into the open Gulf beyond. They found the surface glass-smooth and gleaming white under the strong slanting morning sunlight, and the only suggestion of movement, shifting the bits of grass and other debris in a sluggish fashion, was a gentle undulation of the water.

No other boats were in sight.

But birds were!

"Over there," Buster pointed. Jerry looked left and right. Not knowing what to look for, he didn't see.

"What? Where?"

"Man, you must be blind! Don't you see those birds diving and soaring over there? Must be hundreds. You can see that. Now, come on!" Buster for the first time showed a slight irritation, which quickly evaporated. "I'll head toward 'em. Looks like a pocket about an acre square!"

All at once, Jerry saw. "Gosh! Look at that! Look at the fish cutting the water, flashing and jumping. Is that what we're after?"

"Yep! That's it. And it's all ours. No other boats that I can see. We'll bust into those little beauties and give 'em a fit. A right smart, royal, honest-to-God fit! Hold on." He increased the throttle and the little boat skudded over the calm water.

Jerry was checking his rod and reel when he felt the boat lose speed and sort of squat in the water, at the same time continuing to move slowly forward. He glanced up and was horrified to find the Gulf calm, the birds dispersed and not a fish in sight.

"What happened? What did you do? They're gone! We've lost 'em." He was so disappointed he moaned.

"It's okay," Buster said, already letting line overboard. "Mackerel disappear all of a sudden, and then reappear just as sudden. Don't worry. The water's full of fish. But you can't catch any if you're gonna sit there like a bump. Fish, man. Time's awastin'!"

Then, it seemed, the bottom of the world erupted! The water, far as the eye could see, foamed and boiled, fish slipped and slid over each other in a mad frenzy to catch tiny silvery bait, which tried unsuccessfully to escape by darting first this way, then that, and leaping out of the water. The birds collected again in seconds, screaming and screeching their raucous calls, diving for the bait, plopping into the water and soaring away with a shining tidbit in their beaks, only to be attacked in midair by the late-comers. Buster was yelling in abandoned glee, busily reeling in the first catch, which thrashed and struggled at the end of his line, trying to escape.

It was too much! Jerry sat dumbfounded, unable to absorb all the frenzy, the fury, the raw energy that filled the air ... the fish, the birds, the noise, Buster ... it was overwhelming. He sat stock-still, mouth agape, eyes staring. Slowly, slowly, in a daze, he started easing his drone into the water. Almost a once, before his lure was well behind the boat, a mackerel struck hard. Jerry came alive!

For the next ten minutes there was no time to think. Just let out line, bang, gasp, reel in ... let out line, bang, gasp, reel in. Fish were everywhere, all over the water, bumping each other and the sides of the boat, flying through the air as lines were yanked in, flopping in the bottom of the boat, thrashing, shaking, shivering with the last gasps and spewing blood. The boat was slippery with the filth and it was difficult to stand. Several times Jerry nearly pitched overboard.

"Watch out. Brace yourself. No time now for excuses, so be careful and don't fall out." Buster yelled in warning.

When the fish sounded and the Gulf calmed, both of them sighed with relief. Their arms ached and the back of their necks felt strain. Jerry reached for a scoop and a rag to clean up the mess and bail the sea water slopping about in the boat, and Buster repaired twisted leader wire. The little boat moved lazily in a large circle. Everything was ready. Would the fish reappear?

They would. Jerry was the first to spot them.

"There they are, over there. More! Seems more!"

Several hundred yards off to their left there was a tremendous boiling. Thousands of fish, cutting, thrashing, lunging, striking each other as well as the bait, their vicious toothed mouths open in anticipation of food, slicing the water in a wild, ferocious orgy. Birds screamed and dived, and Buster screamed along with them and reached for the tiller.

Suddenly, they were back in it. Line out, bang, gasp, reel in ... line out, bang, gasp, reel in. Arms aching, fish flopping in the bilge, filth and bait flying around, the boated mackerel vomiting in the air as they thrashed about and died.

"Be careful, Jerry, when you lean over to grab a wire to lift one in, that you don't stick your finger in the water. If a mackerel strikes it, it'll be open to the bone. Watch out, hear?" Buster never stopped for a second hauling in fish and steering the boat.

Jerry nodded back. "I'll take care."

Then he spotted a larger form, slicing a path straight through the schooled fish, and called out.

"What was that? Buster, look. What's that big thing streaking back and forth? What is it?"

Buster stopped winding in and left the mackerel on his line some distance behind the boat. A calm settled over him as he peered out at the school. Then he glanced at Jerry and quietly said, "That's the boy I've been waiting for. Now, we'll have some real fishing. Kings! They're down there, under the surface fish, maybe six-eight feet down. You keep fishing as you are. I'm gonna put a heavier lure, a number eight drone, and go down and get me one."

Suiting his actions to his words, Buster reeled in his catch, put a larger lure on his line, cut the boat motor down a bit and plopped his drone overboard. It sank out of sight.

"Jerry," he called. "Let's do this. Reel on in and give me your rod and you take this. I'll put a number eight on yours, too, and we can both grab us a king."

Jerry reeled in and handed his rod to Buster, who held his own out in one hand to Jerry. As Jerry reached out, Buster's rod suddenly bent nearly in half and flipped and flopped about as if it had a life of its own.

"Grab it. For God's sake, grab the thing!" Buster screamed. "I can't hold onto the rod this way. Grab it!"

Jerry grabbed. Such a commotion! The huge fish went deep, peeling line off the reel with a loud zinging sound, against the drag. The line was first loose, then taut, as the fish rose suddenly, then ran deep.

"Keep the line taut. Wind in. Wind in. He'll get off if the line sags. Don't hold the rod all out there in front of you. Put the handle under your left arm, in your armpit. Grab onto it with your elbow. There. Like that!" Buster wasn't too gentle, rearranging the rod.

"Now, fight the damn thing. Yipee! Yipee!" Buster jumped up and down in excitement.

Jerry didn't. Gritting his teeth and pursing his lips, he hung on for dear life, switching about in the boat as the fish pulled him this way, then that. Buster increased speed enough to keep the action to the rear, as he didn't want the fish to maneuver crossways under the boat and foul the line. Jerry hung on and pumped the rod to increase pressure on the fish, reeling it when he could and bracing his feet when he couldn't. The schooled mackerel, apparently scared off by all this action, had disappeared, as had the birds. It was just the calm Gulf, the hot sun, the little boat and the two men, one holding fast to a large fish that showed no sign of tiring.

In no time Jerry was soaked to the skin with perspiration and he shook his head to clear his eyes.

"Buster, I can't hold on much longer. When will this thing give up? My arms are coming out of their sockets. I'm too tired to keep going!"

"Okay." Buster said. "I'll take it." And he reached out for the rod.

Jerry twisted away from him. "Don't you dare touch that pole. I'll do it by myself. Leave me be. Leave me be!"

Buster looked astonished for a second at Jerry's vehemence. Then he smiled as he remembered himself and his first big fish. "You go ahead, boy. I'm not going to touch it. He's all yours. You're doing fine. Just don't lose him."

By this time the fish was tiring and Buster steered the boat in a large circle, keeping the fish and the action centered. Then, all the tugging and thrashing stopped and a dead weight seemed to hang on Jerry's line. He heaved and pulled, heaved and pulled, and slowly the big fish rose to the surface, on it's side, trailing the boat.

"Wow! Look at him. What a beauty." Jerry nearly released pressure in his excitement, leaning far out over the stern and pointing.

"No!" Buster yelled. "Don't slack off. Keep the tension. This fight's not over yet. As he comes alongside he may spring to life and the pulling and thrashing will be stronger than ever. That's when you'll lose him, if you do."

66

But Jerry didn't. Very slowly, like a veteran fisherman, he tensed the line and maneuvered the fish broadside to the boat. Buster, waiting with gaff ready, leaned down and hooked it under the gill and out the mouth and lifted the king aboard.

The two rested a few minutes and then Buster revved the motor and headed for the pass.

"All this filth to clean up and the fish to clean. Best we go home now, if that's okay with you."

Looking at a blister forming on one hand, Jerry nodded in agreement.

"Can we come back again? That's the most exciting time I've ever had. Can we, huh?"

"Sure." Buster said. "We have to, you know. I haven't got my king yet."

Jerry was sitting in the prow, looking back across the Gulf, as the little boat rose and fell in the gentle undulations and worked its way towards shore.

"Hey, Buster. Are you sure we want to go in? Look out there. The mackerel and the birds are back!"

Buster's eyes followed Jerry's pointing finger, as he automatically cut the throttle. For a quiet moment he watched the birds. Then he looked at the boy's eager face. Without a word, he swung the boat about and headed back out.

Hours later they dragged into Murph's dock. Roy had been watching and he met them as they tied up. He was in a testy mood.

"Not very smart, Buster. First time and all. Miss Agnes has been here several times. She's worried sick. Good Lord, look at you two. And the boat." He relaxed a bit and smiled. "Got into a mess of 'em, did you?"

"Roy," Jerry slid out of the boat and grabbed his friend's arm. "You wouldn't believe. You just wouldn't believe. Man, fish everywhere. I mean, everywhere! I'm pooped! My body aches. But we've got mackerel and kings for everybody."

A horn tooted. Agnes was sitting in her car at the end of the dock walkway, beckoning.

"Oh, oh. I'm in trouble." Jerry breathed. "Big trouble." He ran along the walk to the car.

All three ladies were there. Agnes at the wheel, Cora beside her and Maude in the back.

"I'm only going to say this once, young man!" Agnes was frigid. "Pay close attention."

Jerry looked down and fidgeted his feet.

"Kindly do me the courtesy of looking at me as I speak."

"Yes'm."

"Your actions today were irresponsible! I don't know who is to blame, you or Buster. It doesn't make any difference. You were both there. Absolutely irresponsible! And unacceptable! Here on the island, where lives are closely interwoven, one must be dependable. There can be no question about that." Agnes was tapping her finger on the steering wheel for emphasis. "One cannot shirk duties, cannot drop commitments at a whim. People will not trust you. Do you know it is three p.m.? The mailboat has come and gone. What happened to your deliveries? People were depending on you. Their food was spoiling!"

Jerry gasped, and his face fell. He'd completely forgotten.

"I'll go right away." he mumbled, and started to pull away.

"Wait just a second. Your friends covered for you, and that, too, is unacceptable. We three met the boat and were going to make your deliveries for you but Roy was also there in case you didn't get back and he took the packages around. Do you understand? This is not right. My life, Cora's life, Maude's life and Roy's schedule, all were disrupted because you wanted to fish a little longer. I'm very disturbed and must think seriously about any further association between us if I cannot depend on you. No, don't say a word, please. This is the way the three of us want to handle this matter. We have discussed it. You are to return to your friends and assist in cleaning your fish and that boat. Maude will drive Cora back in this car, I will drive your truck. You are to walk. Walk back and think. All three miles of it. You've some thinking to do."

Agnes climbed out of her car and got into the truck. She stuck her head out of the window, without looking at Jerry, and called over her shoulder.

"Did you enjoy yourself?"

"Yes'm."

"Well, that's good."

The two vehicles skidded down the sandy road. Just before they disappeared, Cora surreptitiously reached out and dropped a mosquito swisher.

7

As with other remote areas emerging in the 40's as budding winter resorts and dependent mainly on a brief three-month tourist season, the tranquil lives of the permanent island residents were seriously disrupted each year — not so much by the arrival in mid-December of the first northern visitors as by the arrival in late October of the vanguard of the winter invaders, the merchant element. The two inns, the shops, the restaurant, all needed cleaning, painting, repairing. Cisterns needed purifying. All the yards had to be scuffled and raked, and the beaches needed tending. There was a two-month period of intense activity that exhausted everyone long before they greeted the first vacationers with nods and flashing smiles.

During this strained period there always developed friendships and free exchange between the natives and the merchants, bound in most cases by a genuine camaraderie, in spite of the underlying knowledge that the October people never actually belonged. No one spoke of this but should a latecomer step too far beyond the line, or presume too insistently, a simple glance and raised eyebrows between two islanders was usually sufficient to return the offender to his proper place.

Captiva offered two inns to the public.

There was Mid-Island Inn, located at the center of the island at the narrowest spot, where Gulf and bay were a scant 500 yards apart. It was owned and operated by the patrician and beautiful Cordelia Winslow, and its select clientele returned year after year — more, it was often said, to bask in the glow of the Richmond-born beauty than to oil and sprawl under the warm tropic sun. Wearing her hair in a Gibson Girl upsweep, and with her narrow waist revetted and stayed, Mrs. Winslow circulated among her guests, dispensing charm and elegance and a feeling that hers was the only proper way to live. If need be, she also circulated among her kitchen help, dispensing a tight control centered upon a flaying iron skillet. Mid-Island housed twelve guests in six double-occupancy cottages clustered around a central lounge-dining room.

There was Captiva Inn, located on the beach where the Gulf road swung right, bisecting the island and running through to Murph's dock. Adam and Ruth Crisfield owned and operated Captiva Inn not nearly as elegantly as Mid-Island, but with better food.

If Cora's 'Grab Bag' shop was included, though strictly speaking it didn't fit, being on the Sanibel side of the bridge, Captiva, during the winter months, had three gift shops ... The Grab Bag, Matilda Crunch's Shell Shop, and the Sinclair sisters' Fisherman's Creel.

These three didn't really conflict. Cora's shop was souvenirs and woven trinkets, baskets and swishers and so on, with a cozy corner where visitors could sit, rest, sip coffee and, of course, eat key lime pie.

Mrs. Crunch sold mostly shells, both retail and wholesale. A depository for commercial shellers, the Shell Shop did a commendable business accepting burlap bags of sorted shells on consignment and trucking them to commercial outlets on the mainland. For casual droppers-in, Mrs. Crunch had added shell-related decorations, more as local color for the shop than as items to bepurchased.

The Fisherman's Creel, however, was a different matter. Open only three months, January through March, it was not so much a gift shop as a boutique. An occasional item, very expensive, sold to an occasional visitor, very wealthy. Total sales for the three months were surprisingly substantial.

One restaurant and one bakery rounded out the commercial establishments. Both operated only during the tourist season, on a reservation basis, and both were minute. The Bide-A-Wee Restaurant seated sixteen people maximum, four each at four small square tables. The Island Bakery, open nine a.m. to five p.m., was too tiny to be believed. Baking was handled by a bank of three apartment-size gas stoves in a room fifteen feet long by twelve feet wide. It was located deep in a tangle of sea-grape trees and reached by walking down a winding path hung with blooming orchids and caged finches. The over-all bizarre effect was increased considerably when one met the two proprietors, Jack and Ted.

The baked goods were superlative!

Fresh donuts with assorted icings every morning, so light the lid had to be quickly snapped shut on the box or they might have floated away, rhum babas that required no chewing at all, eclairs succulent and sensuous, seven-layer tortes that melted in your mouth — all were grabbed up hot from the stoves. White bread sold for $1.25 a loaf, a price causing disbelief until the bread was tasted. A visitor could request one pecan tart for tomorrow, and a batch of twelve would be made, one for the order and eleven to be sold across the counter. A little sign, waving back and forth in the breeze at the entry to the path, would announce "pecan tarts today".

Jack was the baker, and Ted neated up. It was rumored, never denied, that Jack had trained under the legendary Pierre d'Estange, renowned French pastry chef.

In no time at all the Bakery became the focal point of the island for passers-by. As the three stoves, the glass-fronted counter, the sink with cooling racks, and the two bakers so crowded the inside area that only one customer could enter the shop at a time, chairs and little tables had to be scattered about outside the building to accommodate the munchers. More orchids were hung about, more finches ... and umbrellas, in case of rain. The gossip was free, and endless.

Seemingly overnight the little shop was known as far north as Tampa and south to Everglades City. Yachts included in their itinerary a stopover at Murph's dock, where they gassed up and filled their larders with baked goods, ordered the week before by mail. Murph and Pearlie profited along with the bakery, which was soon running day and night, with the two bakers reduced to working double shifts. They became haggard and more irritable than usual as the ` season' wore on, but nothing stopped the baked goods, which continued to pour out.

Sundays, all shops were closed. The Fisherman's Creel Girls, the Bakery Boys, Marge and Stan Brown, proprietors and owners of the Bide-A-Wee Restaurant, all could be found fishing together somewhere in the back bay, drifting about on the quiet water, snoozing under the warming sun and commiserating over their difficult lot.

With more work than they could handle inside the bakery, Ted pressed Jerry to take over their deliveries around the island. It was arranged that Jerry would stop in at the bakery immediately after his mailboat deliveries were completed and make a one-time pickup. Anything not yet ready would have to be delivered later by the bakers. This added substantially to Jerry's afternoon chores, and also his income, as he charged a fee to the bakery and was usually tipped by the recipient. He had to move along, however, without pause, in order to meet his standing three p.m. swimming date with Roy.

●

"Roy, look here!" There'd been a heavy blow all that morning and the Gulf was rough. The swimming was great and as they bounded about together, Jerry unloaded his concern. "Roy, look here. Awhile back, when I started picking up stuff from the mailboat and delivering it, there was hardly anybody here. Now, with all these people and a lot more to come, and the bakery stuff and all, well, I'm too busy. Mornings I give to Aunt Maude and Aunt Cora. They need help. Then the mailboat. Then the bakery. I won't give up this swim with you. Some nights I'm too tired to fish with Mrs. Thigpen on the bridge, and I hate missing that fun. It's all getting to be too much."

"Hideaway island with nothing to do!" Roy chuckled as he said it. "Just remember, Jerry, come April, it's all over and there's nothing much to do 'til next October. Six full months. That's a lot better'n most other places."

Jerry stopped jumping waves and flopped out on the sand to rest. "Yep, I guess so. And then, there's always Sundays. They seem to roll around quick, somehow."

Roy pointed up the beach. "Here comes Mrs. Upton. Now she's got it made. Nothing to do all day but stroll each morning along the beach for special sand for her cats, and again each afternoon. Gets the sand from the base of a certain pine tree on the beach in front of Mid-Island. Claims the cats won't go in their boxes unless she puts this special sand in first. I tell her she's making up an excuse for exercising. The last time I mentioned it that way, she got angry, so I leave it alone. It's about a mile and a half each way, twice in the morning and twice in the afternoon. That's about six miles all told. Must be great sand!"

Mrs. Upton had reached them by this time and Jerry stood up and walked a few steps toward her.

"How do, Mrs. Upton."

"Jerry. Roy." Mrs. Upton nodded and would have passed but Jerry went on.

"Excuse me, Ma'am, but do you know anything about Amanda? I've been delivering packages to her, leaving 'em on her porch, and for about the past two weeks I haven't seen her once. I'm worried about her."

Mrs. Upton stopped walking and assumed her beach-gossiping stance ... left hand on hip, feet braced slightly apart, and right hand twirling the button at the center of her blouse, just below her chin. In her high nasal twang she told Jerry that Amanda had been sick but that she was now well on the road to recovery.

"Is it her foot? Is that still bothering her?"

Mrs. Upton nodded her head. "Yes," she piped. "The foot is still sore, and then her stomach got upset. She'll be fine."

Mrs. Upton went on down the beach and Jerry crouched on the sand at the wave-break, watching the lacy water flow in with a little rush and then sink into the sand as it turned to flow back out. Roy floated over to join him.

Jerry stared at Roy. "Maybe I should go see how Amanda is."

"Oh, don't worry," Roy admonished. "She's always having stomach up-sets. Eats the damnest stuff. Not too long ago, before this foot episode, I came across her knee-deep in the bay, with a long pointed stick. She was stalking stingarees. She'd shuffle along, not picking up her feet, and scare one in the mud and plunge her stick into it when it scurried off. She'd toss the damn think into a croker sack and drag it in to shore."

"Aren't they dangerous? Everybody warns me to stay away from stingarees!" Jerry looked at his friend with apprehension.

Roy shook his head. "Don't worry about 'em. Like everything else, they're not that bad. Give 'em an edge and they'll high-tail it away from you. If you're messing about in the bay, or around the flats, best put your feet down real careful the first time, then move along pushing ahead without lifting. Stingarees can be nasty but only if you step down on 'em. They have a defense gadget on their back, a bone lined with backward-set barbs, at the base of their tail. Like scorpions, they react by converging upward. If that barb gets stuck into you and gets ripped out again, it'll leave a ragged hole deep in your leg or foot, stuffed with slime. It's the slime that causes infection. The ache is unbelievable!"

"Then what happens?" Eyes wide with dread, the boy waited for Roy to continue. "How do they fix it?"

Roy was poking holes in the sand with his finger. "It ain't pretty at all." He went on. "I don't know what you'd do. I don't know what they do over on the mainland, now that there's doctors and hospitals. I only know what they do here on the island, where there's no help of any kind. The guy stung, it's not really stinging as much as poking, the guy stung hobbles to shore and makes it home. Then he takes a sharp knife and cuts a circle of flesh out of his leg a bit larger than the puncture. He packs it with tar and lights it, and lets it burn. Cauterizes it!"

Jerry felt like fainting.

"Are you serious?"

"Never more so."

Jerry was quiet for a long time. Lying on his back, elbows in the sand, gazing out to sea between his feet, he let the hot sun sooth away the horror of this latest evidence of island stoicism.

Finally he turned to Roy. "I couldn't do that. I just couldn't. No matter what, I couldn't cut a hole in my leg."

"Nobody knows what he can do, until he has to. Don't worry over it, Jerry. Let's go back in the water and rinse all this sand off. We gotta get home."

"Wait a minute. You were telling me about Amanda. She speared a stingaree and dragged it to shore. What did she do with it then?"

"Ate it."

"Ate it?"

"Yep. Sliced off it's flippers while it was still alive, and took 'em home to fry. Says they taste like scallops. Gave the rest of the stingaree to Gustave Kroen who chopped it up for fertilizer for his bananas. Great bananas, too. Best I ever tasted. Come on, last one in's a three-legged pig."

●

The ladies were busy when Jerry parked his truck under the hibiscus and rushed into the house. Unfinished mosquito swishers in various stages of completion lay all about. Cora was in mid-sentence as he burst onto the porch, slamming the screen door behind him.

73

" ... ran out last winter. These will give us fifty swishers, which should be enough. Please don't slam the door, Jerry, it startles me. If we need more, of course we can make 'em up later. Don't you think fifty's enough, Ag?"

"To start off with, anyhow. Jerry, will you carry that bunch over to the shop for us, please, and supper will be along soon's you clean up." Agnes motioned to one corner of the porch where finished swishers were piled high.

"Aunt Ag, wait'll I tell you what happened to me." He was so full, he bubbled over. "I was swimming with Roy and you'll never guess what he told me." He dragged up a chair and sat facing them. "Did you know Amanda eats stingarees?"

Agnes's head shot up. "Of course not. Who's filling your head with that nonsense? Nobody eats stingaree."

"Roy says she does, and he doesn't fib. Cuts off the wings, fries 'em up, and claims they're better'n scallops."

Cora had put down her work, and was listening. "Maybe they wouldn't be all that bad. Skinned and diced. After all, folks eat snake and conch. I had an uncle who kept a little box filled with ants by his plate. Would wet a finger, flip open the box, squash his finger down on the ants and plop 'em into his mouth. Claimed they tasted peppery. Then there was old Aunt Rizbah, she liked fish eyes and ... "

"Cora, <u>please</u>." Agnes said, not wanting a trip through all Cora's relatives. "Jerry, take along those swishers, please. I'll get supper."

Maude moved over to her special 'look out' spot, binoculars in hand, and settled back to check things out. Suddenly, she stopped rocking.

"That's odd! Hey, you two. Come over here and look. Seems little orange stakes are stuck all over that small triangular piece of ground between Amelia Armstrong's lot line and the foot of the bridge. Wonder what that's all about. I didn't notice them before."

"I did," Cora said. "I saw the men this afternoon, pounding the stakes in, as I went back and forth to the shop. I didn't go over, I just saw 'em. Their truck had 'Lee County surveyors' on its side."

"Why didn't you mention it?" Maude's voice had a sharpness to it.

"Why should I?" Cora's eyes were wide and innocent. "Just a few men and a bunch of stakes!"

"Just a few men and a bunch of stakes." Maude was beginning to bristle. Agnes jumped in before the other two got out of hand.

"Wonder what Amelia Armstrong is up to? Funny, I talked to her yesterday but she never mentioned this. It's not at all like her to be so silent."

"If it is her!" Maude stuck in.

"Of course, it's her. Who else could it be?"

Maude polished her binoculars and put them back on their shelf. "We will soon know." She said. "Amelia is on her way over here right now. Seems in a hurry."

Mrs. Armstrong flopped into a chair, gasping for breath after the sprint from her house, and gratefully accepted the cool water Cora offered her.

"Agnes, what is going on? she wheezed.

"Then it isn't you?"

"Of course it isn't me! I rushed right out and confronted those workmen and their orange sticks and demanded to know what was going on. But all they could, or would, tell me was that their orders instructed them to survey that teeny piece of land. My living room looks right out on top of it. I want to know what's going on. Cousin Abby, on my mother's side, works in the tax office. I want to go in and talk to her. She'll find out for me, quick enough. Agnes, are you by any chance planning a trip to town any time soon? Like tomorrow?"

Agnes looked closely at Amelia, whose face now was so flushed Agnes feared she might faint. "Well, Amelia, we always need things. I suppose I could drive in. Maude and Cora, with a whole night to plan, will undoubtedly come up with lists each a mile long. Yes, if it's important to you, we can go in. I'll pick you up at 6:30 sharp. We'll catch the first ferry."

The following morning Agnes dropped Amelia at the entrance to the Tax Office at 8:45 and set off to whittle away at the long lists of musts on the front seat beside her. The morning progressed uneventfully, though exhaustingly, and just before noon Agnes swung her car to the curb at the tax office and picked up Amelia, who was fuming.

"Who do you suppose it is? Just guess! Who do you suppose?" she sputtered.

"I couldn't possibly" Agnes demurred. "I haven't a clue."

Amelia was apoplectic. Gesticulating wildly in the air and squirming about in her seat, she was all but incoherent.

"It's that poisonous MacDuff! That monster! Him and his common-law blonde jade!"

"Amelia! Mercy! I didn't know you even knew that word."

"Well, I do! And she is! And he is! Imagine! He's <u>bought</u> that triangle! A lot of good it'll do him. I gave a piece of my mind to that stupid tax man, bawled him out to a fare-thee-well for not alerting me when MacDuff first showed interest. I've been assured he can't use it. Can't build anything on it. The lot's too thin. Something about lot-line restrictions or some such. But just to know, to sit there in my living room and look out on that lot and <u>know</u> he owns it ... well, I'll fence. That's what I'll do."

Agnes was concentrating mainly on the road, as they were driving along at a good clip. Without lifting her eyes, she asked "If you fence, won't that cut off your air from that side? Your house is very close to that lot line, you know."

"Well, I'll do something. I'll think of something."

Later, at home recounting this exchange to Cora and Maude, Agnes added "I suppose the old coot is up to something. Well, as I said at the time, Amelia would have been far ahead of the game if she hadn't tangled with a dyed-in-the-wool British pukka sahib type, and MacDuff certainly is one. It's her own fault. She should have been more worldly, more understanding. Her New

England upbringing doesn't fit in down here. Doesn't fit in most anywhere, anymore, for that matter."

"Why is it Mrs. Armstrong's fault? Jerry wanted to know. "What'd she do?"

Maude took up the tale. "It happened last winter, and I agree with your aunt. Amelia was stupid to lock horns. Can't win. Not against a man like MacDuff. Memory like an elephant. Looks like one, too."

"No he doesn't," Cora interjected. "Looks like a walrus! That fat, round, florid face and those long droopy side whiskers. Exactly like a walrus."

"Anyway," Maude went on, "Colonel MacDuff arrived amid fanfare last winter, in his jeep, with his wife on the seat beside him and a huge English bulldog in the back. They put up at Mid-Island for several weeks, during which time MacDuff purchased a house on a nearby island and floated the thing down the open Gulf and had it re-erected on a lot he'd bought on the Captiva beach. In no time they were installed and Colonel MacDuff threw a party ... a "bash" he called it ... for all the islanders to see the house and to meet Mrs. MacDuff. Amelia Armstrong was quite smitten by Andrusa MacDuff and the following week had a tea party in her honor. All the ladies on both the islands were invited, and most came. Several days after the tea party it leaked out — I've always thought that Bertha Wiggins was the leaker — that MacDuff and Andrusa were not married at all but just living together in what the Good Book refers to as a condition of sin. Well! You should have seen Amelia Armstrong when she found out. She ranted and raved all over the two islands that she had been duped, that her unsoiled reputation had been compromised, that not only she but her momma and all her relatives had been insulted ... "to seat myself and have tea beside a loose woman! I cannot dwell on the outrage of it. Me, Amelia Standish Armstrong. I go all the way back to Miles, you know ... eating crumpets and sipping tea beside that creature! I will not have it. I simply will not have it. They shall pay for what they've done and pay dearly. Mark my words!" We all told Amelia to laugh it off but, no sir, she was fighting mad and without mercy."

Jerry was fascinated by Maude's narrative and pantomime. He could see Mrs. Armstrong stomping about in outrage.

"What happened next?" he asked.

"It all ended up pretty quick," Maude went on. "Though it might not be over yet. Amelia buttered up to Andrusa and got herself and some cronies invited to a special "commemorative" tea the following week. And Andrusa, confident that she was now solidly in and accepted by the Captiva High Society, went to a lot of trouble and expense. Her house was cleaned and flowers were dragged in. A maid was brought in for the occasion from the Mainland. Lots of food and drinks. All for nothing. Amelia and her gang boycotted the MacDuffs. Nobody showed!"

"Oh, how awful for Andrusa!" Cora was near tears.

"What's the matter with you, Cora? "Maude was abrupt. "You already know all this."

76

Cora was wringing her hands. "I know. I know. But the way you tell it, it all seems new. How awful for poor Andrusa. What happened? I can't wait to find out."

Maude looked unbelievingly at Cora. "As you know, nothing happened. By nightfall the entire island knew that Andrusa had been put down, and that old MacDuff had been bested. Andrusa was mortified. MacDuff was outraged and swore vengeance. And life went on. Now, it seems, a new chapter might be opening up." A little smile of delicious anticipation flitted across Maude's face.

●

While all this furor was stirring things up at the southern end of the island, and Amanda's successful recovery and Buster's wickie were the current topics of discussion toward the northern end, the center was agog with excitement over Boojee's Birthday Party!

"I must try to do something to pay him back for all the love and kindness he's given me all these years." Mrs. Upton was talking to Bertha in the post office.

"You feed him don't you?" Bertha commented laconically. Her own day was crowded with unpleasant chores. The mail had been extra heavy, what with all the October people rushing about and so busy. Upsetting! Little Too-loo had the sniffles, which usually turned first into croup and then a chest cold. Upsetting! She was late with that complicated State Postal Quarterly Report. She really wasn't in any mood to gossip, and when Tabitha Upton got started it took the Borax 20-mule team to shut her up.

"Of course I feed him. Don't be silly, Bertha. However, he's been living with me seven years. Seven years this 23rd. Actually, he first moved in on October 31st but not relishing all the tales people tell about old ladies and their cats I felt October 31 and Halloween an unfortunate time for him to have a birthday, so I moved it up to the 23rd. You understand?"

"Not really." Bertha wasn't paying attention. "Why not move it up a full month, to the end of September? Wouldn't that be easier to remember?"

Tabby sucked in her breath with a little gasp. "Oh, my dear, no!" I couldn't do that. It would change his sign. Boojee is a Scorpio. To move him to the end of September would make him a Libra. That might be distressing for him, and possibly even change his personality. He's been a good, good boy all this time. Only gave me one problem, really, when he ate Maria Callas."

Bertha was bustling about, filing and packaging. "Ate who?"

"Maria Callas! My canary!"

"Oh, yes, I remember now. I thought you were never sure if he ate her or not."

Mrs. Upton twirled her button in agitation. "I wasn't at first. I didn't want to dream of it. Even to think of it was too distressing. But then I had to conclude that Boojee <u>did</u> do it. The other two don't chase birds ... like 'em, in fact. Boojee lies in wait. And then, when I found Maria's tiny claw behind Boojee's litter box, I knew! It was quite some time before our relationship returned to normal."

Bertha nodded her head, and her eyes rolled heavenward. "I'll bet", she murmured.

"Anyway," Tabby went on, "I'm planning a party for Boojee for next Saturday, three to five. Can you come?"

"Me!"

"Of course, you. And bring Tiger with you."

"Oh, no. Tiger's an alley tom — he'll tear the place apart."

Mrs. Upton reached out an admonishing hand. "No he won't. He'll have a good time. I'm inviting very few others, the ones with cats. All the cats can play together and have a good time. You'll see. Can you come?"

"Wouldn't miss it for the world!" Bertha was all attention at last. "What else can I bring? Except Tiger, of course. Want my macaroni salad?"

"No, that won't be necessary." Tabby had turned toward the door, preparing to leave, much to Bertha's relief. "Just the two of you. I'll have everything else. Remember, Saturday, three to five!" And she was gone.

Bertha spread the word that afternoon, along with the mail. By dusk everyone was speculating on just who the favored few would be. Those without cats were automatically eliminated. Those with cats, but who were known to be cool about cats, were in a sort of back-up category, in case the real cat lovers couldn't make it. In no time, the islanders threatened to choose up sides, to stage a pro cat and con cat protest. Emmy Kramdon, a vocal cat-hater, discussed having an anti-cat party at the same time at her place, and inviting all the left-outs. There hadn't been anything as intensely controversial since the nationwide search for Scarlett O'Hara.

●

Dennis and Tabitha Upton lived on the bay-side just north of Mrs. Crunch's Shell Shop, in a neat New England salt-box house. A short dock jutted out into deep water and here Dennis moored his small sailing boat. They had no children. They had three cats. They had had a canary until its uncertain demise. Dennis worked all morning on his stamp collection and sailed most afternoons. Tabitha walked the beach and mothered her cats.

Boojee was a Persian. A large Persian. Soon after his arrival, following continued night escapes through clawed-out porch screening, Tabitha carted him over to town, to Dr. White, the favored vet and had Boojee 'fixed'. Ever afterward she shuddered at the thought. She felt as though she'd reached beyond her station ... had, in fact, played God and changed a life. Now, after seven long years, she was subconsciously still trying to atone.

Boojee stayed home. Stayed home and grew fat. And big. At the time of the birthday party he was huge. While Fifi and Belle Ami lay stretched out on the patio, snoozing the hours away in the warm sunlight, Boojee was to be found crouched on the dock, fishing. He was very good at it. He'd lie flat out on the decking, his right front leg drooped low to just above the water, the paw under the surface. As investigating minnows and an occasional pinfish swam about, Boojee would work his claws in a seductive, enticing manner. When a luckless fish ventured too near, drawn by the claw action, swoop and up on the dock it would go. Boojee would then pounce and gobble it up. He would sit and rest a bit after that, licking his whiskers. Soon, he was flat on the dock again, after another tidbit. It was beautiful to watch, though Dennis didn't think so. Sitting at his desk, sorting and pasting his stamps, he'd watch Boojee out of his window. "Hate that damn cat. Hate it!", he'd mutter to himself. "Hate 'em all!"

Occasionally, due to excessive zealousness or an incipient catnap, Boojee would lunge and overreach himself, slipping off the dock and into the water. A great splashing and shaking would follow, with much paw jerking and more whisker licking. Dennis would mutter "Hope the damn thing drowns."

These occasional dips into sea water stiffened and fluffed Boojee's coat as he dried, producing a balloon effect many times his actual size. As he returned to the patio, and the two females welcomed him with purrings and lickings, Tabitha would beam, simpering "They love him so. Just look at them, licking him all over in delight." Dennis was much closer to the truth when he'd exclaim "Nonsense. All they want is the salt from the baywater!" They got the salt and all the loose hairs and both female cats were consequently subject to frequent hair balls.

With all the intrigue circulating about the island, Mrs. Upton felt it would be prudent to issue written invitations. Dennis was reluctantly pressed into working these up and did a beautiful job, in three colors, with lots of swirls and flourishes. Each invitation carried a request to please bring the feline guests in a tote-box. Bertha Wiggins was invited, and her Tiger; Matilda Crunch and her Princess; Ida Benson and Black Boy; Ruta Barstowe and Cuddles. Mrs. Upton stopped there as the attending four animal guests, plus her own three, totalled seven, which was her lucky number.

The Sinclair Girls, though cat-less, were also invited. Faye and Nan were distant cousins of Dennis' from New England, and Tabitha had her eye on a Lalique figurine for sale at the Fisherman's Creel, though she and Faye hadn't yet come to terms on the price.

Jack, the baker, was up to his elbows in a double batch of bread dough, and Ted was at the clean-up sink when Tabby Upton burst into the bakery.

"Jack, Jack." She shrilled, all out of breath. "I nearly forgot. I'll need a birthday cake. Not too big. Actually a small one. Enough for seven. Can you bake it?"

"Sure. What kind? Round or square? Tall? What flavor?"

Mrs. Upton looked doubtful. She wasn't at her best with this kind of decision-making. The button twirled madly in agitation.

"Oh, dear. I don't know. What do you think the kitties will like?"

Jack stood stock-still, his hands deep in dough.

"Cats? A cake for cats?"

From the sink, Ted echoed, "A cat birthday cake?"

"Couldn't you bake <u>something</u>?" Mrs. Upton questioned, agitatedly. "There'll have to be a cake! And as there'll be eight people, I'll want a special savory, some sort of a sweet. I don't know exactly what."

"What about meringues?" Ted stuck in. "And it's such a nice French word!"

Jack shot him a withering glance, but Tabby picked up on it. "Yes, I think meringues would be lovely. Eight, please. And will you do something about that cake? Please do." And she flounced out of the bakery.

Both bakers immediately collapsed into paroxysms of laughter and were bent double when Tabitha peeped back in. She didn't seem to notice.

"Don't forget to deliver everything by two, Saturday afternoon. People are arriving about three, and we'll have to set up. Maybe you can bring it all over, Jack, and stay?"

"Yes'm. Wouldn't miss it," Jack said, not knowing he was echoing Bertha. He was having difficulty with his face. Ted had simply turned to the window.

After she had disappeared out the winding path both bakers turned to each other in consternation. Fertile minds were busy, tearing at the problem.

"Meringues are no problem" Jack mused, making notes on a pad and spreading bread dough about. "And pistachio ice cream as filling. So attractive, the brown and green color combination."

"With the nuts carefully picked out. Those old biddies will mostly arrive having forgotten their false teeth." Ted was back at the sink, slopping soapsuds and scraping brownie tins, which he especially hated. "I suppose you'll pick out the nuts and get to eat 'em. You get all the really good jobs, seems to me. And you seldom throw a thought my way. Like these brownie pans. You <u>could</u> line 'em, and I wouldn't have to waste all this time and effort scraping the damn things. But no you couldn't care less."

Jack was red in the face. "For Gawd's sake, lay off the bitching! You can pick out the pistachio nuts for all I care. That'll be a dandy chore for you. Come over here a second and help me figure this cat cake thing. What in hell will cats eat? At a party, yet?"

"Are you expecting to use one cake to serve two purposes? A cake, say, that the cats and the humans both will eat? From different sides, I hope!"

Jack glanced up, worry lines etched across his forehead.

"I don't know. Maybe two cakes. What do you think?"

That's the way they finally handled it. Meringues and a small round white cake for the people, and a special cat concoction. The people cake would sport mocha filling with vanilla icing, and written in red around the rim would appear 'Happy Birthday, Boojee.' Seven little red candles would be stuck in the center.

The cat cake presented difficulties. Books were read. Other islanders were consulted. A controlling clue was stumbled over in an expensive, lushly illustrated cat volume Faye had purchased especially for Tabitha Upton to buy, which made Tabitha's choice of a Lalique figurine so very distressing. Faye planned to set the figurine price so sky-high that Tabitha would be forced to buy the cat book, or Faye might be left with the thing, God forbid, once the season closed. Frances Fontaine would buy up the Lalique as soon as her home was ready and she arrived on the island later on.

The book mentioned that all cats liked fish, with a special leaning toward sardines and anchovies. That gave Jack his clue and his mind raced away in flights of fantasy. A round cake, so the cats could all nibble at the same time, with thin, thin layers of filleted fish ... a round fish, so Roy would have to produce some sheepshead, which would be perfect ... a paste of sardines mixed with canned salmon, pink and white mixture, quite lovely. More thin fish, two layers in all, topped with anchovies, unrolled and with the capers removed, placed in a squiggly fashion like little fish swimming by. It would have to be made the day before, and frozen down, then defrosted at the final moment, or the fish smell would be over-powering. No problem at all, really.

"A piece of cake," Ted threw in, tongue in cheek.

Friday morning, the day before the party, Faye Sinclair drove into the Upton's yard in a rush, her car skidding a bit.

"Tabby, we're so sorry. We just heard that our dear friend, John Wurlie who is up on Boca, will be here this afternoon and spend the weekend with us. So Nan and I won't be able to attend your party tomorrow afternoon. We're desolate!"

Mrs. Upton pondered this new development for a moment and then she smiled at Faye.

"My dear, bring him. By all means, bring him along. Love to have him. You've spoken of him so often, and he's from Boston, isn't he? He and Dennis will adore each other. Of course, bring him along."

Saturday, October 23rd, arrived, one of those crystal-clear, cloudless, balmy days Chambers of Commerce brag about. Jack had asked Jerry to turn up at the bakery by two p.m. to go with him and hold the cakes, and together they drove to the Upton's. Dennis seemed already in a mood and had little to say, but Tabitha effervesced.

"Come in, come in," she gushed. "Sally-Anne was to be here but at the final hour she got sick, so maybe both of you will stay and help." She didn't wait for an answer but hurried off, arranging flowers and plumping pillows.

There was a wide serving-bar separating the kitchen from the dining room and here Jack placed the two cakes and the meringue shells. The ice cream went into the refrigerator. Jack busied himself retouching the cakes and getting out the forks, napkins and dessert plates. Jerry, at loose ends, wandered about the house. In the living room he came on three large slatted boxes with small malevolent eyes peering back at him.

Then suddenly, it was three p.m. and the guests arrived. Bertha was driving Matilda Crunch, and Ruta Barstowe drove Ida Benson. All had boxes. Mrs. Upton welcomed each one, and the party got under way. Nan from the Fisherman's Creel arrived with John Wurlie, who was wearing a dark pinstripe suit. Faye Sinclair was having, it seemed, a rough day and would be late, if at all. She tippled and had apparently misjudged.

Mrs. Upton seated everyone, introduced Mr. Wurlie, and shut the bottom half of the entryway Dutch door. She placed all the boxes properly in front of each owner.

"So nice of you all to come. I just love parties and I've talked at length to my three, explaining the goings-on, so that they will be on their best behavior. I know each of you had a nice, long chat with your own."

Jack came in with the cat cake, which was passed around and commented on. Then he placed it center of the coffee table.

"No. Not there." Mrs. Upton swooped and picked it up and repositioned it center of the fire-place hearth. "I've cleared this spot specially, as the birthday celebration focal point. Why don't you get the other cake, Jack? It can go on the coffee table. Where did I put my bag of gifts?" She looked around and finally found it. Then rummaging around deep in the bag, she drew out a small wrapped package.

"Ah, this is for Cuddles Barstowe," and she handed it to Ruta. On she went until all the guest cats and the three Upton cats each had a gift.

With a little self-conscious giggle and working her button overtime, she motioned generally about the room. "We'll have to be good sports and open the presents. We can only expect our kitties to do so much, you know." There were little fuzzy mice and catnip sacs and one or two sticks wrapped in bark for sharpening claws. The ladies sat around the room, looking self-conscious, each holding the gift and with her cat in a box at her feet.

Mr. Wurlie was sitting stiffly upright on a little ladder-back chair in one corner, with Nan Sinclair next to him. The two of them were deep in a continuing discourse on the effect of the Truman administration on Wall Street.

"All right, now." Mrs. Upton apparently saw herself as director, readying a Broadway show. "All together, now. Open the boxes and let them out. Whee!"

The boxes snapped open, and cats were suddenly everywhere. Snarling at each other, spitting, clawing, cats on the table, cats on the people, racing round the walls, entangled in the curtains. Mrs. Upton raced after them, yelling "Now behave, behave. Don't do that! Get off of there. Boojee, come control your guests. Come on, now, be a host. Dennis, help. Dennis! Where is he? Dennis!"

No one knew. He'd been leaning against a doorjamb until the opening of the boxes, when he quietly turned to one side and rolled around the jamb and disappeared. Jack was heard to yell "Jerry, come get these damn cats off the divider. I'm fixing the cake."

One especially large dark-brown cat, Ruta's Cuddles, hid herself up against the lower half of the Dutch door just as Faye, bleary-eyed and shaky, leaned through the open top half. "Oops," Faye exclaimed, reaching down. "Somebody dropped her muff!" She touched Cuddles, who hissed and fled. Faye rolled her eyes around the room, thinking nothing had really happened, that there had been nothing there, that it was all just one more boozy dream, and hoping no one had noticed. No one had, as everyone was busy trying to dodge cats.

Then suddenly, all was quiet. The cats had all hidden themselves ... except one, Tabby Upton's Belle Ami. She was center-room, heaving and gasping, her rib-cage showing as she rocked back and forth in obvious distress. Except for John Wurlie's monotone, there wasn't another sound in the room.

"Oh, dear!" Tabitha exclaimed, wringing her hands. "Belle is having a hair-ball. How awkward!"

The gasping and heaving culminated in a reverberating hiccup and Belle produced a slime-green concoction about the size of a golf ball. It rolled around a bit and came to rest beside the coffee-table just as Jack arrived with the people cake.

"I'll get the forks and the plates and Mrs. Upton, maybe you'll serve?"

"Not just at this moment, Jack," she replied, eyeing the wet mess on the floor. "Could you bring me the dust scoop from behind the kitchen door, please?"

John Wurlie and Nan Sinclair, with heads together, continued without a pause their intense discussion, now focused on the actual benefit to England from Roosevelt's gift of fifty destroyers, and had the pound gone up or down.

Boojee, gingerly emerging from behind the sofa, rushed to the cat cake just as Mrs. Upton sank to her knees with the scoop.

"Oh, how divine!" She smiled around at her guests. "Birthday Boy is eating his cake!"

As if a signal had been set off, cats came from everywhere and pounced on the fish. Growling and spitting, making little chewing sounds, crunching up tiny bones, fighting over anchovies and bits of sardine-salmon paste, the cats were having a splendid time.

"Isn't it lovely? They're all eating. Isn't it lovely?" Mrs. Upton cried, waving aloft the scoop with the hair-ball.

Matilda Crunch ducked and shifted in her chair. "Careful," she cried, looking up. "Don't drop that thing!"

Jerry was in the kitchen helping Jack, and had just placed the platter of ice cream on the divider, when Black Boy leaped up and landed in the ice cream.

"Get that damn thing off of there," Jack hissed in a whisper. "Shoo it off. Away! Go!" And he swiped at Black Boy with a ladle.

Spitting in dismay and shifting feet so he could shake the free paw, the cat proceeded to drip ice cream across the counter, across the kitchen, out into the living-room, into John Wurlie's lap and up across his shoulder to a perch on the back of the chair, where he proceeded to clean himself. Mr. Wurlie leaned slightly forward, ignoring the ice cream paw marks across his legs and up his lapels, and was heard to remark to Nan Sinclair "But, my dear, about the Picasso that sold last week at Southeby's ... "

Jack picked cat hairs and fish droppings off the ice cream, smoothed the foot prints, slapped scoops between meringue shells and shoved the plates at Jerry.

"Out they go, and don't you ever dare breathe a word, you hear?" Waving his hand, he dispatched the dessert.

With both cakes and all the meringues eaten, and the cats sleepy now from the food and easily caught and returned to their boxes, the birthday party was over.

As the guests clambered into their vehicles, Mrs Upton stood in her doorway, beaming.

"Same time, same place, next year." She called.

Bertha, turning to Matilde Crunch who was riding with her, said under her breath, "Over my dead body!"

8

November

S and spurs are an integral part of the natural stabilization system of southern beaches. They are also menacing to both people and animals. Growing along the landward edge of the beach, serving as a ground cover around and among the graceful sea oats and the gentle pastel blue railroad vine, their flat, thin leaf-structure traps the fine white airborne sand, blown from the lower beach. Thus they play their role by adding to the beach and increasing the outlying islands' main defense against buffeting storm action.

Sand spur seeds are encased in tiny pods covered with needle-sharp barbs which penetrate, break off, and fester in the feet of the unwary. Clinging tenaciously to the soles of shoes, the pods get dragged in from the beach to the yards of island homes and here they flourish. Requiring little or no moisture, in no time at all they put down roots, spread out their distinctive leaf patterns, and busily produce ever-increasing crops of the burry spur pods.

The undisputed sand spur queen of Captiva was Ida Benson. She was out to get them, and they all knew it. At least so she claimed. Whenever she accepted a new yard to scuffle, she always first walked all over it, brandishing her hoe. The sand spurs hated her, she said, and the weak ones would give up and die. No one ever checked the truth of this, though there did seem to be a great amount of withering going on in the "Benson" yards.

Ida, now in her sixty-third year, had suffered a devastating childhood. Born to a poor German housewife in 1884, she had roamed the back alleys of Berlin in classic Oliver Twist style with little or no parental guidance. In 1901 she married Gustave Veital. Her lot improved in affection but not in finance, and the young couple grubbed along for years.

As the upheavals of World War I approached, Gustave, thoroughly disenchanted with the German State, took his wife, small child, and Ida's younger sister Olga, first to London and then to Chicago. Here Gustave found employment in a German restaurant as Second Cook, and prosperity momentarily raised her head.

Not for long. Gustave ran afoul of the Chicago gang element and was hacked to pieces in a vicious street fight. The two sisters, with true German persistence, refused to accept defeat and together opened a sewing shop.

The Veital Shop was so successful that Ida and her young son Karl were soon able to vacation during the summers, leaving Olga in charge back in Chicago. They went south, searching for solitude, and found it on Captiva Island. They camped summer after summer on the northern tip.

Ida lived for the summers and fell more and more in love with the simple island life. It was far removed from the seething humanity of Chicago and the dreadful state of affairs back in Germany, where her mother and two youngest sisters continued to eke out an existence. Feeling that she had abandoned them, guilt constantly gnawed at her, and to assuage this feeling she, for years, mailed them seventy-five cents of every dollar she made.

In the middle 30's, Ida remained on the island permanently, leaving young Karl in Chicago to finish his schooling. She met and married Neal Benson, a rangy, free spirit many years her junior and for ten years they had a marvelous time ... not much money but great fun. They fished and swam, hunted and played cards, and drank away their hours. Life was good!

But not for long. Disaster struck again in the winter of 1945. A curvaceous blond visitor lured young Benson onto the mailboat, on which they headed north, never to return.

To support herself, Ida took up yard-tending, at a dollar an hour. She was conscientious and her customers, the winter home owners, enjoyed neat, sand spur-free yards while in residence, and had the comfort of knowing that their decorative plantings were lovingly watched over the other nine months, while they were north. Later, they additionally employed Mrs. Benson as caretaker, paying her to hold house keys and watch property. House openings and closings followed in due course, and came under the dollar-an-hour fee, and Ida prospered. It was backbreaking work in the bugs and the heat. A lesser person would long since have given up. But Ida stuck. Disheveled, her face dripping perspiration, and a dank cigarette dangling from her lips, day after day she weeded and scuffled, mowed and raked, and sent off her money orders to Berlin.

●

The day had been unusually hot for the end of October. All through the early morning chores with Maude, squeezing several hours before lunch to drive Cora to an upper beach for heart shells, the double delivery business of mailboat and bakery ... through all these duties Jerry kept anticipating the cooling afternoon swim with Roy and possibly Buster. When he reached the turn of the road at Captiva Inn he was dismayed to find Roy fully clothed, leaning on two scoop-shovels, waiting for him.

"No swim today." Roy called as Jerry parked and climbed down from the flatbed. "We have `civic' chores to do, and it'll do you good. Introduce you to some real work for a change. Give you a taste of how the other half lives." Roy chuckled as he talked.

"Okay," Jerry said somewhat reluctantly. "I guess I gotta say yes, huh?"

"Nope. But it might be fun. This'll give you a chance to help a couple of people and who knows, later on, when you need help, there they'll be. Evan Wiggins is loading his truck at his shell pit and I told him we'd give him a hand. Once a year he hauls two truckloads of shell to Matilda Crunch's shop for her driveway. He usually gets five dollars a load, but Matilda hasn't that kind of money, so he and I haul it for her free. You can help. Okay?"

"Okay."

"Leave your truck. We'll take mine."

"Where're we going?" Jerry asked, tossing the shovels into the truck bed and climbing up beside Roy.

"Evan has a rutty road cut out onto the beach halfway to the pass, north of here. You'll see."

"You said a couple of people. Who else?"

Roy inched his truck gently through the soft sand shouldering the road and concentrated until the roadbed firmed up. Then he glanced at Jerry.

"While I was talking to Evan just a bit ago, waiting for you, Ida Benson came by on her way to Replogles. She tends their place. Says she's having trouble with their cistern and asked me to help. I said we'd stop by later."

Jerry looked doubtful. "I really don't know Mrs. Benson."

Roy chuckled again. "You'll know her after this, wait and see. By the way, we don't get paid for any of this, you know."

"You mean it's all for free? No dough?"

Roy slowed down a bit and looked seriously at the boy. "Jerry, work here on the island falls into two categories. The work you're paid for, pre-arranged and satisfactory to both sides, and the work we do for each other, to be good neighbors, to just be kind. There's never any charge for this last, but the dividends are there and they keep coming back when you least expect. Course, you're free to refuse." He prepared to stop the truck.

"Oh, no. It's fine. I'll help," Jerry said quickly. "Come on, let's go."

Around the final bend in the sandy road, where it straightened out to run alongside the Gulf to the end of the island, they found Evan on the beach, humming to himself and heaving shovelfuls of shells onto his dump truck. Many weeks before, knowing that the winter people would want new shells for patios and driveways, Evan had constructed a pathway for his truck leading from the roadbed across soft sand onto the hard-pack by the high water line, and laterally to a huge ridge of shells stretching a quarter-mile or so and some four feet high. Tumbling in with each wave at this location, due possibly to some odd formation of the outlying sandbar, the shells lay all about in thick, deep profusion. Those removed by truck during the day left only minor gaps in the ridge, which were filled in by the night tides.

Evan's roadway was nothing to brag about ... two tire ruts filled with old boards, palm fronds, discarded sheets of tin, anything he could find around the island that might give his truck tires sufficient purchase to prevent bogging down in the sand.

Watching Evan from a distance, with his wide shoulders and ropey arms, rhythmically stooping and heaving, stooping and heaving, Jerry thought it looked so easy ... Evan seemed to be swaying to unheard exotic music. At the shell ridge, however, pushing a square-point scoop shovel into the mound, with each shell seeming to fight back against being disturbed, it proved very heavy labor. Jerry's arms and back soon protested, and a blister the size of a nickel formed in his right palm. He said nothing but continued to stoop and heave alongside the others.

Matilda Crunch enjoyed the unusual excitement of three men and a truck in her curved driveway, and offered iced tea and corn fritters to each of them.

"You've never stopped in, Jerry, to see my shop. You just rush in with packages and off you go again. Some day, stop by. Let me know a bit ahead and I'll find some cookies for you. Wouldn't that be nice?"

Jerry, fighting heat and the blister, was in no mood to gossip. He smiled back, nodded, and continued spreading the dumped shells.

With the second load hauled and spread, Evan called out "Okay, Matilda all done. Hop in, boys, and I'll run you back to your truck." Turning the key, he ground the starter, but the truck wouldn't catch. The motor turned over and over, but it wouldn't fire.

"Sounds like you're out of gas, Evan." Roy was peering around under the hood. He glanced under the body and lifted his head. "I see the problem. Your cork's out!"

"Cork's out?" Jerry'd never heard of such a thing.

"Yep. I've been at Evan for months to have his gas tank soldered but he claims it's too much of a hassle to take the tank off, wash it and dry it out an' all. So he just stuffs a big cork in the hole, and it must have jiggled out on the bumpy road somewhere."

"Well." Evan shrugged and smiled. "No problem. I've got a spare, but we'll need some gas. Roy, you go get your truck and Jerry and I'll hoof it to Murph's with this can and fill up. Meet you there, okay?"

Roy nodded and headed off up the road.

"Now, ain't this a hassle?" Evan said to Jerry as they trudged along.

When they got to the dock they found that Murph was off somewhere fishing and Pearlie was standing under the outside shower-head in bra and panties, all over soap-suds, scrubbing busily at her legs. She nodded brightly as they walked up, Jerry all eyes.

"What's the matter, boy? Ain't you ever seen a lady take a shower before?" She yanked at her bra and soaped down inside, shifting her voluminous bosoms from side to side. Perky over the lad's obvious embarrassment, she laughed and tossed back her head, letting the shower spray her face. "Go on, now, both of you. Go grab a beer. I'll be done in a few minutes, all dry and spruced up, and we can visit."

When she later appeared, with hair combed back and in fresh bra and panties, she shook her head at Evan, as he brandished his gas can.

"No gas, Evan. Tank empty! Murph's raging and I sent him off for some mullet to cool down. Some bastard, 'scuse me, Jerry, some bastard stole our gas. Never happened before. Things are getting rough over here." She rang up the register, dropping in the quarter Evan gave her for his beer and Jerry's soda. "I just don't know what things are coming to."

Evan looked at Pearlie and shook his finger in the air. "I've been after Murph for years now to lock that tank. There it sits, way at the end of the walkway. You can't even see it from inside here. Whadda ya expect?"

"I expect things to stay the same. To stay like they always was. But things don't. They change, and I hate it. We keep track. We know how much gas we have. We know how much gas gets sold. We're not idiots, you know." Pearlie was heating up. "I can't be running all that distance every time someone wants gas. The tank stays open. People help themselves and come out here and pay me. We've got a separate register for gas invoices and sales. When the tank gets low, we know it from the register, and we send for more. Good system. Works fine." Her chest heaved as she gasped for breath. She slapped hard at the bar with her hand. "Now, it's all gone. Murph says we'll have to lock the tank. I'll have to trot back and forth. I ain't got that kind of time. I'm already busy up to here." Her hand was way up over her head. "Early up and drag out here, gotta cook and clean, keep up the books, ice the drinks. Gotta cool off now and again with a beer and listen to the juke. Shower and laundry." Her voice trailed off as she pondered all these chores, and the beer can emptied. "Now," she continued, "that's all gone. We have to lock. I suppose next we'll have to lock our truck and the house. It'll spread like a disease. Where do you keep all those keys? They'll fall out of pockets and get lost. I just can't stand it. It's a mess. Time, I told Murph, to sell out and get us another island, farther out somewhere." She reached for another beer.

"What do we do in the meantime?" Jerry wanted to know.

Evan put his hand on the boy's shoulder. "Oh, that's no real problem Jerry. We've all got spare five-gallon cans stashed at home. This would have been easier than going all that way, that's all. When Roy gets here, he'll drive me home and I'll grab one up. Maybe we'd better get back to the road. Come on."

As they left, Pearlie called. "Evan. I forgot. Murph wants you and Roy and the others to stop by out here after seven tonight, so's you men can plan how we face up to this mess. Don't forget. And thanks for the quarter."

Roy and Jerry were late getting to Replogles. Ida was bustling about inside the house when they drove in the yard, and she hunched down around a mop handle to hear about the shells and the gas situation.

"That'll make things tougher. More walking. I'll have to leave my mower cans at the tank, walk out the dock and get Pearlie and walk back and fill the tanks and walk back and pay for it and stay long enough with Pearlie to drink several beers. That's an added expense I really can't afford. I agree with Pearlie. It's a mess. Still, life goes on." She shrugged fatalistically. "And I've a problem here. Mr. Replogle put in an electric pump to pull cistern water into the kitchen sink. You know, Roy. You installed it last winter. Well, it won't work. Also, I think the line coming in is plugged. Maybe the cistern needs cleaning. Lord, I hope not. It's too late in the season to get into all that now. Could you both come back tomorrow afternoon? Most of our time is gone today."

Roy and Jerry glanced at each other and nodded.

"Sure," Roy said. "An' we can still catch a swim today. Let's go, Jerry. Wanna come along, Ida?"

She smiled and reached for another cigarette. "No, not this afternoon, Roy. Some other time. Thank you for asking me. See you tomorrow."

"Does she ever swim with you?" Jerry wanted to know, as they drove along toward the beach.

"No. Never does. It's a little game we play. I always ask. She always refuses. I like Ida Benson. You know exactly where you are with her. She works hard, like a horse, really, and tends to her own business. Not overly friendly, but always kind. Still, if you get to know her, stay away from that German thing. She's sticky on that, sure enough."

"What German thing?

"Well, she feels Hitler was a saint, and she can be very loud about it. Refuses to believe any of the horrors connected with the war. Claims it's all Washington propaganda to discredit the German race, so that our boys could go in there and stomp all over those sweet, innocent, little German lads. Real twisted thinking. Still, she has a point, I suppose, from the German view. They had nothing after the first war, and along comes this creep and gives everything back to 'em. They got fat and sassy under Hitler. I suppose they'd think of him as a savior. Like the French with Napoleon. Still, you'll be better off on this little island to stay far away from that one."

Later, around the dinner table, Jerry blurted out "Aunt Ag, did you know Mrs. Benson thinks Hitler was a saint?

Aunt Ag looked nonplussed. "No, Jerry, I didn't know that Ida Benson thinks Hitler was a saint. Did she say so?"

"No. Roy told me."

"Well, I doubt it very much."

Cora looked up, a forkful of mashed potatoes mixed with green peas poised in the air. "It's true, Ag. I've heard her say so. We were talking at the post office dock one day and she got pretty hot about it."

"Cora." Maude pointed with her knife. "Why in heaven's name do you always squash up peas in your mashed potatoes? They get all mixed together and you can't taste either one. Just tell me why."

Cora never reacted sharply when Maude was testy this way. The belligerent edge to Maude's voice seemed strangely to calm Cora, as if she'd gotten a rise and won the battle, so why press it.

"Maudie, that's just it, dear. I don't really like either mashed potatoes or peas — the taste that is. But I just love the squishing in my mouth with those surprise little balls rolling around and popping when I crunch down." She smiled indulgently. "I think the consistency of food is half the fun of eating. Don't you?"

Agnes was watching this exchange out of the corner of her eye, but her attention was on Jerry.

"I always felt ... and if you two would stop sparring and listen, I'm about to be profound ... " Agnes smiled. "I always felt that everyone doesn't have to agree about everything to get along. If that is a sore spot with Ida, then don't discuss it with her. She's had a very tough time of it, all her life, as I understand, and now she's the only woman on the island doing a man's work. Bertha tells me never a week passes that Ida doesn't mail out a money-order to her aged mother back in Germany. Maybe she has had to convince herself that the Germans were blameless just to hold on. The only way we could possibly understand is if we'd led parallel lives."

Cora took a deep breath, preparing to interrupt, but Agnes held up her hand and shook her head slightly. "I feel the necessary thing is to remember that Mrs. Benson is a part of our small community here, an important cog. She is a quiet, trustworthy, kind friend. Let her have her peculiarities. If you probed deep enough, I'm sure you could find some in me, too.

When Roy and Jerry turned up the following afternoon at Replogles, Ida was slumped over a low table in the living-room, rearranging photographs in an album.

"I keep my best ones down here. This house is dryer than mine and the snapshots don't fade so soon."

While she got each of them a cool drink, Jerry flipped through the photos. There were many city shots ("Chicago"), several of a sweet-faced woman ("my sister Olga"), a series of a small boy growing progressively older ("my son Karl") and a large pile of unsorted ones.

Ida grabbed a handful of the loose shots and hugged them to her chest. "These are my very special ones, all here on Captiva." A diffident little smile came and went on her face. She seemed suddenly embarrassed, as though she were sharing something dear, private memories that others might not appreciate. This girlish attitude from the weather-beaten old woman seemed strangely out of place.

"Gee" Jerry exclaimed. "These are great. When were they taken?"

"In the 20's. We used an old box camera." Ida took each shot from him, after he'd looked at it, and built a neat pile on the table. Roy was in the kitchen, checking the cistern pump motor under the sink.

"We used to camp up on the north end of the island. Every summer for years. Here's one of our camp sites." She shoved a fistful across the table, toward Jerry, and then stared silently at the floor. "Best part of my life," she murmured. "I loved those summers."

Jerry sucked in his breath and handed one shot back. "Are those alligators lying there in the yard? Really? It looks like a bunch of alligators."

Ida chuckled and nodded. "Yep. That summer, boating tourists took to bothering us. Somehow, word got about that we were camping there, and people would pop out of the bushes and stare. We hated that. All the trouble we'd gone through to be alone, and here they'd be. Karl decided the best way to scare 'em away was to catch some 'gators and stake 'em out on long ropes, so they could roar and snap at the tourists. It worked, too, though mostly the 'gators slept in the shade."

"Who gave 'em to you? How'd you get 'em?"

"We caught 'em. We went down to Sanibel Prairie and caught 'em. We tramped all over during those camping trips, and one time found a little stream running through parts of the saw grass down on Sanibel ... I think it's fed mostly by the run-off rains, and in the winter it gets pretty shallow. But the summers we were here it was always full and deep ... inky black water, from all the tree roots and muck it ran through. Well, we knew there were 'gators living in the stream banks, as we could see signs everywhere. Flat places along the stream edge, and on top of the banks where they sunned themselves, and holes in the bank, half in and half out of the water. We'd tramp along until we came to a fresh hole, then reach in and grab Mr. 'Gator and drag him out!"

"Gee! Weren't you scared? Don't they bite? Everybody warned me, back home in Evanston, never to tangle with an alligator. Gee! Was it exciting?"

Ida looked intently at the lad. His face was flushed with enthusiasm and he had difficulty sitting still. She leaned toward him and dropped her voice.

"Would you like to go, sometime?" she whispered. "We could take off some morning — mornings are best — and drive down in your truck to Rabbit Road and the prairie's just off to the south. We'll just creep off by ourselves and see if we can find us a nice, plump, young 'gator."

"Could we? Yippee! Wouldn't that be great? Yes, 'course I'd like to go. When? When could we?"

Ida glanced toward the kitchen door, in which Roy had just reappeared. They all spoke at once.

"We could hustle down that way tomorrow morning if Roy's fixed that motor."

"Ida, I think it's okay, now. Broke wire made it short out."

"Golly, I can't go tomorrow. Maude and Cora both need me in the morning." Jerry's face fell into his lap.

Straightening up a bit slowly, Ida smiled as she beckoned Roy to follow her. "Don't worry, Jerry. If not tomorrow, then the day after. Alright?" When Jerry nodded, she added "Good. We've got a date. Day after tomorrow you be at my door at dawn. Don't forget, now."

The shorted motor was repaired, greased and oiled, and working fine, but only a weak dribble of water issued from the pipe lip into the sink. Ida looked at it ruefully.

"Just as I thought. Pipe plugged. Good Lord, I hope the cistern won't have to be drained and cleaned. It's too late in the season now. Not enough rains due to fill it up again. I should have checked it during the spring."

Roy was tugging at his pants. "You bustle off and get me a couple of towels. I'll climb down into the tank and take a look."

"Oh, migod." Ida looked abashed as the pants slipped off. "Wait. I'll get towels. Jerry, come with me, please. You can carry 'em back to Roy. Hey, Roy" she yelled over her shoulder. "Don't go climbing down into that cistern before you shower real good. All over. You hear?" Turning to Jerry as they went together into one of the bedrooms, she shuddered a bit.

"I always hate this sort of thing. That's drinking water. Now here this big ole sweaty man climbs in with his big ole sweaty body and he'll poke around and stir up all the varminty stuff laying on the bottom. Mr. and Mrs. Replogle will drink this stuff. Well, it can't be helped." She shrugged. "We just won't talk about it, now will we? And later on, as Mr. Replogle mixes his friends' drinks, they'll smack their lips and tell each other "best damn water I ever tasted!" She chuckled and squinted up her eyes, her former depression over the situation cleared away by these happy thoughts of island game-playing.

She tossed two towels toward Jerry, who grabbed them in his right hand, and winced.

"Ouch!"

Ida was there in a second.

"What's wrong with your hand? Let me see that."

She checked the fat blister and clucked her tongue. She poked it gently with a finger.

"We'll drain that little beauty. Run those towels in to Roy and I'll get a needle and some thread."

"No." Jerry drew his hand back. "Aunt Maude said, when I showed it to her, not to slit it open. She said the hole would close up again and more water would collect and it'd be sore for weeks."

Ida pushed him toward the kitchen door. "Your Aunt Maude is a very wise lady but she never lived in Germany. Hurry back now."

Roy was crouching behind the outer kitchen door, naked as a jay-bird.

"Where is she?" he hissed, as Jerry came up. "Don't let her in here. Gimme the towels and you stand guard." He slipped outside, lifted the wooden frame protecting the cistern entrance, and slid down the inside ladder. There issued sounds of splashing, and gasping, and water sloshing around. Roy's hand reappeared out the opening, holding a wad of old leaves, sticks, little things that looked like lizard legs, and a squashed-up dead frog. He followed the hand up and out of the cistern.

"She's okay, now. Pipe intake was plugged solid with this stuff. She'll pump good again now." Water cascaded from his head to his feet. "Damn thing's deep. That intake pipe stretches all the way down to within an inch of the floor, you know."

Back inside, Ida waited in the living room, needle and thread poised.

"Stick out your hand, Jerry. Palm up, now. Hold still. This won't hurt at all." She carefully thrust the needle just under the skin on one side of the blister, worked the point along slowly and drew it out the far side. leaving darning thread dangling out both sides. She tied a large knot on one end of the thread and slowly pulled up the slack until the knot was just at the edge of the blister. Then she snipped off the needle and knotted the other end. Giving a gentle tug, she evened the knotted ends dangling in his palm.

"There! The thread will keep the two holes open, and syphon out the water all night long. By morning, you'll be dry as a bone and no hurt. You'll see." Turning to Roy, "Is Replogle back in business?"

"Yep." Roy smiled. "He's back in business."

As they drove back to the Gulf to swim, Jerry squirmed around in the truck seat to face Roy.

"Ida's taking me out to hunt alligators. I've got to be at her place at dawn, day after tomorrow. Isn't that great?"

Roy smiled. "Sure is. See! Dividends already."

Back at Agnes' house, the three ladies closely examined the hand operation.

Agnes nodded and offered, "Should work. I've never seen this before, though."

Maude merely snorted "Humph!"

Cora picked at the knots a bit and gave one of her brightest smiles. "See, Maudie," she said gaily. "More than one way to skin a cat!"

Reactions were tepid at the news of the pending alligator hunt. A very early breakfast would be no problem, as Sally-Anne and Doobie were due that day and they always arrived well before dawn. Agnes would leave Sally-Anne a note and she could get Jerry something to eat.

"I'll pack a lunch, enough for two, and leave it all in the fridge." Cora offered, as Jerry climbed the stairs to his room.

Maude was silent and Agnes was watching her.

"Maude," she said, "you'd like to go, wouldn't you?"

"Love to, but can't." Maude stared out the window. "Yep. I'd love to. But this is Benson's show. We wouldn't hunt the same way. Her feelings might get stepped on. Too small a place. Not worth causing hurts."

"Well, I hope she watches out for the boy." Agnes was worried in spite of herself. "Be terrible to have something happen to him. And I wish he'd remember her age and call her Mrs. Benson."

"Oh, she'll watch over Jerry, never fear. She's done this so often before." Maude smiled reassuringly at Agnes. "Not lately, of course. I'm not worried about the 'gator hunt. Most likely won't turn up anything, anyway. The worry lies in one or the other tromping on a rattler. About your second point, Ag, his calling her Mrs. Benson. Here I think you're wrong. The boy should call her Mrs. Benson to her face, and I'm sure he does, during normal daily exchange around the island. But this is an adventure. They are pushing into the wilderness like old Daniel Boone, and it should be first names and no age barrier. The companionship of the unexplored, you know." She nodded her head to emphasize her position.

Cora leaned way back in her chair and intoned toward the ceiling "Ah, the camaraderie of the open road ... "I'll build my house by the side of the road, and let ... "

"Really, Cora! We were talking sense, and you bring in all that singsong stuff! Besides, you've got it all wrong." Maude twitched irritably and abruptly left the room.

Cora made a little face toward Agnes. "She's so touchy these days. Wonder why?"

Agnes glanced in the direction Maude had taken. "Yes, I agree. She's been all tensed up lately."

●

Rabbit Road cut through Sanibel, from Bay to Gulf, about halfway down its length. Scarcely more than a wide wagon trail, it served two main purposes. Doobie and Sally-Anne Denkins lived in a small clapboard and tin shack about halfway in, on the northern side, and the Captiva people could get to the Sanibel beach for shelling without motoring all the way to the ferry slip, and crossing to the lighthouse point. Even during the summer, traffic back and forth seemed to be heavy, island style. Two cars came through during August, and the Denkins family talked about this strange event for several weeks.

Just past Sally-Anne's home, Ida signaled to Jerry to pull the truck over and stop. They were each encased in full night-fishing regalia, and they were already hot, though the sun was scarcely up. Ida had explained earlier that they had to be prepared for mosquitoes though, once deep in the cord grass and with the sun fully beaming, then maybe the bugs would disappear.

They climbed out of the truck and checked their gear. Jerry had the lunch and a water bottle. Around his neck he had coiled the rope Maude insisted he carry, and her pig-sticking knife was shoved under his belt. Ida carried an old tin bucket from which protruded a machete handle. She carried a long staff, stretching over six feet, forked at one end and with a metal crook lashed to the other. She had a long, heavy rope wound around her waist. A snakebite kit was in her pants pocket, with a ball of heavy twine and the inevitable cigarettes and matches.

When Jerry first saw the crook, he'd laughed.

"You'll look just like Bo Peep with that thing."

"Ah, we've got to have this," Ida replied. "It's my old one. Had it stored under the house." She pointed at the forked end ..." Snakes! "... then at the end with the crook ... 'gators!" ...

They'd been sipping coffee at her house that morning, before leaving for the prairie, and Ida had explained procedures.

"I don't know if I'm right, Jerry, but I figure it this way. A 'gator wants a home, so he travels along the slough 'til he finds a wet spot in the bank where the digging will be easy. Varmints hate to waste energy. He digs a good, deep hole with a dry chamber at the end large enough to turn around in. When he comes back to rest, after feeding or sunning, he goes in and flops down. Okay? Then, along I come. First I unwind this big rope and tie it to the forked end of this staff. Then I shove the end with the crook deep into the hole. It scratches along Mr. 'Gator's back and the crook pushes across his snout and I twirl it. This makes him furious. Maybe he thinks it's a big snake. He thrashes around in that hole and snaps down on my staff ... and I yank. And I yank! Migod, it's exciting. You have to watch out for the pole in your hand — it can bang around pretty fierce. Mr. 'Gator will either back out, or turn in his den and come out headfirst. It's always easier if he comes out headfirst."

"Then what do you do?"

"I fight. We both fight. And we pull! And we watch not to get tangled in the rope. That's for Mr. 'gator. If he's small, we drag him up the bank. If he's too big to drag, we leave him in the water and get out ourselves. Once he's on the bank, we bunch up this rope and toss it onto him and like as not he'll tangle himself. They roll, you know. Over and over. Violently. When they're all tangled up and can't run away, we slip in careful-like and get a noose over his snout and tie his mouth shut. Have to be very careful here — he's quick with that mouth and it's powerful. Have to watch his tail, too, which will be thrashing side to side."

Now, here they were, standing on the edge of Rabbit Road, and Ida had final instructions.

"I'll go first. You follow, and walk in my footsteps as much as you can. If I hold up my hand, you stop and stand dead-still. Don't move again 'til I motion. Okay?"

"Okay," Jerry answered seriously. "I'll be careful."

They stepped off the road and into the tall grass.

●

Long before the coming of the white man, Indians named Florida's vast inner lake of waving saw grass Pa-hay-okee. Today it is known as the Everglades. It stretches some hundred miles southward from the foot of Lake

Okeechobee to the open Gulf, and is forty to seventy miles wide, cut by endless narrow water-lanes that repeatedly lead into and out of lakes within lakes. It is studded with small protruding islands of collected debris, silt and hard woods termed hammocks by the natives. The area in reality is a huge, steaming, pulsating swamp, heavily overgrown with lush, coarse, tall grass. This grass, more correctly a sedge, is thickly matted vertically as well as horizontally, interwoven so tightly as to be almost impenetrable. Each folded leaf-sword bristles with hundreds of upward-growing, needle-sharp serrations, an effective guard against intrusion as the grasses are twisted and beaten, lashed back and forth in an endless waving dance by the gale winds that wander the expanse.

Underneath the saw grass, which can reach twelve feet in height inland where the murky, slow-moving water is deep, but which grows to a more modest four to five feet along the shallow-watered edges, all manner of swamp life creeps and crawls, swims and lies in wait. Each is an important element of an ecosystem so perfectly balanced that the Everglades will endure as long as Man permits.

One moves with caution into this alien world. Hacking at the grasses and looping vines, stumbling through muddy, knee-deep ooze from hammock to hammock, movement is impossible without a flailing machete, a strong arm and grim determination. Even then, progress is slow.

There is no other area on earth comparable to the Florida Everglades. There are, however, imitations, and three of the offshore barrier islands of the Gulf coast harbor mini-Everglades, similar areas of moving creeks, swamp and lush grasses, with overall size determined by the island's age.

The Sanibel mini-'glades, verdant and healthy, covered most of the eighty-five square miles of the island, except for the sandy Gulf beaches to the east, and the mangrove-fringed western bay shores. It had been purged and cleansed in 1930 by an encompassing brush fire. Ignited by lightning, whipped by strong winds, the fire raged across the area with flames twelve feet high. Days later, when it had smoldered itself out, blackened palmetto trees everywhere stood sentinel to the passing carnage. At ground level, shrubs and grasses had been reduced to a thick ash, which following rains beat into the soil, signaling a resurgence of life that completed the revitalizing circle.

During the ensuing seventeen years there had been no repeat conflagration, and the mini-'glades flourished as before, with the tall, matted grasses protecting and guarding.

●

Ida cautiously led off, with Jerry following closely. For the first few minutes it was comforting to the lad to see her moving slowly just ahead. Then he stumbled, and when he looked up, she was gone.

"Hey. Where are you?" he called nervously.

"Up here. Wait a minute, I'll come back." To suit her words, the grass parted and Ida reached out. "Give me one end of that rope around your neck, and tie the other end to your waist. It'll keep us from getting separated. Okay? Now, try to keep up."

They inched forward, hacking and tearing, slipping and stumbling. The sweat poured down Jerry's face and he felt he was smothering in his hood. Finally, Ida called back. "Not much farther, now. The grass is much taller, so the slough is nearby. And just beyond should be the prairie."

Jerry gritted his teeth and wondered how he ever got himself into any such fix. Never again. If the Good Lord helped him get loose ...

"I'm out! I'm on the prairie. Hurry up." Ida sounded miles off but in reality was just ahead. Jerry limped on, and broke through the grass.

They crouched down to rest, placing their equipment all around them. Testing cautiously for bugs, Ida lifted her smothering head-covering and gasped with relief. Not bad. Not many at all. With a hot sun well up and climbing, the heat would soon force the few buzzing insects back into the cooler shade under the grass. She motioned to Jerry to pull off his hood.

"Gee! I thought I was going to pass out. Pretty hot, huh?" Jerry swiped at his face to clear his eyes.

They were in a shady area about two acres square. The southern edge sloped down to an inky-black stream, edged with cattails in thick clumps. Fiddler crabs scurried about, in and out of the water, up the gentle slope to their holes in the wet loam, visiting and gossiping in groups of thousands, or sat silent, eyes on antennas, staring at the intruders.

Jerry was ready to rest awhile and enjoy the quiet scene, but Ida was again on her feet.

"I can see a 'gator den from here. Look along my arm. See?" She held out one hand, pointing.

Jerry looked and could see the top half of what must be a tunnel into the stream bank.

"Careful where you step if you're coming with me. Watch where you put your feet," she called over her shoulder. "This hole looks pretty new. Somebody's home in there, sure enough." She clambered down the bank and into the murky water, shoes and all.

Jerry was horrified.

"What are you doing? Something's going to bite you, down in that water," he called.

Ida pushed on, waving one hand to keep him back.

"You stay there, Jerry. Gather up our stuff and drag it over to this bank. I'll only be a minute." She reached the hole and shoved her arm into it up to her shoulder.

Jerry rose. Any minute he expected to see Ida's arm yanked forward and Ida herself snatched down that tunnel. Instead, she calmly withdrew her arm and rinsed mud off it in the slough. She climbed back up on the bank beside Jerry.

"Just as I thought. Not a very big hole, but it's new. You can tell by the amount of mud stuck to the sides. If it's old, the water sloshing back and forth scours the rocks and sides till they're stoney. This one's slick with mud. Mr. 'Gator's there, sure enough. Be a small one, just right for us."

"Did you feel him?" Jerry was still aghast. "Maybe there's two. Did you feel any?"

"Of course not. I wasn't reaching in to feel 'gators. Lose an arm that way." Ida lit a cigarette and inhaled deeply, smoke snorting out her nostrils. "I was feeling the sides of the tunnel. No danger at all if you reach in slow-like and keep to the sides. Wanna try?"

"No, siree, bob!" Jerry drew in his feet as if there were critters all about. "I sure don't."

Ida chuckled and worked on her cigarette. "Give me a second to rest and plan and then we'll attack. Okay, soldier?"

"Okay."

The sun was high and the morning nearly half over as they crept toward the 'gator den. Ida had her staff, and the cord was in her hip pocket. Jerry carried the rope looped around his neck, across his shoulder and under one arm. The old woman and the young boy slid down the slough bank together, never sensing any incongruity. Intent on their purpose, to do battle in the wild, each knew the other would perform as best he could, and that was enough.

Ida reached the den and paused, looking back at Jerry to share the thrill of it all. Shhhing him with a finger across her lips, she raised her shoulders around her chin in delight, a wide grin on her face. She made little poking motions at the hole, as she unwound the heavy rope from her waist and tied one end to the staff.

Jerry nodded back, and grinned.

Slowly, slowly, Ida pushed the staff, hooked end first, into the hole, keeping it at water's height, about center of the opening. She twirled it gently, sensing whether the hook scraped anything. Slowly she pushed and slowly she twirled. Suddenly her eyes widened and the staff in her hands came to life. A thrashing deep in the den boiled the water at the entrance, and Ida yelled, "We got him! We got him! Come on — help pull!" She grabbed the staff handle and yanked with all her might. Setting her feet against the slough bank, she yanked a second time.

For a moment, all was still. Both sides, woman and 'gator, seemed stunned, unbelieving. Not for long! The water boiled again. The 'gator pulled. Ida pulled. Jerry, reaching the scene, grabbed the rope on the staff handle and he pulled. Very slowly, bit by bit, the 'gator gave ground and was drawn from deep in his den to the entrance.

"Watch out, now. He's coming out head first. We must have him hooked in the mouth. Leave be for a minute. Jerry, stop pulling! Let him lie."

Ida sagged back on her haunches.

"Jerry, listen. This is the worst part. Once he starts out of that hole, we have to work like hell, dragging him out and across the slough and up onto the prairie away from the water. He'll struggle to stay in the slough. He's better in water, you know. So we can't stop. You understand?

Jerry by now was so out of breath and overexcited that all he could do was nod.

"Okay," Ida cried. "Here we go!" She threw herself backward, pulling with all her weight, feet slipping and sliding under the water, trying to find purchase. Jerry was dragging right along with her. The 'gator came sailing out of the hole, hit the water, tried to spin, was up the bank and flopping on the sandy loam before he knew what had hit him.

Keeping pressure on the staff, Ida went into action. She took the excess rope and flung it across the 'gator. As it rolled and tangled itself, she ran over to a palmetto stump and threw the rope around it in a double loop, and drew it tight. Then, grabbing Jerry's rope, she was back at the trussed animal, working a noose around its jaws. Suddenly the 'gator was snuffed tight, body and jaws.

"How'd you do that?" Jerry yelled, jumping up and down. "How did you?"

Ida sank down on the sand, exhausted.

"I don't know. I really don't know how I did it. I didn't stop to think. The mouth had to be tied off, and I didn't want either it or the tail to get me. So I did it. And there he is!" She pointed with one hand, and searched for a cigarette with the other. Suddenly, she was very tired. Slumped over on the damp ground she thought to herself. "Thank God, it's a small 'gator. A large one would have done me in for sure." Gratefully she accepted the water jug Jerry held out.

He went over and squatted by the alligator, tentatively touching its scaly hide with one finger.

"How big would you figure, Ida? What do ya think he weighs?"

Ida, still hunched down, made small figures in the sand.

"I got my own method for sizing. Might not be anybody's else. My rule is, one part head, one part body, two parts tail. His head is about eighteen inches, so his body is about the same, and his tail is another two and a half feet. He's about five feet long. Not too big. Come on." She straightened up with an effort. "Let's cut him loose."

"No!" Jerry cried. "I want him! We've got to take him home! Maude and everybody will never ... Roy and Buster ... they'll never believe we got one unless we show 'em.

Ida studied the boy. Remembering her young son's excitement over the first 'gator he'd caught, she finally smiled and nodded.

"Okay, then. We drag it home. But only on one condition. You must take care not to hurt it, and you must bring it back tonight and release it right here. Okay? Agreed?"

Jerry nodded his head, but Ida shook hers.

"That's not good enough." She brandished her machete. "Promise. You must make me a firm promise, or I'm gonna cut him loose right now."

Jerry crossed to where she sat and squatted down. Taking one of her hands, he patted it gently and looked deep into her eyes.

"I solemnly promise, Ida Benson, to take special care of the alligator, keeping him wet and shaded, and I promise to bring him back tonight and set him free!"

"Thank you, Jerry. Do you understand why it must be set free? Years ago, when Karl and I were hunting and camping here on the islands, we always ate what we caught or freed it. Once in a great while, we'd butcher a 'gator for the hide, if we needed money to eat. You could get two dollars for a hide back then. But we never, never just caught and killed. You can't waste God's creatures. Something happens to you, deep inside, when you allow yourself to go around killing for no reason. You can see it in a man's eyes. They get dull and flat, all the excitement of living gone. I can always tell if I want to know a man by just looking at his eyes. No! You have to bring it back and let it go just where we caught it, so it can continue living out its life. Roy will help you, I'm sure, if you ask him."

Getting the 'gator out to the flatbed was tedious but no great problem. Ida explained what they were doing as they went along.

"We'll fix ourselves a travois, and tie him to it. We'll cut two long poles, branches from that tall pine back there, and three short ones. Let's go get those first."

Back again in the clearing, Ida took her cord and retied the 'gator. With Jerry steadying it, she wound the cord around its snout, just behind the bulge on its lips, and tied a knot.

"The snout is so top-heavy, it can't open its mouth against that cord," she explained.

Next, they folded the front legs up and over the back and tied them. The hind legs got the same treatment, and the 'gator was secure except for the tail.

Ida then laid the two larger poles on the ground about two feet apart and taking Jerry's rope, lashed the three smaller poles across the long ones ... one at the front and the other two midway down and fairly close together. Then, jumping about as the tail slashed from side to side, they carefully rolled the 'gator over onto the travois and tied him firmly ... head, body and tail. Ida motioned Jerry to step in behind the front cross-pole and lift up. Handing him his share of the scattered gear, and grabbing up the rest, off they trudged, the boy dragging the travois and the woman following, to keep watch that the 'gator didn't slip.

It was just after noon when they drove into Aunt Ag's yard, and the three ladies piled out to hear firsthand about the hunt. Jerry talked at breakneck speed, while Agnes and Cora leaned over the side of the truck and examined the prize.

Maude went up to Ida.

"Good job! No snakes?" she questioned gently.

Ida shook her head.

"I kept a sharp eye out but we were lucky. Migod, Maude, I'm so tired. Never again. This is my last hunt!"

Maude noticed the slightly quivering chin and patted Ida's shoulder.

"Nonsense. Wait 'til you're rested. Lots more hunts in you yet."

With a slight shrug of her shoulders, Ida turned aside and fumbled for a smoke.

9

The following morning Jerry overslept. He was deep in a dream-tunnel when Agnes climbed the stairs to the second floor and rapped on his door.

"Good morning, mighty hunter, up and at 'em! Your breakfast is getting cold. We've all eaten and everybody is waiting for you." Hearing sounds of reluctant stirrings, Agnes smiled and went back down to the others.

"Seems such a shame to wake him," Cora said. "It was very late when he and Roy got back from Sanibel last night. An hour more wouldn't hurt." She was standing by the sink, aimlessly repositioning the spices. "Though I can't get into much this morning without help."

Maude glanced up from the cast net she was repairing. She'd rummaged around and had found it in a box under the porch. The leads, all double-bound, were in position around the outer edge and soundly lashed in, but the fretwork of the netting was rotting and the net itself was in sorry condition. She'd decided to repair enough of it to teach Jerry to throw it, and later she'd ask Mr. Jackson to rework the entire thing.

"What's so different about this morning?" she wanted to know.

"I've a date with Evan." Cora simpered, grabbing the edge of her skirt and pirouetting around the room.

"Dearie me." Maude was unimpressed, and simpering made her uneasy. "At your age, how do you know?"

Cora continued to spin about.

"That wasn't nice, Maudie. Evan is supposed to stop by this morning and start building the shelves in the shop." She glanced at Agnes. "When Jerry is through his breakfast, he and I have to drag all that stuff out of Evan's way. I want Jerry to dust that area extra special and knock out every last mosquito. It's overcast this morning and they'll be out by the millions."

"They'll be out in the grove, too," Maude added. "Can't dust there. Not with that little pipe arrangement he uses. If Wesley Richards ever decides to open that mixing station on Sanibel and gives us one of his jeeps, then maybe we can do something."

Agnes turned to Maude. "What do you mean?"

Maude settled back in her rocker. "Had a long letter the other day from Sarah Douglas. You know, she and her friend run that real estate office in Myers. She's after me to open a branch office over here. Imagine! Here on Captiva. I keep telling her she's crazy. Maybe on Sanibel though. The tourists crossing on the ferry all mostly head for the beach right there. They don't get down here. Our traffic, if you can call it that, is mainly home owners and their friends, and the couple of Inns and their guests. I keep telling Sarah to get someone on Sanibel. That cute little wife of Salter, the postman, what's her name, Norma? She'd be a good one. But the whole business is a pipedream. Nothing'd ever come of a real estate office out here on these islands. Never work!" She rocked complacently back and forth.

Agnes, used to these conversational tangents, waited a second and then steered the discussion back on track. "And Wesley Richards?"

Maude chuckled. "Right, Ag ... I got off the subject. Anyway, Sarah writes that this Wesley Richards, who was appointed Lee County Mosquito Control Agent last year, has developed a de-bugging system that seems to work. Jerry, you know, dusts DDT powder. If he blows it about on the leaves and ground while everything is still damp with early morning dew, the powder sticks and breaks down. Or on a wet morning like now. But the effect is soon gone once the sun is hot and has dried everything out. This Richards blows wet fog from the end of a jeep — some kind of anti-bug spray suspended in diesel oil. That fog seeps in everywhere and the effect lasts all day. Sarah says it's messy, as the mist gets into the houses and into the drapes and so on, but the relief of no bugs is worth the extra cleaning work. I don't know. I've never seen it."

"Maude." Agnes continued to steer. "Did you mention a mixing station on Sanibel?"

"Yep. This Richards is a new broom and he's sweeping clean. Talks of bringing real relief to the out-islands. Plans on an experimental setup on Sanibel, which is the worst mosquito breeding area in the entire United States. Did you know that, Ag? By Federal count, Sanibel was way out in front, more than Padre Island and all the Texas coast — more, even, than the Keys. More than ... "

"So he talks of doing something on Sanibel." By this time Agnes was snipping string beans for supper and Jerry was eating his cereal.

"He will, too." Maude was positive. "Sarah says he's planning on building this mixing station and putting a fogging jeep over here to see if it'll do any good. Can't wait. Maybe I can get the driver to scoot in and fog my limes." Maude stared out the kitchen window, past the big gumbo-limbo, and off across the sound, into a rosy, bug-free tomorrow. Then, resting her big hands on the table, she pushed herself upright, patting Jerry's arm as she rose.

"If you're lugging for Cora, lend me your truck and I'll drive myself to the grove. I'll be back long before you and Cora are done."

Cora was spreading little bits of colored paper on the kitchen sink. She glanced at Agnes. "Can you put aside your bean pot a second, Ag? I need your opinion. Remember, we discussed last year doing something to make the shop more visible. I thought Evan could paint the eave board and the window trims orange. Maybe pomegranate. Or pink. What do you think?"

Agnes was immediate attention. If a house of hers was going to be painted anything but white, she definitely wanted a voice in the choice. Yet she didn't want to hurt feelings.

"Cora, all those colors are nice. Heavenly, really, but ..."

"But you don't like any of them!"

"Well, no. Not really. We want to point up, and take care to do it muted. Those colors, I mean pink and flamingo and so on ... they scream!"

Cora toyed with the thought of a small pout.

"I didn't even mention flamingo!"

"Don't you think, maybe, a rust-red, a shade or two below barn red, would say what we want? It would weather into a nice warm brown-red and blend nicely with all the sleeping hibiscus."

"Oh, Ag, how lovely. Yes. Oh, yes. A rust-red is exactly what we want. As a matter of fact, that's the color I really had in mind but I feared mentioning it because I thought you'd rather have yellow or puce or something. I'm so glad you like my idea of rust-red."

Evan painted the facia board around the shop and all the window trims and a signpost at the parking area. The rust-red pleased everybody. When he was finished, the little building could easily be spotted, nestling in the shrubbery, as motorists came bumping down the Sanibel road and slowed to turn onto the bridge.

Maude worked on the cast net most of the afternoon and by sundown had it sufficiently pieced together to stand being tossed about. After supper, she and Jerry went across the bridge to the beach.

"I'm not much good at this, Jerry," Maude explained, as they walked along the shore to her favorite spot by the fallen tree.

"I can explain the idea, but to learn to throw a net properly takes practice. Lots of it!" She took the net from him and dropping the leaded fringe to the sand, casually flipped the remainder over one shoulder. Squatting on the sand she slowly poked at the weights with a piece of driftwood, forming a circle, but her attention was off somewhere down the beach.

"You know," she said softly, "I've always felt that net casting, along with ice-skating and ballet dancing, is one of the truly beautiful accomplishments of man. To me there is something so satisfying, so peaceful, so somehow uplifting, watching a net cast against the sky, that my throat can close off, and I almost gasp." She turned aside, suddenly bashful at this inner exposure. She went on in a quieter voice. "Somehow, I feel safe and secure, as if there couldn't possibly be any danger or evil anywhere as long as this simple, beautiful act goes on."

She had stopped fiddling with the net, and they were side by side on the warm sand, their hands close together.

"The setting has a lot to do with it, of course. Ice-skating needs its rink and the gleaming surface, ballet needs its orchestra and the stage and the framing proscenium. Net-casting needs the sea, the sand, a setting sun, palm trees, a muscular satiny figure swaying and twisting. The moment before the cast, when the thrower braces and his back and arm muscles tense, is so filled with expectation it's difficult to breathe. And then the throw! That glorious moment when the figure stoops and twists and reaches upward all in one liquid motion, and then the net soars skyward, up and up and up ... flaring out so lazily into a full gleaming circle, hanging for a moment at the highest point, and then slowly floating down onto the waiting water." She fell silent, embarrassed at having disclosed feelings usually kept hidden.

Jerry had been watching her face as she exposed herself. He reached out involuntarily and put his hand over hers.

"It's fine, Maude. I understand." Neither noticed the salutatory omission. "I'll practice for you. I really will. I'll get good. Even better, I'll get great and we'll come out here together. When the sun sets we'll come out, and I'll throw and you can correct me."

Then, suddenly, it was gone. The delicate warmth that had bound them for a moment fell away. With an inaudible sigh and an all but imperceptible straightening of her shoulders, Maude reached over and picked up the net and handed the bundle to Jerry. It was surprisingly heavy.

"Spread it out flat on the ground, now," she said, "and we'll take a look at it. Mind you," her voice had a gruff edge, "just now, when I was so fired up, I wasn't referring to this itty, bitty net. I was talking about the huge ones they use in the south Pacific. Real fishing nets."

"I know." Jerry nodded, as he scrambled about, spreading the net.

"This is a bait net." Maude explained. "And that's what it's used for, catching bait. It's only eight feet in diameter, but the principle is the same as with those tremendous ones. You throw it out, twisting it to make it flare. It strikes the water all edges at the same time and these weights here sink it to the bottom, trapping bait under the spread-open net. When I lift up the net you might think all the trapped bait will escape. Not true! It's not made that way. Look close, now. See these little thin strings tied at equal distances around the outer fringe? They feed under the net and up through this small metal collar, and tie into the pull-rope, which you hold fast onto when you toss the net. Then, when the net is spread out flat on the bottom, you pull in your rope by short jerks and it draws these strings together and the net folds under itself. It sort of forms a pocket of netting up off the bottom, with the bait in it."

Jerry looked puzzled and Maude added "Somewhat like your Grandmother's reticule, only upside down. Here. Pull on that rope while the net is spread out there on the sand, and watch what happens. See? The edges fold under."

Jerry was fascinated. Several times he ran around, spreading out the net and drawing in the strings so that the net bunched up.

Maude watched and waited.

Tiring of this flat action inshore, Jerry grabbed up the net and raced to the edge of the Gulf.

"Here goes. First throw," he cried, and spun around and heaved. The net, in a tight bundle, rose in the air and plunked into the water.

"It didn't open, Aunt Maude. It didn't open. What did I do wrong?"

Maude laughed out loud. "Everything. You did just about everything wrong. Quit cutting the fool now, and go in and get that thing. You knew all along it wouldn't open. You just wanted to sneak in a dip in the Gulf. Bring it back here, now, and I'll explain what I know about throwing it." Still chuckling, Maude took the net and stood up. "Remember now, all I can do is explain this throwing business as I know it. It worked for me, a long time back. Like I said, it's the same as with everything else ... if you want to get good at it, you've got to practice."

They spread the net full open on the sand and Maude picked up the pull rope. Opening the loop plaited in the end, she handed it to Jerry.

"Here. First thing, slip this over your left wrist. Then the net won't get away from you if you get rambunctious with it. Now, step by step, here's what you do. Okay?"

Jerry nodded, all attention.

"Next, coil the hand rope in your left hand until you reach the metal collar. Hold all this in your left hand. Okay?"

Again Jerry nodded. The rope was now coiled around his left arm and he held the metal collar in his left hand. By raising his arm as high as he could, the net hung bunched tightly together almost off the ground.

"With your right hand, grasp the full net two feet from the leads, and put that part of the net also in your left hand." Maude was moving all about the boy, chuckling as she circled, amused by his strained expression as he concentrated.

"Don't get confused, now. Seems everything is in your left hand ... and that's okay. Your left hand is the anchor and the right does the actual throwing. Next, and this'll surprise you. You ready for this? Sure?"

Jerry bobbed his head up and down, though his eyes were wary.

"Hold the net up high enough so that the leads swing free. Twist your left wrist <u>counter-clockwise</u>. At the end of the twist, just before the net spins back clockwise, grab the leadline and place it in your mouth."

"Mouth? Did you say mouth?"

"Yep. In your mouth! Between your teeth! Now, with your right hand, flip some leads over your <u>right</u> forearm, until the spin is out of the net. I can't tell you exactly how much. You'll have to practice. It's not the same for everybody. Last, keeping some of the net looped over your right arm, reach down and grab the leadline, where it hangs free. Good. Now, <u>throw</u>! Swing the leads as far as they will go to the left, then stoop and swing upward from left to right, letting the net fan out as the leads take over. Don't forget to open your mouth at the same time."

They were still tussling with all this as the dusk changed abruptly to ink-black night, and they had to head home. They trudged back to the bridge talking quietly and planning, when suddenly a station wagon loomed out of the dark, skidded to a violent halt, and showered them with sand. Two round figures, encased in netting, leaped out.

"Bud, I wish you'd drive slower. You almost hit that tree back there."

"Now, Bud. Don't pick. It's your turn to drive tomorrow and then you can hit trees."

"I'm not criticizing, Bud."

"I know you're not, Bud. Forget it. Help lug this gear out. You take the lantern and I'll drag the net. Where's Ellie? She should be here somewhere. Who are those two, standing like bumps over there and staring? Never mind. Let's go. I can hear those beauties popping already."

Maude leaned her head toward Jerry and whispered.

"It's the Twins! Must have gotten in this afternoon. Always the first of the home owners to arrive. Isn't it dreadful? Before long, everybody will be back and there goes our peaceful little island."

●

Jessie and Ginger Comstock were in the final quarter of long lives dedicated to fishing. Identical twins, they grew up in the Michigan lake country amid muskellunge and trout and doting, wealthy parents. At an early age they captured the Michigan State Brown Trout Flyrod Championship, to which they clung tenaciously and which they defended year after year. They were built like parabolas, and seemed to roll along instead of walk. No one could ever be sure which was which, and the comment was often heard ... "Migod, how do they even tell themselves apart." They referred to each other as "Bud" and communicated mostly in syllables, with one starting a sentence and the other finishing it, with lots of grunting and nodding along the way. This convenient telepathic capability had stood them in especially good stead when they won substantial funds crisscrossing the nation as a duplicate bridge team ... until it was discovered that they could read each other's hands. Then they were barred from any further participation. Years later, still indignant at this seemingly cavalier treatment, they could often be heard by passing islanders discussing this mis-adventure, as they rocked on their porch by the bay, sipping tall, ice-cold juleps.

"Every time I think of it, Bud, I bristle. Just because we had this small advantage was no reason to throw us out. We lost a fortune."

"We also made a fortune, Bud. Don't worry about it. Unreasonable as it was, maybe it's for the best. We might still be playing bridge, and I'd rather fish. It's just as well, Bud."

"I suppose so, Bud. But it still makes my blood boil!"

Their back yard sloped gently to the bay, where there was a boat shed and a tee-end dock. Here they moored a small plywood boat with a ten-horse outboard motor, available at a moment's notice to scoot them out into the open water in pursuit of that day's catch. Each morning, from the first of November until the end of April, there they were, far from shore, drifting about on the gentle bay water, gathering in bait and wearing identical nautical outfits with matching hats. Because old habits die slowly, they used fly-rods and hauled in pinfish after pinfish and plopped the catch in the portable bait well floating beside the boat, to be later used as bait for the snook and redfish they caught in astounding numbers.

During the winter months, when gassing at Murph's dock, those in the know would comment "Thank's, Murph, for the gas. Which way did the Twins go this morning? South, you say? Well, they'll catch everything out that way, so I'll go north."

Ellie Thigpen was edgy every time the twins arrived to fish the bridge. "It's not so much that I actually dislike 'em," she once said to Agnes as she dropped off snook fillets. "They're so bombastic! Maude and I can fish all night, with hardly a sound. Those two shout back and forth to each other, and all that grunting and 'budding' ... get's annoying after a bit. They run roughshod over everybody. And they can get nasty-mouthed if you get in their way. I know. I know. They can fish. Catch more'n I do. Maybe that's part of why I hate to see 'em arrive." Ellie gave an embarrassed little chuckle. "I wish they'd stay all winter down at that Key-way-din place on Marco Island they go to each Christmas. Bet those folks down there hate to see 'em pull in, too."

●

Every spare second he could squeeze from his chores, Jerry practiced with the cast-net. On the beach, off the dock, the open spaces in the back yard, everywhere there was sufficient space, he could be found tossing and gathering in. His throws got better and better. By the end of the second week, watching approvingly, Maude felt it was time to take the frayed net over to Buck Key and ask old Mr. Jackson to repair it. After talking it over, they decided that the coming Sunday, just past lunch, they'd take Agnes' little boat and make the trip.

Sunday proved another golden day, and shortly past noon they pushed out from the dock and headed across the pass and into the channel opposite. The

109

little Johnson Seahorse motor moved them along slowly, causing gentle ripples about the prow as the small boat parted the water.

"Don't know why Agnes' husband ever bought this motor." Maude was sitting in the stern, steering, and she shook her head in irritation. "It's so puny we couldn't even make this trip if the tide was going out. Thank heaven, it's running in. He used it to drift-fish around the inlets, I think. But it really makes no sense for trips of any distance."

Jerry was trailing one hand over the side, watching the water bubble and boil around his fingers. "You know, I've seen this channel from my bedroom window and I always wondered where it goes. Is it deep?"

Maude took up one of the oars and poked it straight down into the water. It disappeared from sight up to the end she was holding. "Yep, it's deep. About eight feet most all along. 'Course, there're shallow spots and the deepest water is mostly in the center, except where the channel turns. Then the deep water is along the far side, where the tides have scoured it out. It's called Roosevelt Channel and it meanders along a couple of miles to opposite the post office. It separates Buck Key from Captiva proper. Only two families live on Buck Key, far as I know. Daddy and Mammy Farlow have a sprawling hut-cow-barn-pigsty kind of home at the northern tip, opposite Bertha's dock, and old Mr. Jackson has a cottage on the south side of Hurricane Hollow. That's a small inland lagoon on Buck Key where most everybody takes their boats when hurricanes threaten. It's shallow and completely protected from the gales by dense mangrove growth all around. There was a Mrs. Jackson once upon a time, but she's not there now. Never did hear tell what happened to her."

The little boat chugged slowly along, and the heat and the passing mangroves, the startled egrets fussing at the passing boat in muted protest, the lazy cormorants perched on branches with widespread wings drying in the sun, the mullet jumping and splashing ... all contributed to a feeling of drowsy peacefulness. Coupled with his full stomach, Jerry found it difficult not to snooze.

"Why is it named Roosevelt Channel?" he asked in a sleepy voice.

"Well," Maude adjusted the lime pie Cora had insisted they carry for Mr. Jackson so it was more in the shade. "This is one of those island tales, dear to us all, but there's no proof now to the truth of it. Seems way back, when life on Captiva was really simple, somewhere about 1904-5, a huge devilfish moved into the bay and set up house-keeping. It hung around and hung around. Its presence ruined the local mullet fishing. Also scared the fishermen, if the truth be known. Well, word of this monster ... I was told it stretched eighteen feet from wing-tip to wing-tip ... reached up-water to Boca Grande where President Teddy Roosevelt was on a fishing vacation. It fired up the old boy and down he came to do battle, trailing all manner of hangers-on, the F.B.I. or whatever it was called in those days, small boats with newspaper reporters and photographers, and half the boating population of Boca Grande. Well, darned if he didn't hook the thing at the mouth of the

Channel, and off it took, heading south, dragging the President of the entire U. S. of A. behind it. Great excitement, and splashings and doubling back when the Channel narrowed down. Finally it tired and Roosevelt hauled it in. I suppose, if the truth were known, someone shot it. Anyway I read somewhere that there's a picture of the President in the Roosevelt Archives, standing beside a huge scaffolding on which the monster is strung up. He came to get it, and he got it! That was the story of his life, it seems. He fought and he won. Remarkable man. Too many teeth, though." As an afterthought Maude added, "Ever since, its been called Roosevelt Channel."

They had moved along about half the channel length when it widened considerably, to some 500 yards. Maude veered sharply to the right and ran straight for the mangroves. At the final moment, with Jerry braced to ram the shore, she cut the motor, lifted the forward mangrove branches, and they drifted through a narrow overhung canal into a broad, quiet lagoon.

"Gee!" was all Jerry could say as he gazed about.

Maude nodded, and chuckled out loud. "Isn't it something? No one would ever guess that little entrance exists unless they knew." She'd been watching his reaction and was delighted at the boy's obvious surprise. She reached up and grabbed a mangrove branch. The little boat barely rocked as they sat and observed the scene before them.

The lagoon water shimmered and sparkled under the hot midday sun. Along the southern shore, where they were, it was about five feet deep, but it shallowed out into exposed mudflats in all other directions. Directly ahead, a short, sturdy dock jutted out from the bushes with a wooden skiff tied to the end.

"Look at the birds feeding over there." Maude gestured generally at the mudflats. "I love this place. It's so quiet and peaceful and protected. The birds feel it, too, I'm sure. Look at 'em. Hundreds."

Jerry pointed at one large scarlet-winged bird that seemed to be sticking it's bill deep into the shallow water and then shaking its head from side to side.

"What is that? What's it doing, anyway?"

Maude looked for a second at the bird in question, and then answered quietly.

"That's a very special bird. It's a spoonbill, a roseate spoonbill. There aren't too many left, these days, so we're in luck to see it. Notice the greenish head and those magnificent scarlet wings. When a flock flies overhead they look like a moving rainbow. Spectacular. Just spectacular. The bill is long and ends in a flat spoon, instead of a point. They move it from side to side through the mud, searching for worms and water-bugs and small crabs and things. The spooned end is very sensitive, like our lips, and can feel its food."

Jerry glanced over at Maude and his face showed awe.

"Gee, Aunt Maude. You know so much! Everything about everything!"

She shook her head. "No, not everything. I've lived quite a time, that's all, and most of it here in south Florida. It would be strange indeed, now wouldn't it, if some of it hadn't rubbed off on me?" Still gazing at the birds feeding on the flats, she talked on in a low voice. "Actually, I know a very little bit about a very small corner of the world. I know the local birds, and the fish, some trees and flowers. I haven't any other family, so I use these. A body has to have something to lean on. I use Nature. It's important to me."

There was a little silence. Then, straightening her back in a deliberate motion, Maude smiled at the boy. "Wonder how many different kinds I can call off for you? Over there, on that old piling, the one standing on top with it's wings akimbo, that's a cormorant. Funny bird. It flies about the air and roosts in bushes and trees, but it feeds under water on fish. It can swim like a streak, outdistancing its prey. It breathes air, of course. It has no oil in its feathers as ducks do, so it has to sit somewhere and dry off or it will become waterlogged and drown. That's why that one is holding its wings out like that. Over there, in the mangrove bushes is another. See?"

Jerry nodded.

"Also, in the mangroves, just below it and sitting very, very still, is a bittern. See that small greenish-brown bird, with its head held straight up? It's difficult to spot, it blends in so perfectly with the background bushes. See it? Do you?"

Jerry was having difficulty. Not knowing what to look for, he missed it entirely. He shook his head.

"Never mind," Maude went on. She ticked off the others. "I see a snowy egret, and a little blue heron. Bobbing about in the mud are some least terns and a Wilson's snipe. I see several plovers and a flock of sandpipers. And look, way back under the overhang is a gallinule. Of course, now, there's others I've missed. Everybody over there is so busy and rushing back and forth so fast, I get mixed up. Isn't it lovely to sit here and see all of 'em? They don't seem to mind us at all. I love that feeling, of being part of nature, not always on the outside looking in. That huge brown bird with the leathery face and strange accordionated beak is a pelican. But you know pelicans. Have you ever watched 'em closely? I mean, very closely? When they dive for fish they turn quarter-circle in the air, usually to the left, and turn another quarter-circle just as they hit the water. Once the bill-pouch fills with water, it more or less remains in that exact spot, with the bird's body flipping over it. When it surfaces again, the pelican is facing in the opposite direction. If it didn't go through all that twisting and flipping business, the pouch would rip open. Think of it. Isn't nature really wonderful to have worked out all these different things?"

Maude maneuvered the boat broadside to the dock and twisted the bow rope around a post in a half hitch. Then, carrying the pie, she climbed up and motioned Jerry to follow. She crossed to a big pine tree and yanked hard on a hanging rope. From above rose a clatter like pots and pans banging together. She chuckled at Jerry's look of disbelief.

112

"Mr. Jackson's door-bell. He tied a bunch of empty gourds together and hung 'em up that tree. When you yank on the rope they jiggle and jangle. He hears the clatter and knows a friend is approaching."

Jerry pondered a bit.

"What happens if you don't 'ring' but just walk in on him?"

"If you're a friend, you ring. If you just appear, like as not you'll get a load of buckshot fired at you."

"No kiddin'? Really?"

"Really!"

The little path twisted off through the bushes and shortly they came to a clearing in a stand of Australian pines and a few tremendous coconut trees. A small ramshackle cottage of clapboard and tin, gray as Spanish moss from lack of paint, with a wide eave jutting forward covering the little porch and rickety stoop, sat off to one side, perched on cement blocks as if a single-winged bird was poised in flight.

Fishing nets were scattered about, some on the ground in heaps, some spread on drying racks. An ancient lapstrake skiff was propped on its side, waiting long overdue caulking and a coat of copper paint. Under it, cats snoozed or stretched. In the shade on the porch an old hound-dog lay half asleep, his legs twitching and his eyes fluttering and squinching over some long-ago chase he lived again in his half-dream.

Mr. Jackson was also on the porch. He was sitting on a three-legged stool with a beaked fishing cap pushed back on his head, and an aged corncob pipe clamped between yellow teeth. White whiskers framed his ruddy face. His pant legs were rolled to his knees. He was bare footed, and was running a net through his gnarled hands. He bobbed his head and tipped his cap to Maude.

"Howdy, Miss Maude," he called in a surprisingly deep and firm voice. "Come on up and set a spell. When I heared my gourds I figgered it'd be Seth, after his net here, and I'd a had to disappernt him as it ain't ready yet. Glad it's you and we can jest gossip some." He motioned toward the old rocker on the porch beside him.

Maude sat down, the pie on her lap. She introduced Jerry, explaining he was Agnes Trumbull's nephew, visiting for the winter.

Mr. Jackson thrust out his right hand and shook Jerry's. "Glad to meet cha, young feller. Come on in and set down. Plenty o' room." He reached back through the open cottage doorway and dragged forward an old peach crate. He upended it and signalled Jerry to sit.

Jerry placed the net he'd been carrying on the ground and gingerly eased down onto the box.

After a lengthy quiet time, during which Maude rocked and Mr. Jackson picked at the net but nobody spoke to break the friendly warmth of silent communion, Maude cautiously leaned forward a bit.

"We've been worried about you, Mr. Jackson. It's been a long time since any of us have seen you. We wondered if you are all right."

Mr. Jackson continued to work the net. Every now and then he'd change a lead, or tie off a snag with strong new linen line. "Well, now, it's mighty comfortin' to know three sech pretty ladies 've been fussed about me. Makes a body feel real important." A fleeting smile played around his face. "Nothin' wrong with me, I 'spect, 'ceptin' my hearing's goin'. Pretty soon, I'll be as deef as old Ned lying there. He's deef as a post, else he'd have been yapping and stomping at you down at the dock when you came aside. Can't hear nuthin' less than a gunshot no more. Pity, too. He's been a good hunter, a good friend. Ain't no use to me these days, deef like he is. Just another mouth to feed. Still, once a friend, always a friend. I sure can't turn agin him now. He'll be safe here with me till he dies. Or I do. One tuther bound to."

He lifted his head and looked long at Maude. Then his rheumy old eyes twinkled and he took the pipe from his mouth, using the stem as a pointer.

"I still sees fine! I can see Miss Cora didn't forget me. That's a lime pie, ain't it? My favorite. My, oh my, how I loves lime pie." He leaned back against the wall and chuckled contentedly.

Maude rose and was taking the pie indoors when the old man stopped her.

"Miss Maude, let's eat her right here. It's been a coon's age since I had lime pie. There's plates and some forks inside there, somewheres. And a knife. Don't forget the knife. But hurry up. I'm drownin' in my tasters!" He smacked his lips in anticipation.

Maude cut the pie in half. Then she cut the half in half. Then she cut one of the quarters in half. Mr. Jackson got the quarter and she and Jerry each got an eighth. She put aside the full uncut half. Mr. Jackson had been carefully watching every move, and nodded in agreement when she'd finished.

Later on, after arrangements had been made for the net repairs and there had been a bit more gossip and Maude and Jerry were walking back to their boat, she laughed and turned to Jerry.

"If I know old man Jackson, we were no more than around the corner than he attacked that leftover pie. By now I'll bet it's mostly gone, every crumb!"

"What does he do for light?" Jerry kicked at a shell in the path. "I don't see any electric wires."

"He uses kerosene lamps, same as we all did before the R. E. A. people brought in electricity awhile back. Actually, it's much cozier, you know. Soft glow. Lantern swaying in the breeze. All that sort of stuff. I always liked it. The kerosene smell seemed to help hold down the skeeters, too. 'Course, with electricity, we picked up real refrigeration, among other necessities. But the Mr. Jacksons, they manage. They get by just fine. He uses a bucket buried deep in the wet sand out by his dock. Keeps things dry and cool and fresh, providing he doesn't leave 'em too long. He told me once if he wraps a cooked mullet in tinfoil it'll stay good for several days, buried there in the sand. Must work. He's healthy and sturdy. Besides, both Bertha and Pearlie feed him. He brings 'em mullet and they cook him up a meal now and again. He does fine."

They rowed the little boat slowly back out the hidden canal and onto the broad channel. Before cranking up, Maude maneuvered tight under the mangroves and broke off several roots festooned with oysters. Rummaging about in a box under her seat in the stern she lifted out two pairs of old gloves and two metal-handled blunt-shafted knives. Handing the gloves and knife to Jerry, she pointed to the oysters.

"Might as well eat up before heading home. That lime pie is gurgling around in my belly and could use a bit of settling. You've never eaten coon oysters, have you?"

Jerry shook his head. Actually, he'd never eaten oysters of any kind, coon or otherwise, but he didn't want Maude to know.

The oysters were small, about as round as a quarter, and clustered tightly together. They smelled dank, like a damp cellar, and wild wet, like exposed mudflats, though the clusters were dry. Using the point of her shucking knife, Maude showed Jerry the difference between the top and the bottom. Holding the entire cluster in her gloved hand, she explained.

"Be very careful. The edges are sharp as razors and will slice you up in no time. Wear gloves, and still take care. Understand?"

Jerry nodded.

"The top is a little smaller than the bottom. See? I always crack the outside edge with my knife. Just bang it off, like this." She swatted at the oyster with the knife handle, crushing the outer edge a bit. "Then insert the knife, running the blade along the lower shell and well in. Wiggle the knife from side to side and you'll separate the muscle that holds the top and bottom together. Did you follow that?"

Jerry nodded again.

Maude then lifted the top shell and exposed the oyster lying inside. It was small, about a half-inch across, grayish, floating now in milky juice, and surrounded by a fluted, brownish membrane. She leaned forward and slurped the oyster down, juice, membrane, everything.

"Ah!" she exclaimed, lifting her head. "Nothing better, Absolutely, nothing better! Sweet as honey. Warm. Salty. Delicious!"

She attacked a second one.

There was no way out. Jerry didn't want to say no, for fear he'd drop in Maude's opinion, but there was no way he was going to eat those slimy things. His piece of lime pie flipped around in his stomach and threatened to come up.

Maude continued swatting and cutting and slurping in delight, all the time with one eye on Jerry. She could well remember her first introduction to raw oysters. Big they were. Big channel ones, not these small coons. With the burly lumbermen all gathered around her, she couldn't back out. She'd taken a deep breath and swallowed. It stuck in her throat, just behind her tongue ... and came back out. "Go on, gal. Try again" they'd yelled. With it stuck in her throat a third time, Bull Dawson, the gang foreman, slapped her hard on the back ... and down it went. That time, it stayed down. The salty tang lingered in her memory and she developed a taste.

"Had my fill! Let's go back. Okay?"

Jerry nodded. Back sounded good. Maybe, later on, sometime when he was alone and could approach the things slowly and on his own terms, maybe he'd experiment with one or two. Maybe!

10

oy spoke without looking up. "If you two are going night shrimping in the back bay, like you been talkin' about, you'd better get to it. Not much time left, you know, before winter chores set in."

The three of them, Roy, Buster and Jerry, were lolling on the beach late one afternoon. Buster was playing with Jerry's cast net, now repaired and in good condition. Jerry was stretched out on his stomach in the water by the wave-edge, propped up on his elbows, his body rising and falling with the motion of the Gulf, watching Roy, who was sitting cross-legged in the sand, picking at his feet with an auger shell.

Buster looked up, interested. "I can go tonight. Nothing ever very pressing here of an evening that I can't just rip myself away from, you know."

Jerry shook his head. "I can't. It's been a tough day and it'll be late by the time I get home, eat, and finish a few things I promised Aunt Cora I'd help with. Saturdays or Sundays are best for me. Could we go this weekend, maybe?"

Buster was fighting the net and getting irritated. "Damn thing just won't open for me. Sure. How's about Saturday afternoon? Let's get away by 4:30 and you bring food. I'll be at Roy's, waiting. Okay?" He heaved the net, which fell into the water in a tight tangle.

Jerry laughed. "I told you to hold the first few folds in your mouth and loop most of the rest over your arm. You'll never get it to open the way you throw it."

"Don't be so damn smart. Awhile back, you couldn't throw it, either."

Roy winked at Jerry.

"Just imagine it's a mermaid out there, Buster. A beautiful, young mermaid, with flowing blond hair." Roy made curvy lines in the air with his hands.

Buster snorted. "With my luck she'd be 150 years old, and wear a wig!"

117

"What would ya do with her, Buster? I mean," Jerry was chortling as he glanced first at Roy and then at Buster, "if you got one, what would ya do with it?"

Buster folded the net into a neat pile and remarked, "Well, now, I guess I'd do exactly what everybody else does who nets a mermaid. I'd set her up on the mantle and dream."

"And be careful you didn't knock her off ... and bust your dreams, eh?" Roy played along with the idea, still picking at his callus.

"Right."

"Okay" Jerry cried. "So we've got a date, huh? Saturday afternoon, at 4:30, I'll meet you at Roy's. What should I bring besides food and water?"

"You don't need water. There's water in a jug already on the boat. I keep it there. Bring extra food instead. You know how hungry I can get, and poling around those inlets is hunger-making work. Get Miss Cora to make more of those egg sandwiches she made before. And cake. Don't hardly ever get any cake. All Roy cooks is mullet."

Saturday afternoon found them gathering at Roy's home. As Jerry came into the yard, he called out "Hey, Buster. I didn't bring anything at all, 'cept food."

"That's okay. I've got everything. I've got lamps and a dip-net, a gig and my own seine net. The gear's already down in my flat-bottom, so let's get goin'. The tide's full and'll be runnin' out 'til past dark an' that's just what we want. Come on."

Jerry stowed the food under a side seat in the stern and helped push off into the bay. The wide-bottomed boat was heavy and clumsy. But it floated in only inches of water and proved as steady as a bed. Buster had nailed a two-by-four from gunwale to gunwale, about two feet in from the bow, and had screwed down a piece of tin over the resulting triangle. Under this protection, he stored whatever he wanted to keep dry, including two head lamps and batteries, and a spare pair of pants. Inside the boat, besides the inboard motor and its cover, was an amazing variety of equipment ... a long pole for pushing the boat in very shallow water, an anchor, a tin container full of gas, a pile of netting, a water jug, assorted buckets and lidded jars, several long wooden poles with metal prongs at one end, and now, Jerry's cast net. Old rags, several beat-up gloves, a short wooden staff with a whittled hand-grip and a length of galvanized pipe were shoved around in convenient gaps here and there. A large dip-net was propped against the forward hidey-hole.

"Not much room, but we'll need all this stuff. Push things out of the way and sit down. I'll be ready soon's I gas the motor." Buster spoke over his shoulder as he fiddled with a gas can.

Jerry hadn't noticed the motor. It was in the center of the boat under a hinged cover that swung up and to one side, forming a handy work shelf.

"This is a swell motor," Buster said. "She speeds up great." Thrusting forward on the throttle, the exhaust roared. He eased back and the motor dropped to a quiet hum. "She'll barely creep along at this speed, which is better than poling it all around, ain't it? She draws only three inches, which is great, as I want to get up into shallow water in the inlets, up against the grassy shores, where the turtlegrass is all bunched by the tide as it drops ... that's where the big shrimp feed. If the boat had an outboard, it would drag bottom and force me to stay in two-three feet of water, and you can't shrimp way out there. Not at night, anyway."

They were floating well offshore by this time, and Buster started the motor, steering to the left, toward Redfish Pass. He cut into the first small bay they came to, and immediately they were in a school of mullet. He signalled to Jerry, who grabbed up his net. Moving deliberately and thinking over all Maude's instructions ... straighten out the net, check the lines, hold high, grab a third of the spread and clasp in your teeth, flip over the left arm, spin to the left ... he twisted and threw. The net arched high, opened respectably and landed with a series of little plops right on top of the feeding fish.

Buster was jubilant. "Pull it in. Pull it in. I think you got some. Yank it!"

"Oh, migod!" Jerry hung his head far down, between his knees, and began beating on the gunwale with both fists. "How could I be so stupid? Buster! I forgot to slip the draw-rope over my wrist. I've got no end to yank on. Maude will kill me. I've lost her net!" He was so furious at himself his lips quivered.

Buster was overboard in a second, standing in less than three feet of water. He plunked along till he got to the net, felt around, grabbed the draw-rope and yanked it in. The net bunched in proper fashion, trapping three fat mullet in the pocket. He slung it all over his shoulder and trudged back to the boat.

"Here ya are, none the worse for all that. Do ya want to keep the fish?" Jerry nodded frantically.

Buster grabbed first one, then another, and laying the heads on the gunwale, took up the wooden staff and smashed down on the fish. The heads squashed and the fish flopped about. Buster filled one of the buckets, tossed the dead fish in, covered it all with a wet croker sack and shoved it forward.

"They'll be good as new time we get back." He rinsed his hands and reached again for the motor.

"Keep your eyes peeled, an' we'll get some more," he yelled over at Jerry.

Later on, moving slowly across the mouth of Chadwick's Bayou, Buster cut the motor and squatted down in front of Jerry.

"There's a narrow channel in there." He pointed to the west. "It feeds into a deep lagoon still further back. As the tide floods, the inside lagoon fills up and lots of large fish — snook, redfish, snappers, jacks, everything — they move in to feed in that protected area. I've always wanted to stop-net that channel. How's about now? We could run in, bottle up that channel and catch whatever leaves the lagoon as the tide drops. It'd be great! Think of all the stuff we'd get." Buster's eyes shown with excitement.

"'Course," he added, "it's a little illegal."

"What do you mean 'a little illegal'? Maude told me it was against the law to stop-net. She said you could use a cast net anywhere, but if you're using a seine net from shore, the end must return to the same beach the front starts from. In open water it's okay to seine in a full circle, but it's illegal to cross from one shore to another, blocking off a channel, like we're talking about. So it's not a little illegal. It's flat out against the law."

Buster's eyes went dead, and he turned back to the motor. "Okay. Guess it was a bad idea, anyway."

"No. It's a great idea!" Jerry was gazing into the bayou as he savored the possibilities of this new adventure. Already he could feel his excitement mounting in anticipation. "Let's do it, if you think nobody'll catch us. Oh, Lordy, what if revenuers or somebody like that ... there's a man on Sanibel, I heard the ladies discussing him the other day, named Elgin Bigelow and he's a conservation man or something, and he has a plane with wheels and pontoons and he flies around and catches folks breaking the poaching laws ... suppose he lands here and catches us, and we get dragged off to jail ... Oh, Lordy!" Then Jerry's pessimism faded out. "Still, wouldn't it be great? Just great! Where's that net?"

By now, Buster had crossed over to the other side of the boat. "I don't know, now. Maybe it wouldn't be right for me to lead you into my wicked ways. If it was just me, of course, I'd take a shot at it." He pulled the starter rope on the motor, which coughed into life, and they began to move slowly deeper into the bayou, heading for the channel.

"Tell me to stop, now, if you're scared."

Jerry shook his head. "Let's go. I'm not scared, really. Let's see what we can catch." Then he held up his hand and pointed up-bay. "Wait a minute. Here comes a boat. Golly! It's really moving fast."

A little boat was speeding along, heading south toward Murph's dock. Moving at a furious clip, the bow thrust high in the air, smacking the top of the wave-chop and making a noise in the late afternoon air like distant drums beating, it cut across their line of vision from left to right and was gone in a cloud of spray.

Jerry was speechless. Buster chuckled.

"It's okay. That's Gustave Kroen. He's been shark fishing. Told me the other day that he had to get out and catch some, as his banana plants needed feeding. He catches the shark, chops 'em up an' buries 'em around the plants."

Jerry made a mental note to visit Mr. Kroen at a later date, and check into that shark business. But for now they were heading deeper into the bayou and that alluring narrow channel.

"Better grab a bite to eat — this little deal might use up a lot of time." Buster was munching on one of Cora's egg sandwiches, and repositioning the seine in the bottom of the boat. They moved along slowly, deeper into the bayou, past Chadwick's old dock, rotting now and listing far to one side. As the water shallowed, the drifts of turtle grass suddenly thickened and fouled the motor.

"Almost easier to pole the rest of the way," Buster grunted, leaning far out from the stern to clear away the grass. "It's just ahead a bit, over by those mangroves."

When they reached the side of the channel, they tied the boat broadside under the bushes, and eased overboard. The water was three to four feet deep except in the center of the channel, where it dropped to five feet. It was difficult to stand on the muddy bottom, as the tide was running strong, and Jerry kept a hand on the boat prow as he tested his footing. Buster was dragging the net to the side of the boat, readying it to feed overboard.

"Help here, okay? It's tricky right at the beginning. You grab hold of the bunched net and I'll tie one end to the boat. Then we'll stretch her out across the channel and both hold the other end. Remember, the corks are up, the leads are down. She's six feet wide, so that's enough to drag the bottom, and there's enough length to let her belly out from the channel mouth into the bayou for quite a spell. It's gonna be tough, though, draggin' her in and tyin' her off, if she fills up. Don't know exactly how we're gonna do that. We'll wait an' see."

Buster produced the galvanized pipe, some eight feet long, from the floor of the boat, and handed it to Jerry. "Use this as a steadier as you cross to the other side. Don't worry about stingarees, the water's too swift for 'em. Use the pipe with one hand and help drag the net with the other. Let's go." He set out from the boat and slipped and slid across the channel mouth. The tide grabbed the following net like a hungry lion with a fresh kill. Peeling from the boat in perfect order, it hit the water and seemed to come alive. Pulling and pitching, heaving and twisting, it reminded Jerry of some huge sea monster fighting for its life. Little by little, dragging the net, the two fought their way through the deeper water and up the far shore.

"As the tide moves on out, it'll get shallower and shallower." Buster was so out of breath he could hardly talk. Jerry leaned for a second on his pipe pole and said nothing. He was exhausted. The net continued to tug but with the floats holding the upper edge even with the surface, and the leads stretching the seine to the bottom, the open-work of the net body offered little resistance to the rushing water, and the pull was manageable.

Buster jammed the pipe deep into the muddy bottom and with Jerry bracing the end of the net, he lashed it firmly to the pipe.

"There. At least now for a bit we don't have to stand here and fight that thing. We can watch. Look out there!" He pointed to the furtherest bulge of net. "See? We've got ourselves somebody already. Look at the water boiling! God! Ain't this exciting? Can you see what it is?"

Jerry peered intently, but the fish was well below the surface and the water was brown with tannic stain from the inner lagoon. He couldn't tell. He glanced over at Buster.

"Hey, with one end of the net tied to the boat and the other over here on this pipe, suppose the whole net fills up. We can't hold all that. What do we do then?"

"How do I know? I've never done this before. I suppose I'll have to jump in there with 'em, and spear those we want with my gig. A good-sized red and a few large snook is all we want, ain't it?" He glanced at Jerry, hoping he'd agree. All he'd wanted to do, actually, was to see if it could be done. And it could. The channel was bottled off, and the net continued to fill up with fish. How they were going to detach it from the pipe and drag that end back over the muddy, slippery bottom to the boat, with the tide pulling and the fish adding all that extra weight, how all this was supposed to happen was beyond him. Maybe they'd just have to cut one end loose and let everybody go. But first he wanted a few.

Buster slid hesitantly over the side of the net, and inched back toward the boat. He motioned Jerry to stay with the pipe and continue steadying it.

"Where ya goin'? This thing's getting mighty hard to hold." Jerry was edgy. This whole experience was getting out of hand, and a part of him wished now that they'd never gotten into it. Still, his heart pumped overtime with excitement, and his breath was short.

Buster had reached the boat, found the gig, and was heading back.

"Holy smoke! So many things in here they keep bumping my legs. Look out there where the net stops. They're piling up. Look! Some are already flipping out of the water, pushed up by those underneath."

Suddenly his eyes bulged and his arms flailed at the dark water as he struggled back toward Jerry.

"Oh, migod! Oh, migod! What do we do now?" He started picking at the net where it was lashed to the pipe.

"What is it? What is it? Did something bite you?" Jerry was wild with uncertainty, and he almost loosened the pipe.

"Don't let it go. That would make things worse," Buster yelled at Jerry. "The net will still be tied to it and the fish will still be trapped. I gotta untie the net and let it go free. Just now, in that pile-up of fish, I saw a baby porpoise flopping in and out of the water. By now, he's called his ma and she'll steam back from wherever she is and there goes my net. I can't get these dang knots loose! Murph says never net a baby porpoise!"

"Look, Buster! Out there!" Jerry pointed to the mouth of the bayou. "A big ripple and it's coming this way. Fast."

"Oh, migod!" Buster stopped picking at the knots and grabbed his head in both hands. "Too late, now. Nothin' we can do but watch. Here she comes!"

The ripple streaked toward them at tremendous speed, and a sleek, dark-grey form rose and fell as it split the surface. Like a torpedo, the grown porpoise struck the net and tore a large hole in it. Back and forth in a frothy fury it lashed first this way, then that. Then, in a sudden calm, two ripples headed side by side across the bayou, one big, one small, and they were gone, back to the sea.

In the boat, Buster looked ruefully at the torn-up net. "Paid $150 for her! Now look at it. What a mess. I'll ask Roy. If he can't mend it, we'll just throw the damn thing away." Then his gloom vanished and he smiled widely. "Boy, that was some fun, eh? All those fish. We did it. For a minute there, I felt like God. I was in total control. Not for long. Just a second. But what a feeling! I felt way up there, in the sky, looking down, like a huge bird. Lord over it all! I was Big Boss! Boy!"

Jerry grinned.

"Yeah," he cried. "It was sure exciting, all right."

The sun, setting in a brilliant splash of color over the entire sky, seemed to hang stationary in the glory for a moment, then dropped like a stone tossed into a pond, and darkness fell over the bay. On their way back to the open water Buster handed Jerry one of the headlamps with its portable battery.

"Slip this sling over your head with the bulb and reflector pointing straight ahead and hang the battery on your belt. When you switch it on, it'll throw a beam of light fifty feet ahead. Go on, try it. Keep the wire connection dry or it'll short out. Okay? Now, let's get us some shrimp. Sure hope this part of the trip proves out better'n the rest. Pretty no-account, so far. We'll mosey on over to that big mud flat up toward the pass and see if we have any luck around there."

The night was between moons and inky-dark. Skuddy clouds blocked out most of the stars. A good breeze had stiffened in, adding slightly to the difficulties of poling but holding off all the bugs, which was a blessing.

"Hope this little breeze stays fresh. We'd really be hurtin' without it," Buster commented, killing the motor. He was poling now, reaching well forward of the prow with his prod and pushing backward. The flat bottom boat moved slowly along, trembling slightly in the wave chop.

"What should I do?" Jerry was squatting aft, hesitant about procedures. "I can do that pole-pushing, if you want, and you can get your stuff ready."

"Okay," Buster handed over the prod and moved a bit sideways, busying himself with the second headlamp and battery. Jerry went forward with the prod, stuck it deep into the muddy bottom and thrust sharply down and rearward, as he'd seen Buster do. The boat moved forward under this push, and though Jerry moved swiftly toward the rear, yanking at the prod, the muddy bay bottom held it in a firm grip. In no time at all it had slipped through Jerry's fingers and had disappeared from sight behind them.

"Oh gosh, Buster! It's gone! It's back there, somewhere in the dark. Shine your light back there. We're stuck out here without a pole." The anguish was thick in his voice.

With a loud guffaw, Buster jumped overboard and splashed back through the shallow water and retrieved the prod.

"Look, Jerry!" He exclaimed, climbing back into the boat. "Every time you thrust down and back and want to remove the prod for another thrust, you have to twist the pole. Not shake it. Twist it. Actually turn the end that's in the mud. That breaks the suction and then you can pull it out. Wait'll I tell Roy how you leave nets and poles all over the bay!"

Jerry reached for the prod.

"Gimme the damn thing! I'll do it right this time. And don't you tell Roy nuthin'. You hear?" He grinned a little to take the sting out of his words.

The pickings were slim. At the end of the first hour they'd netted only a dozen shrimp. Of any size, that is. Buster stood straddle-legged forward, shining his light out over the matted, undulating grass, scooping with his net at the tiny specks of light reflected from the shrimps' eyes, and managed to miss most. Jerry wasn't sure if the shrimp darted out of the way or if Buster was clumsy. He only knew that this was hard work. Dragging the second net alongside the boat, holding it deep enough to scrape the bottom, he'd brought up all manner of little wiggly life, including lots of small shrimp clustered in clumps of grass.

"Those ain't worth a thing," Buster said, shining his light into Jerry's net. "Called glass shrimp and they're too tiny. Murph won't take anything that small. Have to be at least three inches long and 'most the size of your middle finger 'fore he'll buy 'em." He leaned forward suddenly and scooped up a beauty. "See how their eyes bulge out and their face is all whiskery. This one's perfect. About four inches and fat. Just right for a redfish."

"Will they stay alive for long, in that bucket we're dragging?"

Buster nodded.

"Sure. That bucket's lined with small mesh wire and has holes all around. It drags on its side and that forms a pocket of water half-way down and new water flushes in and out all the time and they're safe there. Maybe a bit shook up, but okay. All the shrimpers keep 'em this way an' take 'em to Murph's or some other fishhouse nearby and sell 'em. Get twenty-five cents a dozen. Murph gets fifty cents a dozen from tourists. He keeps 'em in a large, covered wooden trough on his dock with bay water pumpin' in an' out all day long. Nights, too, of course. The tourist fishermen buy up all he can get. Still, you see how long it's taken us to get this dozen, so you can tell it's no path to a fortune. It's rough work. Especially if there's no breeze an' the bugs get fierce ... or it rains. The worst, of course, is a gale. When it storms, the netters come in."

They'd circled the flat by this time and were heading down-bay toward the northern end of Buck Key.

"We'll try in there a bit. That shoreline lays 'twart the tide, an' it may be calmer for 'em there. If we catch some, we'll stay a bit. If we don't, we'll head back to Roy's. Okay?"

Jerry nodded, though it was too dark for Buster to see.

"Buster, these fishermen. What do they need to live on? I mean, without counting beer and smokes. What do they need? Food money, you know."

"You can't cut out smokes an' beer, if you're figurin'," Buster answered as he shook his head," 'cause that's more important to 'em than food is. Maybe somewhere 'round four bucks a day. Especially if you include gas an' oil for their boats."

"Golly! Figuring shrimp at twenty-five cents a dozen, that's a dollar for forty-eight. They'll need 192 shrimp to make the four bucks. At that rate, it'd take 'em all night."

"Often does! But there's several thing's wrong with your figurin'. In the first place, there's some five-six commercial fishermen supplying Murph. They don't all drag in 200 shrimp a night or he'd be overloaded right off, an' stop buyin'. They shrimp while they're doing other stuff, like mullet fishing or troutin'. That Seth, now. He always trouts and shrimps at the same time. Keeps him pretty spry-goin', too. He has four pole-keepers fastened to the inside walls of his skiff, at different angles, two to a side. He uses different length poles, so the lines don't foul as he poles along. He baits up with shiners, tosses the lines overboard and poles along, huntin' shrimp. The motion of the boat jerks the shiners about a bit and that excites the trout. When one strikes, Seth leans back for the pole, straightens it in the air, and the line is just long enough for the fish to clear the gunwale. The trout sails through the air and hits him in the stomach. Its mouth rips out and it flops into the bilge. Seth can do all this with one hand while nettin' shrimp with the other. He wears an oilcloth apron so he can wash off the fish slime when it gets on him. Pretty interestin', huh? We're just playin' out here, now. I've never done much of this an' you ain't neither, so we're playin'. But those boys are serious. They don't waste much motion, no sirree!"

"Who's Seth?"

"One of the locals. Lives by himself over on Indian Key. That's a small mangrove island just t'other side of Buck Key. Has an Indian burial mound on it, a big pile of horseconch shells. Seth's about forty-five years old, and he's pretty ugly. Smashed-in face and scraggly teeth. Says he got messed up when he was younger, in a fire or something, an' a burnin' building collapsed on him, but I don't believe none of that, not for a minute. I think he ran afoul of rummies down in Cuba. He used to gang up with several others ... pretty tough men .. there was Dawson Ecker from Sanibel, and Ransom Diggs from up Boca Grande way. One or two others. A big lumberman named Dusty from Perry joined the gang for a bit, 'til he got drowned. And there was Seth. Real tough bunch. They ran rum from Cuba into the ten thousand islands area and on up here and over to Punta Rassa and the bayous behind Fort Myers Beach. The revenuers were always after 'em. Some escaped time and time again. Some didn't. Seth did. He's Ruta Barstowe's lover."

Even in the dark, the remark hung in the air. Buster made a little face at himself and muttered under his breath.

"Damn," he breathed, "shouldn't have said that." Too loud, he went on. "I mean, he and Ruta ..."

Jerry interrupted quietly. "It's okay, Buster. I'm not a moron. I know what a lover is."

They poled and netted for awhile in silence, without much luck.

"Wrong time of year. We should be out here middle of June, when the starfish and seahorses are matin' and there's plankton in the grass. That's when the shrimpin' is good." Buster was tired and ready to head home.

Jerry worried the bone.

"Which one's Ruta? I think I've met her at the mailboat. Is she the small lady with the little girl body and the old woman's face?"

"Yep. She really has a fine little body, all right. Short. Narrow hips. Beautiful small legs. She wears those little girl clothes and if you're walkin' behind her ya'd swear she was a teenager. Then you pull up beside her and she looks at you from under that wide-brim hat, and it shock's you, if you're not prepared. Poor thing. Such an awful face. All pock-marked and red patches and scars. Story goes that when she was young she had a bad case of chicken pox which left her face all pocked up. Later, she went to a skin doctor and he sand-papered her face to remove the pocks and smooth it out, but he cut too deep all over and she's looked like this ever since. If she's going into town she slaps make-up on real thick and with her face in the shade of her floppy hat, she gets by. Here, on the island, she just lets it go. I remember, one time she and I were drinkin' beer down at Murph's dock, and Seth was out at the end of the walkway, fiddlin' with his boat, and Ruta was watchin' him, and she was smilin' gently. She looked up at me and said ... 'I suppose you wonder why we go together, him being so ugly and me, too. In the beginnin', it was hard. Hard on us both. Then, after a bit, I figured if he could stand me an' my terrible face, I could stand him an' his. Now, we don't even see. I love Seth an' he loves me. We both need that. We let it be, right there. The only time, now, when there's peace in my soul and I don't want to run away an' hide is when he's holdin' me.' ... We best be headin' in."

●

The ladies were rocking on Agnes' porch, sipping iced-tea and talking quietly, enjoying the cool evening breeze, when Jerry drove into the yard that evening. Questions flew and eyes sparkled as they asked for details of the trip.

Maude nodded and murmured over the porpoise tale.

"I've heard tell of that," she agreed.

Cora clucked her tongue.

"Just too dear, taking care of her baby like that. Just too adorable!" There were tears in her voice.

Maude glanced at Cora.

"Could have been a him, you know."

"Oh, I don't think so. Male things don't seem to have that mother-love instinct. At least, I doubt it, dear." Cora paused a second, then added, "Still, of course, it could have been. Did you see, Jerry?"

Jerry glanced at Maude, who rolled her eyes high in her head.

"Aunt Cora, it was all so fast. The sun was setting and the water was shimmering. No, I didn't see. I wouldn't have known what to look for, anyway."

Cora took a deep breath and raised one hand. She seemed about to launch into a detailed discussion on porpoise anatomy, but Aunt Ag quickly took over.

"I think, Jerry ... " Agnes' voice was quiet and she chose her words with care. "I think it's just fine that you had all those experiences with Buster. I'm sure he's careful and can teach you a lot, share with you. But I hope your sprees are over for awhile. You see, we're creeping up on the tourist season and both Cora and Maude will need extra help. I don't mean to be ... "

"Oh, no'm." Jerry broke in with a warm smile. "I understand, Aunt Ag. I won't be running off on long trips for awhile. I'll be close by, and I'll be glad to help."

11

December

One evening, during the first week in December, while the three ladies and Jerry were eating supper, Agnes dropped a bomb!

Glancing around the table and smiling innocently, she announced in a grand tone "We're having guests at four tomorrow afternoon, for tea!"

There was a stunned silence! The other three stared at each other. Then Maude, always the first to recover, jumped up and paced about.

"Agnes, how could you? What do you mean 'we' are having guests. I'm not! I <u>hate</u> that sort of thing. Just hate it! I won't come," she added like a small child.

"Agnes, I've nothing to wear to a tea party," Cora exclaimed petulantly. "You should have asked us first. I'll make you some lime tarts but I'll have to decline. I'll have to stay away. Why didn't you let us know?"

"There was no time." Agnes seemed somewhat chagrined by her friends' reactions. "I stopped by the post office this afternoon and Cordelia Winslow introduced me to Ambassador Drinkwater, Hugh Drinkwater. A lovely man. He was Ambassador to the Hague for years, you know. Retired now. Very handsome. Tall, polished and so warm. As we chatted he mentioned knowing your mother, Jerry. Seems they were close friends back in their college years. So I had to ask them over, both of them. His daughter is down with him. She's just about your age, Jerry. They're at Mid-Island right now but Cordelia says that they've taken the old McClain house for the rest of the winter. Don't worry. They won't stay long. He mentioned that they were going somewhere else for dinner, thank goodness. You'll like him, I know, and I hope you'll all be sweet and be here. No frills required. I told him he'd catch us in our work clothes, so you don't have to dress, Cora."

Jerry was shaking he was so agitated, and his fork rattled on his plate. "Golly! A girl? Golly! A whole girl?" Then he added with a sly smile, his eyes darting around but landing nowhere. "Anyway, I'll be busy all afternoon. Captain Bob warned me that lots of stuff will be coming over on the mailboat ... and I've got to meet Roy later."

Agnes shook her head. "Roy won't mind if you miss swimming this once, Jerry" she admonished. "I really think you have to be here with us, or the Drinkwaters might feel slighted. He mentioned your mother several times."

"Aw, Aunt Ag! What will I say to her? She'll probably be tall, with pimples and greasy hair, and braces on her teeth. Golly! Will I have to wear shoes?"

With an understanding smile, Agnes nodded her head. "Shoes ... and a shirt ... and long pants. No shorts! I don't know what Dorothy Deirdre looks like. She wasn't at the post office with her father. It won't be so bad, now. Only a short time, and I'll make lots of little nibbles, and Cora has already promised tarts. You'll see."

Muttering to himself, Jerry wandered aimlessly about the room. "Dorothy Deirdre! Dorothy Deirdre Drinkwater! What kind of a name is that? Sounds like a cure for indigestion, or a mouthwash. What will we talk about? What can anyone say to a girl named Dorothy Deirdre? What do I call her? She can call me Jerry. That's simple. But do I call her Dorothy or Dorothy Deirdre? Miss Drinkwater? Miss Dorothy Deirdre Drinkwater? Aunt Ag, this is awful. Can't you tell 'em I had an accident as a little kid and haven't been able to talk since?"

Jerry didn't sleep well that night and woke early with a throbbing headache. How could he get through the day? The tea thing hung over the morning like a cloud of doom. He and Maude scarcely spoke while choring at the grove. Just for spite he hadn't dusted the yard and the bugs were fierce. The deliveries were soon done, as he'd fibbed to Aunt Agnes and only a few packages arrived. He lay on his bed awhile, trying to control his agitation. Then it was time to wash up and get dressed.

Ambassador Drinkwater was prompt. Exactly at four p.m. he arrived on the porch ... alone.

Agnes introduced everyone as she escorted him inside. "Where's your daughter?" she asked. "I was hoping to meet her. Not sick, I trust?"

"Oh, no," Ambassador Drinkwater answered. "She'll be along. She ran over to Mrs. Thigpen's for a minute, to invite her to join us this weekend on a short fishing trip to Boca Grande. Mrs. Thigpen knows all the snook holes, or so I'm told. In a few seconds, Dorothy Deirdre will turn up."

And in a few seconds, she did. There was a gentle knock at the door, which then swung inward and a low voice, throaty and resonant, floated into the room.

"Hi, everybody. Can I come in? I'm Didi."

Jerry rose slowly to his feet and faced the doorway. Suddenly something seemed wrong with his eyes. He couldn't see clearly. Everywhere, there was a shimmering, shining mist, through which a lovely face seemed to float forward one second and retreat the next. He had a fleeting impression of tawny golden hair and blue cornflower eyes, of a wide red mouth and gleaming teeth, of sun-browned arms and a tiny waist. His Adam's apple seemed to block off his throat. It had plunged downward and seemed stuck. He tried to move toward the door, but his legs refused to work. Bells were clanging in his ears.

"... Can I come in? I'm Didi ..."

Aunt Ag turned a moment from Ambassador Drinkwater and said "Jerry, please ask Dorothy Deirdre in."

His shoes were three feet long and so heavy he couldn't lift them. His knees buckled and he longed to lie down. Why was his heart pumping so hard? As from a vast distance he heard,

"... Can I come in? I'm Didi. ..."

"... Jerry, please ask Dorothy Deirdre in. ..."

He'd have to move. He'd have to go toward this shining creature, have to say something proper, something worldly, something elegant.

"Can I come in? I'm Didi."

Jerry gulped, took a deep breath and said "Yeah. Sure."

Later, after the Drinkwaters had gone, the four were sitting around the table eating leftovers. Maude contemplated a ham tidbit and observed "Well, thank heaven that's over. They both seemed nice, though. Too bad Jerry can't stand girls. She looked a pretty little thing, all Kansas corn and bluebells. Didn't you think she was nice-looking, Jerry?"

"Yeah. Sure."

"I thought they were both just wonderful," Cora enthused. "The Ambassador is the handsomest man I've seen in ages, and Didi is unbelievable. So beautiful and so polite. Just lovely. Did you two have a chance to talk, Jerry? Didn't you like her?"

"Yeah. Sure."

Aunt Ag was smiling. "I think our first afternoon tea went pretty well. Jerry, maybe, later on ..."

"Excuse me, Aunt Ag. I'm going upstairs and take a shower." Jerry headed for the stairs.

"But you just had a shower, Jerry."

"Yes'm. Now I'm going to take another one." He disappeared toward his room.

Maude laughed aloud. "Well," she said, "that one sure got knocked off his feet, didn't he?"

Agnes gazed speculatively at the stairwell door. "It just could be ... maybe, now, if all goes well ... I mean, here on this small island and so few people ..." She wiped her hands on her apron several times and reached for the dirty dishes. "I can remember so clearly, when Will and I first met, he was tongue-tied for a full week. Couldn't peep! I thought he had a problem." She chuckled. "I should have counted myself lucky. Soon enough, he was talking my ears off. Such a sweet man!" She paused, halfway to the sink, and turned slightly. "I miss him. Terribly. It's not the same, at all, you know." A long, deep sigh shook her body.

Cora pushed in, fearful that approaching sentimentality might touch them all. That would be embarrassing. She hated to look back. Grabbing up a votive candle from the mantle, she plunked it down on the table and danced around it.

"I'm Madame LaSogna and I can see the future." Her dancing quickly got a little wild, as she dipped and twirled and spun around. Then she steadied herself by grabbing the back of a chair. Leaning over the candle, she stared unblinkingly into the flickering flame.

"I can see ... I can see ..."

Agnes watched her, smiling indulgently, but Maude seemed to get edgy.

"Ah. There! A filmy screen is moving aside and I can see this house ... this house ... but it's crushed and sagging. Agnes is leaning against one wall, wringing her hands. It disappears." She waved her hands violently and leaned closer to the candles. "Ah, I see Maude, but something is wrong with her. She's in a swirl ... she's sinking ... twisting and sinking, and her hair is floating about her face, and she's crying out. I can't hear ... I can't hear ... Ouch! You pinched my hand." The spell was broken and she spun around toward Maude. "You pinched me, Maude!"

"I sure did." Maude had jumped up from her chair, had grabbed one of Cora's hands and had pinched it sharply. "Enough of all this nonsense. I don't want to hear any more. You get carried away every time you do this and are sick all night, which keeps me up and I need my sleep. And that's exactly where I'm going ... to bed. Stop whimpering. I didn't hurt you." Maude stomped off and her heavy footsteps could be heard crunching down the shell path.

"She pinched me. Look, it's all red and funny. I can't believe it." Cora's lips quivered.

"Come on, now. It's not that bad." Agnes was at the drainboard, rinsing and stacking. "Maude can be a bit demonstrative but she has her side of things, too, you know. Bring that hand over here and put it into this hot soapy dish water and it'll be good as new in no time. You wash. I'll dry!"

For several days, Jerry couldn't eat. All the excitement of living was somehow gone. He moped about and spent lots of time looking out of windows and staring off into distances. He didn't know what was wrong. A depression had him firmly in its grasp and he hated it. Carrying a large armload of packages from the mailboat to his truck he spied Didi leaning across the engine hood.

She waved.

"I thought maybe you'd let me ride around with you. Can I?" She opened the cab door.

"Sure. I mean ... yeah, that'd be great. Yeah, sure!" Jerry flung the packages onto the flatbed and climbed into the cab.

As they bumped along, Didi twisted around to look through the rear window.

"Everything is banging around back there," she said. "Skidding into each other. What do we tell folks if something gets broken?"

"Never has. At least, no one has ever said so. Gosh, I'm starved! Are you hungry?"

Didi shook her head. Looking straight ahead, she said nonchalantly "I've got my swim-suit on under these culottes."

The truck swerved dangerously at this announcement. Jerry couldn't believe his ears. She wanted to go swimming. With him! He'd have to get his trunks ... as soon as these deliveries were made, he'd have ...

"Hey!" he said, much too loudly. "Let's go for a swim. When the deliveries are done, let's go for a swim. Okay?"

Didi smiled at him.

"What a nice idea." She nodded a bit. "Whatever made you think of it? Let's go."

Bless Ellie Thigpen. Not one to usually 'shop' through the mailboat, this day she had a large package. Jerry saved it 'til last, and then drove into Aunt Ag's parking lot. They climbed out and headed for the house. Cora was peeping out of the shop window as they passed. She called over her shoulder to Maude.

"There goes Jerry, with Didi. They're heading ... "

"I saw." Maude snapped her off.

Where to swim? Mid-Island Inn's beach would be crowded, as the Inn was now full for the Christmas holidays. The beach in front of the old McClain house, which the Drinkwaters were occupying the following week, was covered with boulders, in an effort to slow erosion, and wasn't pleasant for swimming.

"What about that beautiful beach where the road turns toward the bay by Captiva Inn? Don't you usually swim there?"

Oh, migod! Roy! Buster!

"We could swim awhile with your friends, and then stroll along the beach, looking for shells. I've got to get busy on a collection. Everybody seems to have one." Her smile was guileless as she gently maneuvered.

Roy and Buster were stunned when Jerry and Didi parked the truck and raced down to the beach. But not for long. Didi was tact itself, conferring with Roy about this and that shell, discussing fishing at Key West with Buster, and firmly nailing the lid on these new acquaintanceships by an offer to maybe stop by some day and sweep out Buster's wickie.

"Who cleans that thing?"

"Nobody."

"Heavens! Maybe I'll stop by some day and sweep out. Got a broom?" She tossed back her golden hair and smiled at them both.

Jerry drove the truck into the parking area at Mid-Island just at dusk. Didi climbed out carefully, as she was carrying the shell specimens she'd gathered in her shirttail. With one foot on the ground and the other still up on the running board, she glanced back at Jerry.

"If you'd pick me up here on your way to the mailboat, I wouldn't have to walk through all those bugs. "Bye! Loved the swim!"

"Lord love you, boy," Aunt Ag exclaimed that evening at supper. "Are you hollow? Where are you putting it all. I trust this is a onetime catch-up, or we'll have to double the food budget."

"Fill him up, Ag. He'll need all his strength. Tomorrow morning is the deadline, you know. All the fun and foolishness is over and it'll be work, work, work!" Cora nibbled at a bite of fish as she spoke. "Just as well, too. We've played long enough."

Maude's head shot up. "Who's been playing? Not me! But I know what you mean, Cora. Tomorrow is exactly three weeks to Christmas and everything will have to be in order and lined up by then or we can just forget it. Don't fret. We'll make it on time."

●

A subtle change permeated the island. The easygoing, languid, rather sleepy existence changed overnight, and an urgency hung in the air. With the arrival of Christmas, the winter 'season' began and stretched until just after Easter. During that short period a full year's income had to be gathered in by most of the merchant element, or they would face a difficult time during the ensuing eight months. Everyone knuckled down in a final rush of activity, in order to be stocked and cleaned and presenting a serene, calm, smiling face toward the first tourists who meandered along the sandy paths.

Paint was splashed about. Clorox and cleansers were in heavy demand. Tablecloths were bleached. Murph's dock was turned inside out, with the floor restained, the tables repainted and the counter resurfaced. Only the huge jukebox stayed as before. This year Murph and Pearlie were stocking wine for the first time.

Being more or less a 'fresh-order' set-up, the Bakery and Marge and Stan at the Restaurant could do little advance cooking, but each added a small waterproof storage bin and stuffed it full of staples and dry provisions. The two Inns, both full now with repeating guests, had previously gone through this refurbishing procedure and were bubbling merrily along, smiling toward the front while frowning toward the rear. Matilda Crunch's Shell Shop, with its freshly-shelled driveway, was polished and dusted, aired and fumigated, and Matilda herself sat just inside the entry door, waiting!

Of all the small businesses and cottage owners, only the Fisherman's Creel girls seemed impervious to the bustling about. They'd arrived early in October and their relatively few offerings, all expensive, were polished daily and ready for sale. So there was calm at the little gift shop. Besides, both girls saw themselves as Vogue models, and wouldn't dream of allowing themselves the slightest agitation. Too wrinkle-making!

Bertha Wiggins announced in a firm voice to husband and children ... "So stay clear of the living room. Understood? No exceptions! I need that space for post office overflow, packages and backed-up mail, an' I don't want little feet, or big feet, pushing around in it. You hear? Don't make me say this again, now!"

Ida Benson enlisted Jerry "... whatever time you can spare. I'll pay a dollar an hour, same as I get. All the houses to still be cleaned and opened and those yards to be scuffled and raked ... it's more than a body can face." Didi, when she heard of all the work, offered to give some time, and Ida eagerly accepted.

"We'll clean, us two, and Sally-Anne. Jerry can scuffle. Pay's one dollar an hour."

Didi started to object but Ida pulled back. "We all work ... we all get paid. That's it. No discussion!"

Ida was anxious to have this initial house-opening, yard-cleaning work finished and done with as she was planning on opening a grocery store in an abandoned building on Palm Avenue, halfway between Gulf and Bay, just a short distance from the bakery and the Bide-A-Wee Restaurant. The owner had offered the building rent-free for a full year. If the store paid off, Ida would pay rent from then on.

When Jerry heard about this, he questioned her.

"Have you ever run a grocery store? Do you know anything about stores?"

"No and yes, and in that order," Ida answered. "No, I've never run a grocery store ... and yes, I know something about all that. About stores, and shops at least. My sister Olga and I ran a dressmaking shop for years and this couldn't be so different. I mean ... thread and needles, pins and ruching ... cans of beans and so on. Loaves of bread — what's so different?"

"Do you think you'll have it open by next winter?"

Ida laughed out loud, long and hard. "Jerry, my friend," she said, after quieting down. "You can't think that way, here on the island. You have to reach out, quick-like. That old saying 'opportunity knocks only once' is true. You have to hear it and grab. If the opportunity isn't exactly what you expected or what you want, you have to grab it by the throat and shake it hard, and make it fit. If you sit back and wait for it to fit you, it never will, and will go on down the road to the next fella, or the next ... till someone reaches and grabs and shakes. That store will be open and I'll make my first sale by February first, this coming February! It's all arranged. Roy will fix the wiring, and he'll wait to be paid 'til I can afford it. Evan will do all the shelving and make the main counter ... and wait to be paid, also. I told him everything was to be as simple as can be. I want blocks stacked one on top of another and boards run between the holes. Shelves! I want several boards up on trestles. Counter! Bertha has an old refrigerator-freezer she says I can borrow. I think she figures that, later on, Evan will be ashamed to take it back, and will buy her a new one. My cash register will be a shoe box, to start. I'm in business. See?" And she beamed at him, a wide smile spreading across her lined face. "I can sew, remember. Curtains and counter tops and shelf drapings ... in no time it'll be as cozy as can be. I'm going to put my old record player in one

134

corner and soft music will fill the air. Coffee will be brewing. And Jack and Ted have promised to keep me full of fresh baked goods — on consignment. Isn't that sweet of them? I don't know exactly how that will work. I'll buy from them whatever I sell, but what will they do with what doesn't sell? Anyway, we'll work it all out. The best part is that, once the back room and bath are fixed up, I'll move in there during the winter months and rent my house. That money'll go against the store expenses. So it'll be like starting off subsidized. Ain't that grand? I can't wait. Maybe, during the winter months, later on, when it's freezing up in Chicago, Olga will close the sewing shop and come down and be with me. I'd really like that." She reached out spontaneously and grabbed his hand. "Will you help me fix it up?"

●

For northerners, Christmas on the island often proved disappointing. There were none of the familiar trappings. There were no lead-in days of crisp, cold weather, with a bite in the air and gray, lowering clouds that either dropped snow or threatened to do so ... no bundled-up children with mufflers and mittens and apple-red cheeks and runny noses ... no shoppers piled high with colored boxes, leaning into the icy winds and hurrying home to blazing wood fires and smells of ginger and cinnamon drifting in from warm kitchens. Thrown back on their own resources, the northerners sensed a loss. Somehow, the hot, brilliant sun, the warm languid air, the glistening Gulf just beyond their windows did not compensate. They ached for a 'white Christmas' and everything on the island seemed out of step. The islanders, however, born in the hot country, or having voluntarily adopted it as a way of life, felt no such disparity. Dependent on the winter visitors and bustling without pause behind-scenes to keep the tourists satisfied and happy, the natives welcomed Christmas as a single-day celebration, a quiet, restful day with family and friends, with simple remembrances and good food and a long afternoon nap, as children played outdoors in the sand, all reminiscent of that First Christmas, under its Shining Star, in the hot mud-brick village deep in the sandy desert, with its gentle people, and its dusty caravans, and its visitors from foreign lands.

●

Cora had been busy for several nights, stringing tinsel and hanging colored cut-outs about the living room, in one corner of which stood a fir tree Jerry had fetched from Rigby's store on Sanibel. The slender tree patiently waited to be festooned with gaudy balls and glitter. A large wreath of twisted pine branches and holly, with a fat red candle in the center, hung on the front door.

"Don't anybody plan anything for Christmas Eve, as we'll trim the tree then." Cora announced. "I love Christmas Eve, even more than Christmas day." Her eyes were shining and there were bits of colored paper stuck in her hair, which she swiped at ineffectively. "At home, we always gathered around then, and the tree was huge, from floor to ceiling, and it seems as I look back that it took us hours to decorate it, and Mother gave everybody eggnog with nutmeg sprinkled on, and plates of cookies. The sand tarts, with a pecan half on top, were special. Lovely! Crunchy and sugary."

"Maybe Jerry has other plans." Agnes looked up from the popcorn she was sorting and threading. "There'll be parties at the Inns and at some of the homes, I suppose. Maybe you'd rather go to those. Don't feel you are bound, now." She smiled at Jerry.

Jerry smiled back. "I don't know any of the home owners well enough to be asked to a party. Didi and I plan to look in at Captiva Inn and, of course, Mid-Island — both of those are open to anybody. But that's all. Didi wants to be with her father later, as she says this is a bad time for him ... something to do with her mother. We didn't discuss it. So I'll be back here in plenty of time to help trim. And drink eggnog. And munch on those sand tarts."

"Who said anything about sand tarts," Cora asked archly. "I don't even remember the recipe."

"Don't worry, Jerry." Maude boomed. "There'll be sand tarts, even if I have to go out and drag in the sand. Maybe Tabby Upton will give us some leftovers." She roared with laughter.

Cora joined in. "We can call 'em 'kitty litter sand tarts' and sell 'em in the shop! Oh, dear!" She clasped her bosom and gasped for breath.

So late Christmas Eve they munched cookies and sipped the rich eggnog, and decorated the tree. A glistening angel glowed from the top, and yards of gold tinsel were wound all about. Icicles hung in silvery clusters and colored balls swung from the tips of the branches. Agnes had used food coloring on her pop-corn and the reds and golds showed brightly as she wove them in and out. Jerry bunched green tissue paper around the wooden base and Cora dropped pinches of cotton here and there on the green.

"A little touch of snow ... so festive!" she murmured.

When it was finished, they all stood back and marvelled at the lovely, peaceful scene. For a moment they were all lost in their own thoughts.

"Oh, I almost forgot!" Cora exclaimed and left the room in a rush. She returned in a moment, carrying a small round object, which she placed deep in the tree branches.

Maude was standing beside Jerry and she reached out and put her arm through his. "Don't laugh, now, or make a funny comment. This means a lot to her." She gave a bit of pressure to his arm.

Cora looked back at the group watching her.

"I do hope it's secure. I wouldn't want it to tip over." Reaching into her blouse, she took out two tiny white, oval-shaped items, and put them in the nest. She motioned Jerry over. "Look, a bird's nest! And two eggs. How do you suppose it got there? It's the Christmas Dove! Comes every year. I feared it might forget us this year, but there it is!" She pointed to the snug little nest, secured deep in the protecting branches, and the two tiny eggs nestling inside. "If all goes well, they'll hatch and have flown away by morning, on their way around the earth, carrying a message of peace and good will."

Maude turned to Agnes and breathed ... "Hope they drop in on Harry and Old Joe!"

Agnes breathed back ... "Now, don't be nasty, Maude Appleton. If Cora wasn't in and about with her silly remarks and her dreams and her fey little whimsies, it could get dull as dishwater around here. You and I are pretty stodgy stuff, you know."

Jerry had bought sun-glasses for Aunt Agnes, with a little strap fixed to the handles so they could hang around her neck. She was always losing glasses and would welcome a secure pair. He'd found a quaint, handmade necklace for Aunt Cora, of pebble-size cowry shells, each separated from the other by bright beads. A present for Aunt Maude had proven a problem. He finally decided on a pair of tortoise shell combs for her hair. Maude's one vanity was her hair. Chestnut brown and full of red glints, it grew thick and luxuriant, and hung below her hips. During the day she wore it plaited and in a large pretzel-shaped bun on the back of her head. At night, after vigorous brushing, it usually swung about her shoulders in a lush red-brown cloud. Just before retiring, she gathered it into a pigtail which hung down her back. Maude would love the combs.

All the gaily-wrapped packages were pushed under the tree and everyone said good-nights and went off to bed, tired and excited about the morrow.

Jerry was up before the rest and banged first on Aunt Agnes' door and then raced over and woke the other two. Breakfast was a happy time, with all the presents gathered from the tree and brought to the table and sorted into proper piles. Everybody opened at the same time. Egg and bacon and wrapping paper and colored bows got all mixed in together. Agnes tried to keep order but soon gave up. Cora thrust a red bow behind one ear and fashioned a boat-hat for Jerry from bright package paper.

As the excitement quieted down and they were finishing their food, Aunt Agnes smiled over at the boy. "Jerry, there were loud bangings and shufflings late last night, out back, and I think Santa must have stopped by. Maybe you'd better look out on the back porch."

Jerry stared for a second at Aunt Agnes. Then he looked at each of the others. All three were beaming at him, with expectant expressions. Slowly, he pushed back his chair and peeped out the back door. A huge package was off to one side, up against the porch wall, and in big letters on its side was written "Merry Christmas, Jerry. From the three of us." His throat caught and he felt strangely shy.

"Go on." Cora couldn't contain herself one minute longer. "Go on. Open it! Open it!"

Jerry moved slowly to the package and reached out. He knew it was going to be something expensive, way beyond their agreement of casual gift-giving. He looked back at the ladies. Cora was jiggling with excitement. Maude was smiling a gentle, quiet smile and Agnes made quick motions with her hands.

"Go on. Go on, now. Open it. We all decided to throw in together because you've worked hard for months and you've been very sweet about it, and because we love you."

Jerry tore off the wrappings and there was a spanking new ten-horse Johnson Outboard motor. He was speechless!

"Gee!" he exclaimed. "Gee! I'm flabbergasted. Oh, Gee! Golly! Hey, thanks." He went to each one and gave her a tentative little kiss and a hug. "It's not fair, you know, but I'm sure glad you did. Think of all the places I can go now. All the exploring. Can I use your boat, Aunt Ag?"

"Yes, you can. Put it on and store the small one under the house, for a later spare. Jerry, listen now. There are two rules that go along with this motor. You must agree to abide by them. One is, you are never to go out into the open Gulf unless the tide is coming in. Schedule your Gulf trips to fit that rule. Okay?"

Jerry nodded.

"And the second rule is," Agnes went on, "you are to report to Murph or Pearlie every time you go out. Anywhere. In the back bay, or the Gulf, or anywhere. You are to let one or the other know where you're going and when you'll be back, and then stop in there on your way in and report. Understand? Murph keeps a chart of who's in and who's out and where they're going. Then, if they don't come in on time, he takes his big inboard and goes out for them. He's dragged in a number of boaters who otherwise would have spent a bad night drifting about or anchored on some offshore sandbar."

Cora had gone back inside. Suddenly, there was a cry of "Oh, dear! Oh, dear!" followed by a loud moan. The others rushed in, to discover Cora sitting at the table, her head on her arms, sobbing uncontrollably.

Jerry squatted down beside her. "What is it? What's the matter, Aunt Cora? Can I help?"

Cora shook her head. "No. It's too late, now. Nothing anybody can do. I've missed them again. I'm just getting too old, that's all. I'm not quick enough."

Maude, having been through all this before, looked steadily at the floor for a second. Then she raised her head and went toward Cora, and gathered her in protecting arms.

"There, there, dear friend. Don't take on like this. So you missed them again. Next year will be different. Next year, we'll sit up all night with you and we'll watch real close. Now, dry your eyes and go take Jerry over and show him!"

Sniffling and wiping at her face, Cora took Jerry's hand and steered him over to the Christmas tree. Pointing to the dove's nest, a sob escaped her throat.

"See, dear. They're not there. They've flown away!"

Jerry peeped inside and the eggs were gone. A few bits of egg-shell were scattered about in the nest. He didn't know what to say, and glanced back across Cora's head at Maude, who nodded her head up and down several times. Jerry's eyebrows raised and his eyes widened. He thought for a few seconds.

"But, Aunt Cora. Weren't they supposed to fly away? You told us they were Christmas doves." Then remembering the tale of Noah and the Ark, he added, "Maybe they're whistling through the air right now, swooping down and dropping their olive branches all about."

Cora brightened. "Do you think so? Oh, I hope so. Yes, that's their mission, of course." She gazed tentatively at the nest. "But I do so wish they'd hatch out more slowly!"

Later that afternoon, the three women were quietly repairing the damages of the huge Christmas meal, when Roy Coggins drove into the shop parking lot and crossed to the house.

"Merry Christmas, everybody," he exclaimed, sticking his head in the back door.

"Come on in," they all called together. "Merry Christmas to you."

Roy sat down and Cora put a cup of coffee and a dish of cookies in front of him. Munching, he said, "I can't stay. I really wanted to see Jerry. Is he here?"

"No," Agnes replied. "He and Didi left some time back to drive to Sanibel. They're crossing on the ferry to Punta Rassa so Jerry can phone home to his mother. They'll have to catch the last ferry back, so he'll be here about 5:30. Anything wrong?"

Roy shook his head. "No'm. Not really. I wanted Jerry to keep an eye out for my mother and aunt who'll be on the mailboat tomorrow. I can't meet 'em, as I'll be working up at the lighthouse on Sanibel. He can take 'em to my house and they'll be all right 'til I get home."

Cora smiled brightly at him. "Roy. How lovely. How nice for you. You'll enjoy them. Will they be here long?"

"Only a week. 'Course I'll be glad to see 'em but I'm not all that excited about it, I guess." Roy was on his feet, ready to leave, and he was twirling his cap in his hand. "Thank heaven for Ida Benson. She cleaned up my shack, and she's letting me bunk in that shed behind Replogle's. There's a right nice room there. It's inconvenient but I couldn't say no to Momma, you know. Only one week. I'll make it." He smiled and added, "Leastways, for a week I'll eat good. The mullet will be relieved, too." They all chuckled along with him.

"Don't worry, Roy," Agnes patted his shoulder. "We'll tell Jerry. And if you get stuck and would like to bring them to tea one afternoon, we're all right here. Remember, now."

There were only two passengers on the mailboat next day. Dressed in gray linsey-woolsey from neck to toe, with ruffled gray bonnets on their heads, they sat tight together back in a corner and peered out apprehensively at a threatening world.

"They were scared to death of me," Jerry later told Aunt Ag. "At first, they didn't even want to go with me. It was good Didi was there. She coaxed 'em off and we got 'em to Roy's. We were both wondering how women that meek ever ... I mean, they're so scared of everything, it seems unbelievable that they'd be able ... " Jerry was suddenly all confused and blushing red. "Course, Didi and I didn't really discuss it. We just sort of touched on it. I wouldn't want you to think we talked about stuff like that." He shifted his feet.

Agnes smiled, and looked directly at him. "Well, Jerry. That's a very complicated situation you've touched on. It has to do with women's role down through the ages. How they see themselves. How they see their duty. The world is full of meek women still today. Europe. Asia. South America. Only in the 'enlightened' west are women free, so to speak, and more or less able to take care of themselves. I've a book somewhere by Emmeline Pankhurst that goes into all that. You can read it if you're interested."

"Thanks, but I'm not really interested."

"I didn't think you were."

●

It was Ida Benson who got Didi all fired up over dredging. Ida had a splendid shell collection and one morning she and Didi were dusting and oiling the shells and Ida was explaining what each was called and where it lived and why it was the color it was. She picked up a fine tawny sponge pectin.

"This is a favorite of mine. Feel the raspy outside, rough and coarse so it can anchor itself deep inside a sponge. I got this out in the Gulf, off Sanibel. There's a rocky shelf about five miles out. One time my son Karl and I were dredging out there and we got all sorts of stuff ... shells, some brittle starfish, sand dollars, teeny little fish. It was great fun."

"Dredging? How do you mean? What did you use?" Didi was all attention, her mind clicking.

Ida reached for another shell, oval, fat in the middle and pointed at both ends, and covered with brown markings. "This is a junonia. Queen of the shells! Isn't it lovely?"

"Did you get this dredging?"

"No. I found this beauty on the Sanibel beach after a heavy blow. Alive. I found it alive. Actually, the place I found it is in a direct line in from that rocky ledge. Maybe it's really coral. I don't know. Karl got the idea of dredging and made one out of wire and ropes. We borrowed Elmer Wright's inboard. He was a mullet fisherman camped down the beach aways from our camp that winter and we'd gotten friendly."

They chatted quietly on, polishing the shells. Didi's attention wandered. Her shell collection was puny. There hadn't been a storm recently and the beaches were picked over by the tourists. She had good specimens of the commoner shells, like augers and margenellas, lacey murex and hearts, turkey wings and sun rays, rose petals, fans. She had a sorry Scotch bonnet and half an alphabet, but not one of the more exotic, really exciting shells. The answer would be a dredge. Jerry had this new motor and they could go out easily. Maybe Roy would help him fix up a dredge. Ida poked at her and held out a large conical shell, with markings that resembled Chinese writing.

"This is a Chinese alphabet cone. Big one, isn't it? Perfect. I got it alive, too. They live back in the bay, in the mud. There's a large flat about halfway down Roosevelt Channel where they grow. I always think of shells as growing." She chuckled. "Course, that's not the right word. Something about the consistency of the mud in that one flat that they like, them and rose petals. Lots of 'em. It's a special place. Ruta Barstowe showed me. She and Seth used to shell a lot, commercially. I suppose Ruta has forgotten more about shells than the average person will ever know. I promised not to tell, so you must keep it a dark secret."

Didi nodded and promised. "I'll have to tell Jerry, though. I can't get there by myself."

"Okay." Ida agreed. "But nobody else. It's special. If word gets out, in no time the tourists will trample all over that flat and the alphabets and rose petals will all disappear for good."

Didi looked puzzled. "I thought the alphabets and rose petals washed in from the Gulf."

"No. They live in the bay. 'Course, they do wash in but they've had a long trip by then ... from the back bay out one of the passes tumbling along with the tide and later they wash in. You won't very often find a good bay shell on the beach, unless there's been really heavy winds and waves, and for several days." She glanced up and one of her special little-girl smiles flitted across her face. "I just love shelling, after a blow. We will go, sometime!"

Didi was on fire with this new venture. That afternoon, after deliveries and chores, she dragged Jerry down to Roy's to discuss the dredge. They found him in his workshop behind his house, sputtering with rage. Slapping electrical equipment around, and flushed in the face, he was furious.

"I'll kill her. I'll shoot her dead in her tracks. Who does she think she is? I'll get even if it takes my last breath. After all I've done for that nasty old woman!"

Didi drew back in alarm. If Roy had had a fight with his mother, she didn't want to get involved. She crept toward the door. Jerry, more outspoken, moved right in.

"Who? Who did what? What's the problem?"

"It's that Matilda Crunch! Filthy old hag! Where does she get off, being mean to my Momma. And me, too. To my face! I tell you, she's not heard the last of this. No, siree!"

"But what happened?" Said Jerry, soothing his friend by patting his arm.

Roy shrugged off the friendly gesture. "My momma's old," he said. "She's fat, and heavy. Her feet hurt. Hers and Aunt Sookie's, both. They've been here several days. There's nothing to do. I figured they were bored, just sitting in that little room, staring at each other, waiting for me to come home." Roy was short of breath and had to pause for a second. His mouth kept opening and shutting in fury, and his hands clenched up. "I suggested they go shelling," he went on. "Knowing they couldn't walk all the way to the beach and stroll along for miles like everyone else, I told 'em to shell next door, in Matilda Crunch's driveway. After all, you and Evan and I just hauled in all those fresh beach shells, and the old ladies would have been perfectly happy picking over the stuff there. They'd have been busy for hours." Roy's face was so contorted Jerry feared he'd cry.

"So," Jerry prodded, "what happened?"

Roy picked up a slat and banged it up and down on a counter. "So ... off they hobbled! And in no time, back they hobbled, both in tears and shaking with fright. Seems they'd hardly got squatted down but Matilda came barrelling out her door and screamed at 'em, to get off her property. Momma said Matilda yelled 'Scat!' at 'em like they was cats or something! I ran over and there she was, standing on her saggy stoop, with her arms folded, glaring at me. 'What do you think you're doing?' I cried. She rushed at me and stuck that pointy face up at me and I thought she was gonna bite me or something. 'Don't give me none of your sass, Coggins' she snarled. 'And keep those two harpies home. Do you think I want 'em sitting in my drive, pawing at my shells, scaring off all my customers? They look like a pair of vultures, all over gray and with those damn old-timey bonnets. Keep 'em home.' And she made at me with those skinny hands and those long fingernails with dirt packed under 'em. Frightening old bitch. Excuse me, Didi. And as for scaring customers, ain't one in miles that'd be caught dead in that shop, anyway." He walked around for a time, shaking his head. "I will dream up something. Have to put my mind to it, real proper. I'll get even if it's the last thing I do. Momma and Aunt Sookie are still crying. This'll ruin their whole visit.

Didi looked sympathetic. "Poor dears," she said, "do you want me to go over and comfort them?"

Roy shook his head. "No. Don't bother to go over. Just leave 'em be. They'll quiet down. But how about that Matilda Crunch? Somehow, sometime, she's gonna get a good one. You mark my words!"

12

They knew the dredge would prove a great success even though it was no thing of beauty. No one else would ever have claimed ownership. It was twisted and lopsided all at the same time. They'd used whatever material was at hand, and they'd coped.

That was a favorite word of Bertha Wiggins'. When met in the morning and asked politely how she was, she'd like as not answer ... "I'm copin', I'm copin'". One time someone asked her what the word meant and she replied ... "Well, now, that's a pretty small word, copin', but its got a real big meaning. It means when you're tired out and the kids are screamin' and you want to just sit a spell and rest, instead you keep on goin'. It means when there's no money and no food, you scrounge around, a little of this and a little of that, and pretty soon the young'uns have something to eat. It means when your man drags home and the world's been beatin' on him and he needs comfortin', you comfort ... even if you're near broke down with worry yourself. It means laughin' when you want to cry, smilin' when you hurt, buryin' your own wants and needs under everybody else's. It means bein' a mother, a wife, a friend. It means makin' do. Copin'!" ...

A few wood laths for a frame, hardware cloth as a covering, an old machete blade as a front scraper, and there was the dredge. Roy explained about the pull ropes.

"Tie 'em about a third way down each side. If you tie 'em even with the bottom, when you pull she'll fill up with sand right away. Tied in the middle, the blade won't scoop. Tied high this way, when she pulls she'll tip a bit, with the knife scratching along the bottom and the back end'll be raised up. It'll work great. Don't forget your trip rope. I suppose there's a real name for it but it's gone by me. I know the shrimpers all have release ropes tied to the end of their nets. Then, if they get hung up on a big rock or a wreck or something, they yank on the release and up-end the net by pulling the back end forward. They lose whatever is in the net at the time, sure, but they save the net and those things cost like smoke. Okay. There! You're all set."

Didi found an old aquarium stored away in the McClain boathouse. She and Jerry tested it for leaks and installed it on Aunt Ag's porch. She also found an aquarium pump in a corner of Rigby's General Store on Sanibel. With sand in the bottom, and bits of staghorn coral half buried here and there, a bunch of turtlegrass from the bay, and the pump bubbling merrily to aerate the water, the aquarium was soon ready for tenants.

Cora watched all these preparations closely.

"What are you going to keep in there?" She asked.

Jerry laughed. "Ask Didi. She's the big push with the dredging effort. I'm just along as man power."

"Oh, come on, now. That's not fair." Didi, with her sleeves rolled high, had one arm deep in the aquarium, rearranging the sand and coral. "It's as much your idea as mine. You want to go, don't you?"

Jerry nodded and smiled at her. "Sure. I was only kidding."

"We don't know what we'll bring back, Aunt Cora. Ida says she used to drag up all sorts of interesting things. Live shells. Starfish. Urchins. Maybe a sea horse. Jerry, wouldn't it be great if we got a sea horse?" She withdrew her arm, settled back on her heels, and wiped stray strands of hair from her face. "A big male. Pregnant. Then we could have babies!" She giggled in delight at the idea.

"What about dumping?" Aunt Ag had come up and heard all the talk. "What are you planning to do about that?"

Jerry looked at his aunt. "What do you mean, Aunt Ag?"

"I mean, you can't haul in that dredge full of mud and crawly things and dump it all in the bottom of the boat. You've got to have some way of getting rid of the mud and the mess you don't want. After you've finished feeling around in it, of course."

Jerry nodded. "You're right. You're right. Didi, we've got to have some sort of dump platform across the stern of the boat. We could first pick around in the gook and get the stuff we want, and then slush off the junk and the mud with sea water. Couldn't we do that?"

"Sure" Didi agreed. "And little sides of some sort would keep it all from running down into the boat. That'd work."

"And we need some hooks or something to tie the pull ropes to the boat. Can't just sit there and hold it by hand."

"Eye bolts. You need a couple of good-sized eye bolts." Maude called across the porch to them. She was rocking in her chair, binoculars in position, scanning the bridge area for anything of interest. "I've a couple you can have. Roy left a few the last time we had him here wiring the shop."

Didi flopped back onto the floor, her arms folded under her head. "Let up for a bit on this fiddling and let's plan the first trip. I simply can't wait. When can we go?"

Jerry looked at her, and his breath caught. She was so lovely, with her eager face and her shining eyes. Her blond hair was pushed back any old way, her blouse was torn under one arm, her shorts had been made by hacking off

144

the legs of a pair of denim pants and a tantalizing fringe of fray hugged her thighs. There were dirt smudges along her forearms. She was beautiful! Glancing up, she caught his expression and blushed.

"Come on, Jerry." Her eyes fell. "Don't just stand there. Help."

"What do you want me to do? We're all done. Later on, I'll fix the pulls and the platform. What else is there to do?"

Didi was still flustered. "You don't have to stand there, staring at me like a goof," she murmured under her breath. "Do something. Like ... I don't know, exactly. What were we talking about? The date. That's it. When can we go out dredging? Which day?"

Before Jerry could answer, Maude stiffened and called out. "Uh Oh! Something's a-brewing. There's a lumber truck just pulled off the road onto that little strip of land Amelia Armstrong says Colonel MacDuff owns. They're readying to off-load. Wonder what that's all about." She smiled with gleeful expectancy. "Better put on the coffee pot, Cora. Amelia'll be running over, once the delivery truck's gone, that's for sure."

"He really works quick, doesn't he?" Cora crossed over to Maude and took the spyglasses. "Yep, they're unloading. They got in late last night."

"Who?"

"Colonel MacDuff and his wife, and a big dog. In a jeep. They were all in a jeep. The dog was in the front seat beside Colonel MacDuff, and Andrusa was in the back, clutching that huge floppy hat. They roared around the corner spraying sand all over and tore across the bridge at breakneck speed. Lucky no one was approaching from the other side. I heard the tires squeal as they disappeared. Poor Andrusa. That really is a difficult man."

"Where were you when all this happened, and why didn't you tell us?" Maude glanced at Cora with irritation. She prided herself on being up on all the goings and comings, and now she felt slightly out of touch. Her sovereignty was being threatened.

Cora was at once solicitous. "Oh, Maudie! I'm sorry. I didn't mean not to tell you. I was in the shop with a customer and saw all this through the window. Then I got busy selling and forgot all about it, 'til now. I'm sorry."

Maude was only somewhat mollified. Cora simply was not trustworthy. You couldn't depend on her to recognize what was important and what wasn't. Imagine forgetting to tell a juicy tidbit like the MacDuff's return simply because of one more sale. But then, Cora was Cora and one had to make allowances. She returned to her scoutings.

A bit later, Amelia Armstrong could be heard panting up the path. Jerry caught Didi's hand and murmured "Come on. Let's get out of here and finish fixing the boat. This woman can talk the ear off a brass monkey."

Didi chuckled, and they slipped away.

·

The tide would be low by ten a.m. By nine, Jerry and Didi were crouched in the little boat, checking the motor, which was purring quietly, a thin jet of water squirting from the escape pipe. Equipment was stored all about, so thick there was scarcely room for the youngsters. Oars and anchor, buckets and glass jars for specimens both dead and alive, water, two Mae West life preservers, spare gas and spare parts, the dredge, all the various ropes, food, a change of shirts which Aunt Ag insisted they carry, Didi's little bag with lotion, sunglasses, and a billy in case some slimy monster came up in the dredge and slithered around in the boat. Didi took off her watch and put it in her bag. The dredge platform for dumping leaned against one side of the boat.

Maude steadied them against the dock. Leaning over, she handed Jerry two pairs of old gloves, and said quietly but with authority, "You'll need these. Put 'em somewhere handy."

Jerry thanked her and prepared to leave, but Maude wasn't finished.

"Remember," she continued, "by the time you get to the Blind Pass exit it'll be 9:30. That gives you a half hour, more or less, of the out-going tide, which will help you on the trip out. You must stop whatever you are doing and head back in by three o'clock this afternoon ... sharp! I'll be down at Blind Pass with my glasses, watching. If I don't see you by 3:30 I'll head for Murph and he'll come out. So, if you have trouble, drop your anchor and sit it out. We'll get you. Do you understand all that?"

Both Didi and Jerry nodded solemnly. They were so excited they'd have agreed to anything just to get going. They laughed delightedly at each other. Squashing their hats down on their heads, they pushed away from the dock.

Aunt Ag yelled after them "Don't go out of sight of land. Do you hear?"

Again they both nodded and waved good-bye. The Great Adventure was under way. Didi perched on the prow and they moved smoothly along. When the Sanibel shore was only a dim line behind them she called over her shoulder.

"How can we tell when we're five miles out?"

"I've been wondering, too." Jerry's face was creased in thought. "There's no way I know but to take a stab. Let's drop the dredge about here and see what we get. Want to?"

Didi crawled back toward him. "Sure," she said. "Let's do it."

They slowed the motor to trolling speed and pushed the dredge off into the water. The rope fed out and the dredge sank from sight. They were about to congratulate themselves when the boat stopped with a sudden jerk, and they nearly fell overboard. The boat, dead still, rocked with the gentle rise and fall of the Gulf water.

146

They looked at each other silently for a moment. Then Jerry said, behind a little lop-sided smile, "We're anchored! The dredge has filled up and we're stopped. We didn't think of that. Damn!"

Didi was leaning out over the stern, one hand holding the pull rope. She raised the other, cautiously.

"Try a little more speed."

Jerry advanced the gas feed. Nothing!

"A little more."

Jerry slowly twisted the gas feed until the motor was running almost full speed. The stern of the boat sank deeper and deeper into the water from the strain but they didn't budge. Then, suddenly, with tremors like an athlete strained to the limit, the little boat inched forward.

Didi yelled aloud in glee and clapped her hands.

"See! See! It's going to work! Oh, Jerry, I'm so proud of you! We are going to get lots of stuff, I just know we are."

Jerry was glad his hat was flopped down over his eyes. He didn't want Didi to see his delight at her outburst.

"Don't fall overboard, now," he called, his voice suddenly gruff.

After dragging the dredge a hundred yards or so, they idled the motor to haul in. This was tricky business. The small boat had six inches of freeboard, at best. The platform had to be clamped at the rear but at one side, to accommodate the outboard motor. If they both stood in front of the platform and pulled in the dredge, the boat would tip dangerously and might ship water and sink. The dredge would have to be brought in from the stern, over the motor, and only one of them dared to stand back by the motor at any one time.

They heaved and tugged, fighting their footing in the Gulf swells and the dead weight of the dredge. Bit by bit, hand over hand, in it came. Between gasps, Didi muttered, "Thank heaven for Aunt Maude's gloves. Our hands'd be a mess without 'em."

Jerry gritted his teeth and reached down into the water and grabbed the edge of the dredge.

"This is <u>work</u>! We've got to figure out an easier way than this. Here, help. Lift up with me on the count of three. Ready? One ... two ... three."

The dredge, dripping water and sand and lumps of old shells, flopped into the boat, and soaked everything within reach. They got a better grasp and upended it onto the platform.

With little wheezing, breathy sounds they both sagged back against the gunwale. Neither wanted the other to know how tired he felt. Didi lifted her head.

"I've an idea, Jerry. Before we let that thing back out, why not tie knots every yard or so in the pull-rope. That way, the rope won't keep slipping through our hands. The knots will give us a hold."

"And," Jerry nodded to her, "two other things. One, we won't drag it such a long time, and two, once she's up off the bottom, how's about running the boat a bit and sort of rinsing some of the sand out?"

Excitement, however, returned and fatigue was forgotten when they started pawing through the debris. The mounded wet sand was rinsed back into the sea bit by bit, leaving the dump platform covered with worn calico pectins and broken sand dollars, one or two starfish and a pin cushion. Both tried to conceal his disappointment as Jerry filled a bucket with water to rinse the last of the sand away. As he reached out to fling the water, Didi squealed. Quick as a flash, she reached out and grabbed a small oblong shell tumbling toward the platform edge.

"Look! Oh, look! Isn't it beautiful? And it hasn't a break or a scratch, and both the points are perfect." She held out the little gleaming prize nestled in her hand.

"What is it?" Jerry hadn't studied up on shells as Didi had, and was puzzled.

"It's a small olive. And look at the color. Gold. It's a golden olive. I read about these. The natives of Hawaii have for centuries used olives as the center of their shell necklaces, in the place of honor. Olives are usually mottled gray and brown, with a haze of green. A golden one is special. The Hawaiians exchange golden olives just before leaving on a long trip. The shells carry a message ... 'Wait for me. I love you. I'll be back!' ... Those left behind save it carefully and when the traveler returns, it's given back, and this time the message ... 'You're back. I love you. I waited!' ... Isn't that lovely? It's a very, very special shell! I'll treasure this above all the others I have, and I'll remember each time I look at it where we were and how we got it, and that you were here with me." She threw a brilliant smile at him as she carefully put the golden olive in a glass jug for safe-keeping.

Jerry started the motor and as they got under way he turned to Didi.

"Since we don't know where we are, or where that rock formation is, how about running straight ahead for five minutes and then dropping the dredge? Is that all right with you?"

Didi nodded. She was squatted down in the bottom, peering into the jug at the olive. Without looking up, she murmured, "Course, that was mean of me, just now. This shell is just as much yours as mine. Why don't you keep it?"

Jerry wouldn't hear of this. He shook his head violently.

"Nope. That's not right at all. You're the one building a collection, not me! Let's do this. I'll keep all the live stuff we get, if any. For the aquarium. And you keep all the shells. Okay?"

The hours flew by. Their arms ached. They were burned by the relentless sun. Not until well past noon did the dredge bring up anything at all special. They learned to drag the bottom for only a short distance, so the dredge was less heavy. Jerry knotted the rope, which made hauling in easier, but getting the dredge pulled in and lifted up and over the motor took all their strength each time. Didi's face began to show strain.

Then one haul brought up bits of sponge mixed in with the worthless debris. Jerry quickly dropped the anchor.

"We must be over rocky formation of some sort. I don't think sponge lives in just plain sand. Doesn't it have to hold on to something solid?"

Didi thought so. She wasn't sure.

"I think it does. Maybe not rocks. More like a coral reef. Here's more proof we're over something. This reddish-purple growth is called gorgonia, and it does grow on rocks and coral. It's also called a sea feather. Isn't that strange?"

"Sure is," Jerry agreed. "And these little pieces of sponge, some yellow and some red. Are they alive?"

"Yes. Not an animal as we're used to ... more like a plant growth. Sponge, sea fans, gorgonia, they're all alive. You know, if we are over a reef, it could be covered with all kinds of stuff. Isn't it great?"

Jerry sat back on his heels, watching her feel through the remaining sand on the platform. His eyes brightened.

"Let's drop the dredge right here again before I pull up the anchor. Let's drag it forward a little and then turn around and drag it back again. Then haul it in."

The resulting haul was the best of all. Didi was already squealing with delight as the dredge broke the surface at the edge of the boat. Bits of staghorn coral could be seen poking above the mottled gray sand, and the corner of a yellow sponge showed off in one corner.

"Oh, Jerry, careful, now. Don't spill it. It's full of things. I know it is." In her excitement she bumped his arm, nearly causing him to drop the dredge.

"Don't jump around so. We'll capsize. Grab hold and help lift. Come on, now. The damn thing is too heavy. I'm gonna drop it!"

Upended on the platform, with little streams of sea water trickling sand over the sides, the mounded haul was tantalizing. Bits of coral showed here and there. The corner of an old sand dollar thrust out, and a large purplish clump of sponge was poised on the top, about to roll back into the sea. Didi grabbed it and put it on the floor, off to one side. Then she reached out toward the wet pile of sand, as if to plunge her hand in, but drew back sharply.

"Jerry," she said quietly, "we must work slowly. This mound is full of great things. I can feel it in my bones. We'll finger through one handful at a time, okay? And push the sand we don't want down to the platform edge and then rinse it away. Shall we start?"

"No. You start. You paw around and separate stuff, and I'll rinse the sand off for you. Go ahead, now."

Gasping and squeaking with excitement at each new discovery, Didi first uncovered a live calico pecten. She held it out to Jerry for inspection.

"Look. See how all the little indentations fit so snugly? And it's so glossy. Let's see if we can keep it alive in the aquarium."

He took it and put it in one of the glass jars. He was adding a little more sea water and a handful of sand when Didi shouted.

"Come here. There's so much stuff wiggling I can't handle all this by myself."

They found small greenish glass shrimp, tiny marginellas, several lacy murex, and bits of staghorn coral that had been broken off from its base by the dredge. Several kinds of starfish were wiggling their arms in an effort to escape, the thin ones with the small round bodies, from which five twig-like arms radiated, called brittle starfish ... and one fat, stubby Atlantic starfish, fleshy and gray-white. All the live things were carefully placed in the specimen jar.

Jerry found a porcupine fish about two inches long, and very carefully picked it up. Those horn-like spikes on its head and back looked sharp. In the jar, it rested quietly on the sand on its little flat bottom. A black sea urchin moved cautiously toward the platform edging, its many stiff little leg-like protrusions moving in every direction at the same time. Didi grabbed it up before it fell overboard. Jerry had gathered a large handful of sand and was carefully rinsing it away when a tawny shell edge showed.

"Here you go," he said to Didi, plopping the entire mound of sand into her hands. "There's somebody in there. Its shell is sticking out."

Didi washed away the sand and uncovered a large golden-brown lion's paw.

"Oh, how beautiful. It's only the top half, but it's perfect. And it's so large. Look at the wonderful markings, Jerry. It's a huge sea scallop, you know. It's really great. Mrs. Thigpen told me that Dr. Louise Perry told her that once, after a heavy three-day northeaster, so many live lion's paws washed in on the Sanibel shore that Carla Wilson served 'em that evening at the Sanibel Inn for dinner!"

Jerry was bent over the platform, busy with the heap of sand still to be sifted through, and didn't take time to react to this remarkable statement.

"Here's something. Two things, really. A spiky white shell and an old mess of green moss." He was about to toss the moss overboard, when Didi yelled and grabbed it.

"Never! No! Don't throw anything back, 'til we explore it. Look!" She carefully pealed back the fuzzy growth and exposed a small shiny green star shell. "See. You never know. Wish it was alive, but it seems to be perfect. I'll be Queen of Captiva. Nobody else will have one of these, I'll bet. That white shell you're holding is a thorny oyster. Its a beauty."

Finally they were finished. The mound had given up all its treasures and the platform had been rinsed clear. They sagged against the gunwales and rested.

"Wasn't that exciting?"

Jerry grinned at her enthusiasm, and nodded.

"Yeah. It sure was fun. Come on, now, drink some water and let's drop the dredge again."

But Didi had taken out her watch and her face was long and woebegone.

150

"Jerry, we can't. It's almost three o'clock. Maude said she'd be waiting, so we must go. We promised!"

"No. I want to drop the dredge one more time. Can't we?"

"Jerry, we promised!"

"Oh, all right. Damn! We're in exactly the right spot. We'll never find it again, ever."

"Yes, we will. And if we don't, we'll find some place just as good." Didi smiled over at him and nodded her head once or twice. "Come on, now. After all this fun, don't go sour."

Jerry reluctantly nodded back, and turned to pull in the anchor.

"If you say so. If I'd been alone, though, I'd have stayed. Better toss that old sponge back. It'll just stink up the boat, and we'll smell bad enough as it is." He reached down into the bilge slopping around in the bottom of the boat for it.

Didi beat him to it. She grabbed the sponge and gently kneaded it.

"I'll dry this out and rinse it in bleach. It'll be great for sponging down things. Like this boat. It sure could stand ... Jerry!" She glanced up, startled. "There's something inside here. Don't start up yet. Come over here and let's see."

Back at the platform, they bent over together and slowly pulled the sponge apart. The purple tinge changed to a rose red as they poked deeper and deeper. Didi gasped as she exposed a small yellow sponge pecten, firmly held in the depth of the sponge by the raspy outside of the shell, alive and perfect.

"Oh, how beautiful. How beautiful. Except for my golden olive, this will be my very best shell. How really beautiful. Let's add it to the live jar!"

"And this!" Jerry had his hand folded back into a loose fist. "You will never guess what I have. It plopped out of that sponge and I grabbed it just as it ran for the edge. Look!"

He carefully opened his fist one finger at a time and Didi peered in.

"What is it? Oh, golly! Oh! It's a baby octopus, isn't it? It's a little octopus! Isn't it?"

Jerry slowly closed up his fist and nodded. Reaching for the jar of live things, he pushed his hand inside down the neck and carefully unfurled his fingers. The tiny thing, the body no bigger than a nickel, sank toward the bottom and then darted sideways and affixed its eight little legs firmly to the sides of the jar. At the base of the bulbous head, slightly above the joining of the legs, they could see two tiny bright eyes.

"Do you think it'll live, Jerry? It's not damaged, is it? Wonder what it eats?"

"We'll ask Aunt Maude. She'll know. Most likely bits of sea life, all ground up. I can't wait to show her this stuff." He had the anchor up and they were heading in.

Didi had the specimen jar in her lap and was peering down inside.

"You like her a lot, don't you?" She didn't raise her head.

"Like who?"

151

"Aunt Maude."

"Sure. Don't you?"

Didi was silent for a moment. Jerry swung around and looked at her.

"Don't you like her?"

"Of course, I do. Lots. But I don't think she likes me."

"Why not, for heaven's sake?"

"Oh, I don't know. It's just a feeling I have. Every once in a while I catch a look on her face. Then she'll smile and everything will be okay again. But that look seems to hang in the air, somehow."

Jerry's face had turned serious.

"Are you sure, Didi? You're not imagining things?"

"I'm not imagining." Didi looked straight at him disquietingly. "It's not just once. It's often."

Jerry pondered these unsettling remarks as the little boat ran toward land.

Some fifteen minutes later, Didi exclaimed, "I can see Aunt Maude now, sitting on that old fallen pine. Can you see her?"

"Yep. She's still pretty far away, but it's Aunt Maude all right. That old tree is about a mile north of the Blind Pass entrance. We'll run for that. Then, in the pass, when we get opposite the pine, we'll nose in and pick her up."

Didi moved things around in the bottom of the boat, to make sure Maude would have enough room, but when they drew up behind the tree, she was gone.

"That's strange. Why do you suppose she left?"

Didi didn't know what to answer. She feared it had something to do with her but she didn't want to say anything. The day had been too splendid to end it with problems. She looked over at Jerry and squeezed his hand.

"Didn't we have fun?"

Back at the house, the three ladies exclaimed and chattered over the shells as the youngsters spread them out on the kitchen table. Each shell was held up, turned over and minutely examined. The live specimens were of special interest.

"I'll help you transfer all these to the aquarium." Cora was shivery with enthusiasm and bubbled over like a boiling kettle. "Isn't all this grand? You'll soon have the best collection on the island, Didi. How I wish I could have been with you. All three of us." She included the other two in a grand sweeping gesture. "Of course, we'd need a bigger boat. Maybe we could get Jed Staines to rig up his and take us. Could we, Ag? Do you think we could, maybe?"

Agnes, intent on enticing the baby octopus into a small net, nodded her head and smiled. She adored Cora when she was in one of these little-girl moods.

Maude was quietly cutting screened wire and creasing it into a rectangle that would fit the top of the aquarium.

"Have to keep this wire on the tank," she said, "or some of that stuff will climb out. Especially that octopus. He'll be all over the house in no time, and we don't want that!"

"Ooooh, I should say not!" Cora gave a little shudder and drew in her feet. "Two things I don't want crawling around on the floor ... snakes and octopuses! Is that the proper word?"

"What will he eat, Aunt Maude? What can we feed him?" Jerry had taken the little net from Aunt Ag and quietly laid it over the small animal as it stuck to the side of the jar. Then taking a knife from the table, he pushed the blade under the edge of the net and gently prodded the baby. With a convulsive move, the octopus left the side of the jar and rushed into the net, all legs moving at once, and settled into one corner, tightly wrapped up in itself. Jerry carefully transferred it to the aquarium.

Maude looked thoughtful. "Well, now, I don't know. I never had to feed an octopus before. But let's see. If it was living down one of those tubes in that sponge, and feeding on what happened by, it must eat very small live things. I suppose we could mash up sand fleas and small shrimp and try that. We could ball up some of that kind of stuff, and it would feed the other things, too. Small bits of flesh would drift about and the live shells would maybe absorb some. And juices would also permeate the water. We could always hatch out some brine shrimp. Dwarf sea-horses eat those, I know. Maybe the little fella would like those. Rigby's store has some cans. I saw 'em just the other day."

"Could we, sometime? Ag, you're not listening."

"Could we what Cora?"

"What we were taking about. Could we get Mr. Staines to take us all dredging some time?" Here eyes sparkled with anticipation.

"Of course we can, dear. Of course." Agnes replied, placatingly. "You remind me, next time I go to Sanibel, and I'll ask him."

"Brine shrimp?" Didi called across the room. "What are those, Aunt Maude? I never heard of them."

Maude paused so long, Didi thought she wasn't going to answer. Looking slightly past everything, everyone, and at nothing in particular, Maude answered very quietly and in measured tones.

"You buy brine shrimp eggs. They look like dust. They come in a small cardboard tube. You take sea water and spread a small pinch of the eggs on top and put it away somewhere in the dark. Twenty-four hours later, the sea water will be full of teeny, teeny little live shrimp, darting this way and that, no bigger than dust motes. You can dip spoonfuls of that water into the aquarium."

When she was finished, Maude looked directly at Didi, no expression on her face. The look lasted too long, and Didi flushed. Agnes caught Maude's look and Didi's reaction and a frown furrowed her brow.

●

Jerry missed the swimming. There was no time during the winter months for the late afternoon visiting with Roy, the camaraderie of the quiet gossiping together as they paddled in the warm Gulf water. Roy was too busy. Jerry was too busy. There was a feeling about the island, a sense of everyone being bowed down, bent over, from the burden of 'the season'. The little shops ran frantically from nine 'til five each day, with the proprietors continuing breathlessly until late at night, readying for the morrow. The bakery ran straight through the night, with Jack and Ted splitting the twenty-four hours into shifts. The mailboat arrived slightly late each day and so loaded it squatted deep in the water. The deliveries took more time than usual and Jerry seldom got back to Aunt Ag's from the bakery run until nearly supper time.

Didi often accompanied him on his rounds and, if Ambassador Drinkwater was away, as he often was, she would eat at Aunt Ag's and generally fit in. She'd straighten up the kitchen after the meal, chattering all the while. Cora might need a hand in the shop. There was seemingly always something with the aquarium. Night after night the two youngsters crouched in front of the tank, heads nearly touching, hands reaching over the sides, murmuring together as they rearranged the sandy bottom, repositioned the coral, fed the collection.

Maude rocked and watched, her binoculars lying forgotten in her lap. Somehow, when Maude was present, a strange tension hung in the air, like tonight.

"She keeps staring at me," Didi whispered to Jerry.

"She's watching us both, not just you. She's interested in what goes on." Jerry was dipping shrimp water into the aquarium. "You know, these things are okay for everybody but the baby octopus. I never see him eat."

"No. Only at me," Didi persisted. "Wonder why? Makes me jumpy."

Jerry pointed at the side of the aquarium, at the little octopus.

"Didi, look closely at him. Really look. Do you get the feeling he's looking back? Do you? I think he sees us. Aunt Maude, come over here a minute. Look at this thing."

Maude got up and crossed the room. Agnes also joined them. Cora was busy in her shop.

Didi moved slightly and motioned to Maude.

"Aunt Maude, squeeze in here beside me. You'll be right in front of the baby."

"Everybody look close at him." Jerry had drawn back a bit to give more room. "I watch him all the time and I keep getting this strange feeling he's also watching me. Not like a fish. A fish sees motion and light and reacts to

154

that but you never get the feeling a fish actually sees you, like a dog, for instance. But that baby octopus actually sees me. Understand what I mean?"

"Oh, yes," Didi piped up excitedly. "I see. I see what you mean, Jerry. It's really looking back at us, like another person. Ugh. That's weird! I don't think I like this."

Jerry reached out and touched the side of the aquarium, just to the left of the baby. Slowly he moved his finger along the glass to the right. The tiny bright eyes moved with his finger.

"Let's see if he'll ink. That's how the big one's hide, you know. When they're in danger they squirt out a cloud of blue-black ink and hide in it." He put his hand deep inside the aquarium and wiggled his fingers slowly toward the little octopus.

"Don't hurt it, now," Didi cried.

"I won't. I won't touch it."

As his hand neared, the baby repositioned itself slightly, as if to see better, and seemed to tense up. Then, suddenly, it shot away, trailing wisps of pinkish ink. Jerry kept his hand moving behind it as it propelled itself around the aquarium. All at once, the little octopus abruptly up-ended and sank to the bottom, trailing its little legs behind it.

"What happened?" Didi exclaimed.

"I think it's dead," Jerry answered, in a quiet tone.

"It can't be dead!" Maude said, leaning forward, gazing intently into the aquarium. "You didn't touch it. You weren't even close."

"Its dead. See." Jerry poked the little creature with an extended finger but it just lay on the bottom, a crumpled blob.

Didi, distressed at this turn of events, involuntarily grabbed Maude's arm, but Maude gently disengaged herself. Agnes caught the byplay and, straightening up, leaned back against the sink. She stared at the floor for a second with a serious expression. This had gone on, now, long enough. Much as she disliked intruding, she'd have to get involved.

Everyone was surprised at how late it had gotten. Didi had to go.

"Will you run me back, Jerry?"

He nodded. "After I get this thing out of the aquarium. It can't stay in there. It'll rot and sour the water. Wonder what really happened to it?"

"Maybe we can get another." Didi had the little net and she gently scooped up the small dead creature. "Here. You take it." She held out the net for Jerry to take. "Don't tell me what you do with it. I'd rather not know."

The drive down to Didi's house was silent, the only sound being the squeaks and protests of the old truck as it bumped along the rutted road. As they drew up to the front of the house, Didi opened the truck door and turned in her seat toward Jerry.

"I'm upset with Aunt Maude. I don't know what the trouble is. I'm not imagining all this you know. And it's such a pity because Aunt Maude is very likeable."

Jerry fiddled with the steering wheel. "She's more than that. She's very lovable. I love Maude Appleton." There was a pause and Didi thought he was through, but he went on. "She never talks about it, but I think she's had a tough life. There's often a lot of hurt and ache deep inside her eyes. When she doesn't know I'm watching her, I can see it peeping out."

Didi nodded slowly. "I think maybe you're right. I'll be extra kind to her from now on."

"No. Don't do that. She'd hate that. Just like her. Somehow, let her know you like her, without telling her. She's very special."

With one leg out the door, Didi leaned back in, and reached toward him. Her eyes were filled with moisture. "Laddie," she murmured, "You are kind of special yourself." She ran a finger gently down the bridge of his nose. Then, light as a feather, she was gone, leaving an embarrassed little laugh hanging in the air behind her.

●

Back at Agnes', Maude rose to leave as soon as the young people had gone, but Agnes turned from the sink.

"Could you stay for a few minutes, Maude? There's something I'd like to talk over with you. Maybe we can have a cup of tea together?"

Maude nodded and drew out a chair. As she settled herself at the table, Agnes put on the kettle and reached for the cups. How to start? Any opening she could think of seemed awkward, unfriendly. She sat opposite Maude and looked at her. Maude looked back.

"Dear friend," Agnes plunged. "We've known each other a long time now. It's been months since you appeared on the dock that day, when Cora and I were nailing decking. All that time we've never had any sort of problem or disagreement between us, you and I, and I certainly don't want one now. Oh, dear. This really is difficult. I don't know what to say."

Maude's gaze never waivered.

"Why say anything, then?" she asked slowly.

Agnes shook her head. "No, that's the easy way. Something's wrong and I want to get it out in the open, on the table. There's a nasty tension building in this house, and it has to go. Otherwise, we'll all be miserable."

Maude was stony-faced.

"I don't know what you mean, Agnes."

"Yes you do. I think you know exactly what I'm referring to. What is the problem Maude? Are you jealous of Didi? Is that it?"

Maude reacted like she'd been slapped. She jerked her face to one side and her neck turned red.

"No! Of course not!"

She spoke much too loudly and her head lowered. Reaching for her tea cup, it rattled on the saucer as she picked it up. Agnes watched. After a period of silence, Maude's belligerence seemed to evaporate and she quieted a little. Slowly she raised her eyes and glanced over at Agnes.

"Yes, Agnes. I'm jealous of Didi." She paused a moment, and then went on. "But not in the way you mean. And I don't know what to do about it. It gets worse and worse. I didn't think it showed."

"It shows! How could it not show? Every time the child makes a move in your direction you snap her head off. Even Cora has remarked. I feel we should discuss it openly, just the two of us, and resolve it, somehow. This house, even the island, is too small for unpleasantnesses of this kind. If we can't look at things as they really are, if we can't remove these tensions, then I ..."

Maude swiftly lifted a hand.

"No, Agnes, don't lay down ultimatums, please. Once they're said out loud, they hang in the air and things can never then be the same. Maybe if we just talk a little ... this is my problem, really. I'll have to handle it myself. Maybe talking will help."

The kettle hissed. Agnes rose to get the tea, and filled the cups. Trailing her spoon listlessly back and forth in it, Maude sat for some time, gazing deep into the steaming amber liquid. Agnes waited.

"It's not so much that I'm jealous of Didi, I suppose, as that I resent her. I think that's it." Maude's voice was scarcely more than a whisper and she spoke slowly. "You see, these past few months, ever since Jerry came, I've been so happy. I'm not a happy person, actually, but I've been happy around him. The enthusiasm, the sparkle, the newness, the excitement of everything. I've loved seeing it all again through his eyes. He has drawn out of me the little girl I've always kept hidden. Through him, I've glimpsed the childhood I never had. Now, I'm afraid of losing him, of losing all that." She was leaning on one elbow, softly sipping the warm tea. She kept her eyes down. "It would be so much easier, Ag, if she weren't so incredibly beautiful! It's like no matter what I do, I can't possible win."

"Maybe there's no battle," Agnes interjected, but Maude didn't hear and went on.

"I've always wondered what it would feel like to be beautiful. Just for one day, to be beautiful. To have people look at you and smile just because your face pleased them. To hold back your shoulders and hold up your head and to know, to _know_, that you were the handsomest one there. Just once! For one day! I was always ugly. Even as a tiny baby, I was ugly."

As Maude talked on, Agnes' face softened and her eyes shone too brightly. She shook her head and started to object, but Maude raised her hand.

"Oh, yes I was. I was always ugly. Even as a baby. I can remember like it was yesterday, my earliest memory in fact. One time when I was tiny, Poppa was leaving to go to a new camp. Ma and I were leaning against the door jamb, watching the crew walk away. Poppa came running back and swept Ma

157

up into his arms and kissed her good-bye. Then he was gone. I ran down the path after him, crying my eyes out. When I finally caught up with him, I grabbed his pant leg. 'Poppa, you didn't kiss me goodbye. Kiss me goodbye, Poppa'. He stopped and looked down at me and glanced at the men around him. Then he said, 'Little girls as ugly as you don't deserve to be kissed'. Then he and all the crew went on down the path, laughing. I just stood there. I stopped crying. I dried up. Ever after, I've stayed dried up. Sometimes, at night, even now at this age, I dream of his face thrust into mine, saying 'too ugly ... too ugly'." The only sign of emotion was a little quiver to Maude's chin, quickly come, quickly gone.

A silence hung in the room and for the longest time they both said nothing. Just sat. Maude finally gave a great sigh, and glanced at Agnes.

"I've never been able to fully cast aside that remark. I think most everything I ever did all those years was to get Poppa to smile at me and say 'come over here, little girl, so I can kiss you.' He did smile at me once. As he was dying. Ma had long since passed on and I'd taken her place as I grew up, tending the camps and making some kind of a home for Poppa. He had pneumonia, I think. He'd been awful sick, and he was sinking fast. I heard this deep rattle and Poppa lifted halfway up in bed and reached out toward me and his hands beckoned and he had a great big smile on his face. Before I could cross the room he fell back and was gone." She paused a long time. "I've always wondered," she went on, "was he reaching for me ... or Ma? Late at night, when I think about all this, I tell myself it was me. But I don't know. Never will!"

In the quiet that followed, not knowing exactly what to say, Agnes rose and got more tea and some cookies. They sat, remembering and munching.

Jerry suddenly burst into the room at a dead run, all ready to visit. Agnes stopped him.

"Jerry, please excuse us. Maude and I are discussing some important personal matters and we're not quite finished. Please understand, but could we be alone, if you don't mind? Please!"

Jerry nodded and disappeared upstairs.

Maude, hardly aware of the interruption, was watching a miller moth that had flown into the room from the porch. It landed on the table and flexed its little wings up and down. Carefully, with great tenderness, she reached out and pinched the wings together. She pushed back her chair and took the moth to the porch door. Leaning down, she whispered "Little one, don't be so foolish next time." Opening the screened door, she released the moth into the night.

Maude returned to the table. Gazing at her friend but not seeing her, looking deep into a distant place, she softly said, "It's not her fault she's beautiful, you know, and it's not my fault I'm not. I'll try to look at it that I'm not losing the boy, but am gaining a new friend. That's the advice they give you, isn't it?" She smiled a little wanly. "You know, I'm not good at this confidential stuff, Ag. I'm just as clumsy with my tongue as I am with my feet."

"You're doing fine. I understand."

Maude looked at her for quite some time. "Do you, Agnes? Do you really? I'm not sure I understand myself. Maybe it's not in the scheme of things for any of us to understand anyone else. Or ourselves. I don't think on it very much. Too disturbing. I try not to think of anything emotional. I've always had to bind in my emotions like my bosoms. Safer that way. Then people can't know."

"What do you mean, Maude? Bind in your bosom?" Agnes asked gently.

"Poppa really wanted a boy. No place for a girl, stomping about in woods with all those men. It was easier for Poppa if I looked like a boy, no matter what it did to me. Even as a little kid I had to wear my hair cropped close, like a boy's. Then I started to grow up. All the glands started changing around, or whatever they do. My body wouldn't stop growing. I got tall, and then huge. My bosoms got big and stuck straight out. Poppa made me wear a wide strip of canvas, binding 'em flat. All the time. I could never take it off. Hurt like hell." She lifted her face to Agnes and her mouth smiled but her eyes didn't.

Agnes reached out and grasped her hand.

"My dear, I'm so sorry. I'm so sorry."

"Don't blame Poppa, Agnes. I don't. He did the best he could, under the circumstances. He had problems, too, I suppose. At least I tell myself that. And during the daylight hours, I believe it. At nights, I don't. The nights are bad."

Agnes nodded. "I agree," she said. "Nights are bad. Some are so long I think dawn will never come. I lie there and twist and turn. Awful."

"Doesn't it ease up as time goes by?"

Agnes nodded. "Yes, I suppose, on the surface it eases. I'm comfortable now, in the mornings, with my lot. I wasn't at first, but I am now. The day stretches ahead with the possibility of exciting, unexpected little pleasures. All of you, my new family, are about and busy and need to be cared for. The boy remains a delight. I'm in full control of my self all day. But as the light disappears and the night approaches, I can feel myself begin to fall apart deep inside. A restlessness comes on me — a vague discontent, a distrust of my strength to continue. I feel trapped, locked in. Is this all there is for me now? This sitting alone in my room each evening, staring at my empty bed? Is this all? It's then that I need Will so much I almost cannot deny it. I have to clench my teeth to hold in my agony. No, Maude, it doesn't really ease. I miss Will more than before, it seems. It doesn't go away." She put her head down onto her clenched hands on the table. "I feel, sometimes, that it would be far easier to not hold on, to just forget. But that, somehow, doesn't seem fair to Will."

"Yes. Yes, I know what you mean," Maude whispered, and her hand clenched and crushed the cookie she was holding. "We all have our dragons."

Then, after a pause, she went on. "At least, Agnes, you had your Will. I never had my Dusty!"

Agnes looked up, compassion filling her eyes.

"So! So, you too, Maude, have been in love. Tell me."

"So long ago. Yesterday, only. We had a base camp in the middle of the state, back in the piney woods behind Perry. There was too much work, and Poppa had posted a notice in town for extra hands." There was a pause. Maude fiddled with her tea. When she resumed, her voice caught and she had to clear her throat. "One day I looked up from the pots and pans and there he was, leaning against a stump. Standing there, bare-chested, in his cutoff pants. So young, so strong, so handsome."

A tear forced itself out of the corner of one eye, and trembled on her lashes, glistening in the light. Agnes was fascinated, watching it. For the longest time it hung, like a tiny bird about to fly. Then it broke away, and ran down her cheek, alongside her nose. Maude swiped at it with the back of her hand, embarrassed.

"Ag, from the first moment, from the very first second I laid eyes on him, I wanted him. God! The feeling was so tremendous. I seemed to be yanked ten feet in the air and left hanging."

"What did you do?"

"What did I do." Maude brushed at the crumbs in front of her and then glanced up shyly. "I reached back under my dress and released that damn canvas. I turned loose my breasts, Ag, and I never bound 'em again, ever. And I let my hair grow! As the months went by and we drew close, he'd creep up behind me as I cooked or cleaned up, and he'd reach around and cup me in each hand and breath into my hair ... 'So much. So much. And all mine' ... I'd lean back into him and rest my head on his chest, and I felt safe. Here was someone stronger than me, against whom I could lean and be weak. His whole body, what I could see, was covered by a glorious dusting of golden hair. I called him that ... Dusty ... and soon the whole camp was calling him Dusty."

Agnes, so encased in sympathy as Maude went on that she could hardly speak, finally asked in a voice little more than a whisper, "His whole body — what you could see. Didn't you ever see him naked?"

"No!"

"Not even once?"

"No!"

"Didn't you two ever ... I mean, didn't you even once ..."

"No. Never. Not even once."

"Why not?"

"Dusty had principles. He was old-fashioned. Said we shouldn't be intimate 'til we were married. We set the date and all."

"What happened?"

Maude seemed to go into a trance. She turned her head and gazed out of the kitchen window, past the gumbo-limbo tree, past the dock, off across the open bay. For a long time she didn't speak. When she finally did, it gushed out all at once.

"Dusty claimed we needed more money. He knew how he could make a lot. Then he could build us a regular house and we'd marry and have kids and all. He left camp and joined several other men, one of 'em from Sanibel, old Dawson Ecker. They were gonna run outlaw rum up from Cuba. He'd make several runs and get out. But the revenuers got him first. Other side of the Isle of Pines. They bottled him up, sank his boat and he was never heard of again. Oh, Ag" it came out as a heavy moan, "They got my Dusty!"

Agnes was so affected her face was wet. She reached out and patted Maude's hand.

"Oh, Maude. I'm so sorry. I didn't know. I didn't know."

"Of course you didn't" Maude lifted her head and looked at Agnes. "Nobody knows. I've never said, before." She'd made a little steeple with her two hands and had rested her chin on the thumbs. "You know, Ag, I still see him. As I sit out on the beach, on my old, fallen-down tree, if someone comes into sight, walking toward me, I straighten up, thinking ` maybe it's Dusty ... maybe it's Dusty ...' My heart leaps and my breath catches and runs short. I stare at the feet. I'll know him at once from how the feet go down. His went down special-like. Isn't that dumb? After all these years, to still yearn so. I wouldn't really want to see him again, actually, not now. He'd be so young still, so beautiful, and me this old bag of bones. No, I don't really want to see him. That'd just burst my bubble. I'll keep my dreams."

Maude pushed back her chair and got up.

"It's late, Agnes. I've got to get home. I appreciate that you let me talk. It feels better. It really does. I'll straighten out that Didi thing tomorrow. I'll handle that. She'll never know we talked."

Maude crossed to the porch door. As she started through she slumped against the jamb and stared at the floor.

"You know, Ag. It wasn't meant that anyone should have to die ... not knowing."

The screen door opened, and shut. Maude was gone.

Agnes sat for a long time, alone at the table. Then she rose and took up the dishes. "You're right, Maude," she breathed at the empty room. "No one should have to die ... not knowing. Especially not a woman."

13

January, 1949

During the winter season, as cars were lining up at the Punta Rassa ferry slip about 4:45 any afternoon, Captain Bumpter could be seen climbing laboriously down from the wheelhouse and weaving a painful path alongside the automobiles, peering through each front window. If he recognized anyone he'd smile and say "Howdy. Ten minutes to go." If he didn't know the travelers, he'd smile and say "Howdy. Last trip today in ten minutes. If you ain't got reservations on the island, you'll be spendin' the night on the beach. No boat 'til 7:30 tomorrow mornin'. Skeeters are ferocious. Better think on it."

Some people would pull out of line and head back toward town at a fast clip. The stalwart ones would smile back and stay in line, braving it out. Repeating visitors judged whether they had finally become part of the local scene by which greeting Captain Bumpter gave them.

Jean and Frank Culpepper decided to brave it out. They'd spent two weeks of their 1948 vacation 'doing' Florida and had been advised by friends not to return to New York without visiting Captiva.

"The island is enchanting. But the natives are apt to be quirky. Strange things can happen. You'll kill yourself if you pass it up."

They sat hunched low in the car, third in line, munching on O'Henry bars and eagerly anticipating whatever life held out for them.

The first shock was when Captain Bumpter nonchalantly motioned the lead car aboard and the tiny ferry listed badly under its weight.

"Migosh," Jean exclaimed, leaning forward. "The damn thing's gonna sink right there. Frank, we can't get on that!"

Frank bit down on his candy bar and cast a meditative eye at the flop-down boarding ramp.

"It should level out again when the next car drives on. If that old man loads it on the other side, of course. If he feeds it on behind the first one, the whole bloody business is a goner."

Miraculously enough, when the second car was maneuvered into place alongside the opposite railing from the first, the little boat seemed to level out. It had an expectant air about it, as though it didn't know exactly what was next.

Frank and Jean were next. Just as their front wheels ran onto the ramp a wave heaved the ferry up, then dropped it back down and the ramp flopped with it. The car lurched sickeningly.

Jean scrunched down and closed her eyes.

"We're done for," she said. "If we drown over this, I'll never forgive Millie Shapiro for telling us to come here."

Frank was intent on following the captain's directions. A waving hand sent him first to the left, and then to the right. Then stop. The captain approached.

"You ain't far enough over. Won't ask you to back all the way off. We'll see-saw ya a bit." He grabbed the door latch to keep from sliding down the sharp sideways incline. "Careful now. Don't crash my railin'. If we don't get ya just right, snug over, I can't get that truck behind ya aboard."

Jean looked behind, and gasped.

"That thing's huge! Couldn't squeeze into the Lincoln Tunnel without grease. We really will sink. Look how the boat's leaning to one side. No wonder that old man's so gimpy. He could be Heidi's uncle!"

She watched as the captain limped off the boat and motioned around the truck for the last car in line to move up and board.

"Oh," she said, nodding her head in agreement. "I see what he's doing. Smart. He's gonna load opposite us to even the raft ..."

"Ferry boat."

"... and then put that huge truck on between us. That way, the ferry won't tip over on its side."

"See!" Frank grinned over at her irritatingly.

"It'll just plunge down the rear and catapult us all the way back to Fort Myers. Great!"

But it didn't. After a lot of backing up and moving forward, and grabbing hold of anything available to keep his balance, the captain threw Jean a little smile and patted her arm.

"See. All aboard. Here we go." He glanced at a pocket watch. "And right smack on schedule, too." He headed for the wheelhouse.

A brass bell clanged as the captain tugged on a leather thong, and boomed "All aboard. All aboard." Then he limped between the cars and climbed off the ferry and up onto the shore.

Jean had slumped so low in the seat only the top of her head showed.

"You watch, Frank, and let me know. I'm afraid to look. What's he doing now?"

"He's at a winch, turning the handle, and the ramp's slowly lifting off the boat. It's about a foot up now and hanging there. Must have ratchets on it. He's coming back. It's okay."

The captain paused by the open window and patted Jean on the top of her head.

"It's all right, girlie. We'll be on our way in about one minute. But I'll need your help, young fella." He leaned in the window across Jean and pointed past Frank. "Give me time to turn up the engine so's I can squeeze the nose up against the slip, then you lift that big rope off that piling there and we'll be free." He hurried toward the wheelhouse.

With a great boiling of water and engine noise the ferry inched forward until it was jammed tightly between the slip pilings. Frank was out by now and standing against the railing. He leaned over the edge and heaved the heavy hawser off the piling and onto the deck just as the captain threw the engine into full reverse and the ferry lurched backward into deeper water. Caught off balance, Frank pitched across the railing, his arms chopping the air, as he tried frantically to keep from falling into the water below. Jean gasped and thrust a fist against her mouth.

When Frank later climbed back into the car, windblown and out of breath, Jean looked straight at him for a second, a blank expression on her face.

"My husband just fell overboard. Who're you?" she asked.

The crossing, however, was serene. The water was calm and glistened a deep blue in the later afternoon sun. The gray clouds edging the horizon were far off and unthreatening. The tiny ferry, a bit heavy in the stern from the weight of the truck, nosed ahead into the sound, pushing foamy waves to each side as it moved unhurriedly along.

Jean snuggled up against Frank.

"Isn't this lovely? So peaceful. Don't you just adore Millie Shapiro? She was so right! We're going to have a great time over there. I can feel it in my bones."

Frank nodded, and opened the door on his side. "I'm going up to the wheelhouse a minute and ask the Captain about places to stay." He eased out and turned back to Jean. "Don't get out and climb around. Please! You know how you are. Promise? I'll be right back."

Jean wasn't about to get out and climb around the cramped little ferry boat. A porpoise had appeared, riding the prow wave, sinking and lifting with the curl of the frothy water, and Jean was entranced. She rested her head on the back of the seat and let her mind drift. Half asleep, she gave herself up to the languorous moment, the soft, salty air, the warm sun, the slap of the water against the thrusting little boat, a distant bird cry, the exciting, enticing, pine-crowned, unknown island that loomed just ahead. She had a fleeting spasm of irritation when Frank climbed back into the car and brandished a slip of paper at her.

"All here. Nice of the old guy. Are you listening? What's the matter with you?"

"Nothing. Nothing at all!" She yawned. "I just want to be left alone, to drift forever up here ... no body ... no problems ... no husband ... just drifting along. I never want to come back down!"

"Well, let me know when you decide to return and I'll clue you in on what we're gonna find over there!"

Jean sat up. "I'm back! What did old gimpy-puss say?"

Frank gazed at the dashboard for a second. "I wish you'd be kinder, you know. It's all very well to be crass and nasty-mouthed up in New York, with Millie and her gang. They can strike back at you. These are simple people, very gentle, and if you're gonna streak back and forth, being clever and brittle, they're gonna hate both of us."

Jean smiled and stroked his face. "Yes sir. Comment noted. I'll be on my best. Now, what did you find out?"

Frank grinned as he glanced back ... "Why do I put up with this strange creature" he thought to himself ... "So mercurial. Up one minute, down the next. Unpredictable. Stylish. Intelligent. Thin. Much too thin. New York east-side thin. How does she stay that way? Eats through the kitchen three times a day. If I eat a salad, it shows. Getting a small pot belly from that damn O'Henry bar. Stuck with her. Love her to death. Have from the first moment ..."

Jean was picking at his arm.

"Hey! Where are you, now? What did he say?"

"He said by the time we get off the ferry it'll be pushing early dusk and we'd better not zig-zag around Sanibel looking for lodging ... said it's booked solid, anyway ... should drive straight through to the lower island, Captiva, and maybe we'd be lucky there. Said the road was open all along, whatever that means. Gave me two names to see ... Miriam Hallman and/or Emmy Kramdon. Said in a pinch Miriam Hallman, if we can find her, will get us in from weather for the night. Also mentioned to get busy on all this as bad weather is heading this way. Something about that gray cloud mass off there'll be on us soon after dark. He's very knowledgeable."

"'Course he is" Jean nodded. "This ferry business is a gossip pipeline. He's got a monopoly, if I've ever seen one."

The ferry slip on the island, like the one on the mainland, was two irregular lines of huge pilings, wider to seaward, narrower to land, into which the little ferry pushed its nose. Incoming tide, flooding around the eastern end of the island, caught the boat and slammed it against the westernmost piling with a heavy crunch. Cars rocked and passengers' eyes flashed open with apprehension, but Captain Bumpter looked confidently from the wheelhouse window, obviously in full control, as he eased forward on the throttle and worked over his pipe-stem.

The ferry inched into the slip, bumping and scraping from piling to piling, until its prow was against the slip revetting. The throttle went full forward and a boil of water churned at the rear as the engine strained to hold the prow tight in place. Calmly, and in no apparent hurry, the captain climbed down onto the loading deck, heaved heavy ropes from each side to respective piling, and half-hitched them snugly. Returning to the wheelhouse, he reversed the

165

engine and the resulting strain on the hawsers swung the ferry evenly into place, the nose just under the forward lip of the waiting ramp.

Frank chuckled. "Couldn't have been better handled if it'd been the Queen Mary. Look at him. He doesn't even know how spectacular all that was. And by himself. What a wonderful old man!"

Nodding to each driver, and taking time for a word of gossip as he passed, Captain Bumpter slowly worked his way toward the prow and the ramp. He scrambled up, released the ratchet and motioned the lead car off as the ramp touched the deck.

Jean sighed in relief.

"Whew," she breathed. "That was sure bumpy. I can understand why his name's Bump ... ter!" She watched him moving about, bobbing and weaving as each car drove past him. "Poor old boy. He needs someone to help him. Suppose, just suppose he has a heart attack sometime ... halfway over ... good heavens!"

The Sanibel road, a mixture of sand and shell, followed a ridge along the center of the island from the eastern end with its lighthouse the full seventeen miles to the western end with its little humpback wooden bridge crossing Blind Pass to Captiva.

Doc Jessup was employed by the county to ply this stretch of unpaved road with his tractor-scraper and he made a daily pass from one end to the other, knocking the top off the humps and ruts made by each passing car. His scraper was just wide enough to tend half the roadway, so on those days he felt poorly, and only worked half-time, the road would be smooth on one side and rough on the other. The result was erratic driving, as cars going in both directions sought the smoother side and would zoom toward each other in a cloud of dust and skid abruptly aside at the last possible moment to avoid a crash. Occasionally two cars traveling in opposite directions on the smooth side would skid to a halt nose to nose, neither driver willing to give an inch.

Jean and Frank, driving along the rutty right side, slowly passed such a confrontation on the smooth left side, and Jean turned to glance out the back window.

"What an odd way to park! And way out here in no-man's-land. Those two men were shaking their fists at each other. Wonder why they don't just climb out and talk?"

"Too many bugs, most likely." Frank was eyeing the road ahead with ferocious concentration. "Is your window wound up tight? The car's full of mosquitoes. Did Millie Shapiro mention these bugs? This road is impossible. We'll be bumped to death in no time. No matter how slow I drive we bounce up one side and down the other of each of these damn ruts ... and they're only about three feet apart. Did Millie Shapiro mention these ruts?" His voice dripped irritation.

Jean flung up her head. "Stop bitching and drive. I'm no more entranced with this bouncing and these bugs than you are. Where's that pump gun with the spray? It's back here some where." She twisted in her seat, rummaging in the back. "I'll give 'em a blast!"

"No! Don't! You'll fog up the inside of the windshield with oil and I won't be able to see out. Not that there's much out there to see. This endless wagon trail they call a road and those dreary trees overhanging it on both sides. Big bushes, really. With round, flat leaves. Hideous! Did Millie ...?"

"Frank!" Jean spoke through clenched teeth. "Why don't you leave off Millie Shapiro! I don't know what she said or what she didn't say! Just drive. Or if you'd rather, go back and we'll get off this godforsaken place. Oh ... " she reconsidered ... "we can't, can we?"

Still gazing out the back window, Jean rested her chin on the back rim of her seat. "Frank, do you remember, last winter, when we were in the Arizona desert? Do you remember those tumbleweeds blowing around?"

"What's that got to do with anything?" Frank wanted to know.

"Well, those little darlings were nothing, compared to this whopper coming up behind us!"

Frank glanced in his rearview mirror. "What the hell is that?" He slowed almost to a stop, staring behind them.

The huge tumbleweed, increasing in size every second, loomed nearer and nearer ... and zoomed past them on the smooth side to their left.

"That damn truck that was on the ferry with us! Did you ever see such a cloud of sand and dust? Must be traveling sixty miles an hour. Well, I've had about enough. My nerves are shattered ... this place beats me." Frank's head sank down onto the steering wheel and the car came to a standstill.

Jean started to giggle. She leaned over and squeezed his arm.

"I'm sorry I snapped your head off just now. Millie is a dear, and she's the absolute last word on Balenciaga bags ... but apparently she's not so hot on islands. Come on, let's go. We can't just sit here, you know. Try driving on the left side, and maybe, Frank, we should drive fast, like that truck. Maybe that way we'll bump along over the tops of the ruts. Come on, now. It's getting to be beddy-bye time!"

"God! I don't know whether I hate you more when you're hostile or when you're in this goodie goodie, itty bitty mood." Frank started the motor and let the clutch out all of a sudden and the car leapt forward.

"That's a good lad," Jean exclaimed, letting a warm, vacuous smile spread over her face, and grabbing at the nape of her neck as her head snapped back. "Just the way mother told you to ... nice and easy!"

Some fifteen miles later they jiggled around a broad curve and passed a house.

"Back up! Back up!" Jean stuck a hand past Frank's face. "I just saw a house. Maybe we're there!"

"Aw, come on, Jean. That was one house. Just one. I saw it, too. Had a sign on it said 'Armstrong'. Look, there's another. Says 'Thigpen'. And over there, see that little sign. It says 'Grab Bag'. What do you figure that is?"

167

"Must be something to do with that little white house with red trim stuck back in the bushes. See, Frank, I was right. We've arrived. Pretty small place, huh? Three houses!" Jean's face had lengthened and she sounded a little downcast.

The car continued to bump forward and they rounded a curve to the left and confronted a narrow wooden bridge.

"Ah," Frank breathed. "The ferry captain told me about this bridge. Connects the two islands. He said we'd most likely find those two ladies he mentioned about three miles farther on." He inched the car onto the bridge. "Look at this thing, will ya?" Can just barely scape between these railings, and the center hump is so high I can't see if anything is coming at me. Suppose that truck ..."

The truck wasn't, but an ancient flatbed was. As Frank and Jean crested the hump a rickety old open pickup was easing onto the far side, heading toward them.

"What the hell do I do now?" Frank wanted to know, as he slowed down even more.

Jean's competitive spirit surged. "<u>Don't</u> slow down!" she cried, leaning so far forward her nose just missed the windshield. "Go on! Go on! Ram him! Push him off the bridge. We're farther on than that thing is. Go on, Frank. Smash into him!"

There was no need, however, for all that excitement. The little truck's horn went 'beep, beep' and a hand was thrust out of the driver's window and beckoned them on, as the truck slowly backed off the bridge and moved to the side of the road.

Frank pulled even with it, and leaned out. "Thanks a lot. Nice of you."

A young boy grinned back at them.

"That's okay. I'm the youngest, you know. Not by very much, though," he added, glancing at Jean, who preened noticeably.

"Ah," she said smiling. "That was very sweet. Where are you from, young man?"

"Illinois. Evanston, Illinois."

"No, I mean where are you from around here?"

Jerry pointed behind her.

"The other side of the bridge. Next to that little place with the red trim. My Aunt's. I'm visiting my Aunt."

"Oh, that's nice." Jean nodded again and kicked Frank's right leg. "Let's get moving." she muttered under her breath. "It's getting dark."

The road ahead ran between gigantic Australian pines that grew close together and towered some 40 feet in the air. The interlaced branches canopied the sandy lane below, and as their car entered this dark, feathery tunnel Jean sighed audibly. Forgotten were the bumpings and joltings and the stinging, buzzing insects. She gazed ahead, enthralled.

"This is unbelievable, Frank. An absolute fairyland! What a shame the light's fading. It must be glorious in the full daylight." She absentmindedly slapped a fat mosquito on her neck, leaving a little smear of blood. "No wonder Millie ..." she stopped and glanced guiltily at Frank.

"That old guy was right, Jean. It's blowing up out there, and it's turning chilly. The Gulf must be close by. I can taste a tanginess in the air. Funny. No houses. No people. No traffic."

The sandy road veered suddenly to the left for a hundred yards, then back to the right, and they found themselves bumping along between pines that bordered a wide sandy beach, with the open Gulf just beyond.

"Oh, my," Jean sighed again. "Back there I thought it couldn't get any better, but this is unbelievable. I don't suppose we could stop a minute?"

Frank shook his head. "Nope. Look at that water. It's riled up and there's a mist blowing in. I want to find us some place out of all this where we'll be dry and warm."

"You've got no soul. I've known it for some time, Frank. You've just got no soul!"

"Maybe not, but I'm going to take all my deficiencies and tuck 'em in somewhere safe, if at all possible. You can 'oh' and 'ah' all night on the beach if you want to, but not me."

A short drive further along they passed a little sign just off to the right announcing 'Mid-Island Inn' and blowing in the breeze below, hanging from two small metal hooks 'No Vacancy'. Several small huts were clustered tightly around a larger cottage like baby chicks around a mother hen. A few people milled about and one or two were out on the beach, stooped over at the water's edge.

"Let's try here. At least, there're some people about." Jean found her usual buoyancy returning. But Frank shook his head and drove on.

"Frank! Maybe that no-vacancy sign is from last winter and they've just forgotten to take it down. Come on, let's go back."

But Frank refused. They drove on, past Mid-Island, and past several driveway entrances leading to hidden homes with identifications signs like 'Dunrovin' or 'Crab Hollow' or 'Gopher Knoll' or 'Trail's End'.

Jean wanted to discuss this immediately.

"Frank, suppose you'd worked hard all you life and saved your pennies ..." She paused to swat a persistent mosquito.

Frank never took his eyes off the road. "I have worked hard all my life and I have saved my pennies. Except what you get your sticky little fingers on."

"No. I mean, really. Don't make fun. If you had and were able to build a home on a secluded island like this, would you name it some horrible name like those back there? Wouldn't you try to use some imagination?"

"Yeah, I would. I agree. Now be still for a few seconds. I think the road ends up ahead. I can see a sign up there."

Jean was aghast. "Oh, no. It can't be! That long, jolty ride and this is it? What about all those little old ladies that were supposed to be sitting in rocking chairs alongside the road, waiting for us?"

However, the road didn't end. It turned an abrupt right-angle away from the Gulf and ran cross-island toward the bay. A lopsided sign read 'Palm Avenue'. Around this turn, some 1000 yards, they found Miriam Hallman shaking a dust mop from the stoop of a small white cottage.

Frank pulled up beside her and leaned out of his window.

"Pardon me, but we're looking for a Mrs. Hallman. The ferry captain told us to contact her."

Miriam paused in her shaking and leaned on the mop handle.

"I'm Miriam Hallman. What can I do for you?"

She was a mid-western farm wife, severe and tense, with a stiff, straight back and no-nonsense hair parted in the middle and drawn tightly back into a small screw-knot.

Frank shuffled irritatedly as Jean breathed against his neck ... "How do you suppose she ever escaped Grant Wood?"

"We need lodging for the night. Can you help?"

"One night, or longer?"

Frank decided to be cautious.

"Just the one night."

Mrs. Hallman looked hesitant.

"Both of you?"

"Of course, both of us. I mean, here we are, aren't we?" Frank strove to hold down the irritation creeping into his voice.

Mrs. Hallman continued to look hesitant.

"I haven't any rooms open." She paused and then went on. "Of course, there's always the living room. I could put you up there, I suppose."

The living room aspect alarmed Jean.

"What kind of a bed ... flop down, or pull out?"

"Oh," and Mrs. Hallman's face creased in what was meant to be a smile. "I haven't any beds in the living room. Certainly not. But I've two real nice over-stuffed chairs. You'll be comfortable. I've rented 'em before, and folks compliment me."

Frank didn't know whether to be affronted or laugh. Suppose this was all. Ye gods!

"What do you rent 'em for?"

Mrs. Hallman, smelling a deal, relaxed considerably.

"Five dollars each. For one night. 'Course, I can reduce that to four dollars each if you stay longer."

Jean's fingernails were digging into Frank's back. He could feel her shaking. He didn't know if she was crying or laughing.

"Captain Bumpter also mentioned a Mrs. Kramdon. Is her place nearby?"

Mrs. Hallman stiffened again.

"Just down the road a piece. Other side. Palmetto Lodge she calls it. I think she's full, but you can check. 'Course, I don't promise to hold these chairs for you. Folks snap 'em up pretty quick this time of year."

At Palmetto Lodge they found a haven. Emmy Kramdon was scurrying about her back yard, trying to cover a lumber pile with an old, torn tarpaulin. Every time she spread it out and reached for a brick to weigh it down, the squally wind would tear it from her grasp and drop it in a heap to one side.

Not realizing he was addressing his destiny, Frank clambered from the car and ran toward her.

"Here," he called, "I'll toss it and pile on bricks, on the corners first. Then we'll work our way round with more bricks, and it'll soon be fixed."

Emmy sighed with relief. "Thank you, young man. Evan just dropped this off and Charlie'll kill me if it gets wet. He's almost finished fixing up our old garage. Should be done in a week or so. Has to be. We've got it rented from the middle of February on. He's over on Sanibel. I'm all by myself. Evan couldn't stay. Had to get on with other lumber deliveries." This all came out in one stream, without a pause. She ran out of breath toward the end and had to bend slightly over, like squeezing a bellows, to force out enough air for the final sentence. She straightened up with an audible intake, and smiled gently at Jean, who'd joined them.

Jean smiled back. "This Evan person ... was he driving a huge truck with lumber sticking out the back?"

Mrs. Kramdon nodded.

"Charlie needs this stuff for tomorrow and Evan offered to drive to town and get it for him. Charlie's my husband. 'Course, he'll pay Evan but it won't be much. He's such a sweet man, Evan is, and so's his wife. Sweet, I mean. Both Bertha and Evan. Always ready to help a body. Drives too fast, though. Like the wind." She was bending again, and squeezing around for air.

Jean found herself bending, also. Emmy's voice had gotten weaker and weaker as she ran out of breath and Jean had to lean down with her to catch the ending.

"We are familiar with this Evan. And his truck! You're right. He does drive like the wind. Or like a tornado!"

"Better come inside for a cup of tea. This wet, windy weather chills a body right to the bone, doesn't it? Close your car up tight, now." Emmy scurried off ahead of them toward a substantial house in the background.

Settled down and warm again, Jean balanced a steaming cup of strong tea on her knee and examined her hostess. Emmy Kramdon was eighty if she was a day. Spare, new pin neat, she was spry as a wren, which she resembled, with her thin hair twisted up in a top-knot, her starched white apron, and an ancient, shapeless wool sweater draped over her shoulders. Her ways were quick and bird-like, and her round brown eyes missed nothing.

Frank introduced them, and was well into their plight when Mrs. Kramdon held up one hand.

"Don't worry for a second. You dear children can stay in my garage. It's not finished yet, but you can use it. You'll be warm and dry and out of the bugs. Did you stop by Mrs. Hallman's place on your way down here?"

Jean nodded.

"She hasn't a room open. I know. Everybody always knows everything about everybody. Did she try to rent you her living room chairs?"

Jean nodded again.

Emmy threw back her head and trilled a high-pitched little laugh.

"Isn't she the very limit? Last winter a man and his wife spent two full weeks in those chairs. Imagine! And she got the same rental fee as if they had a whole room with a bed. How she can look folks in the face is beyond me."

Jean held out her cup for more tea.

"What is your rental charge, Mrs. Kramdon?"

Emmy's brown eyes twinkled in warm friendship.

"Land's sakes, I wouldn't dream of charging you anything. The garage isn't finished, as I told you, and Charlie will be back there most likely come daylight, sawing and hammering. If you can stand it, the noise and all, you can stay as long as you like ... for free. 'Course, you'll have to be out by February 12th as I'll need to spruce it up for the folks due February 15th, and I'm not as handy as I used to be." Bending and quivering her arms, she gasped for air.

The garage, a small building off by itself, proved to be a single, large open bedroom, with an incomplete kitchen in one corner and a bathroom in another. One entire wall consisted of two swinging garage doors firmly bolted on the inside. Jean busily began unpacking while Frank explored.

"Nothing comes out of the shower-head!"

"How do you know?"

"I twisted the knob."

"What about the toilet?"

"That's okay. At least, there's water in the bowl."

"Thank Heaven for that," Jean said, unfolding and hanging clothes on nails stuck in a wall. "Did you ask our little fairy godmother if there's anywhere to eat? I'm starved."

"Yep. Next door. A small restaurant called Bide-A-Wee. Just 500 yards down the road."

"How handy! Wonder if there's any food in it?"

Frank sank to the corner of the large double bed.

"Remember, Jean, you promised to be sweet." He patted the mattress. "This feels great." He flopped onto his back. "I could stay just like this for the entire night. I'm exhausted!" He started to laugh. "That ride. Wasn't it unbelievable? Worst part is that we have to do the whole business in reverse tomorrow."

A sudden banging and clattering on the roof, like a herd of wild horses stomping about, drowned out Jean's reply. She raced across the room and fell on the bed beside him, her eyes wild. With her mouth pressed against his ear she screamed "What is that? Make it stop, Frank!" Suddenly there was an abrupt silence which Jean wasn't prepared for. She continued to yell into Frank's ear at the top of her lungs. "I can't hear myself think!"

Frank rolled away and rubbed his head.

172

"Damn it, Jean. You nearly broke my ear-drum! Must you always be so damn demonstrative? Damn! Damn!"

Jean was hunched on the bed, her knees drawn up to her chin and her arms wrapped around.

"I hate this place! I want to go back to peaceful old Madison Avenue. Why were all those horses prancing around on the roof?"

"Rain. The roof's tin and it was rain." Frank was at a window and he beckoned her over. "Look! It's wild out there. Trees and bushes blown almost flat and every so often rain pelts down, then stops. Here it comes again!"

Rain fell in such sheets that they couldn't see across the little yard to Mrs. Kramdon's house. The noise from the roof was unbelievable. Talk was impossible. They sat on the edge of the bed and just looked at each other.

When the squall passed and the turmoil outside eased up, Jean reached for her poncho and headed for the door.

"Come on, Frank. Let's dash down the road before it starts up again. That dinky little eating joint won't know what's hit it."

The Bide-A-Wee Restaurant was cozy and warm. Two tables, in opposite corners of the little room were occupied. The owners, Marge and Stan Brown, were bustling about behind a counter, and everyone seemed to be talking at once. They quieted down as Jean and Frank came through the door and sat on bar stools at the counter. Jean looked about expectantly, and drew back. She thought she was having double vision. She nudged Frank.

"Look behind us, over there in the corner, where that old lady is sitting by herself. She's doing something marvelous with mirrors."

Stan handed each of them a cup of coffee and a little handwritten menu and said "Hi," and Marge waved a floury hand. Frank responded and then glanced behind him. He leaned toward Jean and hissed ... "Don't you dare make a scene. That's two old ladies back there!"

"Thank God," Jean breathed back. "For a minute I thought my eyesight was going. They're exactly alike."

"Well, face front and stop staring, will you please."

Jessie and Ginger had finished their meal and were ready to leave. They stood at exactly the same time, as if hoisted on strings by an invisible hand, and gathered up purses and cigarettes. As they called good night to Marge and Stan, Jessie stooped over to tie her shoe.

"You go ahead, Bud, and start the car," she called to Ginger. "It's your turn to drive." Then, in stentorian tones she added, "Don't you just hate New Yorkers! They're so rude!"

"See?" Frank stuck a finger in Jean's ribs. "We've only been on this island a few hours and already they hate us. I knew you'd do it. Did you have to stare like that?

Stan had come up with coffee and he laughed as he put it down.

"Oh, don't mind the twins. Everybody stares the first time they see 'em. They're used to it."

"What was all that green netting they were carrying?"

"Bug gear," Marge called from down the counter. "They're heading for the bridge to snook fish and they wear that stuff to keep the bugs off. Great fishermen. Keep me stocked all winter. Better have some."

They had fish. And more coffee. And pecan pie.

"That's the best fish I've ever eaten." Jean smiled as she said it, looking full and contented. "I'm just sorry I'm so stuffed or I could eat it all over again."

Frank was pushing a small piece of pecan around his plate. He grinned down at Marge.

"You know, I didn't realize pecan pie could taste like that. The closest I've come is Lindy's back in New York ... but this is better." With a grand gesture he bowed to Marge. "You're to be congratulated, Madam."

Marge chuckled and wiped her hands down the front of her halter-apron.

"I don't make the damn things. We get 'em from Jack and Ted across the street, over there."

"What's over there?" Jean wanted to know.

"The bakery. Great stuff. Really great, ain't it, Stan?"

Stan nodded. He was delivering beer to the other two customers, off in a corner, two mousey little ladies huddled together.

"I'm sorry Ida. I'm fresh out of Lowenbrau. All I've got's Pabst. I'm real sorry."

Ida snuffed out her cigarette in a cereal dish full of sand. "That's fine. Let me have the Pabst. Ruta and I've got to go then anyway. So it's no harm. I like Pabst." She smiled over at Jean and raised her beer in a tentative acknowledgment. "Too bad the weather's so wild and blowey. For you, that is. We love it. Been waiting for weeks for a nor'-easter like this."

Jean was full and warm and felt expansive. She left the bar and crossed to Ida's table.

"What do you want filthy weather like this for?" she asked.

Ida laughed and lit another cigarette. Ruta answered for them. She squashed her floppy hat well down on her head and peeped out from under the rim, her face well hidden in the shadows.

"It's the shelling! The beach will be covered with new stuff and lots of it will be alive. Ida wants to go now but I'm draggin' my feet. It's too clumsy in the wind and the rain. My hat keeps blowin' off. We get soaked. The flash-light'll get wet and short out. Best wait for dawn. 'Course, if it wasn't rainin' I'd love to go now. We've been waitin' a long time for this."

"Shelling? What's that?"

Ruta and Ida exchanged quick glances. Ida tapped her cigarette against the sand ashtray.

"If you didn't come over here for the shelling, what're you here for?" There was no rancor in the question, just interest.

Jean shrugged. "Friends back home suggested we come. We don't know nothin' from nothin', except we hate it. How do you stand it? The bugs.

That terrible road. This filthy weather. Our shower doesn't work and we can't even take a bath. I feel dirty!"

"Did you have reservations?"

Jean shook her head. She was beginning to feel sorry for herself again. "No. We just drove over."

Ida was all concern.

"Have you a place now?"

Jean nodded.

"Where?"

"A Mrs. Kramdon is letting us stay the night in her garage."

"You poor dears." Ida clucked her tongue. "Not knowing the islands and getting into all this. Emmy Kramdon's garage isn't done yet. Not fit for a pig, actually. Oh, my!"

Jean sighed and said in her best Pollyanna manner ..." Oh, we'll be all right. We'll make do. And tomorrow the sun will shine." She wished she believed it. Sure, the sun would shine ... on the ass-end of their car, because she and Frank would be waiting for that first ferry off the island.

Ida was still conciliatory.

"'Course, Emmy is sweet as can be. She'll take as good care of you as she can. You'll be fine. Why don't you come along with Ruta and me tomorrow morning. Best way to get a quick taste of shell gathering. Will it be all right with you, Ruta?"

Ruta nodded.

"Sure. I don't care."

But Jean drew back.

"Oh, I don't know. I don't think so. Thanks, anyway. It was very kind of you to invite me. But Frank and I are heading to the mainland on that first ferry, so I won't be able to. Will I, Frank? Frank! Frank!"

Frank didn't hear. He was leaning on the bar, his head close to Stan's and they were both talking at the same time. Jean frowned slightly, then looked puzzled. Shelling? Something new? Why not? She could find out what it was all about and then pack up and by noon they could leave for the ferry.

"What if it's still raining?"

"Oh, no. If it rains, we don't go."

"Bugs? Are there bugs on the beach?"

"Not apt to be after this blow. The wind's heavy in from the Gulf, right now. It'll most likely drop during the night but still be strong enough in the morning to keep the skeeters off the beach. Come on." Ida smiled expansively.

A little voice deep inside Jean's mind cautioned "Careful, careful ... you'll hate yourself ... you'll wish you hadn't," but she shook her head in irritation.

"Okay. Sure. I'll come. What time?"

Ida puffed on her cigarette. She was about to reply but Ruta pushed her chair back and stood up. Gathering her things, including a strange-looking stick with straw hanging from it, she announced that they'd meet there at the restaurant at seven in the morning, sharp.

"We gotta beat all the other shellers if we want a crack at the best stuff. Meet here at seven, grab a cup of coffee, maybe a doughnut if Marge has any, and we'll be off. You have one of these?" She thrust forward the stick with its straw danglers.

Jean pulled slightly back.

"No. What is it?"

Ruta swooped the thing this way and that about her body, her head, her back, her legs. Jean noticed, as she watched in amazement, that Ruta was barefooted ... tiny little feet, like a child's ...

"It's my bug swisher. I made it out of palm fronds. Cora Chisholm down across the bridge sells 'em for a dollar each but I can't afford that so I make my own. I've extra. I'll bring you one. Gotta go." The door opened and shut and with her swisher swinging she left, not seeming to mind the pouring rain.

Ida followed but at the door she turned and with a hint of Old-World formality, nodded to Jean.

"Pleased to know you. We'll meet tomorrow. If you're a little late, don't worry. But not too late, now." She smiled again. "Good night."

Back at the garage, standing in the center of the room and shaking rain drops all about, Jean wanted to know what was so all-fired important about Frank's talk with Stan that he hadn't heard her call.

"Here I was, facing a major decision in my life and not knowing which way to turn, and there you were, lost in a gossip session with a cook in the middle of a forsaken island!"

Frank grinned at her.

"I heard you. I didn't answer on purpose. It's time you face head-on these sticky little situations you get yourself into. Stiffens the character, you know." He'd shed his wet clothes and was shivering in his shorts. "Where's a towel?"

She threw him one and stood there laughing, arms akimbo.

"You know what? I think ..."

"Hold that thought, Jeannie. I'll be right back. I've gotta go potty." He ducked into the bathroom.

Seconds later he reappeared in the doorway, crestfallen and shoulders slumped. Jean could see wet footprints stretching behind him to a slowly expanding puddle.

"It overflowed?"

"It overflowed."

"It's plugged up?"

"It's plugged up."

"You're walking in it?"

"I'm walking in it!"

"Barefoot?"

"Barefoot!"

"Great!"

"Let's kill ourselves!"

As they started to mop up with bath towels, Jean gave a snort of laughter. His voice dripping irritation, Frank asked what was so funny.

"Remember where these towels came from? Millie Shapiro! Oh, I can't stand it." She chortled on.

"No shower! No toilet! And it's getting cold. I suppose there's no heat, either. Is it getting cold or is it my imagination?"

"It's chilly," Jean agreed.

"I'll have to go see old what's-her-name."

Jean shook her head.

"You can't. Her house is dark. She's not home."

"She's home!" Frank struggled into his wet pants. "Where th' hell else would she be, on this godforsaken, bug-ridden sandspit in the middle of a rain forest?"

Jean's compulsion for neatness, even in conversation, rushed to the fore.

"It's not exactly a rain forest. True, there are a few trees and the rain ..."

"Jean! Let up! Just don't poke around with all that semantics stuff and make things worse. Gimmee your poncho. I could use some galoshes, too. Why didn't I remember to bring 'em?"

"Well, dear, at that time you never expected to be slopping about in a rain forest with sand ... and bugs ..."

Frank stomped out, slamming the door and scattering raindrops as he went. When he came back, Jean was in bed.

"Mrs. Kramdon was home. See! We had a long talk. I think she was very happy to have company. We can use her john if we need to and she'll leave her door unlatched. She also said her husband Charlie hadn't yet worked out any heating arrangement so she gave me this electric heater. Thank God we have lights. She'll get a plumber first thing in the morning. Move over. I'm coming in. Or do you want to visit Emmy's facilities?"

Jean was deep in bedclothes.

"No," she mumbled. "Don't have to!"

"Damn camel," Frank said, plugging the heater into a wall socket. Immediately darkness fell.

"Great! Oh, great! I blew the whole system! Where'd you go?"

"I'm right here. Haven't moved. Really don't care about anything any more. I'm going to sleep." She turned back one corner of the covers. "Come on, climb in. I want to snuggle."

Frank nodded, though Jean couldn't see. "We'd better. It's gonna be a long, cold night!"

It was just breaking dawn when Frank sat up.

"Damn. Can't wait any longer. Have to see Emmy. Are you awake?"

"No."

"Want to go with me?"

"No."

"Don't you have to?"

"No."

"I don't see how you do it."

"Do what?"

"Go so long."

"Don't you mean that you don't see how I go so long <u>without</u> doing it?"

"That's what I said."

"No. You said ... 'don't see how you do it'. I suggest that what you really should have said was ... 'don't see how you don't do it.'"

"For God's sake, Jean. Let up, can't cha?"

Jean scrunched lower under the covers and made a little tent over her head with one corner.

"Be careful. Don't hurry, now." Her voice trailed off.

"I'll be careful and I'll be right back. Don't go leaping about, okay? Just stay."

"I don't wanna."

"Don't want to what?"

"Play."

"I didn't say play. I said stay."

"I thought you said play. If I'm gonna play at this midnight hour, it'll have to be with somebody really spectacular." She snoozed off.

Tony Gallegar, the plumber, <u>was</u> spectacular. Emmy Kramdon, early to bed, was also early up and before the sky lightened she had run across her yard, down Palm Avenue, past Marge's restaurant to the Gallegar's home and asked Tony to stop by and unplug her garage toilet. She failed to mention that she had tenants. Tony was scheduled for a job on Sanibel that day so he decided to leave home earlier than usual and fix Emmy's toilet first.

Jean was drifting along on a delightful, gauzy shopping trip through Bloomingdale's when the door slammed and snapped her back to life.

"My," she said. "That was quick."

"I haven't done anything, yet," a rumbly, masculine voice answered. "Oh, Migod! What're you doing here?"

Jean cracked open one eye. "Oh, boy" she breathed to herself. "I must still be in Bloomies. I think I'll buy two of these!"

"I live here," she answered, looking him up and down. Standing six feet two inches tall, with shoulders like Atlas and arms like piano legs, Tony was imposing indeed. Jean eyed him cautiously, drawing the bedclothes up under her chin. "I'm married," she announced, not realizing that this admission was inane and he hadn't asked.

"So'm I." Tony replied.

"What do you want?" She was ashamed of the tremor in her voice.

"Oh, I'm sorry. I'm Tony, the plumber. I'm supposed to unplug your toilet."

"Is that all?" Jean was furious with herself. Why couldn't she just duck under the covers and leave well enough alone.

"Are you having other problems?"

"No-o-o-o. But if I do, where can I find you?" What was her problem, and without any make-up yet.

By this time, Tony was in the bathroom, rattling tools and flushing water. "Oh, just let Mrs. Kramdon know. She'll get me."

"That'll be fine. Oh, Mr. Tony, there is one other thing. I think Frank fused the electric box last night when he plugged in a heater. Is there an electrician on the island?"

"Sure is." Tony had reappeared, and stood calmly at the foot of the bed, just as if he was used to unplugging toilets at 5:30 in the morning for unknown ladies still in bed. Who knows? Maybe he was, Jean thought. "Roy Coggins. I go right past his place. I'll tell him. Your toilet's fine, now. I gotta go. Bye. Nice meeting you." And he was gone.

"Well," Jean thought to herself, "wasn't that something. Soon's I quiet down, think I'll snooze a bit longer. Maybe I can return to Bloomies and see where they stock their Tonys."

Jean was sound asleep again when a long electric drill plunged through the wall slightly above the bed, buzzing like a swarm of angry hornets. It barely missed her head and scattered sawdust all over her face.

She lay for a second, frozen in fright, one eye staring at the twisting, throbbing monster only inches from her face. Then she went into full action. Jumping out of bed and grabbing a chair, she pounded on the wall.

"Stop that! Stop this instant. Who do you think you are? Take that thing out. NOW! Do you hear me? Pull it out and leave me be!" she added inelegantly.

The drill stopped spinning and slowly withdrew, as though it had been bested in battle and needed to regroup to fight again.

As soon as it disappeared from the wall, Jean glued her mouth to the hole.

"Who's out there? Who are you, rushing around, drilling innocent women still in their beds?" She tossed back her head and yelled "I hate you. I hate this place!" She started to sag down the face of the wall. "I'm tired ... and filthy ... and hungry. Why is all this happening to me?" She moaned and collapsed in a heap on the floor.

Just at this moment, Frank returned from Emmy Kramdon's. He found her lying there, sobbing.

"What in hell are you doing now? Can't you be good for five seconds? Get up!"

"I can't," Jean whimpered. "I'm paralyzed!"

"Paralyzed? Well, we'll see about that!" He grabbed one arm and hauled her upright. As Jean started to sag again, Frank hissed between clenched teeth ..." If you don't stand on your own two feet, I'm gonna drop you on your head." He dragged her to the bed and cuddled her in his arms. "What's the trouble, Jeanie girl? Had a bad dream?"

Jean lay back and dragged Frank down beside her.

"Hold me, Frank. Hold me tight. Maybe it was all a bad dream. You'll never believe ... kiss me and tell me the sun's shining."

"The sun's shining!" He was planting a long, lingering kiss as Roy Coggins bounded in the door. Roy took one look at the two intertwined on the bed and recoiled.

"Oh, boy. I'm in the wrong place, that's for sure." He turned and rushed back toward the door. Then he stopped. Staring into the blank doorway he called over his shoulder ... "Nice to meetcha. I mean don't let me disturb ya. I mean, enjoy yourselves. Oh, God!" and he rushed out.

The two on the bed were frozen, goggle-eyed! As the door banged shut Jean squeezed Frank's arm.

"See! It's been like that all morning. Thousands of people in and out. Take me away! I want to go back to the peace and quiet of Madison Avenue. Please!" She buried her head in his chest. "By the way," she added, "the toilet works!"

By seven a.m., somewhat mollified and wearing sneakers and denims, Jean kissed Frank in a haphazard manner and headed for the restaurant. The sun was up and shining brightly. The day sparked crystal-clear. A stiff westerly wind, nippy and salt-laden, fluttered the seagrape leaves and tossed the rusty palm fronds. There was promise in the air of a warm balmy day.

Left to himself, Frank grinned with glee at being alone. Then he frowned. The morning suddenly seemed to stretch forever. What would he do for five long hours? He decided to explore the island.

Standing by the side of the little road, trying to decide whether to go left toward the beach or right toward the bay, he spied the three women hurrying toward him, bent slightly into the wind. Jean was in the middle and the other two were talking and nodding back and forth across her front. What an odd-looking trio. Frank lifted one hand in a halfhearted salute, but they didn't see him and hurried along the road. He decided to explore the bay-side. After breakfast! First he'd see if Marge had coffee and maybe an egg.

By late morning he'd made the circle and was back at the garage. He'd discovered the post office and chatted with Bertha. He'd meandered out to the end of the mailboat dock and looked across to Buck Key where he'd spotted the corner of the Farlow's cowshed, just visible in the clear, white morning light. He'd visited Jasper Dugan and been shown the coconut "farm", each nut tucked snugly in wet seaweed at the water's edge and sprouting energetically in an obvious effort to escape from nut-hood to stand tall and sturdy as a mature tree. Why does everything want to grow up so soon? In this quiet, lovely place why not strive for endless childhood, instead of the other way around? Frank pondered all this as he wandered on and turned into Gustave Kroen's yard. Gustave was burying chunks of shark around the long line of flourishing banana plants and had little time for gossiping. Spying Murph's dock off to the right, Frank headed that way.

He found Murph sitting on a bench outside the taproom, repairing a net. Unlike Gustave Kroen, Murph was talkative and expansive. As they chatted, Pearlie joined them, leaning against the doorjamb, beer in one hand and broom in the other. It was Pearlie who steered Frank to Boozie Chuffer.

"Name's really Charlene. She's from Tampa. In real estate, I hear. Comes down here regular as clockwork to escape all that bother. Mostly stays drunk. We call her Boozie. She's here now. Owns those two little cottages over there." Pearlie pointed her beer can, and Frank glanced upbay to where he could just see two cottages built right on the edge of the water among swaying palms and tall pines. "If Emmy Kramdon's place is too torn apart for you," Pearlie went on, "Boozie'd maybe rent you the cottage she ain't usin'. Why'n't you drop over an' talk to her?"

Later, in an unfamiliar mood of being suspended in limbo, of being distanced from reality, of sitting off to one side while the rest of the world went by, Frank walked slowly across Emmy Kramdon's yard and entered the garage. He found Jean sitting on the floor surrounded by sand and seaweed and piles of shells.

"Where'd you get all that junk?" he softly asked.

Without looking up, Jean answered.

"On the beach. I know it's junk, but isn't it great?" She held up one shell. "This is called a lacy murex! Imagine! It has a name. Isn't that great?" She glanced up at Frank and her face was radiant. Putting aside the shell, she picked up another and rubbed it between her fingers.

"Where were you? Where'd you go?" she asked.

"Oh, around. Here and there. Met a few people." He paused and slumped back on the bed. "I can see what Millie Shapiro meant. Strange place. All the people I met were different, of course, but they were all the same, too. Their mood, I mean. No, that's not exactly right. It isn't a conscious thing at all. Somehow, this place is all to itself. The real world doesn't get in. It's almost as if the other world doesn't exist at all. Not for these folks. This is all there is. I can't figure if it's them ... or the island. Is it a geographic situation and the island does it, being so far out and cut off? Or is it the people?"

Jean had been watching his face as he spoke, and now she nodded.

"Yes," she said thoughtfully. "I feel it, too. The peacefulness is so complete it's almost palpable. I keep having this strange sense of being in control, of being me, and not having to brace myself for fear someone will rush at me and steal it all away. I've never felt quite like this before."

They fell silent. The wind had died and flower scents drifted in the open window. Jean fiddled with her beach gatherings.

"Are you asleep?" she wanted to know.

"Yes."

"Do you want to pack and leave?"

"No."

"No you don't want to pack, or no you don't want to leave?"

"Neither."

"Stay another day?"

"Yep."

"This is really a ratty set-up. Are you sure you can stand it for another night?"

"I want to move into Boozie Chuffer's bay cottage."

"And who exactly is Boozie Chuffer?"

"I met her this morning. Lovely woman. Tight as a tick, but real nice. She has two cottages built right on the water. She's in one and she says we can use the other, if we clean it."

"If we clean it?"

Frank sat up and patted the mattress beside his leg. "Jeanie, leave all that stuff and come over here." His eyes gleamed with excitement. "It's really great. This woman, pretty grim really, has these two cottages. She doesn't rent 'em, which is why she leaves 'em dirty. Comes down from Tampa on long, extended weekends to 'unwind'. 'Course all she does is drink. She was amusing, weaving around, waving these two keys at me. Said she kept both houses empty, as she always arrived 'exhausted' and never knew which key she'd find first. Whichever one she did, that's the cottage she flopped into. Since she was already here, we could have the other one, at least 'til she decides to leave."

"Is this a one-room shack?"

"No. It's not a shack at all. It's a whole house. Living room, dinette, kitchen and two bedrooms ... bath, porch ... and a dock. I was out on the dock. Little fish everywhere and huge brown rubbery-looking birds flopping into the water after 'em." He grinned from ear to ear.

"You really want to do this?"

"I really do."

Jean looked at him long and hard. Then gathering up his hands in hers, she nodded slowly.

"Okay. Let's go. I'll clean the damn shack. But only on one condition!"

"What's that?"

"That you promise never, ever to tell Millie Shapiro!"

14

The brush fire that charred most of Sanibel that winter started from a cigarette carelessly tossed aside by an Audubon enthusiast as he strolled the southern end of the island, seeking an osprey nest rumored to be atop a dead pine bordering the Sanibel River. The rising wind that discouraged the bird-watcher fanned the little ember into a tiny glow that first licked the undergrowth for a foothold, and then quickly burst into an angry orange-red wall of flame. Hungrily it consumed everything in its path as it bent before the wind and raced westward toward Captiva.

A certain camaraderie which might otherwise never have occurred sprang up between islanders and northern visitors as they battled together to stem the spread of the conflagration. Everything on both islands was interrupted — even Colonel MacDuff's construction on the Sanibel side of Blind Pass Bridge as the workmen laid aside their tools and ran with all the others to fight the fire. The resulting devastation of the vast sawgrass area provided a plausible, if untrue, solution to the later "Great Panther Scare".

•

Charlie Kramdon bumped along on his ancient tractor, dragging a cart heaped high with palm fronds and yard rakings from around the semicircle of little cottages that made up Crescent Hotel. If the protesting cart held together long enough he'd dump the debris in his secret pit a bit farther along the sandy path running through the sawgrass behind his hotel. The cart squeaks got louder and Charlie made a mental note to get his grease gun from Emmy's Palmetto Lodge the next time he went to Captiva. Poor old Emmy. She'd been a good wife all these years. A good wife and a good companion. They'd had great times together. But as she got older she got bossy. Bossy and shrively. Not that it was her fault. She couldn't be blamed for that, God knew. And he'd shrunk, too. But it was different, somehow, with a woman. She'd shrivelled into one little bent-over wrinkle, seemed like, and all the interesting parts had gotten smaller. Never were too big at best. Anyway, he'd lost interest and the bossing got worse, so he'd fixed up that property on Captiva and put her in it. Later, with Emmy safely out of the way, he'd started seeing Prissy. Little ole gal, cute as a button. Lived in a tin shack around by Rigby's Store on the bay side. Not too smart, but that didn't make no nevermind. Every time he'd get anywhere near the store some character'd yell ... "yessir, here's Charlie. Now he ain't no orange man, no sirree. Charlie, he's after grapefruit!" ... and everybody'd guffaw and slap their legs.

Half asleep, chewing the frayed end of a big black cigar, Charlie ruminated on, gazing generally across the sawgrass ahead as he bumped and jolted along. Suddenly his eyes snapped into focus on an ominous column of smoke rolling skyward off to his right. He slammed down on the brake pedal and the old tractor promptly stalled. He sat for a second, wondering what to do first. It'd been so long. There was no fire fighting equipment he knew of on either island, 'cept that no-count water wagon Roy Coggins dragged around on Captiva. Not much anyone could do, actually. Let the damn thing run. Try to contain it with burn-backs. Notify folks. Don't panic. Think ... think ...

Let's see, now. This stiff east wind'd push the burn on down the island. It'd speed along front-wise but expand slowly side-wise. Shouldn't jump the river, if you could call that little creek-slough a river. Rigby and the folks along the bay-side were out of direction and safe. From the position of the smoke, Crescent was too far left, and safe. But Carla Wilson and the Sanibel Inn, midway down the island and on the Gulf, were directly in line. And Sally-Anne and Doobie! It'd eat 'em up first thing as it roared along in front of this wind. Must notify folks. Then try to back-burn. Only way. He abandoned the tractor as too slow and hobbled on foot back toward Crescent and his truck.

●

Sally-Anne had stayed home that morning. For the past six nights she'd helped Ida Benson clean and set up that little grocery store. That and normal work each day had tired her out and she needed a rest. When she rested, Doobie rested. They rocked side by side on their little porch, talking softly of this and that. Sally was commenting on their daughter Pruella's latest pregnancy ...

"Lawsy me, Doobie. She's swole agin. How many's this make ... foteen ... fi-teen ... I lose track. How you 'spose she feeds all them mouths, with her Wallace makin' only a dolla a hour? Beats me. What you 'spose that there smoke is, over yonder? Hit's blowin' this way, too."

"Taint no white man pullin' on his pipe, that's f'sure." Doobie cackled aloud.

Sally snapped her head up.

"I'll cackle yo', Doobie Denkins! Thet's a brush burn, sure 'nuf. An' with this heah wind a'hind it, it means trouble. We'd best git busy!"

"Long way off, Sally. Don't git all riley, now. Let the white folks tend it. They mos' likely started it. 'Sides, it'll take a mighty huge fire to jump clear 'cross that road out there an' the yard you done cleaned last month all round the house. That'll protec' us, like as not."

"No thanks to you. If you'd hep't, we'd have a cleared patch twice as deep."

"Twern't no need fer me to budge. You was doin' fine, all by yo'sef. 'Sides, we only got us one machet." He chuckled again.

Sally was searching her mind for a pulverizing retort when Charlie Kramdon came bumping in from Rabbit Road.

"Sally! Doobie! We got us a burn. Still several miles over to the east but that wind behind it won't help any. Wanted to see if you folks were here, Gonna help us fight it?"

Sally stood up as Charlie drove into the yard.

"Sho 'nuf, Mr. Charlie. We'll be fightin', if'n it gits this fur."

Charlie spun his truck around and leaned out the door frame.

"Oh, she'll get this far. With this wind, no doubt about it. It's good you've got this clearin'. We'll use it as a gatherin' spot. If anybody comes by, tell 'em. I'm gonna run the island and notify everybody." He disappeared down the road in a cloud of dust.

Sally-Anne sat down and resumed her rocking.

"Good we got us that heap o' gunny sacks back in the lean'to with Shadrack. We can give 'em to folks, fer slappin'."

"No, we ain't!" Doobie stopped rocking and banged his feet in a rapid tattoo for emphasis. "No, we ain't! Them's our'n. You can use one, if'n you have to. But the res' stay's jest whar they is. An' you leave that ole mule alone, heah?"

"What about you? You gonna fight?"

"I'll do my fire-fightin' right chere, in this heah chair. You go do yer slappin', gal, an' I'se gonna keep scoah."

●

Carla Wilson untied the linen towel she was wearing on her head to protect her hair from dust and tossed it into a nearby chair.

"Oh, Charlie, how distressing." True to her efficient approach to life's problems, she was immediately all business. "I'll take Mama and run her down to Mid-Island. Cordelia Winslow'll see she's taken care of. And I'll tell that young lad, what's his name, who delivers around down there ... Jerry, isn't it?

... I'll tell him to alert all of Captiva and get those men up here. Gabe'll round up my help and they'll take along shovels and hoes and machetes and all our gunny sacks ... and you run the bay-side and tell folks over there and then get back to Doobie's and Sally's and organize things. Did I miss anything?" She had her purse and was rummaging for her car keys.

Charlie grinned. He admired Carla Wilson, and he loved her, which was more important. She was one of God's good people. Her folks had homesteaded the land where the Sanibel Inn stood, and when her Pa died in '33, some say from overwork, she gave up her school teaching and took over. During the past fifteen years, by grinding away from dawn to dusk with hardly a pause, she'd managed to double the size of the Inn, and build an enviable reputation for hospitality and excellent food that reached far beyond the island confines. The gleaming crystal beach stretching along that section of Sanibel was known worldwide for its superb shelling.

"Got any guests?" Charlie asked.

Carla glanced from the corner of her eye.

"Of course. Haven't you? Why?"

"Maybe you can send the men-folks on over."

"Well, I can always ask 'em. Some are pretty finicky, you know. We will see. Run along, now. We'll get nowhere, jawing here all day."

Jerry was at Mid-Island, loading luggage onto his truck for later delivery to the mailboat when Carla drove rapidly up to the Inn door. He gently carried Miss Josie into the lounge, with Carla bustling along behind.

"Careful, Jerry. Mama's so frail. Easy. Don't bump that door jamb. Here. Put her in this overstuffed. Are you comfy, Mama?"

Miss Josie nodded slowly and raised a veined hand to Jerry in thanks.

Carla explained the crisis, and added ... "So stop whatever you're doing and dash about the island and notify everyone. Evan and Murph. Marge and Stan. Stan will want to help fight. But first of all, find Roy and get him started up to Rabbit Road with that water wagon. Hurry along, now. Off you go."

"Miss Carla," Jerry said, "there're two carpenters working down at the bridge. Maybe, as you drive by, you could stop and tell 'em."

"Certainly. Of course," she answered. "Hurry along, now. Find Roy first off. It takes him so long to drag that contraption up the road."

Jerry nodded and raced off. He found Roy's truck parked in front of Ida Benson's new store.

"Come on down to my shack and help me connect the wagon," Roy said. "I just loaded her up yesterday, thank God. She's a real bitch to hitch when she's loaded."

The water wagon was off to one side of Roy's clearing, facing out. A large wooden tank bound in brass binding and painted fire-engine red, it lay on its side on a sturdy wheeled cart. Hoses were lashed to both sides and two gas-fired pumps were positioned front and back. The forward pump sucked water into the barrel through one hose, from any convenient source, Gulf, bay, slough ... and the rear pump forced water from the barrel out through a second long hose onto the fire. A complicated series of hand-operated valves controlled the flows. A triangle of hefty steel bars was bolted to the front cross-beam, the forward point drilled to receive a bolt. A similar barred contraption was affixed to Roy's truck and when the holes were aligned and a sturdy carriage bolt dropped through, the truck and the wagon could lumber together slowly along the road.

"Remember, she holds 500 gallons, so she's heavy. And all that water slopping back and forth, wonder she doesn't pull the ass end of my truck right off."

Jerry nodded in sympathy, but felt pressure from the urgency of the situation.

"Gotta go. Have you seen Evan anywhere?"

"Yep. Saw both Evan and Murph just a bit ago, talking out on the dock. You go on over there. We're all set here, so I'll head on up to Sanibel."

Returning from the dock and heading back along Palm Avenue, Jerry saw Marge standing in the restaurant doorway. He turned into her parking lot.

"There's a fire ... "

"Yeah. I heard." She motioned for him to go along up the road. "Go along. I'll tell Stan soon's he gets back from the post office. He'll be up and will bring Ted from the bakery with him."

Jerry backed out, almost running over Jean and Frank who were ambling up to the restaurant for breakfast. How'd Marge know about the fire? Hadn't been any time at all since Miss Carla told him. How'd she know? He drove on up toward the Gulf.

"What was that all about?" Jean asked, as she and Frank reached Marge's door. Jean was swishing bugs at a great rate. Marge was inside, swishing at her side of the door as they came in and sat at the counter.

"Fire up on Sanibel. Jerry says he heard from Carla Wilson that it's a big one. The men-folk'll collect and beat it out. Hope it doesn't burn anybody up in the meantime."

"Could it? I mean, is it apt to?"

"Can't tell. I recall years ago, back behind Sarasota or somewhere's up there, a fire burned a whole island ... homes and livestock ... everything. It all went. Could here, too, I suppose. How you want your eggs?"

Jean reached over and grabbed Frank's arm.

"Let's go! Let's help 'em fight. You go get the car and I'll help Marge pack us a brunch. Go on, now!" She pushed him out the door.

Adam Crisfield was raking the front yard of his Captiva Inn as Jerry turned the corner at the Gulf. He slowed and called ... "Brush fire on Sanibel" ... and Adam waved one hand, signifying he understood.

Jerry next ducked into the old McClain house and picked up Didi.

"We gotta rush. Damn thing'll most likely be out by the time we get there and we'll miss all the fun."

But Didi was serious.

"Might not. The breeze is stiff and getting stronger. And think of all the wildlife. Rabbits and deer, if there are any, can all bound ahead of the fire. But what about all the land turtles and the snakes and baby birds ... they'll all cook. Ugh! How sad!"

"Thought you hated snakes." Jerry grinned at her but she didn't grin back.

"I do. To touch. Or if any should crawl on me. But not to just kill or to slowly cook to death. The wildlife balance will be all upset. What about that?"

By this time they had crossed the bridge and were pulling into Aunt Ag's driveway. The three ladies were sitting on the porch and seemed to be expecting them. He didn't answer Didi but clambered out of the truck.

"There's a fire ..."

"We know. We heard," Agnes interrupted ..." Maude wants to go with you. Cora and I'll stay here."

"Can you squeeze me in, Jerry?" Maude was in her fighting garb, her belt and hatchet already strapped on, and she leaned forward eagerly.

"Sure. Plenty of room." Ye Gods! Again. How'd they know?

"How'd you know?" He vocalized his thought.

Agnes was vague.

"I don't know. I'm not sure. In the air, I guess. Actually, I think Maude heard it from Carla. Maude was pruning that big hibiscus out there when Carla pulled into that thing, whatever it is, that MacDuff's building across the road, and told those carpenters. They took off up the road right behind her. As they drove off they asked Maude to put up a sign for Colonel MacDuff."

"Aunt Ag, will you meet the boat and tend to the deliveries if I'm not back in time?"

Agnes agreed and Maude climbed into the truck with Jerry and Didi and off they went, bumping down the sandy road, trailing a swirling cloud of dust. In no time at all they drew up behind Roy, lumbering slowly along with still a good distance to travel. As they passed him Roy smiled wanly across at them and waved.

Minutes later, as they turned right onto Rabbit Road, they could see smoke not too far off to the left, and now and again a lick of flame shooting high above the waving sawgrass.

"Mercy," Maude breathed. "Looks like a big one. It's gonna be nasty, bottlin' that thing up."

Charlie Kramdon was standing spraddle-legged in front of Sally's and Doobie's shack as Jerry pulled up. Dispatching fighters up and down the road, the line stretching out now for better than a half-mile in each direction, Charlie repeated at the top of his lungs his attack plan ...

"Fan on out, down the road. Stay twenty-five feet apart and hack at the brush alongside the east edge. If the wind dies down, we'll light what you hack and let it back-burn toward the fire. Don't bother about the west roadside. If she jumps, we'll beat her out. Widen the road eastward. Keep in touch. Watch out for varmints, especially snakes. Don't get caught in the smoke.

Watch that careful, as the burn gets nearer. In this wind, the smoke will swirl up and down and if you get caught it can be bad. Widen the road to the east. Widen the road to the east!"

He coughed. His throat hurt. He was already tired. He wished he had a bullhorn.

Just at that moment Colonel MacDuff roared up in his jeep. He <u>had</u> a bullhorn. Standing erect and steering with the fingers of one hand, the bullhorn in the other, he bellowed into the wind.

"Hold on, now! I'm in charge here! I'm taking over, see. Mobilize around me, men! Collect on my jeep! Over here! I'm in full charge, now!"

As the fire fighters within earshot seemed to waver, Maude rushed over to Colonel MacDuff and yanked the bullhorn out of his hand.

"You old fool! You aren't in charge of anything. Shut up and get down off that jeep. Fight alongside the men as a man or leave us be! Here, Charlie, take this thing and save your throat!"

Colonel MacDuff was speechless. Buzzing and sputtering, he spun his jeep ninety degrees and plunged off the road toward the fire and disappeared into the tall grass. People close by heard his cry ... "silly little fire. Snuff it out all by myself. When I was in the Punjab ..." and the brush closed behind him.

When Roy Coggins and his water wagon finally reached Sally's house he pulled off on the downwind side and went to find Charlie.

"Want me to start wetting the east side of the road?"

"No, no. I want you to locate a water source, first off ... where you can get your wagon near enough to reload. Actually, if you can, find two. One halfway to the bay and the other halfway to the Gulf. Use this yard as midpoint. When you've found 'em, then find me. And hurry. Not much time left. An hour at best. That smoke is heavier than before, and so's the wind. If it doesn't settle some, my guess is that this place's a goner." He pointed to the Denkin's home. Sally-Anne, passing nearby, overheard and sucked in her breath. Bracing her shoulders and gritting her teeth, she ran up to the porch and shook a fist in Doobie's face.

"Git up! Git up! Does you heah me, ole man? Git your machet an' come hep. Else we's gonna burn to a cinder. Mr. Charlie sez so!"

Charlie finished instructing Roy.

"Take someone with you. That young lad, Jerry. You know each other an' he'd be a good one. He can be your tie-in with me. Don't wet down now. We'll wait 'til later and then we'll wet the <u>west</u> side, not the east. Must keep that sucker from jumping the road." He pointed off to where black smoke boiled up into the sky on an approaching front about a mile wide. Now and again a bright finger of fire stabbed high into the smoke.

Turning to Maude and Didi, who were standing around trying not to get in the way, Charlie beckoned them over.

"Good," he smiled. "Two beautiful ladies. Just like the doctor ordered. Good. I need more eyes. Why don't you two go up and down the road and look for trouble. Any trouble at all. Stay together and also keep your eye on me. Especially when the fire is almost on top of us. I'm countin' on that burn to reach us on an uneven line. Can't imagine it'll come up onto the road all at once. If it comes up a bit at a time, we'll lick it. We can slowly beat it out and withdraw, beat it out and withdraw. Oh, my Gawd! Look there! What in tarnation is <u>that</u>?"

Down Rabbit Road to the left the grasses had been crushed aside and Colonel MacDuff had staggered out. His clothes were torn and muddy and his pith helmet was gone. He stood for a second, swaying from side to side. Then, spying Charlie, he moved unsteadily toward him.

"Jeep's stuck. Deep inside there, somewhere. One wheel's in the muck. Spins. No traction. Need help!"

Charlie, unbelieving, shrugged.

"Can't help you now, man. We've got nothin' that can haul you out."

"I has." Sally-Anne had come up unnoticed. "Kennel, suh, my Doobie kin tug ya out." She turned to Doobie, standing dumbfounded behind her. "Git Shadrack. Ya heah me, boy? Go git Shadrack an' drag this Mr. MacDuff out. Don't stan' theah thinkin' sass at me. Git!"

A bit later Roy spotted Colonel MacDuff recrossing the road, heading into the sawgrass, followed by Doobie leading an old mule. He turned to Jerry and muttered ... " Boy! Now I've seen everything. I mean everything!"

The fire first touched the road along the south side of the mile-wide front. The men had to give ground and pull back toward the northern side to escape the black smoke swirling in suffocating billows along the ground as well as high in the air. Embers were blowing all about, singeing hair and eyebrows, dropping across the road and producing little curls of white smoke in the thick brush along the down-side. Flames soared high and bent before the wind with a furnace heat and a strange hissing sound. It was horrifying and frightening, but oddly exhilarating.

Charlie eyed the approaching searing carnage, the speed with which it ate across the grasses, the height of the flames, the swirl of the ember-filled air, the tar-laden smoke, and his shoulders sagged in defeat. There was no way. Roy couldn't take the water wagon into that cauldron. If the down-side wasn't wet, the fire would jump the road, even with the men leaping forward to pound each new tongue of flame starting up. He was fearful of them getting trapped, and had been forced to pull them back faster and faster. He was heading back to Sally's to tell her and Doobie to evacuate ... when the wind died. All of a sudden! The smoke ceased roiling and rose instead in well-contained columns. The flames dropped from twelve to sixteen feet to a manageable four to six feet. The resultant heat pulled back sufficiently for Roy to run the road. The men could fight. Charlie wanted to sit down somewhere and cry. Instead, he looked where the men were pointing as a great cheer went up. Doobie Denkins was coming slowly up the road leading Shadrack, pulling Colonel MacDuff inch by inch behind them in his jeep.

When the fire was under control, Carla Wilson borrowed Charlie's bullhorn and drove slowly up and down Rabbit Road, issuing a general invitation to everyone to stop by the Sanibel Inn for food before disbanding.

"I know you'll be setting watches all night long, 'til dawn — but on your way home, stop by. I'll keep the kitchen crew on all night and there'll be plenty of food. Gabe'll bring coffee and sandwiches up here for those who have to patrol. Great job! Great job! Every one of us owes every one of you a huge debt of gratitude."

Roy decided to stay all night with his water wagon handy, just in case, so Jerry gathered Didi and Maude and they headed for the Sanibel Inn. Everyone was filthy but it didn't seem to matter. When they reached the Inn, Carla wasn't there. A little round man they'd seen fighting the fire was bustling about the kitchen, helping Hanna, the cook, make sandwiches.

"Come on in," the little man called, "and grab a seat somewhere. I'm Billy Burke and I'm practically a member of the family. Carla said she'd be back soon. She's gone down to Mid-Island to get her mother."

Maude introduced everyone and asked Mr. Burke where he was from.

"Massachusetts. Cambridge. Harvard University. I'm Assistant Curator of Mollusks there. I fly down here every time there's an interesting blow, like several days back, to check Carla's beach for specimens. Didn't expect all this exercise, though." He chuckled delightedly. "Once the threat was over, I found I quite enjoyed all the excitement."

Didi's interest was captured.

"Mr. Burke," she called from the corner where she was washing up in the vegetable sink, "we had a strange experience a few weeks back. Oh," she paused and looked shyly at him. "I'm sorry. Maybe you aren't called 'Mr.' ... Would it be 'Professor'?"

"Well, now, let's see. Up in Cambridge ... students and all ... discipline ... they call me Professor. Down here, where everything is so much more ... shall I term it democratic ... I'm just plain Billy. Billy Burke. Do you think you can manage that?"

Didi was peeping at him over the top of a towel, with dirt smudges all over her clothes and her face half washed. She was a fetching sight.

"I'd feel better if we compromised. How about Mr. Billy? Can I call you that?"

He nodded and beamed back.

"That would be delightful, my dear. Now, what about this odd happening? What was it?"

Others had come in and the long kitchen table was filling up. Hanna was bustling back and forth, piling sandwiches all about and joshing with everyone. The talking and laughter increased.

Jerry, Didi and Mr. Billy moved to one end of the table, in order to talk quietly, and here they were joined by Jean and Frank.

"Jerry and I," Didi continued, "had been dredging out in the Gulf not too far from here, more toward Captiva, and we pulled up a baby octopus. If you know all about mollusks maybe you know about octopuses." She turned briefly to Jerry. "Oh," she whispered, "that's not correct is it?"

"No," Jerry shook his head. "It's octopi, I think. O-c-t-o-p-i." In turn, Mr. Billy shook his head. "Actually, you're both right. I think you'll find that Mr. Webster shows both, with 'octopuses' listed first, in the preferred position. I suppose that's why we use 'pi' up at Harvard. Correct, if eccentric." He paused to remove a piece of ham gristle. "Now, what was your question . I know a bit about the octopus. We've had an ongoing study on them for years. Fascinating creatures."

"Well ... " Didi turned to Jerry. "Do you want to tell him?"

Jerry was tackling a piece of cold chicken. "No, you go ahead. You're doin' fine."

"Well ... " Didi pushed at a lock of hair that was hanging across her cheek and took a deep breath. So many people were listening ... "Well, we took this tiny thing, not much bigger than a quarter with all its eight legs spread full out, and put it in our covered aquarium. It stuck itself to the glass side, and looked at us. It seemed to be watching. I mean ... it saw us, somehow."

Mr. Billy nodded.

"They do," he said. "Up at college, we have several big ones. We keep 'em in huge tanks and they've gotten quite tame. They do look back. We've often remarked about it. You're right. There's a definite give and take. Quite alarming, first time one encounters it."

"Yes ... " Didi had stopped eating and was staring at the professor. She was lost in thought, and a little involuntary shiver chased around her spine. "Yes, so-o-o ..." She dragged the word out.

"So, what? Is there more?"

"Oh, yes! I'm sorry. I was thinking." She smiled cautiously. "So, we decided to see if it could ink. You know ... protect itself."

Professor Burke nodded.

"So ..." Didi went on, "Jerry put his hand slowly into the water a bit to one side of the octopus and wiggled his fingers. It quickly shifted so it could watch his hand. Imagine. That tiny thing. As Jerry moved his hand closer to it, it suddenly shot away and I had this feeling it was panicky."

"It was." Professor Burke nodded. "It was afraid Jerry would hurt it." The professor was listening carefully.

"Then," Didi went on, "all of a sudden it curled up its little legs and drifted down to the bottom ... dead! How could that be?"

Professor Burke smiled.

"It had a heart attack. Jerry scared it to death."

Jerry joined in, eager to explain that they'd been careful.

"I didn't touch it. I didn't get very near at all. I was real careful."

"Just the same, it died of fright."

Maude had joined them when this conversation started and now she spoke up.

"Professor, it was very strange. I was there, too. The little fella was alive one minute, perfectly all right, and dead the next. Strange! It didn't seem frightened like a fish at all, startled and darting about, you know. It was frighted more like ... like a human." Maude's voice had dropped to little more than a whisper. She didn't like where this conversation seemed to be going. She toyed with a crust of bread on the table. "Do you mean ... are you saying ... if that little thing died of fright, it had to imagine danger. Nothing can imagine unless ... I mean, imagining isn't the same thing as instinct, is it? Something can't imagine unless it can ... "

"Think." Didi blurted out.

Professor Burke looked at the three questioning faces and smiled gently. "You're perfectly correct. They can. Octopuses <u>can</u> think. We've known that for some time. And they can communicate, too. How we don't know yet, but they can."

Didi drew in her breath in a long slow gasp, and shivered in dismay.

"Oh, how awful! How awful! Ugh! A brain trapped in that hideous slimy body! You must be joking, Professor?"

Billy Burke shook his head. "No, I'm not joking. For several years now we've conducted tests. They're quite intelligent. We figure, on the evolutionary scale of progression, that octopuses are right up there with elephants and dolphins. We don't know how it happened, or why. Mother Nature is inscrutable." He smiled. "We feel the octopus is a major retrogression. At one time, eons and eons back, buried in the millennia it takes for adaptation to occur, the octopus emerged from the sea and lived on land. For some reason, through the years, its progression reversed, and it returned to the water. By the way, it's not slimy at all, and if you study it closely, it's quite beautiful."

"That, sir," Maude interjected softly, "is the opinion of a scientist!"

Professor Burke acknowledged the remark with a little nod and went on.

"We don't yet know at what level the brain works but they can reason. They can learn tricks, simple tricks, like a dog. And they have a remarkable ability to change shape. They are able to 'ooze' through openings smaller than their body. Not too long ago, we conducted quite an interesting experiment. A large-necked bottle was submerged in an octopus tank and food was placed down inside. We fed the octopus this way for several weeks, until it was thoroughly familiar with this feeding procedure. Then we substituted the original bottle with one with a slightly smaller neck opening. Then, a bit later on, we substituted that bottle with a smaller-necked one, and so on. No matter how small the opening, the octopus would 'flow' into the bottle, providing it could get its beak through the neck. The first time I saw this I couldn't believe my eyes."

Didi leaned toward the Professor rapt with attention.

"You mean ..."

"I mean that there's an elastic factor in an octopus' body structure that allows for reshaping, much like when you squeeze a filled balloon. There are

193

other evidences of this ability in nature, to a lesser degree, mainly with snakes. They often swallow prey larger than their heads. To a much smaller extent, ostriches do the same. The octopus, however, is the most advanced in this feature."

"What about communicating?" Jerry asked. "You mentioned something about them communicating. Do they make noises?"

Maude had given Professor Burke another cup of coffee and he paused for several moments as he stirred it.

"Well, now ..." he went on, "we know very little about this. We're trying to devise experimental testing. We know whales talk to each other, and sing. We know porpoises chatter away at a great rate, clicking and squeaking to each other, and our experiments show that they understand this exchange. We believe — and I stress that it's more a scientific awareness and we're not supposed to allow ourselves the privilege of sharing it — that the octopus can communicate. Of course, they could employ either taste or scent, like a shark. We don't know." He paused to sip his coffee, then went on. "With a brain of high caliber, it would seem rather a travesty of nature to leave their locating each other to mere chance. Nature is not haphazard, and there is very little seemingly left to chance." He smiled at Didi's eager face. "What you and your young friend should do, my dear, is to return to your dredging area and capture another. Best, more than one, if possible. Set up several aquariums and study them. When they're used to you and comfortable in their new setting, conduct simple experiments. But don't frighten them. You have to gain their confidence, like with everything else. I'll tell you what. Why don't we set up a joint dredging expedition. Captain Jed often takes me out and his boat is large enough to accommodate several more shellers."

Didi sucked in her breath and glowed with delight.

"Yes. Let's." She cried. "Wouldn't that be great? When?"

Professor Burke shook his head, as he pushed back his chair.

"I'm sorry to disappoint all of you, but not now. I have to return in two days to my studies and my students." Seeing the forlorn expression on Didi's face he quickly added ... "Next year. We'll go next year. I won't forget. Meanwhile, study ... study ... study ..."

With a comical little bow, he left the room.

●

Maude had her binoculars glued to her eyes. She was crouched half in, half out of her rocking chair.

"Pssst! Ag! Come over here a minute and look." Maude crooked a finger vaguely at the sink without removing the binoculars from her eyes. "Unless I miss my guess," she murmured, "those carpenters are finished with that little building. They've hung a door in the opening and now they're packing up. I think they're getting ready to leave."

Agnes crossed over, wiping soap suds from her hands. She peered through the glasses, and nodded.

"I think you're right," she murmured back. "Why are we whispering?"

"Don't know," Maude murmured back. "Seems proper, somehow, when you're spying on folks."

"But we're not spying." Agnes returned the binoculars. "We're watching! That's much different. Spying is secretly gathering information to do hurt. We're not hurting anybody. We're observing what's going on."

"There they go! Whoops! Gone!" Maude settled back in her rocker. "I was right. Did you notice that half-moon cut in the top of the door? I seem to recall ..."

"No. Let me see." Agnes peered through the glasses again, adjusting the focus knob. "Yes. You're right, Maude. A little half-moon in the door. And what's that little arm coming off the wall at an angle? What do you suppose that's for?"

Before Maude could answer Cora burst in, slamming the porch door in her rush, and holding aloft a fist full of money.

"Look, girls. Did we make a killing today, or what? There's better than fifty dollars here." She came to a full stop when she realized she'd interrupted something. "What're you doing? You're talking about me!"

"No. No, we're not." Agnes spontaneously clasped Cora around the waist. "We're speculating about Colonel MacDuff's little building over there next to Amelia's house."

Maude suddenly sat bolt upright.

"I remember now. We don't have to speculate any longer. I know what it is!" She returned to her rocking, a smug little smile on her face. "It's a biffy!"

"A what?" Cora was now looking through the glasses. "A what?" She repeated.

"A biffy ... a john ... a loo, as the British say ... a chic sale."

Cora stared blankly at Maude.

"What do you mean? I don't know what all those things are. What is it?"

"It's an outdoor toilet, dear." Agnes told her and then turned to Maude with a devilish grin. "That old scoundrel! All this time and trouble and now he's going to win after all. Amelia will be apoplectic!" They both started to laugh. Cora's continuing dazed expression added to their delight.

"I don't understand! What are you hooting about? Tell me." Her lips puckered and she seemed about to cry.

Maude leapt up and headed for the door.

"Ag, explain to Cora. I'll be right back."

"Where are you going?"

"Over to Amelia's. Inviting her to four o'clock tea. We can't miss this!" Grabbing a swisher from the peg beside the door, she was gone.

Amelia <u>was</u> apoplectic! When she later arrived, she was short of breath and her face was fire-engine red. Agnes was alarmed as she handed around tea, and wondered if she should slip something more bracing into Amelia's cup, but things moved along at a fast pace and she forgot her apprehensions.

"I cannot stand it! I cannot stand any more!" Amelia began to whimper and the tears coursed down her face and dripped onto the lace jabot of her starched linen shirtwaist. She didn't seem to care and lifted red-rimmed eyes to the ceiling. "Lord only knows I've taken more than most, and now this loathsome creature continues plaguing me. When will it ever end? I can't look any of my friends in the face. How dare he? Who does he think he is? I've never harmed a hair on his head!"

Maude was merciless. This was all too juicy not to press.

"Ah, dear, but you have!" She gave a quick little shake of her head toward Cora, who seemed about to interrupt. "I told you before not to challenge Colonel MacDuff. He's a dangerous type, and they always plot and connive to win. You should never have insulted his wife."

"She's <u>not</u> his wife, and I wanted to rub his nose in it!" Amelia sniffed in righteous affront and jabbed at her eyes with a square of lace.

Maude nodded.

"You did. Why you felt it necessary, I don't know, but you did, and this is the result. Did you expect him not to slap back?"

Tears affected Cora, and now she was all sympathy. Leaning toward Amelia, she slowly rubbed her arm.

"There, there. Don't take on so, dear. Maybe if you apologized and asked him sweetly he'd take the little building down. Do you know what it is? Ag says ..."

"Of course I know what it is. I was raised with those things. As a child, back in Massachusetts, we had them all over the place. Well, not exactly all over, but two anyway, behind the main house. Nasty, smelly things. Even back then I couldn't bear to think about them. And now here I am, with one in my front yard. Right in my front yard!" The tears again began to flow.

"Of course," Agnes interjected," Cora is right. You could apologize and maybe, then ..."

"Never! I'll never apologize." Amelia banged her little fist so hard on the table that all the cups jumped up and down. "I'm a Standish! We never apologize! Its never been necessary. We're never wrong!"

Maude was back at the window, busy with her glasses.

"Of course, if you wanted to apologize ... mind you, I'm not saying you should, but if you did want to ... now would seem a good time to do it."

Amelia sniffed and threw back her head.

"Why?" She asked.

"Because they're both over there right now. Colonel MacDuff just drove up and Andrusa is with him!"

"No! I don't believe it! If my Daddy were only here, God rest his soul, he'd shoot them both dead! Don't tell me a single thing more." Then, in a complete reversal ... "What are they doing?"

Realizing that Amelia actually was consumed with desire to learn what the MacDuffs might be up to, Maude smiled broadly and held the glasses to her eyes.

"All right," she called, "I'll give you a step by step report. First off, the MacDuffs drove up in their jeep and skidded to a stop in their usual cloud of dust. Colonel MacDuff was driving and Andrusa was in the back seat, one hand grasping the side bar, and the other holding that huge floppy hat down on her head. Colonel MacDuff has now gotten out and is inspecting the building. He seems to be screwing something on the door ... a lock, I think. It glitters in the sunlight. Now he's back beside the jeep, talking to Andrusa. She's reaching around on the floor for something. It's a ball. A white ball. MacDuff has taken it and is fixing it on that little wooden arm sticking out beside the door. Oh, my, it isn't a ball at all." Her voice dropped. "It's a ... it's a ..." Maude sat back in her chair and stopped talking.

"It's a what?" The three others called out together.

"Toilet paper! It's a roll of white toilet paper!"

With a gentle moan Amelia collapsed across the table, upsetting the tea cups and scattering cookies. Agnes ran to her, calling to Cora to bring towels and ice. Maude resumed her travelogue.

"He's walking back and forth, like he's rehearsing. Now he's in the jeep and they're driving away. Mercy, he drives like the wind. I can hear them squealing across the bridge all the way over here. Can't you? That poor woman!"

An ice cube on the back of her neck had revived Amelia and she came up snarling.

"Poor woman, my foot! I'll poor woman both of them. I'll have that shack torn down if it takes the rest of my life." Her self-pity had gone and she was suddenly Eleanor of Aquitaine charging the infidels. She pulled her shoulders squarely back and her eyes flashed. Her little bosom heaved with indignation.

"I'll put the Health Department on him. He can't do that out there in public. It's ... it's ... unsanitary! Cora, when does that Health Inspector visit you next?"

She paced up and down the room, one hand on her hip, the other raised off to the side. Maude was so taken by the performance that she almost missed Colonel MacDuff's return. Alone this time, he roared up in his jeep, leaped out, paused, glanced right and left, gave two loud toots on the jeep horn, sauntered over to the chic sale, unlocked the door, put the toilet paper under his arm and hung his pith helmet on the peg in its place, glanced to his right and left a second time, then entered the building, closing the door behind him.

As Maude finished relating all this to the others, there was a dead silence. Everyone seemed frozen in place, waiting. The clock over the sink ticked loudly.

After what seemed an age, Maude breathed audibly.

"He's emerging! He's put the toilet paper back up on its peg and his hat back on his head. He's turned toward your windows, Amelia, and seems to be fumbling. His back is mostly to me, so I can't see clearly ... I think he's ... I think he's ... buttoning ... up ... his ... pants!"

As Agnes reached for Amelia and Cora ran for more ice, Maude glanced at her wrist-watch.

"Five minutes," she announced matter-of-factly to the room in general. "Exactly five minutes. Not bad!"

15

The days following the brush fire on Sanibel came and went as if packaged by the Chamber of Commerce. Gone were the blustery winds and the scudding squalls. Pink-tinged dawns crept over the eastern horizon followed by huge orange suns. Billowing, fleecy clouds played tag with each other across azure skies. Gentle breezes, salty and intimate, cooled the beaches, ruffled the Gulf, rustled the palm fronds and tossed the flamevine clustered lushly up lattice-trunked palmettos. Hummingbirds darted from blossom to blossom seeking the sweet delight from deep inside each vivid bloom. Elderly tourists rose late in this strange land where no outside influences disturbed the serene progression of quiet hours, and they retired early, exhausted from the burning sun, the laving, seductive zephyrs, and the unfamiliar, upsetting need to amuse themselves. Bertha, busy at her post office, was hard pressed each day to dispatch the extra mail traffic in glossy postcards, all written, apparently, by the same hand ... 'arrived safe, resting up, wish you were here, sending oranges'...

●

Amanda Johnson ran down her pathway, heading for the post office, to mail her monthly meter reading to the Rural Electric Association office in Fort Myers. She always waited 'til the final day of the grace period, telling herself she was buying an extra month of time before she had to pay, and having lost once again the battle to cheat and falsify the wattage information to be shown on the little pasteboard printout the R.E.A. office supplied each month. She would stand before the meter, pencil poised, struggling mightily against lying. Her breath would seem to be caught in her throat and she would be all atremble as the pencil point approached closer and closer to the paper. But at the final moment, always the same — visions of starving Armenian children would flash before her eyes, and in a private agony she would quickly note down the correct reading. She didn't know why Armenian or, for that matter, why children. Neither had been important in her background. But there it was. It happened each month. Maybe she should paint the impressions. Tortured purples would be nice, and magentas, with a swirling overlay of violent greens.

Puzzling this intriguing combination she turned the little curve by Matilda Crunch's Shell Shop and, heading south, almost stepped on the panther tracks. Actually, she stepped over the panther tracks and proceeded some thirty feet beyond Mrs. Crunch's yard before she realized that back there, at the turn, she had seen something odd. She came to a full stop just as Jean Culpepper came barreling out of the little pathway on Amanda's left that led to the bay and Boozie Chuffer's cottages. Jean was bent over the handlebars of an ancient bicycle she'd found in a shed on the Chuffer property and was now pedaling laboriously along the sandy lane on her early morning constitutional. Head down and grunting audibly with each pedal push, she glanced up just in time to avoid smashing into Amanda, standing stock-still in the middle of the road, lost in thought. Jean gave a violent twist to the handlebars, skidded in an abrupt half-circle and fell into a clump of periwinkles.

"Oops," she exclaimed, dusting herself off, "I almost ran into you! Sorry! Did I scare you?"

Amanda turned slowly toward Jean, a distant expression on her face. Seemingly unconcerned over the near accident, she pointed vaguely with one hand.

"Back there, something is wrong."

"Where? What?" Jean looked at this shy creature standing diffidently before her. There was an air of flight about Amanda, even when she stood still, and now she seemed about to dart away into the underbrush. What a lovely face. Beautiful, flashing white teeth. Immense brown eyes. A wood nymph! A startled fawn! Jean was afraid to breathe for fear of causing alarm.

"Back there," Amanda repeated softly. "At the turn. I'm sure I saw something."

"Was it alive?"

"Oh no. Patterns. The patterns were wrong. The lines upset. You understand."

"No, I'm afraid I don't." Jean looked doubtful. At this early hour there was little Jean did understand, and what this fey creature was murmuring at her was definitely not part of it. "I don't understand at all."

"Everything is a pattern. Everything. All of life. All about." The arms gestured as gracefully as swans' necks. "It's all lines and patterns. Otherwise, there'd be no substance. No form. To anything. No order." The large brown eyes crinkled at the corners, and a fleeting smile edged in and out. "When something disturbs these patterns it's like a loud bell ringing in my head. It's ringing now." She cupped both hands over her ears. She thrust her head forward, pointing with her nose ... "Back there, the patterns are disturbed. Something is out of place."

"Well, let's go and see," Jean exclaimed. All thoughts of a constitutional were now gone and already she couldn't wait to share this conversation with Frank. He'd never believe it!

Side by side, eyes on the ground, together they crept back along the sandy road. Jean was just about to excuse herself and break away ... at seven in the morning this was too weird for anyone ... when Amanda pointed.

"There! You see! Tracks! They're not supposed to be there. The normal road patterns are disturbed. I knew I'd seen something."

Jean looked where Amanda was pointing. There were, indeed, tracks. Large animal tracks! They emerged from the heavy brush on the bay-side, crossed the road, hugged the bushes bordering the Shell Shop yard, and, crossing to Mrs. Crunch's house, disappeared around the south corner.

As they followed carefully, bent nearly double, Matilda appeared on her stoop.

"Lose something, Amanda? I ain't got it!" She folded her arms righteously across her bosom.

"You'd better look at this, Matilda. It seems to have crossed your back yard. Some kind of a big animal. Looks like panther tracks."

Matilda joined them and all three bent down.

"Cat! It's a house cat!" Matilda stated firmly.

Jean shook her head, and straightened up.

"No," she commented. "I've always had cats, and these prints aren't cat. Too big."

Matilda sniffed.

"Has to be. What else can it be? Some big old Tom has been pushing about, courting my Princess. That's all. It's a house cat!"

Amanda had pulled off to one side and was flicking the corner of her R.E.A. print-out.

"It's panther. I've studied Florida wildlife and I know. A panther has been prowling around your house, Matilda, and a big one too."

"Well, we'll see about this!" Matilda ran back into her house, jammed a pointed shapeless black felt hat down over her beehive and grabbing a mosquito swisher headed down the road toward the dock. "We'll see about this," she called over her shoulder as she scrambled along. "I'll just get Murph to come have a look."

"It's a panther, sure 'nuf." Murph later announced in a decisive tone. "That fire up on Sanibel must have flushed it out. Didn't know there was any up there, but could be. Acres and acres of brush back in there." He turned to Roy Coggins who'd spotted the small gathering and had sauntered over to investigate.

"It can't be! I won't have it!" Matilda was indignantly hopping up and down. "In my yard? Next it'll be snarling at me in my shop."

"You can always snarl back," Roy called to her laconically, and then grinned at Murph.

No telling where this exchange might have gone if Jerry and Didi hadn't appeared in the old delivery truck and called out ... "Redfish schooling in front of Captiva Inn. Right in to shore. Thousands of 'em. Thick as sand-fleas!" ... and everyone ran off to get gigs and rods.

As luck would have it, Frank was cleaning their two fishing rods when Jean rushed in out of breath and began rattling incoherently at him.

"Stop. Stop. Whatever you're doing, put it down. No, I mean grab it up. Come on or we'll be too late! Where're the car keys? Move! Come on!"

Frank wondered if she was demented. He never should have let her go off on her bike without coffee and orange juice. Now she was having some sort of fit, which he didn't recognize. Jean had turned red in the face, as she continued yelling.

"Come on! Fish don't wait! We'll be the last ones there! Well, then, damn it, sit there with your mouth open if you want to. I'm going." Grabbing one of the rods and the car keys, she headed out.

"Wait! Wait! I'm coming." Frank grabbed generally at the equipment and joined her.

There was already great excitement along Palm Avenue as Jean and Frank rushed toward the Gulf. Ida was leaning out of one of the windows of her new store, dust rag in hand, and she waved. Marge and Stan were standing alongside the road, looking toward the Gulf and two customers were emerging from the restaurant, napkins in hand and jaws working. Emmy Kramdon was standing with Miriam Hallman, talking at a furious rate and gesticulating. A stream of Captiva Inn guests dribbled up the road in all manner of early morning garb. Faye from the Fisherman's Creel Gift Shop had had such a disastrous night she was much too much under the weather to walk, but her sister Nan hurried along with a pole on her shoulder. As if there were a huge magnet on the beach, and the people were merely slivers of steel, everyone who could move was being irresistibly drawn swiftly to the water's edge.

●

To the studious mind, the cause-and-effect cycles in nature are discernible, if not always understood. Like cogs falling into place in a revolving engine, when conditions are right, certain occurrences will follow. When mayflies hatch and flutter low over sylvan brooks, trout will leap. When the creeping drought finally desiccates the Serengeti plain, the wildebeest will migrate. When the atmospheric pressure drops and cold northern air flowing south meets warm southern air flowing north, gigantic storms will boil and roar in the heavens. So it is along southern shores ...

This night, toward dawn, the barometric pressure fell, causing discomfort to the sand fleas busily feeding several inches down in the sand, the females large with maturing yellow egg sacs. They instinctively repositioned themselves to just below the surface. Incoming waves undulated gently up the beach slope and receded again, leaving a moist, lacy foam blanket that seeped into the sand, warming and wetting the sand fleas. Plovers and sandpipers, also sensitive to pressure change, collected in large active flocks, eager to take advantage of this easily accessible food. So long as the wave action stayed gentle, and broadside to the beach, conditions remained calm. However, soon after dawn, with the first warming of the land, a stiff breeze rose, the waves increased and swept inshore at an angle, scouring the beach and riling the surface sand. Each receding wave now carried with it glistening sheets of the feeding sand fleas.

Also sensitive to pressure change and wave reverberation, the redfish schooled just offshore, and were facing in, awaiting this bounty being swept so effortlessly toward their ready, eager mouths ...

●

Adam and Ruth Crisfield owned Captiva Inn. They were from New Hampshire where they operated a small hotel in the White Mountains during the summer months. They'd searched south for a small inn for the wintertime and during the lean war years they bought Captiva Inn. Adam was large and bluff and gregarious. He liked small inns. He could be his own repair man and still have time to give individual attention to his guests. He loved that, and what he loved, Ruth loved. She ran the kitchens in both locations with a minimum of hired help. They prospered.

They now stood together at the edge of the shore, under a twenty foot palm tree, smiling and waving, watching the frenzied action up and down the beach. In both directions, people were rushing about, dodging the waves, hauling in fish, screaming at each other, slipping and sliding up and down on the wet sand. Birds were also screaming, screaming and diving. The commotion disturbed the tiny silvery alewives, and pelicans and terns dived and fought each other for these glittery tidbits. The shore birds piped sharp penetrating disapproval at being disturbed and circled and landed in swift cutting flights as they searched in vain for a private spot. Way up the beach, propped against a fallen palmetto, Adam could see Amanda, sketch book on one knee, capturing the scene in sure swift strokes.

"Look down there, Ruthie. What an introduction to island life for that New Yorker fella and his wife. What's their names? Haven't met him yet."

Ruth nodded to Matilda Crunch, who'd just hurried up before she answered.

"I think it's Culpepper or something like that. I think that's what Emmy Kramdon told me. Well, Matilda, and how are you? Look at all the goings on out there. Isn't it just splendid? We'll freeze down and have redfish all winter."

Matilda, still with the felt hat jammed hard on her head, hadn't regained her composure.

"Hmmmph! Not if that old panther gets into your pantry."

Adam didn't hear this remark and they all talked at cross points.

"Jerry and that pretty little Didi Drinkwater have just joined those Culpeppers, Ruthie"

"Matilda, whatever do you mean panther? That's nice, Adam."

"I mean just what I say. There was this big panther in my yard just awhile back ..."

"Ruthie, do you think maybe I should get my gear and go out and catch some too? Or ..."

"How do you know it was a panther, Matilda?" Ruth held a hand up toward Adam, who seemed poised to join the revelers.

"Murph and Evan saw the tracks. They studied 'em. Both agreed it's a panther-cat. Big 'un too!"

"Adam, do you hear this? Matilda had a panther in her yard this morning. Says it was a huge one!"

"That's good." Adam answered off-handedly. His attention was on the fish. Then, like having been struck by a bolt of lightening, his head snapped back.

"What? What did you say, Matilda? A panther? A _panther_?"

"Yep! Big! Tawny brown!" Matilda got a bit carried away. "Saw it go bounding off into the bushes by the corner of my place, heading for the canebrake down by the Upton's. Snarling! _Huge_ teeth!"

Adam was stunned.

"Evan and Murph said," Matilda went on, reluctant to release the spotlight, "Evan and Murph said it won't be safe to walk around after dark!" Evan and Murph had said no such thing, but this little discrepancy didn't bother Matilda. She suddenly felt much better than she had all morning.

"Good Lord, Matilda!" Adam glanced this way and that, fearful their conversation had been overheard. "Don't say such things, unless you're sure. We wouldn't want folks getting scared and leaving the island, now would we?" His mouth smiled at her but his eyes were wary.

"Oh, we're sure." Matilda raised her voice and said loudly "A - big - old - panther - cat!"

Adam became solicitous.

"I'm sure it was, Matilda. But let's just keep this between ourselves, just us, for a bit, and I'll run down and talk to Murph."

"Oh, I won't say a word to anybody. My lips are sealed. From now on I won't say a single word!"

Matilda could afford to be generous about her future panther-gossiping, as she'd paused on her way to the beach and talked to Emmy Kramdon and

Miriam Hallman. The story was now winging its way along the grapevine from one end of the island to the other. And also out onto the beach!

Adam was distressed to notice that people were suddenly gathering in small groups, their heads together, glancing nervously over their shoulders at clumps of seagrape, collecting their equipment and drifting in off the beach. Good Lord, a story such as this could ruin the season, only just begun and stubby at best. Merciful Heavens!

Jerry offered to haul fish for those so laden they couldn't manage, and then he and Didi dropped off a large, perfect one at her house.

"I'll freeze it whole" Didi said. "Then, later on, when we've time, we can run it in to Fort Myers to Phil Boyle, the taxidermist. I'll ask him to mount it. Can we?"

Jerry nodded. "Sure," he agreed at once and carried the beauty into the pantry for her.

Oddly enough, Aunt Agnes and the other two ladies hadn't heard about the redfish run, but had heard about the panther. They were delighted with the large haul and fell to at once cleaning and scaling. Everyone talked back and forth except Maude, who took Agnes' car and rode over to confer with Murph. When she returned, she was thoughtfully serious.

"Murph says sure enough it is a panther. That's all nonsense, though, about Matilda seeing it. Nobody saw it. Just the tracks. And they did lead across the road in the direction of those overgrown acres to the north of Upton's. It's rather unsettling, thinking maybe there's some ferocious varmint out there, hungry and slavering all about. I suppose it could pounce." She gave a little shiver.

Agnes was thoughtful, also. This wasn't a situation to play around with.

"Did Murph mention where he thought it came from?" she asked.

Maude nodded.

"He thinks it more'n likely was flushed out by the fire on Sanibel. What it might've been doing up there's anybody's guess. The thing would have plenty of food, of course ... deer, rabbits, coons and all. Murph mentioned he's seen deer on Sanibel. But Captiva is so small. Half a mile wide at its widest and not quite five miles long. And people dotted here and there, especially now with the tourists and winter people. When it gets hungry it could be a problem. I stopped by Bertha's and talked with her about not letting her kids play outside, especially little Too-loo. She'd be only a mouthful for a hungry panther!"

"Maude! Stop! Don't say such things!" Cora was wild-eyed and covered with goose bumps. "Ugh! I'm not going to sleep a wink tonight. You on that screened porch and me just inside." She gave a sudden nervous little laugh. "At least, you'd be more than just a mouthful. It'd have to drag you away and down the road and stuff you up a tree, or whatever panthers do, and there'd be a trail of blood. Ugh! Awful! Awful! And who'd take care of my limes and help with all this stuff? I can't do all this work by myself, Agnes. That was never part of the plan, you know." Cora sank into a nearby chair and covered her face with her hands.

"Well! That sure disposed of me in a hurry." Maude commented.

●

Frank and Jean Culpepper returned home just before noon, groaning under the load of fish they'd caught. Previously, Frank had constructed a sturdy little table-high platform at the end of Boozie Chuffer's dock, and now they stood there together, scaling and gutting the redfish.

"Aren't they beautiful," Jean commented, turning one over and examining it closely. "Seems the reddish blush is fading as they dry out, but the round black spot on either side remains bright and clear. I'll bake one or two and fillet the rest. How about that?"

Frank nodded. He was watching the gulls diving for the entrails and was lost in thought. Jean nudged him.

"Hey. Come on. Scrape, at least. I'll do all the dirty stuff."

Slowly Frank dragged himself back.

"Wasn't that unbelievable, back there? All those fish boiling the water ... and the birds ... and the people dashing about ... and now this, and the sky so close up above and spreading out forever, and the few fluffy clouds, and the gulls diving around our heads, and you standing there all brown and messed up. I never knew. I never dreamed. I've never felt so peaceful."

Jean smiled at him and impulsively leaned over and kissed him on the cheek, leaving some sand and a few fish scales on his face.

"Yeah. You're right. It's sure different down here. I love it. But I can love it just as well in by the sink, so help drag these monsters in there. How's about a flaky fish salad for lunch? Lots of hard-boiled eggs, crisp lettuce, boiled fish and potato chips. Sound good?"

Later on, at the table, Frank toyed with the lush salad, heaped high with mayonnaise and doused liberally with lime juice. His eyes wandered beyond his plate and off out the window.

Jean looked at him several times, reaching for his mood.

"Something's bothering you, isn't it?"

He nodded slowly and glanced over at her.

"I don't want to go back!"

"Go back where?" She mumbled, her mouth full.

"Only two days left of our vacation — and I don't want to go back to New York!"

Chewing slower and slower, Jean studied his serious face for some time before she spoke.

"Neither do I!"

"Let's stay."

"How can we?"

"Let's just stay. If we stay, we stay. Don't go back."

"You mean, get an extension to our vacation?"

"No." Frank stared deep into her eyes, and took one of her hands in his. "Let's both get a six-month leave of absence, and if we still feel the same way at the end of it ... we'll stay permanent. Whadda you say?"

Jean was rocked.

"No fair," she cried. "I can't answer that, right off the bat. You've been thinking about this for a long time, but it's a brand new idea to me. I gotta work my way along it, carefully." She twirled her fork and shoved at a piece of fish. "It's pretty simple for you, you know, to turn your back on your desk out there in Bethpage ... Some other engineer can slide into your seat. But it's different with me. Without complimenting myself, Benton and Bowles won't be the same if I pull out. Of course, I suppose that's not truly accurate, is it?" She pondered silently, stirring her tea. "I mean, none of us are indispensable. Someone else will come along and be better'n me." She was silent again for a bit. "I'd love to just stay. Of course I would. And I'd also love to finish the Gaines Dog Food thing I've been working on for months now. It's all packaged and all I need is a sure-fire slogan. They're for naming it 'gravy train', can you believe? Dreadful! If I'm not there to stop it, they'll most likely use the damn name, and if they do, they'll never sell another pellet of dog food!" Her voice trailed off.

"Jeannie," Frank still had her hand, and he massaged her fingers and smiled at her. "It's so simple, really. Do we want to stay ... or not? Remember that old wife's tale about opportunity? Well, listen closely. I can hear it knocking. Can't you?"

Jean looked back at him with a long, calculating stare, and slowly withdrew her hand.

"Well," she said gently, with her practical approach, "maybe you'd better high-tail it over and charm that sweet old drunk next door into letting us stay through 'til August. Don't put any money on the barrel-top, though. This all depends on New York."

Frank pushed back his chair. His grin was wide and somehow shy.

"First, come over here!"

"What for?"

"Sit on my lap!"

"You're kidding!"

"On my lap!"

"Culpepper, you've lost your senses. You've always hated this mushy stuff."

"In New York, maybe. But not down here. Down here, I want lots of mush."

"In the middle of the day?" She was inching toward him.

"Shut up and sit."

They wrapped their arms around each other and held tight. After a time, Jean lifted her head.

"What about that lion? If he gobbles me up, will you rescue me?"

"It's a panther! If he gets you, I'll tear his heart out while it's still beating!"

"With your bare hands?"

"With my bare hands!"

She lowered her head and sighed.

"That's my bronzed Aztec warrior!" Then, as an afterthought ... "And what will you use for muscle?"

"I have a little." He grinned. "And after a couple of months here, I'll have lots."

"I can't wait," she murmured into his chest.

●

Pushing the papers to one side of her desk, Kate O'Hearn made room for the Spartan lunch due any minute now from the kitchen. It was irritating that the phone call she'd placed to her St.Paul office an hour earlier hadn't yet been returned. She made an entry in a black fold-top notebook to look into this sluggishness immediately upon her return north. Things seemed, lately, to slack off up there once her back was turned, and it had to stop! It was also irritating that the decision at Minnesota Mining, of which she was Chairman of the Board and controlling stockholder, had been to again split stock, though she had specifically requested — ordered is closer to the truth — that any such action await her return. There had already been sixteen stock splits down through the years and she was delighted the company was flourishing and her fortune along with it, but she had specifically asked, and they'd all moved against her request ... and that, too, needed serious examination. She made a second entry in the little black book.

Helga placed the fruit salad and orange juice on the desk, and then stood a bit to one side.

"Miss Kate, Sam says to please tell you that your office has been phoning but something is wrong with the ship-to-shore. As soon as he gets a clear connection, he'll buzz your extension."

Kate nodded her thanks and smiled gently after Helga's retreating back. Such a consolation. She simply couldn't live without Helga. A blend of secretary-housekeeper-cook and companion, the large Minnesota farm girl had been tested down through the years and their association was true and sincere. Lars, Helga's husband, on the other hand, wasn't of the same caliber. His assignment to outdoor chores taxed both his enthusiasm and his intellect, but Helga doted on him, and where she went, he went. The household of four was quiet, efficiently and smoothly run, and she could work, even if she wasn't allowed to eat! She contemplated her lunch with distress. You couldn't live on lettuce. Rabbits got more than this back home. But as the years went by she had gotten pudgier and pudgier and now, at 68, the doctors had given

Helga firm instructions. What could she do? She nibbled at a piece of pineapple, and gazed out of the window. Sam Wooten, the fourth member of her Captiva household was visible in the wheelhouse, fiddling with the radio-phone. He'd been her Captain for fourteen years, ever since she'd commissioned Wanigan II. Together they'd poured over plans, designed and redesigned, fought over some features, laughed aloud over others, both dreaming of the perfect small yacht. Small? The damn thing was seventy-six feet long, longer than this house, and had cost half a million, just a bit better than $6,000 a foot. Anyway, she adored it, and there it was, swinging gently from its main hawser, lifting and sinking with the waves in her lagoon, right outside her back door. Her guilt at having so blatantly indulged herself was somewhat assuaged when she reminded herself, as she always did, that she didn't drink or splurge on clothes or entertain lavishly like others in her crowd. After all, that boat wasn't a toy. It was an expensive investment. She could always sell it and recover.

So she mused to herself and worked halfheartedly at the stack of papers in her in-box until Sam sent a message by Lars that the ship-to-shore was repaired. Almost at once the extension on her desk buzzed and there was Minneapolis-St. Paul and reality. She was still on the phone when the first limousine purred up her driveway and deposited Frances Fontaine at her door.

Helga knocked gently and then walked over to the desk.

"Please excuse me, Miss Kate."

Kate held up a cautioning hand and for a few more seconds poured instructions into the phone. Then she said "Wait a minute. Helga wants me." and turned around.

"I think maybe you've forgotten, Ma'am, but it's four p.m. and today's Thursday ... the third Thursday ... "

"Oh" exclaimed Kate. "You're right. Damn! I had forgotten. Can you please lay out my culottes. I'll be right with you." Then back into the phone, "Ed? Hello, Ed? Can you hear me? Well, I must go. It's the Sycamore Club thing. Meets today. Right now, in fact. Anyway, you've now got all the instructions necessary and can handle things at your end. Please phone me again tomorrow morning. I'll tell Sam to expect your call. At ten a.m., my time. Must go! Good-bye."

●

It took so long for the limousines to creep down the main road and feed into the O'Hearn driveway that Roy's old truck almost stalled. On his way home from work, he'd stopped at the bridge and picked up Jerry. They were going mullet-netting in the back bay, and now this hold-up.

"Seems to be some doings this afternoon on the Gold Coast."

Jerry had never heard about any gold coast.

"What's that? Gold Coast?"

"Oh," laughed Roy, "that's what a few of us nasty-mouthed natives call 'em. Gold Coasters. Miss O'Hearn, she heads it. Then there's three other households, and their guests and some spill-overs that stay up at Mid-Island. You know, all the winter millionaires. Four houses full of 'em. This driveway where we're stopped and the next three. Miss Kate's Pa, old Black Strap Bart, oil wells in Texas, he first found Captiva thirty-forty years back and built a fishing camp on that ridge right down that driveway. When he died, Miss Kate had the rough cottage tore down and built that nice place instead. Her cronies came later. She's from St. Paul, Minnesota. Nice lady. Sweet and kind. Does lots of good things for folks here on the island. Up on Sanibel, too. Keeps it all quiet. Never no chest-puffin' atall. Real nice lady."

"What sort of things?"

"Oh," Roy shook his head. "I don't know. Various stuff. That time Pearlie and Murph's daughter Becky needed an operation, some kidney business, and they'd no way of handling the cost. Damn near killed Pearlie. Then, all at once, things cleared up. A doctor friend of Miss Kate's, vacationing up on Boca Grande, came in to Myers and did the operation for free. We none of us ever believed he actually did it for free but that was the story. No one poked around in it. Becky's been dandy ever since. Married and two kids of her own. Interesting, huh?"

●

Four shiny limousines, each chauffeur-driven, turned one behind the other into the driveway lined with royal palms, and drove slowly toward the imposing dwelling standing well in from the Gulf. Each single occupant was deposited at the carved wooden entry-door exactly at four p.m. this third Thursday in January, and the Sycamore Club of Minneapolis-St.Paul's first monthly meeting of the New Year was in session.

Each club member wore identical White Stag culottes but of varying hues, blending harmoniously with the latest hair tints, and carried small matching briefcases from Abercrombie and Fitch. These outfits were club issue. There was a certain amount of 'ohing and ahing', kissing and hugging, as if they'd not seen each other for years though, in fact, they'd all attended a lobster dinner the preceding evening at Sanibel Inn.

"Ladies, ladies. Quiet down now and find your seats, please." Kate O'Hearn, Chairman of the Club, rang a little hand-bell and seated herself center on a large sofa, from which several overstuffed chairs stretched both left and right. A small glass-topped table stood beside each chair.

She tinkled the bell a second time.

"Quickly now. Your name is on each table. If you sit back like I am, and drag the table around between your legs, you've a little desk for taking notes."

She was sitting spraddle-legged on the edge of the sofa, and the need for the culottes was apparent. They afforded a maximum of leg activity with a minimum of unseemly exposure.

" We'll skip roll call and minutes of the last meeting, as all that'll have to be carefully gone into and properly noted once we're north again. I've asked Helga to take notes of this meeting, which she can handle and still get drinks and keep the hors d'oeuvres going, if we break every so often. Can't you Helga?"

Helga had quietly entered the living room and she nodded.

"I hope," Kate went on, as the other members sank almost out of sight in their deep chairs, "that we can wind up the reports on events back home in about an hour, so I've asked Tabby Upton to join us about 5:30 and bring us up to date on island doings. All right? So noted." She motioned toward Helga, who scribbled on a pad.

The northern activities were discussed at length, each the specific responsibility of a different member. The new wing of the St. Paul Municipal Hospital was on schedule and on budget and due for completion next year.

The Home for Wayward Girls, located on Elm at Center, downtown Minneapolis, had twenty-two girls in residence and would soon need expansion. It was hoped that a campaign ... newspaper, radio, billboards ... could educate and guide the wayward girls from being quite so wayward.

The Twin City Flower Mart, established along both sides of the river, and of special interest to Frances Fontaine, seemed to be flourishing. During her accounting, and inching forward so enthusiastically that her little table teetered, Fanny reported that 10,000 trees had been planted in and around the two cities the past year ... "and enough money is left over to pay rents and restock, with only the barest infusion from me! Isn't that splendid? She beamed around the group.

The fourth club project, a new venture of a summer camp for underprivileged children still in the planning stage, was being tossed about when Tabitha Upton joined the group.

"Ah, Tabby. Good to see you." Kate called, waving toward a vacant chair. "Join us and have a drink. Tell Helga what you'd like. We want a rundown on what's been happening the past nine months on our little piece of paradise."

"Well, now, let's see." Tabby sipped at her gin and tonic and twirled the large button on her chest. "It's all pretty much the same, Kate, as you know, year after year."

"Well," Fanny Fontaine piped up, "that recent fire on Sanibel was pretty frightening."

"Yes, there was that. And now, as a result of it, seems we've got a hungry panther prowling about." Tabby looked around the group of ladies, all now at full attention. "Dennis says there's no doubt of it at all. It's a panther."

The chattering and exclaiming reached a high peak before Kate could quell it.

"Please. We'll never get the story if you don't all quiet down. Tabby, who's seen it and how many times?"

"As I understand it, no one has actually seen it. Lots of folks have seen the tracks, but the animal seems to be deep in the canebrake north of me, which isn't too attractive."

In her soft, hesitant manner, Tabby told them all she knew about the scare.

"Have the men any plans?" Fanny was on the edge of her chair. "I mean, we've all got lots of bushes right up to our doors, and we don't want to be pounced on every time we go out."

"Dennis had a meeting day before yesterday with Murph and Evan. They've organized a neighborhood watch, so to speak, and are systematically prowling the panther." She gave a little high-pitched laugh. "My, that's humorous, isn't it? ... prowling the prowler ... Anyway, they looked yesterday and this morning and didn't find anything."

Kate motioned to Helga. "Let me have your pad, please. Maybe you can slip away and start our supper. This is about over, anyway." She flipped to a clean page and noted at the top in her broad, flat strokes 'Captiva — check:' Then she added underneath "panther".

Tabby continued.

"The Inns are full."

"We know all that."

"The Fisherman's Creel Gift Shop is open again."

"We all know that."

"The bakery and Marge's Bide-A-Wee are doing fine."

"We all know that."

"Do you know that there's a new delivery service throughout the island?"

"No. What sort of delivery? Who's operating it?"

Tabby preened a bit. She'd found a subject no one knew of and she relished her moment in the sun. She reported that Agnes Trumbull's nephew, Jerry, had come down in September, had quickly recovered from some sickness she wasn't sure about, pneumonia, she thought, and had started up a delivery service with Roy Coggin's old truck, and everyone was very pleased. He met the mailboat each day and delivered packages around the island for 5 cents each.

There was an instant excited discussion, as it had long been customary for the chauffeurs to meet the mailboat.

"Well, that won't affect us ... you've Lars, Kate, and I've got William ... and I've got Samuel ... and I've got Rupert ... and I've got Achmed ..."

Alice looked at the last speaker.

"Achmed?"

"Yes. Well, I mean, Thurmond left me and I found this lovely, young, I mean this highly recommended young man from Morocco ..."

Kate frowned and tapped her teeth with her pencil.

"Really, Doris," she said staring straight at the lady in question, "you're much more dangerous than any panther. You'll have us all slaughtered in our beds some night, you and your sloe-eyed sinister young drivers. You really should control your emotions!"

The excited talking started up again but Kate wasn't finished. Shushing them into silence, she continued to speak.

"I would like to put before this meeting the suggestion that the Sycamore Club goes on record acknowledging this new delivery service as a community improvement and beneficial to our life here on the island." There was a breathy ` hear, hear' and she went on without pause, writing swiftly on her pad. "And as such, the Club will offer full support while each member is in residence." She looked up, her pencil raised. "That means none of us sends our help to meet any mailboat deliveries from now on. Give your yard men and chauffeurs something else to do. Lord knows they all can use the extra chores. And let this young lad make his deliveries. To be certain this sticks, I want a vote. I vote Yea." She raised her hand.

All the others signified agreement except Doris Lockwood.

Kate stared at her.

"And what about you, Miss Adventuress? Do you vote with me, or shall I have your Achmed's Moroccan activities checked into?"

The vote was unanimous!

"Good," Kate went on. "I think it unfortunate that I had to railroad this agreement. If we don't support new ventures in the village, where are we? The plumber and the electrician and the little restaurant and so on are <u>needed</u> by the community, and by ourselves also. How can we expect these people to meet their bills and be there for us when we want them if we don't support their efforts? Is there anything else, Tabby?"

Mrs. Upton nodded.

"One thing more, Kate. I think this will be another benefit for the community. Ida Benson is opening a grocery store!"

"Really? Where? How soon?"

"Tomorrow one week. I stopped in for a minute on my way up here, and honestly, you can't imagine. You should see what she's done. Unbelievable. Do you remember that little eye-sore building where the two lanes cross just below Marge's restaurant?" They all nodded and leaned forward. "Well, its got a new coat of white paint, and the yard's been cleaned up, and you'd never recognize it. Inside, it's adorable!"

"That's an odd phrase to use for a grocery store, isn't it?"

"Wait 'til you see it. It's tiny and yet there's so much room. There's a quaint foreign flavor to it. Curtains everywhere and little tables. She says she'll serve coffee. Think of that!"

"Smart!" Kate mulled this news. "Very smart! Those Germans have many admirable traits, in spite of this recent conflict. I believe she was born in Berlin, wasn't she? Diligent. Imaginative. Thrifty. She'll catch the mailboat visitors each day and the coffee will be a great attraction. It's really a brilliant idea." She glanced around the room. "Any of you have a problem adjusting your shopping plans? I thought not."

213

As the others tossed this new idea around among themselves, Kate turned back to Mrs. Upton.

"Tabby, you live down that way and pass her little store every day on your cat walks ..." Mrs. Upton nodded. "Pop in and out and keep an eye open. If Mrs. Benson hits any serious problems, like bills she can't pay or anything like that, let me know." Again Mrs. Upton nodded, and Miss O'Hearn closed her pad and gazed thoughtfully out of the huge windows facing the Gulf. "All year, Tabby," she added softly. "If she hits rough spots, it will be during the off-season months. No matter where I am, get me. Ed Hopkins in my St. Paul office, he'll know how to reach me. I'll give you his number and you can phone when you're in Myers. Will you do that, for me, please?"

Before Mrs. Upton could respond, Fanny Fontaine spoke. She was packing her little briefcase, and shaking her head. Her shiny black culottes blended exactly with her startling inky-black hair, swept back from a dead-white forehead and hanging to her shoulders in a filmy cloud.

"Kate. I have no argument with any of this and we'll all get behind all these new ventures and push ... and push. Of course we will. But I want to go on record, please make note, that I'm dead against all this ... this metropolitan expansion. Do we really need all these things ... electricians and plumbers, and bakeries, and now a grocery store and a delivery service? Where will it stop? What's happening to the uncomplicated, simple, hidden little island we've known for so many years? I mean ... next it'll be taxicabs and police. And soon some fool will build a bridge to the mainland. Hordes of people will pour over and there goes our little hideaway."

Kate O'Hearn nodded and smiled softly across the room at Mrs. Fontaine. "Calamity Jane, Fanny!"

"What?"

"I suppose Jane said the same thing to that big man of hers ... was his name Hickok? ... every time a new wagonload of easterners drove into Dead Man's Gulch or wherever. It's called Progress, Fanny. Things move on. Think how lucky you are, with your millions and all. If things get too crowded for you, you can pack up and move somewhere else. The villagers have to stay. Try not to be so insular, dear!"

As they all kissed and hugged and prepared to hurry away, Miss O'Hearn slipped her hand under Tabby Upton's arm.

"I'll walk you to your car, Tabby, if I may. By the way, I noticed a strange small building on the other side of the bridge. What's Amelia Armstrong putting up?"

"Oh, it isn't Amelia. She's up in arms about it, threatening to sue. It's Colonel MacDuff. Apparently he bought that little slice of ground and he's built a privy there."

"No!"

"Yes. And he uses it. As he goes back and forth, up and down the island, he uses it. To be sure Amelia knows he's occupying it, he rings a loud little bell as he goes in."

"No!"

"Yes. She's enraged. She's been to Fort Myers several times about it, involving the Health Department and the zoning people and everybody. Swears she'll force him to tear it down."

"No!"

"Yes."

Miss O'Hearn, well aware of the previous winter's clash between Mrs. Armstrong and the Colonel, was now convulsed.

"Imagine him going that far? Unbelievable! Is Miss What's-her-name with him again this winter?"

"Andrusa? Yes."

"Oh, dear. It's really too amusing. But that's one little situation I'm not going to touch. I don't want him building his privies all over _my_ beach." She leaned in the open window of Mrs. Upton's car and kissed her cheek. "Thank you, Tabby, for joining us this afternoon. It was sweet of you. Bye, bye. See you soon."

●

Ida Benson felt pressed for time. The days were clicking by at an alarming rate and there was still a lot to do. Most of the shelves were stocked and priced, with the final shipment due from the mailboat as soon as Jerry picked it up. The windows along the big wall were curtained and the six tables underneath had matching covers. There was enough material left over to make two dirndl-aprons ... skirts of material gathered into little pleats and stitched to a wide belt, that'd tie 'round her waist ... and it would give a warm, friendly effect, all the windows and the tables and herself in matching gingham. Homey! She had Roy hang a kerosene lamp from a pulley screwed into the center ceiling rafter, and at night when she was working it'd give a soft glow around the room. Cozy. Gemutlich. Warm. She still had those aprons to sew, and several more batches of cookies to bake. She'd decided on pfeffernuss. They were round and bodisome and would fit snugly on the saucer with the coffee cup. She'd charge five cents per cup for the coffee and give each customer a free cookie. After everything was done, she'd ask Jerry to bring over the Victrola. One corner of the large room had been saved for the table and the records and the player. She would put potted palms in front, and let the music seep softly through. And then, last of all, of course, she'd mop. She turned slowly in the center of the room, envisioning customers coming in the side door, taking one of the wire baskets that were neatly stacked just inside, crossing to the shelves where the canned goods were spread out, bringing their purchases back to the counter with the little hand-operated cash register, and the money would jingle satisfactorily as she dropped it in the drawer.

She was mulling all this over in her mind when Jerry drove up to the side door.

"Ida. Are you in there?"

"Yes. Yes." She ran to the screened door and held it wide open.

"I finished everybody else first, so I'd be free to help you unpack. Everything came. The list you gave me, it's all here. Everything."

Together they carried in the cartons and stacked them in the middle of the room.

"Hey, why don't I unpack and you get your marker and price 'em right now? We'll be done in no time." He glanced around. "You've really fixed it up great. Everything looks swell. Will you be able to open on time?

Ida nodded, flipping through a price list and beginning to figure costs.

"It's Tuesday and the store opens at eleven a.m. Friday, so I've still got two days. I've decided to stay open only four hours a day, six days each week, off on Sundays. From eleven a.m. 'til three p.m. That way, I'll catch everybody coming and going around the mailboat. How about that?"

Jerry thought it was fine.

"I'll get Aunt Cora to print up several signs. One for inside here, and a large one for down on the mailboat dock. I asked Bertha if we can put one up and she says sure."

The sun was setting by the time they finished, and as Jerry prepared to leave, Ida pushed a stool across to him, and he sat down on it.

"Can you give me a hand on Thursday afternoon? I'll be home sewing and baking all day tomorrow and most of Thursday, so I won't be down here at all. Thursday afternoon I want to move my Victrola and table down and if you'll help we can do it all in one trip."

"Of course I'll help. Sure."

"Then, Thursday night, I'll mop, and we'll be done. Won't that be just grand? You know ... " she leaned across the counter, dropped her head down onto her arms and closed her eyes ... "I'm tired out. Really tired. But I still feel good!"

Jerry looked across at her and smiled. He liked Ida. Even more, he admired her. What exactly was it? He wasn't sure. Never before had he bothered to explore his feelings and wasn't conscious of doing so now. He looked at her and saw her clearly ... a thin, tired, old woman, with a torn dust rag wound round her head and a heavy tobacco smell about her. Her face was crisscrossed with wrinkles. He could see a little pulse throb in a ropy vein running down her neck. Her hands were chapped and careworn. Her shoulders were stooped from worry and heavy work. He wanted to protect her, to help her. His admiration was mixed with love and pity. At an age when most people were retired and rocking on a porch somewhere, here she was, heading into yet another venture, and by herself. All alone. He realized all this as he gazed at her, through her, sensing that there was something more but unable to reach it.

Suddenly his mind pulled back and his eyes focused. With a guilty start he realized that she'd opened her eyes and was watching him watching her.

He flushed in embarrassment.

"Mess, ain't I?" She murmured, her eyes warm and smiling.

That was it! There it was! She'd read his thoughts. His mind flashed back to occasional moments when he'd had a strange sensation that he knew what she was thinking, too. He couldn't remember exactly where or when but it was there. His flush receded and he felt a little shiver. He wasn't sure he liked all this. He felt strangely uncomfortable.

After an awkward pause he spoke quietly.

"Where's the Victrola gonna go?"

Ida sat up and pointed to the empty corner.

"Over there. It'll be out of the way. Waltzes! I'll play Viennese waltzes. Strauss! I love 'em. I've got a whole set. They're heavy, so don't forget Thursday afternoon."

"I won't."

"Promise?"

"Sure. I promise. Thursday afternoon I'll be here. I'll remember."

He had the best intentions in the world and he would have remembered as he promised ... except the panther reappeared.

●

Charlie Kramdon held up the bullhorn and called over to Dennis Upton.

"You'll need this, Dennis, if you expect to direct this gang. They'll be spread out so far they won't be able to hear you on the ends without it."

It was 7 a.m. and the sun was barely up. Everyone free to help was gathering at the post office dock, leaning against the railing or hunched down by their cars. They all carried heavy sticks of some sort.

Matilda Crunch moved back and forth among the group, edgy and tense but enjoying all the attention. She spied Bertha standing in the post office doorway and rushed over.

"This ain't gonna do no good," she cried breathlessly. "We're gonna have to call in the authorities. I can't stand much more of this ... can't live this way, lookin' over my shoulder all the time. Can't get my work done. That thing could pounce any minute!"

"Did you see any sign of it this morning? Any new tracks?" Bertha was apprehensive. Her young ones, usually playing unsupervised all day in her yard, had been bottled up inside since the first scare, and the screaming and the fighting in the house all day was getting on her nerves.

Matilda shook her head so violently her beehive rocked.

"Nothin' this mornin'. Yesterday was quite enough, thank you. All over my yard, and the road, and those two paw marks right on my bedroom window sill! I tell you I'm scared to death ... that thing standin' on its hind legs, peerin' through the window at me while I'm sound asleep in my bed. It's enough to roll the dead! They must do something! I'm at my wit's end!"

Dennis tested the bull horn.

"Everybody gather over here, please, and we'll get organized." Then, as the group tightened up, he boomed again ... "Does this thing work?"

Heads nodded and hands clapped over ears and there was general laughter.

"Okay. I won't use it here, but later on I will. I'll try to keep the line straight. Here's what we'll do. Oh, by the way, did any of you bring whistles?"

Several held up their hands and Mr. Orbison from Mid-Island twirled something noisey in the air.

"I found this old claxon. Makes quite a racket."

"Good!" Dennis climbed onto the hood of a car so everyone could easily see him. "Now here's what we'll do. As much as possible we want to hold a straight line across the island, Gulf to bay. It'll be difficult as it's easy going up by the beach but along the bay edge those mangroves are thick. No need to tramp through 'em, deep inside, that'd be impossible, but we must know that the cat isn't lurking in there. Actually it isn't too likely at best, the tangle and all, and they don't like water, but we'll have to know." He shifted the bullhorn to his other knee. Damn thing weighed quite a bit. Taking a deep breath and talking over the crowd, he went on. "The ladies will walk the beach and the roadway, and the men will stretch from where the ladies end on across the island to the bay. I'll be in the middle, and I'm going to ask Evan to control the line along the bay-side. Where's Roy? I don't see Roy Coggins. He said last night when we were planning this search that he'd be here for sure."

"Roy went bustin' through here an hour ago," Evan called. "Said to tell you there was some electrical emergency at Sanibel Inn and he'd catch up with you about ten o'clock."

"Okay." Dennis went on. "Remember, folks, we don't want an encounter. We're not out to kill that cat. We want to see him. We want to establish that there is a panther. Then we'll get the county to come in. Oh, one thing more. Elgin Bigelow will be hovering back and forth in his Piper Cub. So don't wonder when he appears."

"Who's Elgin Bigelow?" Someone wanted to know.

"He's the official representative of the U.S. Fish and Wildlife outfit. Lives up on Sanibel at the lighthouse. Animals are Federally protected on these islands, remember. We can't kill any. It'll have to be trapped and hauled off. So, are we ready? Let's move out. Keep within hailing distance and eye contact and don't hunch. If you reach an easy stretch, don't go leaping ahead. Try to keep the line straight." He raised the bullhorn and bellowed ... "Okay. Off we go!"

By mid-morning they had reached Palm Avenue and here they took a break. Dennis had arranged refreshments to be positioned along the roadway, and the bush-beaters rested and gossiped. The panther had not been sighted! The

218

only excitement had been the evacuation of Didi Drinkwater by plane to the hospital in Fort Myers for an x-ray of her leg. She and Jerry had joined the line of searchers under Evan, scouring the bay-side where the mangroves were thick, and Didi had caught her foot in a root tangle. Her involuntary cry of pain alerted Jerry and Evan and by the time they'd extricated the poor girl the leg was useless, already swelling and turning black and blue. Elgin Bigelow was contacted by radio, and landed his amphibian plane in the quiet bay and taxied to shore. Jerry gave Didi last minute instructions as she was bundled into the little plane, to wait for him in the hospital main lobby and he'd leave at once in his truck and drive over for her, as Elgin Bigelow had to return to the search.

By late morning the line reached halfway between the Upton's home and the northern end of the island, just south of Chadwick's Bayou. The thickest tangle of undergrowth lay ahead. The line of searchers had now telescoped appreciably, due to the narrowing of the landscape. Dennis was hard pressed with his bullhorn to keep people from bunching up.

The majority of the hunters, by one p.m., had broken through to Redfish Pass, which separated Upper Captiva from Captiva, and were lolling at the water's edge, waiting for the stragglers to come up.

No panther! And no Roy Coggins. This was odd, as Roy's hut was next door to Matilda Crunch's Shell Shop, where all the panther tracks had been found, and he was as interested in the situation as she was. Presumably. He must have been held up at the Sanibel Inn.

It was a tired, disgruntled crowd that slowly wended its way back down the beach and to their various establishments.

"It's holed up somewhere, deep in those tangled mangroves, most likely in an abandoned 'gator hole, and we just walked on by," Dennis Upton exclaimed later to Evan, as they sat out on Murph's dock and drank a cold beer. Murph, in from mullet fishing, spoke slowly, between gulps.

"Seems to me we should stop playing games with this thing. Let me contact Herb Mercer at the Everglades Wildlife Exhibit down in Bonita Springs. He's forgotten more about Florida panthers than all of us put together ever knew. Let's get him up here and check this thing out."

"What can he do that we can't?" Dennis wanted to know.

"Well," Murph explained, "He can tell us once and for all if it really is a panther. And if it is, we'll ask the County Commissioners to mount a proper trapping."

●

One look at Didi, sitting hunched over in a corner of the hospital lounge and Jerry's heart dropped. Her hair, usually so neat and glowing, was messed up and full of twigs, and her jeans were filthy. The leg was bandaged thick as a fence post.

"Anyway," she said, "it's not broken. A bad sprain. Really bad. But no bones damaged. That's a relief, of course. Look at me! Isn't it ridiculous." Her smile was brave but there was pain underneath. "Did they find that panther?"

"I don't know. I left right behind you. We'll find out when we get home."

Back at the bridge, Cora clucked over Didi like a latter-day Florence Nightingale, and Aunt Agnes cooked a huge meal. They sat and talked and ate. Jerry and Didi were preparing for the short ride to Didi's house when Roy Coggins drove into the yard.

"Sorry I didn't get back in time to help look for that critter. Carla was having a real problem over at the Inn. I did get back in time, however, to help Ida drag over that Victrola and table to her store. She says don't worry. She understands about Didi and her leg. Her chores are all done now, and she says she'll be opening on time tomorrow. Thought I'd let you know."

Jerry's mouth had flopped open and he looked distressed. Ye Gods! He'd forgotten all about Ida! That was really dreadful. And he'd promised, too! He'd run Didi home and then go on down to the store. Maybe there was still something he could do to help. At least, he could be with her for a while as they'd planned, even if it was late now, and night had set in.

●

Jerry parked his truck to one side and approached the store building at a half-crouch. He'd peep in and see what Ida was doing, and then he'd call and surprise her. He was chuckling to himself in anticipation of her startled look as he slowly raised his head up over the windowsill and peered into the room.

She had been mopping the floor and was resting now, leaning on the mop handle, listening to music blaring from the corner behind the potted palms. Martial music. Jerry didn't know what it was, but it had a strong beat, and a fife in the background. With a closed fist, Ida was keeping time, swinging her arm high and bringing it sharply down as the cymbals clashed, and her feet beat time on the floor with each heavy rattling roll of the drums. Jerry found his finger keeping time along with her on the windowsill. Suddenly with a tremendous burst of combined horns and woodwinds, piano and harp, with a

220

bass viol thumping and kettledrums rolling, the entire orchestra peaked full-throated into a clash and bang of stunning sound ... and it was over. Silence!

Jerry lowered his head for a moment onto his hand and let the excitement of the stirring music wash through him. Then, straightening up and taking a deep breath, he prepared to call in to Ida, but instinctively hesitated. Ida was moving swiftly. She ran to the wall switch and flipped off the lights, leaving the hanging lantern flickering a warm, soft glow across the floor. She ran to the Victrola in the corner and Jerry could hear records clicking. She ran back to the center of the room and stood in front of the mop and bucket, her hands folded over her stomach and her head demurely bowed.

Softly the lilting opening notes of the Blue Danube waltz drifted over the room, and Ida sank to the floor in a full curtsy.

Jerry held his breath and strained to catch the sound. As from a great distance, he heard a French horn call, answered by a flute, then an oboe. The music swept nearer ... nearer ... and suddenly burst into the room with a rollicking shout.

Ida didn't move.

As if disappointed, discouraged that their arrival failed to alert, the instruments seemed to hesitate, to back off to the far side of the room, shuffling into a quick regrouping. Maybe sixteen bars wasn't enough. Maybe the enticement should be longer. Maybe thirty-six bars. This time, as they started again, a cello, thick and lush, joined in, and a resonate kettledrum pummelled the air. Tendrils of lovely sound ribboned and billowed around the room, beckoning, signalling to the listener ... join us ... join us ...

And Ida heard. One arm lifted slowly, the hand reaching for the mop handle, the fingers extended ...

A wayward little breeze rocked the lantern. Shadows lengthened and shortened and seemed alive. Jerry couldn't see distinctly. A gauzy film encased the room. He inched his head forward until his nose nearly pressed the screening. Everything seemed so hazy ...

The searching fingers found the top of the mop handle, and grasped. Only it wasn't a mop handle! Another hand was reaching down, other fingers were grasping, lifting, raising the little old woman up off the floor until she was poised upright, on tiptoe.

The music leapt in wild abandon, appeared to split into two flowing streams of sound, two arms reaching to encircle the room. The strings raced ahead along the near side, the violins and the harps abreast, and the cellos, with a youthful zither struggling to keep up. The other arm, the winds and the percussions, in competition with the lighter, daintier strings, boomed and clashed, tooted and trilled, as it swept more majestically along the far side. Like a benign coachman holding the reins tightly to his chest, the kettledrum, muted and throbbing, blanketed the entire ensemble with a pulsating, controlling beat. Crashing together in the center of the room, exciting sounds spiralled high to the ceiling and broke into a shower of musical tinsel that drifted in tinkling notes down upon the two figures standing below.

221

Two? Two figures?

Jerry drew back in amazement. What was he seeing? What was happening? The little hairs on the back of his neck seemed to lift and a chill raced along his spine. He was alarmed and wanted to leave, but his feet seemed imprisoned. He pressed farther forward. If only the haze would clear, but it seemed to thicken. Through it, Jerry glimpsed the blue of the young man's tunic. He was bent slightly forward, his head inclined, and he was holding Ida's hand to his lips. An officer ... possibly a hussar. There was a plume on his visored upright hat, and a short sabre sashed to his waist, and spurs were attached to his shiny black boots.

Ida? Ida's hand? But there was no Ida! Standing before the resplendent officer was a young girl, all in white, shimmering and glistening, in a long flowing gown, one arm raised, the other by her side, one foot slightly behind the other, and a little yellow rose over one ear. They gazed at each other in silent tableau as the orchestra started to play the opening bars of the promenade.

Without lowering her hand, the officer led her forward in stately cadence, first to the flower-banked corner, where they both bowed low, and then in a solemn, measured parade around the perimeter of the hall. Elegantly gowned ladies and their manicured escorts became visible as the marchers passed by, and Jerry could hear muffled applause. Chandeliers, with branching clusters of glowing candles, swayed from the ceiling and cast a mellow orange glow about the room as the dancers returned finally to the center of the hall. Here, as the music faded, they assumed their original stance, motionless, slightly bent, one arm aloft, one foot slightly back ... heads erect ... waiting ...

With an exuberant, swift rush, the violins were back, sighing, smiling, beckoning, enticing ... and as if marionettes, strung to an unseen hand, the two figures responded to the insistent, compelling three-four beat.

A quick bend and she had a fold of the voluminous skirt in her left hand, held high, a soft fluffy bird poised for flight. His right arm slipped around her waist and snuggled her body to his. With his left hand holding her right tightly to his chest, they moved forward with a slight dip and a glide, and whirled away across the room as the orchestra wrapped them in soft sensuous sound. Round and round, dip and slide, twist and twirl, swing and loop, swing high, swing higher ... they led the orchestra now, dragging it along behind them in an increasing, swooping, wild abandon. Grasping the back of her partner's neck for leverage, the young girl leaned out farther and farther as she spun in dizzying swirls. Her eyes were fast shut and her lips were parted in a delighted smile and she didn't notice when her hair tumbled loose and fell to her shoulders in a filmy cloud.

All of a sudden the scene filmed over. The room, the audience, the dancers, everything seemed suddenly to fade, to drift away. With his heart in his mouth, Jerry involuntarily cried aloud.

"No! Oh, no! Don't leave. Don't stop. Go on. Go on."

Two tourists, Suzy and Sal Vecchio, strolling arm in arm along Palm Avenue, heard Jerry call out. Suzy nudged Sal in the ribs.

"Go over and see what that kid's yelling about. Nothin' else's happenin' around here."

Sal crossed over to the bank of windows and looked inside.

"Ain't nothin' at all," he called over his shoulder. "Just some old dame prancin' around with a mop!"

Jerry heard him and spun around.

"That's not true!" He shook his head in agitation. "Can't you see?" They're dancing. It's beautiful. One of the loveliest dances I've ever seen. Look. Look."

He turned his head and peered back inside, but it was too late. The spell was broken. Sal Vecchio was right. Nothing was visible inside except Ida. Ida and a bucket and a mop. A scratchy record was playing on the Victrola.

A bit later, when Jerry walked quietly into the store, Ida was standing holding the mop in one hand and gazing intently at something in the other.

"Hi" she called. "Look at this! Wonder where it came from. I just found it on the floor."

She held out toward him a little yellow rose petal.

16

February

T he little wooden building, situated well in from the beach, nestled among a thick clump of sea-grapes and was almost entirely hidden by protecting Australian pines. Its clapboard walls were glistening white. The twisting entry drive was swept clean of the burrs and pine needles dropped by the trees, so that visitors, barefoot from strolling the beach, could approach in comfort. Above the simple doorway, and just below the squat steeple, a sign read "Chapel-by-the-Sea".

The chapel was old by island standards. The land had been donated to the community by Bertha's grandmother, and the first chapel had been built by her grandfather. In the early 20's it had burned to the ground, no one ever found out why, and Evan had built the present building on the same site. Immediately adjacent was the simple graveyard. Bertha had proclaimed herself custodian and every week she dusted and cleaned the little building and weeded around the few graves, and it was here that Jean Culpepper found her.

"Hi," Jean called, climbing off her bike and leaning it against a tree. "Can I help?"

"Dearie me, you sure can." Bertha straightened up and wiped her forehead. "I've been after Evan for ages to rotor this area and cut down some of these weeds. He keeps saying he will but in the winter months he's got to grab every job he can get, you know. I'm almost done for this trip and have to get back to the post office. Boat'll be dockin' in a couple hours and 'course, I gotta be there, you know."

Some time later, when Bertha was satisfied that the reaching weeds had been thwarted for another week, she nodded her thanks and smiled at Jean.

"Want to see inside? I'm mighty proud of our church. Not that we have regular services or anything like that. Can't get a preacher and no one hereabouts wants to take on the job. It's chorey, you know, and if a body ain't used to speakin', it can be pretty frightenin'." She fumbled under her apron and drew out a long, old-fashioned key. "Come on in. Remember, this ain't no northern cathedral. It's just a simple little back-woods country chapel. But it's clean and I like to think that God pauses here and rests a spell as he bustles about doin' all his good works."

The door swung wide on oiled hinges and Jean entered hesitantly. It was clean, all right. Spotless! The windows along both sides glistened in the early morning sun and the pine floor, recently treated to a lye solution mop-down, had the grey-brown patina of old Spanish moss. There was an open space immediately inside the door, supposedly extra room for folks to stand should there happen to be an overflow crowd. An aisle stretched ahead between neat rows of folding chairs, six on each side, and six rows deep. Another small open space and then the pulpit, atop a low platform. A piano stood against the wall on one side of the wooden lectern, and next to the other wall was an overstuffed armchair, plum colored and frayed.

Bertha smiled as she pointed to the chair.

"That thing hadn't oughter be in here a-tall. We put it there some five years back and haven't gotten around to heftin' it out yet. Afraid we might need it again, though Preacher Adams has been dead now for four years. He used it to revive in. Sure was some preacher, standin' there, with his wide-brimmed hat pushed back an' hangin' down his back on a little cord, hammerin' and beatin' on that stand up there. He'd call down on us every drop of brimstone and hell-fire he could muster. He'd get louder an' louder as he got into it, an' then he'd stagger over to that chair and collapse an' we'd have to rush him a glass of cider. Never did know what was in that cider. He'd bring a gallon jug of it with him an' the fumes'd mount once he uncorked it, but whatever it was it'd do the trick an' pretty soon he'd rear up an' struggle back to the stand and go to shoutin' an' poundin' again. My, it was grand! Sure was. While he was restin' an' sippin', my oldest, Rose, she'd play ` Chopsticks' on the piano. Couldn't play nothin' else, an' 'course we hadda have music. At the end of the sermon, with Preacher near dead from his exertions, and that cider, we'd all sing ` The Old Rugged Cross'. All us women, we loved Church. The men folks, 'course they hated it. None of us never did know exactly what killed Adams. It was either the preachin' or that funny business up at his fish camp!"

All through this Jean had been sitting on the first chair in the front row, looking at Bertha across the little aisle.

"What funny business up at what fish camp?" she asked.

"Well, I hadn't oughter tell you this, seein' as I'm not positive sure about it. I mean, I didn't hear or see anything myself. I got it from old man Jackson. Still ... well, Preacher Adams liked his likker and he had an eye for a well-turned ankle, as they say. He had this little hut, one-room affair, built on stilts offshore some 200 feet out in the open bay, up toward the end of the island. Only way to get there was by boat, and weekends he'd chug on out to this fish camp, as he called it. Well, one Saturday morning Mr. Jackson was out troutin' an' a fierce squall come up outa nowhere, as it can out there on the bay, and the only place he could reach for shelter was underneath Preacher Adams' hut. Crouchin' under there, with his skiff lashed to the piling and his motor off, 'course he could hear all the goings on going on. He later got down to our dock and stumbled into the house, where I dried him off and gave him some hot soup. He just sat there dumbfounded-like, mutterin' to himself ... 'Never woulda figgered it that way! Never! Never woulda thought that ole man had it in him. Ain't it funny how different folks is from what we think. Never woulda figured it that way!'"

He just sat there, shaking his head and mutterin' to himself. I later got Evan to boat him over to his home in Hurricane Hollow, and when Evan come back he slapped me on the hip and chuckled.

"Well, ole gal, seems Adams had a little bit of heaven, several little bits of heaven, giggling and carrying on, all to himself up in that fish house!"

"You shut up, Evan" I said. "I don't want to hear about it. Not a word! I don't want the kids to hear about it, neither. And you'd better never set foot near that camp. You hear me?"

"Soon after that time, ole Adams died!"

Jean got up and walked over to the piano.

"You've never had a preacher since then?" she questioned.

Bertha shook her head.

"No," she said. "Not since then. 'Course, once in a coon's age a winter guest'll offer to hold a service and we'll spread the word around and folks'll gather, but it ain't the same. Not like a regular service you can count on."

Jean opened the piano and sat down in front of it. Quietly she started playing "The Old Rugged Cross". Bertha sat stiff in her chair until the end.

"My! You didn't tell me! That was beautiful. Just beautiful. Even with that old piano all out of tune, that was beautiful. Can you really play that thing? Or is that all you know, like my Rose and her 'Chopsticks'?"

Jean shifted into "Nearer My God to Thee" as Bertha crossed to the piano and leaned on the edge.

"Do you know 'Little Church in the Wildwood'? That's my favorite."

When she reached the end of the simple tune Jean looked up at Bertha with a naughty expression on her face.

"I can also play like this" ... and swung into a rousing ragtime version of "When the Saints Go Marching In". Long before she was finished, Bertha was shaking her hands high in the air and twisting her head from side to side.

"No! Not stuff like that. Not in here. That's for outside, not in a church!" Fearful she'd hurt Jean's feelings, she quickly added, "Real catchy, though. It'd be just the thing for our jamboree. In May. We have one every year, you know. End of May. The home owners have all gone an' all, an' then all those places have to be closed up for the summer an' when all that work's done an' we've had a bit of time to ourselves an' our own stuff, then we always have this big bang-up party up here, outside in front where it's cleared. We call it 'The Welcome Back Jamboree'. All the snowbirds have flown away back north an' we've got our island back again. Lots an' lots of food an' singin' an' the kids go swimmin' an' Murph brings up his dart board, an' Roy rigs us up a line for the Victrola." Her face glowed with excitement as she remembered. "But we ain't never had music, live music. Think how wonderful that'd be! We'd move this piano outside an' you could play an' we'd all gather round ..." Her voice trailed away into nothing as she gazed at Jean. "Oh, I forgot. You won't be here, will you? You'll be leavin' in a day or so now." Her face fell.

Jean picked at one of the piano keys, making a soft little bong, bong sound, and slowly turned her head toward Bertha.

"Actually," she said in an undertone, "we didn't want to say anything quite yet, as the arrangements aren't all worked out, but Frank and I are planning to stay. If Mrs. Chuffer agrees, we'll rent her place for another six months, and after that, maybe we'll buy it. So, you see, I'll most likely be here, and I'd love to play for your party. Count me in."

Bertha took a deep breath, and plunged.

"Would you play for Sunday School and Church?"

●

As with most other financially fortunate northerners, seeking escape from frigid weather by residing for several months under warm southern suns, the wealthy winter group on Captiva were hard-pressed to avoid boredom and the resulting ennui of drifting aimlessly from house to house at 4:30 each afternoon. The solution was a monthly 'excitement peak'.

During February, the national celebrations in memory of Lincoln and Washington, followed by the nostalgic sweetness of St. Valentine's Day, seemed insufficient, and each year a fevered attention centered on February 15th ... Mammy Farlow's birthday.

During the beginning of February, Kate O'Hearn mailed the following note to Mammy:

Dear Mrs. Farlow:

As in years before, my friends and I would like to call upon you and Mr. Farlow, at two in the afternoon of February 15th, to honor your birthday.

There will be five of us ... Mrs. Fontaine, Mrs. Lockwood, Mrs. Macabbe, Miss Randolph and myself.

Kindly let me know if this will be convenient.

Cordially,

Your friend, Kate O'Hearn

In due course, Kate received the following brief reply:

Dear Friend O'Hearn:

We is honored.

You and your ladies can hitch up to our dock.

We will be awaiting.

Cordially,

Your friend, Mammy Farlow

Lars was immediately sent around to the four households involved, to invite each lady for lunch. The trip across Roosevelt Channel to the northern tip of Buck Key had to be planned in detail.

Seated at the head of the luncheon table in the huge room, Kate glanced around at the others, all ferociously devouring the chicken salad and creamed vegetables in patty shells as if they'd not seen food for a month. She shook her head slightly. Really, what a worthless bunch. Still, she mused to herself, I suppose they do some good. At least, they try. Pushing back her plate, she folded her napkin and reinserted it in its silver ring. She patted her stomach in sympathy with its approaching difficulties in digesting the rich food not on her diet. She could feel gas building up.

"Girls." She raised her voice slightly to get attention. "Does everyone agree to meeting here on the 15th at one p.m., following lunch at your own place. Helga will be too involved making and icing the birthday cake to fix lunch here. Is that all right with everyone?"

There was general agreement, though Miss Randolph demurred slightly.

"If we meet at one o'clock, and the trip takes all of fifteen minutes, we'll be early, won't we? We surely don't want to spend any more time than absolutely necessary, I wouldn't think, considering we're all so rushed. It'll be boring enough, anyway, once we get there."

Kate kept making notes and replied without looking up.

"Lolly, dear. If you're so tied up with work that your schedule will be interfered with, maybe you should forego the trip this time."

"Oh, no! I didn't mean ... of course I'll go. I just feel that we should try not to be too early, that's all." Lolly Randolph looked hastily around the table but found no supporters.

Not wanting even a gentle confrontation, Kate went on.

"I'd thought of that and we'll take care. Still, I feel one o'clock is a wise choice. You know how you all are. If we aim at 1:00 p.m., it'll be 1:15 by the time everyone drags in, and then Doris will forget something, like she always does, and we'll have to wait while what's-his-name ... what is that smoldering young man's name, Doris?"

"Achmed!"

"Ah, yes." Kate peered speculatively over the top of her glasses at Doris. She couldn't resist a thrust. "Is he proving ... satisfactory ... dear?"

"He's a very conscientious driver."

"Ah, yes." Kate murmured again. She could play this game all afternoon but Doris was showing signs of squirming so they'd better move along.

"As I was saying, this Achmed will be sent back for the dark glasses or the powder or whatever, and by the time we all climb aboard, it'll be 1:30 or later. The trip over will take some fifteen minutes, and to time our arrival exactly at 2 p.m., we can cruise up and down Roosevelt Channel a bit. So, unless there's a real objection, I'll expect you at one o'clock and I'll see that Sam has the tender mopped and bailed and gassed up."

"Will Sam be at the tiller?" Someone wanted to know.

Kate shook her head.

"No, I'll run us over. It wouldn't be fair to Sam to ask him to wait at the dock for us the hour or so we'll be with the Farlows."

"An hour? A whole hour?" Lolly Randolph wouldn't quit. "What will I do for a whole hour?"

"Bring a comic book with you" Fanny Fontaine called brightly, "and you can read." There was a twitter of amusement.

"Plates!" Doris Lockwood called out. "Can't I please bring small plates? It gave me the willies last time, eating cake off those dirty, cracked things Mammy Farlow handed around. And a cake knife?"

"Certainly NOT!" Kate was emphatic. "Honestly," she went on, "sometimes I don't know why I put up with all of you. Where are your feelings, even if you haven't any tact? We're not going over there to insult the Farlows. We'll accept their hospitality and eat on their plates exactly the same as if we were dining with Bess and Harry in the White House. If you can't handle that, then stay home!" Her voice was heavy with irritation. "And," she went on, "this year, please, everybody wear a simple shirtwaist and jeans. That bias-cut tea gown you flounced around in last time, Sara, was lost on me and didn't seem to impress the Farlows at all. For heaven's sake, let's try to be as gentle and gracious as Mammy and Daddy will be. They're special, those two, and I feel very close to both of them. They've been part of the island scene ever since I've been coming down here, for years now, and I tremble when I think of their age and something dreadful happening to either of them." She paused and doodled with her fork on the tablecloth, and seemed lost in thought. "Anyway," she continued, "if there's nothing else to go into, let's adjourn this meeting and release Lolly to get back to her heavy schedule."

●

Amelia Armstrong was so excited she couldn't sit still. She was in and out of her chair, pacing the porch floor and making little stabbing thrusts at an imaginary foe, as Agnes and Cora watched openmouthed. She'd rushed in that morning, calling "Cora ... Cora" and let the screened door slam behind her as she rushed over to Cora and grabbed her by the shoulder.

"Dear me," Cora exclaimed, scattering palm fronds all across the floor.

" 'Scuse. 'Scuse," Amelia said, breathlessly, "but today's the day! Today's the day! I've been living all these weeks for today and here it is! Don't you dare forget, Cora Chisholm, to let me know the very minute Bob Wilson shows up. He and Russell and I, we're going to nail that Lieutenant MacDuff right into the ground!"

"He's a Colonel, Amelia."

"Well, anyway - in Myers the other day, in the Health department, Bob Wilson told me he was scheduled to check your shop this afternoon, Cora, and the Building and Zoning Inspector, Russell Jones, would be with him. They've already notified MacDuff to be at that shed by three p.m. He's got to dismantle that monstrosity. Tear it down! I won't have it a single day longer! I knew I'd win. Papa brought me up to persevere. To organize and wait my time. Well, this afternoon is my time. I've won. I've won!"

Maude and Jerry came in from the lime grove just at this moment and caught the end of Amelia's gleeful statement.

"Won what? What'd ya win?" Maude wanted to know, unhooking her tool belt and letting it clunk to the floor.

Amelia started to launch into her plans of entrapment but Jerry interrupted.

"Mrs. Armstrong they just drove up as we came in."

Amelia was stunned!

"Colonel MacDuff and that woman? They just drove up?"

Jerry nodded and held up a finger.

"Listen. Hear? He's ringing that little bell. Can't you hear it?"

Amelia didn't know what to do to show her agitation. Instinctively she chose not to faint as that would take too much time and she had to know what MacDuff was doing.

"Let's creep out to that big hibiscus bush and peep." Suiting action to word, she was half out the door before she finished speaking. Like large mice, they sneaked out and grouped under the thick bush. It was a perfect vantage point. They could see the little shed and the jeep parked in front. Colonel MacDuff wasn't visible but Andrusa was. She was sitting upright in the back seat.

"What's she doing?" Amelia breathed at Maude.

"Knitting." Maude breathed back.

"Knitting?"

"Knitting."

"Of all the gall! What a cool customer that one is! She's sitting there knitting while he's inside doing God knows what."

"We know what he's doing."

"Please! I don't want to think about it. I won't think about it. I will ..."

But they were never to hear Amelia's next comment, for at that moment Colonel MacDuff emerged. He returned to the jeep and off it roared, Andrusa apparently not dropping a single stitch.

"That filthy creature!" Amelia was near tears.

"Yes," Agnes agreed, shaking her head, "This is all unacceptable. He should be stopped. Wonder what Andrusa was thinking. Oh, dear. All that nastiness on this small island. People just haven't enough to do."

Back on the porch, with Amelia gone, Maude made a general comment as she helped Cora straighten up the work table.

"You touched the exact situation just now, Ag, when you used the words 'small island'. I still say that Amelia is getting her just desserts. On this small island she should never have made an issue of Andrusa's and MacDuff's relationship in the first place. What does Amelia think she is? The National Conscience?"

Promptly at three p.m. the little procession converged on Colonel MacDuff's chic sale. The Health Inspector and the Building and Zoning Inspector, followed closely by Amelia Armstrong, Maude, and the others, grouped in front of the door and the Health Inspector glanced at his watch. Coincidingly, a rumble of loose boards on the bridge could be heard and Colonel MacDuff hove into view, traveling at top speed.

"Right-o." He called as he skidded in a semi-circle just off the road, showering everyone with sand. "To what do I owe this honor?"

Bob Wilson, from Health, took up the reins.

"Sir, we've had complaints about this ... "

"I know. I know." Colonel MacDuff rumbled. "You want to see what rules and regulations I've broken. Right-o." He turned toward Mrs. Armstrong and bowed low. "To you, Madam, I owe this intrusion. Lovely Lady, eh what?" And he dug Russ Jones, Building and Zoning, in the ribs as he straightened up. He reached over, unlocked the door, stood aside and with a gallant sweeping gesture of his right hand, motioned everyone to enter.

There was nothing inside!

Nothing! Just a folding chair, a tiny stand and an old dog-eared copy of Popular Mechanics.

Bob Wilson and Russ Jones stood silently in the center of the little room, a slow smile etching across their faces as the charade became clear to them.

Faces lined the doorway as everyone peeped over each other and under each other for a clarifying look.

Amelia Armstrong was apoplectic!

"As any fool can see, I haven't broken any rules. Any supposed infringements have been the product of the fertile imagination of this frustrated lady." Colonel MacDuff was beside his jeep now, one putteed foot

231

on the step-up, and his pith helmet on the back of his head. "However, Madam," again the gallant bow, "this little game has now run its course. I shall dismantle this cozy little building tomorrow. Not because you have bested me, but because I need the material for my carport. Needless to add, you have acted in this matter like a spoiled brat. Andrusa has never done any harm to you. If you had reservations regarding any irregularities of mine, you should have come to me and laid out your complaints openly. You claim to be descended from Miles Standish, somewhere in the eighteenth century, isn't it ... Longfellow, and all that. Well, my lady traces her line directly to King John and all that ruckus under a tree when he signed that Magna Carta ... 1215! Using your own guide, judge for yourself which is the grander lady!" Turning to the two inspectors, as he climbed into his jeep and started the motor, he called "As for you two gentlemen, may I suggest you return to productive endeavors before I notify your respective offices that you're wasting the taxpayers money." With a roar of his engine and a sudden leap forward as the gears clashed, he was gone.

●

If Matilda Crunch hadn't collapsed that morning from fear, gone into an hysterical fit and fainted on the Shell Shop porch ...

If Darlene Epstein hadn't decided that morning, as she and Abe were packing to head home to Poughkeepsie, to make one last visit to the Shell Shop ...

If Elgin Bigelow hadn't that morning been at Murph's dock, his little plane nosed into the turtlegrass along the shore, while he conferred with Murph and Pearlie regarding rumors of egret hunters working the back-bay bayous ...

If Jean and Didi hadn't previously planned a joint rush trip to Fort Myers that morning so Jean could shop for a secondhand piano to practice on now that she was "church pianist", and so Didi could take her carefully preserved redfish in to Boyle's Taxidermy Shop for stuffing and mounting ...

If Roy Coggins hadn't decided that morning to remain at home cleaning and servicing the fire wagon ...

If Jerry hadn't been helping Ida that morning at the store, just two doors south of the Shell Shop ...

If Herb Mercer hadn't cut short his week-long rattler hunt with Ross Allen in the piney woods behind Ocala and returned two days early to Bonita Springs and his Everglades Wildlife Exhibition ...

If all these apparently disassociated events had not each occurred at the proper time, had not each fallen in line in an orderly sequence ... the Great Panther Scare of 1949 might never have been solved!

For the past week Matilda Crunch had over-nighted with Ruta Barstowe, whose house was a short way up-island from the Shell Shop, as she was too scared to sleep alone with that panther prowling about, peeping in her bedroom window as she slept. This morning she crept down the dirt lane, keeping a sharp eye right and left, and turned into her driveway ... and froze as she climbed the porch steps. There were the tracks again! All across the porch. Clear tracks. In mud! Apparently the creature had even sniffed around the door, as there were muddy scuff marks on the trim. Matilda absorbed all this in a single glance, before she gasped and fell flat out on the porch floor, shaking and moaning, her eyes bobbing about in their sockets.

Darlene Epstein hurrying along, intent on buying that huge alphabet shell she'd seen the day before, found Matilda spread-eagle on the porch, arms and legs stiff out and twitching. Darlene threw back her head and screamed at the top of her lungs. Scream after scream tore through the soft early morning silence. When help didn't instantly appear, Darlene started jumping up and down in cadence with her screams.

Roy was emerging from the Upton's driveway, just opposite the Shell Shop, dragging the fire wagon which he'd just filled with fresh bay water, when Darlene's screams smote his eardrums. He dragged the water wagon into Matilda's drive and climbed out of his truck. Shushing the now incoherent Darlene, he took one glance at the supine figure shaking on the floor and reached for the water hose. Remembering from his training as a medic in World War II that cold water reduced shock, he doused Matilda from head to toe with a steady stream.

In her semiconscious state, Matilda imagined that the water was the panther's breath and her little body jackknifed in a reflex spasm as she fainted dead away.

Darlene didn't shush but continued to scream, and Ida, shaking a dustmop out of the store doorway, heard and called to Jerry ... "Better get up the road and look into this. Sounds like somebody's in trouble ..."

Jerry jumped into his truck and drove toward the Shell Shop at a good clip.

Murph and Elgin Bigelow, sauntering along the pier alongside the dock, heading for Elgin's plane, also heard and hurried through Gustave Kroen's banana patch toward the screams.

Everybody within earshot collected. Matilda seemed to be beyond help. Elgin Bigelow held one wrist but couldn't feel much pulse.

"Murph," he murmured, "she should get to Lee Memorial as soon as possible. Not a second to waste, seems to me. Let's get her to my Cub and I'll fly her over."

A blanket was hauled off Matilda's bed and she was wrapped in it. Then she was pushed onto Jerry's flatbed for the half-mile trip to the plane. As they hurried along behind the truck Murph and Elgin talked about this animal thing.

"We ought to get Herb Mercer up here from Bonita." Murph was saying. "Quick enough to check into these tracks before they're all scuffed out."

Elgin nodded. "I'll get Matilda into the hospital emergency first off," he said, "and then I'll buzz on down-country and see if Herb is home. If he is, I'll fly him back up. Okay?"

Murph agreed. "That's the best way. Thanks, Elgin. Couldn't have handled all this by myself. I'll wait out on the dock with Pearlie."

Everything quieted down as people scattered and went back to their chores. The last seen of Darlene, she was sneaking into the open door of Matilda's shop.

●

Herb Mercer eyed the footprints. He measured side to side and front to back. He knelt and squinted. He examined the yard, the muddy flower bed in which there was one perfect print and he measured ground to sill at Matilda's bedroom window. He kept his peace and chewed on a sea oat tassle all the while. He kept shaking his head. Without a word he walked with Murph and Elgin back to the dock.

As they entered, Pearlie called "Hi, Herb."

"Hi, Pearl" Herb responded.

"Well," Pearlie went on, "do we have a panther?"

Herb Mercer nodded.

"Yep. You got a panther. Measures out a big 'un! Wish I had it down in Bonita. It'd make me a fortune."

"How come?"

"Just would. That's all."

Pearlie shook her head. "That big, huh?"

Herb sucked on his beer bottle, 'til it was empty. Then he pushed it aside and motioned Pearlie for another.

"'Taint that it's so all-fired big, Pearl, but its got only one foot."

The other three silently lowered their bottles and looked at Herb.

"You mean ...?"

"I don't mean three feet, or two feet. I mean one foot. Your panther is hopping around the island on one foot ... the right one. Right front!"

Meanwhile, over in Fort Myers, Jean and Didi quickly chose a secondhand piano that Jean felt was a good buy. The music store, only one in town, also had a contact to a piano tuner. Jean made arrangements for delivery of the instrument and engaged the tuner for later on in the week to come to the island and tune the piano in the church. Then, with the redfish fast thawing in its wrapping of newspaper, they drove to Phil Boyle's taxidermy shop in East Fort Myers.

There were only two decisions to be made ... which way the fish should face, and the choice of wood backing. As they headed out of the shop for the trip back to the island, Mr. Boyle walked with them to the door, and held it open for them.

"Do either of you know Roy, over on Captiva? Roy Coggins?"

"Yes," they chorused. "We both do."

"Will you give him a message for me?"

"Sure."

"Ask him not to forget to return that panther foot I loaned him a few weeks ago."

Sitting in the car, fitting the key into the ignition, Jean stared at the dashboard for quite a while. Then, half-smiling and looking sidewise at Didi, she asked softly

"Do you suppose ..."

Remembering Roy's fury at Christmas, Didi smiled back and nodded slowly. "Yes," she said "I sure do."

●

The loading of the Bonita Catcher, Kate O'Hearn's yacht tender, moved along smoothly. The midday sun was beaming down from a cloudless sky and there was just enough breeze to stir the air and ripple the lagoon. Buck Key loomed lush and green just across the channel. The only hitch in the orderly proceedings was when Sara Macabbe caught her spike heel in a crack between the dock decking and snapped it off.

"Well," snorted Fanny Fontaine, "why in God's name did you wear high heels, anyway? Couldn't you have worn deck pumps, like the rest of us?"

"Oh, dear," Sara moaned, distressed by the misadventure. "I'll just run home and change. It'll take only a sec."

"Why not just break off the other one?" someone called. "Or walk lopsided. It isn't far." Everyone laughed.

Kate lifted her hand and turned to Helga, who was helping Sam steady the small boat. "No, don't go anywhere. I'll ask Helga to root around in storage on Wanigan. We've extra pairs of shoes on the yacht. What size do you wear, Sara?"

By the time all this was organized and the ladies had shifted seats several times and Helga had leaped on and off every time this activity threatened to tip the cake perched on a side support, and the motor had been turned over and was purring smoothly, and Sam had loosened the forward line and tossed it into the boat and had given a gentle shove against the gunwale, it was exactly 1:30 and Kate felt a slight vindication as she glanced at her wristwatch and settled herself at the wheel. She liked to be on schedule. An orderly mind was a peaceful mind, and schedules were to be adhered to. She eased the tender past the big yacht and out into the open channel. She smiled to herself as she had a sudden urge to throw the engine full steam ahead and blow off all their hats, but controlled it when she realized there'd not be enough time to circle about and fish the hats back aboard, and still glide gently up to the Farlow's dock at two p.m.

Two stiff figures were standing at the water's edge as the boat came in. Dressed from head to toe in their best black alpaca, holding hands in a silent reaching-out for mutual strength to carry them through the approaching ordeal, Mammy and Daddy silently waited for their guests.

Mammy waved a gentle hand. Daddy did not react, but stood straight and tall until the ladies reached the end of the dock. Then, sweeping off his large-brimmed flat-crowned black hat, he bowed from the waist. It was a simple gesture of welcome, filled with innate charm and warmth. He and Mammy then turned and slowly led the way down the sandy path edged with bleached horse conchs to the small clapboard cottage just beyond.

"Don't let them pigs sceer ya," Daddy called over his shoulder. "I fed 'em good this mornin', so's they ain't hongry and shouldn't bite none." Pigs were everywhere, grunting and snorting as they rooted about in the bushes. Every so often one would stick its snout out and sniff at a passing foot, which was hastily withdrawn in near panic. Chickens scattered in confusion to both sides of the path as the party moved along, except for one huge iridescent cock with a brilliant comb. He fluffed his feathers and dragged the tips of his bunched-out wings in the dirt as he turned in defiant circles, belligerently standing his ground, cackling and clucking in loud disapproval.

"That theer's ole Tom." Daddy offered. "Can be right troublesome. If'n he attacks, stop and stan' still. Like as not he won't strike ya. I'll keep an eye and shoo him off."

As Mammy held open the porch door, a cow looked over her shoulder from the adjacent shed. Mammy smiled and stroked the broad white band down its forehead.

"Here's ole Dora. Bossie died and Dora misses her. Ain't she got a purty face?"

Dora mooed softly and pulled back as the ladies drew closer.

"My. What a splendid Guernsey!" Sara exclaimed.

"No." Lolly Randolph shook her head. "It's not a Guernsey at all, Sara. It's a cow."

Kate caught this exchange as she went on inside and put the cake on the small table in the center of the room. Her eyebrows shot up and her eyes rolled. "Mercy," she sighed to herself, "this is going to be a tough visit. Wonder sometimes why I drag this gang around with me."

Positioned along one wall were four chairs and one upended orange crate. With her usual tact, Kate sat on the crate and motioned the others to the chairs. Daddy and Mammy sat on a little bench along the opposite wall. Everyone shifted about until they were comfortable and looked around expectantly. Nobody said a word.

After what seemed an impossibly long time, Kate spoke, much too loudly.

"You seem to have done very well, since last year, Mrs. Farlow. I don't remember all this livestock."

236

Mammy nodded in solemn agreement.

"Yes'm. We've made out right smart. We've a gracious plenty."

Another agonizing silence!

Then Mammy went on, just as if there'd been no pause.

" 'Course, Miss Kate you'd never've seen our critters last time, no ways."

"Oh?" Kate was eager to keep this hopeful flow alive. "Really. I don't think I understand, exactly."

"Back las' year, jes' afore you come along, we'd eight-nine days rain. Everything was mud."

Daddy broke in gently. "Twar six-seven days."

Mammy nodded and covered Daddy's large hand with her own small one. "I do believe thet's right, Daddy. Leastways, it rained for a caution, right smart along."

Kate was disappointed when the conversation threatened to lag. She leaned forward toward the Farlows.

"Ah, yes. I do believe I recall. Lots of rain! Can be heavy this time of year. But has this anything to do with the livestock?"

Mammy stretched tall on her bench and smiled at Kate. The cake was between them and Mammy had difficulty seeing over it.

" 'Course it do. When it's all mud the hogs and the chickens is fenced under the house. Else they track it inside, you know."

Poor Lolly fell into the unintentional trap.

"And the cow Dora? Can she squeeze under the house?"

Daddy and Mammy chuckled gleefully over this, rocking back and forth in their merriment.

Daddy took up the tale.

"No'm, Dora can't scrunch low as all that. When it rains she lives in this here room. The cowshed leaks and we'se feared fer Dora and the colic." There was a touch of wonderment in his voice, as though he couldn't understand why such a normal solution wasn't obvious to everyone.

Another impossible silence followed.

"Mammy." Daddy came to life. "I'se been thinkin' on to it. I think you is right." Mammy nodded her head in agreement before she knew what he was going to say. "I think twer eight-nine days! After the party, las' time, an' Miss Kate an' all'd gone, it started up rainin' again and that time twer six-seven days. Right afore I broke my neck!"

Mammy nodded in agreement as the ladies came to full attention.

"You broke your neck? How awful! How did it happen? Wasn't the pain terrible? Are you all right again?" The ladies chorused together, showing proper concern and interest.

Daddy took a deep breath and prepared to grab the spotlight, but Mammy patted his knee and looked up into his face.

"Now, Daddy, don't excite yourself. If'n you don' mind, I'll tell this here story. You was done fer, anyway, through mos' of it, 'member, stretched out there in the mud, gaspin' and twitchin' like a big fish." In her excitement,

Mammy jumped up and began to pace about the little room. The visitors tucked their feet under their chairs to keep from tripping her up. Mammy sucked in a deep breath and launched into the story.

"Well, sir, it was rainin' fierce. Had been fer days. Mud was up to my knees, seemed. There was a big pile o' straw in thet corner over thar," she pointed, "fer Dora. But she was riley. Wouldn't stay lyin' down. Hates rainy weather. If'n I got near, her tail'd wrap 'round my head an' slap me in the face. I were fightin' all this, the mud and thet cow in the house, an' we didn' hev much vittles, some grits an' hog-ass as I recollec', an' I'se thinkin' on all this when I heared this loud plop an' a long sorta moan, an' I knewed Daddy'd done fell outa thet there tree."

"Had he?" someone asked.

"Yep. Sure had! Fell slam blast outa thet thar tree!"

Kate didn't have to worry any longer. The conversation was now flowing at a spirited pace. The party would be a great success, after all.

"What was Daddy doing, up a tree in all that rain?" she wanted to know.

"An' storm! Don' fergit the storm. A right smart wind'd come up by then."

"All right," Kate said, changing her approach. "What was Daddy doing up a tree in all that rain and storm?"

"Feared thet ole coconut'd flip outern the groun' an' smash our cow shed. He'd shimmied up her to cut loose them nuts. They'se most the weight, you know, an' in all thet rain, he slipped an' down he come, splat, into that mud, squar' bang onto his haid. When I foun' him, one leg wuz still pushed up thet tree trunk and his body wuz all bunched up an' his haid were at a funny angle. His free han' was clutchin' at the air, which should'a been goin' down his neck, but I could see at onct 'twerent possible." She let out what breath she hadn't used in a long sigh and settled back, basking in all the attention from the five eager faces.

Lolly had been following this report intently. Clutching her own neck so tightly she could scarcely speak, she moaned in a low rasp.

"Mercy! Mercy! Did he die?"

"Of course not!" Fanny Fontaine was so exasperated with Lolly she almost slapped her. "He's sitting right over there, you idiot!"

Kate was genuinely horrified.

"What did you do, Mrs. Farlow?"

"Oh, she fixed me up right smart." Daddy interjected. "She's real trusty when troubles trouble. Calm and thoughty."

Mammy continued eagerly.

"I plopped down in that mud, astraddle his crooky haid, placed my feets onto his shoulders an' gave a real sharp twist an' tug, and his haid come aroun' straight real nice. Somethin' popped loud like, never did know whut 'twas, an' he had this here lumpy place alongside his neck. Poked out real far. But he could suck in air. Made a loud, rushin' noise, like water in a pipe, an' his han' quit snatchin' at the sky, so's I knowed he was better."

"And then? What did you do then?"

"Then I leant down real close like and I sez 'Daddy, you res' real nice and quiet, now, an' I'll be right back' an' I run out onta the dock an' raised up thet white flag. Bertha made us put it there way back, in case we'd bad trouble. Thank the Good Lord it twas mornin' an' Cap'n Bob, when he come by in thet mail boat, he spied our flag an' tol' Bertha. See, he couldn't git up to our dock. Water's too shaller. Thet mail boat she drags deep. 'Course ..." she drifted off a bit, musing over this possibility ... "'Course, he mighta, if'n he'd not been loaded up. If'n he's empty an' the tides in, then maybe ...'"

Fanny interrupted.

"And they came and got him? Evan and all?"

"Yep." Mammy nodded. "First Evan come an' looked. He yanked Daddy's haid this away and that away." She illustrated with a swift side-wise motion of her hand. "Then he said 'Mammy, I think his neck is broke'. And it were, you know. Then that revenue man up on Sanibel, him an' his airy-plane, they took Daddy to the city an' he didn't come back fer two whole weeks. Near kilt me, worry an' all. but he's fine now. Ain't you, Daddy? Wiggle your'n haid and show the folks."

Daddy duly demonstrated.

"'Course, thet lumpy place onto his neck, it ain't never gone down. Can most hang yer hat onto it. Show 'em, Daddy."

Doris Lockwood waved a frantic hand.

"Never mind. Never mind, my dear. We'll take your word for it. How awful. Truly awful. Horrible. All that pain!"

"Oh, taint all thet bad." Mammy was by now fully relaxed and felt expansive. "Taint near as bad as a tooth ache. Daddy here's real good with pliers. Quick, you know. But it hurts like smoke when he twists an' yanks. I'm not real spry with pliers. Keep slidin' off an' I lose my grip. I usually jest grab up a board an' a hammer."

"Oh! Oh!" Lolly Randolph moaned.

Kate interrupted quickly.

"Yes, my dear. We understand. Well," she twisted around on her orange crate and nodded to the others, "shall we present Mammy with her cake?" Turning back toward the other two across the room she half-raised up, but Mammy got there first.

"An' twern't long after when Daddy nearly losted me. When I was hexed, you know!"

A hush fell over the room. Kate was glad she didn't have a late afternoon engagement. This little get-together seemed destined to stretch on longer than anyone had planned. With a certain trepidation as to where this might lead, Kate cleared her throat.

"When you were hexed?"

She glanced with a touch of guilt at her companions.

Mammy leaned forward and thrust a long finger at Kate.

"This heah were Enos' doin's, Miss Kate. Hates me! Always has! Ever since his mammy died and his daddy wed up wit' me, Enos has hated me. Got the evil eye. Plans onto killin' me. Works at it hard. Daddy won't let him live here no more, or ever set foot on this heah property. But he sneaks around, tryin' to ketch me by myse'f. 'Bout las' June, twer, an' Daddy'd gone off trackin' Dora. She hadn't been heah long an'd take to lopin' off, and this heah afternoon, she loped. Daddy were out huntin' her an' I were in the bedroom nex'," she pointed through a doorway, "when I felt somethin' starin' at me an' I glanced up an' there were Enos standin' in the doorway, leanin' onto one side, an' he had a little ole soap doll an' he was jammin' pins into it!"

Mammy paused and shuddered. She didn't seem inclined to continue without prodding.

"Then what?" someone breathed.

"Then I felt this cold feelin', creepin' all over my body, startin' with my feets an' slowly creepin' up an' up an' aroun' my ches' and my arms. They got heavy, an' my neck started to close off an' my eyes got all milky an' I couldn' see. Enos, he started to laugh real loud, an' the ice crep' up over my haid an' iceprickles stuck up from my skull ... an' I don' recollec' no more." Mammy subsided into little twitches and shakes. Daddy put his arm around her shivering shoulders and patted gently.

"There, now. He won't never come back. I done hung that cross atop the door edgin'. He cain't pass thet by, you know."

Turning to the visitors, Daddy nodded his head with great solemnity. "Yessiree. Thet Enos is evil. Born with a cowl all over his face. All the way down to his chin. Woulda died right then an' there if'n I hadn't yanked an' tugged at it 'til it tore off. Maybe I shoulda jes left it be an' let him smother ... I was a-chasin' Dora when I sensed this heah misery back with Mammy an' I come hustlin' home. Never did find Dora. She come stragglin' in on her own self coupla days later. Bossie was in the shed, an' Mammy was stretched out on her bed, stiff as a pole an' cold as ice. I knew right off hadda be Enos. I was dumfoun'! I sat 'til moon-up watchin' Mammy but she never moved a-tall. Jest laid out thar on thet bed, stiff-like an' pale white. The moon shine in the winder lit the bed-pos' an' thar I spied a hat. Twas Enos' hat! I grabbed it up and sailed it outer the winder. It landed in the cowshed."

He came to a full stop and there was a breezy little sound as the audience slowly expelled. Fanny Fontaine recovered first.

"Is that all?" she asked. "There must be more."

Daddy nodded gravely.

"In the mornin' Mammy was all right." After a short pause he added as an afterthought ... "The cow Bossie was daid!"

In the silence that followed, Kate decided to push the cake. The cracked plates and the tin forks were handed around while Mammy sliced. Sara kept swiping at her plate with a hankerchief and muttering to herself, "I can't. I just can't."

Kate overheard and spun on her. "Oh yes, you can!" Then, to the general assembly, "Helga made this delicious cake especially for Mammy Farlow and her birthday, and each of us will eat a generous slice, even if it <u>isn't on our</u>

diet!" She stressed the last four words and nodded to each one. They all nodded back and accepted large portions. Mammy and Daddy fell to with relish. There was no talking as they all munched.

Then, refreshed, Mammy seemed rejuvenated and once again full of talk.

"But twern't all bad doin's fer us, Miss Kate. Bes' thing is that Sally is doin' fine, at las'."

"Sally? Who's Sally?" Sara whispered to Kate.

"Salome. Daddy's and Mammy's daughter," Kate whispered back. "Their only child. About 45 now, I'd guess."

"We's been thet worried fer years, but now, praise be, seems she's at las' got her bed made. She's up Tampa way, an' writes regular now. Says she's happy as ken be. Ain't thet gran'?" Mammy smiled expansively all around, and sneaked another piece of cake.

"What does she do?" Lolly Randolph wanted to know.

Kate shushed her with a little frown.

"Don't ask. Don't ask." she whispered to Lolly.

"Why not? She must do something. What does she do?"

Mammy picked up on the question.

"I don' know exactly what she do do. Walks a lot. Works at night. Complains all the time that her feets hurt. Writes now, regular as clockwork. Onst every month. Sends money, too. $30.00 each an' every letter. Always in $5.00 bills. We's mighty proud she's turned out so good, ain't we, Daddy?"

17

March

The third week in February was bookkeeping time for Adam and Ruth Crisfield at Captiva Inn. Each year, with March just around the corner and only four short weeks left of 'the season', Adam would bring the Inn books up to date and project their finances on to April. They liked to know exactly where they were and the end of February was, for them, the proper time. Otherwise, paper work became a chore and got in the way of the partying and the packing-up for heading north, and their attention was apt to stray from the hot southern breezes toward the more refreshing Spring climate of New Hampshire. Snow would still be on the hills when they got back north by the first of May and crocuses would be thrusting out of the ground. The lovely old hotel, nestled back in the hills, would seem to smile and nod as they drove up the curving driveway between the elms and the chestnuts. Best to get this Florida paper work out of the way.

Ruth was perched on a high, three legged stool just inside the kitchen door, busy with the week's batch of homemade mayonnaise. Tricky stuff! She didn't really enjoy the work of making the dressing but she did enjoy her guests enjoying it. Well worth the trouble! She turned the huge bowl in her lap and ticked off in her mind ... egg yolks, vinegar, salt, pepper, sugar, dry mustard, a pinch of cayenne ... all in and well mixed. She was reaching for the olive oil when Adam called.

"Ruthie, can you hear me? Can you listen for a minute?"

She leaned back through the kitchen door into the dining room, and looked across to the adjacent office, where she could see Adam fussing with the ledgers.

"Yes," she called back. "What?"

"Things look pretty good to the end of February. We're full up and all the bills are settled, so I can figure fairly accurately. March is what we don't know for sure."

"I thought we were booked solid."

"We are, and paid in advance. <u>But</u>, will they all show? If they don't, I'll have to refund, you know."

Ruth shook her head.

"Adam," she demurred, "there's something very wrong with your refund system. When it gets this close to the first of the month, if people change their minds, we should keep something ... half, maybe. If someone cancels now, we'll lose out. We'll never be able to fill the space at this late date. Still ... it's your problem."

Her attention reverted to the mayonnaise. Oil. One drop at a time. Forty-five beats between drops. Keep an eagle eye out for curdling. Drop. Forty-five beats. Drop. Forty five beats. Drop ...

"They all look solid." Adam was leafing through the stack of reservations. "All repeats, except these two rooms we're holding for Blackstone. What did you finally find out about Blackstone, huh?"

"Stop, now, Adam. See! You've made me lose count. If this stuff balls up and curdles, it'll be your fault, and you'll have to eat all of it. Let me finish. Where was I? I'll have to start this beat all over again, and that might, just might, spoil the whole batch!"

"Why don't you use the electric mixer?"

Ruth carefully wiped the wooden spoon on the side of the bowl and laid it across the top. Settling back against the wall, she folded her arms over her chest and stared straight ahead. In quiet, measured tones she then spoke.

"Adam, stop! I need another five minutes here and then I'm free and we can talk. I don't use the mixer, as you know, because any fool can do it that way. I feel my love and concentration flow down the spoon handle and spread out all over the ingredients and that's what gives mine its special flavor. It's the tender loving care." She smiled gently. "So you sit there like a nice boy and be good. Dream of June, and the jonquils, and dallying with Eulia West over in Concord."

"I don't dally with Eulia. Never have. Why you always bring her up like this I'll never understand. But it might be fun at that, you know. I'll sit here and dream. Take your time."

Ruth wasn't sure she liked where this conversation was leading. She grabbed up the spoon and twisted the bowl.

"I'll hurry!" she said.

●

The reservation had arrived back in November, together with a covering check. It was noncommittal. Without the usual filigree of gossipy exchange, it zeroed in on the essentials ... "Please hold two rooms, full month of March, for Blackstone. Corner, if possible. Check enclosed." It carried a flowery signature ... "Leticia Blackstone."

At Adam's request, Ruth had asked around, but nobody seemed to know anything about any Leticia Blackstone ... not until old Mr. Rostand up at Mid-Island recalled hearing years ago an Austrian piano virtuoso named Blackstone.

"That's the only Blackstone I've heard of. Think the first name was Bettina ... could have been Leticia, I suppose, or she could have changed it. Very Fine! She was really very fine! Heard her in Bonn when I was a lad. She was touching middle age then. Would be dead by now. I mean, I'm seventy now and I must have been fourteen-fifteen ... so we're talking fifty years or so. Of course, she could have been somewhat younger, you know how the young see older folks. Anyway, she'd be dead by now. I don't know of any other."

Bertha snapped the lid on the speculation by suggesting they all wait until Arlene and Reuben Stowell arrived in February. Arlene'd know. She 'pianoed' and though her talents were meager she studied and read and prided herself on knowing all present and past piano greats. The Stowells owned a small two room, two-storey house on the Gulf just north of Mid-Island Inn. All three were tall, spare and weathered ... Reuben, Arlene and the house. The single downstairs room contained a large piano, endless canvas covered cushions, and the touch-down landing of a narrow staircase leading up one wall to the bedroom above. Guests squatted on the cushions, which proved surprisingly functional, as they were large and firm. If a visitor had leg problems, sufficient cushions could be mounded one on top of another until a comfortable height was reached. Only occasionally were there difficulties, as when General Beauregard Jones happened by. General Jones was so gimpy he walked stiff-legged with two canes. The cushions had to be stacked table-high, which was fine until tea was over and the General prepared to depart. There being no arms for him to lift against, he finally had to roll sideways onto the floor, quite a jolt, and claw his way erect by pulling on the staircase balustrade.

"Well," he murmured as he dusted himself off, in what must have been the understatement of the month ... "that was a bit ... unsettling!" He never returned.

On being questioned, Arlene Stowell looked puzzled for a moment and then her face cleared.

"Blackstone? Blackstone? Leticia? Let me see! I've a book somewhere. Can I get back to you on this?" She peered myopically at Ruth and gnawed at her lower lip. "I'll stop by at Captiva Inn this afternoon and give you the results of my investigation, if that will be satisfactory?"

"Perfectly," Ruth replied. This poor, thin creature! With the sun shining on those thick glasses and blotting out her eyes, she looked for all the world like a tall, stretched-out Orphan Annie. Straightening her shoulders and shaking off this uncharitable thought, Ruth smiled warmly. "And when you come by, maybe you can stay for tea and cookies. I'm going to make a fresh batch of ginger snaps around three."

Later that afternoon, with a teacup teetering on a bony knee, Arlene corroborated old Mr. Rostand's recollections.

"I have found just the one Blackstone. First name Leticia. Austrian. Concert pianist. Born 1867. Renown for her exacting interpretations of Beethoven. Nothing in the glossary after 1939. Jewish. Both parents. Maybe she was swept up in the Holocaust, which would explain why no death date is listed." Arlene fingered the reservation letter. "She'd be eighty-one years old by now. She _must_ be dead. This _can't_ be her."

But she wasn't ... and it was!

●

March first, long past the last ferry and well after the dining room had closed for the evening, an insistent knocking rattled Captiva Inn office door. Opening it, Adam was confronted by a short, middle-aged woman wearing a visored cap perched at a jaunty angle atop flaming red hair. In a guttural boom the woman announced:

"Madame Blackstone haf arriv-ed! I am companion ... und she is hongry."

Adam hustled out to the parking lot. Spread out across the back seat of a long, baby-blue touring car, Madame refused Adam's proffered hand and smiled disarmingly.

"Thank you so much. Valia Uganova will assist me. She is familiar with all the necessary manipulations. We take longer than most, but we always manage."

Valia Uganova reached forward and turned the handle in the middle of the limousine's side section and two doors opened, one right, the other left. Little steel steps folded down like a 17th century carriage, and Madame Blackstone laboriously descended. With one hand draped imperiously on her companion's arm, and a long black cape sailing behind in the fresh evening breeze, her large, heavy figure bore down on the Inn dining-room like a clipper ship under full sail.

Ruth wiped soap suds from her hands onto her apron, patted her hair, and prepared to be gracious. Thank heaven the evening leftovers were still on the pantry table, and there was plenty of food. In no time she could produce an excellent meal.

Once the guests were seated, and muttering to themselves in a gutteral language Adam took to be German but which was Russian, he excused himself with a little bow and scurried through the kitchen. As he went he passed Ruth.

"Must get down to those rooms and take the slats from under the mattresses. Thank God I've those extra two-by-fours."

Ruth was dishing salad. She nodded.

"And don't forget to put in the bedboards. Why did you bow just now?"

Adam looked puzzled for a second, his hand on the screen door latch. "Bow? What do you mean? Oh, that! I don't know. Seemed the thing to do, I suppose."

The island immediately buzzed. A low murmuring could be heard by a discerning ear, building momentum from the Fisherman's Creel Gift Shop immediately behind the Inn, to Miriam Hallman's cottages next door and down Palm Avenue to Emmy Kramdon's. A short time later, returning from a stroll along the beach in front of Mid-Island Inn, Arlene Stowell kissed the air beside Reuben's face as she always did if separated from him for even five minutes, and glanced at him over the tops of her glasses.

"Seems I was wrong, Reuben. Leticia Blackstone is not dead after all. She is eating supper down at Captiva Inn this very minute! Isn't that something? Think of the stories she can tell!"

The following morning Madame Blackstone breakfasted in her room and appeared on the Captiva Inn lawn only at noon. As the other guests were filing into the dining room Ruth went out to greet her.

"My dear, don't worry about me." Madame said. "I'll rest here and take the sun. So peaceful with no one around. I don't lunch. I am under orders from my doctor to lose weight. Pounds and pounds he wants, a perfect Shylock! Since being put on notice I've deprived myself of lunch. At this age I don't mind, really, but it is a bit hard on Valia Uganova. So possibly you could find a corner somewhere for her. Run along, now, Valia. I will sit here and dream."

Alas, there was no dreaming for the kind old lady. Circling several miles out of her way, as she returned home from the post office, Arlene Stowell spied Madame Blackstone alone on the lawn.

"How awful!" Arlene spoke aloud to herself, as she did now more and more as the years went by. "She's so lonely! I'll pop by and cheer her up." She leaned her bicycle against an Australian pine and crossed noiselessly to the front of Madame's chair, where she stood, silently gazing intently down.

Feeling someone close by, Madame Blackstone slowly opened her eyes and then heaved upward in a tremendous start.

"Oh!" Arlene was horrified. "I didn't mean to ... that is, I saw you sitting here ... what I mean is, I never dreamed you were asleep. I am so sorry if I alarmed you."

"But you didn't, my dear." The old lady smiled. "I'm rather used to it, you know. People staring at me. When I was young, they stared because of my music. Now that I'm eighty they stare because of my weight. Would not you suppose there'd be a difference, somehow, in the stare. There isn't! During those early years, they stared, wondering. Now they stare, still wondering. I've always felt like a freak. I'm quite used to it." Again the lovely, gentle, disarming smile, and Madame had found herself an acolyte.

In no time the two new friends, the immense old lady at the end of an exciting life, and the emaciated middle-aged introvert crying for fulfillment and vicariously living the great musical triumphs, became the nucleus of afternoon gatherings that included at first a few musically inclined islanders, and then quickly expanded to include everyone around Captiva Inn. Adam put out lawn chairs and little tables with umbrellas and Madame Blackstone quickly became the toast of Palm Avenue.

The Gold Coast pouted!

"Why do you suppose she stays down in that rather awful place," Fanny asked of Lolly Randolph, "when twice I've sent her invites to tea here in my house? But she always refuses."

Lolly clucked her teeth in full sympathy.

"What excuse does she give, Fanny?"

"Nothing, really. Both times she said the same ... 'Thank you but it wouldn't be convenient.'"

Doris Lockwood was more understanding.

"Maybe it wouldn't. She's so huge, just getting around must be a chore. Maybe you're better off, Fanny."

Mrs. Fontaine was tapping the floor with an irritated foot.

"Exasperating! That's what it is! I always have all visiting luminaries to tea. I pride myself on it."

"Maybe she's not all that luminous any more." someone said.

Always anxious to assassinate by innuendo, Sara Macabbe smiled and dropped her eyes demurely.

"Maybe she never was," she smirked.

"That's where you're wrong, Sara." Kate O'Hearn put her cup firmly on a handy side table. "She's one of the few really greats. Until the war, her concerts were sold out completely. I can remember, back in my Goucher days, a group of us 'did' Europe all one summer. The only event we couldn't get near was a Blackstone concert. It was held, of all places, at La Scala ... to my knowledge the only time that huge Opera Hall has presented a single artist. She was mobbed!"

While this conversation was taking place on the Gold Coast, another was in progress a mile and a half northward, on the Captiva Inn lawn. Arlene Stowell was passing a plate of tea sandwiches and offered a tiny one on a napkin to Madame Blackstone, who pulled back, shaking her head.

"No, my dear. I'm so sorry. My doctors, you know. I can't eat anything sweet during the afternoon."

"But they're not sweet. I made them myself. Vegetarian. Nothing false. Nothing chemical. Homemade bread from the bakery, water cress, cucumbers, no dressing, just natural lime juice."

Reuben Stowell, who by now had become a permanent member of the afternoon gatherings along with old Mr. Rostand, leaned over toward his elderly friend and murmured softly.

"Not much taste, either!"

Mr. Rostand bit into one, and grimaced.

"What do you mean ... 'not much taste' ... None! None at all!"

Madame Blackstone took the offered tidbit and held it until Arlene had moved along around the circle. Then she hid it carefully among the bowled flowers by her side, and glanced quickly around to see if anyone had noticed. She spied Mr. Rostand watching her. Their eyes twinkled and they chuckled together over their little secret.

The general conversation quickly picked up.

"You were telling us, Madame Blackstone, of your escape from Europe just inches ahead of the Nazi police. It must have been so thrilling!" The vacuous remark hung in the air.

Madame Blackstone stared at her hands, folded and lying in her lap. She answered the speaker very softly and very seriously.

"Thrilling ... is hardly the correct word. It is not ... thrilling ... to have your roots torn up, to be forced from your home and your friends, to leave behind a whole life, mementoes, clothes, familiar surroundings, to have to search the unknown for a safe haven ... I wasn't telling you of those days as I never speak of them. I never allow myself to even dwell upon them." She gazed off across the Gulf, her eyes distant. With an obvious effort she pulled herself back into the present. "I merely said that I was one of the lucky ones. I had friends in high places throughout the free countries and they helped me. I crossed the Italian Alps into Geneva, then to Washington where I knew Ghia Manning. Ghia was at that time an indispensable part of Voice of America, broadcasting four times daily into Germany and Russia, all over the Axis countries, as it continues to do today. Such a dear person. She steered me to her Aunt, Alexandra Tolstoy, who was doing good works in the refugee field and who had an expansive settlement, a farm actually, of seventy-five acres ... chickens, pigs, cows, horses ... up in the hills above Nyack, along the Hudson, some twenty miles northwest of New York City. Alexandra welcomed me with open arms, as she did anyone needing help, and I had a peaceful, rewarding two years there. The days were difficult. I didn't then speak Russian. On the other hand, the nights were splendid. We would gather in one of the large halls, a renovated barn actually, where there was an old piano, and we'd give little concerts, I on the piano and Alexandra strumming her guitar. What a tremendous personality she is ... the most decorated American woman after Mrs. Roosevelt. Medals and awards from everywhere. She would often laugh and tell me that if she pinned them all on her bosom at one time she wouldn't be able to stand up. She heads an international refugee organization, highly thought of by the State Department. She has five books published ... and she cheats at cards!" Madame Blackstone chuckled as she remembered down the years. "In the evening we often played Canasta. She would cheat! Not hidden or nasty at all. Quite openly. She'd just cheat. If I called her on it she'd openly admit it and laugh loudly. If I went out and caught her with a handful, she'd snarl ` sobotka' at me, Russian for ` dog', you know. Such a strange blend of child/woman. I love her and admire her more than I can possibly tell you." She dreamed again of yesterday, a little smile playing around her mouth. No one spoke, hoping she would continue. With a sudden deep breath, she did. "After two years there, I left. Anna Landowska, a childhood friend of mine, had bought a lovely small house in Lakeville, Connecticut and asked me to join her. Soon afterward I bought a little place there also, up in the lovely green hills, with a wide, deep lake at my feet. That's where I hide. I've a piano and a spare room for an occasional visitor or two. Valia has her own apartment on the floor above. We are happy now, and content. I often call on Anna and we play together the stirring old music. I boom on the piano and Anna tinkles on her harpsichord. Sometimes, when we pause, there'll be a burst of applause from outside where the tourists have gathered, and we'll cross to a window and wave. So like the old days. Lovely. I like my new home. I like my new country." Her eyes glistened with moisture.

"So you still play?"

"Of course I play. All the time. I couldn't live without playing. Music is my life, my soul. I don't give concerts any more but I play." She gestured in front of her. "That's the one drawback to this lovely place ... no piano!"

Arlene Stowell straightened up in her chair so abruptly her eyeglasses slipped to the end of her nose. She moved over to Madame Blackstone and knelt before her, one hand on the great lady's arm.

"Oh, Madame. We have a piano! Would you use it? I mean ... we'd both feel so indebted to you if you would ... I mean..." she waved one hand vaguely in the air ... "there it is. It's an old Baldwin but it's in perfect tune. We'd be so pleased."

"How very kind of you." Madame Blackstone looked at the eager face before her with its tense, expectant expression. She reached out and patted Arlene's hand. "Maybe we can work something out."

So it was that the March afternoons were filled with music. With the Stowell cottage as the focal point, people gathered on the beach from north and south, swam and fished or just lolled on the sand, while beautiful sounds flowed about them. And so it was that Arlene and Reuben prevailed upon Madame Blackstone, but only after persistent pressure, to give a recital.

"This is all nonsense, my dear," the old lady said to Arlene as she practiced scales. "I'm much too old, and my fingers are much too stiff. See, I can scarcely stretch an octave. It's been so many years. My mind is brittle, also. I will forget."

Squatting on a handy cushion, Arlene lifted clasped hands in an imploring gesture.

"If you forget, you can fake. No one will know."

"I will know! No, we won't speak of dishonesty." Madame shook her head violently. "All of my life I've despised dishonesty. At my age I can't change that, now can I? I am exceedingly reluctant about this whole endeavor. Will anyone come? People down here are vacationing. They want to fish and swim and eat and relax ... not sit around listening to a fat ... sitting? Where would people sit? Not on those cushions, certainly!"

Smelling victory, Reuben jumped into the conversation.

"Ah," he exclaimed, "we'll fill the room and the porch with chairs. We'll borrow those in the Chapel-by-the-Sea ... and the Sanibel Church has as many or more, and we can ask people who have little chairs to bring their own ... just like concerts in parks in large cities."

The Blackstone Piano Concert was scheduled for the last Tuesday in March ... from 8:00 until 9:30 in the evening ... at the home of Reuben and Arlene Stowell.

As the great event approached there was frenzied activity behind the scenes. Reuben enlisted Jerry's help collecting all the chairs and with revetting the piano bench and staining the new wood to blend with the old. Didi and Arlene arranged potted palms in strategic locations and collected old netting for atmosphere, on which they hung shells, dried sea horses and pieces of sponge. Bertha produced a cousin, Elmer Gant, conveniently employed by Englehart Funeral Parlour in Fort Myers, who arranged the loan of an entry-way canvas canopy. Erected side-ways across the front of the Stowell cottage instead of perpendicular, it doubled the porch area, making room for an additional twenty chairs. Little signs were handprinted and scattered throughout the island ... at the two Inns, at the Bide-A-Wee Restaurant, at the dock, Ida's grocery store, Matilda Crunch's Shell Shop, the gift shop and the bakery. There was no question, as the day drew near, but that everyone on Captiva knew of the Musicale ... nomenclature changed from 'concert' at Madame's insistence ... "The performance will be much too short and much too informal to be classed a concert. Please indulge me."

The Gold Coast mounted pre-musicale cocktail parties and dinners, vying strenuously for influential guests. Adam found tiny toy pianos in Woolworth's on the mainland and placed one on each table in the Captiva Inn dining room that evening in honor of the event. Everything was in order and under control as the clock hands pointed to five p.m. ... except the weather. The clear, warm, sunny day had clouded over and a cold breeze blew in from the Gulf. By seven p.m. the wind was increasing, and by 7:30, as the guests began to assemble, the first few rain drops fell.

It seemed to Arlene Stowell, peeping around the side of the building, as if people would never stop arriving. The living room was soon crowded, with every seat taken, and people were seated in corners, on the floor, and all the way up the staircase to the top landing. The porch was filling up quickly. The roadway along the Gulf was choked with cars, and more were honking and racing their motors to get by. The wind had increased, and the rain drizzled.

Out on the back porch, Reuben was bent solicitously over Madame Blackstone, who was wrapped in a warm blanket against the chill air and whose hands were soaking in a tub of hot water. She reached up and pushed back her kerchief.

"Mr. Stowell." Her eyes were wary. "I really do not want to go in there. I am not ready. I need weeks of practice still. What time is it?"

"Quarter to eight."

"Oh, dear me!"

At eight o'clock people were still collecting and Reuben, after a conference with Arlene and Madame, decided to postpone until 8:15.

"But not one minute past that," Madame cautioned, calling on past experience. "The audience will hold fifteen minutes but will then get so fidgety I will never be able to quiet them down!"

The chattering and calling back and forth had mounted, and there had been little scatterings of applause by the time Arlene entered the living room through the back porch screen door, and rapped the corner of a glass tumbler with a dinner knife. She cleared her throat and pushed up her glasses.

"If you will all quiet down, please, the program will commence." Her voice was weak. Just at that moment a strong gust of wind blew rain mist into the room and everybody jumped up and circled about, putting on raincoats and throwing capes around their shoulders. Through this confusion Arlene continued to tinkle on her glass and Reuben leaned through the screened doorway.

"Speak up!" he hissed.

"Are you ready?"

"Yes. Speak up."

Arlene rang her glass and spoke loudly.

"It is so nice of you all to join us this evening. Thank you for coming. If I may explain. In order to provide as much room as possible for seating, we have pushed the piano tight to the staircase wall. Madame Blackstone will sit with her back to the audience. She will follow each offering with only the barest pause, so please reserve your appreciation until the end." Arlene gave a little half-bow, then continued. "It is now my great pleasure to present to you Madame Leticia Blackstone!" Her arm swung wide toward the porch door.

Following a moment of silence Madame appeared, and paused in the opening. There was polite applause. Inclining her head imperceptibly, she blanketed the audience with her warm, glowing smile. The applause mounted.

Madame stretched out a hand toward Jerry, crouching at the foot of the stairs.

"Young man, will you assist me, please, to the piano. Ah, you are too kind." They walked slowly over and Jerry adjusted the bench for her.

With one hand on the piano, Madame eased down toward the bench, then stood straight again and turned slightly to the room.

"As you can see," she seemed serious but her eyes danced, "Mr. Stowell has seen fit to reinforce the piano bench. Such a wise man!"

There was a shout of amusement ... and Madame Blackstone had her audience in her hand. Turning back to the piano, she again prepared to sit, only to rise once more and face fully front.

"I would like to take these first few moments to share with you my predicament. I do not play publicly any longer. I am too old now and too grotesque to appear on the stage. I am also weak-willed. I have been swayed against my better judgment by Mr. and Mrs. Stowell, who have pressured me unmercifully." Again the lovely smile. "So I finally agreed to a short program." Rain pelted down, drumming on the tin roof, and she glanced upward. "I see I am going to have competition!" The squall passed over. "I will offer you tonight only four rather short works, all special favorites of mine. A Brahms lullaby which you will readily recognize and which was made popular by my great friend Madame Ernestine Schuman-Heink. I thought we would have a little fun with it. I will play it first in skeleton form, so to speak ... just the barest melody with a few lower chords. Then I will dress it up in lace and filigree as if it were a showy production number. If we last through all that," she gave a low chuckle, "I have prepared a youthful air of no particular value except that I hope it will thoroughly soften you up." She paused as laughter broke out again. "A simple but quite lovely Austrian folk song and a short work by Beethoven will bring us ..." The rain returned in the increased wind and pounded the roof. Little fingers of lightning stabbed through the dark night ... "to a close."

Madame sat before the piano and raised both hands, but a sudden commotion occurred in the audience. Those outside, grouped around the windows and under the canopy, pressed forward, trying to squeeze into the already crowed living room, as the wind, laden with rain, swooped through the Australian pines, flapping the canopy and banging the window shutters. Misty drops glistened from their heads and shoulders, and expensive hairdos started to droop dispiritedly. There was a muted disturbance as people pushed into each other, stumbling over feet and excusing themselves and those safely seated leaned forward and hissed "sshhh." Then, as suddenly as it had come up, the squall raced on, the audience settled down and Madame nodded once, dropped her hands and her fingers fluttered across the keys. The gentle, lilting strains of the Brahms lullaby wrapped around the room.

At the end of the simple melody, as the final soft note drifted upward, the old lady's right hand suddenly slid from high E toward low C in a swift downward stroke and her left hand accompanied with a recurring base chord. With a devilish gleam in her eyes, she was off into a dazzling virtuoso display of runs and slides, arpeggios and glissandos, wild dashes among the sharps and flats. Her left foot kept time as her fingers blurred in their mad racing up and down the keyboard.

Jean Culpepper plucked at Frank's arm and leaned close to him.

"She can't do that. The tempos are different. She can't do that!"

"I know," Frank breathed back at her. "Just like Lily Pons can't sing two notes at one time!"

"But this is different," Jean insisted. "She'll lose the melody."

But she didn't! With great subtlety the melody was woven in and out of the bombastic display and became again the dominant theme as Madame eased the bravado and slipped once more into the appealing, soothing lullaby. With a final pounding chord and a swift thrusting of both hands high over her head, it was over.

The gathered islanders applauded loudly ... and thunder rumbled outside, ominously close. The pines and seagrapes tossed and twisted, bolts of lightning forked, and the electric lights flickered.

Reuben Stowell signalled to Arlene, motioning for her to join him out on the back porch.

"Have we any candles?"

Arlene blanched, and drew back.

"I didn't say," Reuben rushed on, "that we need them, just have we any and if so, where are they? Better to be prepared than sorry, you know!"

Back in the living room, the talented hands were poised above the keyboard while Madame, her head slightly sideways and a hesitant half-smile on her face, waited for quiet. When it was to her liking, and signalling her readiness with a finger jabbing the air, down came the hands and "Beer Barrel Polka" poured from the piano. She rushed through it with no particular style, just racing along, enjoying every minute. Outside, the rain pelted down and the din on the roof was unbelievable.

"Sing along with me," she called, leaning far back, her hands moving like pistons back and forth on the keys. "Sing with me!"

At first softly, then louder as the thundering rain masked those who were off-key and gave them confidence, the audience took up the verse and "Roll out the barrel" competed with the storm. As soon as she sensed the audience with her, and with a huge bounce on the bench, Madame abandoned the traditional rendition and broke into a rollicking, bouncing ragtime. The islanders sang and stomped and kept time with their hands. As she reached the end, Madame cried "Again ... again..." and started through a second time.

When it was over the applause was as deafening as the storm outside, and the audience laughed together as they clapped and called back and forth. Everyone was exhausted except Madame. Fresh as when she started, bent low over the keyboard, she was dreamily drifting into that gentle, shimmering paean to an Austrian wildflower, Edelweiss, when the storm outside broke in full fury. The rain poured down, pummelling the cottage roof and drowning out the piano. Madame quietly rested her hands on the keyboard, waiting for the deluge to subside. She smiled over at Didi and Jerry, crouched at the end of the piano by the staircase landing.

"Will it all pass?" she mouthed.

The youngsters were shrugging to answer when it stopped. All in an instant, as Spring squalls often did on the island, it was gone. Everything was quiet.

"Well," old Mr. Rostand said loudly to no one in particular, "thank heaven that's over. Let's hope it's gone for good!"

Evan Wiggins was leaning against the front door jamb, and he shook his head as he looked outside, speculating. He didn't like the stillness. It was too heavy, too thick. No breeze followed the cessation of rain, just an oppressive darkness.

Madame began again and the sweet, simple song gently massaged the air. When she reached the end she twisted on the bench and faced her audience.

"I hadn't planned on all the disturbance outside when I decided to offer you this next work." She was kneading her hands, twisting her palms and bending the fingers back and forth. She looked down at them for a moment, then raised her eyes. "But maybe it's fitting. All my life, from when I was a tiny child, I have been in love with Ludwig Beethoven. True, he died in 1827 and I wasn't born until 1867 but he talks to me through his music and I have loved him all these years ... passionately and consumingly. He has always seemed an actual presence to me. My reputation, if I may be allowed to phrase it that way, has been based on his genius. For the next short while I will share him with you." She turned back to the piano and raised both hands high above the keyboard.

A searing bolt of lightning forked from the frowning heavens and struck distressingly close. Thunder boomed at tree-top height and the people sitting nearest the windows winced. Madame didn't seem to notice. Still as a statue, arms aloft, head thrown slightly back and eyes closed, she dreamed a private dream, reaching for that exact moment when muscle and mind blended exactly with emotion and allowed artistry to flow. Then, with a tightening of her shoulders and an imperceptible tensing of her neck, her hands crashed down in the opening bars of the peerless "Appassionata."

As if on cue, with the piano thundering and booming inside, the tempest outside peaked in violence. The gale-force winds tossed and twisted the seagrapes, snapping the tangled branches like matchsticks. With a loud ripping sound, the canvas awning tore from its bracings and sailed off into the inky darkness. The brittle Australian pines bent moaning and creaking as they fought to remain upright. The Gulf pounded the nearby shore and rose threateningly, as if pushed by gigantic, unseen hands.

Through this chaos, the old lady at the piano never paused. As a thoroughbred, with the bit in its mouth, heads down the home stretch, she was off and running. Her head jerked up and down marking cadence, her torso swayed left and right, and her hands seemed detached in their frantic rush over the keys as her blurring fingers traced the exalted tonal tapestry. She was well into the heartbreak of Gethsemane when a bolt of lightning struck the tallest of the nearby pines, severing a large limb. As it split from the mother tree and crashed down, the limb swept with it the electrical wiring ... and darkness fell inside.

"Light! Light! I must have light!" shrieked Madame, never pausing at the keyboard. "Someone give me light!"

Muttering to himself ... "Thank God I had sense enough ..." Reuben Stowell quickly placed a candle at each end of the piano, inches from the flying fingers, and momentarily there was light. However, with the next gust of wind tearing through the room, the candles wavered and flickered out.

Old Mr. Rostand leapt forward, newspaper in hand.

"Light 'em again. Quick." he instructed Reuben. "We'll hold the paper up to stop the wind."

The piano throbbed on. Outside, lightning forked and thunder boomed.

"Light! Light! More light!" Madame cried, pounding away.

The candles were quickly relit and little paper barriers were held up. The heavy wind coursing through the room flicked paper corners into the candles and flames shot toward the ceiling.

"Thank heaven," Madame yelled, "you've given me enough light. Now I can see." She bent deeply over the keyboard, fingers working away in a blur, as she traveled the path to Calvary. People screamed and pulled back into each other. Kate O'Hearn reached deep into the shoulder bag she always carried and came up with a large flashlight, which she handed to Mr. Rostand.

"Gather more," she yelled in his ear. "There'll be others."

Madame, enwrapped in her musical saga, never noticed personal danger but proceeded consummately from the Agony of Betrayal in the Garden through the Humiliation of the Trial, the Distress of the Procession to the Cross and on to the Torture of Golgotha. There was no stopping her. With her head thrown back and her eyes glazed half-shut as if in a trance, she poured forth the exalting, heartrending music. Outside, in a wild savage counterpoint, the tempest raged on. Lightning, thunder, deluging rain peaked into a shrieking demand for attention, but the little audience did not hear. The old lady was painting a wondrous picture of the Ecstasy of the Resurrection, and tears were streaming down her face. Then, with a low sob and a final rumbling chord, it was over! Finished! Her head sagged to the keys between outflung arms, and her shoulders heaved.

Reuben Stowell and Jerry helped Madame up, across the room, out the back door and into her limousine which Valia had waiting.

As the storm abated, the applause soared. The audience stood as one, pounding their hands and stomping their feet, crying "Bravo... Bravo ..."

Madame never heard. Exhausted, she rode slowly away into the wet night, sitting by herself on the back seat, wrapped in the aching loneliness of the truly great.

18

April

Helga Helgarson leaned in the doorway of the Bide-A-Wee Restaurant and gave Marge a wide Minnesota grin. "Good morning, Marge. Have you enough chili on hand to give both Jack and me a large bowl? We'll be here most of an hour I guess, so a piece of lime pie will taste good later on."

Marge nodded and smiled back.

"Sure. Come on in. How soon you want it? This your yearly get-together with Jack to stock that ole yacht?"

"Yep. We have to start planning as early as this if Jack's to have time to bake all the things Miss Kate needs. He'll be along in a few minutes, soon as he takes a batch of pecan tarts out of his ovens. How do you suppose he manages on those three itty, bitty apartment-size stoves?"

Marge shook her head in disbelief.

"Never did understand. Him an' Ted! Coupla characters, ain't they? Work like dogs, though. All year long. When the bakery shuts down, all summer Jack scoots around the island gathering seagrapes and carissa fruit 'n he gets watermelons from the mainland ... makes enough jelly and pickles for the whole coming season. Ted grubs in yards, usually with Ida. Tough life. Anyway, when are ya-all pulling out. It's early yet, ain't it?"

"Not all that early. We'll leave by the end of the month, so we still have almost four weeks. What's today?"

"April 5th."

"It'll be an easier get-away than usual since we're not closing up the house. Miss Kate is going back to St. Paul on the Wanigan instead of dry-docking her in Tampa. I suppose there'll be lots of guests. Don't know who. Don't think Miss Kate has decided yet. There'll be herself and me ... and I'll have to have a helper ... Sam will pilot, of course ..." She began counting fingers. "He'll need two men to help him. How many's that? Six already. Wanigan has crew's quarters for four and guest rooms for six. With herself and me, that's a total of twelve, which is right. She accommodates twelve."

Marge was dusting shrimp with flour and nodded absentmindedly. The lunch loomed just ahead and she was puzzling over her menu. She took time to place a steaming bowl of chili in front of Helga, and a plate heaped high with saltines, and returned to her fryer.

"Lars isn't going with us!" Helga toyed with her chili, and her lower lip pushed forward in the beginning of a pout. "I'm already upset over that. I tried to get Miss Kate to change her mind but she can be set once she's decided. I won't see that big old Swede for a month or more, can you imagine? That's how long it'll take Miss Kate and her friends to make the jaunt ... you know, poking along, putting in at various ports, changing guests all along the way ... Lars has to stay here to chauffeur the Worthingtons. He'll drive the Rolls up to St. Croix middle of June. Mady'll ride up with him. So you see ..."

"Whoa! Whoa!" Marge interrupted, leaning on her elbows on the counter, floury hands held up beside her head. "Back up! You're goin' too fast. Mady? Who's she? And who're those Worthingtons? Tell it slow so's I can understand."

"I'm sorry. I'll go slower." Helga dipped a spoon into her chili and tasted it. Too hot! She cooled it by lifting spoonfuls into the air and letting the chili drip back down. Glancing out of the picture window facing the road she could see Jack hurrying over from the bakery. "As I said, Miss Kate is turning the house over to Mr. and Mrs. William Worthington. He's a big Wall Street man, tycoon or something she called him ... tons of money ... Miss Kate is giving them the house for the month of May, complete with housekeeper, chauffeur and the Silver Cloud, her Rolls Royce! Can you believe it?" She pushed out a chair for Jack as he joined them.

Marge rolled her eyes heavenward.

"Thems that has ..." she murmured.

"My sister Mady will fly down about the 21st," Helga went on, "and will cook and tend for the Worthingtons 'til they leave, end of May. Then she and Lars will close the house and drive north to St. Croix. Got it?"

Marge nodded.

"Miss Kate and I and Sam and two crew and somebody to help me and whatever guests get dragged along will pile on the Wanigan the end of the month. We'll cruise up the Caloosahatchie past Fort Myers, Alva, Olga, and into Lake Okeechobee, on out to Stuart and follow the Intercoastal Waterway all the way up north to the St. Lawrence. Then we'll veer west down the St. Lawrence Seaway through the Great Lakes. That's so beautiful. We'll tie up at Duluth. Five weeks! No Lars!" She drifted off for a moment, then shrugged. "However ... I'm here now so Jack and I can figure what baked goods we'll need."

Jack's mouth had fallen open. He stared at Helga.

"You're expecting me to provide enough baked stuff for twelve people for five weeks? Even if I can, where will you keep it?"

Helga nodded her head.

"Twelve people ... five weeks! Correct! I'll keep it in the deep-freeze on the Wanigan. The biggest thing on that yacht is the freezer ... huge! Walk-in, you know. Just like for a big hotel. You bake the stuff ... I'll find space for it."

Spooning chili into his mouth at a good rate, Jack tried to talk around a huge bite, swiping with a paper napkin at the little bits that tried to ooze out. He nodded his head.

"Good idea to leave Lars with the Silver Cloud. If it breaks down he's the proper one to repair it."

Helga snorted.

"You're wrong there, Jack." she exclaimed. "On two accounts. First, Lars wouldn't make any repairs, even if he was permitted to. He's much too lazy. Repairing mechanical things isn't where he shines!" She preened a bit and giggled. "And second, it's not allowed for anyone anywhere to repair that car. Miss Kate has had it some five years now and only once has there been a problem. A strange clacking sound. She telephoned the Rolls head office in England for them to recommend an American representative. Instead, they flew a mechanic in from London. Can you believe it?"

Marge's eyes were now so far up in her head Jack wondered if they were stuck permanently.

"Wait'll I tell Stan that!" Marge patted a platter of breaded shrimp and pushed it into her cooler. "Did the Queen stop by to check it out?" she tittered.

Helga grinned at Marge as she spread out some papers on the table.

"It's over my head, too, Marge. But way up there, on that money level ... it's interesting how they live, isn't it?"

Pushing his empty bowl off to one side Jack was already planning on rotating his ovens. Rolls Royces weren't part of his life. Or Marge's, either. She had her soups and fish and he had his pies and cakes and that's where their reality lay. Full of chili, he was ready to go to work.

"Okay! Let's go. Have you figured what you'll need? Breads first."

Helga smoothed out a long list.

"Breads. Okay. We'll need twenty loaves of each... white, cheese, oatmeal, pecan, and rye. On second thought, better make that thirty white and thirty cheese. They love that cheese bread, though pecan is my favorite." Helga was lost in thought for a bit, tapping her teeth with her pencil. "Makes the best toast. Course, cutting all this stuff is a chore."

Marge had left her stove and was counting up.

"Good Lord, Helga! That's 120 loaves. That'll take two full gurneys in your freezer."

"That's okay. I've got six of 'em. I can handle it fine." She reached out a finger and touched Jack's notebook. "Are you with me?"

"Ay-yeh!"

"That does the breads. Now, cakes. Better give me ten mocha tortes. They freeze fine and with ice-cream, make a good dessert. And at least twenty angel food ... think you can handle that?"

"Ay-yeh!"

Helga glanced sideways at him for a second, a puzzled expression flirting with her eyes. Then she went on.

"Mix up the angel food. Some white, some chocolate and a few of the orange. Pies! None of the squashy ones and no meringue. Don't freeze well. We'll stick to the firm ones, like apple, pecan and pumpkin. Let me have fifteen of each." She crossed off her list. "Is that okay?"

"Ay-yeh."

Helga tilted her head to one side.

"Where do you come from, Jack?"

"Binghamton."

"New York?"

"Ay-yeh."

"Oh, that's why."

"Why what?"

"That 'ay-yeh' stuff! I had a girlfriend in high school from Binghamton, New York, and she was always saying 'ay-yeh' just like you. It's funny, eh?

"Oh, I don't know." Jack pulled slightly back and turned edgy. It had been a rough morning, what with that upsetting squabble with Ted and the ruined batch of apple pies, all because the dry-goods delivery man had forced on him those new-fangled pie tins with that ridiculous card-board insert ... supposed to be the latest baking gadget on the market... pies slice up and lift out easier ... all it did was soak out all the butter from the shell, leaving it so leathery even a sharp knife wouldn't cut it ... had to throw out twelve pies ... and Ted laughing his head off ... he's gotten so irritating lately, always bitching at cleaning the pans, and gobbling down all the icing drippings and the spilled nuts ... getting fatter each day ... won't be able to squeeze in between the stoves or the sink pretty soon ... damned irritating ... and here Helga was, picking on him. He liked Helga but that didn't give her any right to criticize. He needed a vacation.

"Yeah," he muttered. "Up there, we all say it. Sorry if it upsets you."

"Oh, no ..." Helga's voice drifted off. If he wanted to be touchy, better leave it alone. She returned to her list.

"And Miss Kate says she'll take whatever pickles and jellies you have left. Especially the lime marmalade and the mango chutney. Really great. And that tart carissa jelly. Perfect with meats. Everybody always gobbles up the green tomato and the watermelon pickles. Whatever you have, we'll take it all. Just charge us, okay?"

"You better believe it! You'll get a bill, never fear."

•

The sound of hammering drifted in the kitchen window and soothed her concern. Agnes liked to know where everyone was. It was most likely a blemish in her personality, but there it was ... she just felt calmer if she could place people. Cora was over in the shop with Sally-Anne, dusting and cleaning, beginning the long process of packing away for the summer things that might mildew or discolor during the hot weather. She could see Maude and Jerry laughing together as they repaired the dock, and the comical pelican Hiram, skipping sideways when they came too close. Maude had handled her problems with the young folks, and the tensions and jealousy were behind them, thank goodness. Even old Doobie seemed busy, digging and chopping around the base of the gumbo-limbo tree. She'd finally given in to Maude's repeated requests to have the tree trimmed back, especially that gigantic, gnarled, sagging old limb that hung across the kitchen roof, and Roy and Evan were due the end of the week to take care of that problem. Roy'd said to fertilize the tree ... "If you're gonna chop off one end, better feed up the other. Helps it stand the pain" ... She'd never thought of it that way. Maybe Roy was right, who knows. Anyway, she'd asked Doobie to free up the roots a bit this morning and there he was, poking at the ground and leaning on his hoe-handle, most likely moaning to himself about his sad fate. She smiled as she watched him. Poor Doobie. He was exhausted by the end of the day from having struggled so hard not to work. Still, hers was a good life, really. Not at all what she'd planned when she and Will married. She'd planned children, and there were none. She'd planned on Will's companionship on through the years, and he was gone. She'd rushed blindly away to escape the pain and the combined feeling of loss and fury at being left alone. She'd asked this quiet, tiny island for protection, and it had wrapped her in soft warm sunlight and gentle breezes and had lulled her into a semblance of well-being ...

A boisterous shout of laughter came from the dock. Agnes interrupted her ruminations and crossed to the window. Jerry and Maude were both flat on their stomachs, poking at something under the dock, and Jerry was drumming his feet in excitement. What a thorough joy that boy was. He'd grown tall and filled out. Bronzed by the sun, with red-gold glints flashing from his thick hair, what a finelooking lad. And in love! There was no doubt about his being in love with that enchanting little Didi. He most likely didn't know it ... and he'd be miserable when she went back north in a few weeks. Maybe there was some way she could ease things for him. Wonder how Didi felt? And what about her own feelings? What would she do, how would she handle the loss, the emptiness when he returned to Evanston? He couldn't stay down here forever. One year, she'd said to her sister Peg. One year! It seemed such an endless time when she first thought of Jerry's coming down, and now here it was, two-thirds gone. She'd learned to value the lad more than she'd thought possible. He was like the young son she had wanted and never had. How would she handle his leaving, when Will's leaving was still so new? Another loss was impossible to think of. She'd have to get more to do, something more important, something that really contributed to the total effort of all three of them. Somehow, though she'd never planned it that way, she'd drifted into the position of housekeeper/cook. Somebody had to, of course, but it got tiresome. Frustrating. Maybe it was time to get that kiln and get back into ceramics, like she'd done years before. Basic pottery. So many new products on the market. She could turn ashtrays and dishes patterned on seagrape leaves, and lamp bases with driftwood to hold the shades and sand-dollar clusters around the pedestal. She'd talk to Roy when he came with Evan on Saturday and see if he could bump up the electricity. Somewhere, in an old magazine lying about, there was an article on kilns. She'd seen it just the other day ...

Agnes was startled out of her reverie when Maude and Jerry burst into the kitchen and Doobie banged the front porch screened door. A sudden squall, which Agnes hadn't seen approaching, pounded rain in a steady downpour and immediately tiny rivers coursed through the sand, forming little canyons as the water rushed across the yard into the bay.

Maude shook herself dog-fashion, and raindrops scattered across the kitchen.

"Always a silver lining," she exclaimed with a laugh. "Lunch time! We had to come in anyway. What's for lunch, Ag?"

A little frown started to form on Agnes' forehead. See! There it was! Chief cook and bottlewasher! She'd have to work on this and ease out of it, somehow. Still ...

"It's a huge lunch, but a secret. I'll surprise you. Jerry, could you brave the tempest and run over and collect Cora and Sally-Anne. If we don't call 'em, they'll both work straight on through."

The rain fell in sheets all afternoon and everyone stayed inside. The dock repairs were held up and Doobie couldn't return to his hoeing. Agnes felt heavy from the sudden humidity.

"Cora, can you spare Sally-Anne? I'd like to have her clean up the kitchen from these lunch things and turn out the cupboards. Unless, of course ..."

"Oh, no, Ag." Cora nodded and smiled. "Of course, Sally-Anne can work over here. I'm mostly caught up in the shop, anyway. Lots of tagging and wrapping left, but everything's pretty clean now."

Maude moved slowly from the table to her rocking chair, and called to Cora as she went.

"I'll be cleaning the fishing gear until the rain stops, and can always help you Cora, if you need me. Jerry, this'd be a good time to mend that net. The two of us should be able to figure out how, don't you think?" Her eyes were half-closed and she rocked contentedly, letting her food digest. "Have you heard anything about the O'Hearn picnic, Ag? It's getting on to that time.

Last year there was quite a buzz. Not a word so far this year. Maybe O'Hearn won't repeat."

"Oh, Miss O'Hearn will surely have it." Agnes had her mending in her lap and squinted through a needle eye at the window. She made little jabs with a piece of thread. "I've been told the April regatta is more or less a fixture. I know that folks certainly had a grand time last year. Amelia Armstrong told me it's really her way, Miss O'Hearn's I mean, to do something a bit out of the ordinary and nice for the County Commissioners and the Directors of the R.E.A., and so on. Everybody comes over to the island and she takes them on her yacht to Upper Captiva for an afternoon picnic. All the home owners and islanders who have little boats trail along, and there's lots of food and people fish and swim and lie about. An old-fashioned outing. Very nice." Her voice died out as she finally had the thread through the eye and could knot it. Maybe she should have her eyes checked. It seemed to get more and more difficult to see the needle. She glanced over at Maude, who had stopped rocking and was nodding in her chair, snoring gently, with one cheek fluttering a bit.

Jerry moved closer to his aunt so they could talk and not disturb Maude.

"Do you suppose I could go along, if there is a regatta? I've got that boat of yours and my motor, and Didi'd go, too."

Agnes glanced at the boy's eager face, and smiled at him.

"Of course you and Didi can go. We'll check around and see what the plans are. I suppose Helga will close that big house by the end of the month."

"No, I don't think she will. The other day Captain Bob gave me several packages addressed to Worthington, care of O'Hearn ... and Bertha told me that Miss O'Hearn has turned her house over to a Mr. and Mrs. William Worthington for the whole month of May."

Sally-Anne backed out of one of the lower cabinets which she was cleaning, and looked up.

"Maybe they's gonna need a maid?"

Jerry shook his head.

"No. No they won't. Helga's sister is flying in toward the end of the month and will cook and clean for 'em and she and Lars will close up. Lars is staying to drive for 'em and they'll have the Rolls, too."

"Ye Gods!" Maude sat straight. "Who are these people? King and Queen of Sheba?"

Agnes went quietly on with her sewing.

"I thought you were asleep."

"Well, I wasn't!"

"Your eyes were closed."

"I was restin' em."

"And you were snoring."

"I never snore!"

Jerry chortled, and Maude threw up her head.

"What's that supposed to mean?"

"Well," Jerry laughed, "if you weren't snoring, you were making funny noises with <u>something</u>."

Sally-Anne giggled out loud and Maude threw a glance her way.

"And don't you get into this, Miss Skinny." She grinned at Sally-Anne. "Doobie tells me," she went on, "that you rattle around so much at night that he never gets any rest."

"If'n he neva gits no res', tain't from <u>my</u> rattlin' roun'." Sally-Anne giggled again.

A voice from the porch called, "I neva sed no sech thing!"

Sally ran over to the screened door.

"Git along, you Doobie Denkins. Tain't rainin' all thet hard, naoh. Git alon' back to thet hoein'. Slap thet rainy hat onto yer haid an' git. You needs anothah haircut, boy. Yer hair's all peasey agin!"

There was a nip in the air as a misty fog blew in from the Gulf, and Agnes brought some hot tea. Maude toyed with her spoon and looked dreamily at her cup.

"Can you imagine having all that money? What do you suppose it would be like to have millions ... able to have anything, <u>anything</u> you wanted whenever you wanted it?"

"Oh, I don't know, Maude." Agnes rested the sock she was darning on her lap and sipped her tea. "Actually, what would you want? I mean, what would you do with a million if you had it? You'd always be worrying about someone taking it from you. You know, I've never known a really happy wealthy person. Not on our level of happy, that is. Something about all that money that lifts them so far above our level of existence that they can't possibly know what it is to have pressing bills, or no food, or not enough money to clothe your children." She was sewing again as she talked. "That's why it's always so absurd to me when yet another millionaire becomes President on promises of helping the poor. The poor is a faceless mob to him. There's no way in the world he can understand the problems of the poor, peering down on them from the height of his great wealth."

"Sure, sure, Ag ... but we can dream, can't we?" Maude nodded generally at everyone, and moved her rocker more toward the center of the room. "Let's play a game! Let's play 'what if'... what if you had a million. Not with all those problems you've listed, which are very real, of course ... just what if someone suddenly gave each of us a million. What would you do with it? Cora, you're first."

Cora's eyes flashed big. She'd been sitting, she thought, on the sidelines and now here she was, suddenly thrust center stage. She drew a deep breath.

"Good heavens! Why, I don't know. I haven't thought. I mean, you must give me a little time. Let's see. Put it in a bank, I suppose, and hire a lawyer." Cora was too flustered to continue.

Maude jumped in, wagging a finger in the air.

"No. Not that stuff, Cora. Not what would you do <u>exactly</u>, step by step. What would you use it for. Don't ponder. You <u>must</u> have a few things you'd use unexpected money for. Come on, now!"

"Well," said Cora, "if you mean just quick like ... I'd get a nice present for you, Maudie. And something for Ag. And you, too, Jerry. Sally-Anne and Doobie need a car. Oh," she shrugged, "I don't know, I'm really not good at games like this."

Maude looked at her for a second and then reached across the table and patted her hand. There was a little silence. Turning toward Agnes, Maude nodded.

"Your turn, Ag."

Agnes put her sewing on the table and looked at it for some moments. Then she lifted her eyes to Maude.

"You know, Maude, you're asking a very difficult question. The prospect of having great money is unlikely and I'd have to think and plan for a very great time. There's this place, of course ... all the bills, and the repairs. I'd want to see what Peg needs, up in her home, if anything. I'd want to set up for Jerry in wherever he's going. Like Cora here, I really don't know. There actually isn't much I'd want, for myself that is. I can't think of anything I really need ... except a new stove, maybe." She smiled, a bit embarrassed.

"That's exactly my point!" Maude leaned forward, eyes dancing with interest. "There's nothing we'd use it for. We don't really need lots and lots of money. Oh, of course, we'd pay our bills and toss some around among our friends like Cora said ... but we don't <u>need</u> anything. It would ruin each of us if we fell into a fortune. We'd spend all our remaining days being selfish, thinking of ourselves, trying to entertain ourselves, trying not to be bored. Here we sit in the pouring rain and we've lost sight of just how lucky we really are. We don't need anything at all."

"Ken I play? I need things!"

They'd forgotten Sally-Anne, but she hadn't forgotten them. She was leaning against the kitchen sink, facing them, and wringing the dishrag in her hands. Her head twisted to one side and a surprised expression flitted across her face in startlement at her own boldness.

"S'cuse me," she murmured.

Agnes made an involuntary gesture toward the little woman, including her in the group.

"No, you please excuse us, Sally. Of course you can play. We didn't mean to exclude you." She pushed back a chair at the end of the table. "Sit down for a few minutes and rest. Tell us what you'd use a million dollars for."

Sally-Anne inched hesitantly toward the table and slowly perched on the very edge of the chair, resting her hands in front of her.

"If'n I gits a millyun ... if'n somebody done give me a millyun dollahs ..." She ducked her head slightly and chuckled. "'Course, ain't no possibleness u' thet!"

"But if they did?"

264

"If'n theys did ... fust off, I'd do like Miss Cora sez. I'd get me to town an' push all thet money straight into Lee Bank. Then, I'd git me 'cross to ole Mr. Strayhorn's office an' I'd hire him up. I'd need a lawyer-man sure'nuf, to handle ma bisnez, all I wants to do." She was silent. Her fingers beat a gentle tattoo on the table and she pursed her lips.

"Then, I'd 'tend fer Doobie!"

"Doobie?"

"Yes'm. He ain't had no 'tention fum no-body his whole life. No-body thet counts, that is. Nobody 'cept me. Doobie's a good man. Always wuz. 'Cept he wore out. An' he's little. All the white mens has mo' money an' all the black mens theys bigger. Doobie ain't neveh say so, But I knowed he hates thet. I'd have ole Mr. Strayhorn fix it so Doobie don' hev ta hoe an' chop no mo'... git money each week, like he does now, only raise it up a quarta. A man's gotta git at leas' one raise in a lifetime. Ain't decent he don'. Then, he could stay home an' res'. An' maybe thet way, I'd git me my piazza screened in." She chuckled and bobbed her head. "Annnn'" She drew out the word as she sucked in a huge breath. "Ever' one o' my gran'kids would go to college. It ain't now like it were when I wuz a youn'un. All this here pickin' cotton an' rollin' 'bacca leaves, thet's mos' gone an' kids needs edication now. No two ways 'bout thet! They needs it to git alon', to be somebody, not like Doobie an' me. An' I'd give it to ever' one, so's they could walk aroun' wid theah haids held high."

Agnes was following all this carefully.

"How many children do you have, Sally?"

"I'se got me a whol' passel. Ten! Doobie keeps tellin' me we's got nine but he keeps forgittin' Ruthie. She's always quiet an' settin' off to one side an' if'n Doobie's gonna forgit one of 'em, she's the one. But it's ten. An' a whol' slew o' gran'kids. Mostly all over in Myers. When I gits to town an' theys all skittlin' out ta kiss me, seems a whol' town-ful. Each an' ever'one mus' git schoolin'. An' I'd take thet money an' fix 'em up." She paused and no one else spoke. A thoughtful speculation settled around the table. Sally-Anne ignored the cup of tea Cora had gotten for her, and pondered on. Then in a low voice, almost a whisper, she continued.

"I wants me a weddin'! A real weddin'! In a church. A white folks church an' a white preacher-man!" She threw up her head. "Mind ya, ain't nuthin' wrong wid whut Doobie an' me done. We made our plans an' tuk 'em ta God an' He tol' us we could be man an' wif' an' fum thet day to now thet's been bindin' on us an' I ain't nevah strayed oncet. If'n Doobie done, he ain't nevah sed an' I don't want to heah it, nohow. But it ain't right fer our kids. They don' complain. Wouldn' dare. I don' hol' wid complainin'. But I knows! Under the white man's law, ain't good fer 'em. I wants real bad ta fix it." She glanced around the table and in her excitement the years fell away. An eager young girl shown through the crinkled old eyes. "An' I wants ta wear a flowy dress. Not white, 'course, but a flowy flowery dress, an' Doobie'd hev a big ole posy onto his coat, an' music'd play ... hev ta hev music! An' ever' body'd be invited. Oh, I'd be careful 'bout all them feelin's ... the black folks'd sit on one side an' the white folks on t'other, so's nobody'd feel bad. An' I wants a lil' gal throwin' flowah petals in front o' me as I walks down thet aisle. An' at the end, at the finish, when hit's all over, I wants me a paper ... a paper wid Doobie's name onto it, an' mines ... an' signed by thet preacher ... an' it mus' say we's legal wed!"

Sally smiled and bobbed her head in deference to each of the others as she sipped her tea. The eager little girl slipped away.

"An' after all them doin's, I'd take me all the moneys lef' in thet bank an' I'd buil' me a church!" She turned to Agnes. "You know, Mis' Agnes, we ain't got us a church. Not a real one. We meets of a Sunday in Iona, up a ways fum the ferry dock, but thet's not a real church. We needs us a big church, wid a steeple an' a roun' glass winder, all shiny colors glowin' in the sun. Think o' thet!" She smiled quietly to herself for a few minutes, and the others sat silent and watched her. Then, with a start and a guilty expression, she stood quickly.

"Gotta git back to wuk!"

As Sally-Anne returned to the kitchen cabinets and busily pushed around a cleaning rag, Maude sighed deeply.

"My," she breathed. "Wasn't that something? Imagine knowing so precisely what you want."

●

"Are you going to leave them your electric go-cart, too?"

"Who?"

"The Worthingtons."

"No. Of course not. We'll need it to poke around those little towns we lay up in overnight. We'll take the cart on the Wanigan with us. It has its own little elevator and a hidey-hole below deck."

"Really, Kate, you thought of everything when you planned that yacht." Fanny Fontaine took a long sip of her mint julep and smirked inwardly. She was delighted the boat wasn't hers ... all that bother and fuss ... endless days of planning food and trying to balance guests so people didn't clash or get bored. Not for her. She'd just ride along and not have to get involved, thank heaven.

Kate picked up on Fanny's smug mood. "One of these days Fanny, I'll haul you along and just drop you off in Podunk or some such place."

"You wouldn't dare!" Fanny swizzled her little stick and sucked loudly on a piece of ice.

"Oh, yes I would. Don't press me. And if you're sucking that ice cube loud like that, thinking Helga will hear you and leap to attention, forget it. There'll be no more kowtowing to you, old chum. If you're going all the way to St.

266

Croix with me, you'll have to work for it ... and now's a good time to start. Get yourself another drink. You'll be bartender on the way north -- Helga'll be too busy to mess with that. Alright?"

Fanny shrugged and tucked in a stray lock of inky-black hair.

"Nothing ever comes easy in this life. One needs to slave for even the smallest blessings." She allowed what she thought was a beatific expression to creep over her face.

"Really? Listen to who's talking. What've you got now, Frances, after that last pirate deal of your husband's ... thirty-five million? Not too difficult to pay for life's little blessings, as you term them, backed by thirty-five million!"

"Now, Kate, you know what I mean. But I didn't drag all the way over here," she smiled and poked her friend's arm so there was no sting to the remark, "to nitpick with you. You asked me to take over the farewell regatta business, remember. So I'm here. Let's plan. What do you want me to do?"

Kate reached across to the little table on her right and picked up a pad and pencil.

"Here," she exclaimed, holding both out to Fanny, "Make some notes and we'll wind this up in a jiffy. You know, Fanny ..." She paused and sloshed her drink around in her glass for a minute, as she stared out of the big window. "I'm getting old. Tired all the time. This trip north'll be a sad occasion for me!" Her legs spraddled wide and she put her hands behind her head and leaned backward. "I've decided to sell the Wanigan soon's we tie up in Duluth. Sam's really disturbed and I'm sorry about that. But it's too much bother, and I've just grown tired of all the hassle. I should be able to sail easily through the arranging of this regatta business <u>and</u> plan the trip home but suddenly it seems too much. I don't know. I'm just tired, I suppose. Always pushing on ahead and dragging everybody along behind. I want to be behind for awhile and have somebody drag me." Her glasses had slipped to the end of her nose and she peered over them at her friend. Then she smiled. "Oh, come on, Fanny. Your mouth's wide open."

"Sell the Wanigan? <u>Sell</u> her? Whatever for? Put her up in drydock some place. What would you get for her ... half a million? It's not like you need the money, Kate."

Kate shook her head.

"No. It's not that. I certainly don't need any more money. But to dry-dock her seems to say I'll use her again some day and I won't. I'm not going to get any younger as time goes on. And it smacks of reaching back, somehow. I never reach back! Anyway, there it is. I've decided. This'll be the final cruise, and I want it a good one." She smiled and reached for a potato chip. "Okay. Enough of the sad stuff. On to the regatta. Let's see. We'll schedule it in three weeks ... Saturday ... the last Saturday in April. That's the 24th, which will leave me six days to wind up readying our departure. I want to leave here promptly at 10 a.m. April 30th. Sam tells me the tide's high at that time, and we can slip quietly out the channel. No blasts. No horns. Just here one minute, gone the next. I like that, somehow."

"Well ..." Fanny's pencil was poised over her pad ... "if this is the end of the Wanigan, then this will be the last regatta, too. You should appoint yourself Queen this year, Kate. That would be only proper."

"Oh, no! No, no, no! Fanny, are you out of your mind? This picnic isn't for me. I'm never out in front that way, and you know it. We'd best let it go by. We just won't have a Regatta Queen this year, that's all. We'll just leave the tiara and scepter stuck away in the game closet on Wanigan and say nothing about it. And don't you say anything about it, either, Miss Chatterbox. You hear? Not a word about not having a queen ... and not a word about this being the wind-up picnic. You hear me, Fanny? Promise, now ..."

●

They'd dragged the little boat out of the water and up the bank on pipe rollers. Then, carefully, Jerry and Didi had flipped it first on its side and then completely over. The bottom was heavily encrusted with barnacles.

"No wonder we can't get up any speed, carrying all that extra weight. Watch your hands as you scrape this stuff off." He handed her a pair of heavy leather gloves. "Those barnacles are sharp as razors and'll tear your fingers to the bone."

Jerry had an old paint scraper and Didi held a putty knife. They scraped and poked and the little shelled creatures squashed and fell to the sand. In no time sand flies, gnats and no-see-ums collected and buzzed in their faces.

"Ugh. Let's hurry. This isn't all that pleasant, is it?" Didi was edgy. She hated bugs that flew up her nose and into her ears. And the teeny no-see-ums bit like fury. When the boat bottom was finally clean, rinsed and the barnacle trash had been shoveled into the channel, both youngsters were filthy.

"Let's run across the bridge for a swim." Jerry had washed the gloves and was spreading them on the dock to dry.

"I haven't got my swim suit on."

He started off, beckoning her to follow.

"Oh, that's okay. We can go in with our clothes on. Get rid of all this slime and guk. We won't stay long. I want to get the bottom coppered soon as it dries."

She ran after him.

"Wait up. Where're you going so fast?"

They raced across the sand when they reached the beach and plunged into the warm water.

The Gulf was placid, blue-green and friendly. Didi spread her arms wide and floated face down, luxuriating in the coolness. If she opened her eyes she could see bottom ... all those strange little many-colored bits of life, moving gently to and fro with the slack tide. She reached down and poked a conch shell, only to have it scoot off in wild confusion, dragged along by the hermit crab that was living in it. She lifted her head to take a breath, the sea water dripping down her face and beading on her eyelashes. She surprised Jerry staring silently at her, a strange expression on his face, half hurtful and half hopeful. She stared silently back. After a long moment, Didi sat on the bottom facing him, the water up to her waist.

"We have to talk about it sometime, Jerry. Might just as well be now." She reached down for a handful of sand and let it trickle through her fingers. "I've been thinking about it, too."

"Are you going to come back?"

"I haven't left yet." She smiled.

He didn't.

"Yeah. But are you coming back? I have to know."

"Yes. I'll be back." Her smile disappeared and she was suddenly as serious as he was. "What about you? Are you staying or will you go back to Evanston?"

"I'm going to stay all summer, at least. After that, it all depends."

"On what?"

"Lots of things. Like I'll have to do something about school. I've got to finish school, you know." It was his turn to lower his head and funnel sand through his fist. The odd look, half eager-half hesitant, returned and his eyes hooded over as if to block exposure.

"'Course, it really depends on you. Didi, look at me. I've been afraid ... I mean, I've tried several times but it always stuck. I like you heaps, more than anybody, but it scares me, this pressure in here ..." He patted his chest ... "like I can't breathe ... every time I look at you. Like now. As you sit there and watch me, I could just die."

They looked steadily at each other for some time. Then Didi drew in her feet and rested her cheek on her knees. She spoke very softly.

"I like you heaps too, Jerry. I will be back. In the Fall I will be back. I hope you will be here, too."

"I will! I will! If you're coming back, then I'll stay."

There was another long pause, but this time it was without tension. Both were comforted.

"Has your father set the date you're leaving?"

"Yes. At least he's set the date he's leaving ... May 15. But I'm not happy about leaving then. I've agreed to accompany Father to Morocco in July but he has to go to South America in June and I don't want to go there. I want to stay here through June and catch up with him in Spain the first week in July. He won't agree to any such arrangement unless I've a chaperone ... a trustworthy older woman to live with me until I leave, July 1. I've been puzzling ... going over everybody I know. I always come back to the same person. Do you suppose ... do you think, maybe ... what about Maude?"

"Oh! Perfect! She will. I know she will. We can ask her tonight."

"No." Didi shook her head. "Maybe I'd better ask her myself. If you ask her she'll say yes. If I ask her she can say no if she really doesn't want to. Mind?"

"No. We'll do it the way you want. You're smarter 'n me about all that stuff. Whichever way ... Let's get back. I want to get that boat bottom finished before supper. Tomorrow I'll repaint the water mark and she'll be all spruced up for the regatta."

They started back, looking like bedraggled waifs, but their minds weren't on their clothes. At the bridge Didi reached out and took his hand and held it tightly all the way across. At the far end she pulled him up.

"Jerry, listen. If Maude says yes ..."

"She will."

"If she does, then I can stay 'til the end of June ... and that'll give us plenty of time."

"For what?"

"To give Sally-Anne her wedding!"

●

As in former years, Murph's dock was the rendezvous. By noon on Saturday, April 24th, the little boats began to gather. Bedecked with festive streamers and with jaunty guidons fluttering from the prows, they nosed in and tied up to the piling amid shouts and calls of greeting. The ladies were resplendent in tailored slacks, starched shirtwaists with mutton-legged sleeves, and carried lace-fringed parasols. All wore huge floppy hats. The men, looking somewhat uncomfortable, were dressed sedately in blue slacks and white coats. As they climbed up onto the dock and clustered under the wide eaves they looked like a Winslow Homer transplanted from the Jersey coast into a tropical setting.

Those who had no boats but were riding with friends had also collected, and there was lots of kissing and hugging and beer-drinking. Didi and Jerry didn't join the others but were content to drift about, talking quietly and making plans for the future.

Pearlie was nowhere around. Cleo Smith, who often helped out during the winter months at the dock and the Bide-A-Wee Restaurant, was tending bar, popping beer caps and chatting with the islanders. Murph was hauling iced beer up-island to Redfish Pass, the picnic site.

"Where's Pearlie?" someone called. Others took up the question.

Cleo waved one hand in the air.

"Don't worry. She'll be along. She's having a problem with her outfit. She tore something."

"Tore something? What?"

"Her bra!"

"Oh, my God!"

There was a wild shout of laughter. Pearlie was known far and wide for the largest unrestrained bosom on both islands, a source of affectionate amusement in which she readily shared. Standing behind the bar, she would often confront strangers by leaning back against the oversized mirror, holding a bottle of beer in one hand, and thrusting a wet rag, fresh-dipped in the cooler ice, down her bra as she smirked ... 'My land, ain't it hot?' To Pearlie, a ripped bra could be a catastrophe.

The buzz of concern was mounting when Cleo glanced out of the rear window and spied Pearlie hurrying along her path toward the dock.

"It's okay, folks," Cleo sang out. "She's on her way!"

"At the same instant a distant blast of the Wanigan's horn was heard and Pearlie's plight was forgotten as everyone rushed to the forward railing, staring eastward down Roosevelt Channel.

"Can you see her? Ah, there she comes! Beautiful! Just beautiful!"

Pearlie arrived in the bar doorway just in time to overhear these last remarks. She knew she was gorgeous in her new outfit but in her wildest dreams she'd never expected to cause this much excitement. She preened visibly.

"Well, thankee," she exclaimed loudly, puffing her hair. "So nice to see ya! Ain't it gonna be a grand party?"

Everyone turned, and froze. Pearlie had arrived! No doubt about that. There she stood, in flaming, clashing color from head to toe. A bright green Robin Hood cap perched over one eye, a voluminous ruched pink bra, strapless and held so tightly by elastic binding that a shelf of flesh hung over the edge, topped skintight, shiny purple pants. Her shoes were red, with turned-up tips.

"Shades of Maude Adams ..." someone murmured as Pearlie made her way through the gathering to the edge of the dock platform, nodding this way and that with a bright smile. If she noticed people imperceptibly drawing back she gave no sign.

Sam held the Wanigan just off the dock in deep water by churning its engines and Kate O'Hearn called out from its deck.

"Time to go, folks. If you'll stretch out behind us in a long line, we'll be off. Sam will steam slowly so there won't be any wake and remember, there's lots of us, so please don't speed in and out as we go. We don't want an accident."

Everyone scrambled into their little boats, fitting in guests here and there, and the air was filled with the sound of outboard motors starting up. Suddenly the dock was empty ... except for Pearlie. She stood leaning against the railing with an incredulous expression on her face. There was plenty of room in several boats and she couldn't believe she'd not been invited to go along. She turned to Cleo Smith, watching the developments from the doorway, and murmured something. Cleo shrugged and lifted her hands. Then Pearlie slumped a bit and started to walk slowly back down the dock to her house.

None of this byplay was missed by Miss O'Hearn. With Helga by her side and her mainland guests grouped around her, she surveyed the scene on the dock.

"Oh, oh," she breathed in Helga's ear. "We're having a little problem. We've got to move fast. Go tell Sam to lower the side gangway and I'll call to Pearlie."

Quick as Kate was, Jerry and Didi were quicker. They, too, had been watching and now Jerry threw his motor into full speed and circled in to the dock, throwing spray as he skidded up abreast of Pearlie.

"There you are! You were late and we missed you. We want you to ride with us."

Didi stood up and grabbed a piling, steadying the little boat.

"Yes," she called. "There's plenty of room. Step down here beside me. Careful now!"

Pearlie's forlorn expression lifted and a glowing smile creased her face. She looked down at the two youngsters and her eyes melted.

"Do you think there's room?"

Jerry bobbed his head and put out his hand to help her.

"Sure. Just don't jump. Ooze down, sorta. Here, sit in the middle and Didi can perch up front. There! Are you comfortable?"

Pearlie nodded and straightened her hat which had tipped to one side. Didi gave a big shove against the piling and they moved slowly out into the open bay.

Kate O'Hearn, from the bridge of the Wanigan, had watched the little scene play itself out. She leaned toward Helga.

"Did you see the lad? Not a second's hesitation. He spotted an uncomfortable situation building and moved immediately, without thought, to solve it. Tact! You don't learn that, Helga. It has to be bred in. Native diplomacy! What's his name?"

"Jerry."

"I know that. What's his last name?"

"I'm not sure, Miss Kate. Marshall, I think."

"Where's he from? Not here. I know he's staying on the other side of the bridge with his Aunt, Agnes Trumbull ... but where's he from up north?"

"Somebody told me Evanston. Evanston, Illinois. I think that's where."

"Helga, please make a mental note of this and act on it first thing tomorrow. Find out the boy's full name and correct address, and get it to Ed Hopkins in the St. Paul office. Send him Agnes Trumbull's address, too. Tell Ed he's to set a permanent check on Jerry ... have someone responsible keep quiet tabs ... he'll know what I mean ... not to interfere in any way with the lad's life, but when the boy tires of the island, and he will, Ed's to give him a job in my office. That one's going to be a splendid young man and I want him at Minnesota Mining. Don't forget, now."

"No'm. I won't."

"But first," Kate grinned a Cheshire Cat grin, sly and cunning, "there's one other little matter that needs tending to before we sail up to Redfish. So stand by to help me." She reached beyond Sam, who was at the wheel, and gave the alarm lanyard three quick tugs. The horn blasted across the bay and the boaters quieted quickly. Kate then gave the signal to gather round by circling one hand high over her head. As the little boats drew into the Wanigan, she whispered to Helga.

"I cannot abide snobbishness. Plenty of room in most of those boats for Pearlie. There was no excuse for them to leave her out. Watch me fix their little red wagons."

"Folks," she called through the ship's megaphone, "we can't move out without a Queen." Helga gasped, then smiled and ran off to get the tiara and scepter from the game closet. "In previous years, we've honored one of the mainland guests, as you know, but this year we've decided to pick our Queen from our island friends, one of the ladies who live here year-round. Well," she paused a moment ... "that gave us quite a problem as they are all special and all deserving. We finally decided the only fair method was to put all the names in a hat and draw one out. And here it is!" She held aloft a scrap of paper. "I'm happy to announce that this year's Regatta Queen is Mrs. Murph Suggs, our own Pearlie!"

Pearlie was stunned. She sat silently through the applause as Jerry carefully maneuvered the little craft in against the yacht where Kate waited on the lower platform of the gangway.

"Careful, now, Jerry," Kate admonished. "Grab hold of this railing and I'll help Pearlie aboard."

But Pearlie drew back.

"Oh, no ma'am. Thank you for the honor and I'm that touched. But I'll stay put and ride along with these two kids. They was sweet enough to make room an' it wouldn't be right for me to leave 'em now, would it?"

Kate instantly agreed. She gazed speculatively at Pearlie for a second.

"You're correct, of course, Pearlie. It wouldn't be right at all." She leaned far out and placed the tiara on Pearlie's head. "Wear our crown proudly and carry this guidon. And instead of the Wanigan going first, why don't you lead off, Jerry, you and Didi and our Regatta Queen."

And so they went! The tiny boat first, with its new red depth line buried in the water from all the extra weight, followed by the huge, majestic, glistening yacht, trailing a long line of smaller boats, festive with flying pennants and colored bunting.

Cleo Smith watched from the dock and waved as the procession passed by, moving slowly northward, twisting slightly right into deep water, then left between the channel markers and on out of sight toward Redfish Pass.

"My!" she muttered to herself, "don't Pearlie look grand!"

19
May

She was known on both islands as Tarpon Nannie. Pearlie inadvertently named her in an off moment, and it stuck!

Mrs. William Worthington, the former Nancy Scofield of Baltimore, had been born with a gold spoon in her mouth. She couldn't possibly have been fancier. Married to Bill Worthington, Wall Street tycoon, the only thing larger than her diamonds was her heart. For three months out of each year, while Bill was adhered to High Finance, she wrapped her pedigree around her shoulders like an invisible feather boa and highstepped around Biarritz, the Riviera, Cannes, Monte Carlo. Groomed, gay, gorgeous, her exquisite tiny figure, aflame with baubles from Tiffany's, could be seen hurrying into Chanel's or La Scala, or, late, late at night, Maxim's, trailing a broad swathe of perfume, laughter and escorts. For three months ... January through March! Then a month in her home outside Baltimore to recuperate. The rest of the year was fish and chips.

They felt, Bill and Nancy, that three months in the public eye more than paid the year's dues, and the rest of the time they could concentrate on ground level fun. They sought out simple places where they could loll about, fish, swim, put their feet up ... where their winter identity could be packed away along with their formals and fur coats, where phone calls could be made outgoing but could not come in.

The emphasis was on fishing. They had caught tuna off Nova Scotia, and giant trout in Lake Titicaca. They had landed channel bass off Cape Hatteras and sailfish in the Galapagos. Nancy's near-record broadbill swordfish, boated off the Chilean coast only after an exhausting fight, evened once and for all Bill's huge Sacramento sturgeon, encountered at the mouth of the Columbia River. One year they laced back and forth across the continent after manta rays and shark, referred to joyfully in quiet moments when they reminisced as their ` summer among the monsters.'

But never tarpon!

This was a sore point with Nancy. She was the one who pushed.

"If only the kids hadn't given us that article on 'The Silver King, Lord of the Caribbean Waters'. There it lies, up on the mantle there, gnawing at me like a rat with cheese. Bill, how many years is it now that I've begged you to arrange a Gulf trip? If we don't go after those tarpon pretty soon, we'll be too old to fight 'em." She was slumped in a chair, mostly on her back, with her feet propped high on the work bench. "Bill ... please put aside your fly-tying and talk to me."

He glanced over at her. Tiny little mite she was ... a mere four feet eight inches tall and some ninety-eight pounds ... soft and cuddly and so innocent looking ... but steel through and through. He stood and stretched his long six foot two inch frame to its fullest and grinned down at her.

"Why don't you let me get you a special low-built work bench, Cutie, so your feet won't be so high? Can't imagine but your back aches from that scrunched-down position."

"Don't you dare lord it over me, Bill Worthington, you and your lanky frame. I may be small but I can match up to you any day in the week and don't you forget it!" She held out her arms and he knelt beside her and rested his head in her lap.

"Poor boy," she breathed, smoothing his hair. "I've really given you a fit, haven't I? But it's been fun, hasn't it? Hasn't it, Bill?" She fingered his ear, which he loved. "Hair's getting pretty thin. Maybe we should give up chasing around the countryside and you can rest. You stay home and rest ... and grow hair ... and I'll go off to the Indies by myself and catch tarpon. How'd that be?"

Shortly after this conversation, Bill had a long lunch with his great friend "Ding" Darling and the conversation turned to fishing.

"There's this fantastic little island," Darling was saying, "out in the Gulf off Fort Myers, Florida, where the tarpon fishing in May and June is not to be believed. Have you ever fished for tarpon?"

Bill slowly shook his head and his eyes glowed.

"Trouble *is*" Darling went on, "by that time both the local Inns are long closed. You'd need a place to stay. Ah, Kate O'Hearn! Close friend of mine. Has a little place down there. I'll phone her up."

●

Jerry was surprised, when he met the mailboat at 12:30, just past noon, on May 3rd, to see Captain Bob signalling frantically before the boat even docked. He caught the hawser and expertly twirled the end in a half hitch around a piling. Then he leaned over the gunwale into the Santiva.

"You want me, Cap'n?" he asked.

Captain Bob gestured toward the rear and spoke in a harsh whisper.

"Folks back there for ya. Say they're friends of Mr. Darling and Miss Kate, an' they're supposed to stay in her house. Where's Lars? If he don't turn up, you'll havta run 'em up in your truck. Not got much luggage. Guess they don't plan to stay long. Lots of fishing gear, though."

While Jerry was loading the several pieces of luggage securely on the back of the truck, Bill Worthington held the door open for his wife. She scrambled in.

"My, isn't this just fine." she exclaimed, spreading her dress out over the torn seat and resting her right arm along the top of the door window.

"Move over, Cutie."

"No, no, Bill. You sit in the back, on a suitcase. There's not nearly enough room for three up here. Besides, I want this young man all to myself. By the time we get to where we're going, I'll have all the news." She beamed a broad smile at Jerry, who looked back shyly.

The truck wouldn't start. Jerry leaped out to the attack.

"Can I help?" Mrs. Worthington was poised to assist.

"Can I help?" Mr. Worthington was up and preparing to step across the luggage.

"No, thank you. She needs a little jolting, that's all." Jerry was furious at the truck. Why now, of all times, did she have to act up? Thank heaven he was nose into the bay breeze or the bugs would have made it miserable. He kicked the left wheel and bumped around on a fender. Mrs. Worthington turned the key and ground down on the starter and finally the old truck sputtered into life.

"Don't choke her. She needs a quiet moment to collect her wits, and then we'll be off." Jerry grinned from ear to ear. "Did anyone warn you about things going wrong out here?" He climbed back into the cab and meshed the gears. They inched forward.

"Not really." Mrs. Worthington gazed out the window, drinking everything in. "But we're used to islands. Nothing bothers us very much. Did the Captain call you Jerry?"

"Yes'm."

"Jerry what?"

"Jerry Marshall."

She nodded.

"That's nice. Where are you from, Jerry?"

"Originally from Illinois. Evanston. I'm staying with my Aunt, Agnes Trumbull. She has the first house on the other side of the bridge, down that way." He pointed vaguely toward the south.

Mrs. Worthington nodded again as they chugged along. When they got to the intersection of the post office land and the main road they turned left and drove along the edge of the Gulf. The water was calm and deep blue.

"Ah. Magnificent! Bill..." She stuck her hand out where the back window should have been and wiggled her fingers at her husband. "Look. Great looking water! I know it's full of hungry tarpon, just waiting for us. Isn't it grand? Have you caught many?" she asked Jerry.

"No'm Not any. I only got here last September and I've been working pretty steady and I don't think there're any tarpon around just now, anyway."

"Full moon. Full moon this month." Mr. Worthington stuck his head through the window hole. "Mr. Darling said they come in when the May moon is full. By the thousands, so he said."

Mrs. Worthington was watching the youngster's face, and she didn't miss the excitement that flared in his eyes.

"Maybe, if you can rearrange your schedule, you can come along with us now and again. We're going to fish with Captain Staines. Mr. Darling assured us he's the best in these waters. Do you think you can arrange that?"

"Yes'm. That would be fine. 'Course, I'll have to talk it over with my Aunt Agnes."

"Of course." Mrs. Worthington agreed solemnly.

"We're almost there, now. The driveway's up ahead, where those tall palms are. Lars is gonna be mighty surprised."

"Lars? Who's he?"

"Miss O'Hearn's chauffeur. He's been polishing that Rolls for days, waiting to drive to town to fetch you."

A quick glance through the back window at her husband.

"A Rolls? A Rolls Royce? Way out here on this tiny island?"

"Yes'm. A silvery one. They call it the Silver Cloud. Maybe you should'a waited on the mailboat and I should'a gone for Lars. This ain't, isn't, very comfortable for you."

"It's perfect. Just perfect. Isn't it, Bill?" But Bill didn't hear. A bright flash offshore brought his binoculars to his eyes and he was studying the water.

"Here we are!" Jerry turned from the Gulf into the palm-bordered driveway and coasted up to the front door. No one was around.

"Good heavens! Bill, this is beautiful. I thought you said Mr. Darling told you it was a little shack!"

"No, Cutie. He said 'little place'. He said his friend Kate O'Hearn had a little place. I suppose it's a matter of perspective. If you live in a huge mansion, this could be classed as a little place."

They stood in the center of the lovely living room, gazing around, as Jerry put their luggage inside. Suddenly, a swinging door in the rear wall pushed slowly open and a young girl peered around. Then she hurried through and stood, wiping her hands on her apron.

"Are you Mr. and Mrs. Worthington?" She bent her knees in a little curtsy. "I am that sorry, ma'am. I didn't hear. That mixer out there, you know. I'm Mady. I'm to tend for you. Oh, my! This is awful. Lars is down at the boat slip and he'll be that upset. Did you drive over with Jerry in that truck?" This all poured out in her confusion and she looked scared to death.

"No. We came across on the mailboat. Friends told us that was the only way to 'meet' the island and it was a lovely trip. Wasn't it, Bill? Wasn't it grand?" She settled herself on the sofa. "Now, dear, don't be upset. We're fine. Maybe you can tell Lars to come in for a moment, and I'll apologize for not sending word ahead. But we didn't expect anyone to look after us. Arrangements were so quick and haphazard, and we couldn't reach Miss O'Hearn to discuss things. She's off some place, is she not? A trip somewhere?"

"Yes'm. They all left four days back, at ten in the morning, right on schedule. Miss Kate likes to stick to a schedule. Yes'm, I'll get Lars right away."

Mrs. Worthington motioned Jerry over to her side.

"Please sit down here for a minute, Jerry. I want to plan a bit. This is all so unexpected. Bill and I want a simple vacation, you know." Jerry didn't know, but he nodded anyway. "We are on a fishing trip. We can't possibly travel around in a Rolls Royce! Can we, Bill?"

At the picture window, still checking the expanse of the Gulf through his binoculars, Bill answered across one shoulder.

"Well, Cutie, it'll be pretty difficult to carry our gear, poles and nets and bait slopping about in a Rolls. But if that's all there is, we'll just have to make do." He shrugged.

"No. I don't want that. If that's what we wanted, we could have brought the Continental. It's mixing apples and pears and puts everything out of kilter." She frowned for a second, then turned to Jerry, and her face cleared. "Jerry, what about you driving us? In your truck. Wouldn't that be grand? You could drop by after breakfast each morning and see what we are up to, and you'd still have time for your other chores. You could arrange that, couldn't you? And we'd hire you by the month for a nice fat fee. How about that?"

Jerry's mouth had flopped open. He looked at the sweet, motherly face and fell in line, just like all the others. How could anyone say no to this gentle, effervescent little creature?

"Yes'm." He spoke slowly. "I suppose so. 'Course, there's Lars. I wouldn't want to hurt his feelings."

"Oh, I'll explain to Lars. I'm sure he'll be delighted. Fish scales stuck to all that plush, and sand all over the car would give him a fit. He'll be fine." She smiled warmly. "But it is sweet of you to think of him. I like that. And there'll be lots of chores for Lars to do. We'll be renting a small boat and he can tend that. And fetch the groceries. Mr. Darling mentioned a store, Rigby's or some such name, somewhere on a second island. He'll be busy and I'll take special care to make him feel important. Don't you think that's a good solution, Bill?"

"Whatever you say, Cutie. You're the boss."

Jed Staines wasn't home the morning Jerry drove Mrs. Worthington into his yard. They'd driven up Sanibel almost to the ferry slip, and then circled left along the bay past Rigby's General Store with its sign nailed on a post, on through the mangroves for several boggy miles and finally emerged on the edge of Tarpon Bay.

"My!" Mrs. Worthington exclaimed, "what a heavenly spot!" She surveyed the rippling water, the sandy shore sloping gently, the old clapboard two-storied house with its wide encircling screened porch, the three little children playing in the sand, the scampering chickens and the sturdy, large woman hanging out laundry. Busily swishing her horse's tail at the mosquitos and sand flies, Nancy leaned toward Jerry.

"I suppose, with the years, one gets immune to these bugs. To the bites, at least. But the noise. That horrid, high-pitched buzzy whine mosquitoes make! I could never get used to that."

She waved across at the woman as she climbed down from the truck.

"Hello. I'm Nancy Worthington. Can we stop in for a minute?"

"Surely, surely. Run on into the porch and get out of these varmints. Just let me hang these here sheets and I'll be along in."

Mrs. Staines introduced herself and nodded to Jerry.

"Always time for a visit. Don't see many people, ya know. Set. Take that rocker. Can I get ya some tea?" With few wasted motions she placed cold glasses in front of her guests and added a plate of fresh hulled coconut.

"Hold a little piece between your back teeth and let the cold tea slosh around it. Adds a nutty flavor I jest love. No, you can't have none." She slapped at a questing little hand reaching up and over the edge of the table. Then, relenting, she added... "Well, maybe a little piece. Here, take one and take these two pieces out to Essie an' Tom. Careful, now, don't fall." She smiled at Mrs. Worthington and shook her head. "Them kids. They'll be the death of me. Jed ain't home but he knows he's takin' you fishin' soon's the tarpon turn up. Mr. Darling wrote him. He went to Boca Grande this mornin' to talk to the guides up there. For some reason, those fish always seem to turn up at Boca before they do down here. Jed says it's the depth of the pass an' the amount of water runnin' with the tides." She paused and sipped her tea, looking expectantly at Mrs. Worthington, who decided she ought to react in some way. She was having difficulty with the large piece of coconut she had taken. Possibly matters might prove easier if it were a smaller piece. She crunched down on the one in her mouth, and swallowed. Then she reached for a smaller one. Shoving it to one side of her check, she talked around it.

"Mrs. Staines, my husband and I have been on Captiva several days now and though we've kept a sharp lookout, we haven't seen a sign of tarpon anywhere. Mr. Darling told Bill to forget all about tarpon and concentrate on snook and redfish and the like until the middle of the month when the moon is full. Is that true?"

"Yes'm. That's about the size of it."

"Do they come in one or two at a time?" We don't want to have them go on by and miss out."

Mrs. Staines laughed aloud.

"Land sakes, Ma'am, you won't miss 'em. No, them fish don't dribble in. They come all at once. None at all, then there they is ... an' hundreds of 'em. Thousands! More. The passes will be full up to stuffin' out, sure' nuf." She laughed again, a deep jolly sound. "No, Ma'am. You can't miss 'em. An' my Jed, he'll put you on 'em. Best guide anywhere near, my Jed is. You'll see. He left a message for ya, jest in case you come by. He says to keep watchin' an' run up here an' tell us, soon's you see 'em. An' be prepared to go out after 'em the very nex' day. Mornin'. Crack o' dawn."

"What do we bring? Rods? Food? Bait? Drinking water? Ice?"

"No'm, you don' need to bring nuthin'. Jed has rods an' he'll load up with bait an' ice at Murph's. He always has drinkin' water. You can tote some food an' soda or beer, if you've a mind fer it. Jed don' drink but he ain't sticky if'n you wants to. He's easy-goin'. You'll like Jed. Everybody does."

●

Wesley Mitchell of the infant Lee County Mosquito Control District sat in his office in East Fort Myers, checking off the days on his calendar. He circled in red the week May 8th to 15th. He had to stop this grumbling among the commissioners that the money allotted to his control program was wasted, that mosquitoes were a southern way of life and had to be accepted along with death and taxes. If he could just get hold of a secondhand light plane, one of those crop dusters now being used in Texas, he knew he could bring those pesky bugs under control. But first he had to have a pilot project, some positive success to point to, in order to jolt those commissioners, or they'd never get up off the funds he needed. The two offshore islands were the perfect set-up. Sanibel was by far the more heavily infested but it was also cumbersome. Too large a land mass and too much standing water. Laced with sloughs filled by brackish tidal flow, that island year after year placed first in the national mosquito census. The fresh water variety, together with the smaller, more vicious saltwater hatchlings swarmed in such clouds around a person's head it was difficult to breathe. He hated the monthly field trips he had to make over there, stomping around in the saw grass, wearing all that suffocating protective gear, especially the heavy green netting tied around his face.

He'd focus on Captiva! The problem was relatively just as great but more manageable. The island was really little more than a raised sandbar, a mere five miles long and only a half-mile wide. No standing water or swampy bog to speak of, and only a handful of residents, if he waited until the winter influx left. The mixing station would have to be on Sanibel, in the middle, where the ground mounded high enough for the equipment to be safe. The highest place on Captiva, the ridge running down its center like a little backbone, was only some six feet above high tide and that was unacceptable ... too subject to flooding by storm. No, the mixing station would be on Sanibel just east of Rabbit Road, and the jeep would be housed there, also.

He riffled again through his calendar as he planned. The tanks and storage sheds could be trucked over the last of April, erected and ready to function by May 6th or 7th ... and the jeep could start fogging on May 8th, before dawn, when the dew was heavy on the undergrowth.

He needed a driver, an islander, someone who could be trusted and who could make on-the-spot repairs, who wouldn't panic when things went wrong, because, of course, they would. That jeep was a monster, really, and it could be dangerous, especially when the fogger on the back ignited and the whole thing became a flamethrower. It all hung on the driver. He'd go talk to Charlie Kramdon who knew all the islanders. Or maybe Carla Wilson at her Island Inn. Elgin Bigelow, that Fish and Wildlife fellow, was also a good source of information. He got around all over both islands in that Piper Cub of his.

Wesley pushed back his chair and reached for his truck keys. He'd better get on over to the islands and check things out.

A bit later, as he bumped along the rutted back road toward Punta Rassa and the Sanibel ferry, his mind wandered along the odd paths his short life had taken. He hadn't really planned any of it, but seemed, instead, to have been gathered up and pushed along. An inquisitive childhood poking about the Jersey flats and adjacent wetlands had led to a consuming interest in tidal marshes and their fascinating inhabitants. This led to Rutgers and a degree in entomology. After hearing of a small, hot, south Florida town that was seeking a bright enthusiastic young man to head up its proposed mosquito control program, here he was, several years later, bumping along the countryside, heading he wasn't sure exactly where. It wasn't that he harbored any doubts about himself or his own abilities. He knew what he wanted to do and he knew what should be done. He knew mosquitoes inside out! What he didn't know was what the village men who controlled the funds might do. He'd stretched the meager yearly allowance he'd been given 'till he damn near tore the dollar bills in half. The jeep spraying program, in both the town and down at the beach, had been well received and he'd gotten a lot of favorable publicity through it. But at best it was a stopgap procedure. Each spraying was expensive and the benefits were soon gone. You couldn't eradicate mosquitoes, really eradicate 'em, unless the tidal rise and fall in the marshy areas was controlled, as salt water mosquitoes laid their eggs above the normal tide line, which hatched only after being flushed by sea water ... unless all standing fresh water in ditches, stagnant pools, ponds, was either drained or oiled down, preventing the maturing of freshwater mosquito larvae... unless those areas of standing water that were to remain unoiled had larvae-feeding fish introduced in sufficient quantity to combat the tiny emerging wigglers ... unless, coupled with all this activity and while work was in progress and on afterwards, a vigorous spraying program was conducted. That's why he needed those light planes.

Meanwhile, he had the two jeeps. His normal optimism returned as he chugged into the Punta Rassa clearing and lined up for the ferry. He would remain undaunted and if, God willing, he could manage a real breakthrough on Captiva, maybe he could shake up the commissioners into talking sense.

●

Maude and Nancy Worthington saw the tarpon at the same moment. At least, Nancy saw them and Maude identified them.

The day after Maude moved in with Didi she met the Worthingtons at the post office and it didn't take long to see that they were depressed. Nancy was confiding.

"I don't know what I'm going to do about Bill. He's taken to moping about the house. Here on this lovely spot there's so much to do to have fun, but somehow he doesn't seem to care. Keeps muttering to himself 'Never should have listened to that fella. Doesn't know what he's talking about. We should leave and go somewhere else' and so on."

"What's the matter? Is Lars acting up?" Maude's face was set with concern.

"Oh," Nancy Worthington flashed her warm smile, always near the surface, and rested one hand on Maude's arm. "Bless you, it isn't Lars. It's Bill's friend Mr. Darling. He is the real reason we came to fish for tarpon all the way down here. It was his advice that fired us up and now we've been on the island almost two weeks and not a fish. Oh, I've caught snook down on the bridge and several reds but fish like that can be caught so many places. We've been watching religiously and not a tarpon anywhere. Not one. Not even one!" She was feeling somewhat depressed herself, watching her husband wander aimlessly back and forth along the mailboat dock, pausing now and again to kick a piling.

"Would you like to go shelling with me tomorrow morning?" Maude asked. "That might be fun for you. I'm going up to Redfish Pass, at the northern end of the island. There's a special spot on the Gulf side where the beach is scooped out and a little indented bay has been formed. Offshore, across the mouth of the pass, about a half mile out, there's a large sandbar forming just under the water." She leaned over conspiratorially and whispered in Nancy's ear. "Don't mention this 'cause folks have a way of flocking and it'll be ruined. I think that old sandbar deflects the incoming tide in some way and aims part of the flow right into this little bay. And the shells, too. I always find lion's paws and scotch bonnets, lots of limpets. All kinds of good stuff."

Nancy's eyes lit up. It sounded like a new adventure and she loved anything new.

"Bill won't come, but I'd love to. What time?"

"Well," Maude paused to consider. "The tide is dead low, which is the best time, at 11 a.m. I'll pick you up about ten and we'll get up there half an hour before it's full out. Will that be okay?"

The next morning, when Maude came by, Nancy was ready. As soon as they reached the beach they instinctively separated, each going her own way, but staying within hailing distance. They searched the perimeter of the little bay, calling back and forth over each special find. Then, together, with the tide just turning in, they walked the water's edge northward toward the end of the island. When they reached Redfish Pass, they squatted in the sand to rest.

"They tell me it was back in 1921 when this cut broke through." Maude sat spraddle-legged, with her basket of shells between her feet, sorting and discarding. "Until then, this island and that one over there, Upper Captiva it's now called, were part and parcel. All the way up to Captiva Pass and Cayo Costa. The northern end of Cayo Costa, 'course, is Boca Grande Pass. That's a big one and oceangoing vessels ply through it to the phosphate plants on Boca. Used to be lots of trade there."

Maude talked on, bent over her heap of shells. She examined each one carefully and built two piles, the ones she planned to keep and the discards. Nancy had her head resting on one knee, watching. Each time Maude put a shell into the no-good pile, Nancy quietly took it and added it to her basket.

"There've always been those two natural passes ... Boca Grande and Captiva. I say ` always' but 'course I don't know firsthand. Anyway, they go way back in years. Then along comes that killer hurricane of '21 and opens this pass. First it was just a little trickle, and I suppose it tried to heal itself, like we do when we're cut. But the tides were too strong. The incoming water riled the sand and boiled it along into the back bay and disbursed it everywhere. The outgoing flow reversed this action and sucked sand from the pass bottom out into the open Gulf. And that's where the sand comes from that's building the bar out there." She pointed offshore.

Nancy peered out but the Gulf was quiet and glassy flat.

"Where? I can't see it at all." She squinted and shook her head.

"It's out there, though, and building. The top's just a foot or so below the water." Maude stopped sorting and peered out, too. "When the wind's up and the tide's rushin', it foams all over white out there. Real pretty! 'Course, now with the tide mostly dead and the Gulf flat and quiet, it doesn't show at all."

She went back to her shells. Nancy continued to gaze out the pass. Suddenly, she reached over and grabbed Maude's arm.

"Oh, I see it, Maude. Look! Out there! It's beginning to foam, just like you said. All along! Isn't it beautiful, all lacy and glittering in the sun. Sparkling and leaping and flashing ... leaping and flashing ...?" Her voice died away and she squeezed hard on Maude's arm. "Maude! What's happening?"

"It's the tarpon, Nancy! They're back! Here they come! Boiling in across that bar by the thousands. Pushing and bumping into each other as they dash for the back bay. Oh, my. Isn't it thrilling?" Maude's voice was thick with emotion. She jumped to her feet and dragged Nancy up with her. "Keep looking, Nancy. It isn't often a body is blessed by a sight like this."

They stood together at the water's edge, mesmerized. Nancy slowly drew her breath in, a long slow inhalation, and let it out just as slowly, as her eyes shone with excitement.

"I never dreamed! I simply never dreamed! Old Mr. Darling never mentioned anything like this. I thought he meant one or two fish ... to keep an eye out for one or two. There are hundreds out there. Thousands!"

Maude nodded.

"More. Many, many more, Nancy. Thousands. In no time, just hours, they'll fill the passes so thick you could walk across on their backs, dryfooted, if they'd hold the weight. All up and down the Gulf coast, from Key West to Pensacola and on around the perimeter down to Texas. Thick. All the passes. All the back bays. In and out of the canals and bayous. Tarpon all over. And they'll stay thick like this through June and into July."

The fish, migrating northward to spawn, had initially followed the deeper water, splitting around the sandbar just off the mouth of Redfish Pass. Entering the pass proper, the first fish slowed appreciably, possibly to feed in the deep channel, and thousands traveling behind at top speed piled up until there were layers and layers of thrashing, ravenous, hundred-pound scavengers, funnelled by the pass into a tumbling, teeming, thrashing, bumping mass. Those further offshore, unable to follow the deep water, cut across the bar, pushing each other up and out of the shallow water in their frenzy. They flashed silver in the brilliant sunlight like a thousand mirrors, and it was this bright flaring that Nancy had first seen.

"Maude!" Nancy looked toward her new friend as they inched along the shore watching the spectacle, pointing at the fish streaking past them just beyond the beach-dip. "The moon is full <u>tonight</u>! How do you suppose that old gentleman could have spotted this so accurately?"

"It's just one of Nature's timetable miracles, and it hangs, of course, on everything being so-called normal. No raging storms or too little or too much rain ... if everything is normal, then all sorts of natural events follow a strict timetable." Maude was in her element and loved talking about the wonders of nature. She had a simple faith in the goodness of things and the orderly procession of the seasons, the migratory controls, the pull of the moon and the response of the tides, all reinforced by her years in the back country in logging camps and the training she'd received from her Everglades trips with the Seminoles. "When the Florida holly berries are ripe, the robins will arrive. Not later. Not before, Exactly on time. And they have flown miles! Edwin Way Teale, that wonderful naturalist, in his exciting book ` North with the Spring', mentions standing on a tiny wooden bridge spanning a small stream in North Carolina on a certain morning pinpointed by the natives, and watching enthralled as baby eels struggled upstream against the current to the still lake further along. These elvers as they're called, not much longer than your finger and hair-thin, were at the end of a thousand mile journey lasting better than a year and a half. On a certain day, at a certain hour, there they were. Isn't it incredible! On and on it goes, too many examples to name. If the conditions of preceding months haven't been thrown out of gear, these fish will turn up during the full moon in May every year."

Nancy stood stock-still and shifted her bag of shells from hand to hand.

"Maude, would you mind terribly if we went back? I want to find Bill and send him up to see this and I have to get up to Captain Staines and tell him. Mrs Staines mentioned that the Captain would be ready to go out the morning after the fish showed up, and I can't wait! Do you by any chance know where Jerry is?"

"Yes. He's over with Didi. They're fussing with his boat at her dock. Sure, we can go. Come on. I'll send him on over to your house."

●

Didi was giving strong moral support! She was leaning up against the trunk of a pine and watching Jerry drill holes in the stern of his boat just above the water-line.

"Won't that leak when the boat is tied up?"

"Nope." Jerry shook his head and pushed a copper tube through the hole into the boat. "When she's moored, this pipe'll be above water. When we're in her, the pipe will be below water and will allow water in to fill the bait-well. I've already put in an overflow outlet, so when we're moving the water will circulate in through this pipe and out through the overflow and keep the bait alive. Without this we'd have to drag along one of those floating bait jugs and I hate that. Always bumping the boat and scaring the fish. This'll be much better. Shrimp and pinfish will stay alive for days in here."

"What about around the holes, outside, where the pipe doesn't fit snug-like?"

"Caulk. Hemp rope, soaked in oil. Won't leak. We'll sure need this arrangement if those tarpon ever show up."

Maude strode around the corner of the house in time to catch this last remark.

"They have. Mrs. Worthington and I just saw 'em pouring through Redfish Pass and she wants to get to Jed Staines on Sanibel. She asks you to bring your truck, Jerry."

"Sure. Come on, Didi." Jerry dropped his drill and grabbed a pair of jeans to cover his swim trunks.

"No. You go drive Mrs. Worthington. I'll stay here with Maude and we'll help Sally-Anne inside." She smiled up at Maude and then glanced back at Jerry. "Don't forget us while you're gone, now."

Talking together as they strolled into the house, Didi mentioned that she'd asked Sally to clean and dust the guest wing. It wasn't in use but she felt it should be neated up if she was leaving in six weeks.

"Has she ever mentioned again wanting to be married in a church?" Maude turned a questioning face toward Didi. "Remember awhile back, when we were all sitting inside during that rain storm at Agnes Trumbull's? Oh, that's right. You weren't there, were you?"

"No, I wasn't," Didi agreed. "But Jerry told me about it. I suggested that if she really was serious, we should all get together and have a wedding. Wouldn't that be great?"

Maude looked doubtful.

"Maybe so. Maybe not. That kind of venture can lift right up in front of you and smack you between the eyes. Has me, many times."

Later that afternoon, grouped around a table in the back patio, Didi, Maude and Sally-Anne were talking. Didi had a pencil and a big yellow legal-size pad. A cool easterly wind blowing in from the bay discouraged the mosquitoes, and the three planners weren't bothered. Didi was reviewing her notes.

"Now, let's see. We'll need as much time as possible. Yet it has to be before I leave the end of next month. We ought to set the day." She glanced across at Sally-Anne, who was picking at a seagrape leaf that had fluttered onto the table. "Do you want a weekday or Saturday or Sunday?"

Sally-Anne shrugged.

"Whatevah yo-all wants. Whatevah' is bes'."

"No, now, Sally-Anne." Didi's pencil was poised in the air. "It's not us. It's you. What is best for you?"

"Well, Miss Didi, 'pears to me thet a Sat'day is bes'. Folks will be comin' fum Myers an' Sat'day is off an' Sunday don' seem right, somehow, seein' as this ain't a real weddin' or nothin'."

"It will be a real wedding!"

"Yes'm. 'Course it will. But Doobie an' me, we's been married up so long now it ain't a firs' weddin', see. Thet's why I tol' you I didn't want no white dress. Ain't lak I'se a virgin bride ... white is fer virgin brides. I'll sew me up a dress of lilac purple. I'se a right smart hunk o' lilac purple cloth over yonder. An' I'll wear me a white hat. The hat kin be white. A big, floppy white hat wid a white lace trim ..." Her eyes were closed and her voice dropped low ... "an' white shoes. White leather. Button up. Thet'll be nice.

An' I'll tote an armful of white gladyelas. Wid a few purple ones. The gladyelas is special to me. Thet's whar Doobie an' me firs met up, ya know, in the flowah fields." Her eyes opened and she smiled shyly. "He didn' know whut to mak' o' me, back then."

Didi returned to her pad.

"Okay. How about the last Saturday in June?" She consulted a little calendar. "That'll be Saturday, June 29. Will that be alright?"

Both the others nodded.

"You know," Didi went on, "both Aunt Agnes and Aunt Cora want to help, too. Aunt Ag said she'd take over the food arrangements."

Sally-Anne's head snapped up.

"Food. Is we havin' food?"

"Of course. The wedding will be at the Chapel-by-the-Sea and we'll set up trestle-tables outside and there'll be lots of food. Tell all your family in Fort Myers to bring food, too. Do you think they would?"

"Sho! How is they gittin' heah?"

"We'll hire two busses, if there are that many, and have 'em driven over and back."

"My!"

"And Aunt Cora asks if she can sew your dress for you? You know, she sews beautifully."

"My! Yes'm. I'd be mighty proud to have her." Sally-Anne's eyes were damp. "My, my! I'se gonna have me a weddin', sho nuff!"

●

There wasn't a breath of air stirring when Captain Staines cut his motor and eased into Murph's dock an hour before dawn. A dark quiet hung heavy over the water. To the east a brightening grayness slid slowly into view, exposing the underside of the fluffy cloud mass blanketing the sky.

"Gonna be a hot one!" Murph said, catching Jed's bow line and securing the boat snugly broadside to the walkway.

"Yep. You got them pinfish?"

"All you want. Jest got in awhile back. Buggy out there, over that grass an' no air to speak of. Don't know why I do it, some time."

Jed slapped his neck.

"Buggy in here, too. It'll git better, though. All we gotta do is hang in an' hold on. Changin' all the time. Zelma's real happy with that new-fangled dustin' gadget Mitchell's put over here. Says first time ever she can hang out sheets without droppin' 'em in the dirt to swat bugs. That baker Ted does quite a job. He was foggin' when I left my place an hour ago. I've cut me a path clear round my house and he circles us twice each trip, foggin' up such a storm o' spray you can hardly breathe fer a bit. But that diesel oil sure does the trick. Sticks like glue to the leaves an' unless we gits a pour-down, won't be nary skeeter all day long. Zelma says it's a blessin' from high up and she thinks we oughter give a party for Wesley Mitchell to sort o' thank him or something."

They iced the boat and gassed it up. They then netted pinfish and shrimp from Murph's huge bait trap, with its pungent fish smell and bubbling water sucking in from the bay. As they filled two small wells on the boat they counted each bait carefully. Then Jed rearranged the fishing gear so his clients could climb aboard without tripping, and went with Murph into the bar.

Pearlie was sagged across the counter as they entered. Lifting one hand in a desultory greeting, she struggled to keep her eyes open.

"Middle o' the night! Ain't you guys ever gonna straighten up an' fly like other folks? No-body but burglars works all night! An' these bugs! An' the heat, already. One don't git ya, other will. That lil' ol' toot of dustin' Teddy gives us don't do no good. They all talked that arrangement up right smart an' got our hopes high an' it don't 'mount to a hill o' beans!" She took a limp rag, dipped it in ice water and thrust it into her bra.

"Cut yerself a jeep path 'round yer shack," Jed called, "so's Ted can buzz all the way 'round, an' it'll do right smart. Zelma swears by it."

Pearlie nodded toward Murph, slumped at a table.

"Talk to that big ol' bum. Any tree choppin' he's gotta do it. I ain't runnin' around bustin' trees. Can't git all my work done now, as tis." She reached into the ice water for a cold beer.

The sun was just peeping over the horizon when Bill and Nancy Worthington slipped quickly into the bar through the screened door, carrying assorted fishing gear, hats, and protective clothing.

"Good morning. Good morning." Nancy was always cheerful in the morning and glum stares from the others couldn't dampen her spirits. "A beautiful day! Look at the sky! Have you ever seen such a glorious dawn?"

The reaching rays of the rising sun had touched the clouds and turned the entire heavens into a pale pink canopy. As they watched, the color changed from pink to fiery red and the entire world was suddenly awash in a bright blush. The bay water, the dock, the boat, the faces of the watchers, all reflected the sky and shone pinkish-red. Then, as Bill and Nancy stood there, transfixed, the sun seemed to leap into full view and changed from a hot red to a deep gold, the clouds gave up their scarlet tinge and slowly returned to a somber gray ... and the dawn was fully born.

"My! Wasn't that beautiful! I've never seen such sunrises and sunsets as you have here on this little island." Nancy crossed slowly to the counter and perched on a bar stool.

Pearlie responded instantly and smiled. She always reacted to a compliment, if not for herself then for the island, both of which she loved.

"Well, now, that's mighty nice of ya, Ma'am. We think they's purty, too. Have a cold beer?"

Nancy shook her head sharply.

"No, thank you. Not this early." Then, fearful of hurting Pearlie's feelings she quickly added, "Of course, if you enjoy an early beer ..." She smiled expansively, "then you should have one."

"That's how I figger it." Pearlie nodded her head emphatically. "Coffee an' beer, first thing. Coffee gets me goin' of a mornin', an' a ice-cold beer winds my motor." She sipped away.

"Captain, there's more gear just outside the door, food and my parasol and my book, and ditty bag with little things. If you'll put it all aboard, I think Bill and I are ready. Aren't we, dear?"

Bill nodded, and handed a wad of mosquito netting to his wife. Then they climbed aboard and Nancy squatted on a swivel seat and immediately covered herself with the netting. Bill cast off at a signal from Captain Staines, who reversed the boat, pulling carefully away from the dock into deeper water. With a quick gear change and a revving motor, they gathered speed and headed up-island for Redfish Pass.

"Good luck. Take care." Pearlie stood in the doorway as they moved past. "Hope ya catch one!" She watched them out of sight. "Poor ole Jed. Bet he has his hands full with them two. She's so small if she hooks a trout she's like to be yanked overboard." Turning back to Murph, "Do ya want eggs an' ham, usual-like?"

Rounding the bay marker at full speed, Jed swung left and headed straight for the pass. There wasn't a ripple in the bay and the open boat seemed to float on air as it tore along, bow up and stern down, leaving a trail of split water and foam behind it. Just off the pass, still in the bay, Jed abruptly cut his motor and the craft nosed down and lost headway. He left his wheel and walked over to Nancy.

"Ma'am, yer legs is too short, beggin' yer pardon, to reach the stern from that seat. So I brung this ol' peach crate and we can wedge her in like this," he proceeded to demonstrate, "an' yer feets can prop agin it. Try it, now. See. Ain't that dandy?"

Nancy beamed her widest smile at him.

"Ah, Captain Staines, how very considerate of you. I'll be just fine. Thank you." She had emerged from the netting as soon as they'd left the dock and now she swiveled back and forth, scanning the open water. "All we need now is fish, but I don't see any. They seem to be gone."

"No, ma'am. They ain't gone." Captain Staines had the motor in neutral and the boat was drifting slowly with the tide away from the pass and out into the open bay. He was working on the fishing rods, checking line and testing the drags. "They're here. That green water you can just spot in the pass over there, that ain't green water atall. It's tarpon rollin'. Back's are green, you know. No, ma'am, they ain't gone. That pass is full of fish. After a bit, when the tide turns out and we gits up there, you'll see fish, big fish, rollin' all over, even up agin the boat. I just hopes they bite."

Bill was on his knees, fiddling in a knapsack and spreading out lures.

"Captain," he said, "if you don't mind, think I'll use my own gear." He held aloft a sturdy deep-sea rod and reel. "I'm used to it and the line is linen and a hundred-pound test. Is that heavy enough?"

Captain Staines nodded.

"It's heavy enough, but it depends on how much line's on that reel. These critters move fast an' far out. How about you, ma'am? Will you be usin' yer own rod or one o' mine?"

"Oh!" Nancy was diplomatic, laying the ground work for a future friendship. "One of yours, of course, Captain. I wouldn't dream of anything else, thank you. Tell us about these fish. Do they have special habits? And the bait? What will we be using?"

Jed was nodding.

"Well, these here fish are special. Ain't anybody knows all about 'em. I suppose I knows much as the nex' guide, as I've been fishin' for 'em every spring fer years but they can still surprise me. They're big and they're powerful. Average tarpon will weigh in at better'n a hundred pounds an' it's solid bone an' muscle. A hundred thirty's a big fish and more than that's a monster. They can go up to 250 pounds, 'course, but not many of them's been caught on rod an' reel."

Bill and Nancy were hanging on every word, fascinated. Jed dipped a little net into one of the bait wells and took out a fish about the size and shape of his open hand.

"This here's a pinfish. They're all over in the shallow bay water. Up north I think they're called sunnies. You gotta handle 'em careful or that little dorsal fin on its back will raise up and stick your hand ... why we call 'em ` pinfish', I guess." He smiled gently and held the little fish out toward them. "Right here, behind the eyes where there's this little sorta bump, we stick the hook right through, clear to the far side, one of these big hooks, an' we're baited up. Fixed that way, the pinfish will stay alive a long time, and struggle to get off. We'll begin fishin' about fourteen feet deep, with a six foot wire leader just behind the hook, then the line with a cork bobber. We'll head into the tide an' cut the motor an' drift back through the pass, with the bobber an' bait about fifty feet or so off to one side. It'll drift along with us. We keep the bait off to one side like that so's the fish that bite don't land in the boat. Don't want a fresh hundred pounder banging around in the bilge. Can easy break your leg."

Nancy's eyes were bright with excitement and she was glancing everywhere at once, at Captain Staines, at Bill, out across the water. She was eager to get started, but Jed methodically continued his narrative.

"These fish take the bait tail first. Don't know why. They circle the bait an' grab it tail first, an' they then crush it, spit it out an' reverse it an' gulp it down head-first. It's here you'll lose him. Most folks do. When he first takes your bait, an' your bobber goes down ... don't strike! Remember! This is the most important thing in fishin' for tarpon ... don't be hasty! I always tell folks to count to ten after the bobber goes under, an' then strike ... hard! Real hard!

290

Give the fish time to play like he wants with that bait. 'Course, the average person gets all excited and strikes right off an' away goes the fish. Understand you folks've caught marlin an' sails. Well, this ain't that type o' fishin'. There you drug yer bait an' the fish struck <u>you</u> ... here, the fish takes the bait slow-like, an' you strike <u>him</u>. Different game. Ma'am, you'll sit where you are, with the crate an' all, an' Mister, you'll use the other chair, an' you'll each fish off to yer own side. It'll be my job to steer the boat so's your baits don't foul each other. An' when you get a bite, just say so an' I'll tell ya when to strike. Be prepared for the boat to lunge at the same time. I'll throw it full forward or full astern dependin' on where your fish is, as it'll take both of us, you reelin' an' me lungin' the boat, to take up the slack when the fish leaps. 'Cuz it'll leap, way up out o' the water. This is the second most important moment. When he feels that hook as you strike him, he'll fling hisself high in the air an' shake like crazy, tryin' to throw that hook, an' this'll create slack in yer line. If it ain't kept taut, like as not you'll lose him."

Both rods were baited up and stacked so that the pinfish dangled in the bait wells. Jed had previously strung corks on the two lines and now he positioned these some fourteen feet from the hooks. He nodded at his two passengers.

"We'll move on in, now, back toward the pass. Tide's been slack fer a bit an' it's fixin' to turn out. Jest what we want."

Nancy glanced over at Bill and crunched her shoulders up around her ears in delight. Little shivers ran up and down her spine. Bill chuckled and patted her knee.

"Give 'em hell, Shorty. Knock 'em dead!"

The bay water was glassy, milky white, reflecting the heavy cloud cover. Clumps of turtlegrass floated lazily about in the dead tide and split left and right as the boat nosed slowly forward. Brown pelicans dove for little minnows along the inner shore of the upper island, and tiny white terns hovered excitedly just above, plunging into the water for the alewives disturbed by the larger birds. There was no other boat within sight, and there was an eerie sense of wildness, of loneliness all about. They were alone in the vast expanse, the restless water, the plunging birds, the rolling fish, and the insignificant little boat. The sun was up and hot, even at this early hour. Far beyond the pass the open Gulf glistened hazily and already heat waves obscured the horizon.

"The tide's turned, Captain!" Nancy called suddenly, peering down at the water. "That clump of grass is floating right along beside us. See, Bill? We're not gaining on it at all."

Jed grinned at her, and nodded his head.

"Yes'm. It's turned. An' so'm I." He swung the craft broadside to the flow and slipped the throttle into neutral. "We'll fish right here." He took Nancy's rod, released the drag and cast the bait off to the right, snapped back the drag ratchet and handed the rod to her.

"There ya are, Ma'am. Put the handle in that little socket fixed to yer chair, 'tween your legs, an' it'll balance real well. Keep yer eye on that bobber. I ain't expectin' nothin' to happen this early, but if it does, yell real loud."

Nancy sat hunched forward, her legs stiff and her feet pushing against the old peach crate. Jed cast Bill's bait and gave him the rod, and then retired to the little seat back by the steering wheel, his cap slumped over his face and anyone would have thought he was asleep. They would have been wrong. His eyes were as alert as an eagle's darting this way and that over the water, not missing a trick. He hadn't expected any action this early so he wasn't disappointed ... maybe another hour or so, when the tide was running stronger through the narrow pass, washing little fish and crabs from the bay flats out to sea. The tarpon should come alive then ... hope she gets at least a strike and one jump, though what she'll do with it is beyond me. Zelma said she was much too small and dainty to go tarpon fishing, and she is ... those short little legs can barely reach the decking ... thank heaven I'd sense enough to bring that crate ... what in tarnation is she doing now? She's laid that rod cross her lap ... if a fish strikes now all my gear is gone! She's putting up that parasol! I can't believe it. Ah, she's got the rod again, holding that parasol in her left hand and the rod in her right. Scared me there for a second. Oh, oh! She's moving around again. Well, I'll be damned! She's now got that book in her lap. There she sits, parasol, rod, reading a book. Zelma won't believe this. Maybe we can make it a half-day trip. She'll be bored by noon and want to go in ...

By this time they were some distance offshore, out in the Gulf, and drifting right along.

"Ma'am, if you'll reel in and put yer bait back in the well alongside there ... you, too, Mister ... I'll swing around and head back in an' we can make another drift."

"Just a minute, Captain, if you don't mind." Nancy looked back and poured her special smile all over him. "I'm not quite ready."

Jed was captivated.

"Take yer time, Ma'am."

She dog-eared a page and put the book down onto the deck. Next, the parasol was collapsed and laid beside the book. Then she reeled in unhurriedly, reached up and took a few strands of grass off her line and plopped the bait, still wiggling energetically, into the bait well. Again the brilliant smile.

"Alright, Captain. I'm organized. We can go."

Sitting comfortably, sort of sidesaddle to make room for the rod handle in its little flexible pocket, holding her rod and the parasol and sharing a juicy murder with Perry Mason, halfway along the next drift in the center of Redfish Pass, her bobber went down. Captain Jed said very softly ... 'yer bobber's down, Ma'am'... and Nancy nodded.

"I see it, Captain." she answered just as softly.

"Don't strike yet, Ma'am."

"I won't, Captain."

The book got a new dog-ear and was put quietly on the deck. Holding the rod in the crook of her arm, she was closing the parasol when Jed whispered 'Strike.'

"Not yet, Captain," she answered. "I'm not quite ready." She finished closing the parasol and laid it beside the book. she straightened around in her chair, set her feet, took a firm grip on the rod with both hands just above the reel... and struck! Hard! So hard her feet flew up and she'd have fallen over backward if Jed hadn't leaped to support her. As he did he thought to himself, 'What a pity to lose that fish ... she took much too long. That fish is miles away by now. A good, solid bite, too. Too bad. It's gone, sure'.

But it wasn't. Nancy had regained her balance and was reeling so fast her hands blurred. she was giving little strikes to the rod, hunting for pressure against it, but it felt empty, somehow, and a wondering expression formed around her eyes. Suddenly, the bottom of the pass seemed to erupt skyward, as a silver fish leapt full-length from the water, shaking itself violently from side to side, showering sea water all about as it frenziedly tried to free itself from the hook. Then it fell sideways back into the water with a resounding splash.

Belatedly Jed threw the throttle forward and the boat churned ahead until Nancy called loudly.

"Captain, enough. Enough. The line's taut. I can handle him from here on."

But could she? The line sang off her reel in a high-pitched whine as the fish raced seaward. Then the line sagged again, and Jed hit the throttle.

"He's comin' up! He's jumping' agin! Watch the slack. Reel agin' him. Reel in, fast."

Again the tarpon exploded high in the air and thrashed from side to side, its eyes seeming to start from its head, like a fenced-in stallion.

"Oh, how beautiful. Oh, the poor thing. I don't think I can handle this. I can't hold on much longer. What a pull! My arms ache. Maybe we should let it go."

Jed moved forward and reached for her rod, but Bill stopped him.

"I wouldn't, Captain, if I were you. She won't thank you at all. She's okay. I've seen this performance with other fish. If you touch her rod she won't ever forgive you. Leave be!"

Jed pulled back and Nancy hung on. The fish sounded. Deep, deep it went and the line sang again ... and then went limp.

"Oh, I've lost him. Captain, I've lost him." she seemed ready to weep.

"No'm. He's still on. He's restin', that's all. He'll be trailin' us, way down where he is, an' restin'. Suddenly he'll start up agin an' fight you worse than ever. Reel in yer line 'til you can feel it snug, an' let me know if he moves. I'm gonna work us over into the back bay where it ain't so deep. He'll feel trapped back there in thin water an' maybe jump agin."

Like Death itself, Nancy hung on. Bill held out a glass of water and she took a long drink. Little drops of sweat trickled down her forehead, and he wiped these away, chuckling as he did so.

"Okay, Cutie. You wanted to come tarpon fishing, and here you are. So fight it, girl. And when you've had enough, cry 'uncle'."

"I'll never cry uncle," she answered, between clenched teeth. "Uh, oh. Captain. He's moving. I can feel him moving!"

Jed was perched by the wheel behind her and he leaned way forward.

"Don't git scared, now, Ma'am. Keep the pressure on. He'll try to head back to deep water, but that fish is gettin' tired. Keep a strong pressure on him an' pump. Pump him smart an' reel in as you pump."

"He's so far back, Captain."

"Yes'm. He's some hundred yards, but pressure him, pump hard, an' he'll draw in."

Slowly, slowly, pumping and reeling, pumping and reeling, her feet stiff against the peach crate, she drew the fish toward the boat. When it was halfway in it appeared at the top of the water on its side, struggling strongly. As it sighted the boat it gave a mighty surge and raced away, the line screaming off Nancy's reel. With a forlorn glance over her shoulder, all she could do was sit there braced and hold on.

"Yer doin' jes' fine, Ma'am." Jed had an urge to pat her shoulder. "Now, turn him. Pump an' reel an' like as not, he'll draw in."

Toward the end of the struggle, the fish was a dead weight on her line and it was brute strength, pulling and tugging, pumping and reeling, that finally drew it alongside the boat. Captain Jed was ready, leaning over the gunwale, a large gaff in his hand.

"A little more, Ma'am. Jes' a bit ... ah, I got him." Jed slipped the gaff through the gill opening and out it's mouth.

"Don't hurt him, Captain." Nancy leaned from her chair and looked down. "On, my! Isn't he magnificent? Beautiful! And didn't he fight?"

"Yes'm. An' so did you, Ma'am. That was right pert fishin' you did. Do you want to keep him?"

"Nanc," Bill offered, standing beside Jed and looking at the prize. "We could have him mounted. Your first tarpon. Hang him on the den wall, over the fireplace."

"Never! No, never! He's much too ... too ..." she searched for the word she wanted ... "gallant. He goes free! Let him go, Captain, please. Turn him loose. Back to his sea and his wife. So beautiful ... so beautiful." She reached down and gently stroked its shining silver side

Captain Jed quickly slipped a finger under one huge scale and tore it loose. He held it out to her.

"Souvenir, Ma'am."

Then, twisting the gaff from the jaw, he released the huge fish. They all watched as it drifted on its side away from the boat for awhile, then gave a little shudder, righted itself and swam slowly out of sight.

Climbing off the swivel seat, Nancy would have fallen if Bill hadn't caught her. Her legs were trembling and her hands felt like claws, clenched and twitching. She leaned into her husband and smiled up at him.

"That was absolutely splendid. What an experience! What a fight! You know, Bill, somehow this was different from all the other big fish we've caught. There was a strange ... intense ... personal feeling that reached me across the line. I can't explain. Once that fish was hooked, he <u>knew</u> he was hooked, and I knew he knew ... and it became a personal struggle between the two of us. Intimate. Powerful. I don't know ... I'm so tired, I'm trembling. How long was that, Captain?"

"'Bout an hour, Ma'am. You did right good. That was a big fish, yes'm." He was back again, seated beside the gear-housing, and the boat was drifting untended about the bay. "Have you had enough, Ma'am? Want to head in?"

Nancy looked at him and slowly shook her head.

"Of course not, Captain. We came out for the day, didn't we? To fish! Bill has to catch one, now. Bill, you won't believe. There's <u>nothing</u> like it. It's the best ever. My legs seem to be coming back." She did a few knee-bends and flexed her hands. "But not again without gloves! I packed two pairs. Will you see if you can find 'em, Billy? And a sandwich. Why am I so starved so early?" She beamed at Jed. "Just a few more seconds, Captain, and then I'll be ready. Would you care for a sandwich? Chicken or ham?"

She sat on the rear gunwale and worked on her sandwich, her jaws crunching up and down.

"Mercy! I'm ravenous! Maybe now, Captain, you can explain why you didn't help me when I first struck that fish. You didn't move the boat like you promised."

Jed was embarrassed, and he scratched his head through his cap.

"No'm. I sure didn't, did I? You caught me flat-footed. Won't happen again, Ma'am."

Bill didn't fare so well. Two drifts later he got a bite and nervously struck too soon. The fish jumped and swam away. Nancy chuckled.

"You need a little Perry Mason, Billy. Always good in a crisis."

The morning wore on. The sun rose high in the heavens and the cloud cover rolled back, revealing a cobalt blue canopy stretching from horizon to horizon. The Gulf lost its slaty gray and turned a soft azure, reflecting the sky. The only disturbance was the motor of the boat, idling as they floated through the pass and revving suddenly as Jed circled and headed back against the tide at the end of each drift. Fourteen feet below the surface two fresh pinfish darted about in a fruitless effort to escape. Deeper down, where the sunlight was diffused and there was no obstructive turtlegrass or surface debris, large forms circled about or streaked by, nudged into action by the flow of the water or by natural urges to feed. Occasionally, one or two would lift toward the surface, pausing to examine the pinfish as they rose from the depths.

Bill was nodding, half-asleep in the peaceful warmth, and Nancy was hoping Della Street would turn around in time to escape the mad killer stalking her when Nancy's bobber again was yanked from sight. At once she saw and tensed, and the little ritual of parasol-folding and dog-earing began. Captain Staines reached a hand toward the throttle and Bill began to reel in his bait to get it out of the way of Nancy's line when his bobber also disappeared. They both shouted in glee.

"A double-header!" Nancy yelled and struck hard. Jed threw the boat full speed ahead as to the rear her hooked fish leaped from the sea in a spectacular display. Seconds later, just off the port side, Bill's fish also broke skyward, showering the three occupants and the boat in foaming spray. Reeling violently, both fishermen attempted to take up the slack as Jed helped with the boat.

"Keep yer lines taut, now, an' don't bother none about the other," he cautioned. "Keep yer lines taut. Concentrate on yer own fish. I'll try to keep them things from foulin' up. Easy now, yer both doin' fine." His face was drawn in stern lines as he set a course dead center off the two fish.

Grimly holding the bending rods, giving little jerks to further set the hooks, frantically shifting in their chairs as the two fish veered from side to side, they were both soon bathed in sweat and short of breath. Then, unexpectedly, both tarpon leaped high in the air at the same moment, frantically tail-walking the surface of the water, shaking violently from side to side. Bill jumped up and held his rod over his head, fearful Nancy's fish would foul his line as it flopped back into the sea, but it cleared by a few feet. Nancy was glued to her rod, just hanging on, her little arms stiff and knotted up.

"Have you ever... Bill, wasn't that unbelievable? Did you ever think for one moment ..." She tugged and tried to reel but her fish had sounded and was a dead weight on her line. She couldn't budge it. Bill's was active and his reel sang as the fish streaked out to sea, apparently heading for Mexico.

"When he settles down," Jed advised, "an' sinks deep to rest, better check that drag. If you give him more pressure, he'll tire quicker."

Then Nancy called excitedly over her shoulder.

"I can't feel a thing, Captain. My line's slack!" She was frantically reeling. "I've lost him. My line's dead."

"Keep reelin', Ma'am. Keep reelin'." Jed pushed his throttle full ahead and the boat surged forward. "He's swimmin' toward you an' if'n he gits under the boat, we've got troubles."

The movement of the boat added strain to Bill's line and his rod was bent nearly double when his fish again leaped from the water, way behind the boat. Nancy felt weight again on her line as the slack was taken up and she gave it a tremendous strike, and up came her tarpon, high in the air, so close to the boat it nearly scraped the gunwales. Nancy flinched to one side.

"Whoa, there, boy. Not so close. You stay on your side and I'll stay on mine!" She shouted in excitement and shook the spray from her face.

For awhile all was quiet. The contest became a tug of war, both fish pulling against the lines with all their weight and the fishermen just holding on. Bill glanced sideways at his wife, grimly pushing against her peach crate with set legs and leaning forward over her bent rod, and he grinned.

"Hang in there, Cutie. Don't give an inch. If you lose that fish, I'm gonna divorce you!"

Nancy shook her head just a bit.

"Don't badger me now, Bill. This is too difficult. I've got to concentrate. You tend your own fish."

They both jumped as a loud thumping startled them. Captain Jed was banging on the gunwale with an oar, and smacking at the water.

"What are you doing? What's wrong? What are you <u>doing</u>?"

"Shark! Off there. I've been watchin' him. He's circlin' an' comin' in. Tryin' to scare him off. Don't want him in on these fish!" Captain Jed yelled, pounding away with his oar.

A triangular black fin was slicing the water some hundred yards behind the boat, as the monster circled slowly just below the surface. It seemed to be lazing about, biding its time, waiting for the proper moment. Jed's rumpus seemed to have been effective as the fin soon disappeared and the Gulf water was again undisturbed.

There were no more jumps. Bill's fish remained well behind the boat, deep down, and just a dead weight, as Nancy tugged and pulled her fish up and alongside the boat. Jed pulled out the souvenir scale and was busy removing the gaff to release the fish when Bill flopped suddenly backward in his chair.

"Jed, mine's off! There was a huge flurry of action just now, and then my line slacked up." He was frantically reeling in. "See. It's free. My line's free. No! Wait a minute. There's still a weight on it but not that heavy pull. Something's still on it." He continued to reel, as Nancy's fish was set free and Jed straightened up. "See! It's on the surface. It's flopping on the top of the water!"

Jed shook his head.

"Bring it on in, Mister. You got a tarpon head out there. Shark! Damn! Pardon me, Miss Nancy, but I hate them filthy sharks!" Jed slapped his thigh in disgust.

Nancy felt like crying as she looked down at the horror Bill reeled in. The head had been sheared neatly, with no bleeding tendrils dangling.

"Jes' one bite! All it takes, one bite." Jed freed the head and it sank out of sight. "Hope he got his fill an' won't bother us no more."

By mid-afternoon Bill still hadn't gotten a fish but Nancy had hooked and boated two more. Captain Staines leaned over toward her and tipped his cap.

"Don't you think, Ma'am, we best be headin' in? Them four fish has wore you out. We can come out agin in a day or two, when you're rested up."

"Just one more drift, Captain. One more. It's so peaceful and so quiet out here, I hate to leave. It'll never again be my first tarpon trip, you know. Bait me up, but give me that pinfish." She pointed to a half-dead one floating on its side in the baitwell. "That'll be a good one for this last drift. Both it and I, we're nearly dead!"

It proved the perfect pinfish for the final drift and half-way through the pass it intrigued a huge tarpon which struck it. Nancy's bobber plunged from sight and she gasped in dismay.

"Oh, dear. I don't want any more. I've not the strength to fight another one, not today." But she set her teeth, braced her feet and struck mightily. When the fish exploded high in the air they all three gasped. It was huge! Jed threw the boat forward and Bill heard him mutter ... "must be 180 pounds or more. Will yank her overboard, if I ain't careful."

Bill quickly glanced at Nancy, ready to suggest that they cut the line and let the huge fish go, but one look at her intent, straining face was enough. She was hooked just as much as the fish and it would cause a crisis if he intervened. The tiny thing. There she sat, nearly exhausted, her lips trembling as she muttered just loud enough for him to hear ... "I've got you, you beauty. You're mine! Fight away. Go on, pull! I'll win in the end ..." Her arms shook and throbbing little muscles showed alongside her neck. But she hung on! Pumping and reeling, straining against a fearful and steady pull, then reeling and pumping, she hung on until, suddenly, the reel came loose and slipped around under her rod.

"Captain. Captain." Her cry was shrill and plaintive. "The reel's broken. It's broken! I can't reel in. It's underside my rod. All I can do is sit here and hold on. Damn!" Her eyes shot toward Bill, as she never cursed, but he was looking off seaward and pretended he hadn't heard "I want that fish! It's the best all day. I'm so disappointed!"

Jed studied for a second. He looked at the reel, and the rod, and at Nancy. "Do you really want that fish, Ma'am?"

Nancy nodded her head.

"Well, then ..." He cut the throttle and glanced around the area to check their chances. "Then, Ma'am, let's git it! At least, we'll give it a shot. Do jes' like I say, now. We're almost to the back bay an' the tide's not too strong. Don't slack off none on yer pressure, but don't jerk yer line, neither. Let the fish sink an' res'. I'll circle. That way we won't jar him none an' maybe he'll jes lay quiet."

Jed tied off the wheel with a keeper rope so the boat would run in a wide circle and his hands would be free. He took a spare rod and reel and stripped all the line off and let it pile in the bilge. Then, keeping tension on Nancy's line, he opened her drag and handed the tense line to Bill.

"Hold this, please. Wrap one turn round yer finger to keep it tight. Only one turn. If'n that fish comes to life an' strikes out, let it go or else you'll lose a finger."

He quietly fed the line off Nancy's reel until he reached the end, cut the line, fed the cut end through the eyes of the spare rod and tied it firmly to that reel, and took up all the slack. When he had it fully rewound he tested the drag and then handed the rod to Nancy.

"There you are, Ma'am. Git yerself all set, now, an' nod when yer ready. Let's give thet ol' fish hell." He reached for the throttle.

Nancy could scarcely stand when they got back to Murph's dock. As she struggled from the boat to the landing she'd have fallen flat on her face if Bill hadn't held her up. She nodded briefly to Pearlie as she went by and hobbled on down the dockway to where Jerry was waiting with his truck.

"Whatever happened to that one?" Pearlie wanted to know. "She sure looks beat up. Did she catch a ladyfish and get all tired out?"

Jed was sagged back on the motor cover. He took off his long-bill cap and mopped his forehead.

"Pearlie, you wouldn't have believed it. We boated five tarpon ... five an' a half, actually. Mr. Worthington, he brought in the half. Ate up by sharks. And the missus, that tiny, sweet, gentle little lady, boated the other five. Five full-grown tarpon! All by herself. She never lost a strike an' she never lost a fish. That last one was a whopper. Must have been all of 180 pounds or better. Five tarpon. All by herself!"

"No!" Pearlie snorted in amusement and swigged her beer. "No! Jes' goes to show ya! Ya never know. Turned out to be a terror, huh? Five fish on her first trip, an' never lost a one. A real Tarpon Nannie, ain't she?"

20

Murph Suggs and Frank Culpepper were in the bar, hunched over a corner table, studying sketches and designs. Papers were scattered over the floor and snuffed-out cigarette butts littered the shell ashtrays. Pearlie was behind the bar, muttering to herself and shaking her head.

"Don't y'all count on me none! There ain't no way I'm gonna fancy-foot about no marina. I've got more'n I can handle with this here dock an' beer hall." She leaned across the bar and her face crinkled into a plea, belying her belligerence. "I can't handle no more. In this heat an' bugs, I can't handle no more!"

Frank looked over at her and sensed her concern.

"Don't worry, Pearlie. It won't land on you. If we can get this thing going, I'll be running the marina. You and Murph will be silent partners."

Both Pearlie and Murph snorted at the same time.

"That'll be a first." Murph muttered.

"Oh, I don't know!" She tossed her head and swiped at the bar with a damp rag. "I kin keep my mouth shut, if I wants to." She studied her husband for a second, watching him shake his head. Then, stung by his derision, she straightened to her full height and tossed back her hair. "I can, too! It's been almos' two years now, an' I ain't said a word!"

"About what? Murph asked offhandedly, tracing lines along a drawing.

"Okay. I'll tell ya. If'n you've forgotten, I ain't!" She wiped the sweat on her brow with the rag and pointed at Murph with one finger. "Tell the man about when I run onto you an' that filly up under them mangroves. Go on, tell him!" She'd pulled the plug and it all flowed out. "I wuz mindin' my own business, see, moseyin' about the island ...

"You weren't 'moseyin' about no island. You were spyin' on me, that's what!"

"... moseyin' about the island, mindin' my own business, like I jes said, an' I hears this little moany chuckle off in the underbrush, an' there's this gal who shall be nameless, flat on her back, an' this ole boar ..."

"You hush up, now. We ain't got time for all this gossip." Murph thrust back his chair and rose threateningly. He started toward Pearlie and she backed up against the screened door. "Go on, gal. Git back to the house an' clean something. Lord knows it can use a sweepin' out. Go on, git!" He drew back his arm and his fist was clenched, but she disappeared around the corner, chuckling to herself.

"When he gets all riled up, he's sure fierce," she said to herself. "I do believe he'd a struck me jes now, if'n I'd a kept it up. Lordy, how that man loves me!"

Murph and Frank were planning a marina, to be built parallel to the existing dock. They'd been talking about it for several weeks and now Frank was explaining the plans he'd drawn up.

"If we took the present walk-way and widened it, twelve boats could tie up, nosed in, with plenty of space between to keep from fouling each other. There's already gas, water and electricity piped out to the platform here at the end, and we can easily add plug-in connections and faucets. No problem with that. We won't get involved with housing the people. They can either stay on their boats or make their own arrangements on the island. All this new traffic will bump your beer and wine business and everything, the bait and the gas and so on. I'll get the tie-up fees. You've already got that big pile of lumber stacked by your porch. What is that, anyway?"

"Evan carted that stuff over from Myers several months back an' it's been stacked there ever since."

"Was it back in January?" Frank asked.

Murph nodded.

"Yep. Around the middle, or thereabouts."

"I remember. Jean and I were driving along the Sanibel road, our first trip down that road, and Evan passed us like a bat outa hell. He scared Jean half to death." Frank chuckled, remembering. "What's it for?"

"Every Spring I have to repair this dock," Murph explained, "but I'm waitin' this year 'til the Jamboree the end of the month is done. Evan and I will be buildin' a large platform in that clearin' over by the Chapel an' we'll use that lumber. Afterwards, I'll fix the dock with it."

"What about a dredge?" Frank bunched the papers together and lit a cigarette. "I don't see any problems except a dredge."

Murph leaned back in his chair.

"That's all arranged. The other day, in Myers, I dropped in an' talked to ole man Sampson, Sampson an' Sons, cousins of Jed Staines, an' all we have to do is order it in. Sampson figures two weeks maximum for the dredgin', includin' down time when the dredge is broke. Says he can give us a hole twenty feet wide, eight feet deep an' one hundred and fifty feet long."

"A hundred and fifty feet long?"

"Sure," Murph said. "We'll have to dredge out from low tide all along the walkway an' that's better'n a hundred feet, an' we'll have to dredge deeper all across the dock front out here, which is fifty feet. It's so shallow right outside, the mailboat almost scrapes and she draws only three feet. We'll be the only tie-up marina in these parts, you know, an' some big ole boats will be puttin' in. We gotta be ready."

"Yeah." Frank nodded. "Did Sampson give you a figure?"

"Five Hundred a week, plus room an' board. Him an' one son."

"Room and food? Ye gods!"

"Don't worry none about that, neither. Jasper Dugan says if we'll share the spoil with him, he'll put up Sampson and the boy, an' feed 'em, too. I said okay." Murph smiled expansively. "All that spoil's gotta go some place. I figure if we pump it onto my bayside, and Dugan's next door, both of us will add 'bout fifty feet to our property. Not bad, eh?"

Frank was doodling on a sheet of paper.

"A thousand for the dredge. Another thousand for lumber and hardware. As I promised before, I'll cover all costs, keep books on it, and loan you your half. We'll set up some simple monthly pay-back system. Is that still okay with you?"

Murph nodded and reached for a couple of beers.

"Sounds good to me," he said. "Let's drink on it."

●

The Jamboree undertaking fell heaviest on the women. As in former years, Bertha elected to supervise the food. There was no argument about this, as the job was so time-consuming and thankless no one else wanted the responsibility. Besides, only Bertha owned a kettle large enough for the turtle pilau. She chose Pearlie as her helper. Ida was put in charge of everything else. It was necessary to cover so much ground, readying platforms, gathering chairs, stringing electric wires, preparing a latrine and so on, that Ida needed two assistants and this year chose Jerry and Didi. One evening, after supper, just past the middle of May, the five of them met for a council of war in Bertha's big living room. They grouped around the square central table.

Both Bertha and Ida came prepared, and carried lists. After strong iced tea was passed around, everyone agreed that Bertha should lead off.

"Last Spring our Jamboree was so successful and everyone had such a good time and ate so much, seems to me we can't do better'n repeat that menu."

Everyone nodded.

"Then," Bertha slipped on her reading glasses and read aloud from her list, "we'll have two main dishes, both hot ... turtle pilau and fried mullet. We'll have hush puppies with the fish, o'course. Maybe we can get Maude to make a batch of her peanut butter soup, for those with really big appetites, like the kids."

Ida and Pearlie nodded emphatically, and Ida murmured under her breath "Delicious ... best I ever ate." Pearlie caught Didi looking a question at Jerry, who shrugged in uncertainty.

"Jus' you two wait. You won't believe it. 'Specially if she's heavy-handed with the sherry." Pearlie smacked her lips. "Oh, my!"

"Baked yams," Bertha went on, "an' swamp cabbage salad. How about that?" She glanced around the table.

"Don't forget the lime pie ... Cora's lime pie. She'll kill us if we forget that." Ida was so intent on getting this added to the menu she forgot to puff her cigarette.

Bertha's face brightened even more.

"O 'course. I forgot. Cora's lime pie for dessert. Perfect. We can put out all this food and later the piano will be moved out an' we can sing an' dance an' the kids can swim and fight." She giggled in anticipation.

Ida stubbed her cigarette and leaned forward, handing a pencil and pad to both Didi and Jerry.

"Okay. That takes care of the food. Now, let's go through the other chores." Running a finger down her list, she began ticking them off. "Actually, most of these will fall on Jerry. 'Course, Didi can help both him an' me. Let's see. Evan an' Murph'll have to be reminded about buildin' us a platform, an' maybe you, Jerry, an' Roy, can dig our latrine. Roy'll know what's needed. And Roy will have to string an electric line from the church to an outside pole for the Victrola. You men will have to get together about pits an' fires an' angle-irons to hold the big soup and pilau pots. Roy will have to cut palmettos for the cabbage salad. Someone will have to ask Ted to keep the church yard fogged out so we don't have bugs. What have I forgotten?"

"The turtle! I want that turtle several days before the party." Bertha was emphatic. "If I don't get it bled just right, the meat'll be rank. Has to hang at least a day."

"Turtle?" Didi's eyebrows raised high in surprise. "When you said a turtle stew I thought you meant canned turtle."

Bertha laughed. "Never heard o' that. I meant from the Gulf. One of the huge loggerheads. We catch it at night on the beach and after it's laid its eggs, we turn it onto it's back, kill it, and drag it on in."

"I thought that was against the law."

"Tis. But we do it anyway. Elgin Bigelow, the wildlife warden, he helps. Ida, that's another thing for your list. Someone has to ask Elgin's permission to turn a turtle ... an' to invite him an' Piety to the Jamboree."

Nodding in agreement, Ida added a note to her list and motioned to Jerry.

"I'll ride down to Sanibel with you an' we'll call on Elgin an' Piety together. It can get touchy. Elgin's an honorable man, honest and churchgoin' an' all, an' he takes that game warden job very seriously. He does a fine job, too, protectin' all the wildlife and enforcin' the law against poachers from Charlotte

Harbour down past Marco, an' inland. That's a right far piece, you know. An' here we come an' ask him to break the law, or look the other way, while we do it an' this gives him a problem. I can understand that. It can get touchy, so we'll trod gentle."

"'Course, it ain't like we're killin' fer nothin'," Pearlie said. "We ain't jest playin'. I mean, we're gonna <u>eat</u> the thing, you know." Pearlie's voice trailed off on an uncertain note. Bertha glanced around the group and then turned to Pearlie.

"Pearl, it ain't the same thing atall, an' you know it. None of us is that poor, 'ceptin' maybe Amanda, an' we don't <u>need</u> it. Ain't like we're backwoods crackers or some such. We're plain breakin' the law an' we're easin' our guilt by askin' Elgin Bigelow to approve, an' that ain't real fair, is it?" After a pause, she added ... "Anyway we're gonna do it. What's a jamboree in these parts without a turtle pilau?" Bertha was getting restless. She hated meetings, and the kids were squalling in the next room. "Let's set the date, an' then we can all go home. I think ..."

Pearlie broke in.

"Remember last year, Bertha. It was on a Saturday an' some folks had to work an' couldn't come."

"I never swallowed that!" Bertha leaned back deep in her chair. "It wasn't 'some folks' atall. It was old Charlie Kramdon, tomcattin' about Sanibel, an' Emmy didn't want to come alone. I'll tend to Charlie this year, jus' leave him to me."

"Maybe," Ida interjected, to block a possible argument, "we could have the jamboree on a Sunday." There was tentative agreement all around, except Bertha.

"No. No way! I won't agree to that. It's bad enough to use the church area and drag the church piano outside without messin' up the Lord's Day. Sundays we should be in church. The kids are gettin' used to bein' taught Scriptures of a Sunday morning and Jean Culpepper's piano playin' is bringin' folks in to noon service an' we shouldn't do anything to upset all that. We'll have the party on a Saturday ... the last Saturday this month ..." She consulted a calendar ... "Saturday, May 25th, at one o'clock sharp. Nine days from now. Can you all be ready?"

Everyone nodded, and Bertha stood up.

"Good! That's fine! Now, shoo! Run on home. My kids is bawlin' like cattle an' I gotta get busy an' feed 'em."

●

Cora never knew how she managed to get Sally-Anne up on top of the work-bench, but there she was, unsure of her footing and with knees slightly bent to brace against a fall.

"Just stand still now, Sally." Cora mumbled around a mouthful of pins, bending way down so she could squint along the edging. "It won't take us very long if you'll hold still. I don't want to jab you. Stand straight. There!" She folded the material to the length she wanted and secured it with a pin. "Now, turn a bit to your right. Go on, now. Don't skid your feet like that, Sally-Anne. You won't fall. I'm right here. I'll catch you!"

"Yes'm." Sally-Anne wasn't confident. She wasn't sure all this was a good idea at all. She ought to be cleaning up that kitchen, all those dishes stacked sky-high, instead of teetering back and forth way up here on this rickety table, getting stuck with pins.

"I'm very pleased with the way it's coming along." Cora straightened up and clasped Sally by the waist and gently turned her to the right. "This cotton material is such a good choice. The light purpley color is just right for you, and it's going to hold its pleats beautifully. You'll be the belle of the ball." Cora giggled excitedly.

Sally-Anne wasn't so convinced.

"If'n it's gonna be my ball, I's supposed to be the belle, ain't I?"

Cora looked up, surprised.

"What?" she asked. "Oh, yes. I suppose so. Yes. Only a figure of speech, really." She jabbed in a final pin and stood back to view the effect. "Lovely. The hemline is fine! Of course, with that generous full skirt and all those pleats, the hemline travels a bit up and down anyway. Supposed to. Years ago, when I had that little sewing school in Atlanta, I always told my pupils not to fritter away too much time on the hemline of a pleated skirt. When you twirl it all flies out and nobody can tell, anyway. Spin a bit, Sally-Anne. Go on, twist!"

Sally-Anne wasn't too cooperative but moved back and forth just enough to flair the material a bit and Cora nodded her head in a pleased manner.

"Good! Fine! It's going to be lovely. I'll just take in that waist a bit more ... Sally-Anne, you certainly have the smallest waist I've ever seen. You say you're still the size you were when you were fifteen years old? After all these years and all those children, how do you do it?"

"I diets!"

Cora looked at this mite of a woman. Sally-Anne couldn't weigh eighty-five pounds wet. And she dieted?

"Diet? You diet?"

"Yes'm. I dassent put on a single pound else Doobie screams his haid off. Yells I'm gettin' fat. He don' like fat gals ... sez they's unhandy!" She almost simpered.

"Oh, yes. I see. Yes. Of course he would." Cora looked vague and rolled her eyes high in her head. Reaching out a steadying hand she helped Sally-Anne down to the floor.

"Whew! Glad thet's don'. Does we havta do it agin?"

"Only once more, up high like that. I want to finish the shirtwaist first, but we can fit that while you're down here beside me on the floor. Once that's done, we'll have to get you back up and check the entire ensemble."

"Sure takes time, don' it? Maybe it's too much trouble, Miss Cora. Maybe it's bes' if'n I jes' wears me a boughten dress from Woolworth's?"

"Why, Sally-Anne, stop all that gloomy talk. This is no bother. I like to do this, and when we're finished and you walk down that aisle in your lilac gown, and a big picture hat on your head and holding a bouquet of flowers, you'll be a sight to remember. Your children will be so proud of you!"

"Yes'm. Maybe then thet ole dream will go away. That's a right smart part of why I'se goin' to all this trouble, to get rid o' thet scary ole dream."

"What dream is that, now?" Cora was instantly at full attention. Dreams interested her. She pondered her own and always wanted to hear of others.

"Fer the pas' year, seems, mos' every night, soon's I close my eyes, I'se in dis here scary dream ... I'se dead, only I ain't, 'cause I can see what's goin' on an' I can heah. I'se stretched out stiff, lyin' in my coffin, only the lid's not on an' I'se way down in the bottom of dis heah deep hole, an' I keep lyin' theah, scared almos' to death since I knows whut's goin' ta happen, 'cause I'se dreamed dis dream befo'. Know whut I means? An' purty soon, way, way, up at the top o' thet hole, fust one, then tuther o' my chilluns, they peep over the edge at me, deep down in thet hole. An' they's mad! An' they stares! Purty soon dey all calls down at me, together-like ... 'Mama, theah you is, down in thet ole hole, an' we ain't gonna say goodbye to ya 'cause you ain't nevah fixed us up ... fixed us up ... fixed us up! An' it keeps ringin' in my haid ovah an' ovah an' they starts peltin' me wid dirt clods an' the dirt clods hit me all ovah an' falls all 'round in thet hole an' starts to fill it up an' it's ovah my nose an' I cain't breathe an' I wakes up screamin' an' holdin' tight to Doobie." Sally-Anne was quaking from head to toe in terror as she relived her horrid nightmare, and her eyes rolled in distress. Instinctively, needing some support, she reached out and grabbed Cora. "Oh, Miss Cora, does ya thing thet ole dream will leave me be, onst I'se all married up respectable-like in a church? Does ya? An' my chillun, they'll be regular-like, won't they?"

Cora wrapped her arms gently around the tiny trembling woman and squeezed her tightly.

"There, there, now. Of course that nasty old dream will disappear and the children will be so proud of you and they'll love you and everything will be fine. Here, take my hanky and wipe your eyes, now."

Suddenly embarrassed, Sally-Anne squirmed out of the embrace and escaped to the sink.

"Gotta git back ta work," she muttered. "Gotta make up all thet los' time, 'fore Miss Agnes flares up."

306

Thursday evening, May 23rd, was perfect for the turtle hunt. The entire day had been overcast, hot, muggy, with rain threatening. The murky sky-cover carried over into the early evening, breaking somewhat about nine o'clock, allowing a pale moon to show briefly now and again through the skudding clouds. It was made to order for the adventure and so Elgin Bigelow announced as he stood in Didi's doorway, waiting for her and Maude and Jerry to collect their gear and join him.

"It's made to order, tonight. Driving along the beach in my jeep just now I passed several fresh crawls. There are turtles coming in. The Gulf is calm as a bathtub, so heavy wave action won't disturb 'em. Let's go. Bring plenty of bug repellent. A fresh incoming breeze is building but it's not enough yet to blow the skeeters inland. Might, later on. Of course, a heavy wind will also rile the Gulf and we don't want that."

All four carried powerful flashlights and Elgin Bigelow additionally had a miner's lamp strapped to his forehead. They each had heavy gloves tucked in their back pockets and Maude wore the inevitable leather belt with the dangling hatchet. They climbed into Elgin's jeep and headed north, riding slowly along the hard-pack between high and low tide.

"There's that long smooth stretch about half a mile beyond Captiva Inn where very few shells wash in. Something to do with the offshore sand bars, I guess." Elgin explained in a low voice to his attentive passengers as they drove slowly along scrutinizing the beach expanse before them. "Several nights each week, up until the middle of July, there'll be fresh crawls up there. I'm going to park a little south of that spot and we'll walk the rest of the way. I asked Roy to meet us up there."

"Exactly what are we looking for?" Didi wanted to know. She glanced at Elgin. It was difficult to see him clearly in the halflight, but there'd been no problem awhile back on her porch. She had been struck by his presence and had found herself strangely impressed. Tall, wide-shouldered, prominent cheek bones under deep-blue eyes, Elgin Bigelow was a romantic figure in his jodphurs and his pith helmet, and with his deep, resonant voice. How odd, she thought to find a man of such superb appearance on a tiny island out on the edge of nowhere.

Didi's question gave Elgin an opening. He loved to share his knowledge of nature, especially indigenous wildlife, and now, parking the jeep and climbing out, he talked of turtles.

The other three clustered tightly around him as they strolled along the shoreline, flashlights shining ahead and mosquito switchers flicking energetically. Every once in awhile Maude would nod in agreement as he talked.

"I'm not too great on turtle anatomy," he said. "First off, there's greens and loggerheads. Folks tend to lump them together, when they're really quite different. Loggerheads are much larger and the flesh is tougher, with a rank, wild taste, compared to the smaller greens. Their flesh has a delicate flavor. Down in Key West the green turtle industry is well organized ... has been for years. The boats drag big nets and catch them by the dozens. They're kept ashore in huge flooded 'crawls' and sold individually to local restaurants and home owners. Green turtle soup is quite the thing in the Keys. I understand there's a House bill up in Tallahassee to outlaw the practice."

"And about time," Maude interjected. "Though it'll be years, most likely, before it passes and meanwhile the green turtles can be netted out of existence."

Elgin replied cautiously.

"Oh, I don't know about that. It would take quite a bit of netting to wipe out an entire species. But I hate that commercial approach, too. I'd like to see it stopped."

They walked in silence for a few minutes, each lost in his own thoughts. Then Elgin continued.

"Both loggerheads, which we're after, and greens live in deep water. They feed on a wide variety of sea life, and the females come ashore during the early summer months to lay their eggs. They select a spot above the tide line and drag themselves up to it. They leave a wide trail that shows where they've crawled. That's what we're looking for, to get back to your question, Miss Didi. The crawl track of even a medium-sized loggerhead, which might weigh several hundred pounds, is easily identified ... two parallel paths where the front flippers have dug in and the back feet have pushed, with a smoothed-out center section made by the underside of the shell as it's dragged along. In the center of this smooth part will be a small single trace which has been made as the tail drags. You'll know it's a turtle crawl the minute you see it."

Maude was beaming her light all around and it came to rest on Roy Coggins crouched down in the sand by the wave edge a hundred feet ahead.

"Mercy, Roy. You gave a body a start. Why didn't you call or something to let us know you're there." Maude waved her light back and forth.

Roy jumped to his feet.

"Shhh! Be quiet. We don't want to startle her."

"Who?" someone asked.

"That big ole turtle. She's up the beach just a short ways, laying her eggs. I found her and was watching until I saw your lights coming along. She's big, too, and she has been laying for a half-hour that I know about. She was at it when I found her, so there's no telling when she started. We may have a long wait."

"How long does it usually take?" Didi questioned.

"Upwards to two hours, sometimes," Elgin answered. "All depends if this is her first lay of the season. If it is, she might lay 140 eggs, maybe 150. If it's her second or third lay, not so many, and it's over quicker. Where is she, Roy?"

"Right over there." Roy pointed his flash and directed the beam. "Up against that little bank."

"Watch your light," Maude whispered, but Elgin explained, flashing his own and reaching up to the light on his forehead.

"Light won't affect her, or our talking. Actually, once they start to lay, it's very hard to distract them. Listen closely. Can you hear that grunting? She grunts heavily every time she lays an egg."

"I can hear. Look at her. She's huge. All nestled down there in that sandy depression." Didi was mesmerized and bent down low to look. "Her eyes are almost closed, and there are tears ... she's crying! Look! The poor thing! Maybe she's in pain. Do you suppose she's in any pain?"

Elgin took over.

"Don't get up too close, now. Don't crowd her. No, she's not in pain. If anything, she's enjoying it. I don't think those are real tears, crying tears, that is. I read somewhere that sea turtles control their salt intake by emitting extra saline solution through their tear ducts. She's not in pain. It's more likely exhaustion. This is a big exertion for her, you know. She's had to drag herself out of the water, cross the entire beach, find a satisfactory nesting area, then wallow out a good-sized depression and finally scoop out a deep egg chamber for the eggs. The actual laying is a long process. Then she has to reverse everything. The hole must be filled in, the general area must be rewallowed and dug up again, and finally flattened out by heaving herself up and flopping back down all over so predators ... raccoons, dogs, cats, hawks ... can't find the eggs. Then the long trip back across the beach and into the water again. No wonder she has tears."

They watched for some time, as the grunting went on and the turtle was immobile. Then, suddenly, the grunting ceased. The turtle's front flippers twitched and she slowly raised her head.

Elgin motioned them back.

"I think she's finished. Watch what she does now. This is interesting."

With great effort, as if arousing from a deep sleep, the turtle dragged herself backward off the nest. Everything was now in slow motion as she was very tired. The flippers scooped sand into the deep central hole and pounded it for some time. Only when she was satisfied that the hole was filled and the sand was as firm as before she dug did she stop pounding. She sagged down for a bit, her heavy head resting on the sand. Then, urged by an age-old instinct and by the passing night, she crawled back and forth across the large depression surrounding the hole, scooping sand toward the center, lifting herself on her flippers and pounding back down, to flatten and firm the entire area. At last, content that her young would be safe, and exhausted by these wearying exertions, she inched her way back across the wide beach toward the open water.

As the turtle moved slowly past her, Didi reached out.

"Mr. Bigelow, will she snap at me if I touch her? She's been so brave I want to pat her back."

"Go ahead, if you wish. She won't bite. In fact, there's nothing much that will deflect her now. I think her mind is back in the cool, green depths she knows and is used to, and it's only a question of dragging her heavy body back to the mother water that so mysteriously draws us all. You could climb up on her back and ride her, if you want."

"No, thank you. A touch will be enough. Maude, come on. Let's congratulate her."

"What for?" Maude's voice was gruff. "What for? In a few minutes we're going to kill her! After that marvelous performance, we're going to kill her. That magnificent creature! I wish there was another way to get Bertha her pilau meat. I don't want to be part of the slaughter."

Elgin responded at once.

"Maude, why don't the three of you go get my jeep. Here, take the keys. By the time you get back, Roy and I'll be done and we can all go home."

Gratefully Maude took the keys and the three of them scurried away down the beach. The turtle by now was nearing the water's edge. Elgin motioned to Roy and they ran to it and flipped it over. It lay on its back, pawing the air in vain as its flippers were too short to reach the sand, and it could not right itself.

Elgin was moving swiftly now, collecting driftwood and unstrapping his knife. Roy ran up the beach and retrieved an axe he'd brought along.

"This is nauseating business, Roy. I can hardly bring myself to do it. Let's be quick or I'll be sick." Elgin was feeling queasy.

Without another word the two set about their fearful job. Elgin took a sturdy piece of driftwood and banged on the turtle's head until finally she clamped down on it. Roy was standing by, axe raised. As Elgin pulled on the stick, stretching the turtle's neck, Roy struck ... and the head rolled into the water, jaws snapping in reflex. Blood poured over the sand and stained the shoreline as the waves licked gently at it. Off in the distance, heat lightning streaked through a dark cloud. Later, when the jeep rolled into her yard, Bertha looked at the turtle stretched out on the tail gate and nodded in satisfaction.

"A nice big one. Fat as all get out. Heave it into that ole horse trough over there and let it bleed. Lean it agin the edge, neck down. Cover it tight in that tarp to keep the coons off. Evan and me, we'll tackle it in the morning. Thanks!"

The five marauders looked silently at each other for a moment. Then Maude, Didi and Jerry crept away home. As they entered Didi's house Maude shivered and leaned against the door jamb.

"I feel filth from top to bottom. I'm gonna take me a shower, but I doubt if deep down inside I'm ever gonna come clean!"

•

Bertha had no qualms at all as she helped Evan dismember the turtle the following morning. Approaching life from a sturdy stance, feet firmly on the ground and arms akimbo, she scraped and fought through each day, giving no quarter and expecting none in return, providing for her man, her offspring, her friends, and her community, and in that order, as best she could. She wasted no time on sentimentality or reflection. There were appetites to be satisfied and she resolutely set about satisfying them. Now she stood in her yard, looking down speculatively at the huge carcass leaning against the edge of the horse trough, half submerged in thick, bloody water.

"Too much meat in that critter for the pilau pot. No sense wastin' it. I'll use the flippers, the back feet an' one saddle. The other one we'll freeze down an' we can have turtle steaks off an' on fer several weeks. An' we won't mention it even to the kids. Okay?"

Evan grinned and nodded. Bertha was a good planner and since this wasn't a strong point in his makeup he always went along.

"Okay. Mum's the word, Bertha, girl. Let's get on with this business. It's not one of my favorite jobs."

"Mine, neither. But what's got to be is got to be!" She put aside her knife and hefted the axe. "Here, you take this. I'll use the hatchet. Split that thing down the ridge along the center." He hung back. "Go on, swipe it. Evan! Go on!"

Grimacing in distaste, Evan swung a mighty chop. With a loud crack, the axe head was buried to the handle.

"Good!" Bertha said. "Now, twist it some so's I can slip this hatchet in an' I'll work it along under the edge of the shell. Then you axe it further, along down to the tail. Don't pay attention to all the blood. It'll help out an' let our hands slide easy when we reach in an' grab the edges an' tear."

They grunted and pulled, slicing the meat where it held firm, and finally ripped off first one side of the back shell, then the other.

"Okay, now." Bertha was dripping sweat and spattered all over with bloody water. "Better unplug the trough an' let this slop drain out. An' then help me up-end this thing. I'll work on the bottom shell, an' carve off the flippers an' the hind legs while you drag that ole iron pot from under the house an' light us a fire. Drag me that big one, thirty gallons, with the three legs. I'll need every bit of that big one for this critter."

The children had collected as the work progressed. Designating the two oldest as guardians, Bertha banished them back into the house.

"Go on, now. Git! Rose, you an' Lily, take these kids inside an' get 'em some breakfast. Then all of you stay out o' sight 'til your Pa an' me finishes up with this mess. Hear me, now? Off you all go. Once we're done here an'

311

the pot's a-boilin', then you can come on back an' scrub out this ole trough. It has to be spickety clean so's it can fill up agin with rain water. Scoot along, now. That's right."

Evan scrubbed out the black pot with sand and then rinsed it with the hose. Next he scooped out a deep hole in the yard, lined it with brick from the discard pile out back and built a hot fire. Then he placed the iron pot over the fire, braced the legs, and filled it halfway with cistern water.

"Now toss in some salt," Bertha called, watching him out of the corner of her eye, as she added a flipper to the growing mound of oozing flesh.

"How much?"

"Oh, come on, Evan. This ain't the first time you ever boiled a turtle. I don't know. Coupla hands full, I guess. Maybe three, for all that water."

The front flippers, hind legs and feet, one saddle, that thick heavy tenderloin running down both sides of the back, and the tail were dumped into the salted water. Bertha pushed at the remaining meat.

"While I get us some wrapping paper for this mess, how's about you bringin' up that ole wheelbarrow an' see if you can find our iron grate to top it. Makes a handy table for me to skin this stuff an' snatch out them toenails once it's boiled a coupla hours. First, though, poke around in this slimy stomach mess an' drag out the liver. How I love that liver, fried up with a mess o' onions an' some thin-sliced 'taters. Um. Um. I can taste it right now. Can't you? But don't break the bile sac! Poke around in there real easy, now. No! Evan! No! Not with that long stick. Evan! Use yer hands!"

Directing the action like a general on the attack, Bertha was enjoying every minute. She hurried off into the house for the wrapping paper.

While the turtle boiled away, Roy and Jerry were stomping around the back scrub up on Sanibel.

"I figure we'll cut eight palmettos. One heart usually feeds five people, blending out the kids which don't eat heavy with the grown-ups which do. If there's forty folks, that's eight trees."

"Forty people? How do you make out that many?" Jerry was incredulous. "Where'll they all come from?"

"Well, let's count. There's Amanda, Ruta and our dear friend, Matilda Crunch ... and Gustave Kroen. Murph and Pearlie and Ida. Marge and Stan from the restaurant, they're still here, and so are Ted and Jack from the bakery. You and me, your Didi and Maude, Bertha and Evan and their seven kids ... how many's that?"

Jerry had been counting on his fingers as the list progressed.

"That's twenty-four already!"

"See." Roy went on. "And there's your ladies on the other side of the bridge, and Mrs. Armstrong. We forgot Charlie Kramdon and Emmy, and Jed Staines and Zelma always come down and Elgin Bigelow and Piety. And there's Frank and Jean Culpepper ... one or two will bring a guest, maybe ... it'll get up to forty people easy by the time we're done, you'll see. I was right. We'll need eight trees. Let's grab this one. I like 'em six feet tall, tip of the tallest frond. That way the stump is a bit bigger than your two hands can grab and the heart will be solid and tender and white as anything." He swung his axe and quickly felled the tree.

"After we haul 'em back, what do you do then?"

"Nothin' more today, but keep 'em covered and damp," Roy explained. "I'll fix the salad early tomorrow morning. I strip 'em down, choppin' off all the outside layers until I get to the heart. That gets sliced real thin, and mounded into several big bowls. There'll be too much for one bowl. Just before noon, when all the other food is being lugged up to the church, I'll douse the bowls with oil and vinegar. Lots of vinegar -- I like it tart. If it isn't sharp enough, I'll pour some lime juice on it. Fixin' it at the last minute like that keeps it crispy and it'll pop in your mouth like pickled watermelon rind, and it tastes like chestnuts. De--licious!" He smacked his lips. Then he hefted his axe and grinned at Jerry. "Let's get crackin'. After we get these trees, we have to go out an' net us a mess o' mullet. It's gonna be a busy day."

It proved to be a busy day all around. Cora had pie tins spread all over her cottage and was defrosting lime juice. She had banished Maude to Agnes' kitchen as she hadn't room for twelve pies and Maude's peanut soup preparations. Agnes wasn't much involved in the jamboree food as she was saving her energies for Pearl-Alice's wedding at the end of June. She was glad for the company and sat on a stool in her kitchen, talking to Maude and watching her work.

"How are you planning to work this out?" Agnes queried, as Maude made a great show of clattering pans. "You can't make the whole thing today and heat it up tomorrow or it'll taste like paste."

Maude nodded.

"I know. I'm going to make the roux ... flour, butter and milk ... today. I'll bring it all up enough to scald the milk but not boil it, and as soon's it cools to lukewarm, I'll pop it into the back of your refrigerator, and the cold will retard the action and it'll hold its flavor that way. I've done that before and it works fine. Tomorrow, in the morning, up at the church, I'll put in the peanut butter, salt and sherry. The whipped cream topping will be brought up at the last moment. Roy promises me a fire all to myself and a big kettle. We'll use your tureen and ladle, like last year, if that's okay ..." Agnes nodded ... "and Ida and Ruta Barstowe have agreed to rounding up soup plates and spoons. It's all worked out, Ag, so don't worry. The peanut butter soup will be a thing of beauty with a taste divine." She exuberantly bobbed and twisted in a quick little dance, spinning around in a clumsy circle, scattering flour all over the floor. "Oops! 'Scuse! I'll clean that up right away."

●

Emmy Kramdon couldn't settle down. Fluttering more than usual, she scurried back and forth on her screened porch fluffing pillows, straightening ash trays and driving Charlie crazy.

"Emmy! For heaven's sake, stop pacing all over the place. All I said was that maybe I could run over to Rigby's store later this afternoon and get some things I need, and be here tomorrow to go to the Jamboree with you." Charlie's mind was really on that little ole gal Prissy, in her tin shack back of Rigby's store. He'd told her he'd stop by on Saturday but he'd forgotten about the beach party. He'd missed it last year and Emmy had been so disappointed. He didn't want to upset her again. Besides, tomorrow was their wedding anniversary, their 56th. Emmy had forgotten it but he'd remembered. He could run up to Sanibel and pop in on Prissy this afternoon. He was mulling this over in his mind and watching Emmy hopping about like a banty hen ..."Emmy, you're driving me crazy, hopping all over the place. Light somewhere, can't ya!"

"Charlie, I know. I know. I'm already so excited, so pleased that we can go!" She perched on the edge of a chair. "It's going to be special this year!" Bless him, she thought to herself, he's forgotten it's also our wedding anniversary. Makes fifty-six now, I think. Thank heaven I bought him that set of tools he's had his eye on for months. I'll wrap it up and ask Roy Coggins to hand it to him when we're all done eating. He'll be so embarrassed, because, of course, he hasn't gotten me anything. But I don't want presents, or need 'em. He's enough. He's been a good husband all these years and he loved me for a long, long time. I knew exactly when it changed from love to friendship. And I know all about Prissy ... all about the other Prissys, too ... what does it hurt, really. We're a team. Always was, always will be. Charlie and Emmy - Emmy and Charlie ... Her eyes misted over and she smiled gently at him, sitting opposite her and fretting so obviously to be away and into some mischief.

Charlie caught the expression and rose abruptly, his face flushing slightly with guilty embarrassment.

"Best get goin'. I'll be back along 'bout supper. Anything you need?"

She shook her head, and he went out. He thought to himself as he climbed into his rickety truck ... I'll drop into Rigby's store and get her that yellow hat ole Rigby told me she'd tried on last time she was down. She'd mentioned to him how much she was taken by it but it was more than she felt she should spend. She'll be so surprised because, of course, she hasn't gotten me ...

314

The following morning, Saturday, May 25th, the sun was almost the last one up. As it spread its dawn light across the sky and peeped over the horizon between its rose-tinted fingers, it exposed a scene of feverish activity in the front yard of the Chapel-by-the-Sea. Deep holes were being dug. Wood, mostly dried pine, was being hauled in. Fires were being lighted. Electric wiring was being strung. Platforms and trestle tables were being built. There was a cheerful camaraderie in the air as hammers pounded and axes rang. Ted was in and out with his fogging machine and the mosquitos were defeated. By eleven o'clock, when Evan drove in with a truckload of chairs borrowed from the Sanibel Community House, all was in fine shape. By noon, as if the various cooks had practiced the delivery many times, the food arrived in procession. Maude's peanut butter soup was first, and the big pot was positioned over its special fire, reduced now to coals to keep the soup hot but not boiling. The whipped cream was whisked out of the sun and into the cooler church. Cora's lime pies were carried in Jerry's truck, boxed specially to keep off the dust in transit, and also taken inside the church. Ruta and Ida had spread white sheets over the tables, so the bowls of swamp cabbage were set right in place. Roy had his own two fires and two huge frying pans, with oil heating in both. Beside him, on a large table, were mounds of prepared mullet, cleaned, gutted, pre-dipped in corn meal and minced onion, waiting to be fried golden brown. On a second table were equally high mounds of hush-puppies, little balls of corn meal, onions, milk, eggs, baking powder and salt, ready to be fried alongside the bubbling fish. Bertha's turtle pilau was the only problem. Before dawn, Ida, Ruta and Bertha had drained the boiled turtle, saving the liquid, removed any skin that hadn't cooked off, separated the meat from the bones, pulled out any toenails overlooked previously, dumped the cleaned meat back into the strained broth, added quantities of onions, carrots, canned tomatoes, and rice, all from Ida's store.

"Don't worry, Ida. We'll pay you back, later on." Bertha said, beginning to stir the huge pot with a board nearly as big as an oar. "Keep a list and we'll settle up from the Sunday church collections. I've thought it all through an' I think that's fair. I mean, Evan does all the paintin' an' repairin' free, an' I never charge for cleanin', so for a community party we can cover the few expenses from church donations. We can call it a church bazaar. It almost is, you know!" She looked quickly at the others to see if they approved, as she really believed her arguments were on the thin side.

Several hours later, the mixture had boiled down to a thick stew with chunks of succulent turtle meat bubbling up and down. The tantalizing aroma carried across the yard and into the house where all the children sat, expectantly watching the clock. The trick, then, was to get the pot up to the church yard.

The cauldron had to be hoisted to Evan's truckbed and carried over the rutted road to the picnic area, lowered again to the ground and positioned onto the grill over its fire, all without spilling ... and the pot was boiling hot.

It took every available man and Evan's truck winch to effect the transfer. As the huge pot came to rest, the contents intact and not a drop spilled, a cheer went up from the early arrivals. They all collected around to sniff and comment and salivate.

"Not yet. Not yet." Bertha laughed, stirring with a flourish. "Half an hour to go. Gotta wait for the latecomers, ya know."

Promptly at one o'clock, Bertha ran over to the church entryway, with its little bronze bell. She waved at the crowd and called at the top of her lungs, clanging the bell clapper back and forth.

"This here Jamboree is now begun. Come an' git it. Everybody, eat up. Come on, now, while it's hot."

Jean Culpepper, seated at the piano, struck up a lively tune and everyone chattered at once as they gathered around the tables. A welcoming breeze, blowing in from the Gulf, cooled the midday heat and rustled the pines, as the mounds of food seemed miraculously to melt away. An air of contentment and peace settled over the gathering as they ate. Finally, the children, stuffed to bursting, giggling and whispering, ran off down the shell path to frolic in the Gulf, and the oldsters sat in the shade, calling back and forth to each other, gossiping, relaxing and poking fun. Later, after the food settled and catnaps had been taken under slanted hats, there was dancing and singing. Roy Coggins dragged out his Jew's harp, and Evan had his sweet potato. Elgin Bigelow had brought his fiddle and they provided a concert with Jean improvising, hooting with laughter and banging out accompaniment.

During a temporary pause in the festivities, Jerry carried a large package from Roy's truck over to Charlie Kramdon and laid it crossways on his lap.

"What in tarnation is this, now?" Charles was flustered and suspected he'd been bested. He glanced across at Emmy but she seemed completely involved in an intimate discussion with Amelia Armstrong. Their heads were together and they were chuckling and nodding.

Flushing with embarrassment at having been so suddenly singled out, Charlie turned the package over end for end and stared at it.

"Go on, Charlie," came a call, and everyone joined in. "Open it. You've got a secret admirer. Look at me ... I ain't got no present. You must rate, sure 'nuf," and so on.

A little card fluttered to the sand as Charlie tore at the wrappings and Matilda Crunch pounced on it. She read out loud.

"For my darling husband on this, our 56th wedding anniversary. All my love, Emmy."

Charlie looked at the new tools in their box and hefted a large pair of plyers.

"Well, now. Don't this beat the dog. Thank you, Emmy. I'm that obliged." Then, laying aside the box, he raised a finger at her. "But don't think, ole gal, you can best me! I got a little something fer you, too." He hobbled to his truck and took a hat box from under the tarp. Looking around at the gathering, he smiled broadly. "It may not always seem so, but for more years than I can shake a stick at I've had me the best darn gal in these parts an' I love her mightily!"

Everyone applauded and cat-called back and forth as Emmy put on the yellow hat and Charlie leaned over and kissed her.

Knowing Charlie's delight in tinkering with tools and recalling their recent conversation about his adding a room to Emmy's house, Evan called across the crowd.

"What are you planning to do now, Charlie?"

Charlie deliberately chose to misinterpret.

"Now?" He had an arm around Emmy and he pulled her close. "Now? When we get home I'm planning on doing exactly what we did on our wedding night!"

Emmy's response was instant.

"Oh, goodie!" She exclaimed, clapping her hands. "Will I have time to take off my stockings?"

Charlie leaned over to kiss her again and croaked in a harsh whisper that carried across the crowd.

"Knowin' me, ole gal, you'll have time to knit 'em!"

21

June

Heavy rains poured down during the first week in June. Accompanied by gale-force winds and coinciding with the new moon, extremely high water resulted throughout the coastal area of southwest Florida. Outgoing tides could not fully ebb as the normal flow was blocked by the winds holding the water longer than usual in the estuaries and back bayous. The incoming tide, with the winds behind and pushing, piled in on top.

On the island, life was difficult during this period. People walked around in heavy waders as the bay waters rose over the mangrove aerial roots and reached the leafy boughs. Docks were submerged and salt water stood in most yards in puddles and tiny lakes. Boats had to be watched closely as they filled from the rains and were bashed against their moorings by the winds.

Landbound wildlife repositioned itself as best it could. Raccoons and the few rabbits pulled back to the high ridge along the island spine, and birds huddled under large-leafed foliage.

The huge banyan tree in the post office yard grew on a raised mound, a dry island amid the surrounding flood. In among the tangled root-system, far back, high up and out of sight, was the entrance to an abandoned rabbit den. The timid creatures had departed for quieter quarters many months ago when the Wiggins children had hung a swing from a low-lying limb.

The subsequent tenant, a land turtle called a gopher, was accidently squashed one day as it nibbled a tuft of grass in the post office driveway.

The coarse-haired black palmetto rat that next moved in was content for quite some time, foraging for seeds, bottle tops, shiny bits of glass, anything that was movable and that glittered, all of which he lugged back under the banyan roots to the snug round inner chamber for safekeeping. Then, one day, his routine of hunt, eat, sleep, was thrown out of gear when he chanced upon a beautiful little female with a grayish coat and shiny black eyes. They touched whiskers for a few seconds and then scampered off to live together in her home under the post office living room floor.

As the tide level rose, the slough not far from the post office overflowed, flooding an old gopher hole and disturbing the two burrowing owls and the rattlesnake that lived there. They moved out, searching for higher, dryer ground. The snake, a large one with a head as wide as a silver dollar and five rattles on its tail, slithered around a deep puddle and up under the banyan roots, and found the abandoned rabbit hole. Hesitantly, testing for body heat from any possible occupant with its flicking tongue, it inched slowly down the open tunnel.

The June rains stopped as suddenly as they began. Everywhere was a feeling of invigoration, of cleaned freshness. The sun set in a burst of scarlet, and a yellow moon rose high in a cloudless sky.

●

Framed in the shaft of moonlight beaming in through the open window, Bertha combed her long hair and stared across the dock and out over the open bay.

"My, ain't it beautiful," she murmured to Evan, stretched out on the big bed behind her. "You know, when you can stand in this cool night air an' see such a purty picture, the ruffly water glistenin' in all that soft moonlight, it makes a body think. It all seems so suddenly worthwhile, somehow. All the work an' the sweat, the kids an' all their problems ... "

... "Me an' all my demands," Evan stuck in.

... "that, too," Bertha went on, smiling. "We have a good life, Evan. This island has been good to us, you know. I wouldn't want to live nowhere else."

"Why don't you come over here an' tell me all about it?" Evan wiggled down a bit and rested his arm across her pillow, and Bertha chuckled. She began to plait her hair.

"Come on," he said, impatiently.

"Wait a minute, now. I ain't quite ready. Uh oh! What do you suppose this is all about?"

"What now?"

"A rowboat is comin' toward our dock from Buck Key! At this hour, halfway to dawn? Looks like Daddy an' Mammy Farlow. What in the world do ya suppose they want?"

Evan joined her at the window and they both watched as Daddy Farlow tied the boat to a piling and walked stiffly toward the house, leaving Mammy sitting upright in the moonlight.

Bertha reached the porch door as the old man labored up the steps.

"Why, Mr. Farlow. Can we help you?"

"Yes'm. You sure can. I was wonderin' if'n you kin wash Mammy?"

"Wash Mammy?" Bertha looked along the dock toward Mammy, sitting so quietly in the little boat. "Can't she wash herself?"

"No'm."

"Why not?"

"She's daid!"

Bertha sharply sucked in her breath. Beckoning to Evan, she whispered to him.

"Go on out there and check. I'll give Daddy a hot cup of tea."

The old gentleman was distraught. Now that he'd turned the problem over to someone else his sturdy resolve cracked and he sank shivering onto the sofa, twisting his hat in gnarled hands.

"Don't know exactly whut ta do! This ain't never happened to me afore!"

"There, there, now." Bertha clucked, at the same time shooing at the children who were clustered in the doorway. "You kids go back to bed. You can find out all about everything in the mornin'. Lily, put the kettle on. Then you an' Rose run up the path to the McClain place an' ask Maude if she'll come down an' help me. Run along, now. That's a good girl."

When Evan came back he nodded solemnly.

"Is she ...?" Bertha asked.

"As a door-nail! Already stiff, too. Musta been some time back."

Bertha held out a steaming cup of tea to Daddy Farlow and sank down beside him on the sofa.

"How did it happen, Mr. Farlow?" She stroked his free hand, trying to convey her sympathy.

Daddy lifted rheumy eyes and stared vacantly across the room.

"Musta been in the early morning, some time about then. Jes' afore lunch. I'd been repairin' the pigpen, an' I looked in the bedroom an' Mammy was sittin' in her rocker with her back to the door an' I didn't pay no never-mind, as she sat like thet regular. Along about dusk, when she still sat, an' thet wuz longer than mos' times, I goes in an' touches her, but she can't move none. Jest her haid, it sags a bit. I sat on the bed, nex' to her chair, awaitin' fer her to wake up. But she don'."

"Well, now, we're all that upset. Don't you worry any more, now. Evan an' me, we'll stay with you an' tend to everything." Bertha rose and motioned Evan to follow her outside.

"I've sent for Maude. This is woman's work, an' she'll help. It sure ain't pleasant but it's gotta be done. You carry that sweet old lady in from the dock an' lean her up agin the horse trough over there. I'll get Daddy to a spare bed, an' gather the washin' things. See that the kids go back to sleep. An' you stay outa the way, but handy. Maude an' me may need some help. An', Evan, best plan on catchin' that first ferry. This ain't primitive times no more, you know. Mammy'll have to go in to Fort Myers to Englehardt Funeral Home, first thing."

Mammy's body had stiffened in a sitting position. The weight was less than a bag of cement so Evan had no difficulty lifting it from the rowboat. He ran in the dock, holding it extended at arm's length and sat it at the end of the horse trough, where it immediately tipped over on it's side. He propped it back up with a rickety old chair and shook his hands in disgust.

"Whew! Whew! Awful. She's all over mess. You should see that rowboat. Poor Daddy!"

"Yeah," Bertha nodded, dragging a garden hose from the toolshed. "I agree. Poor Daddy. He's got all my sympathy. But I ain't got none for us, so wash yourself off. 'Course the boat's a mess. So's Mammy. Body functions, you know. You take a pail an' go sluice that boat, an' we'll tackle Mammy. Thank heaven, here comes Maude."

●

The meeting on Agnes' porch, earlier that evening, had set the final arrangements for Sally-Anne's wedding. Agnes, Cora and Didi had their heads together and were sorting papers and checking off lists affixed to clipboards.

"I've been over both islands, every house, and I've seen everybody." Didi was a bit short of breath as she had arrived late. "That, and those little notices both Bertha and Jenny up on Sanibel will place in every mailbox will tell anybody I've missed what we're planning. Of course, no telling how many will actually show up. Not everybody, I hope, or we'll never fit 'em all in. How's the gown coming, Aunt Cora?"

Cora smiled expansively and settled back in her chair, anxious to discuss her creation.

"It's already so beautiful! Not quite finished. I still need one more fitting. Sally-Anne thinks it's fine the way it is, but I want to add some lacy frills and scatter little bows around the skirt. We'll be ready on time"

Didi was perched on the edge of her chair and her eyes sparkled. "Now, let's go over the 'procedure list' and see if it's correct. Everything depends on the timing." She giggled excitedly. She loved all this planning and controlling and the other two smiled indulgently.

"I just love this figuring things out. Let's see, now. Mr. Simpson, the preacher, will catch the 11:30 ferry and be on Sanibel by 12 noon and be met by Jerry in Aunt Ag's car. The school bus will follow on the next ferry."

"The school bus?" Cora's eyes opened wide.

"Yes. Oh, did I forget to tell you? I'm sorry. Everything's happening so fast." Didi reached out and patted Cora's hand. "We've had real good luck. The Lee County School Board is lending us a bus, complete with driver. We have to pay him, of course, and the gas and the ferry fees, but the bus is free. Isn't that great? It'll be in East Fort Myers at Billy Bowlegs Park in time to load Sally-Anne's family and still catch the 12:30 ferry. It can haul forty people. We don't expect that many ... we're transporting only the family ... Sally's children and their wives and husbands, and her grandchildren. Marge and Stan Brown have made arrangements with a Fort Myers restaurant to place forty box lunches on the school bus, and that is the Brown's contribution to the wedding. Mr. Simpson will have lunch here and then go straight to the church and get himself organized for the ceremony which is set for 1:30. The school bus will come straight on through and park on the main road by the church lane as we certainly don't want that big bus in the church yard. Well, let's see, now." She beamed at the other two and rearranged a few papers. "That takes care of the off-islanders. Did I miss anything?"

Cora took up the plotting.

"Ag and I'll dress Sally-Anne. Doobie will drop her off here and then drive Shadrack on over to Bertha's yard, dragging that cart. Why do you suppose Sally insists on that mule and that squeaky old wooden wagon? I don't understand."

Ag lifted her head.

"I understand exactly. Sally wants this proceeding simple, as close as possible to her own level of living. No frills. Her children, living in Fort Myers, have cars and fancy clothes and all, but Sally and Doobie don't. They get about in that wagon, pulled by that mule and that's the way Sally wants to arrive at the church. It wouldn't be correct for them to climb down out of a car. I agree with her."

Cora's face showed a trace of dismay.

"But a bride can't arrive in a wagon!"

"That's exactly the point, Cora." Ag smiled gently at her friend. "In Sally's mind she isn't a bride. This is an expedient. She wants to legalize her status, that's all. I've no doubt she'd gladly have settled for a simple civil ceremony at the court house. We've caused all this hoopla, Didi and company. Sally has gone along with us, that's all. I think it's brave of her."

"Oh!" The excitement drained from Didi's face. "Aunt Ag, you don't mean, do you ... ?"

"No, dear. I'm not criticizing at all. I also understand your sympathy and concern and it's very commendable. The affair will be lovely and there'll be a big gathering and everybody will have a fine time. And after the church ceremony there'll be lots of food outside. Thank heaven they left the Jamboree tables in place. At least we won't have to go through all that again."

"Wasn't it sweet of Bertha," Didi said, "to offer her living room for Sally-Anne and Doobie to rest and have a cool drink? You'll be there with them, won't you, Aunt Cora?"

"Of course, dear. I want to make certain Sally looks her best as she heads for the church. Of course I'll be with her."

Agnes pushed back her chair and stood to stretch. She had the evening meal to prepare and her mind had already wandered from the wedding preparations to meat and vegetables.

"Do you want me to drive you home, Didi?" she asked, crossing to the sink and reaching for an apron.

"No, thank you. Jerry'll be by. He's over at my place with Aunt Maude. They're tinkering with his outboard motor, and he promised to fetch me."

"That's good. Then I'll get busy with supper. Thank heaven those rains the front of the month are over. We needed the rain, of course, but those high tides!" Agnes paused and shook her head. "And the mosquitos afterward. Weren't they impossible? Well, things seem to have quieted down. Lets hope nothing else happens for a bit. The moon should be bright tonight. Let's enjoy it."

●

"My, my," Maude exclaimed, joining Bertha in a rush. "Why is it always middle o' the night? Why not at midday or some decent hour, when we can see what we're doin'!"

Bertha shook her head.

"Don't ask me. I don't know. This is gonna be messy. Better take that tool belt off if you don't want to wet it up." She looked quizzically at Maude. "Do you sleep in that thing?"

"'Course not. But I reach for it soon's my feet touch the floor. Comfortin', somehow. I feel naked without it." She unbuckled the belt and tossed it toward the house. The hatchet rang sharply as it struck a large conch shell. "Okay. What's first? I'm not too sure."

"Me, neither." Bertha was walking around Mammy, looking at the situation from all sides. "What we want is to clean her up an' wrap her in a windin' cloth so she stays clean of dust an' sand for the trip to Myers an' the buryin' home over there." She poked with a finger at the body. "First off, maybe we should rinse her down. Pretty disagreeable the way she is. Grab that hose an' you squirt. I'll twirl her. After we get all the mess gone we can slide her into the trough. It's full of good clean rain water."

Silently, with gritted teeth, the two women worked together in the moonlight. The only difficulty was in removing the shirtwaist, as Mammy's arms were folded demurely across her chest and had stiffened enough to pinch the cloth. When the body was nude and comparatively clean, they paused to catch their breath.

"Poor little mite," Bertha murmured. "Hardly weighs an ounce! She's had a hard life. No one who ain't lived in a place like this can understand how difficult it is. An' it was worse when she was young. I sure take my hat off to those old gals. Hard enough, God knows, on the men, but it was murder on the women."

Maude quietly nodded in agreement, as Bertha continued.

"Your man, mos' likely only one fer miles aroun', leavin' of a mornin' to work off somewhere an' never knowin' if he was goin' to get back. Totin' water, buildin' fires, fightin' these damn bugs, childbirthin' an' all that horror all by yourself, slopped up in a corner somewhere like an animal, kids an' their hurts an' sicknesses, findin' food three times a day, every day ... I sure admire all of 'em. I sure do."

Maude continued to nod. Bertha straightened her back with an effort.

"Let's clean ourselves an' this ground around here, so's the kids don't trod in it later on. Then we can slip her down into the trough an' go get a hot cup of coffee. How about that?:

They didn't linger long in the house. The night was passing and Bertha wanted everything tended to properly before the kids trooped downstairs for breakfast. As they returned to the body floating in the horse trough Bertha murmured as much to herself as to Maude ... "mos' likely we's gonna have trouble with those legs. Gotta unbend 'em an' get 'em straight out, somehow. I'll steady her shoulders, Maude, an' you bear down on her knees."

Maude pushed down on first one knee, then the other. The legs slowly straightened but snapped back up as soon as she released the pressure.

"This is spooky, Bertha. Gives me the creeps. Besides, my working her legs up and down, she's seeping again."

"Then we'll have to plug her." With her practical approach, this proved no great problem for Bertha. "Run into the post-office an' on the left side in a corner is a pile of old newspapers. Wad some into a tight little ball, better make that two little balls ... that's all we'll need. An' while you're doin' that, I'll round up two slatty boards an' we'll force them legs down an' strap 'em to the boards."

After all this was done, Bertha produced a clean white sheet.

"'Course, this ain't a proper windin' cloth. Should be more canvassy, but it's all we got. Leave lots of spare up towards the head so's we can fold it down onto her chest, snug-like."

"Bertha." Maude had drawn back a bit and was staring hard at the body. "We really should do something about those eyes. Wide open and all starey!"

"What do you suggest? The lids won't stay down. Every time I close 'em they slowly inch open again. What can I do? Nail 'em down?"

"Of course not!" Maude didn't know whether to shiver or smile. "It just seems somehow all wrong."

"Well, far as I'm concerned, we tried," Bertha said. "We did our best. Just leave 'em be an' fold that sheet down over her face, open eyes or no open eyes." Then she chuckled and glanced quickly at Maude. "Bet it'll give them undertakin' fellers a start, over in Myers. When they unwind her, there she'll be, starin' back at 'em."

"Just one problem, now," Maude stated softly. "We left so much slack at the top of her head, the sheet doesn't reach all the way down. Her feet are sticking out. We'll have to unwind her."

"We'll do no such thing!" Bertha's voice was sharper than she meant it to be but she was tired and dawn was breaking and she wanted done with all this. "We'll stuff the feet into an ole pillow case. I got plenty in the house. You go find Evan an' have him carry Mammy into the storage room aside the post

324

office, and then ask him to fetch Roy. Roy'll have to ride in with Evan and Daddy Farlow."

As daylight strengthened, and with all the kids grouped at upstairs windows, Evan's truck pulled slowly out of the yard, heading for the ferry eighteen miles down the rutty road. Beside Evan in the cab sat Daddy Farlow. Roy Coggins crouched on the open flat bed, one hand on the iron cot with Mammy's shrouded body, and every so often, as the truck jiggled and the cot inched toward the open end, just before it would have slipped over the edge, dumping Mammy head-first onto the sandy trail, Roy would snatch it back to safety.

Maude and Bertha plunked themselves down at the big round table in the kitchen and sipped coffee as the two oldest daughters, Rose and Lily, got everyone breakfast.

"Already, Maude, I'm tired," Bertha sighed. "Not what could be called a good night's rest, eh?" Maude was toying with a plate of grits, eating halfheartedly and glancing around the room at the girls seemingly everywhere.

"There seem to be so many. Are they all yours, Bertha?"

"Yep. Count 'em. There's seven. Ain't they grand? Actually, I've had nine ... two boys more ... but they both died. Up in the little graveyard they are, next to the church. One of the reasons I love to go up there. It's peaceful an' quiet an' I'm near my babies." It wasn't a sad remark, just matter-of-fact. The girls were all over, at the sink, clearing dishes off the table, and one about five years old, Daisy, was leaning tight against Bertha's dress. Bertha absent-mindedly fingered the child's hair.

"With so many I suppose it's hard not to have favorites an' I watch that close. Always have. Don't think it's fair to favor just one. When I gets provoked, I slap 'em all. Same treatment all around." She smiled at Maude. "It's been a lot of work." The two women chuckled aloud.

"'Course," Bertha went on, "with a newborn, that's different. 'Til it can walk it gets special attention an' extra love. Not only from me but from all the girls, too. the oldest ones, they're lots of help, now. With Too-loo, when she come late like, they took most of her care off me. Where is she? I don't see Too-loo anywhere." She raised her voice. "Hey, where's Too-loo?"

Daisy pulled at Bertha's dress and twisted on one foot.

"She's outside, Mama, settin' in that ole trough, playin with her boat."

"In that filthy water? Ain't been rinsed out, yet!"

Bertha jumped up and headed for the door.

"Lily, Rose ... get that child outa there, right now. This instant. You hear me? Land's sakes, she could drown!"

As the children ran outside Bertha returned to the table.

"Really, they'll be the death of me yet. Always something. Too-loo's too little to climb up into that trough by herself. She had help! I'll investigate that later."

After the rescue of Too-loo all the youngsters gathered again in the kitchen, standing around expectantly, wondering what to do. Bertha was more than up to this occasion.

"I just hate when they all stand around, starin' at me," she murmured sideways to Maude. Then she sat straight and organized.

"Go on, now! Shoo! Git outside! Rose, you an' Lily take the whole shootin' match up to the beach an' go swimin' an' find me some good shells. Daisy, you stay here. Put Too-loo's halter on her an' tie her to one of them big banyan roots under that tree outside, an' give her a shell to play with. An', Daisy, you sit on the steps outside and you keep a close eye on her, mind you."

"Yes'm." Daisy answered and did a squat little bow. Bertha beamed and leaned toward Maude.

"Ain't she cute? It's hard to stay mad at these kids. I love each one of 'em so much. Go on, now," she called out, "git goin'. Aunt Maude an' me, we'll clean up this mess."

Too-loo was dressed in her halter and tied in the dappling morning sunlight under the banyan tree, where she cooed contentedly to herself as she banged on a large root with a big shell. Daisy perched on the stoop to observe and the others trooped off to the beach. Finally all was peaceful and the day began.

●

Without ears, unable to hear, but sensitive to reverberation, the thump, thump, thump on the root aboveground alerted the rattlesnake. It raised its head attentively, sensed that this disturbance might be food, and decided to investigate. Slowly, with a flowing motion, it uncoiled and slid from its nest up toward the light at the end of the entrance shaft.

●

"I don't see how you manage to feed and tend to seven kids and yourself and Evan. I don't mean to pry, but isn't it hard to manage?" Maude was mopping up the lineoleum floor and Bertha was finishing up at the sink.

"Oh, we couldn't a done it atall," Bertha said, "but for this post office money. I get $2,400 a year, by the month, an' we never could've made ends meet without that. That's when we figured on all these younguns, when I got that appointment."

Daisey had crept silently into the kitchen, and was pulling at Bertha's dress.

"Mama." She yanked gently. "Mama."

"Not now, Daisy. run along back to the front stoop, like I tole ya." Bertha shoved the little girl toward the door and turned back to Maude. "Now where was I? Oh, yes. Evan an' me! Well, back some ten years or so ago, when I got this job ... Evan is great, an' he works his head off but durin' the nine off-

326

season months there ain't much to do an' he's never made but $1.50 to $1.75 an hour, an' that can go pretty quick, you know. Now Daisy, stop tuggin' at me! Why are you back in here? Your Aunt Maude an' me, we're talkin' an' you've a job to do out front. So git along, now." She pushed Daisy again toward to door, patting the little girl's rump as she went, and smiled at Maude. "She likes to be with me all the time. It's hard to break 'em of that, sometimes. So, as I was sayin', with all this government money Evan decided we'd have jes' as many kids as we could feed. We're both from large families an' love kids. We manage."

Maude put up the mop and strapped her tool belt around her waist.

"I gotta go. Didi'll be worrying why I'm so long. We're through, aren't we Bertha?"

Bertha nodded and put her arm around Maude's shoulder.

"It was real neighborly of ya to come down in the middle of the night like that, an' I appreciate it." She glanced towards the door. "Lands sakes, here's this child again. Alright, baby, what is it?" She stooped down to listen.

"Mama, Too-loo's playin' with a big ole snake!"

"A snake!" Bertha stiffened and a look of horror and disgust showed on her face. "Gawd! How I hate snakes!" She raced through the door with Maude close behind her, and gasped, one hand raised to her mouth. Under the tree, among the roots, the baby sat cooing and gurgling, scooping up sand and trickling it onto a huge rattlesnake stretched out at its feet.

"Pussy ... pussy ... pussy." the baby cooed.

"Oh, migod! Oh dear Lord in Heaven! My baby! My baby!" Bertha was frozen and couldn't move her feet. Slowly she sank to her knees, moaning.

Maude, however, could move. She tensed for the attack. A primeval air of the age-old huntress settled on her as she crouched and inched along the side of the house until she was broadside to the baby and some twenty feet away.

Alerted by the actions behind it and sensing fear in the air, the snake whipped into a tight coil. The rattles on its vibrating tail buzzed like angry bees. The upright head was but a foot from the child's face.

"Pussy ... pussy" gurgled Too-loo, leaning forward and reaching out to pat this interesting new friend.

There was a moment of inaction. The snake's tail stopped vibrating. The buzzing halted. The head ceased its slow side to side weaving and the thick body tensed.

"It's goin' to strike! Oh, migod! It's goin' to strike!" Bertha cried in a hoarse moan.

Maude moved instinctively. Her hand darted to her belt. There was a flash of sunlight on the blade as the hatchet twisted through the air, whizzing within inches of the baby's face. Striking the snake on the upper neck, it sliced the serpent's head cleanly off, leaving the coiled body momentarily upright, gushing blood over the baby's shirtwaist.

Bertha rushed forward, kicking the convulsively snapping head to one side, and grabbing Too-loo into her arms so violently she snapped the baby's halter. She ran back into the house, hugging the blood-soaked infant to her bosom.

"Maude! Maude! I don't know what to say. I gotta clean the mess off this child. Maude! ... Maude?"

But Maude was gone. Still in a half crouch she ran up the back lane toward Didi's house, but collapsed, hysterical, under a spreading pine tree.

"Suppose I'd missed! Suppose I'd struck that child! Oh, Migod, suppose I'd hit that beautiful little baby!" She wrapped her arms around her body and rocked back and forth, tears streaming down her face. "Dear God, suppose ..."

Didi found her there and took her home.

●

On Saturday, June 29th, the noon ferry touched down at Sanibel exactly on time and the Reverend Eugene Simpson drove off first. Jerry was waiting for him in Aunt Ag's car, and one behind the other, they drove down Sanibel to Blind Pass. When they arrived, Sally-Anne and Doobie were already there. Sally was on the porch with Cora and Doobie was sitting in the wagon behind Shadrack. Cora was making shooing motions at him.

"Go on now, Doobie. I'll take care of Sally-Anne and we'll be at the post office in half an hour. We'll meet you there."

"Mis' Cora, you'll mos' likely pass me by on the way. Shadrack can't walk all that distance in no thuty minutes."

"Then you'll have to hustle him up. Make him run."

"No'm. Thet mule don't hustle, an' he don't run. Jes walks."

Doobie crushed his straw hat further down on his head and slapped the reins. After a moment's indecision, Shadrack heaved forward and they rolled slowly out of the yard and headed across the bridge.

"Oh, dear!" Cora wrung her hands and appealed to Sally. "He'll never get there on time. We should have started him sooner."

Sally-Anne shook out her dress and spun a bit to make it swirl.

"Don't you worry none, Mis' Cora. Doobie'll be theah on time. Else he's me to face an' Doobie don' want non o' thet. My, ain't this dress purty! Jes' laik I always dreamed. These heah bowy things on the shirtwaist, they's so starchy an' stick out jes' laik it's me under theah. I likes thet. I'se skimpy up on top. An' the skirt is all flowery an' it's blowy jes' laik I wants. Mis' Cora, I can't ever repay yo' fer all this. Whut kin I do fer yo'?"

"Oh, Sally. You look just grand." Cora circled the tiny woman, pinching here, pulling a bit there. "And those white high shoes look just fine, though they look too small. Do they hurt your feet?"

"No'm. They'se fine. Efen they'se a touch tight, makes my feets look smaller. Where's my hat? My white hat? Ah, yeah. Theah tis." She reverently took the hat from Cora and placed on her head. Cora led her into Agnes' bedroom so she could see herself in the mirror on the back of the door. Sally-Anne was stunned!

"My gracious goodness! I looks jes like I done when I was young."

Later, at the post office, Doobie echoed her words, Somehow he'd managed to push Shadrack along and was circling the wagon to face it toward the church when Agnes, Cora and Sally-Anne drove up to the door. Sally-Anne emerged and preened.

"Me, oh my! Sally!" Doobie was equally stunned and instinctively reached up to pull off his hat. "Yo' is so purty! Jes' like yo' was back in them flowah fields. My! Nex' to yo', I'se jes' no count!" His face fell.

Sally couldn't resist the chance for a good solid dig.

"I'se suppose' to be purty! I'se the Stah o' dis heah she-bang. De folks is gonna be eyin' me, head to toe. I'se suppose to be young an' purty an' smell good. Dis heah is a woman's party. Yo' is jes' a man, Doobie. Yo' is suppos' to look scrunchy an' no-count an' be hid behin' ma skirts." She gave out a high-pitched cackling laugh and flounced toward the living room door. "Ain't thet 'bout it, Mis' Cora?" She called as she climbed the stoop.

"Oh, I don't know, now, dear." The bantering had sailed way over Cora's head. "I think Doobie looks very nice, too. When we pin his white carnation on his coat, he'll look very ...he'll be quite ..."

"'Course he will. I knows thet! I'se jes' pokin' fun." Sally ran back to Doobie and folded him into a tight embrace and gave him a long, lingering kiss. "Don' look so scart, Doobie. It's yo' an' me, yo' know. Jes' liak always. It'll all be jes' fine. I looks purty an' yo' looks handsome an' everybody's gonna be so jealous!"

At the front of the church, to the right of the pulpit and opposite the plush-covered armchair, Jean Culpepper sat at the piano playing soft mood music. The school bus had arrived from Fort Myers with the family, and the small children had immediately scattered to the beach. The older folks stood in small clusters under the trees, unsure of what to do. They nodded and smiled nervously at the islanders, also standing around in little groups and also unexpectedly unsure of themselves. In both groups, the women wore big-brimmed hats and fanned themselves against the pressing heat. Conversation was stilted.

Back in Bertha's living room, Sally-Anne and Doobie were paying close attention to Jerry's explanations.

"It's very important now that everything works out smooth. Didi and Jean and I all have watches and we set 'em to the exact time just an hour ago. I gotta get you two to the church steps in twenty minutes ... exactly at twenty-five minutes to two. Didi will be at the church door then, to help you start down the aisle. Jean will start your entrance music exactly at the same time. So you gotta be there. Understand?"

Both nodded solemnly.

329

"I've just timed it from the church steps to here, walking at Shadrack's pace, and it takes eight minutes. We figure you can climb down off the wagon and cross to the church steps in one minute, so we'll leave here in exactly ten minutes. Got it? I'll walk beside Shadrack and hold his halter. If you've got any freshening-up to do, better get it done."

Sally-Anne shook her head.

"I'se ready!" she said.

"Me, too," Doobie agreed, clearing his throat and reaching out for Sally's hand.

Meanwhile, at the church, Didi was acting as usher. Fifteen minutes before the deadline she clanged the outside bell to summon everyone into the church, except the small special group that would line either side of the entryway through which Sally and Doobie would walk. She stood beside the door, smiling and nodding.

"The first six rows, both sides, are reserved for the Denkins family and their friends. Everybody else, find your own seats. Please sit well front so there's room in the rear for latecomers." She repeated this several times as the crowd filed in. Then Jean, following a quick glance toward the front door and a glimpse of Didi motioning to her, struck the opening chords of Sally's special choice, the melodious spiritual "He's got the whole world in His Hands". Heads turned to watch the rear of the church as Sally-Anne and Doobie came into view, walking hand in hand toward the pulpit. Doobie was hangdog and looked as if he wanted to fall through the floor but Sally was glowing. Her back was straight and her head was high as she moved confidently down the aisle, a proud smile on her face. When she reached the front rows and her family, she paused to hug and kiss her eldest daughter, Elvira, and to pat the nearest children on their heads. As she and Doobie neared the pulpit Reverend Simpson met them with extended hands and slowly and gently turned them toward the congregation. He then motioned everyone to rise and together the entire gathering sang the stirring old song.

The Reverend Eugene Simpson was a Southern Baptist minister, of the self-taught school. As a young man, working in his father's pecan grove in Georgia, he was touched one day by the beckoning finger of the Almighty. Transfixed, and with eyes glazed in ecstasy, he dropped his hoe and set forth into the world to preach The Word. His approach to Heaven was up a path strewn with Bombast and Hell-fire. His sermons always began from nowhere and ended just as vaguely, but in between he thundered, flailed, and exhorted, until the congregation, swaying in time with his gestures and interjecting little moans and wails, was wrung out and left exhausted. Each was now convinced he had sinned every second of every day.

Discovering early on that eye contact was disconcerting and tended to break his concentration, Reverend Simpson would gaze fixedly at a convenient spot on the far wall, above and beyond the assembled heads. Mentally supported by this stationary mooring, he was free to twist and sway as he built from a wide, sweeping base and climbed upward to lofty peaks. He was soon lost in his own rhetoric. He was on his own way to salvation. If anyone wanted to join with him, they could come along. If not, he would make the trip alone. In his enthusiasm he often talked beyond his breath, his sentences running out of sound and ending in empty mouthings, emphasized by fist-pounding on the lectern and followed by a loud, slow, dramatic intake of air. This procedure never failed to daze his congregation, and he soon became known among the irreverent as 'Sucker Simpson'.

This day was no different. It is true that upon contemplation, he had been somewhat hesitant. After all, it wasn't a proper wedding. The usual procedures didn't fit, somehow. Best not be too specific. Wander around a bit and then sweep into the usual wind-up ... 'Do you, John Doe, take this woman, Jane Doe ... ' and so on. He'd done some homework. He'd talked to some acquaintances and had gathered a certain background. Below him on the floor stood these two intent little people. They were no real threat at all. He was above them, safe on his raised pulpit. He lifted his arms in front of him, with his hands face down, to quiet the gathering. Then, twisting his palms over, he reached high above his head and gazed heavenward. Sucking in a deep lungful of breath and reaching low-down for those heavy, resonant, rolling stomach tones, he began:

"Years ago, long before most of us gathered here today were born, up in our fair neighboring State of Georgia, this man and this woman first saw the light of day ..."

He talked for twenty minutes.

Sally-Anne got fidgety. The heat in the little church became unbearable, and she had no fan. She leaned toward Doobie and whispered. Reluctantly, hesitantly, he crossed to the wall and brought her a chair. She sat facing the pulpit, fanning herself with her bouquet. The visitors from Fort Myers, caught up in the verbal wanderings, didn't seem to mind the heat. They swayed from side to side with the cadence, scattering "praise be" and "Amen" as the voice from the pulpit intoned on, rising and falling hypnotically.

Then the Revered Simpson verbally stubbed his toe!

He had painted a splendid picture of the sinning of Man, sweeping from the unfortunate transgression in the Garden down through the complicated vicissitudes of the Old Testament, jumping from the plagues of Egypt to the plagues of the Middle Ages with but the merest pause, probing the outskirts of the First World War, about which he knew absolutely nothing, and swooping grandly into the near Armageddon of the just-past global conflict. His voice was getting edgy. His fist was red from pounding the lectern and was beginning to swell. It was time now to return to the present and get on with the business of this ceremony.

"... And so it was," he boomed hoarsely, "that these two people before me, years ago, with the thoughtlessness of their youth, decided to raise a family without the sanction of the Church or the Blessing of the Almighty."

This statement was too much for Sally. She sprang to her feet and raised a shaking hand toward the minister.

"No!" she cried. "No sech thing! Thet ain't the way it wuz!"

Elvira, in her front-row seat, was horrified.

"Mama! No! No!"

"Elviry, yes! It's gotta be tol' right! Heah, in God's Home, it's gotta be tol' right. Tweren't nobody theah sep' Doobie an' me, nohow, so's only him an' me knows." She turned again to the Minister, standing silently behind the lectern, stunned, with his mouth hanging open. "With all my respec's, Reverend, an' hopin' yo' won't feel put out none, suh, but Doobie an' me, we ain't heah to git the blessin' o' the Almighty. We's already got the blessin' o' the Almighty. Fum the very fust, we's had the blessin' o' the Almighty. We's heah to git the proper gov'ment paper, license or wutevah tis called, so's ouah joinin' will be legal under the law, an' then, maybe these kids'll hush up!" She leaned toward the pulpit and her voice dropped to a confidential note. "They'se the ones whut am causin' all the ruckus. Doobie an' me, we's satisfied. We's been satisfied fum de fust. With yo' permission, suh, I'se gonna tell the folks how it wuz."

Without waiting for a reply, she turned her chair and sat back down, spread her dress until the pleats and bows were just so, reached up and took off her big hat to use as a fan, and searched around in her mind for a place to start.

"'Course, Reverend Simpson, he's right! Way back then, we wuz young. 'Course we wuz. Back then, we ain't had no time yet to live much." The congregation had settled down and was listening closely. "This Sally an' Doobie, squattin' in front o' you now, yo' cain't see airy trace o' them two younguns. Under des wrinkles an' snowy haids, yo' won't fin' a smidgeon. We's jest two skinny ol' folks now, neah done. Yo' won't see nuthin' else. But we kin! We kin see, jes' laik it wuz yestiddy!" She paused a second and her eyes were distant and half closed. "I kin 'member when Doobie an' me, we done hung back an' let that ole truck drive off wid all dem workers, takin' 'em back home. It was a clear, sunny afternoon, no clouds nowhere, an' Doobie he reached out an' took my han' ... "

●

... The day had been hot and the gladiola fields were thick with dust. The field hands, happy that the day's work was finished, were clumped together, laughing and joking, climbing onto the jitney truck that would carry them back to their quarters. Doobie hung back. Since he was holding Sally's hand, she hung back also.

"Y'all betta climb on up heah. We ain't waitin' fer y'all." Someone called out. Another voice answered ... "Leave 'em be. They's sparkin'" ... and the truck pulled away.

They were in no hurry. They wandered between the rows of flower spikes, kicking at the loose dust, peeking sideways at each other, strangely embarrassed, working their way slowly cross-field to the row of brush and uncleared tangle that bordered the edge. Tall grasses nodded fuzzy yellowish plumes in the gentle breeze, and an occasional long-needle pine rose majestically toward the sky. A red-shouldered hawk wheeled high and cried its piercing screech as it hunted its late afternoon meal. Mockingbirds darted back and forth and a bluejay sounded a warning as they drew near the brake. Doobie parted the grass and Sally-Anne crept forward, toward the shade and protection of a nearby pine. The ground, thickly strewn with needles, was soft and cool, and the girl sighed in pleasure as she sank to her knees to rest. Doobie knelt beside her. For a long time they were content. They held each other but didn't talk, just rested and absorbed the silence, the freedom of being alone, the rustling of the pine needles in the breeze, the shafting afternoon sun that cut through the overhead branches here and there and formed little puddles of light on the ground.

Doobie pulled Sally closer and she rested her head on his shoulder. She looked upward and pointed.

"Look, Doobie. Jes' like a church! A big ole church. them branches goin' up an' up an' all peaky. An' the sun shining down in them streaks. Ain't it beautiful? Look, Doobie. Yo' ain't seein'.'"

"I wants ya to marry me." He looked steadily into her eyes. "I wants us to git wedded."

Sally was confused. She smiled and lowered her eyes.

"Sho! Some time. Sho! I'd laik thet." She lifted her eyes to his and they locked there.

"Not no sometime. Now! I wants to wed up now!"

"Now? Right heah?"

"Yeah. Now. Right heah. Can't be no bettah time an' can't be no bettah place."

She pulled back slightly.

"I'se gotta think ... "

"What's ta think? I loves ya, Sally, an' I wants to be yo' man. An' I thinks ya loves me, too. Don' ya? Don' ya? Huh?"

She was frightened now and felt alone and undecided. She resisted the tugging on her hands.

"Don' ya?"

"Yes, Doobie. I loves ya. Have ever since I fust laid eyes on ya. But somehow, I don' know. Seems laik theah'd be somebody to ast. We gotta ast somebody."

He wrapped his arms around her and swayed side to side in a lulling entreaty.

"Chile, chile. 'Course we gotta ast somebody. Yo' mammy ain't heah, an' my mammy ain't heah, but God is. We kin ast Him."

Sally's face lit from within and she beamed at this earnest young man kneeling before her. Yes! Of course! She would ask God. They did not need a man-made church. Here, under the arching pine boughs was a God-made Church, and she would ask Him! She pulled Doobie toward her and together they adjusted themselves until they were kneeling side by side. She took his hand in both of hers and looked straight upward, to where the high branches came together. She started to speak in a voice so low Doobie could barely hear her.

"Mistah God, Suh ... I'se Sally, an' this be's Doobie. We wants to get wed. We wants to vow up, jes' like fancy folks do in church. Only we ain't got us no church. We can't afford none. On whut we'uns make in dem flowah fiel's, takes all thet to jes' feed us. So, heah we is, under dis beautiful tree, an' we knows You is heah, too, so we is astin' You to please heah our vowin'." She paused. The pine tree sighed softly in the breeze and a shaft of sunlight shown briefly through the moving boughs and bathed Doobie's face in a golden glow. It was the sign she was expecting. God had heard and He approved. In simple faith, she continued.

"I loves Doobie, an' I'll be his wife an' I'll be true an' hones' an' love him til I'se daid. Twon't be nary man 'ceptin' him to evah tech me, evah. Jes' him an' me, and if You, God, is pleased, maybe we'll git us some chilluns." ...

●

Slowly and with obvious effort, Sally returned to the present. The congregation was nodding and murmuring in sympathy and understanding.

"An' I'se been true to them vows," Sally continued, "from thet day til this." She smiled, nodding. "We was Holy wed in the eyes o' God and' it was bindin' tight on both o' us. Cain't no church do no bettah." She took a deep breath and stood up. Turning toward the pulpit, with quiet dignity, she nodded to Reverend Simpson.

"I jes' wanted to explain, Reverend, thet Doobie an' me, we ain't been livin' in sin all these yeahs. In our eyes, an' blessed by the Almighty, we's been tight wed, same as if'n wed by a church. 'Course, seems laik the gov'ment don't accep' thet an' says we gotta sign somethin', so's our chilluns will be legal. Well, if'n we's gotta, we's gotta, an' pardonin' my interruptin', Suh, you kin now git on with all thet legal business."

●

This would be their final walk! Neither wanted to mention it, but neither could think of anything else. Jerry parked the old truck on the Captiva side of the bridge and helped her down.

"Let's walk the beach to Maude's old tree." Didi said, trying her best to sound spritely, but with little success. "Shall we?"

334

Jerry was feeling depressed.

"Sure. We can sit there for awhile, but I thought we could go all the way to the end."

"Almost two miles?"

"We have time, don't we? I thought you said you were all packed."

Didi nodded her head.

"I am. All but the small last-minute things. I'll stuff those in somewhere tomorrow morning. You'll pick me up, won't you?"

"Of course. Gosh, I hate all this going-away stuff. What will I do while you're gone!" His face was long and morose.

"Same as I'll do. Stay busy, keep out of trouble and remember." She reached over and took his hand. "You know, actually I'm the one who should worry. I'm coming back. I already know that. Daddy has taken the old McClain house again for all next winter. So I'll be back. By the middle of October. What we don't know is about you."

They were strolling along the water's edge, letting lacy little waves rush in and cover their feet. Holding fast to Jerry's hand, Didi was slowly twisting back and forth, occasionally scuffing water out toward the open Gulf.

"You already know about me." Jerry picked up a shell and skimmed it across the water. "I told you I would stay on the island if you'd come back. If you are coming back, then I'll be here."

They sat on Maude's fallen pine, but conversation was stilted. They were too filled with emotion to talk easily. Both were embarrassed by the silences.

Didi arose abruptly.

"Let's go. Do you want to stroll along, or is there something you want to show me?"

"I've got a surprise. One last surprise for my only girl." He put his arm around her waist and kissed her ... a long, gentle, deeply-felt kiss. Didi let her head rest on his chest.

"Jerry." She looked up into his face and spoke softly through a shy smile. "I think I am in love with you. I don't know for sure. If I'm not, I could be. We've had some wonderful times and mostly it's been because you've been here with me." Her smile disappeared and a serious expression replaced it. "I want another winter. I want to be sure. I know you love me. At least, I know you think you do. But I need more time, we both do, before we make any promises. Do you understand what I'm saying?"

Slowly he nodded.

"Can you agree to our agreeing to being Best Friends ... for now, and this time next year, we'll know for sure?"

Again, he nodded slowly.

"In that case," her smile was radiant, "bend down here and let me kiss you. And then let's go find your surprise."

Slowly they wandered along the sandy ridge where the island continued for several miles. Little more than a finger of sand and shell, this thin stretch of Captiva thrust up from the Gulf floor some three to four feet above the high tide line and extended southward parallel to the northern tip of Sanibel. Blind Pass separated the two islands.

Spreading in all directions on top of the sandy dune formation railroad vine flourished. Pale blue blossoms covered the fleshy runners anchored firmly in the sand by hair-like feeder roots. Undaunted by the broiling heat or the absence of regular moisture, the vines crisscrossed the sand in all directions, and Didi found it difficult to walk. Reaching out for Jerry's support, she smiled up at him.

"I've never been down here before. I don't know why. I just never have."

As he moved along beside her Jerry shook his head.

"Me neither," he said inelegantly.

"What made you decide to come this time?"

"Aunt Maude. She said we should see the birds near the end, that it was a spectacular sight, and only happened at the end of June, and that we shouldn't miss it. It's the terns. The Least Terns. Those are the smallest, you know, the little white bird with a black cap and a yellow bill. Real small."

Didi looked doubtful.

"What are we going to see? What do we look for?"

"Aunt Maude says that they're nesting all over this sand spit. By now the babies will be hatching. Lots and lots of babies and hundreds of grown birds. Usually only the last two weeks in June."

Didi raised her hand to shade her eyes from the penetrating afternoon sun beaming in from her right.

"I don't see ... oh, there! Way up ahead. It looks like clouds sailing around. You know, I think those are birds. Must be thousands. Let's hurry."

The railroad vine had given way and they soon found themselves on clear open sand. The birds were nearer, some hovering overhead. Didi was about to break into a run when a shout from Jerry stopped her.

"Watch out! You'll step on it!"

"What? Where?"

"Down there." Jerry pointed to a small depression behind a bleached horse conch. Didi leaned down, and peered.

"Oh, my goodness! Oh, my goodness! It's a baby bird. A teeny, fuzzy little baby bird. All alone. No, over there is another. They must be together. I'm going to pick it up."

"No! Don't touch it. Aunt Maude was specific about that. If we handle any, the parents are liable to shun it and it'll die. Don't touch 'em. But look around carefully."

Now that they'd seen two and knew what to look for, suddenly they could spot baby birds all about. Tiny balls of fluff, yellowish tan with a splashing of brown, they blended perfectly with the sand. Didi and Jerry carefully moved deeper into the nesting area. The chattering of the parent birds took on a collective shrill note as they focused on the intruders as the enemy. They began to dive at the youngsters.

"Oh, dear," Didi cried, ducking her head to one side as a tern darted past. "They're attacking us." She didn't know whether to be scared or fascinated. "I've never been attacked by birds before. Watch out, there's one after you."

Zoom! The tiny creature zipped by, just missing Jerry's eyes. It then flew in a wide circle, positioned itself high up, aligned itself exactly right, hovered for a moment, then dived again for his eyes, emitting a shrill, high-pitched chatter. With birds suddenly streaking at them from all sides Jerry became apprehensive that Did might be struck. Waving his arms to scare off the attackers, he tugged at her dress.

"This could be dangerous. Let's back off until they quiet down and watch 'em for a bit. Be careful where you put your feet."

There were, indeed, thousands of birds. And thousands of chicks. The nests, mere scooped-out depressions in the hot sand, were side by side and reached in all directions. The usual depression contained two chicks. How the parents knew, among all those thousand babies, which two chicks were their own, was an unanswered secret of nature ... but there were no dead babies lying about. The parent birds would fly off across the open Gulf until they found fish feeding on small fry on the surface. Then, plummeting down and hitting the water with a splash, they would snatch the tiny transparent fish in their beaks, beat their wings frantically to regain height and return to feed their young the tiny morsel.

Crouched side by side, Didi and Jerry watched fascinated. The afternoon wore on and the sun was setting when Jerry finally stood up and stretched. He reached a hand toward Didi.

"Come on. We gotta get back. It's a long hike to the truck. Aunt Maude will be waiting supper."

Didi rose reluctantly. She hated to let go.

"You're right. We gotta leave, I suppose. Only we're not having supper at my place, don't you remember? Aunt Agnes is having everyone at your place. Hasn't this been exciting? What a wonderful last day, Jerry. I'll never forget it. Never!"

Holding hands, they walked down to the Gulf edge and headed back to the bridge.

●

The following day, July 1st, the two young people were bathed in gloom. The brilliance of the morning went by unnoticed and they sagged about their chores in a desultory fashion.

Aunt Maude was helping Didi pack the few last minute things.

"Why didn't you ask Jerry over? You two could have enjoyed a last swim before the mailboat and I could have packed these things."

"No, Aunt Maude. It's better this way. Yesterday was lovely and I enjoyed all of it. But there were strange tense moments. I didn't like those at all." She glanced up at the older woman. "Aunt Maude, how is it that two people can be so close and yet so far apart? There were times yesterday when Jerry and I had nothing, absolutely nothing, to say to each other. And we've been so close. Isn't that strange?"

Maude smiled gently as she folded a pongee shirtwaist and laid it on top of the other garments in the suitcase.

"No, Didi. Not strange at all. How could it possibly be any other way? As long as something visible was happening, you both shared it and talked easily. But then, once it had passed, the invisible, the deep feelings of facing separation that you both dread, that settled in again and took over. You couldn't find anything to say because you were too caught up in your own sadness at being abandoned, at being left alone. Everybody hates goodbyes."

"Yes ... " Didi agreed. "I hate goodbyes! And this one's the worst in my life. Oh, don't pack that little box, please. Leave it on top of the suitcase. It's a little present for Jerry."

Down at Agnes' house, it was the same gloom. Agnes and Cora were busy in the kitchen but Jerry was wandering in and out.

"Honestly, Cora" Agnes pointed a finger after Jerry as he disappeared again up the stairs to his room. "I understand his agitation but I wish he'd stop wandering about. I asked him why he didn't go on over to Didi's and visit or go in the Gulf for a swim, but he muttered something about awkward moments in their walk yesterday, and added ` if she really wanted me around she would have asked me' or some such remark."

"I know," Cora replied. "I know. But there wasn't anything awkward last evening when he gave her that lovely little traveling clock as a going-away present. She was so pleased. Did you see her face, Ag? Just bubbling with delight! Aren't they cute?"

Agnes leaned against the sink, and her eyes grew dreamy.

"Yes, they're cute. Will and I were cute, too. I remember it like it was yesterday." She sighed, as she wiped her hands on her apron. "Young love can be so painful!"

●

As the mailboat came around the end of Buck Key and headed for the post office landing, Jerry and Didi were just climbing down from the old truck and they walked slowly out onto the dock and sat on opposite pilings. Jerry caught Captain Bob's bowline and half-hitched it snug to the end of the loading ramp. He turned back to Didi.

"Will you write?"

"Will you answer?"

They both said "Sure" at the same time and giggled together self-consciously.

There were no incoming packages. Bertha brought out the few letters being mailed and took the small bundle of incoming mail, so Captain Bob was soon ready to leave. He motioned Didi aboard.

Crossing to Jerry, she took his hand and looked deep into his eyes.

"This is for you, but don't open it until I'm out of sight." She pressed a little box into his hand. "Promise?"

He nodded and softly kissed her goodbye. He sat back down on the piling and watched the mailboat chug down the channel and off across the open bay. Didi stood in the stern, one hand held high above her head, as the boat grew smaller and smaller and finally disappeared around the end of Buck Key.

No one else was on the dock. Jerry sat for some time, trying to quiet his emotions. Finally he untied the little box and opened it. Inside, lying on a soft cushion of raw cotton, was Didi's golden olive shell. She'd had a hole drilled in the end and a thin gold link chain threaded through it. Under the shell was a note ... 'remember the tradition' ... His breath caught and a lump formed in his throat. He remembered. Gazing off into the distance, over the expanse of quiet water, he heard again her excited voice ... 'a golden olive is special. The natives exchange them just before leaving on a trip. They carry a message. They say wait for me. I'll be back. I love you'.

He cleared his throat loudly and glanced around. He was alone. He slipped the chain over his head and gently stroked the shell as it rested on his chest just below his throat.

22
July

Roy Coggins was convulsed! He stood just inside the screened doorway, arms braced on opposite jambs, leaning forward into Agnes' porch, and hooted with laughter.

"Oh, migod! He's gone shark fishing with Gustave Kroen? I went once. Never again! Took several months for my kidneys to recover. When Jerry gets back, Mis' Trumbull, better bring out all your cushions. He's gonna be sore." He straightened up and turned to leave. "Please tell him I stopped by, won'tcha? We need him down at the dock." He continued to chortle as he left.

"Yes, I will. I'll be glad to. Roy, wait a minute, please. Do you think it's safe? I've been kind of worried."

Roy turned around.

"Oh, it's safe enough. Anyway, I guess it is. The only real danger is that weird boat might turn over. But Jerry swims like a fish, so even then, he'd get in to shore. Yeah. It's safe. Safe as any of the other things we do down here, I suppose. Only he'll be shook up pretty bad when he gets back." Roy went on down the path to his truck, still laughing.

Later that afternoon, when Jerry got back, he was, indeed, 'shook up'. His legs threatened to cramp and his backbone felt tied in knots. He hobbled around the screened porch, trying to find some comfort.

"Sit down there, Jerry." His aunt pulled out a wicker rocker and fluffed a pillow. "Sit and rock and tell us what happened." Both Cora and Maude nodded in agreement.

"I couldn't. I can't. Thanks a lot, Aunt Ag, but I'll stand up for a bit longer. My bottom is pounded all out of shape. If it didn't hurt so much it'd be funny. I don't know much about boats, but that thing is ridiculous. Gustave just took sheets of plywood and bent 'em and nailed 'em together and stuck a motor out the end, and called it a boat. A big engine, too! Actually, what he made is a sled, a water sled. No keel at all! And it goes like the wind. When he tries to turn a corner it skids sideways in a big circle, throwing water everywhere, and threatens to turn over. I just sat there frozen, scared to death the thing would tip. He didn't seem to notice and kept adding speed and adding speed and we rushed along slapping the wave tops, bump, bump, bump and I was all scrunched up in a little ball in the prow and all that bumping and banging smashed against my tail bone. It's so sore I can't touch it. I think it's broke!" He ran out of breath.

"Why did you go? When he asked you to go with him, why didn't you just say no?"

"Oh, I wanted to go. Before we shot away from his little dock I didn't know all this stuff, and by the time I found out we were in the open bay off Redfish. I was stuck!"

"Oh, you poor dear." Cora was all sympathy and leaned forward in her chair, preparing to rise and administer. "I'll run over to my place and get some liniment."

"No thanks, Aunt Cora. Liniment won't help. I think it's broke. How do you splint up a bone down there?"

In spite of themselves, the three women chuckled, Maude the loudest.

"Oh, come now, Jerry. If your spine was split you'd most likely be paralyzed. You'd be in such agony you couldn't move. Here!" She took the chair and put two extra cushions in it, pushing them high against opposite sides. "Here. Squat on these and they'll keep your bumpo high enough to prevent pressure where you're sore. You've bruised yourself. That's all. But go on, tell us what happened. Did you catch any shark?"

"Yeah. We caught three. Two small ones and one large one. That was as weird as the boat. We got up to Redfish and Gustave headed out into the tide which was coming in. He cut his motor to idle and took a huge hook, biggest I've ever seen, and he wired a bunch of mullet to it. He sliced the mullet up real good so blood oozed out all over. Then he tied the chain on the hook to a half-inch rope that was tied to a big truck innertube and that was tied to a cleat on the prow of the boat. Then he threw everything overboard. The hook and mullet sank out of sight to the bottom, and the innertube floated, like a tremendous bobber. He told me to draw in the excess rope and curl it in the boat. Then we drifted out along with the tide and waited." He stopped, inching around in his chair, grimacing with discomfort.

"Go on! What happened?"

"Well, for awhile, nothing. Then, on the third drift, on the bay side of the pass, the innertube came alive and bounced all around and the curled rope at my feet peeled out and Gustave inches forward and takes hold of the rope and yells 'come on' to me and we both tug and haul and the innertube acts like a reel drag and slows down the shark and pretty soon we can haul it in to the side of the boat. Gustave pounded it on the nose several hefty bangs with a billy and stunned it. Then he reached into a little box under his seat, took out a pistol and shot that shark point-blank. Shot it in each eye! It shuddered a couple of times, and a twitching started at the head and quivered along its body to its tail and then it went limp. It was dead. Then we hauled the thing into the boat. There it was, under our feet!"

"Ooooh, I'm glad I wasn't there." Cora gave a little shiver of disgust. "I hate things like that. The poor fish. Did you later push it overboard?"

"Oh, no. Mr Kroen was after shark as fertilizer for his banana grove. He chops 'em up into four to six inch squares and plants 'em around his banana stalks. Says it's the best fertilizer. Something about the oil in the flesh. He sure has great bananas, so it must work."

Maude was intent on the story.

"You say you got two small ones? How small?"

"About five feet long."

"What about the large one?"

"That was about nine feet. It was big. At least big for that small boat. When it took the mullet bait there was no kidding. That shark meant business and it musta been hungry. It struck hard and the innertube stayed under the surface and pulled all out of shape, into a large oval. Gustave yelled at me ... "we won't pull this one in. Too big! Hold on. We're going for a ride" ... and we did! That shark headed out the pass for the open Gulf, towing us behind, and we just sat there and held on. I was scared stiff! After awhile the innertube popped up, still an oval, and now we could see the shark just below the surface and still pulling strong."

"What did you do? Pull it in hand over hand when it got tired?"

"Yeah. Hand over hand. Several times. As it got near the boat, it came alive and rushed off and the rope ripped out again. Had'a be careful not to hold on or your hands'd get burned. Then, later on, it got real tired and we could pull it in alongside the boat. Mr Kroen shot it like the others and killed it. We didn't try to haul this one into the boat--the other two were taking up all the space. We lashed it to the side and bounced on home. It was fun, I suppose. Interesting. Once, that is. Wouldn't want to do it again. but it was fun. Did anything happen here while I was gone?"

Aunt Ag shook her head.

"Just the usual summer day. Oh, I forgot. Roy stopped by and asked you to see him when you can. Something about Murph and Frank Culpepper needing help with that dredge business they're working on."

"Golly. Things are piling up. I thought when all the tourists went home everything was supposed to quiet down. We're busier now than in the winter. Ida is after me to help with her yard work. Tomorrow morning, after Aunt Maude and I finish tending the lime grove, I promised you, Aunt Cora we'd hunt heart shells. And you need driftwood, don't you?" He looked at her.

"Well, all that's not so pressing, actually." Cora put aside the fronds she was ripping and glanced at Maude. "Maybe Maude will go along to the beach with me, and you can run down to see Roy."

Maude reached her hands over her head and yawned.

"It's all a trap. No different than anywhere else, really." She was feeling old and discouraged. Here it was, another hot, sticky summer, bugs and rain, stretching ahead through August and September. They were the nasty months. Humidity would shoot up. Heavy dews at night would seep through the screening, leaving blankets and sheets damp. Her hair, her one vanity, would droop lankly and little tendrils would be glued to the back of her neck. She hated that. There was no end to it all. Life was a treadmill. She voiced her thought.

"It's all just a treadmill! Over and over. Round and round we go. Those winter people have the idea we just loaf the nine months they're not here ... loaf and swim and fish and move our listless heads slowly to one side so the falling coconuts won't hit us. They've no idea how we have to scrounge and skimp ... how we have to push on, in the most unpleasant conditions imaginable, sweat pouring down our faces from dawn to dusk, just to make a few pennies. They float in with their big cars and their fat pocketbooks in their stupid frenzy to amuse themselves and they think our life is just as easy, just as empty as theirs ... and they never know that, behind the scenes ..." She paused and stared distantly at the floor.

Cora, thrusting a pin into the base of a thick frond and ripping it along toward the tip, prodded the conversation.

"Behind the scenes? What do you mean ... behind the scenes?"

Maude dragged herself up from her sink of depression and rolled a caustic eye at her friend.

"Behind the scenes, Cora, means just that ... behind the scenes. It's self-explanatory! What's so difficult about that?"

"Well, you don't have to bite my head off! I was just commenting. I was just trying to be nice and join in the conversation. I don't really care at all, if you want to know the truth, about anything behind your scenes, or in front of them, for that matter. I was just ... "

"Oh, for heaven's sake!" Maude shrugged with irritation. "Leave it be! I'm sorry! I apologize! I didn't mean to snap! There!" She waved a listless hand in Jerry's direction. "I'll hunt shells with Cora. You plan on running down to the dock."

"That's okay." Jerry had hoisted himself up from his mound of cushions and was leaning on the work table, flexing his legs. "We can squeeze it all in. I can see Roy and the others when I meet the mailboat at noon. What kind of liniment do you have, Aunt Cora? Maybe we should try some. This feels pretty miserable."

The following noon, after he'd met the mailboat and put the few incoming packages on his truck, Jerry drove the sandy lane along the bay to Ida's store and turned right to Murph's dock. He found both Murph and Frank up to their hips in the mud with shells pouring around their legs from the dredge exhaust pipe and tussling with an upright piling. Frank settled back against the old dock as Jerry came up.

"Great," Frank called. "We were hoping you'd show up. Oh," he laughed, "don't look scared. We aren't going to ask you to jump in here and help us with this."

343

The dredge motor was wheezing and clanking, and old Mr. Sampson was leaning out of the wheelhouse window, gesturing to his young son Dick who was up to his neck in bay water and inching still further out toward the equipment.

"Hey, Dicky, back off now," the old man called. "You're too close to the intake pipe. Back away. Wanna get sucked off yer feet? I keep warnin' you an' warnin' you an' one of these days yer gonna get dragged down by that there thing an' drown. Go on, back off, son."

Frank watched this situation and winked at Jerry.

"There's actually no problem. It's Mr. Sampson's way of impressing us how dangerous the job is. He's hoping for a generous tip. Pipe's too small anyway and hardly has enough suction to pick up a dead fish. Jerry, we were hoping, Murph and I, that we could talk you into tying up your boat here for the next several weeks. It's smaller than either of ours, and it would come in handy for measuring where we set piling. We've decided to stagger 'em off the dock, some far enough out for really large yachts and others closer in. Would you mind?"

"'Course not. I'll bring it by later this afternoon. Only thing is, with me down there by the bridge and it up here with you, you'll have to keep your eye on it if it rains. I wouldn't want it to fill up and sink."

Frank nodded and smiled in agreement.

"Sure. I'll keep it bailed. Don't worry about that. I've got mine here, too. Can empty both at once."

Jerry glanced around at the work site, at the piling stacked along the shore, and the planking scattered about.

"How long before you're done?" he asked.

Frank raised his eyebrows.

"Ye gods, we've only just begun. The dredging is the smallest part of the whole thing, you know. That old scow and its anchor ropes, and the discharge pipeline with all the extension sections laying about, all that takes up most of our space, and until Mr. Sampson winds up his work and clears out of here, we can't set the piling for the boats or put down the new dock stringers. If we could run all of that work at the same time, we'd be mostly done in another week or so. As it is, there's still a week of dredging ... the channel leading in to the gas pumps has to be widened and deepened. It'll be another month or so, maybe middle of September, before we're done." He shook his head slowly from side to side, and smiled ruefully. "Seems to always be the case, down here. If you plan a job to be done in a month, it'll take two. Always!"

Jerry nodded. Pearlie had appeared at the end of the dock and he waved to her.

"Mess, ain't it?" she yelled.

"Yeah," he yelled back. Then, to Frank. "I agree. Things aren't very efficient down here. If you want efficiency you should stay in New York." He headed back to his truck, and called over his shoulder.

"'Course, they don't have our beaches ... or the fish ... or the shells ... "

Captain Bob tossed the old gunnysack onto the dock and then stepped up from the mailboat and squatted beside it. He motioned Jerry over.

"Ever seen a heap of scallops like this? He opened the sack and scooped out a handful of the colorful shells. "Pretty, ain't they?"

Jerry nodded, bending over and taking one in his hand.

"Sure, I've seen 'em before. But not in a bunch like this. Singles, mixed in with other shells."

"Matilda Crunch asked me to get her a sackful from the fish market in town." Captain Bob explained, sinking back on his heels. "They're late this year. Usually come along toward the end of July. When the weather's sweltering like it's been and the water up the river and in the sound gets too hot, they hang back in the deeper, cooler areas. Then, all that rain last week cooled the inland water somewhat and now they're thick as fleas all over. Rufus Roe, who runs the market ... " He glanced up and his eyes were sparkly. He slapped his thigh and laughed out loud. "Ain't that good? Rufus Roe running a fish market! Get it! Roe ... fish market." He laughed on and Jerry laughed with him. "Rufus told me that the netters are bringing in so many he had to hire two extra hands to shuck 'em all. Messy job, shucking 'em, and the edges can slice your hands if you don't hold 'em just right." He shook his head decisively. "Shucking bay scallops is not for me! Too fussy! All folks is after, you know, is that little white muscle inside. You hold it top up," he demonstrated with one of the shells still held together by a strip of golden membrane. "This side, with all the spotty colors, is the top and the white half is the bottom. You can slip a knife carefully between the two halves and sort of slide it along the bottom shell, reaching for the muscle that's holding it firm together. When you slice through that muscle, it pops apart. Like opening an oyster."

Jerry turned a shell over in his hand.

"They sure are pretty," he said. "All mottled brown and gold with that little reddish mark here and there. Must be some reason for the colors."

Captain Bob nodded.

"Camouflage" he commented. "They move in from deeper water and feed in the grass flats where it's shallow. Layin' there among the long, skinny turtle grass and the filmy manatee grass waving back and forth, they blend in with the sandy bottom and look like little spots of sunlight. They migrate, you know. They're not like oysters that stay attached to rocks and coral. Scallops move all about." He carefuₗₗᵧ closed the two parts. "Look how tight it fits together. When the shell's alive there's a thin brownish tissue lining the insides of the bottom part and each of these grooves all around has a little blue eye peering out. They lay there on the bottom, in among the grass, with their shells slightly open so that the water washes in and out, which is how they feed. And when they see something that startles 'em, they snap shut their shell so quick that the force of the water rushing out scoots 'em back in the opposite direction. Most of the time, they escape. Wonderful, isn't it?"

Amanda Johnson was talking to Matilda Crunch at the Shell Shop when Jerry drove up to deliver the sack of scallops. She clapped her hands and beamed with joy.

"They're back! Finally, they're back! I've been waiting all summer. They're so late I thought they'd never return." She turned toward Jerry and wrapped her enthusiasm around him like a cape. "Let's go out and get some. We can use your boat. Sometime soon. On a Sunday when you have time. Wouldn't that be fun?"

Jerry agreed instantly.

"How long will they stay in the bay?" he asked.

Amanda was fingering the shells, and she talked on enthusiastically.

"Never can tell. Nobody knows how long they've already been here. Hard to say how long they'll stay. They're not on this side, you know. They're over on the other side of the sound. In all that thick grass over there, stretching for miles along Pine Island. We should go this Sunday. Maybe Matilda'll lend us some croker sacks like this one."

Matilda nodded.

"You can have all the sacks you want, if you'll give me the shells once you've shucked 'em."

Frank and Jean, later hearing Jerry discussing this venture with Pearlie out on the dock, decided to gas up their boat and go along. Early that Sunday morning, just as the sun peeped over the horizon, the four met at the Culpepper's dock and began loading the two small boats. As with any all-day water trip, the equipment was unbelievable. There had to be oars, in case a motor gave out; water, in case either or both boats became marooned; anchors and long ropes; cans of extra gas; jars for captured live specimens; rain proof containers packed with food; first aid supplies, in case someone got stuck with a fishhook or stepped on a stingaree; 6-12 oil mixed with citronella as mosquito repellant; cushions that doubled as life preservers; snorkeling tubes and goggles; the inevitable cameras; assorted and bulky fishing gear; spare parts boxes for motors and reels; and, of course, ditty bags for each person, the small, formless bags into which was stuffed a solution for any eventuality, according to past experience with discomforts on the open water far from home ... extra hats, rain coats, old gloves for shucking oysters, oil for suntanning, cigarettes, matches, chewing gum, bath towels, sun glasses, and little bundles of cotton mesh to be worn over the head and under the hat in case the wind died down and bugs swarmed. Frank additionally carried a large dip net, as he was planning on dragging it slowly through the grass beds for dwarf seahorses. He had set up a seawater aquarium on his porch and wanted to experiment with raising these tiny creatures.

Over coffee and sweet buns, after the boats were loaded, they planned the day.

"Let's just meander. I love that." Jean was alive with anticipation and eager to be off. "I love to drift along in the soft early sunlight, before the heat of the day sets in and not think about anything ... just feeling alive and peaceful."

Amanda nodded solemnly.

"Yes," she added. "That and the glorious feeling that you're off away from everything else. Nobody knows where you are or where you're going. They can't reach you. You're by yourself, under the blue sky and the fluffy white clouds, with just the seagulls and the stretching water ... heaven! It's just heaven!" Her fawn's eyes glanced quickly around the table, suddenly shy over having exposed her private thoughts.

"I want to stop on that long mudflat just back of Buck Key and hunt for Chinese alphabets. Maybe we can find a few live ones and bring 'em back for your aquarium." Jean reached out and patted Frank's hand as she rambled on. "And a few crown conchs, little baby ones. Then, as we head across the sound we can drift over the grass beds and catch pinfish. Wouldn't that be fun?"

Frank got up quickly and headed for the refrigerator.

"Good thing you mentioned pinfish. I'd forgotten to load the chicken gizzards. Did you bring any, Jerry?"

"No. I'm sorry."

"That's okay. I have plenty. We'll keep the boats close enough to share. Not too close. Not on top of each other, but close enough to talk back and forth. And we can share the gizzards."

"And I've brought this." Amanda held aloft an odd-shaped wire with a swivel and hook at one end and a loop at the other.

The other three stared in amazement.

"What is that?" Jean asked.

Amanda gave a soft, low toned laugh.

"It's my sniggler."

"What's it for? What do you do with it?"

"It's for eels. I'll bait the hook with a small piece of shrimp ... there'll be lots of glass shrimp over on the grass flats and I'll catch one and break off its head and the body will ooze and eels love that flavor. Then I'll push the wire down their holes and when they bite, I'll pull 'em out."

"And you'll keep 'em far, far away from me. Ugh!" Jean shivered in horror. "If you so much as touch me with one, I'll drown you on the spot! That's not a threat... that's a promise. Nasty, snakey things!"

Frank was fascinated.

"Where did you learn about that? What do you do with them?"

"I learned about this up in Carolina, in the back bays inside Cape Hatteras. Folks up there clam and eel all the time. What do I do with them? I stuff 'em into my sack and bring 'em home. Then I skin 'em and fry 'em in deep fat, lots of spice. Wonderful. Oh my ... I can taste 'em now." She smacked her lips in anticipation.

"Don't they bite you?" Jean was interested in spite of herself.

"Oh, I slice off the heads soon as I catch them. I always carry a sharp knife."

"Your juker, I suppose," Frank interjected, looking at Amanda sideways and grinning.

"My what"

"Juker. All the hoodlums in New York carry stubby knives," Frank went on. "They're pointed and razor-sharp. The kids wander around in gangs and jab unsuspecting people in the butt and thighs. They think it's fun, juking."

Amanda looked doubtful.

"I don't know anything about that. Why would anyone want ...

"Hey. Come on." Jerry was getting impatient. "Let's go. The tide's way out and that's perfect for the mudflats. They're lying out there, just waiting for us to stomp around on 'em."

The two boats floated through the low water on out into the channel and moved slowly past Murph's dock. They paused long enough for Frank to call in to Pearlie that they were heading across the sound for scallops and should be back by late afternoon.

"If we're not back by six o'clock, ask Murph to come for us."

Pearlie stuck her head out of the doorway and waved them off.

"You won't have no trouble. Enjoy yourselves an' bring back a mess. I'll help shuck 'em, an' we can have a scallop fry."

Jerry and Amanda had pulled a little ahead. He looked down at her feet. "Do those Keds lace up?"

Amanda nodded.

"Of course. But I won't lace 'em 'til we're at the flat. I hate shoes! Never wear 'em. But you can't stalk around mudflats barefooted. If the flat is sandy, then it's okay, but this one's mud and each step we'll sink in six inches or more. If your shoes aren't laced tight, they'll suck off. I don't want that." She grinned shyly. "Only pair I've got."

This was Jean's and Frank's first trip to a bay flat. They'd both walked the sandy beach, of course, and wandered the edge of the bay, but they'd been too busy since deciding to stay permanently on the island to indulge in the luxury of an all-day spree. Now they were set to have a really great time.

When they were broadside to the flat they swung left out of the channel and inched toward the expanse of mud. Frank's boat, slightly larger and heavier than Jerry's, grounded first, still in shallow water. Grabbing the anchor rope, he leapt overboard ... and froze! Standing stock still, his eyes widened in amazement. Then a sly grin covered his face.

"Jeanie, why don't you tilt up the motor and jump out and help me?"

She did! Anxious to show her best scalloping prowess, she put both hands on the gunwale and vaulted over. She landed flat-footed in the water, and her feet sank out of sight. She couldn't lift either one. Struggling, she lost her balance and sat in the water. To support her fall, she thrust down with both hands and they sank in over her wrists. She was trapped! Throwing back her

348

head, she screamed at the top of her lungs to the fleecy clouds high overhead " ... Millie Shapiro, I'll kill you!"

Everyone roared with laughter, and Amanda called out, between her chuckles.

"You shouldn't have jumped. If I'd known you were going to jump, I'd have warned you. You must put your feet down toe first and lean a little forward. Then the angle of your foot will help break the suction. And keep moving at a slow, steady pace. Say to yourself ` toe first ... toe first' until you get the swing of it." To demonstrate, she slid off the prow of Jerry's boat and moved in out of the shallows with no difficulty. "You'll find little mounds of sandy loam scattered about that are firmer than the mud and you can rest there without sinking." Her voice got dimmer and dimmer as she moved away. "Reach down and grab a handful of the mud and see how exciting it is."

With one hand now free, and balancing on the other, which sank further in from the extra weight, Jean followed Amanda's advice and lifted out a handful of the bay bottom. She took one look and screamed again. Hauling her hand back, she flung the mud at Frank.

"It's alive! It's full of squiggly worms. There's all kinds of moving things in there. I can feel 'em moving around my legs. Get me out of here, Frank Culpepper. Get me back into the boat. I wanna go home."

Just then Jerry, following behind Amanda, yelled at her.

"Hey, look," he called. "Look what you passed over. Right where you were walking. An alphabet! A live alphabet!"

In no time at all Jean was beside him.

"Lemme see! Oh, it's gorgeous. I want one. Where'd you find it?

"How'd you do that?" Frank wanted to know. "One minute you were stuck in the mud ... the next you were ... how'd you do that?"

Jean shrugged and grinned at him.

"Just remember, dear," she said, wiping a glob of mud from her chin, "from now on, whenever you find yourself mired down in one of life's little mudflats ... toe first. Toe first."

After an hour or so of slopping about on the flats their legs were exhausted and all four were ready to return to the boats and recuperate. Jean had her live alphabet. Amanda and Jerry were carrying live starfish and sea squirts for Frank's aquarium, and assorted sea urchins that Amanda wanted to eat later.

"This is really delicious," she commented, holding up a large urchin with its hundred spiky legs twitching in every direction. "You crack off the top half of the shell while it's still alive, and inside is a little star-shaped clump of orange-yellow jelly. I scoop it all out and wrap it in a lettuce leaf. I can't tell you how good it is."

Jean felt slightly nauseated.

"What do you do with the bottom half?"

"Oh, you have to put that in a bag or something. If you leave it on the table it'll crawl right off."

"With no top half?"

Amanda nodded, putting the urchin carefully in with the others.

Jean glanced hastily at Frank, and made a heaving motion. She felt she might vomit! Frank shook his head violently.

"Don't you dare! Don't you _dare_! Remember ... toe first."

A morning breeze had come up. Gentle and blowing in from the west, it was just strong enough to nudge them across the sound toward its eastern shore.

"Isn't this thoughtful of the boys," Amanda said as the two boats drifted along side by side. She was working on a slender reed pole with fishing line tied to it. She had a teeny fishhook, no bigger than the head of a hat pin, and was wiring it to the line.

"What boys?" Jerry wanted to know, working on his own pole.

"Up there." She pointed upward. "The boys up there. I call the Fates 'boys', you know," and she smiled bashfully. "We talk all the time. They take good care of me. Like now. If we didn't have this lovely little breeze we'd have to run our motors. So much nicer this way, don't you agree? And it's in exactly the right direction." She tied a knot and shook the little rod. Then, in an undertone, half to herself, she added, "They always take care of me. We're friends!"

The westerly breeze gently ruffled the sparkling, crystal clear water. The pinfish were hungry. Hooks were baited with slivers of chicken gizzard and flung overboard where they were slowly dragged down into the grass by small lead weights. The little pinfish struck hungrily and sailed through the air when caught, wiggling and flopping. They were grabbed by the lucky fisherman, de-hooked, and dropped into the bait wells. The hook was re-baited with more chopped gizzard, and more pinfish were yanked from the water.

"Now, this is fishing! I love this!" Jean was all smiles. Sitting among the pile of equipment and spare gas, she was grinning from ear to ear. "Come on, Frank. They'll get ahead of us. What, in heaven's name, are you doing now?" She looked at him in disbelief.

He had his cap on backwards and was busily fixing hooks to short pieces of leader wire. These in turn, were tied to twelve inches of string which ended in a float. Selecting a good-sized pinfish from the baitwell, he thrust the hook through its shoulder hump and tossed the whole thing overboard. There were a dozen or so of these bobbered, bouncy baits drifting from the boat.

"Watch, Jeanie! Watch what happens now." He bounced up and down on the cross-bar seat, like a young boy. His eyes shown with excitement and Jean felt her breath catch. He was so handsome, so tanned and looked so well. He seemed to grow younger every day.

He pointed off across the bay.

"See all those fish leaping about and flashing in the sun? Those are baby tarpon. Watch 'em go for my pinnies!" As he spoke, one of the bobbers just off the boat suddenly disappeared and then a small footlong tarpon leaped skyward. As it splashed back, another leaped. Frank crowed with delight.

"See! They jump but they can't get off. They've got nothing to pull against. Isn't that funny?"

Amanda ducked her head and muttered something under her breath.

"What?" Jerry asked.

"Nothing. Nothing at all."

"But you said something. What did you say?" He leaned toward her and spoke softly.

Just as softly, she answered back.

"I just said that I hate that. He shouldn't do it. I hate teasing. Especially something that can't tease back. He shouldn't do that. Make him stop!" She lifted pleading eyes.

Jerry didn't want a disagreement. He didn't want to criticize Frank, still releasing his floating lures and still laughing boyishly. Jerry pondered for a few seconds and then found a solution.

"Hey," he yelled. "We'd better be heading on over across the bay. We still have six miles to go and it's past noon. Amanda and I'll go first and you follow." He started his motor and took off, leaving Frank and Jean nothing to do but follow.

"That was very tactful, Jerry. Thank you." Amanda settled herself as best she could as they headed eastward at a good clip.

The tide was flood by the time they reached the far shore and the breeze had died off. The water was glass-smooth and grayish, reflecting the almost solid cloud cover.

"What did I tell you about the boys upstairs?" Amanda said gently, surveying the area. "This is perfect for scalloping. See how they take care of me. I was worried about that wind, however soft it was ... the water surface would've been riled with little waves and that distorts vision. You can't see the bottom clearly with riley water. Of course, that problem disappears once you get your head under the surface. Everything works out." She smiled at the three faces watching her, then turned her head, embarrassed by all the attention.

They dropped anchor about 150 yards from shore where the water was two feet deep, and jumped overboard. The bay bottom was sandy and they could stand. The croker sacks were passed around and tucked under belts. Snorkels and goggles were put on and amid laughter and bantering the four started off. As they separated, each to go his or her own way, Amanda called a final caution.

"Once you're under water, check how the bottom flow is moving ... which direction ... and get in front of it. I mean, you should move into the flow. If the flow is behind you and going in the same direction, the area in front of you will soon be all cloudy by the sand and debris you stir up, and you won't be able to see anything." She flopped on her stomach, her head under water and her snorkel sticking up in the air. She propelled herself along with one hand, grasping her croker sack and her sniggler in the other. Hesitantly, Jean and Frank followed suit ... and entered a strange, marvelous world. They were mesmerized, and lay side by side for a long time, faces just off the bottom and thrust deep into the undulating grass. Everywhere, on all sides, were swarms of live things. There was a sense of fright at first, as these two new 'animals' settled to the bottom, but when they remained quiet and offered no threat, in no time at all the busy life of search and devour resumed. Tiny colored fish darted in and out of the grass fingers, sometimes pursuing, sometimes being pursued. Little glass shrimp, so transparent their insides were visible, flipped by with their distinctive jerky motion. Thick, fleshy starfish, anchored by one leg to the base of stick-like gorgonia, let the tide wash over their four free legs, straining plankton from the water with their thousand minute feet. Hermit crabs dragged their purloined homes over the bottom, bumping and scraping as they moved along searching for a more advantageous location. Little volcano cones of sand spurted jets of water as clams, buried deep in the bottom, syphoned the tide through feeder tubes, and discharged the waste. A lovely pale orange flower bloomed just in front of Jean, gently waving enticing long, filmy, thin petals in the currents. Jean reached out carefully to pick it up, but when she touched it, it snapped shut and withdrew from sight. It was the questing siphon of a deeply-buried mollusk. Sea urchins and sand dollars were scattered about, and Jean watched in amazement as one dollar, paper thin, seemed to float down into the sand. Covered with soft tenuous, hairy spines in constant motion, which set up pockets of current around the sand grains, nudging them gently aside, the creature 'drifted' into the bay bottom and disappeared. A banded tulip shell, abandoning the protection of one clump of turtle grass and moving toward another, drifted across her line of vision. Jean was so fascinated watching it glide along that it disappeared into the grassy jungle before she decided to reach out and capture it. The tide motion soon covered its tracks. Everywhere she looked, tiny creatures were busy with their lives. There seemed no end.

Then, all of a sudden, Jean spied a scallop. It was not far away, off to one side, slightly in front of her, lying on the bottom, one side leaning against a clump of grass at a jaunty angle. Jean had the distinct impression that it was watching her. Possibly it was. For when she reached out it jerked backward, darted high, then low, first to the right, then to the left, propelled by its special reverse thrust. Jean followed close behind and as it settled to the bottom some distance from where it started, she clamped her hand down on it and closed her fingers. She surfaced and pushed her goggles up onto her forehead, eager to share her excitement but the others were under water. She crab-walked over to Frank and poked his back. He surfaced with a gasp, startled, fearful one of the tiny underwater creatures he'd been watching had somehow grown to monster size and was attacking him. When he saw it was Jean, irritation and relief fought each other across his face.

"Don't ever <u>do</u> that! You scared me out of a year's growth. What do you want?"

"I'm sorry!" But she was too excited to be sorry. She held out her hand to show him. "Look. I've got one. Isn't it beautiful? I wanted you to see. This is what we're after. Just so you'd know." She handed him the little shell, about as big around as a quarter, and sank back under the water.

The day moved on. All four had bulging sacks by mid-afternoon and were resting against the boats, munching sandwiches and drinking water. The cloud formation had settled in and blotted out the sun, and they discussed going home.

"Before we go," Frank was rummaging in the piled-up gear in his boat, "maybe I can drag my dip net through the grass. Won't take too long to make a few swipes. Maybe I'll net a sea horse'"

Amanda was eying the sky.

"I wouldn't take too long," she admonished. "I don't like the glassy look to those clouds. And it's too still. I think a squall's building, and if it does, we'll get soaked going home."

Jean laughed out loud.

"We're already soaked!"

"Not the same thing. Not the same thing at all. We're soaked with sea water. I never heard of anyone catching cold from sea water. Rain water is something else. We'll be chilled to the bone if it squalls heavy and we're caught in the middle of the bay. The waves can get huge, too. We shouldn't play around."

"Okay," Frank nodded, "I think that makes sense. Have I time to drag a bit first?"

"Yes. I guess so. But go ahead then, and do it. We'll wait."

Jean also had an eye on the sky and had caught Amanda's apprehension.

"Frank, why don't you hold it down to two drags. No more. Then we go. It's beginning to look ugly."

He nodded and walked slowly through a large stretch of thick turtle grass, dragging the net. It quickly filled up with the long, slender, green leaves, which he drained and dumped into his boat. All four pawed through the heap. They exclaimed excitedly over every find. Starfish, pipefish, several large glass shrimp, one good-sized shiner, marginellas, several Florida bugle shells, a rose tellin, but no sea horses. After sorting the live specimens they wanted and putting them all safely away, the mound of grass was tossed back into the bay.

As Frank swung along on the second drag, Jean held out a large shrimp to Amanda.

"Here. For your sniggler. Oh dear! You never used it, did you. I'm sorry."

"That's alright," Amanda answered and timidly patted her arm. "I didn't see any likely holes. Maybe it's not done down here, or the bottom's not right. I don't know. But people do catch eels. The commercial fishermen are always bringing them in. I'll try later."

Frank returned with a second full net, and this time their luck was better and they found three of the tiny horse-faced creatures. Dwarf bay seahorses are about one inch long when full grown and eat tiny brine shrimp no bigger than dust motes. The two small seahorses were pried loose from their perches on blades of grass and put carefully in the specimen jar. Thin and about three-quarters of an inch long, they were females or half-grown babies. The other was the prize. Large and sturdy-looking, its abdomen was distended. Amanda pointed at it and clucked her tongue.

"Better leave that one ... it's a male and it's pregnant ... better leave it attached to its perch and put leaf and all into the jar. It looks ready to give birth so we don't want to bump it."

Jean looked sideways at Amanda.

"A male? Pregnant?"

Amanda nodded her head and spoke slowly.

"Right. It's a male and it's pregnant. Male seahorses give birth to the young. So do pipefish. The females deposit the eggs in the male's pouch. He fertilizes them there, externally, like fish, and carries them until they're born. Once a seahorse is born it's on its own. But a just-born pipefish will swim back into its daddy's pouch if frightened. Isn't that interesting?"

By the time they reached Murph's dock it was running on to 6 p.m. and Pearlie was edgy.

"Thank God, there you are! I was that worried as the clock ticked away. Murph's out back, ready to go in case you didn't show up. I'll run out and tell him."

"Thank him for us," Frank called, one eye on the heavens as he steadied his boat against the dock platform. "We gotta get home, Pearlie. It's blowin' up and looks nasty."

Before they could unload, the sky opened and rain plummeted down. Squall winds ripped across the bay and as far as they could see through the downpour the open water was pitching, curling whitecaps.

"Didn't that come up quick?" Jean yelled over the noise. She and Amanda were on the dock, carrying equipment into the house as Frank and Jerry handed it up. The two little boats began to pitch and toss and it was difficult to stand. "Better leave all that and come in," she added, "or you're gonna get soaked for sure."

"Already soaked," Frank yelled back. "Here, take this gas can, please. We'll drag in the scallop sacks and you put on some coffee."

Later, sitting around, bedraggled and dripping on the floor, they looked at each other and smiled.

"Well," Amanda had a cup of hot tea and she sipped at it tentatively, "weren't we lucky to get in ahead of this?"

"Timed like the Rockettes," Jean said, nudging a croker sack with one foot. "What are we gonna do with all these? I don't want more than one sack."

Amanda glanced at her, a serious expression on her face, as she tried to smooth her wet hair.

"You know," she said "shucking scallops can be quite a chore. I don't want a whole sack. Maybe a half."

Jerry nodded in agreement. "A half is all I want, too. Let's split one, Amanda, and then we can give Pearlie a sack. She said she wants some."

"With all those kids, maybe Bertha will be glad for the last sack, if that's okay with you?" Jean asked, turning from the counter where she was tossing together cheese and crackers and looking at Frank.

"Sure. Anything's okay with me. I just want to get into some dry clothes. We can drive down to the post office and drop the sack off soon's this squall lets up."

Amanda stood by the window, balancing her tea cup and nibbling a cracker. She watched the rain sheeting down the pane. Reaching out with one finger, she tried to trace the drops coursing along their zigzag track. Turning slightly back toward the room, she nodded optimistically.

"This is good," she murmured. "We need this rain. The island is parched. All the cisterns are low. It'll be over by tomorrow and everything will be washed clean again and be green and lush."

Amanda's prophecy, however, was wrong.

23

August

I t rained for a solid week! For seven straight days, one after the other, it poured. By the third day the islanders were edgy.

Captiva, like all offshore barrier reefs, was primarily an outdoor place. Nerves became frayed when people were hostage to bad weather and forced to remain indoors. Children were underfoot and noisy, their shrill, piercing little voices, darting through the thick air like stabbing needles, penetrated older ears with a throbbing insistence. The houses quickly became uncomfortable, unfamiliar, unfriendly. Built with wide windows on all four sides to catch the slightest cooling breeze in fair weather, water now seeped through cracks and covered floors, furniture, even bedclothes with unwelcome, glistening, dew-like moisture. Green mold appeared along baseboards, thrusting out tiny hair-like white-headed spoor shafts that gave off a pervasive odor of mildew, causing headaches and aggravating allergies. Eyes ran, noses dripped, clothing became sodden. And over everything was the constant, never-ending clamor from the pounding rain, hammering a deafening cannonade on the tin roofs.

Outdoors was soon a shambles. Water that hadn't had time to leach down through the shell and sand ground cover collected in expanding lakes, sheeted across yards and driveways, and submerged the path along the mangroves from the post office to Matilda Crunch's Shell Shop. A strange quiet could be felt under the stretching canopy of the deluge. Birds had disappeared. The twittering and cheeping of cardinals, towhees, redwings... gone. The lilting song of the mocking birds... gone. The splash of pelicans, the overexcited piping of shore birds... gone. The slapping of the bay water against boats and docks, the familiar gentle swooshing of the Gulf waves, foaming along the shore edge, were also gone. The plummeting rain flattened both bay and Gulf, changing the glittering, choppy water into oily, grey, smooth expanses that undulated restlessly up and down like wind under a blanket.

The flowering shrubs, hibiscus, alamanda, bougainvillea, oleander, all pruned and coaxed into brilliant bloom by loving hands, lay flat in the puddles, twisted and torn apart by the sluicing downpour.

Eager for some relief, the grownups collected each afternoon at Murph's dock. After the arrival of the daily mailboat they'd jammed oilcloth hats on their heads, tossed ponchos around their shoulders, shoved their feet into thick galoshes, and slopped their way through the debris to Murph's.

"Ain't it peculiar," Pearlie commented to Ruta Barstowe, putting a cold beer down on the table in front of her," that there ain't no wind to speak of in all this mess? 'Course, we're lucky. If it was blowin' the rain horizontal like it sometimes does, we'd be more miserable than we are. But ain't it peculiar?" She drifted on back behind the counter.

Ida and Amanda and Ruta were playing 3-handed pinochle, each studying her hand with concentrated ferocity. Little tendrils of smoke drifted across the cards from Ida's drooping cigarette and Amanda swiped irritably at it with her free hand.

"Must you do that?" she snapped. "The air is difficult enough to breathe without secondhand smoke!"

Ida snorted two streams of smoke from her nostrils and calmly laid down an impressive meld.

"You're just irritable from all this rain and the fact that I'm winning." She sucked in a hefty drag, snorted again through her nose, tapped her cigarette on the edge of the ashtray and added another fifty points to her growing score. She smiled across at Amanda.

The screened door banged and little drops of collected moisture spattered across the room as Jean and Frank stumbled in.

"Murder! It's plain murder out there. How long's this gonna keep up?" Jean flung her hat and raincape into a corner. "Nobody told us it could be like this. Uncomfortable. Really uncomfortable!"

Frank joined Murph and Evan at the large round table in front of the juke box.

"Pretty disgusting, you know," Frank said. "We can't finish that marina work 'til this is over. Thank God the old man's taken his dredge back to the mainland. How long do you give it?"

Both Murph and Evan shook their heads.

"I don't know." Murph stared out of the window at the flat bay. "I just don't know. I caught Jimmy Norris on the radio just awhile back an' he didn't warn of any storm around anywhere, but it's sure strange out there. An' no wind. Just this low cloud cover and all this rain. The tides ain't actin' up atall, else I'd be real edgy. Barometer's not movin' much, either."

Elgin Bigelow came bursting in out of the rain, his face streaking water, and everyone looked up, startled.

"Good God, Elgin. You ain't flyin' in this weather?" Pearlie spoke before the others. He grinned, shaking himself like a dog.

"Course not. That rain's enough to beat holes through the plane's wings. I drove down in the jeep. Wet drive! Have you any coffee, Pearl? I'm chilled to the bone."

"Why in hell ain't you home with the missus, like a good husband oughter be?" she said, fixing a steaming cup and pushing it across the counter toward him. "Or did that bumpy ole jeep jes' need a bath?"

"Actually," Elgin replied, accepting the hot coffee and joining the group around the table, "I came down to count the waves. I couldn't be as accurate up on Sanibel, where the bottom graduates out more'n a half mile. Down here on Captiva, where you have this deep swash channel just offshore all along the beachfront, the waves are bigger. But not today. This rain has flattened the Gulf so much there's nothing to count!"

Jean looked quizzically at him.

"What do you mean ` count the waves'?"

"Well, this weather's got me puzzled." Elgin looked over at Murph, who nodded in agreement. "Never remember it raining so steady so long. My barometer is broken so the only gauge I've had has been the local radio station in Myers but there's no information coming in from them. Nothing about a storm anywhere near. So I headed down here to look at your barometer, Murph, and decided to check the Gulf waves at the same time. You can usually tell that way."

"How?" Jean persisted.

"In good weather, waves roll in at an average count of one every seven seconds. When a large tropical disturbance is approaching, that action is slowed to an average of one every twelve seconds. If you've an eye for such things, and time them, you can tell fairly accurately if a heavy storm is back of torrential rain like this. Scientists think it's this change in the rhythm of normal wave action that warns the birds and the fish that bad weather is coming."

As Elgin explained, everybody in the bar had gathered around him. They all sat quietly for several minutes, thinking to themselves. Ida finally looked up, a worried expression on her face.

"Are you saying, Mr. Bigelow, that we've a hurricane comin' in on us?"

"No, I'm not. I'm not saying that at all. I'm saying I don't know and I'm saying I'm worried."

Murph had crossed to his barometer, hung by the entrance door on a nail.

"This thing's not too accurate, either. Never shoulda bought one with a control knob on the front. Folks play with it. Near as I can tell it's pretty steady at 29.7... which calls for rain an' we sure as hell got it."

Ida was mulling her problem.

"If there's a hurricane back of all this, I gotta get busy, rain or no rain. All the keys I'm holdin' to all them houses! Folks depend on me. Every one of them places'll have to be boarded up. There's my own place. An' now I've got that store. Stuff that can blow around is scattered all over up there. I gotta go!" She pushed back her chair and struggled into her rain gear. "What do I owe, Pearl, for the beer an' all?" She paid and waved as she slipped through the door and out into the torrents.

Murph looked long and hard at Elgin and his face showed his concern.

"If there is anything bad behind this, Pearlie an' I gotta empty all this stock, all the beer an' wine an' stuff... we gotta haul it all inshore to our house. An' the boats gotta be tended." Pearlie was staring at him, her mouth wide open.

But Elgin was shaking his head.

"Don't everybody go flying off the handle, now. I don't know anything. If I did, I'd tell you. I think we'd be wise to keep our radios on and share whatever information we get. Maybe this rain'll quit and everything will be fine again."

The rain did quit! Early in the afternoon of the eighth day, the rains suddenly ceased! One minute it was pouring, the next it was not. A cloud cover stretched over the land, threatening to spill more water from billowing pockets, like tarpaulins spread over wooden framework. Angry, gray, menacing, seemingly just beyond arm's reach, the sky hung silent, and watchful, like a ravening beast marshalling its strength for the final attack.

The islanders were as stunned by the cessation of the noise as they had been by the thunderous progression of the rainstorm. They stood around, uncertain, listening to the lack of sound, hesitating to venture outside for fear the deluge would return. When it didn't, they slowly picked up their lives and moved on.

●

"It's so difficult to breathe ... like a cloth is binding in my lungs!" Cora took several long, deep inhales and grimaced over at Maude. "See? It hurts. If a wind would only come up and blow away all these murky clouds, maybe that'd change the air."

Maude was rocking, her hands folded in her lap. She nodded.

"I agree. With this humidity and pressure, I can't lift a hand. What's that little barometer read, Cora?"

"Twenty-nine point six. It's dropped a little. It was twenty-nine point seven early this morning."

"Rain!"

"What?"

"Barometric pressure down that low signifies rain."

"Well, we've had that."

"Yes. And could have more." Feeling slightly like the Oracle of Delphi, Maude rocked on, her eyes closed, her afternoon nap not far away.

Cora watched her for a time, an affectionate smile on her lips. But Cora was not one for long silences.

"Where's Ag?"

"Over at Amelia Armstrong's. Jerry's with her. Amelia says there's more to come and she wants to take this break in the weather to board up. She's leaving early tomorrow to go up-country to friends in Carolina."

"Who? Agnes?"

Maude flopped her tongue against her teeth and made a little clucking noise. It was so exasperating trying to carry on a conversation with Cora, whose attention span was about two seconds long.

"No, Cora, not Ag! You <u>know</u> Ag isn't going anywhere. Why can't you go along with a conversation instead of running all about like a leaky pot? Amelia, <u>Amelia</u>, is going away to visit friends and wants to board up her house before she leaves, and Ag and Jerry are helping her. Got it? Really, you're difficult to talk to!"

Cora was miffed and felt she wasn't at fault for not understanding. She wanted to pursue the subject.

"Well, why didn't you say 'Amelia'"... you just said 'her' and there are two of those over there. There's..."

"Oh, for heaven's sake, Cora. Stop! It's not worth all this. As a matter of fact, I didn't say 'her' at all... I said 'she'. What difference does it make? Anyway, they won't be long, only eight windows in that house and Amelia has plywood shutters that hang from little hooks and cleat down. Jerry has to get back as he promised Ida he'd help her. He... Jerry... got it? ... will come back here after dark and he and I... Jerry and Maude... got it? ... will board up our cottage and this house. Now, enough. I'm going to sleep."

After the seven days of rain and the threatening afternoon, the sunset that dusk, as can happen in the tropics, was brilliant. The cloud formation rolled back and fingers of crimson and gold shot up from the western horizon behind the setting sun and painted the frowning sky with glory. Those who saw felt their breath catch as they watched in awe. In a few minutes the light was gone, but it had been long enough to reassure the watchers that all was again in order and that they could sleep the night through, confident that the morning would again be bright.

During the night the wind hit! At first, it was just a stirring, a pulse of unseen flow, moving in gently from the east between low-hung clouds and the land. The flattened bushes lifted a little, the foliage trembling, as if called by a distant voice. Seagrape leaves fluttered, palm fronds rustled. There was a feel of expectancy all about. After days of pounding rain beating down, it was time now to revive in these warm, friendly breezes. This feeling, however, was short-lived. Behind the first gentle puffs strong winds lurked. Striding swiftly up from the horizon on sturdy feet, these stronger winds strode swiftly across the heavens, rolling back the murky, water-filled, oppressive clouds, while towing behind them ever sturdier gales that quickly rose to thirty-mile blasts.

●

Bertha's nose was pressed firmly into the small of Evan's back as they slept in their huge bed. She stirred and raised her head. Settling back down after a bit, she murmured to her husband.

"Blowin' up out there, Evan. Maybe it'll push those suffocatin' clouds away an' we can breathe for a change. Hope it keeps up. No bugs can fly against all that." She dozed off.

●

Ida sat staring out of the large front window of her store, puffing on a cigarette. A worried frown creased her forehead. She'd have to see Roy first thing when daylight broke and ask him to drive down to the bridge and rouse Jerry. She had to finish up the winter houses tomorrow before this blow got worse. She could sense in her bones that trouble was building.

●

On the other side of the bridge, Maude and Cora, unable to sleep, sat side by side on their small screened porch, listening to the wind whip the hibiscus bushes and seagrapes bordering their parking lot. Cora leaned across and patted her friend's arm.

"You're worried, aren't you, Maudie?"

Firmly but gently, Maude shrugged off Cora's hand. She hated expressions of affection.

"Not yet. Not while it stays like it is. But this rose all of a sudden and I don't like that. I was sleeping peacefully and suddenly, here's this blow, out of nowhere. If it increases, we might have problems. I'm especially concerned about that tree limb handing low over Ag's kitchen roof. We <u>must</u> get it trimmed back."

"The gumbo limbo?"

"Yes. Of course, Cora! There's only one tree growing tight up on Ag's cottage. The ground's so soaked now and spongy from all the rain, I'm afraid that tree might tip over if this wind gets stronger."

"Are you going to go back to sleep?"

"No, I guess not. It's most four a.m. now. In a couple hours, it's dawn. I want to be here, in case. If it blows itself out, I'll go back to bed."

361

Pearlie roused and reached across the bed for Murph. She came wide awake when her hand encountered nothing and she realized he was gone.

"God! How I hate this gettin' up business," She muttered to herself. "Every bone in my body aches. Where do you suppose he is?" She struggled to a window and spotted a light out on the dock. Pulling on bra and panties and throwing a large bath towel around her shoulders, she stumbled out into the wind. The bay water, riled and slopping up through the decking, wet her feet. Shaking them angrily like a cat, bending her head into the gale, she pushed on. Somewhere, near at hand, a shutter banged.

She paused for a second just inside the door and glanced at Murph, who was staring at the barometer, chewing his lower lip. Then she crossed to behind the bar and rummaged in the melting ice for a beer.

"What's the trouble? Jes' a blow, ain't it? she asked.

Murph shook his head.

"Don't know. This damn thing's droppin'. Down now to 29.5." He flicked the casing with his finger. "Wonder if this is workin' right? Can't really tell, hangin' like it does in all this damp and people playin' with it."

"Nuthin' on the squawk box?'

"'Course not. They don't open 'til 6:00."

Pearlie took a hefty gulp from her beer, and gestured at him with her empty hand.

"No, I don't mean now. I know they ain't up at this hour. I meant las' night afore we went to bed."

"No. Nuthin' atall. Never said nuthin' about no storm, an' that's a funny thing. Shoulda at least mentioned a squall area. Where in hell'd this blow come from? It's a good thirty-five miles out there. It's my guess some of them gusts is upwards to fifty miles at least."

●

At six o'clock WINK came alive! Instead of Douglas Thomas languidly giving farm news, Jimmy Norris' voice boomed into the room.

"Hey, sweetie," Pearlie yelled above the radio and the wind. "Turn him down some. Don't need all that squawkin' an' screechin' at this hour."

There was a note of urgency in Norris' voice.

"Good morning. It's six a.m. We are interrupting our usual early farm program to bring you a weather advisory bulletin just in from the National Hurricane Center in Miami. During the night a tropical disturbance developed in the Gulf of Mexico, some 700 miles southwest of the Florida mainland. Located at 24.2 degrees north and 92.0 degrees west, this disturbance was first discovered as a squall area with little cohesive pattern. In a matter of hours, however, it has increased to a well-defined tropical storm with winds now at gale force of fifty miles per hour. It is traveling east-northeast at twelve miles an hour. We are advised that this disturbance, because of its freakish nature, bears close watching. Due to its location and no land mass between it and the Florida coast, it can increase in strength with dramatic suddenness. The entire west coast from Everglades City to Apalachicola has been put on standby alert. Instead of our usual broadcasting schedule of advisories every six hours, we have been instructed to bring you up-dates every three hours. We will further advise at nine a.m. I repeat, this disturbance now at coordinates 24.2 degrees north and 92.0 degrees west, and traveling toward the Florida mainland at twelve miles per hour, bears close watching. There will be a further bulletin at nine a.m. Here now is Doug Thomas with the farm report."

Murph snapped off the radio. He stood for some time gazing across the white-capped bay. Pearlie, behind the bar, was frozen.

"Well, at least, now we know." She expelled a whole lung full of air and sagged slightly. "Jes' what we need. A storm! Even a small storm could do damage, what with the ground so wet an' all. An' I suppose the rain'll come back. What'll you do?"

Murph shrugged.

"Gimme another cup o' coffee, Pearl. I suppose I'd best gather in the men. I'll round up Roy, an' Evan, an' Jasper Duggan. Maybe Gustave Kroen...

"Don't forget Frank Culpepper. He'll want to help." Pearlie stuck in.

"... an' Frank. We'll hold a meetin' here at 7:30, an' you cook up a mess o' flapjacks an' bacon an' eggs. An' lots of coffee." He threw on his poncho and eased out the door.

Later, at 7:30 that morning, nobody was very hungry. They sat clustered around the large round table, apparently waiting for Murph to take charge. Roy Coggins pushed half a pancake, soaked in Karo syrup mixed with molasses, back and forth on his plate.

"Do you think this one's comin'?" he asked Murph.

With a serious expression, Murph looked up.

"Roy, we gotta think somethin'. It won't do to sit back an' say it <u>ain't</u> gonna hit. We gotta be ready, or as ready as we can get."

Frank was figuring on an old pad.

"If it was 700 miles off at six this morning, and traveling twelve miles eastward each hour, and today's Wednesday ... it'll hit land by six p.m. Friday." He leaned over his pad to check his figures. "Yeah. Somewhere about six p.m. day after tomorrow."

Roy slurped down a forkful of pancake and mumbled around a full mouth.

"What?" Frank questioned him, glancing up.

"I said `providin' it don't speed up'."

"Or slow down!" Murph stuck in.

"It'll gather strength over all that warm water and no land mass to soften it up." Thinking of his wife Peggy, still ailing and in bed most of the time, Jasper Dugan was worried. "Course, it can go up. Some have. Just gone up an' disappeared. Not long ago a storm, a big one, too, plowed on in out of the Atlantic and crouched to hit Miami. Then it blew itself up and disappeared. Two days later it come back down again, on the Carolinas, an' raised hell."

"That's my point," Murph added. "We don't know, so we must get ready. We gotta board up."

Mr. Kroen hadn't contributed much. Being Russian, he had a language barrier but he could understand. Now he nodded in agreement and breathed ` da, da' under his breath.

"You gotta plan? How do you think we oughta begin?" Frank asked.

Murph worried the coffee grounds in the bottom of his cup, stirring them around with one finger.

"I think we should work as a gang, all six of us. An' Jerry. Where's Jerry, anyway?"

Roy spoke up. "He's helpin' Ida. I drove down to Mrs. Trumbull's at 5:30 an' got him. He an' Ida are boardin' up the Gold Coast."

Murph thought this over, then went on with his scheme.

"Let's do this. We'll all band together as a team an' start at the first house north an' work south to across the bridge, boardin' an' protectin' each house as we go. If the owner is here, that's all we'll do... they can gather in their own outside junk and store it. If no one's at home, we'll police the grounds. We'll finish each place before going to the next one an' with any luck at all we'll be done by nightfall. We'll leave the dock 'til tomorrow. I'd like to know that the thing's actually gonna hit before evacuatin' all this beer an' wine. That can be a real hassle."

Evan smiled. "We'll all turn up an' help with that... ya can bet on it. Where do ya want to haul it?"

"Don't know, yet. Pearlie can talk to Ida. Maybe we oughta drag it all up to her store. She's got plenty of room."

"An' plenty o' food." Pearlie yelled across the room. "I'll haul up the ice an' we can have us a hurricane party. Everybody can donate food... an' can <u>buy</u> my beer.: She grinned widely.

"We'll see. We'll see." Murph was itching to get going. "Pearl, maybe you can keep an ear to Norris an' WINK an' write down each advisory. We'll forget all about it 'til we get back tonight, but then we sure want to know what is goin' on. Anybody disagree with any of this?"

Nobody did.

"Good! We don't have to go up to South Seas. The caretaker and his grove gang can take care of those few cabins an' the manor house. We'll start with Ruta Barstowe, then Amanda, then Matilda Crunch an' so on. Let's get crackin'!"

Frank raised his hand, and smiled at Murph.

"Just one question, Murph. Where do we get all the lumber we'll need?"

364

Murph nodded as he responded.

"Every home owner has plywood sheets, already cut to size an' numbered by window, stored under or beside their houses. All we gotta do is haul 'em out, sort 'em an' hang 'em. Don't take long. But it ain't wimmin's work."

By nightfall the weary, windblown gang was back at the dock. All the houses, including Agnes Trumbull's and Mrs. Thigpen's down across the bridge, were boarded up and as safe as could be managed. The crew welcomed the beer Pearlie set out on the counter.

"On the house. All on the house!" she beamed as she yelled over the howling wind.

Digging sand out of his eyes, Murph crossed to his barometer, and squinted at it.

"It's down more. It's showin' 29.3. Ain't good. Ain't good atall. What'd Norris tell ya durin' the day, Pearl?"

Pearl preened. Everyone was looking at her. She was the center of attention. She felt the importance of the moment course up her spine and her bosom expanded as she gulped down a huge breath.

"Well, sir, now let's see. They've named her... she's Fanny. The sixth storm of this hurricane season. They ain't classed her as a hurricane yet, but they will... they will." She patted her hair, and reached down to stir the ice in the cooler bin. Savoring the moment, she dawdled behind the counter.

"Pearl, I'm gonna slug ya! Where is the damn thing?"

"She's jes' where they said she was. I got it rit down somewhar's. Oh, here 'tis. At six p.m. she was at coordinates 24.5 north and 90.0 west an' scootin' straight as a beeline fer us at twelve miles an hour. Winds still at fifty miles. So the only thing new is they named her. Fanny! Kinda nice, huh?"

"Yeah. real nice! Great!" Murph threw a sarcastic grin at her as he crossed to the big table where Frank Culpepper was again figuring on his papers. All the others were grouped around, undecided about what to do next.

Frank tapped the paper with his index finger and glanced up.

"Right on course. She's covered 150 miles in the last twelve hours... she's now about 550 miles off. What puzzles me is if she's still classed a tropical storm, with top winds at only fifty miles an hour, she can't be too wide. I mean, the storm circumference would have a radius stretching out from the center maybe only 100 miles or so. Then, how is it that we're getting all this wind way over here some 600 miles away? Can't be from that storm, can it?"

"No," Murph agreed. "You're right. Can't be. But maybe this unusual stretch of hot, muggy rain we've had this past week could'a been the northern fringe of a storm system much further south. Storms, big tropical storms, hurricanes, they're strange things. Once, years back, when I had more of a mind..." He looked over at Pearlie who was slicing bread for supper. With an affectionate, endearing smile, she saluted him with her carving knife.

"An' when I was purty an' had me a figger," she tossed into the conversation.

Murph smiled back at her.

"An' that, too. Anyway, as I was sayin'... back then, as a youngster, I guided out of Miami one summer, an' Professor Bob Gilbert fished regular with me. He was with the Weather Bureau down there an' we discussed storms an' such all the time. He told me that these things start up in the tropics followin' a long period of very calm weather. Seems the water gets too hot an' the heated air over it rises higher an' higher an' then two things happen." He paused, embarrassed that he'd been talking so long. He glanced at Frank and raised his eyebrows.

Frank leaped to the rescue.

"A low pressure builds inside the column of hot air rushing upward, which in turn sucks cooler outside air toward the center... and then the entire huge disturbance begins to turn slowly counterclockwise as it is caught up in the influence of the earth's twist. As it spins faster and faster, the interior winds increase, and it feeds on itself. Something like that."

The others had gotten bored with all this technical talk and were restless to leave.

"Bertha's gonna kill me," Evan said, as he moved toward the door. "I gotta get home. What about tomorrow, Murph? Will ya be wantin' help?

"Sure, unless this thing veers off. I'll check Norris at six a.m. an' we can decide then. If it does bear down on us, the island is as safe as we can make it. Drinkin' water's no problem except haulin' it. After all this rain the cisterns all over are full. If we pool, we got plenty of food. Tomorrow we gotta take care of all the boats an' somebody should check on Daddy Farlow an' ole Mr. Jackson. We can do that when we take the bigger boats into Hurricane Hollow. An', of course, I gotta cart all this stuff outa here an' can sure use a hand or two."

●

When Jerry got back to his aunt's house he found all three ladies outside in the wind, fighting lumber and shovels and a sledge hammer.

"What's going on?" he called, leaping from his truck and racing over to join them. "Here, let me do that. What are you doing, anyway?"

It was a chaotic scene. Maude was grim and determinedly pounding away. Cora was near tears, fearful Maude would hurt herself. Agnes, for once, dithered on the sidelines.

"Thank heaven you're back," she exclaimed, throwing an arm around his shoulder. "Please take over. Cora has to get out of there. She's going to injure herself trying to protect Maude. I declare, Maude is a wild thing. She has decided, at this late hour, mind you, to prop up that huge limb. Says it's too heavy and might split off in all this wind and crash down onto the house. Of course, it might, but we should have done something about it long ago.

366

Now it's too late. But you know Maude. Once she gets an idea she holds on like a bulldog."

"Could do this all by myself," Maude grunted as Jerry went over to help. "If all these females would only go back inside, I could manage. I'm afraid to sledge really hard for fear dear Cora will stick her head in the way and I'll squash it like a melon. Send 'em both away. Here, grab this two by four... what I'm trying to do is prop up this limb from underneath to take some of the weight, and then lash it to that hefty seagrape over there so if the limb does crack off the sideways strain will maybe twist it as it falls and it'll miss the house. This is all my fault. All my fault. Shoulda <u>insisted</u> months ago that the tree be trimmed. Too late, now. Never get anything done crying over spilt milk, though. Cora, get out of the way! Cora! Git! What are you after, under here with me? There ain't enough room for even one and now here we are, three! I'm not makin' another move 'til you get out!"

"I only want to save this bird feeder!" Cora's face was crinkled in despair. Tears glistened on her cheeks. "It's right in line with the fall. The poor birds!"

"Poor birds, my foot! There ain't no birds' They all flew off into the interior somewheres, soon's they sensed a storm. Shore birds and land birds... all gone. Snakes and gopher turtles still around, but buried deep. Get your damn bird feeder and get out. Please?" She added the last to soften her vehemence. Cora grabbed the feeder upright and tugged it from the sand. Then she crossed to the house wall, undecided about further action, the feeder propped against her leg.

When the tree limb was braced and lashed to Maude's satisfaction, Jerry went over to Cora and gently took the feeder from her.

"Where do you want it set up. Have you figured out a spot, Aunt Cora?"

"Not really," Cora replied. "It's such a problem you know. If we put it up too far from where it was the dear little birdies might not find it. If it's too close to that limb it could be knocked down. Oh, dear!" She wrung her hands in uncertainty.

"I see a nice spot right over here." Jerry retrieved the sledgehammer and pounded the feeder pole back into the sand. "See. It's out of line with the tree, and you'll be able to see it from the living room side window once the shutter is off, and the birds will love it."

"Jerry!" She exclaimed, kissing his cheek. "You're such a dear. So kind and thoughtful. Not at all like Maude." She kissed him a second time as he wiggled to escape.

●

The six o'clock weather report the following morning placed Fanny at coordinates 25 degrees north by 88 degrees west, or some 430 miles southwest of the Florida mainland, traveling on a direct line toward Fort Myers.

"... have increased to sixty-five miles an hour," Jimmy Norris was in mid-sentence when Murph snapped on his radio, "with gusts to 73 miles an hour. The National Hurricane Center in Miami is monitoring this storm by plane and cautions that Fanny is a decided threat to the western coast of Florida. The impact point, unless she veers, will be Fort Myers. With winds reaching some 350 miles outward from the center, the outlying islands will feel the impact by mid-morning. People there are urged to evacuate. Fort Myers Beach should take all precautions. Sanibel, Captiva, Cayo Costa and Boca Grande should be evacuated. People should move inland. I repeat, Fanny is now a large storm, brushing full hurricane status, is 430 miles off the mainland, traveling toward Fort Myers at twelve miles an hour. The Miami Hurricane Center advises evacuation of all low-lying offshore areas at once. Bulletin! Bulletin! Just in, a local advisory. The Kinsey Brothers Office announces that the Sanibel-Punta Rassa ferry will discontinue service at five p.m. this afternoon, allowing the ferry to move up-river past Fort Myers to safe harbor in the Orange River. I repeat! All those leaving Sanibel and Captiva must do so today, before five p.m. This entire weather advisory bulletin will be repeated at nine a.m., with an update report out of Miami at noon. I repeat, this is a serious storm..."

Murph reached over and snapped off the radio. He glanced at Pearlie, seated for a change at the central table, desultorily stirring a cup of coffee.

"Better get all this packaged up. Ida said she'd help. I'll go tell her and then get to the boats. Just before this thing hits, if she does, an' it sure looks like it will, you an' I can duck over to Ida's an' ride it out with the folks gathered there. Bertha an' Evan will have old Mr. Jackson an' Daddy Farlow, an' most likely Jasper an' Peggy Dugan, an' with their own kids they'll have a crowd at the post office. Gotta go." He turned up his collar, crushed his hat firmly on his head and ducked out the door into the winds.

It took all morning, with every available man helping, to take care of the boats. Twelve large fishing craft, all with inboard motors, were relocated down Roosevelt Channel to Hurricane Hollow, where they were tied fore and aft to piling still in place from former storms. Then they were lashed sideways to each other, with sufficient free rope to allow each to move up and down without ramming its neighbor. On the final trip, old Mr. Jackson was picked up in Murph's swift inboard and dropped at the post office dock. He would weather the storm with Bertha and Evan. Daddy Farlow was fearful of leaving his livestock unguarded and decided to stay on Buck Key.

"If something happens, fly yer white flag," Murph yelled into the gale as he backed away from the Farlow dock. "If we see it, we'll try to get over an' help ya."

Daddy nodded as he stood leaning into the wind and holding on to the dock railing.

"Mistake," Roy shouted into Murph's ear. "We shoulda insisted more."

"Can't tie the old man up. Still a free country, storm or no storm." A rolling whitecap slapped the side of the boat, throwing chill foaming spray over everyone and halting further conversation as they settled down to the grim business of buffeting the bay waves back to Murph's dock.

Next came the small boats, the little outboards and the rowboats. Motors were taken off, wrapped securely in tarps and hauled to storage sheds. Then these small boats were lined up under docks and filled with water until they sank. Once on the bottom the hulls were weighted down with non-buoyant debris such as broken building blocks, cement discards, and scrap iron. Finally, each little boat was lashed sideways to piling.

This work was exhausting. In water shoulder deep, with a driving wind beating choppy waves into their faces and cutting off their sight, the men gritted their teeth and labored on. Roy Coggins caught the brunt, as he could hold his breath longer than the others. As soon as a boat was in position, and while the others were tramping into shore and back out with whatever ballast they could find, Jerry would brace the sunken boat with his feet while Roy submerged and tied off the hull to nearby piling.

By noon, with the winds steadily increasing, the work was done. All boats except two were secured and as safe as possible. Murph's large inboard boat was hauled out of the water and lashed onto a steel repair ramp so it would be available at a moment's notice should it be needed, and Evan's sturdy outboard with it's fancy battery-operated starter was left afloat in the covered boat slip to one side of the post office property. Lashed fore and aft, and half-hitched sideways, she would be snug and safe, able to ride out any storm, unless the entire slip blew away. Gustave Kroen dragged his ramshackle shark skiff up to his shack near Ida's store, and lashed it between two palm trees. He was afraid the plywood would warp and separate if the skiff was sunk in sea water for several days.

The bay water was an inch over the dock as the men walked back out to the bar. Whitecaps were everywhere in the bay and salt spray, snatched by the gusting winds from the top of the wave-curls and flung sideways, pelted them like horizontal rain. They dashed into the safety of the bar and stood together inside the door, dripping a large puddle on the floor.

Pearlie tossed Murph a mop with hardly a break in her activity. She and Ida and Ruta Barstowe were packing beer and wine bottles into cardboard boxes.

"Suppose these'll all get soaked as we carry 'em to the store, an' the bottoms'll fall out an' we'll lose everythin' overboard!" Clearing out the bar and its two storage rooms was such a depressing chore Pearlie had become discouraged. Her mood was not improved by Ruta's forced gaiety or the cloud of cigarette smoke that all but hid Ida.

As he wrung out the mop into a nearby bucket, Murph glanced at the wall clock over the bar. One-thirty! They'd missed the weather report.

"What did Norris have to say?" he asked.

Pearlie motioned toward the bar.

"It's all there, on a piece of paper. Nothin' much new. She's a little closer, that's all. About 360 miles out. Still headin' slap-bang fer us at that twelve

369

miles an hour. Norris mentioned high tides an' kep' tellin' us to evacuate. How in hell can we evacuate?" She leaned back against the counter and brandished a bottle of red wine. "How the hell can we leave? They must all be nuts. Everythin' we got, everythin' we own is here. If we left an' went to the mainland the uncertainty'd kill me faster'n drownin'!"

"What'd he say about the wind?"

"Fer Gawd's sake, Murph. You've been out in it. You've jes' come in. It's blowin' out there. You know that!" Her irritation at all these extra difficulties mounded on top of an already difficult life saturated her voice. With a shrug she went back to boxing bottles. "I don't know. Read my note. He said the wind'd increase all afternoon, an' that we'd be feelin' heavy blows by six p.m. What's he figure we've had so far, pea-shooter puffs?"

Murph glanced at his barometer and noticed that it now read 28.98. He didn't comment, figuring everyone was already nervous enough.

By three o'clock that afternoon the winds reached storm strength of sixty-four to seventy-two miles an hour, with gusts well in excess of hurricane force.

The little procession of workers found it tough going, lugging the boxes through the rising tide and fighting the wind the length of the dock to the waiting truck. Murph banished the women, sending them in to Ida's store, and insisted that the men lug only what they could carry in one hand, leaving the other free to hold the dock railing for balance. Never stopping, in and out, in and out, by 5:30 they were finished and the bar was empty. Then they gathered at the store with the women.

As Ida handed around cold beer, Pearlie chortled out loud.

"Well," she laughed, "Lawdy me, ain't this a twist?" She took a long swallow and smacked her lips.

The talking and cat-calling died abruptly at six o'clock as Jimmy Norris' voice sprang from the radio.

"Good evening, Southwest Florida. Here is the six p.m. weather advisory just issued by the National Hurricane Center in Miami. Fanny continues to roar along her predicted path. Since this morning's advisory, Fanny has increased in strength and in size. She is now a fully established hurricane. Located at coordinates 25.4 degrees north and 86.2 degrees west, and some 288 miles west-southwest of the Florida mainland, with internal sustained winds of 85 miles an hour, and gusts to 100 miles an hour, this is a dangerous hurricane. The storm influence reaches out some 300 - 350 miles from the eye. I repeat... this is a dangerous hurricane. All precautions should be taken. The Miami Hurricane Center warns that Fanny will continue building during the night and early morning hours tomorrow and should make landfall tomorrow evening about six p.m. with winds in excess of 130 miles an hour. A storm surge as high as nine feet is predicted. On her present course, and there is little reason to expect any change, the storm eye will cross Sanibel and Captiva islands by 3 p.m. tomorrow and the mainland just north of Fort Myers by six p.m. Torrential rains are forecast from noon on tomorrow. We have been instructed to broadcast the following information pertinent to hurricane centers or eyes, as they can be deceptive to the uninformed. The eye of Fanny is some 22 - 25 miles in diameter. It is a huge vacuum. It will take approximately two hours for the eye to clear any given point. During those two hours, as the eye crosses from west to east, there will be no wind. The vacuum can possibly contain clear, quiet weather, even sunshine. Wave action in bays and rivers will rapidly decrease. Tidal influence will return. Do not be fooled. This is not... I repeat... not the end of the storm but the middle. Once the eye proceeds on by, hurricane-force winds will return with alarming speed... but blowing in the opposite direction from the first half of the storm. As this action starts, you should close all windows facing west and open all windows facing east to relieve pressure inside your homes, even if boarded up. While within the influence of the eye, excessive activity is cautioned against, as breathing will be difficult. The evacuation of the outlying islands proceeded smoothly, with a minimum of traffic snarling, and those people wishing to remain in the general Fort Myers area are now safely lodged..." Norris' voice was cut as the radio was flicked off.

Jerry crossed over to Ida.

"Bertha asked me to bring her some candles, if you can spare any. I'll drop 'em off as I go past on my way home."

Ida nodded and took a box off a shelf, and Jerry slipped out into the storm. Later, down at the post office, Bertha called after him as he left her and ran for his truck.

"You take care, now, drivin' through this mess. These Australian pines is brittle an' snap off, an the seagrapes will be whippin' about in this wind. Remember, if you need anything, I'll be glad to help. There's plenty of space up here, if anybody needs any."

Jerry thanked her and inched out the post office clearing, down the dirt lane, and turned south along the road bordering the beach. The Gulf had turned ugly. Huge waves were slapping the beach and coursing wildly into the erosion overhang along the road. They fell back onto themselves with thunderous uproar, casting spume high in the air. In several places the Gulf had cut the bank and crossed the road, the waves expending themselves far inland. Pine boughs lay strewn about. Bertha's warning about the seagrapes proved true, as the long branches whipped and flailed about in the storm. Jerry had never seen such fury. Driving slowly, staring straight ahead, braced for a falling branch to plunge onto him at any moment, he crept through the tempest and sighed with relief as he came up on the bridge. Moving carefully toward the far side, he had an odd sensation of too much space, a feeling the sky had increased. He allowed the old truck to roll to a stop as he looked around, wondering. Then, suddenly, he understood. There was an unfamiliar opening over Aunt Ag's house, where tall, leafy limbs should have been. The huge tree! The gumbo limbo! It was gone!

He found the three ladies cowering in a corner of the living room, holding each other, stunned by the catastrophe. The entire kitchen and back porch were crushed in. A large green-bronze limb protruded into the living room, the leaves waving gently in the wind blowing down through the torn roof.

"Are you all alright? Is anybody hurt?" He rushed to his aunt and tried to lift her into a chair. She was limp as a rag and her face was dazed. For a long period she looked straight at him, a vacant expression in her eyes. Then, with a start and a small shiver, her eyes cleared.

"Seems like an awful difficult way to get a new stove," she said, with a fleeting half-smile. Jerry felt a rush of joy. Aunt Ag wasn't hurt. She'd be okay.

He crossed to Maude, now slowly straightening up and groping for her rocker.

"I'm alright," Maude murmured softly, and gestured toward Cora. "See to her. She's scared half to death!"

Cora wrapped Jerry in thin, quivering arms and hung on.

"Oh, Jerry! It was awful! Horrible!" With eyes rolling and fingers curled into claws snatching at his shoulders, she gushed forth the story. He eased her onto a bench and knelt in front, his arms in her lap, trying to comfort this tiny, frightened creature.

"We were sitting here around the table, with the radio in the middle ... it's still there ..." She pointed "... waiting for Mr. Norris to come on and tell us where this thing is, when all of a sudden great gusts of wind started to swirl outside and the sand twisted up in spirals and then there was this tremendous loud bang like a huge cannon going off, and the roof split and then ... sort of slow-motion ... that giant limb out there sank slowly through to the floor, squashing the entire kitchen and most likely the back porch and our little storage shed out there. Now I'm fearful the whole house may come down. We have to get out of here." She grabbed his head and held fast. "We can't stay here. The rest of the roof can collapse any minute and trap us!"

Jerry pulled back in momentary panic, but Maude reached out a restraining hand.

"It's not going to come down. There's nothing wrong with what's standing. It's sturdy enough. The roof was smashed in. It didn't rot or anything like that. But Cora's right. We can't stay here. Thank heaven it's not raining. This is all my fault. I should have known enough, after all these years, when something has to be done, do it. I didn't. I'll have to fix it somehow. But we gotta get out." She looked toward Agnes.

"Don't look at me," Agnes said, slowly shaking her head. "This time I don't know what to do. I usually do, but this time I don't. I'm not thinking clearly." Her head sank in uncertainty.

"Well, I know!" Jerry was decisive. "We all get out of here!" No one noticed his authoritarian tone, or if they did, they didn't react. "Both of you, Aunt Cora and Aunt Maude, help Aunt Ag collect the things she'll need, like clothes and money, her check-book and so on ... and Aunt Maude, you lead'em across to your little house. When you get there, wait for me. I want to look around. Aunt Cora, maybe you can make some tea."

"But the stove is flattened! Look at it!"

"Not here. Over in your house. Go on, now. I'll check out the damage as good as I can and come right over. I'll be careful, so don't worry about me."

He first threw off the main electrical switch. Then he checked his room on the second floor. It was not damaged, nor were Aunt Ag's bedroom and bath, most of the dining room and the long screened porch across the front of the house. But the kitchen was wrecked. The stove and the sink, torn from the floor, were twisted out of shape and lying crushed under the huge limb. Jerry checked the bottled gas line which, luckily, had been crimped when the stove twisted. He had to go out the front screened door and around the side of the house to the back to reach the bottled gas tank, which was unharmed. He twisted down the valve, shutting it off. The rear of the house was a shambles. The back porch roof had collapsed in the middle, leaving the edges flaired upward. A second limb, torn from the main trunk as the first split off, lay atop the little tool shed that had formed one wall of the porch. He couldn't get inside because of the tangle of wires, pipes, shattered boards and screening, and the tree limbs lying all about. The wind, increasing every minute, whistled shrilly through the jack straw lumber, adding a bizarre quality that unnerved him. He studied the hole in the roof, expecting the remaining tin sections to peel back and sail off into the night. But, miraculously, they didn't. There was nothing he could do about anything right at that moment. He bent into the wind, squinted his eyes against the blowing sand and crept across the yard to Cora's cottage.

The three ladies were seated in the small kitchen, staring silently at the doorway, and they spontaneously leaned forward as he came in.

"Aunt Cora, did you make tea?"

"Oh, I'm sorry! I forgot! Do you think this place will blow down next?" She looked all around, terror creeping into her voice.

Maude got up and crossed to the stove. She smoothed Cora's hair as she passed.

"Now, now. Don't take on. We're gonna be fine." As Cora responded and quieted somewhat, Maude lit the stove and filled a pot from the five-gallon water bottle in its tipper beside the little sink. "I'll make the tea, and there's bread and sliced meat in the fridge. We'd all better eat something. It's gonna be a long night. And crowded..." she added as an afterthought. "How'll we sleep? I can't use the porch, not in all this mess outside. I suppose we can put down blankets..."

"No!" Jerry interrupted. "We'll get something to eat first. Then we'll all climb into my truck and I'll drive us to Bertha's. She told me she had lots of room."

Aunt Ag looked doubtful.

"Oh, Jerry. I don't know. That would be imposing. We can't just land on Bertha. She has her hands full already.

"In this storm?" Cora looked aghast. "We're going to drive in the dark through this storm? In an old open truck? To a tall, wooden shack stuck in a grove of oak trees, all slashing around and crashing down? We'll be killed for sure. I won't go! I just won't go! Why can't we use Ag's car?"

Jerry shook his head. When he spoke there was a no-nonsense edge to his voice.

"We'll use my old truck. Aunt Ag's car is locked in Mrs. Armstrong's garage, and it'll be okay there. Later, we will need it. The storm can't damage my truck."

After a quick supper, clothes and food were hastily stuffed into suitcases and boxes and strapped to the open bed of the truck. Then the four of them crushed into the cab, with Jerry at the wheel, Aunt Ag next and Maude by the door. Cora sat gingerly on Maude's lap. Each tightly clutched a bag of personals.

As Jerry revved the motor and fought the gears, Maude suddenly cried out... "I'll be right back." She wiggled out from under Cora and fought her way back into the cottage. Returning in a few minutes, she brandished aloft one hand and clambered back into the truck.

"My combs! I almost forgot my combs! The ones you gave me for Christmas, Jerry. Can't go anywhere without 'em. Okay, let's be off!"

Cora leaned down and breathed in Agnes' ear.

"I think she's enjoying this!"

The trip from the bridge to the post office, so familiar in good weather but unknown now in the inky dark with the tempest roaring just inches away, was fearful. As they reached the center of the bridge, wind-borne spray from the whitecaps in Blind Pass drenched the truck, obscuring the windshield and flooding in the open window. Both Maude and Cora were soaked. The little truck rocked in the buffeting gusts and several times threatened to tip over. As Jerry turned off the bridge and headed north along the island road, the headlights exposed a bewildering scene, and Jerry was shocked by the debris that had accumulated in the short time since he passed this way. Everything seemed to be straining westward toward the Gulf. The giant pines whipped back and forth like monstrous fly rods cast by a crazed fisherman. Every so often a branch would break loose and come crashing down. The longer-limbed seagrapes, growing lower than the pines and usually clumped in benign clusters, now stood on end, reaching skyward in a wild frenzy, branches tangled together, bending and swaying like sea snakes gyrating in a macabre dance. Palm trees swept the ground in sudden gusts, only to whip upright again as the winds momentarily lessened. Coconuts rolled about all over the road, jerking the steering wheel abruptly from Jerry's hand each time a wheel struck one. A huge strip of bark, ripped from a pine tree by the wind, sailed through the air and struck the wind shield with a resounding crack. Cora screamed and ducked her head. Several times the truck had to be stopped to allow Jerry and Maude to lug limbs from the roadway. Sand was everywhere, piled in windrows along the road, swirling about their faces and stinging like angry bees.

An hour after leaving the bridge, the little band of bedraggled travelers inched into the post office yard, exhausted from the trip. Jerry drove around the house to the side door, out of the wind, and Bertha rushed out to greet them. With the instinctive understanding of the Florida native that unexpected visits late at night stem from catastrophe, she wasted no time in questions but herded the four out of the storm and into the warmth and security of her kitchen.

It was already crowded. Over in a far corner Peggy Dugan was resting on an old wicker chaise, while Jasper hovered nearby. Several of the older children were busy in a canasta game on the floor. Evan and Mr. Jackson were talking together and working over a bait net and the rest of the Wiggins children were spread around on the floor. Bertha bustled at the stove and Agnes and Maude helped her. No one noticed the old house creaking and groaning in the wind.

"Will ya have to tear down the whole place?" Bertha wanted to know. She stirred a big pot, and lowered the burner. "When anyone eats, everyone eats." She smiled as she spoke. Reaching for two loaves of bread she began slapping each slice with peanut butter. "With everythin' goin' on tonight, I'm late with this food."

"I thought it all looked pretty hopeless," Agnes said, "but then Jerry assured me on that horrible trip over here that only about a third of the roof is damaged. He thinks the three of them, Roy and your Evan and Jerry, can do all the repairs necessary except for the plumbing. We will have to call someone in for that. The worst part will be removing that tree. Unless, of course, it rains. Then everything will be soaked. Anyway, we'll see."

"Well," Bertha smiled. She loved to mother the unfortunate and now she felt expansive..." you all can bunk in here with Evan an' me for as long as you want. Once this ruckus is over there's plenty of room in this ramshackle ole place. It'll be a little bothersome for everyone for a day or two, 'til this mess blows itself out, but then, when the others go home, we'll be real comfy. You'll see."

●

The following noon, Friday, the storm was at its peak. The weather report, all but unintelligible because of static, placed the eye seventy-two miles west-southwest of Fort Myers, or a mere forty-two miles off Captiva. Winds at its center had been clocked at a constant 110 miles an hour with gusts to 135. The outward thrust reached 350 miles around the eye, and the island was catching the full fury. Fanny roared across the Gulf, struck the tiny unprotected island and shook it fearfully. The surf, plunging into itself from several directions at once, peaked and foamed, sprang high, then rolled back, then rose in towering waves as it rushed toward the beaches. Driven by the

375

twisting gales the spume blew about in sheets, soaking everything in its path. Reaching shallow water, the waves arched high, then plunged down onto the sodden sand with sledgehammer blows. Carrying a weight of 1500 pounds for each cubic yard of water, the beaches reeled and shook under the tremendous onslaught. The surf soon flooded well beyond the high water line, sluicing around fallen trees, undermining and sucking them back into itself, only to lift them high on incoming waves and plunge them shoreward once again as crushing battering rams. The beaches could not long stand against this attack and began to crumble. Erosion started slowly at first, then increased in speed, as retreating water sucked the roiling sand seaward. The passes, unable to contain the additional surge of the high water, widened and deepened as the sandy sides collapsed into the rushing tide. Tons upon tons of sand washed either into the bay or back out into the Gulf.

Inland, trees twisted and snarled and ripped from the ground. As they fell, they tore down electrical wires and knocked over poles. Bushes blew about like western tumbleweeds. This accumulation of undergrowth and fallen trees bunched together, tangled with the wiring, covered the roads and paths, and mounded high along the center of the island. Acting as a barrier to the onslaught of the winds this mass of debris deflected somewhat the ferocious violence of the gales as Fanny galloped along on her relentless charge toward the mainland.

On the bayside, the shoreline remained comparatively stable, as the bunched mangrove aerial roots and low-spreading limbs absorbed much of the wave action. Where there were no protecting mangroves, or where they had been axed out, erosion occurred as bay water penetrated inland.

●

The islanders in Ida's store were grouped around the windows where they could peek out between the shutter cracks and watch... watch the storm... and play pinochle... and eat... and drink. What was a hurricane party without booze and cards and food! They greeted Evan with open arms and raucous shouts when he joined them. By mid-morning he'd become bored with all the women and children crowded into the post office area and had escaped out the back door. Bent nearly double in the wind he had slowly worked his way along the lane bordering the bay to the store. It took him the better part of an hour of double-nipping to catch up to the others, who were now somewhat glassy-eyed and talking too loudly. A few danced. Someone had put a record on the player and couples were circling about. An air of increasing hilarity spread throughout the room and no one noticed when the bay waters, riled and furious in the driving wind, sucked out all the newly-dredged sand along the shore-line between Murph's and Jasper Dugan's, carried off two sections of the new dock and tipped over the metal repair slide Murph's boat was lashed to, wedging the craft on its side.

●

The women at the post office were more alert. It had been a dreadful night. The children had been overexcited and restless, everywhere under foot. The old house trembled and shook to such an extent that sleep was impossible. By five a.m. everyone was out of bed, hungry and in the kitchen once again. Bertha was back at the stove.

"It's gonna be a long day," she said to Cora who was helping with the cooking. "This thing came up so sudden-like I didn't have no chance to stock up proper. 'Course, we got plenty o' staples, rice, potatoes, carrots an' the like. We'll just hafta keep the soup pot boilin'. The bread's short but we can bake more this mornin'. Milk's already give out. I'da laid in lots if I'da known. "Course, ain't no tragedy. If this thing outside follers a usual course, it'll be blown way up-country day after tomorrow, an' the river an' the bay'll be calm an' Captain Bob'll boat over gallons of milk for both o' us, Sanibel an' here. So the kids'll jes hafta go two days without." She shrugged.

Cora stirred the huge soup pot in front of her and poured in the rice Bertha had already measured out.

"But that'll be Sunday. He doesn't make a run on Sunday."

"He will this Sunday." Bertha nodded her head emphatically. "As soon as the water's flat, he'll be over. All the grocery stores in Myers they'll be open. Folks over there'll need food, too. Bob'll gather up all sorts of supplies, heavy on bread an' milk, an' he'll be here smack at noon. Wanna bet?" She smiled at Cora.

Agnes stood for some time gazing out a side window, the only one without a shutter. She didn't see the thrashing oaks or the whirling debris. She was off in some distant place, mulling over her situation. She had a firm grip on her nerves. She wouldn't panic. Experience told her that things would smooth out. Time would smooth it all out. Experience also told her that time didn't solve anything by itself. One must reach out, grab hold, and make it work. But how? She couldn't see where to start. If the house was stable, if it could be shorn up safely, then she and Jerry could at least sleep there. Cora and Maude would be safe in their small cottage. Everyone could eat in Cora's small kitchen. Repairs could be lived through. It all came down to the boy. She'd promised Peg she'd keep the lad only the one year and it was fast running out. He should return home! It would be a terrible wrench, nearly as bad as when Bill died, but it was her duty and she'd never shirked her duty. He must go! Actually, of course, it was his decision ... his choice ... she'd not try to sway him one way or the other ... could the Didi thing be strong enough to keep him... She puzzled on.

377

Tiring of the "Popular Mechanics" he was leafing through, Jerry noticed Aunt Ag at the window and crossed over to her, slipping his arm around her waist.

"Exciting, isn't it?" He watched the oaks whipping in the wind, the fierce wave action in the bay, as the water peaked and spilled onto itself in a frothy tumble, slapping over the dock as it rushed shoreward and pounded the wooden seawall. "It's horrible, of course, with all the force and the danger and the mess. But it's also exciting. I never knew anything like this. It's just... it's just... exciting! Isn't it?" He gave her waist a little squeeze.

"Yes, it is. Agnes agreed, and tilted slightly toward him. She glanced quickly at his eager, alert face. "Yes," she repeated, "it is exciting! But how do you suppose..." Her voice broke off as she realized Jerry wasn't listening. Nor should he. All those worries could now wait 'til later when the storm was blown out and plans could be made. "I should be helping with the cooking, not standing here, dreaming." With a warm return caress, she moved away and crossed to Bertha and Cora.

●

Down through the years so few hurricanes had hit the island head-on that no one had previous experience with the phenomenon of the eye. The little group at the post office was dumbfounded. They stood around the windows, peering out through the shutter cracks in utter disbelief. One moment the storm had been on top of them, twisting and tearing at the trees like a giant run amok, heaving the bay water skyward, grabbing the spray and hurling it against the houses in a frenzied rage that peeled the paint from the boards, and the next moment the fury had died... and was gone! An eerie, unexpected silence suddenly settled over the island and they were in a strange, unfamiliar world. The hurricane-force winds, roaring in from the east, ceased abruptly. The trees and bushes hung without motion. Nothing moved except in the bay. With no wind pushing it, the water settled swiftly and in minutes the tumult died down, leaving a quiet, familiar undulation across the sound. At full flood, the water began to run out, caught again by the age-old tidal influences. A pale, uncertain sunlight bathed the island and small, puffy clouds could be spotted miles above the storm reaches, moving slowly about, nudged along by gentle upper winds.

●

"Mama, can we go out? It's all safe out there, now. Can we, Mama?" Housebound for several days, the children raised a clamor to escape, and Bertha nodded in agreement.

"Yes, you can. But stay close to the house."

"But, Mama, we want to go to the beach. We want to see how much it's been cut."

Lily's face was lit with excitement and a chorus of "beach... beach" rose behind her.

"Okay. For fifteen minutes. You lead'em, Lily, you an' Rose, an' y'all stay in a bunch. No stragglin' around, you hear me? Stay together, an' Lily, you bring 'em all right back here in fifteen minutes, else I'll skin you alive!"

With cries of 'yes'm,... yes'm...' off they trooped, and Bertha expelled all her air in a huge sigh. She squeezed Maude's hand.

"My gosh! I'm sure glad for a breather. So many of 'em. Always at me. I love 'em, but the Good Lord knows I get tired. Let's wander out in that strange air outside an' see what it's like. Sure is hard to breathe."

Echoing Bertha's last remark, Peggy Dugan, still stretched out on the wicker chaise, grabbed her chest and wheezed at her husband.

"Jasper! Jasper! Push me over to the doorway. Can't breathe!"

Jasper dragged the chaise to an opening and Bertha thrust a palmetto fan into his hand. The women grouped around solicitously until Peggy rallied somewhat, then stepped hesitantly outside. Jerry had preceded them and was circling the house and the yard, checking for damage. It was difficult to walk. Tree branches lay thick on the sandy ground, intermingled with sea grasses and mounds of bayside debris, all of which had to be pushed over in order to step.

Recalling the recent rattler episode under the huge nearby banyan tree, Maude called out in a cautionary tone.

"Watch out for snakes!"

With a little gasp, Cora drew back.

"Where? Where is it?"

"I didn't say there were any. I said 'watch out'. Don't get excited, Cora. Just be careful." Maude moved on across the yard toward the dock, and stood staring down at the water. "Doesn't look friendly, somehow," she called over her shoulder. "Looks dirty and threatening."

The other three, Agnes, Cora and Bertha grouped themselves on the post office stoop, facing the bay.

"Some mess, huh?" Bertha pointed generally around. "It'll take us days to clean up, even if we come through the rest of this thing without damage to the house. Anyway, can't be helped, an' it'll give the kids something to do." She looked up, counting heads as the children wandered back from the beach.

Cora was desultorily tracing lines in the sand in a little spot she'd cleared. she spoke without looking up.

"Shouldn't take the men all that long, should it?" she asked.

Bertha shook her head.

"The men won't do it. They'll be out from dawn 'til dark with their chainsaws, tryin' to open the roads. They'll have to clear all of this island an' on up the Sanibel road 'til they meet a crew clearin' down, an' that'll take days... maybe more'n a week. Can't get on or off the island with a car 'til the road is open. Milk trucks an' food an' medicine an' ambulances if needed, nothin' can come or go, you know, 'til the road is open. The electrical repair crews can't get in. We'll be isolated for several weeks at best. Always are."

Agnes had put aside her personal problems and was studying the odd situation around them.

"This is really a queer experience, isn't it? Of course, the whole business has been unusual. For me, anyway. That strange period of heavy rain, all those days... then that stopped and we had all that wind for no apparent reason... then this storm out of nowhere... the horrifying, distressing situation with my house... now this stillness and pressure. It's as if something was pressing a huge blanket down on us. Nothing moves. It's so eerie. I like this least of all. I feel very uncomfortable -- threatened!"

"Why don't we go back inside and start up that bread we were going to bake?" The idea sparked a flicker of life in Cora's eyes as she spoke.

Later, as they mixed and kneaded, flour up to their elbows and scattered across the big table, Cora settled back on her heels and glanced at Agnes.

"Wasn't it strange out there, Ag? Did you notice, in all that mess, how clear the atmosphere was? I could see all the way across the sound, and that's seven miles or so. Daddy Farlow's dock was clear as anything and that little white flag hanging on it. I could see it all just as if I was right beside it. I always thought ..." She glanced around and her voice trailed off as she saw that the others were standing stock-still, staring at her.

Bertha wiped her arms without looking down, and spoke softly.

"What? What little white flag? Where?

"On Daddy Farlow's dock. Up on that little flag-pole there. It's a small white flag and of course it's not fluttering or waving now. There's no breeze. But when there is, I'll bet ..."

What Cora might have bet was lost on the other three. They rushed back outside and stood staring across the water. Sure enough, there it was, a small white cloth, hanging from atop the flagpole, limp in the passing storm-eye.

"Oh, Migod!" Bertha's voice rang with distress. "I never noticed! I wasn't lookin'! He needs help. That poor ole man needs help. Somebody'll have to get over there and help him, see what's wrong." She looked around frantically. "Evan ain't here. Jerry's too young an' Mr. Jackson's too old."

Maude was already crossing to the covered boat slip.

"I'll go! I'll borrow your boat, Bertha, and I'll go. Can be over there in ten minutes. It's quiet now and it won't be any problem at all."

Cora was distraught.

"You can't go by yourself, Maude. Somebody should be with you. I'll go, too."

"Good Gawd, no!" Maude was emphatic. "No, just let me go by myself. I'll have all I can do running a strange boat and tying it up. I know a bit about first aid and I can care for Daddy til Murph gets there." She'd been ready to climb into the boat but faced around. "Jerry, please fetch me my tool belt. It's in the kitchen on the chair by the far wall. Then you work your way along the path to Ida's store and tell Murph and Evan to follow me over. Hurry on, now."

Agnes cut in.

"Jerry you go along to the store. Maude, I'll get your tools. I'm worried about you alone. Let me go with you."

"Nope." Maude was firm." Don't worry, Ag. It won't be any problem. I'll be fine. Bertha, steady this thing while I get in, and help me unlash it. It's got an electric starter, hasn't it? An' I suppose that's all connected."

Bertha nodded, holding a line snug so the boat was tight against the slip. "You have to connect the gas line, there. Turn the motor handle to 'start' an' mash down on that little button. She steers from this handle, like mos' all outboards."

"How much time's left on this storm quiet?" Maude asked, busy with the gas line with one hand and detaching mooring lines with the other. Her foot rolled on an oar and she pushed it to one side.

"If the motor don't catch, let up on the starter button for a second and push that little primer button." Bertha pointed it out. "You got almost a half-hour left on this eye business, if Jimmy Norris is correct, an' he's been right about all the rest of it. Here's Agnes with your belt, so go on an' we'll send Murph an' Evan behind ya. An' Maude," she yelled as the motor coughed and caught... "Maude, you take care, now. Hear?"

Maude nodded and moving the gear lever to forward she steered the little boat smoothly out of the slip and headed across the open water toward the Farlow dock on the northern end of Buck Key.

Half-way across, the engine sputtered and died!

Maude began a frenzied dance around the boat and those watching from the post office dock nearly collapsed. She could find nothing wrong. She plunged down on the starter. No response. Several hefty pushes on the primer, and another plunge on the starter. No response. The tide caught the boat, and it began to drift southward toward the mouth of Roosevelt channel, at the end of which lay the open Gulf.

Bertha cupped her hands into a little megaphone and screamed at the top of her lungs.

"The anchor! Throw out the anchor!"

Maude heard and began another frantic search of the boat. Agnes grabbed Bertha's arm and pointed at the boat slip. There, on one side, lay the anchor.

"Oh, my god!" Bertha moaned, "Evan took it out!"

The speed of the little craft, drifting sideways, picked up... just as Fanny returned in full force. Within seconds, swirling winds from the west churned the bay water into a heavy chop, then riled it into heaving whitecaps. Maude crouched in the little boat, hands locked on opposite gunwales, as white waves sloshed over the sides, and the light craft, pitching and tossing and with the winds behind it, drifted through the storm into the swift waters of the channel, and out of sight.

●

Jerry reached Ida's store as the storm returned, only to discover that Murph, Roy and Evan were all down at Murph's dock, tugging and hauling at the inboard boat, trying to free it from the tangle of lumber and twisted metal it was caught under. Murph was again booming instructions.

"Everybody get back here an' grab hold of the stern with me. We'll inch her up an' twist her sideways. Then we can tackle the prow. Jerry, come on over here an' tug with us."

Jerry passed along Bertha's message and Murph grunted.

"Okay, okay, we'll try to follow Maude over to Buck Key once this boat's freed. If she does free up, and if we can then get her into the water. Wind's comin' up strong agin."

Some half-hour later, when they had the boat free and in the water and lashed to the lee side of the dock, they were all able to climb aboard. Murph patted the hull and grinned broadly as the powerful motor purred into life.

"Everybody stay down, now. This is gonna be a wild ride," Murph yelled over the tempest as, with a roaring engine surge, he flung his boat into the waves. Shaking a clenched fist at the open bay he called against the wind... "Okay, Storm! Let's see who wins this one! Yipee!"

As they drew up to the lee side of Daddy Farlow's dock, the old man was frenzied. Holding to the railing with both hands and leaning into the wind, his scraggly hair was blowing straight out from his head and his pants were ripped and torn.

"It's Dora!" he yelled over the storm. "She's under it! She's bein' crushed to death. I cain't lift that barn off'n her all by myself. I tried, but I cain't!"

Dora wasn't hurt. She was frightened but she was safe. As the barn had collapsed in the storm one wall had hung up on the edge of the house, forming a protection over the cow. They found her in this flimsy lean-to, wedged in among crushed planking, her eyes wild and rolling in fright. As they pried up the wall she struggled free and loped off into the scrub.

"Maude! Have you seen Maude?" Jerry yelled at Daddy Farlow as they leaned up against the shack to catch their breath. "She was going to come over and help you."

"Ain't seen nary a sight o' Mis' Maude," the old gentleman yelled back. "Ain't been nobody here 'cept me. Me an' Dora. Now, she's gone!"

"She'll be okay, fendin' fer herself out there," Murph told him. "Don't worry about her. But Maude?" He had Mr. Farlow by the arm, and steered him toward the shack door. "You ain't seen Maude?"

The old man shook his head.

"Maybe she never came over," Roy suggested. "That's rough stuff out there. She most likely never came over at all."

They waited while Daddy Farlow collected a few belongings and then they all climbed back into the boat. Murph circled carefully into the waves and headed for the post office dock. As they drew near they could see the three women, signalling and holding on to each other.

Bertha, Agnes and Cora all talked at once as Murph maneuvered up to the dock. They were so hysterical the men couldn't understand a word.

"Whoa, now. Slow down." Murph grabbed a piling to steady the boat.

Evan pointed at the empty boat slip, and yelled "where's my boat? Did it break loose?"

The wind was howling so loudly the three women, clutched together, had difficulty projecting. Bertha's voice rose above the others.

"Maude took the boat. Maude took it, Evan. She was goin' over to Daddy Farlow.."

"It was calm then." Cora screamed. "The wind wasn't blowing and the waves were quiet and ..."

"Motor trouble!" Bertha was so agitated she seemed about to fall off the dock, Evan reached out a restraining hand. "Halfway across, the motor conked. She didn't have no anchor!"

"Oh, God!" Evan yelled back. "I took it out. Didn't want it bangin' around in the boat in the storm. Did she drift?"

"Yeah. Fast, too. Down Roosevelt! An' the winds come crashin' back an' pushed her faster! An' she jes' disappeared, headin' for the Gulf!"

Murph had the boat motor going again. Without a word he boosted Daddy Farlow up onto the dock, motioned the other men down and gunned the boat in a wide circle. Spray shot high in the air, where it was caught by the storm and sheeted back over the occupants.

"Dear God!" Agnes murmured to herself as she watched the boat disappear down the bay in the gathering dusk. "Dear God! Please let them be in time. Let them find her, stuck somewhere but safe. Please, Dear God, let her be safe!"

They soon found the boat. Jammed prow first into the overhanging bushes, wedged in under the arching prop roots of the mangroves 100 yards north of the entrance to Hurricane Hollow, they found the boat, but not Maude. Silently, holding tight to the gunwales of both craft as the boats rose and fell in the choppy waves, they stared at each other as the hopelessness of the situation settled on them.

Jerry climbed silently into Evan's boat and reached into the bilge, awash with sea water. From under an oar he retrieved a small object, which he gazed at steadily, turning it over and over in his hand.

Evan silently signalled to Murph and Roy, and pointed to a large overhanging branch. Along one side was a streak of red. Running his finger along the streak, he held his hand out to Murph.

"Blood!"

●

It was old man Jackson who found Maude. Several days after the huge storm had passed, poling his flat-bottom mullet boat along Roosevelt Channel just in from Blind Pass, he glimpsed a large pale object under the water.

Later, tied up at Murph's dock, Mr. Jackson bought a beer and sat quietly on a bar stool. When Pearlie went into the store room he signalled to Murph to join him outside.

"I got Miss Maude! She's there, in the bottom of the boat, under that tarp. Heavy! Had a right hard time draggin' her up over the side, an' her loose hair kept snaggin' on the roots. Best not let anyone see her. She's chawed up right smart. Crabs has got to her."

●

The day was winding down and Cora had produced iced tea and cookies. The three of them sat around the large work table on Agnes' screened porch, each lost in private thoughts. Thoughts and remembrances.

The house repairs had moved along rapidly. The roof had been patched, the interior repaired and painted, the kitchen sink and stove replaced. Tomorrow the plumber was due to connect the piping.

There had been no frivolity, and little talking, these two weeks since the storm. Each had gone about whatever chores needed doing with efficiency but little communication. Cora's face was puffy and her eyes red but she held herself in close check. There had been no emotion in front of the others.

Jerry had been stoney-faced.

Aunt Ag lifted her glass to sip and looked at him across the edge. He was all bottled up. If only he'd break and cry. Let the grief wash away. Cora obviously wept when she was alone. She, herself, was now used to silent mourning. The lad was too tense. She ached to comfort him. But he was withdrawn, locked away somewhere. She couldn't reach him. He sat there alone, twisting that thing in his hand. Agnes put her glass back down on the table and it rattled as she did. She placed her hand on top of it in irritation.

"What are you twirling, Jerry?"

"Her comb."

"Where did you get it?"

"I found it on Evan's boat ... in the storm."

Cora gave a pathetic little gasp. Rising quickly from the table, she crossed hastily to the window and leaned against the framing.

Jerry slowly raised his head and looked at his aunt.

"Aunt Ag, I don't understand! Why? _Why_?"

He continued to look at her through the long minute before she answered.

"I don't understand, either, Jerry. I never have understood. Why Will and not me? I don't know. Maybe it's not for us to understand. We just have to accept."

"She was so good! So kind! She never hurt a single soul. Now, she's gone, all because of a cow. We've had to exchange her for an animal!"

Agnes responded quickly to this outburst.

"No, Jerry. That's not true. We shouldn't try to even things up like that. Maude _was_ good. She _was_ kind. She gave her life helping someone else. To look at it any other way is to minimize her value. No, it wasn't because of an animal. That was incidental. She was following her pattern ... reaching out to help someone ... possibly the greatest of all human traits."

His eyes were set on hers. He strained to understand, to accept. Then, suddenly, his face broke. It was devastated, and tears coursed heavily down his cheeks. As he slowly lowered his head to his arms, Agnes heard him moan.

"I loved her so much. I never told her but I did. Now she'll never know."

She reached out and stroked his hand.

"Jerry," Agnes said, her own eyes wet, "this terrible pain you feel, this sense of not having done enough, of being left all by yourself, it will ease with time. You won't forget... none of us will ever forget Maude. We will wrap our memories carefully and store them in a special place in our hearts where she will always live. And our lives will go on. Things will move along. We must go on. I thought when Will died ... I knew I'd never be able ... but I did. We all must." A slight pressure from his thumb against her hand told her he heard. "Which brings us to another difficult situation." Her words almost stumbled and she had to clear her throat. "We must make arrangements for you to go back north. Back to your mother and your family up there. Soon now. We must."

After a long moment, Jerry lifted his head and faced Agnes. He swiped one hand across his cheek, clearing off the glistening tears.

"I'm not going back, Aunt Ag. I've thought about it very carefully. I'm not going back. You need me here. Aunt Maude would agree. I'm staying on the island with you."

Agnes was afraid to react. She was searching for a proper retort when Cora beckoned and called from the window.

"Ag, come quick. Come over here and look. Quick!"

Agnes crossed to the window and slipped her arm around Cora's waist.

"Look, Ag. There's a redbird on the feeder! See! They're back. Do you see?"

Agnes gave her a gentle squeeze.

"Yes, dear, I see!"

ABOUT THE AUTHOR

Ted Levering was born in 1915 in Towson, Maryland. At age 18 he enrolled at the Academy of Radio and Drama in Cincinnati. After graduating he worked for a year at WLW radio station in that city as one of a stock company of young actors.

In 1937 Ted relocated to New York and worked in the theatre on and around Broadway until World War II exploded in Europe. Ted enlisted in the 29th National Guard Division when that unit was mobilized in 1940. When the Allies invaded France in 1944, he was with the second wave of infantry onto the Normandy beach, and fought with the 29th through to the Elbe River.

After the war, while fishing through Florida in 1947, Ted discovered Captiva Island, and remained there until 1962. He then accepted a position with the Tolstoy Foundation in New York and spent 12 years working in International Relief. He returned to Florida in 1974.

Now retired, Ted lives inland in East Fort Myers.

ABOUT THE ARTIST

Ann L. Winterbotham was an art instructor in Massachusetts before moving to Sanibel Island in 1965, where she became a founding member of the Sanibel-Captiva Conservation Foundation. She served as its chairman for seven years.

She was appointed to the first Sanibel City Planning Commission which she served for ten years, eight as its chairman. During that period her dedication to nature preservation on the islands, in Florida and the world was a driving force.

Her illustrations have appeared in books and periodicals over a period of many years.

This book is available from

Willowmead Publishing Company
4030 Skates Circle
Fort Myers, Florida 33905

Price of book $14.95
Shipping Cost   2.00
                        ———
Total $16.95*

*no c.o.ds. -- no credit cards